A GRAAL QUEST
UNLIKE ANY OTHER BEFORE IT

Arthur's voice was hushed; the wind died as he spoke, even the trees above us seemed to bend to hear him.

"Morgan fears Marguessan is creating a Black Graal."

A Black Graal, a Cup of darkness. . . The mere idea was an uncleanness out of the seventh hell; but I had to admit that the possibility was no new one. For all things and persons of power, there are things and persons of equal and opposite power—as above, so below; as without, so within; as the Light, so the Dark.

It is not the good in a sacred thing that makes it holy, it is the power. And power can be used for good or for ill, as we have all by now seen. If no Black Graal yet existed in our Keltia, be very sure it has existed since time began, on the inner planes or in a Keltia that is not the one we know. And if Marguessan had found at last a way to bring it through to our world. . .

A BOOK OF THE KELTIAD
Volume III of The Tales of Arthur

THE
HEDGE
OF MIST

PATRICIA
KENNEALY-
MORRISON

HarperPrism
An Imprint of HarperPaperbacks

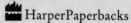HarperPaperbacks
A Division of HarperCollins*Publishers*
10 East 53rd Street, New York, N.Y. 10022-5299

Limited edition prints of the artwork on this book cover, numbered
and signed by author Patricia Kennealy-Morrison and artist
Thomas Canty, are available from Mithril Publishing, 4060-D
Peachtree Rd., Suite 291, Atlanta, Georgia 30319. Please call
(770) 662-7574 or write to receive a complete catalog of prints and posters.

ISBN 0-06-105604-9

 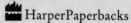
Cover art by Thomas Canty
Maps and other art by the author

A hardcover edition of this book was published in 1996 by HarperPrism.
First mass market printing: January 1997

Printed in the United States of America

Visit HarperPaperbacks on the World Wide Web at
http://www.harpercollins.com/paperbacks

❖ 10 9 8 7 6 5 4 3 2 1

Visit Patricia Kennealy-Morrison on the World Wide Web at
http://www.wwonline-ny.com/~lizardqueen

For my brother Kevin James

ACKNOWLEDGMENTS

A Keltic Triad: The Three Great Influences on my
writerly life—Rudyard Kipling, Lord Dunsany
and E. R. Eddison.
All praise, thanks and honor, pen-beirdd all.

KELTICHRONICON

In the Earth year 453 by the Common Reckoning, a small fleet of ships left Ireland, carrying emigrants seeking a new home in a distant land. But the ships were not the leather-hulled boats of later legend, and though the great exodus was indeed led by a man called Brendan, he was not the Christian navigator-monk who later chroniclers would claim had discovered a New World across the western ocean.

These ships were starships, their passengers the Danaans, descendants of—and heirs to the secrets of—Atlantis, that they themselves called Atland. The new world they sought was a distant double-ringed planet, itself unknown and more than half a legend, and he who led them in that seeking would come to be known as Saint Brendan the Astrogator.

Fleeing persecutions and a world that was no longer home to their ancient magics, the Danaans, who long ages since had come to Earth in flight from a dying star's agonies, now went back to those far stars; and after two years' desperate wandering they found their promised haven. They named their new homeland Keltia, and Brendan, though he refused to call himself its king, ruled there long and well.

In all the centuries that followed, Keltia grew and prospered. The kings and queens who were Brendan's heirs, whatever else they did, kept unbroken his great command: that until the time was right, Keltia should not for peril of its very existence reveal itself to the Earth that its folk had fled; nor forget, for like peril, those other children of Atland who had followed them into the stars—the Telchines, close kin and mortal foes, who became the Coranians, as the Danaans had become the Kelts.

* * *

Brendan had been twelve centuries in his grave when a time fell upon Keltia at which the Kelts still weep: a reign of blood and sorcerous terror, civil war and the assassin-murder of the reigning king and the toppling of the Throne of Scone itself, all at the hand of Edeyrn the Archdruid, known ever after as Marbh-draoi, 'Death-druid,' and rightly so.

Edeyrn fastened round Keltia's throat the iron collar of the Druid Theocracy and Interregnum; and, with the help of traitor Druids, collaborating Kelts and the terrible enforcers called Ravens, kept it locked there for two hundred fearful years. The royal House of Dôn—such of it as survived the Marbh-draoi's methodical slaughter—was forced into hiding, while a great resistance movement, known as the Counterinsurgency, was raised to fight against the Theocracy's forces.

Yet even iron collars may be broken by a single sword-stroke, so that the sword be sharp enough, the blow well enough placed; and if the arm that wields the sword be strong enough—and so fated. . .

In the year 1946 of the Common Reckoning were born in Keltia three children: a girl and two boys. As has been already told in *The Hawk's Gray Feather* and *The Oak Above the Kings*, Gweniver Pendreic, Arthur Penarvon and Taliesin Glyndour—princess, prince and bard to be—grow up in the Marbh-draoi's despite, to lead the Counterinsurgency and to rule Keltia in what are to be its most fated times.

Arthur and Gweniver, royal cousins, are also co-heirs, equal lawful inheritors to the Throne of Scone. Though initially loath, they wed and rule Keltia together after the death of their uncle the High King Uthyr and their own overthrow of Edeyrn Marbh-draoi and all his forces; and eventually they even fall in love.

Taliesin, Arthur's foster-brother, reared with him by Ygrawn, Arthur's lady mother, becomes the greatest bard of Keltia since the order's founding, and himself weds Arthur's half-sister Morgan, as mighty in sorcery as her mate in bardery or her brother in war.

But Merlynn Llwyd, teacher to Arthur and Taliesin in

their youth, and the great enemy of Edeyrn, has laid a doom on them all before his own mysterious magical vanishment; and when it is learned that Arthur's other half-sister, Morgan's twin Marguessan, has stolen away the great Cup that is known as the Graal and is one of the Four Hallows of Keltia, a quest is launched to bring it home again.

And Arthur and Taliesin both alike must find themselves at the last upon very different quests of their own; while Morgan out of her might as sorceress raises for Keltia a protection for all time. . .

Twelve musics we learn in the Star of Bards, and these the twelve:

Geantraí, the joy-song,
> whose color is gold and whose shout creation;
> whose number is one, and one is the number of birth.

Gráightraí, the heart-lilt,
> whose color is green and whose descant rapture;
> whose number is two, and two is the number of love.

Bethtraí, the fate-rann,
> whose color is white and whose charge endurance;
> whose number is three, and three is the number of life.

Goltraí, the grief-keen,
> whose color is red and whose cadence sorrow;
> whose number is four, and four is the number of death.

Galtraí, the sword-dance,
> whose color is black and whose blazon challenge;
> whose number is five, and five is the number of war.

Suantraí, the sleep-strain,
> whose color is gray and whose murmur calmness;
> whose number is six, and six is the number of peace.

Saoíchtraí, the mage-word,
> whose color is blue and whose guerdon wisdom;
> whose number is seven, and seven is the number of lore.

Créachtraí, the wound-weird,
　　whose color is brown and whose burden anguish;
　　whose number is eight, and eight is the number of pain.

Fiortraí, the honor-hymn,
　　whose color is purple and whose banner justice;
　　whose number is nine, and nine is the number of truth.

Neartraí, the triumph-march,
　　whose color is crimson and whose anthem valor;
　　whose number is ten, and ten is the number of strength.

Dóchtraí, the faith-chaunt,
　　whose color is silver and whose crown transcendence;
　　whose number is eleven, and eleven is the number of hope.

Diachtraí, the soul-rune, sum of all before it,
　　whose color is all colors and whose end perfection;
　　whose number is twelve, and twelve is the number of God.

—Taliesin ap Gwyddno

THE HOLLOW MOUNTAINS

ST. CLEARS'S WELL

METHVEN

THE LITHERLANDS

MOUNT KELTIA

THE DRAGON SEA

FAIRLIGHT

THE EASTER ISLES

GAP OF ARMOY

ARMOY

WINDRED

PLAINS OF LISTELLIAN

THE CHINNS OF KELLS

SIENNEGA

THE COBBLER

INISGUIDRIN

THE HAND

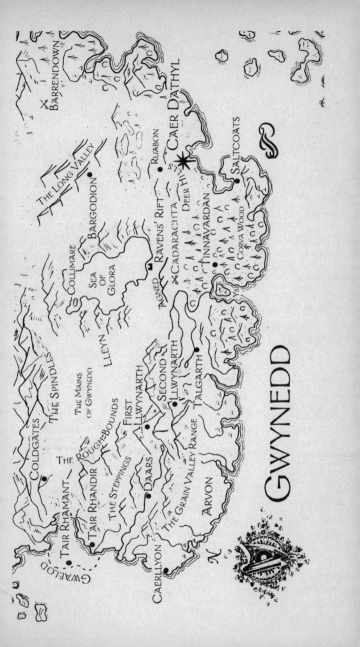

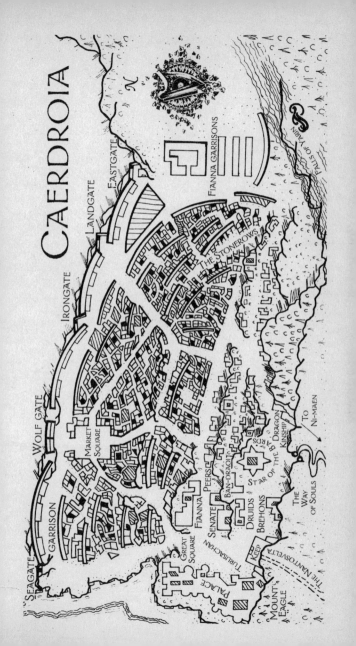

Clod ior, angor gwlad.

(The fame of the ruler is the anchor of the land.)

FORETALE

Say of the lastlight: that fierce fiery beam, straight as a lance or a lasra, that shoots green and clear and cold out of the West where the sun has gone, one final glint like an arm upraised, valediction and benediction both together.

I have come now almost to the end of my telling, if not perhaps just yet to the end of my tale. All the others who began this running with me have finished before me, and I alone am here to speak the last truths of them and me. It did not turn out altogether as we had planned it, or had hoped it; but neither did it fall out for the most part as we had feared it, and for that we have ourselves to thank, as much as the gods who so willed it.

We have a new High King these days, Arawn Ard-rígh, son of my beloved friends; he has ruled for some years, and shows the best of both parents—and that is considerable. Far away on Aojun, his halfsister Donah reigns as queen over her own folk. I see my friend and brother in them both, my Artos, that grave and joyous soul; and their mothers also, those two great queens, so different and so very much alike. Arawn my nephew has himself wedded a strong and worthy consort—yet another Gwen to be queen over Kelts, this one Gwenalarch, a daughter of the Clannrannoch—and they have given us a Tanista, Arianwen. As for Arthur's other daughter, Arawn's fullsister Arwenna, she too has wed, and will in time be the ancestress of royal dynasties yet to come; for did not Merlynn Llwyd tell us that the line of Arthur should never fail, not in Keltia nor among far stars?

Merlynn himself never failed us, though he fell in strange fashion and many think before his dán demanded; but then, one who knows better than any other has told me a bit more of that seeming fall, and of what shall come of it long centuries hence. Said too that I myself would see it, I Taliesin, in a life of mine yet to be, and I find that thought both comforting and unsettling. My folk do not hold with the sad and terrible doctrine of one life and one only, and eternal punishment should we get it awry. Nay! She Who Made All has ordered things far better than that, with more mercy, more grace, more love for Her creation and Her creatures. She never wasted a grain of sand; how much less then would She be spendthrift of a soul. . .

But for this life as now is, I am come at last to the lastwords, my life having been lived for words; those, and the songs I made to frame them. As I review what I have so far chronicled, I am for the most part pleased, with both the events and the chronicling thereof, though from time to time I stand gape-mouthed that things should have fallen out as they did—both words and deeds alike. Every Midsummer comes to my ears the ancient shout: "Is it peace?" And the joy of the answer as it rings back from every world of Keltia takes me out of myself: "Peace it is!"

Too long was it until once again we could make that honest declaring, that proud and happy boast; and I am prouder still and happier that I myself had a hand in making it so, I and all the others. Well do we deserve the joy of it now. . . Still, even Edeyrn Marbh-draoi gave us peace—of a sort—in the two hundred years of his dominion; but it was a black and a bloody peace, not worth the having, nor the price it cost us all. We are graced that it and he are gone.

I will go now too, I think, very soon; my beloved Morgan has set out before me, as I knew she would and prayed she might. At the least she was spared what I myself have known since she went—the loss and the silence, the tears and the dreams. . . I have left word in my will that I would be given the Fians' ending, to be disatomed by the crystal scadarc upon the wicker bier, but, I tell you now, that is not how it shall be, though to oblige the poor teller of the tale you will keep it beneath the Horns. Of all those I leave behind, only my closest blood-kin—all I have left to me, my soul-kin are already moved on—shall know the truth of my real road. And Cathelin, my son's daughter, she who was named for the Terran mother I never knew in this life—shall know more than that. For she is bard, my Cat-lass, my heir in art as well as in estate, and she will sing of it to such as are inclined to hear, and so will all of it be kept alive. What better end, or successor, could one ask?

This tale I now complete is by volume far enough advanced as to make recapitulation perhaps a touch boresome, for teller and hearer alike. One cannot harp forever on the same string for those who through no fault of their own have come late to the story, but that is after all why ballads are constructed as they are, and I pray earlier comers be patient with them and with me . . .

If you have attended, then, to the previous of these chronicles, you will of your grace recall how it stands with us in tale-time: how Arthur the young came up from the Caer-in-Arvon to challenge Edeyrn the Marbh-draoi, and I came with him from the first; how he triumphed, and restored his uncle Uthyr Pendreic to the High Kingship so long usurped; how he wed his cousin the Princess Gweniver, to share with her the Ard-tiarnas of Keltia, she as Ard-rían, he as Ard-rígh, and though they were wedded they were not truemates, not yet anyway; how we his Companions went with him on all his roads, following him into legend; how he loved Majanah, queen of the Yamazai, before he came to love his own wife, and had by her that Donah who now is Aojun's queen (and some there were who even then believed that she was not his firstborn, but that he had gotten a son by his first wife, the loathly Gwenwynbar, who now is slain, and rightly too); how the sacred Cup of the Treasures, called by us the Graal, was stolen, or at the least was sore assaulted, by Arthur's halfsister the Princess Marguessan, my own wife's twin; and how the High Sidhe-folk did charge me with the carrying of these terrible tidings to Artos and to Gwen, so that quest might be made to restore the Cup. . .

Ah, I make but a bad hand of it, now as then. If it is hard to be a legend, as Arthur himself learned to his sorrow and wrath and utter cost, harder still is it to correctly tell of one—in especial when that legend you would tell of is to you not just a legend but also a man you love above all other souls.

My mother, who was as I have said of Earth, had a saying in her journals that I now know came from her homeworld, and it is this: that the pen can be mightier than the sword. And I have always wondered: Whose pen? Whose sword? Whose the hand on both or either?

But you shall hear all now, of swords and pens alike full measure, to the end—or what shall pass for ending. And I pray you, as all bards pray all hearers, disremember not of the telling, nor of the tale's poor teller, nor of the great love and loss that live in tale and teller both.

For remembering is all that we can hope for at the last.

BOOK ONE:

Dochtraí

CHAPTER 1

Darkness a long time, or so at least it seemed. Then, it seemed also, I awakened; or my body awakened, if not just yet my mind. I had no memory of how I had come to this place in which I found myself awake, or of my own past, or of this place's name, or of my *own* name. Even so, I could not think of any state or place or space that seemed to me better, or even other. I was comfortable, very; I was alone, right enough, but nor could I recall the names or faces or voices of any whom I would have wished beside me in my isolate condition. I might have been a prisoner—I guessed I probably was—but I was not sure even of that.

I was by no means ill-treated, nor even ill-kept. Food, good and hot and plentiful, if simple, arrived at amply satisfactory intervals, left by an unseen hand while I slept (or, to be accurate, while I was unconscious); clear clean water-springs, cold and hot, bubbled out of two stone founts in one corner of the stone-walled chamber in which I was resident. I had an easeful, well-furnished sleeping-couch; comfortable raiment laundered fresh in regular rotation; thoughtfully supplemented by warmer or cooler garments when the season warranted; even my own harp, Frame of Harmony that had accompanied me through so much down the years. Yet for days, or maybe years, I could not recall even so much as this; could not call to mind, even, how to

play my harp—far less how came I here in the first place.
You will think it strange; and you are so right to think it.

But, as I say, I was not unhappy; not even much distressed. It was as if I slept waking, undemanding, unde-
manded of, and was dreamless and thought-bereft withal.
After a while, though, bit by bit, through no action of mine,
my state began to change, and I began to begin to remember. . .

Nothing much at first: It started with the light. Perhaps it
had been there all along, and only later did I come to notice
it—a cool blue light even in daytime, or what I took for daytime, since I could see not sky nor sun nor star to mark the
hours. There was a small high window through which the
light seeped down to me; the window, though stoutly barred
and grated, also sifted fresh air into my place of confining.
There were many days led up to that moment, and many
more before I became gradually 'ware of faint sounds
beyond my chamber's ambit. Again, naught much, naught
dramatic: just the natural small sounds of life and those living it, shouts of folk, tread or call of beasts, far tiny cries of
birds. But even when at last it dawned on me that I might
try to raise myself up to the window, and after another
seeming eon I did in fact succeed in so doing, I still could
see nothing. It was as if beyond the stone walls and iron
grate—no door, you will note—that marked my world, only
echoes existed.

I cannot tell you how long it was, much less seemed—
only later did I learn the true duration of my captivity; for
such indeed it was, but as yet I did not know even that,
though you would think that the bars and doorless cell
would have given me the clue. . . Once I did remember, or
was permitted to remember, how to harp, I consoled myself
with that, playing unceasingly, until the harper's calluses, all
but worn away with disuse, returned to my finger-ends. But
nothing new did I make of song; all music that came to me
in that time came from a former time.

You may well imagine how this interested me, how I
speculated madly on even the smallest thing. Had I been a
bard, then, before I came to be shut up here? I could not
say. But it seemed at least possible: There had been the

harp's mere presence, for one thing. Most of our folk, however much we love music (and almost all of us do), would not possess such an instrument at all, let alone so fine a one, with its inlaid runes and gemstones adorning the soundbox. If bard, though, why could I not now create—unless of course that was the reason for my punishment?

I was full ready to accept that; but still it seemed only part of it. I did not appear to have been a warrior; the scars of that trade were utterly absent, save for two or three small white relics, long since healed, marks that any user of a sword, however casual, might easily have come by. A Druid, then? When I got to this possible former profession I was suddenly seized by a kind of formless dread: a sense of something untapped, something tremendous and potentially liberating, shut away behind a barred door far more unassailable even than the walls of my physical chamber. But if it were indeed magical skill that had been sealed off so, it had been sealed off by a far greater talent than I, and I could find no way to come at it. If I were Druid, belike I was not a very gifted one. . . Perhaps I *deserved* to be here.

As time passed and I felt myself gradually awakening, one thing did come to mind, and it troubled me greatly: a feeling as of some terrible and urgent task left undone, a charge upon which lives and even kingdoms turned, and I the only bearer of the tidings. When first this thought came floating into my ken, I dismissed it as mere vainglorious ravings: How could I, this humble dullard who could not even recall his own name and life and profession, shut up in a place unknown for offenses unguessed at, ever be thought worthy to bear such a message of menace as this that I imagined?

But the thought would not leave me; and then, night after night, day upon day, the dreams began to come: of people mostly—a kingly man with hair like the red oak in autumn; a woman bright and dangerous as a blade; another woman— and from dreams of her I woke weeping—with clear eyes that seemed to offer her love and soul and spirit to save me, to bring me home, her hands outstretched, on one finger a ring of gold in form of two intertwined serpents with ruby eyes. Other faces there were, too, and beings that were

shapes only, shadowy and faceless; but though I knew I
knew them all, I did not *know* them, and it was torture not.

If they had messages of help for me, I could not hear
them, and in my dreams I strove mightily to tell them so, to
pray them speak louder, longer, clearer. And whether
because of my prayers and my tears, for pity of my asking,
or for some other, greater reason, every now and again I
broke through to the truth, I burned through the fog that
bound me, my mind unclouded and I knew all; for a
moment, only, but I *did know!* And then the slow soft dark
would claim me again, and I forgot not only the knowledge
but also the knowledge that I had remembered, and I fell
back into dullness and stolid stuporous daze.

Who knows how many times I almost breached the walls
of my mind-prison? Certain sure I never managed to make
the smallest crack in the equally substantial walls of stone
that held me just as surely. But after what might have been
a month as easily as a millennium (though it was to prove
something rather more than the former, if much less than
the latter), real change came. I had a visitor; and for all of
me I cannot now tell you, nor could I even then, whether I
was glad or sorry that she had come to me at all.

It was on an afternoon of late winter or early spring; I know
not how, but I had learned somehow to distinguish times of
day and night even in that chamber cut off from outer time,
and some sense in the very air told me it was thawing-time
in the world without—the first weeks of March, maybe, the
early days of the Wolf-moon that is full of winds and weath-
ers unlike all other months. A significant month too, I had
the feeling, though not my own birthmonth—*that* I knew
from the runes tattooed upon my left shoulder. According
to those, I had been born in the Badger-moon, in the second month of our year, the dying-time of the sun and its
returning; so, not *my* birthmonth, but someone else's, someone very dear to me? One of the shadowy dreamfolk: the
woman with love in her eyes who tried so desperately to
touch me, or that other woman, the dark-haired one whom
lately I had dreamed wearing a crown. . .

Any road, the woman who so suddenly stood before me in my chamber-cell, as if she had come there by magic (and so she must have, for no door had opened to admit her), was no woman I had ever seen before, not even in my dreams. And yet, and yet. . .

"Do you know me?" she asked, and her voice was low and thrilling; but also full of menace, as if it burred just below my hearing, like the nathair's evil buzz before it strikes.

I stared and stared, and shook my head. "Nay, lady," I said in all honesty, for her look compelled me, and any road it was the truth. Or so at least I believed; it seemed that never would I have forgotten such a one as this: She had a haunting look of that ringed woman I saw in dreams; but was not so tall, and more rounded, with curling light-gold hair, and the most extraordinary eyes I had ever beheld—blue they were, and startling, with broad black rims round the irises, almost as if she had taken a paintstick and drawn them there. The brows and the heavy lids were painted too, as were almost every woman's in Keltia—Keltia! I had remembered the name of my world! I opened my mouth to speak the name in joy, but some warning brushed feather-soft over my cheek, and I shut my mouth again before I could say what I now knew I knew.

The woman stiffened a little, frowning, as if she perceived I knew something I had not known a moment since; her eyes fought into mine, striving for the knowledge, but I would not give it up, and after a minute or so she released me. But she looked most ill pleased.

"You are quite certain you know me not?" she asked again. "Our paths have never crossed before this instant?" The honey in her voice thickened, but there was poison there too. "Tell me this then: What is *your* name, my master?"

At that question my bones went to water, and I sagged all over, a mannikin whose strings had been cut; for of course I had not the faintest *idea* what my name was. But I was wary now; and if I had no resources with which to defend myself, was as a naked unarmed child before a war-witch in battle armor, still I had the one weapon of my honest ignorance. And I employed it, shaking my head and slumping down upon my couch as if in bewildered despair—which had the additional safeguarding advantage of being my true state of mind—and shielding my thoughts as best I might.

It seemed effective: She appeared convinced I did not know her, nor yet even my own identity, and to a very great degree she was certainly correct to think so. But if I did not know as yet who she was, I surely knew now *what* she was; and if the knowledge feared me, I also knew, just as surely, that she and I had indeed met before, and not for the better.

After she had gone, as abruptly as she had come, one instant there, the next gone (well, now at least I knew for sure it was magic afoot), I stretched out upon my couch, my arms extended to either side as if in some half-recollected ritual, and stared up at the rough-hewn rock ceiling. I was shaking a little in reaction: What in all the seven hells had just happened here? Who was this woman? This sorceress—for that much was plain by now—why was she keeping me here? Even *my* addled senses had computed by this time that she and no other was my jailer. . . And the question above all others: Who was I to be so jailed?

A face formed before my eyes: the man's face, the King, as I thought him. Dark-red hair to his shoulders, or just a bit past, deep-set eyes the color of peat-stained water, beard just beginning to be touched with gray: The vision cheered me, but vexed me more, for I knew I knew him, and knew him well, and loved him well—better perhaps than any living soul—and yet I could not say how, or even who.

I felt just as sorry as vexed, a poor case to be so used, for whatever, or whosever, reasons. Not to make great bones of it, but I was well aware there was a vast matter here, and that I, however grave or pitiable I thought my present case, was by no means the center pirn of the thing. Nay—I was merely a messenger, an errander, but with a commission of staggering import, and I was being kept here so that my message should go undelivered. That much I had puzzled out. But there was so much more to it than that—why, for example, did not my captors simply kill me, and stop my message then and there?—and that was why the woman had visited me just now.

All at once I felt perversely cheered. If she felt the need to reinforce my captivity, to assure herself of my ignorance, to shore up the spells I now knew were at work upon me to keep me in that ignorance, then perhaps in that outer world—*Keltia,* I said to myself, savoring the name as much as the regained knowledge of it, *out there in Keltia*—some force was at work against her, a force she feared, a force that could, perhaps, defeat her; a force that even now was set to save me.

My hand dropped to my tunic neck-slit, and I absently thrust my fingers through to scratch my chest. To my surprise, for I had not noticed this before—or, if I had, I had not remembered—there was somewhat lying there beneath my leinna: a chain, apparently, and upon it a pendant of some kind. How I had managed to miss this—for I stripped twice daily to bathe, as was the cleanly habit among all my folk—I could not imagine, save that I had been *made* to miss it. . .

But I tugged now on the chain, and it spilled out into my hand: a beautifully crafted piece of work, each fine link of yellow gold hand-forged and soldered. And upon that chain— I stared in wonder at the pendant piece, and for no reason I could name tears started in my eyes as I gazed.

It was a feather of gold, every part of it most carefully carven, barb and quill and down and shaft lovingly detailed, strangely heavy for its dimensions. I turned it over in my fingers, and saw that it was cunningly hinged along one edge, and fastened with a tiny boss and catch on the other. A reliquary of some sort? I ran a fingernail along the latch edge and popped it open.

Inside was a clear crystal of what looked like white sapphire, shallowly faceted, forming a domed cover for what lay beneath: a hawk's feather, gray and silver, brown and black. The gold casing that housed it so magnificently in its own likeness bore slight signs of age—the fine lines of the vaning were a touch blurred here and there, as if from long wear—but the real feather seemed new-plucked from the bird's own pinion.

I stared at it a long time, but no message or memory came to me, and finally I snapped closed the locket casing,

defeated and more than a little frustrated. Why had this one
thing been left me, when so much else had not? Was it a
kindness, or merely more subtle torture? But before I put it
back safe beneath my leinna, I touched the case to my lips,
and felt from somewhere very far and yet strangely nearby,
very soft yet very clear, a wave of love and comfort and
promise. Whoever had gifted me with this had loved me,
long and greatly; and I was glad indeed to have even this little certainty of knowing.

And perhaps the discovery of the locket set free my
chained memory in other directions as well, for of a sudden I
felt coming upon me the words and the burden of a song, and
I reached as if by instinct for the harp that stood against the
wall. The music came more readily to my fingers than ever
before in my time here; the words took longer, as if I were
wrenching them to me past some arva-draoi or rann of hiding.
But they came, oh aye, they came.

   "'Sleep through thunder—
    We sleep shining like silver
    And heavy like silver. . .
    My life is turning eastwards
    Since you and I were wed
    My side warm with your
      white breasts touching
    You promised me magic
    And logic
    And love;
    I have peace now
    And power
    And you beside me
    breathing in an iron dawn
    Your promises are well kept.
    O love! Stir not yet!'"

I paused, astonished and barely daring to breathe, lest I
disturb the stream of song; but I need not have feared. As I
played, the stream grew to a torrent, and I was carried far
from my prison on the strength of it.

   "'My kinsman is content with his ragged mantle,
    My kinsman has two tents and is pleased.
    He took a woman of the camp to wife.

I have done better.
I carried off a maiden from a distant tribe
Surprised her at the well
And found she was their queen.'"

I drew breath for the verses I knew came next, the
rounding-off of the song, the resolving of the mood that the
song's maker had set out—though who that maker was I
knew not, save that it was not I—but I sat there, my chest
that had been filled to chaunt sinking now in little gasps as
the breath left it, driven out of me by the dwimmercraft
that was on me, and I had forgotten all, yet again.

I huddled there motionless a while, too hurt and sad to
move; then suddenly yawned hugely. Whether it was the
spell renewed upon me or the work of the song upon my
soul or maybe even the locket ensuring my safety, I was all
at once tired beyond words, wearied as if I had been battling
all day in fíor-comlainn. Perhaps I had; but I drank off
thirstily all the slightly musty water in the quaich beside the
bed, then went over to the fount to plenish the cup again
with fresh.

Sipping small of the stingingly cold water, I lay down
again, pondering the brief encounter with my captor, wondering at the song that had come to lift my heart, fingering
the reassuring outline of the locket through my shirt and
tunic. Perhaps it was an omen of better dán to come, that I
should have recalled this particular song, should have
become 'ware of the locket when I did. Perhaps the dream-
faces tonight would have answers for me; perhaps, at the
very least, there should be a respite from questions and
from fears.

I rolled myself up in the pieced sheepskins that served
me as coverlet, feeling the small but definite weight of the
gold feather against my chest, and gave myself over to sleep,
the music still sounding somewhere far within, like the rush
of a stream heard from a distance on a quiet night of fog
and mist. How wrong, and how right, I was, would soon be
proved; and in no uncertain manner.

CHAPTER 2

I was lying upon my couch, trying to recall a particularly tricky bit of fingering for an alternative chord, when suddenly there came a blur and vibration in the very air, and a haze began to form in one corner of my cell.

I was on my feet in an instant, my fingers moving as if of their own will in a pattern my conscious mind could not frame, a warding-spell of some sort. I was almost as astonished at this hitherto unremembered evidence of Druid training as I was at what occasioned it: Someone else was joining me in captivity.

Whoever it was, he or she was not arriving in the same easy manner in which my previous visitor had contrived to join me. This new arrival was probably but another poor bodach doomed to the same forgetful, and forgotten, existence as I myself had been seemingly sentenced to. Still—I brightened a little even in the face of the unknown cellmate's misfortune—it would be someone at least to talk to, maybe even someone who had known me of old and could at last give me that little trifling detail of my own identity.

I had not long to wait: Almost as quickly as it takes to tell of it, the thing was done, and I was no longer alone. And I stared as if my eyes were on sticks, for the man now cutting a very sharp glance round the chamber was the man I had so often seen in dreams, the tall bearded lord with the air of a king.

He saw me at once, and stopped where he stood. Then a look of the most unutterable joy and sorrow together came over his handsome countenance, and he reached out a tentative hand to me where I lurked over against the far wall. He made as if to speak, but instead an extraordinary smile grazed the edge of his beard, and he seemed to settle back within himself.

His first words were an uncanny echo of those my last surprise visitor had spoken.

"Do you know me?"

I drew a deep shivering breath, and let it out again before I felt able to answer him.

"I think I must. . . I have seen you, often, in dreams; I feel, I *know*, that we have met—but nay, I cannot put name to you. Nor yet to myself, if you must know; so if you are looking to me to tell me who you are, you must look again, and we both be nameless together."

He smiled again, but now there were tears in his eyes, which astonished me even more. "Nay, that knowledge is nothing I need ask of you. But, truly, do you not know me—Taliesin?"

I wish I could say that at his pronouncing of what I knew at once to be my own name I remembered everything; but that would be a lie. Still, I was immediately certain of the truths in his words: I was Taliesin, and he and I knew each other well.

He was a little hurt, I could see, that I did not remember him; but he put it by at once, and turned with a devastatingly refreshing air of practicality to the greater matters at hand.

"Well, I know *you*, braud"—and the endearment somehow gave me a deeper pang than it seemed to warrant—"and I will prove it withal. . ." He was running that all-seeing glance of his into every corner of the stone chamber, searching for I knew not what.

"You will find no way out, I fear, save the one you came in by," I said presently, but I was by now shaking a little. "Will you not tell me who *you* are, and what I might be, before we are many minutes older?"

He laughed then, in real amusement, but did not for an instant cease his searching. "All in good time, my Talynno... I know you have been here long and long in forgetfulness, but it is not yet safe for us to speak."

Oh, was it not? When, then? But I asked no question more, and withdrew to my couch to watch him complete his inspection of the chamber. He quartered every inch like a hunting-dog, peering into every corner, running his hands over the cold stone walls, even dipping cupped fingers into the waterfounts. At last it seemed that his curiosity was satisfied, for he sat down opposite me, on the pile of furs and bedding that had appeared at the same time as he himself, and which was apparently intended to serve as his place of repose, and looking straight at me he smiled.

"Not so ill as I had feared, though less good than I had hoped," he said, half to himself. "Any road, we are here, and we are together, and that alone is more than I had prayed so long should be..."

"*How* long?" I asked. "Have I been here such a span?"

Now he was no longer smiling. "Aye, braud, my sorrow for it... You have been two years in this place, and only a fortnight since did we learn that you were here at all."

When I made no immediate response to this rather staggering bit of information, he leaned forward, as if he were trying to reach me across that two-year chasm in his life and mine.

"Your name is Taliesin Glyndour ap Gwyddno," he said in a clear slow voice. "You are the youngest of the seven children of your father who was Lord of Cantred Gwaelod; your mother was Cathelin, a lady of Earth." He paused to see if this struck any strings, but I shook my head; it was as if he told me the tale of an utter stranger, or else a legend of old, and after a moment more he went on with a kind of desperate patience, as if he were trying not to fright me but knew also how greatly it mattered that he get through.

"You are my fostern since we were five years old, and you are wedded to my mother's daughter, Morguenna, with whom you have a son called Gerrans."

I stirred restively, but I could not say I had been touched

by an actual *memory*, just so, at the mention of my mate and son; yet somehow it did not seem so unfamiliar as before.

"What was I, then, before I came here? What was my calling? And how came I here at all? And where *is* 'here'?"

He seemed to choose his words now with even greater care. "You are the Chief Poet of Keltia. Folk sing your songs on all our worlds, and on worlds far among the stars, and for your great gifts they have named you Pen-bardd."

Taliesin Glyndour ap Gwyddno, Pen-bardd of Keltia. . . It sounded far too grand for the likes of me as I was here, in my well-worn (if clean) garb and untrimmed (if also clean) hair and beard. I pondered it all for a while, and he respected my silence; then I remembered that he had not answered my last questions—and did not appear disposed to do so just yet—so I asked another instead. "Who, then, are *you*?"

An expression I had no words for crossed his face, a vivid shading of love and ruefulness, sorrow and amusement, pity and care, hurt and patience and impatience all together. Then he did something extraordinary: He reached forward and pulled my recently rediscovered gold locket out from under my leinna. But when he spoke, his voice was even and his manner plain.

"I made this for you, braud, for one thing. But for the rest of it, I am Arthur Penarvon, son of Prince Amris Pendreic and the Lady Ygrawn Tregaron, and I am Ardrígh of Keltia, King of Kelts. I have come to this place— have allowed myself to be brought here—only to bring you out of it. This is the castle of Oeth-Anoeth, and it is my mother's other daughter, Marguessan, who has kept you here."

Well! This was a parcel of news and no mistaking, rather a lot to take in all at once, as you will doubtless agree. Yet what he had said carried the immediate bright ring of truth. He *was* the High King. He was Arthur, my brother by fostering and by marriage, and his sister—who was presumably also my wife's sister—had shut me up here, for reasons I could *not* imagine. . .

"It sounds—correct," I said at last, still thinking furiously. "A touch *unlikely*, I grant you, but correct—"

At that he laughed—*Arthur* laughed. "Now that sounds more my Tal-bach—but are you not wishful to know the rest of it?"

"Oh, perhaps just the tiniest bit curious; no doubt Your Majesty will tell me in royal good time."

Still grinning, he leaped up and began to pace the chamber, and—it is hard to explain—it was as if a shutter had blinked open inside my head, just for an instant, and I knew him. *Truly* knew him, *knew* I knew him: That pacing was a thing he often did when he needed to work things out, and very often I myself had been there to watch him do so. . . But then it was gone again, and I settled back expectantly on my pillows and some piled-up cloaks, hands behind my head, to listen.

"You had been sent," he began cautiously, "to a place I think I shall not speak of aloud just yet, for fear of who might be listening. There it was you had the truth of your mother, her name and arms and origins—for you had not known of her before—and also you were given a message, information of the most terrible purpose and consequence, to bring back to me and to the Ard-rían—"

"Gwennach." The name was out before I even knew I had spoken, and Arthur shot me a glance like a lasra.

"Oh aye, *her* you remember—" The tone was teasing, exasperated, mock-annoyed, but the delight in the dark eyes was very real; and so too the tiny gleam I saw of relief along with it. "Well then," he continued, "when you came to leave that place and return to us at Court, you simply—vanished."

I was enormously interested, and inverted my position, head to the bedfoot, flat on my front to listen in greater comfort.

"Where did I go?"

"We had not the smallest idea. You had departed, as I say, in good order and good time, and should have been back with us within hours. But you did not come, not then, not later, and we began to fear almost at once."

"What did you do?"

"We had another messenger in your stead—again, I think I will not name him, or her—who came to tell us what had befallen: that you were gone missing, and that your horses had been found wandering on the outskirts of Drum Wood. Now were we alarmed in good earnest, for Drum is many hundreds of miles from where you went missing. We mounted a search for you all across the planet, but there was no trace."

In some perverse way, I was much enjoying this. "And I was here?"

Arthur was still pacing. "Aye, but we did not yet know it. Even Morgan, your own wife, could not find you with the strongest of her magics, and she is the greatest sorcerer we now have. All she could learn was that you yet lived; no more, save that whoever held you also commanded mighty magics, and had a place to keep you proof against all comers."

At his mention of Morgan's name, an image of the woman in my dreams, the one with dark-gold hair and the serpent ring upon her hand and the urgency in her hazel eyes, flickered across my sight. *Ah, my Guenna, how could I not know you, of all folk else?*

"This place—Oeth-Anoeth, you name it—where is it?"

"On the planet Gwynedd, in the Old North, on the lands of Irian, who is Lord of Lleyn. He is wed to Marguessan—" Arthur spoke the name quietly enough, but there was an undernote of icy anger that caused me to look sharply up at him. No love lost here, then, between brother and *this* sister; therefore, I wondered—

I said, choosing my words with care, "I take it that Marguessan is not our favorite amongst our kin."

His laugh was grim. "Nay, not by a far cry. . . But Talynno, we have not the time to rehearse all our lives just now. Marguessan it is who put you here, and she too who has sent me to join you; and I do not think we have time to waste in doing aught not aimed to free us both."

My excitement and interest had been steadily growing as he spoke. "But what can we do? You have not said so, not in so many words, but clearly it is only by magic that Marguessan has got us here at all. I am no sorcerer; are you?"

His eternal credit that he did not laugh in my face; but

he did allow himself that faint grin again. All he said, though, was, "Enough of one to open the door on a crack for one who truly is. . . Listen, now—"

He spoke urgently and to the point, and when he had finished I nodded; what is more, I understood.

"You are beginning to remember," he said approvingly. "A Druid Merlynn made does not so easily forget—"

At that name I started violently; and if a shutter in my mind had been chinked before, now it was as if someone had set shoulder to it, had flung it back and light had come flooding in. He had the right of it: I was beginning to remember, and also I had not forgotten so much as I had feared.

"What shall we do?" I asked, with a certain deference to my manner, for now I also remembered rather better just how much of a sorcerer he was.

"We wait," he said with a grimness. "Marguessan will be along presently; until she arrives, let us try to fill in the gaps in your mind."

It turned out that I had been to visit the Sidhe-folk—those whose name Arthur would not speak, and as things turned out it was as well that he had not—had disappeared while en route back to Caerdroia, and had wandered in impenetrable forests for some weeks before Marguessan, who had engineered my going astray, finally reeled me in and set me down here in Oeth-Anoeth.

It has a fell sound even now: Oeth-Anoeth, a stronghold of the Marbh-draoi Edeyrn, up in that ancient quarter of the planet Gwynedd called the Old North. I reflected that it said much for Marguessan's connections, as well as her magical abilities, that she was able not only to arrange my long and involuntary rambles, but that she had managed to get me off the Throneworld entirely and here to Gwynedd, all without the best sensers in Keltia being any the wiser.

And here I had been, for nearly two years' time; though, as I told Arthur, it seemed less, and I had had to my knowing only that one interview with Marguessan, or the woman I assumed was Marguessan, at least. . .

"But why?" I asked at last. "Why me? You have said she and I had a long history of unfriendliness, but what use could I be to her here? Or was it merely to plague and fret you and Morgan and the rest of my dear ones? Just simple revenge, and no more?"

Arthur lifted eloquent eyebrows. "Revenge is never simple—you must know that by now—and almost never is it merely 'no more.' There is almost always more, and I think"—he had come silently to his feet, and had assumed a stance of combat-readiness; it was all done unthinking, beautiful to see, and I was most impressed—"I *think* she is about to answer your questions for herself."

I saw no reason to stir me from where I was ensconced— Arthur seemed to have that covered—so when Marguessan all at once was in the chamber with us, I was still lying comfortably on my pillowed bed.

She spared me the briefest of glances, then turned on Arthur a stare as straight and as potentially fatal as a spear. For his part, he seemed unconcerned, if wary, but I suddenly sensed peril, and very quietly began to shift position so that I might help, if help was called for.

Arthur, however, appeared to be, if not master of the situation exactly, at least in the position of one with much in reserve—a fidchell player whose pieces give no hint to his opponent of the sainn-an-rían to come. Encouraged obscurely by his air, I turned my attention again to my sister-in-law.

Now I looked at her closely, I wondered that I had not known her at once, no matter how she had contrived to cloud my mind. The eyes with their eerie ring of darkness round the blue—surely they should have stood unveiled even to *my* memory, however tampered with. When one encounters evil, looks it straight in the eye, as it were, one generally finds it fairly unforgettable ever after. . . I was beginning to remember more bits and pieces now: From incalculable depths of years swam up a sudden vivid darting image—Marguessan as a child of ten or twelve years, she and I in a great vaulted underground cavern full of gleaming technological tools and artificings, and she stirring water in a silver bowl, most *un*technological, and on one of

the viewscreens a picture of a doomed birlinn heading for
fanged rocks on a distant seacoast. . .

If Arthur was recalling any similar memory, he gave no
outward sign of it, merely watched his sister's face with
sharp and close attention, his stance easeful and his outer
mind a blank. Then, out of the ease and blankness, came a
question like the point of a sword.

"Where is the Cup, Marguessan? Where is Pair
Dadeni?"

She laughed, and her eyes somehow sharpened to match
his words, as if she had set tiny knives in there amidst the
black-rimmed blue.

"The Cup is not for you, Arthur."

"Nor is it for you," returned her brother without heat.
"As you well know. . . Or is it that, not being Ban-draoi,
you would *not* know?"

Now that stung, clearly, though I of course did not recall
just why; but I did wonder—why in all the hells was Artos
(I had remembered how I called him!) asking her about a
cup, of all things? I had heard how he spoke the word—*the*
Cup, as a proper name; not just any old mether, then. And
then suddenly I saw it, or rather I Saw it: the great hall in
Turusachan full of richly clad folk, and the glowing, blazing
quaich with pearls round its rim, spinning like a triskell
above our astonished heads and vanishing in a flash of fragrance and flame. The Cup indeed: one of the Four Chief
Treasures, the Hallows, one of that great and sacred
Quaternity upon which all Keltia was founded, a corner-
stone of our faith. And I looked again at Marguessan, and I
began to be afraid.

Though Arthur still seemed untroubled, at least outwardly, it was far otherwise with his sister: She had drawn
herself up like a hiss-cat at his barb, even her hair seeming
to crackle with spite.

"You throw my lack of Ban-draoi skills in my face," she
said calmly enough, "but you forget that when that training
was denied me, I found for myself another teacher in
magic—a teacher mighty enough to suppress all magic in
Keltia for twice a hundred years."

"Aye, and you learned well his lessons, I have no doubt;

as we all saw at Kerriwick." Arthur suddenly seemed beaten and weary, and Marguessan could not forbear a small smile.

"Taught me well enough so that I could bring both you here," she said with a touch of complacency, "and you will learn still better what he taught me, now that you *are* here." She glanced aside at me, then back at Arthur. "Be welcome in Oeth-Anoeth." And she was gone.

Arthur's seeming weariness went with her. "Come, Talyn, we have much to do, and time is not on our side in this one."

He was rummaging through the depths of the leather travelling backsack that had been slung across his shoulders when he arrived in the cell—Marguessan for some reason had not relieved him of it, or of whatever were its contents—and he soon found the object of his rummage, for he straightened with an air of pleased triumph.

"Do you remember this?"

I stared at the thing he held out on his open palm. It was a clear sphere of rock crystal, of the size of a small fruit; two bands of rune-incised silver circled it at poles and equator, as it were, and there was a soldered ring at the top through which was threaded a leather cord. Oddly enough, it seemed *most* familiar—

"Morgan," I said, though I did not know why, and Arthur smiled.

"Morgan indeed. Come sit by me."

I obeyed full eager, for the crystal drew me powerfully; once I was well settled on the pile of furs by his side, Arthur held up the stone before my eyes. It caught the vague blue light from outside, prisming it into shifting colors and sparkling motes, and I could not look away.

Arthur's voice came warm and golden to my ear, but that was all the contact I had with present reality: The stone seemed to pull me into it, and at the same time to pull me out of myself, or what for so long had passed for my self. The sensation was distinctly unpleasant, but often healing can be so, or feel so, even though we know very well it is for our own weal.

Any road, I saw naught before me but the light of the stone; I felt dizzy and sick, as if I were being spun about, blindfold, and though I could not comprehend Arthur's words, those words were the only thing I had to cling to, and I did.

It did not go on very long, perhaps not even so long as I have taken here to tell of it. Or perhaps it went on for hours, days even, time being what it was within these walls; I never found out. What I do remember is that all at once, without warning, Arthur ceased to speak, and the light went out, and I fell forward onto my knees, as if I had been suddenly set free from, well, chains. Not all shackles saw a smithy.

I took a deep uneven experimental breath. My mind was full again: over-full, brimming. There were names and faces and colors and memories and words, places and people, in a long vivid procession reaching back as far as I could see. And I *could* see, I could; and I almost sobbed, so empty had I been, to be now so full.

I raised my head and looked at Arthur. Slowly, tremulously, the same smile began to form on both our faces.

"Well," I said. "I am back."

CHAPTER 3

And not, it would seem, a moment too soon. . .
After Arthur and I had spent all the time we dared on the joy of a real reunion, we began to lay plans for escape from Oeth-Anoeth, before Marguessan could put in train other, less wholesome plans of her own. Even explanations and accounts of what had happened in my absence must wait a safer time, so I put my myriad questions aside and gave Arthur my whole attention. Indeed, there was no other choice.

He had different concerns. "Do you feel up to this now? We could perhaps afford to wait a day or two—"

I laughed grimly. "A day or two in this place might well be another year or three out there. . . Nay, I will make shift to follow and to help as best I can. Only tell me now, how is it with my lady? And my son?"

Arthur grinned. "You shall see. . . I know that you are feared and weary and troubled, Talyn, but it is best, truly, that we remove ourselves hence as soon as may be. Not only for what may happen here, but for what may happen out there." He gestured vaguely toward the high barred window.

I made no answer, but I was thinking hard. Whatever it was that he was so reluctant to tell me of just now, it must be terrible indeed, if only to know of it would so unsettle me that our escape might be put in peril. Still, it was no joy to work in ignorance— I shook myself. What was wrong with me? Arthur had arranged his own imprisonment, had allowed Marguessan to entrap him and throw him in here with me, all to bring me out with him; I was being a petulant ungrateful churl, at the very least. With my newly restored memory, I called to mind innumerable instances in our long shared history where one or the other of us had done likewise, for ourselves or for others of our Company. . .

"Is the Company still strong?" I heard myself asking in spite of my resolve and his, and he smiled even as he focused on his working.

"Aye, stronger than ever. We have even taken to formal assembly, each fullmoon; there is an old table in a disused Council-room of the palace, that Daronwy and Elenna thought would serve the purpose."

For some reason the image caught my bard's fancy. "A table? What of rank and precedence? The seating arrangements—"

Despite his fears and preoccupation with graver concerns, Arthur laughed aloud with real amusement. "Raighne, whose table and Council-room those once were, must have had much the same kind of mind as you. . . Nay, the table is shaped like the rim of a wain-wheel," he continued with exaggerated teasing exactitude, "open in the middle, and the chairs are ranged in a triple row along its edge. So there is no head to this particular table; no assigned places even, save one alone. Nay, not for Gweniver or for me, even, and thus all are equal at the Companions' table. But we can discuss furniture another time, Talyn; now we must get ourselves away from here, and swiftly too."

"Well, aye; but how? There is no door to work on, as you did in Kerriwick, as I am sure you have noted; or even that time in the Nantosvelta, when Guenna—" I broke off and stared at him. "That is the trick you plan to try here, not so?"

"Well, as you say, there is no door of the more usual sort," said Arthur reasonably. "We have seen how Marguessan comes and goes, how she put us here in the first place. We must try to leave by the same road she uses."

Magic, then; why was I not surprised? I left off questioning, and joined Arthur where he sat cross-legged on the floor in the center of the cell. He had placed a quaich of freshly drawn water to his left, had poured a small quantity of salt into my pottery food-dish and put it on his right; above these and in the center, between us, he set now the crystal sphere. He motioned me to follow his lead, whatever he might do; my Druid training having come back to me with the rest of my memories, I felt an inward pride and confidence to know that I could help, and prepared myself to do so.

The one worry I had not dared voice, neither inwardly to me nor aloud to Arthur, nevertheless naggled at my newfound faith and sureness: What *of* Marguessan? She had been clever enough and skilled enough to get us here and keep us here; surely she would sense any attempt to escape, particularly if it were done by means of magic—and crossics to cribbins she would not be sitting back with her feet up while it went on without her. . . I set my fears firmly aside. Uncertainty is a great killer of spells, and this enterprise had already enough elements of chanciness that my faintheart doubts might cause it to perish before ever it had been fairly begun. No more.

And, as I thought so, I felt almost as if a dammed passage had been made clear again, as if a river choked by ice had all at once been unblocked, so that the torrent might once more run free. As I watched Arthur begin the working in earnest, and myself began to feed power and support to him, I heard Morgan's voice come clear to me, and I was glad. She it was who was doing the real work here; Arthur and I were merely vehicles, conduits of her power to where it was needed, supporters of her effort with the mere fact of our being and the raw strength we could lend her. Our success, and hers, would depend largely on how skilled Arthur and I were at being so used, how well we could subdue our own selves and wills and skills and let hers, so boundlessly greater, move through us.

Now that I knew more or less what was toward, I was happier, and I settled myself to Arthur's acts and Morgan's might. And, I have to say, it very nearly worked: The spell Morgan had sent in the stone, the clach, the course that

Arthur and I had prepared for her to send in upon, it was
all very nearly enough. As we sat there, the walls around us
began to shimmer and tremble and dissolve away, and I felt
Morgan's presence in the chamber. Looking over Arthur's
shoulder, I could see hallways beyond, and dimly glimpse
spaces that seemed to be rooms and chambers in Oeth-
Anoeth's further reaches. It would take only a little more
time, a few more touches upon Marguessan's evil web, and
we would be free. . .

But this was Marguessan on her home ground, in her
master's stronghold, and it was not to be so simple after all:
All at once there came a shudder beneath us, as if an earthshake had broken loose under the castle. The walls that had
been fading became solid again, and across the chamber the
water of the stone fountain sloshed wildly in its basin.

I threw a glance of pure terror at Arthur, all the time trying even in my panic not to break the link, not to lose touch
with Morgan's presence and power.

"It is Marguessan," murmured Arthur, though he surely
did not have to tell me, and he never for one instant withdrew his attention from the focus of the stone and its blazing blue light. "She has twigged what we are attempting—"

I hardly dared breathe. "And can she prevent it?"

"Maybe, though I think not entirely. Any road, we have
other help as, for all her boasts of Edeyrn, she does not."

With an effort almost physical, as if the very air resisted
him, Arthur straightened his shoulders and lowered his
hands, resting his wrists upon his knees. I followed suit; and,
closing my eyes the better to order my own attention, I suddenly saw with a warm incredulous shock of emotion and
recognition a vision before my inner sight. *Merlynn...?* Then
a flare of doubt: Was it rather Edeyrn? Nay, surely it was my
Merlynn, my Ailithir, our beloved teacher and friend and
guide! His aspect was not as we had known in life, but as I
had last seen him: a beautiful white-haired, white-bearded
man of years, asleep, peaceful, yet also somehow awake and
strong, and aware of us and our need, sending of that
strength to us as we struggled here against Marguessan,
whom he had ever coldly loathed. One thing only differed
from my last sight of him, under the hill in Dún Aengus of

the Sidhe: He lay now upon a bed of gold, not within the crystal tree in which Edeyrn had entrapped and entombed him at the fight of Nandruidion; and yet the crystal tree was also somehow there. . .

I blinked and shook my head to clear it. *Was* it Merlynn, after all? Now the sleeping countenance bore a look of Uthyr Ard-rígh, or rather Uthyr as he might have looked, had he been given to live out his span, Uthyr in the hale old age he had never reached. Or was it in truth some other—Amris, Leowyn, Gorlas, Gwyddno—all these together, or some king or lord I knew not yet?

Without warning the vision faded, and the same instant that it fled I felt Marguessan's angry force thrown back for good and all. The walls thinned to vanishment yet again, and this time they stayed vanished; the floor had ceased to rock, was steady and firm beneath our feet. I looked at Arthur, and he nodded answer.

"Get your harp and cloak, go and do not look back for me. I promise I will be close upon your heels."

I heard the confidence in his voice and trusted unquestioningly. Of course he had to follow me out, he had to close down the magic: to break the link, scatter the salt, spill the water, dim the light of the stone. . . I dived across the couch and seized Frame of Harmony in its travelling bag. Coming onto my feet again, I stooped to catch up Arthur's cloak and my own, his leather backsack, a few oddments that might come in handy after—

And as my hand closed on a small pouch of my own that had lain unnoted in a corner of the chamber, I startled to feel through the soft green leather the unmistakable outline and weight of a blade. Had I been weaponed all the time I had been here and known it not? It would seem so; but now was not the time for further investigation, and with all my strength and hope, a prayer to the Goddess on my lips and trust in Morgan in my heart, I flung myself through the wall of the cell as if it had been mere air.

And so in fact it was: Without even the shock of contact I found myself in a broad dim corridor that ended in a door a long way off. Moments later, Arthur was beside me, unruffled if perhaps a touch grim; behind us, the cell seemed to contract into darkness, folding in upon itself in a way my waking mind could not understand. But some other, deeper sense understood very well indeed, and I was away at once, following Arthur as he raced down the hallway to the door at the distant end.

Though that door, when we reached it, proved to be a stout thick one of ancient findruinna-strapped oak, it had neither lock nor bolt to it; Arthur, raising his brows at the apparent ease of it, raised the latch also, and we stepped through—into what?

At once the source and origin of that strange blue light that had seeped in through my window were apparent: No sun, no sky, no faha or court, no distant skyline or bordering forest were visible to us as we stood there. Oh, the castle was real enough behind us—I laid a hand on its rough mossy stones just to be certain—but before us and above us was naught but mist. A wall of sorcerous vapor, a fence of fog, a mist-hedge enveloped all that should have been seen, and I drew a steadying breath of even such freedom as this, and glanced at Arthur. For there is at life's first end a border we all must pass—in some faiths a river, in others a wall of stones or gates of pearl or gold; in ours a hedge of mist—before the great journey may begin. Was this where our escape had brought us? If so, well enough; I only wished to know.

Arthur saw my question and doubt. "Nay, not yet," he said with a smile, half to himself, half to me—or perhaps to someone else I could not see. Then he lifted his arm, and blue fire shot from the crystal sphere he held in his right hand.

The flash of light must have been a prearranged signal of sorts, for no sooner had its lancing rays pierced the fog than came to my straining ears the sound of a horn. Not Gwyn's horn, that horn of the Sidhe I knew so well, fearing and loving it together; but an earthly horn, its sound no less lovely or welcome for all that.

And with the horn's cry the mist began to break. It shivered and tattered, it fell away in rags, revealing what it had heretofore cloaked: a faha, then an orchard full of flowering apple trees, stretching away before us, and far in the distance a range of blue hills. A wall ran randomly in front of the trees, enclosing the green grassy space of the faha; it was built of the same gray stone as the castle—

I looked over my shoulder and leaped back in astonishment, for the castle that had been at our backs was as vanished as the mist. We stood now on a grass-covered knoll, unmarked by stone or ditch, nothing to show that a castle had ever been there. Oeth-Anoeth had simply—ceased to be; perhaps it had gone back to whatever place it inhabited when its mistress did not wish it discovered, and perhaps that too was why I had not been found for so long a time. My whereabouts had not been discovered because none could discover the place where I was. . . But then, where had it, and I, *been?* What 'there' had we both dwelled in?

I discovered I did not really wish to know the answer to that, and turned again to Arthur, who had never moved. He did not meet my glance, but pointed, directing my gaze to one side of the green-grassed faha, before the walls and the trees began.

I looked and gasped: Marguessan was seated in a chair of solid gold, her arms along its arms, upon her head a golden fillet. She was not looking at us, but at a gate in the faha wall, broad and high enough to admit a mounted rider. And beyond the gate—

I drew back a little, appalled and yet not at all surprised. Arthur, it seemed, had seen already, or perhaps he had been made to see earlier still, on his arrival at Oeth-Anoeth. . .

In amongst the trees of the orchard, half-veiled by the foam-white apple-blossoms along the boughs, were set smooth stakes of peeled gray wood, each of the thickness of a woman's arm and of the height of a tall man; and on each of those stakes was impaled a human head. I could not look to see detail, not more than a quick brief glance through lowered lids, but it seemed that there were men and women both in that savage orchard. Some heads were helmed, some bare under the sun, some with hair streaming, some with Fian war-braids; some all but skulls, some freshly mounted. . .

When I had finished being as sick as I felt I could reasonably be at this particular moment, I stepped forward again to stand at Arthur's side. Again the horn sounded from beyond the faha wall, and this time Marguessan raised her hand. When she lowered it, the gate in the wall was open to admit a rider on a blood-bay warhorse. Both rider and mount were full armed and caparisoned for combat; their armor gleamed dull gold in the newly revealed sunlight. But I did not recognize the horse, and the rider's helm was closed; I could not see the face.

The rider paid no heed to either Marguessan or ourselves, but rode at a slow parade trot to one end of the faha and turned, drawing to a halt in combat stance. I looked round for the opponent he obviously expected, but saw no one. Then Marguessan raised her hand again, and another rider appeared in the gate.

He wore silver armor, and was mounted on a tall, powerfully built black horse whose tail swept the ground; I saw a small gold horn fastened to the saddle roll just by his left knee. He paused as if to survey the scene—unlike the first knight, this one seemed to look long on Arthur and on me, but the silver beaver was down, and I could not say for sure—then rode in, turning to the opposite end of the faha from the warrior on the bay.

I opened my mouth as if to speak, for somehow it seemed that I *knew* this second knight, this one who rode the black horse; there was something familiar about him, the set of his shoulders, his seat on the horse, his bearing— But Arthur closed iron fingers upon my arm, and I closed my mouth.

But an unspoken signal had apparently passed between the two knights, and also between Arthur and Marguessan, for he nodded, and she lifted her hand a third time; when she let it fall, the two horses, the blood-colored and the black, surged toward each other with a sound of thunder.

It was not a joust, as I understand the single combat is often practiced on other worlds, and as I later came to read in my mother's books and journals was once the custom on Earth her homeworld. Rather it was a swordfight ahorse, and the chargers used in such contests are trained as long and as carefully as their masters, for they are equal partners with their riders in the fight.

They met with a clash of blades, the horses going up on their hind legs with a scream like to that of sword against sword. Marguessan's champion—for so he was, the rider on the blood-bay horse—won the first exchange, and as they drew off to make another run I saw that the knight in the silver armor, *our* champion, had taken a wound in the arm.

"He is hurt," I said to Arthur, all unnecessarily, and Arthur nodded.

"The horse will make up for it," was all he said, for just then the fighters spurred forward to engage again. Our eyes went at once to the black charger, who seemed to know just what weakness his rider now labored under, for he backed and danced and reared so that it seemed the knight on his back was wielded by him like a blade, the rider merely a means to hold the sword so that the horse itself could fight the opponent charger.

And indeed the horse made up his rider's lack, and more beside, for at the end of this exchange it was the gold-armored knight who drooped and sagged in his saddle. Even from where Arthur and I stood, we could see blood running down the gleaming breastplate, and another stream of bright red issuing from the cuissed leg above the boot-top.

The black's rider seemed to know he now held the mastery, and the horse knew too, for barely had they wheeled this time before they were charging again. This time the gold knight was theirs; even the bay's skill could not save him, and as the other struck, he went top-for-toe over his horse's shoulder, to lie very still upon the ground.

Marguessan had watched the combat with her face impassive, only her hands clenching and unclenching upon the dragon's-head armrests giving evidence of her state of mind. When the gold knight fell to the earth of the faha, and lay unmoving, Marguessan slowly rose up out of her chair, and turned her face to Arthur.

Astoundingly, she was laughing. But it was not mirth that moved her.

"Brother, to you!" she cried in a hawk's voice. "This time, to you! Glyndour, farewell! I enjoyed your guesting with me, if you did not—greet my sister from me, and tell her she fought well today. But her teacher has yet to stand against mine; tell her that too." She lifted her arm in salute to the rider on the black horse. "Kinsman, to you! So it can be, when dragon fights dragon—but you will yet follow wandering fires!"

She raised both arms above her head, palms flat and facing, fingertips just barely joined. Arthur made one uncontrollable move forward, the black horse half-reared, from the saddle the silver knight winded his horn yet a third time— and Marguessan was gone. Gone too the fallen knight, the bright bay stallion, the gold chair, the gray wall, even the terrible orchard and its trees that bore the ghastly fruit of Marguessan's champion's other, more successful combats. All had vanished even as the castle Oeth-Anoeth, leaving only the clean grass underfoot and the distant skylined mountains.

And ourselves, of course. . . I felt myself all over, gave Arthur a long hard scan—I felt I could not be too careful, the way things changed and shifted around here—and then turned with him to face the oncoming rider on the black horse.

I knew him before he had unlaced the silver helm; said his name with love and pride.

"Gerrans. My son."

Geraint Pendreic ac Glyndour ap Taliesin looked down at me out of Morguenna Pendreic's eyes. I had not seen my son for two years, true enough, and before that not for another year more: He had been from home, training with the Fianna that was his first love and for which he had the greatest talent. He was not yet of age, being some years short of his full majority; but I saw with pride and pleasure that he had grown into a tall, lithe, well-made young man, who this day had surely done full credit to his training and his bloodline.

And speaking of blood. . . "Are you badly hurt?" I asked with swift paternal concern. "Shall I help you down? Shall we do a healing rann? Can you—"

Gerrans laughed and leaped down from the saddle. "I am well enough, athra, now that you are back with us!" He leaned into my embrace, a fervent bear-hug of love and relief, and, on my part, gratitude for both my deliverance and his own safety; then he broke off and looked at his uncle the High King, who stood indulgently by.

He bowed formally to Arthur, who bent his head in equally formal acknowledgment.

"I have been fighting against myself, Lord," said Gerrans then.

"Then thou hast conquered thyself," came Arthur's calm reply, in the stately High Gaeloch, and I wondered at the sudden formality that chilled the moment.

But just as swiftly the frost was gone, and Gerrans leading his splendid black horse went down the grassy slope with me on one side and Arthur on the other, to where the wall had been that bounded the faha, and beyond to where the evil trees had stood—and perhaps still did, in some other realm of the real.

To my surprise, four horses waited there for us, two patient pack beasts and two riding horses fully tacked, a little nervous and lonely, and glad to see us. Gerrans gave each of us a leg up—my bones and sinews, two years out of the saddle, would be howling their protest long before night-fall—then stripped off all but the minimum of armor and vaulted up again upon the black.

As we rode away, I carefully refrained from backward glances, and said no word to either of my companions. There would be time enough for talking, to catch up on the events that had been in Keltia in my absence; for the moment it was enough to know that I was free, and that Morgan my lady and Geraint my son and Arthur my brother had been the means of my deliverance. And Marguessan and the gold knight were gone; that, also, was enough for my satisfaction as I rode.

CHAPTER 4

"Well, they are not gone, just so," Arthur had said. "But for the moment, and for our purposes, they are gone enough. We will find out where in good time."

But that was earlier; now it was just before sunset on the day of my liberation. We had ridden at an easy pace away from Oeth-Anoeth—or where Oeth-Anoeth had been—and were now well out of Marguessan's lands into a rolling country of hills and open chases and cleared woods. Across ploughed fields there were just visible the lights of a substantial farmstead beginning to glow through the blue dusk. We could have claimed hospitality there with perfect right had we been even the simplest and humblest of travellers, and they who dwelt there would have been glad to entertain us. As it was, the High King, his matebrother and his nephew would have been given the warmest and most lavish of welcomes, the neighbors called in from several farms around— But by tacit agreement we turned our horses' heads from the farmlands and made our camp under a roof of red oak leaves and heavy maple boughs, in a stand of ancient trees in a small hollow sheltered from the wind.

As we pottered happily about, making safe and soft our campsite, preparing a hot supper, caring first of all for our horses' needs, I kept unbroken the silence I had maintained for the greater part of that unsettling day. Oh, not for ill humor or anything like; but as the three of us had wished and needed to keep ourselves *to* ourselves just now, so I wished and needed to keep myself to myself a little longer, apart if not away from my fostern and my son.

There was much that I wished to say to them, truly, and much more that I wished to hear them say to me; but I had been two years in my own sole company, all but the last few hours of it in ignorance even of my own identity, and I needed a while longer to grow used to myself and others— even dearly loved others—once again. Needed, too, time to make real to my soul and senses the fact that I was free again, was me again; and to their credit, the other two saw this and did not press.

But they were not refraining from cheerful speech between themselves, and this too helped me: Gerrans had ever enjoyed a loving bond with his royal uncle, and for his part Artos had dealt with him as if he had been more son than nephew. I had ever been delighted by their closeness, as was Morgan; considering the full slate of young relations on the Pendreic side consisted of Gerrans and Marguessan's three brats—Mordryth, the eldest; a lass called Galeron, whom I had ever held to be a sly-eyed piece of goods; and the youngest, a lad named Gwain after his grandsir, Darowen Ard-rían's consort, and of whom we as yet knew but little—I was thrilled that the High King and my son were so fond of each other.

So Arthur and Gerrans chatted casually and amiably as they readied our nightmeal, and I listened contentedly with half an ear, as it might be to a running stream, and took comfort in the sheer normalcy of the sound.

We were just finishing our supper of grilled beef and roasted buttered framachs and toasted bread—one of my favorite bills of outdoor fare, the savor of the meat and the framachs and the flavor of the woodfire in both are incomparable—and were washing it down with cool cider when Arthur, answering a query of Gerrans's, caused me by his words to snort cider up my nose in utter and complete 'stonishment. When I had finished choking and coughing and wiping cider from my chin, I turned to stare at Arthur.

"A *son!?* Since what time? Why did you not tell me? Is Gwennach—"

Arthur laughed and filled my mether where I had let it fall in my excitement. "There were somewhat more pressing things for us to deal with and discuss than even your new status as uncle," he said, still smiling. "But aye indeed, there is now a new Tanist for Keltia, Arawn by name, and he will be a full moonyear old this very week. He and Gweniver are both well and happy, and the folk are most pleased. So too his halfsister and her mother, I might add."

"I daresay, I do daresay." I grinned like an idiot for a few moments more. "What else have I missed out on whilst Marguessan's hospitality ruled my life?"

"Well, you are named godfather to the Prince, needless to tell; Grehan stood proxy for you with Morgan, and she herself is goddessmother, so that keeps it all nicely in the kindred."

I saluted him with the mether, and we drank a belated toast to my new nephew and his mother. Arawn. A likely name, if perhaps but little used heretofore in the House of Dôn; in the bardic speech it means 'Lord of the Summer Stars,' and is the name of one of the mightier deities in our Keltic pantheon. Arawn Ard-rígh: It would sound most fine when the time at last came for it. Good that Arthur and Gweniver had an heir at last; good too that they had gotten him in love, for they had not always had a match of the heart. And best of all, it meant that Marguessan was no longer Tanista presumptive, and her brat Mordryth was thrust yet another place farther from the Throne of Scone—

"Arawn Amris Taliesin Gorlas, to give my new cousin his full due," said Gerrans, and I felt tears sting my eyes at the redoubled honor my beloved friends had done me. It was a real honor, too, not just a sop to convention and ties of blood; in Keltia those who stand godparents to a child have specific obligations and rights and privileges with respect to their ward. They have legal standing, to be consulted in major decisions regarding the child and its schooling and fosterage and career and eventual marriage or liaison; often the child will make use of them as surrogate parents, or even as allies against its parents when circumstances may require.

Though of course a royal heir-apparent will have many to look to in time of need, still it will be to goddessmother and godsfather that any child will turn all life long, and I was deeply and humbly happy. Happy too for that the boy bore also Gorlas's name; but then Arthur had ever paid attention to details another might have missed.

I looked across the fire at my own son—who was, as it happened, gods'-child himself to Arthur and Gweniver. Gerrans, unaware of my covert study, was industriously and skillfully mending one of Arthur's stirrup leathers, broken in the afternoon's ride. His arm that had been injured in the combat was healed now, lightly padded against the soreness that would be in it for a day or two. Otherwise he was hale and whole and seemed happy, and I beheld him with a strange new pride. He was dark-haired like me, hazel-eyed like his mother, with a small gap between his front teeth that gave him the most engaging grin imaginable. As I said earlier, his aptitude, quite unlike my own, was clearly for soldiery, and already the Fianna had tagged him for officer placing. As for other talents, so far both Guenna's gifts and my own had shown utterly lacking in him; a more literal-minded, unmagical person, seemingly, had never been born in Keltia. But if that had been cause in time past for some wistful or indeed wishful moments, on my part or Morgan's or his, the future would show different, to Keltia and to worlds beyond. . .

"Now we shall speak of that which we have not yet spoken of," I heard myself calmly pronouncing, in the bard's voice of command, and I felt Arthur's surprise as well as Gerrans's.

But the King obeyed me equably enough, first smooring the fire, then settling back upon his sleeping furs and padding his saddle with his cloak to serve as pillow, and began the whole terrible tale. . .

It seemed that I had been captured by Marguessan almost as soon as I had ridden out of Glenshee and long before I reached Methven, the market town from which my trek to the faerie lands had begun. Perhaps she had had spies about, perhaps it was mere mischance; but any road, I was taken and magically transported by her to Drum Wood, where after my monthlong stay beneath the hollow hill I had wandered houseless and nearly foodless and just about witless for a full month more, until I was exhausted and spent in body and mind and spirit, defenseless before her. Since none yet knew I was kidnapped, rumor of my disappearance did not reach Caerdroia until well after Marguessan had whisked me off the Throneworld and brought me in secret here to Gwynedd, where in the rough lonely lands of the Old North, her lord, Irian Locryn, had kept me close until she immured me in Oeth-Anoeth. And there I had been kept, myself not even knowing my own plight, for a full two years... I stared bleakly into the flames, but said nothing.

"We do not know just when she had you brought to Oeth-Anoeth," said Arthur, divining my thought as he usually did. "But Oeth-Anoeth having been one of Edeyrn Marbh-draoi's magical strongholds, it was many months before even Morgan's magic could find you, and longer still before we could mount a rescue."

"But how then did you learn where I was, or even that I had been taken at all?" I asked quietly, and drank some more cider, for I found myself shivering a little. Gerrans saw, and put his arm round my shoulders, but Arthur continued the tale as if he did not see this, though of course he did full well.

"Gwyn told us," he said simply. "The Prince of the Sidhe came to Caerdroia to tell us you had left Glenshee safely, but had not come safe away. By then, of course, we knew that you went missing, but no real word had come until Gwyn brought it."

I stared at him, then into the fire, caught by the picture: Gwyn son of Nudd at Caerdroia! To the best of my knowing, the Shining Folk had not been seen in the streets of the Crown City for centuries...

"Not since Edeyrn, that is certain," said Gerrans, who had been following my thought. "But before that? Uncle? Do you know?"

"Centuries since," said Arthur. "Athyn Anfa was a great friend to the Shining Folk, and they loved her dearly, and came often to guest with her and Morric her lord; but after their time less often, and in these latter days not at all. It was a great honor, and a thing of great dread, for Gwyn to come so—and the folk are still not sure what to make of it."

"Nay, not even those who had been at Nandruidion, and seen the faerie rade," put in Gerrans eagerly. "I have only heard of that, of course, and as you have sung, athra, and as my mother has told me, but *this*—"

Arthur smiled at him. "Even for one who *has* been beneath the hill, my sisterson, let me tell you, it was a daunting moment to see Gwyn son of Nudd ride through the Wolf Gate and up to Turusachan."

I wanted now every tiniest detail, of course, furious and jealous beyond *belief* that I had not been there to see it myself, forgetful in that moment that of course if I *had* been there, then Gwyn would not have. . .

"Came he alone? Was he attended? What did he wear? Did he ride his white stallion? Who—"

"Peace a moment!" Gerrans was laughing. "He had with him two others, two only. Birogue of the Mountain, whom you know, tasyk, and the other—" Gerrans turned abruptly to Arthur, conscious of having trodden upon the tale, but Arthur only grinned and gestured him to continue. I was merely charmed that Gerrans in his excitement had called me by the childname 'tasyk'. . .

"Well then," he began again, "the other was a lord of the Sidhe, by name Allyn son of Midna. Gwyn rode in the center, upon a great white stallion with mane and tail of gold; and the Lady Birogue, who was my mother's teacher at Collimare, *you* know, rode on his right—her horse was black, with a white star and snip on his muzzle. And the Lord Allyn was on the Prince Gwyn's left hand, on a horse the color of old bronze. They were all three of them cloaked in gray, and the horses bore neither saddle nor bridle, only jewelled and plumed headstalls, and martingale breastplates with silver and opals for adornment."

I was impressed; for one supposedly not bardically gifted, Gerrans was making a fine job of painting the scene.

"And then?"

"Gwyn and his folk would not come within walls," said Arthur, "but waited ahorse in the Great Square, and Gweniver and I ran out at once to him. I say 'ran,' and we did, I promise you! Then Gwyn told us what had befallen: that Marguessan had taken you, though he did not tell us how he knew that. Or would not—any road, he told us where to find your horses, and then he gave us the message he had given you to deliver concerning the Cup."

I went suddenly cold and still. In my prisonment, I had been made to forget that direst and most desperate of messages, and in the few hours of my new freedom I had to my shame and sorrow not thought of it once, all my mind being filled with longing for my Morgan, my life back again. . .

"Marguessan has taken it," I said dully. "So Gwyn said—"

Arthur nodded. "Aye, but Nudd his father thinks there is more to it. What, he knows not, or tells not; but Marguessan is preparing some blackest working, of that there is no doubt. And since the Cup would never permit itself to be used so—"

"But it has been *two years missing!*" I cried out in anguish. "Two years unsought—"

"Not altogether so," said Gerrans to soothe me. "Gwyn told us how you were charged to tell the Ard-rían that she must lead a quest for the holy Cup, and that women and men of art should assist her. Companies were sent out, but—"

"But it seemed that whilst Marguessan had you prisoned, any quest was doomed to failure. Though I admit it took us all a while to puzzle that out," added Arthur gloomily. "And lives were lost, and much time, and all the while healing has been slowly leaching from the land, since the Cup is gone from us."

"Nay, we healed Gerrans's arm only this afternoon!" I protested. "We had sufficient magic to do that—"

"Oh aye; and only thank the Goddess he was not more sorely hurt," said Arthur. "For any much graver wound we could *not* have healed. . . All of us have seen it so these two years now. And unless we find the Cup, in time *all* healing will be gone from Keltia, and we will be as poor primitive worlds who have not earned or learned that sacred gift."

But that had reminded me of something. . . "What then of the other knight, the one Gerrans fought and vanquished?

He was hurt badly, if I miss not my guess. What fate must be his tonight?"

Arthur looked uncomfortable, and he and Gerrans exchanged glances before he spoke again.

"Have you not guessed who that knight was?"

I shook my head. "Some champion of Marguessan's, I had thought." Then, as I suddenly recalled a thing Marguessan had said in the faha, and another thing Arthur had said, after, to Gerrans. . .

"It was—it was *Mordryth?*"

Their silence confirmed it, and I thought about it for a moment or two. Mordryth, Marguessan's son; Arthur's nephew, Morgan's nephew, Gerrans's cousin. . .

"No wonder she said dragon fought dragon," I remarked then. "It was Pendreic against Pendreic today—"

"Fighting against myself," said Gerrans somberly, "or at the least against my own blood and House. I could wish. . . well, no matter now. It is done."

"Marguessan will see to his healing, wherever it is she has betaken them both," said Arthur, who was drawing little patterns in the dirt around the fire with the handle of his sgian. Gerrans marked them not, but I did, and was keeping a close eye on them; if Arthur thought we needed runes of warding, he must surely have good cause to think so. . .

"With the *Cup?*" I asked aghast. "Does she then have it, in truth? How did she get it, how was it taken from Dún Aengus?" I tried to keep despair out of my voice, but I do not think I was successful.

"As Gwyn told you, aye and nay. As to how she came by it, we do not know, and if the Sidhe know, they have not told us. But that is where Nudd's fear comes into it: The Cup will not allow itself to be harmed, or to work harm, but it is powerless to prevent its own power from being turned. The thing Nudd fears is the thing your lady fears, and she being the sorceress she is, she most rightly fears it. . ."

I closed my eyes briefly, opened them and looked straight at Arthur. "And that would be?"

His voice was hushed; the wind died as he spoke, even the trees above us seemed to bend to hear him.

"She fears Marguessan is creating a Black Graal."

The fire went out in front of my eyes, and I believe I nearly fainted away right there; it felt that the earth heaved in protest beneath me—certain it was my guts had writhed and knotted, though I did manage to keep my supper where it did me most good. After a while I sat up, running a hand over my face which was clammy and cool, and in that moment probably white as milk.

A Black Graal, a Cup of darkness. . . The mere idea was an abomination, a filth, a pollution and defilement, an uncleanness and a stench out of the seventh hell; but in the calmness to which I now forced myself, I had to admit that the possibility was no new one. For all things and persons of power, there are things and persons of equal and opposite power—for every Morgan, a Marguessan; for every Merlynn or Gwyn, an Edeyrn. Whether or not those things and persons of darkness ever come into ascendancy, or even existence, on this plane is a matter for the Pheryllt, or for the Reverend Mothers of the Ban-draoi, to debate in their conclaves.

But as above, so below; as without, so within; as the Light, so the Dark. It is not the good in a sacred thing that makes it holy, it is the power. And power can be used for good or for ill, as we have all by now seen. If no Black Graal yet existed in our Keltia, be very sure it has existed since time began, on the inner planes or in a Keltia that is not the one we know. And if Marguessan had found at last a way to bring it through to our world. . .

"What would happen, do you think?" I asked at last. "If Marguessan succeeds?"

Arthur shook his head, and his eyes were haunted. "No one knows for sure. Even the Pheryllt disagree, and the Reverend Mothers. . . Morgan believes that the Graal and its opposite cannot exist in the same plane at the same time, that one must surely destroy the other. In such a plight, Keltia itself would be destroyed; for we cannot allow the Dark such purchase, such a foothold in our Light."

"We as Druids are not bound to destroy the Dark," I reminded him gravely, "but to take the evil from it, to restore it to the balance it had once at the Beginning, before the evil came. This is the charge of Kelu to all those who are of the spirit; and until we come to that, without Darkness there can *be* no Light."

"Oh, do not quote Merlynn Llwyd at *me,* Glyndour!" snapped Arthur, and I knew by that very snap just how deeply frightened he was at the prospect before us. "That is as I have said a thing for the highest of the priestesses and priests to work out; I am only Ard-rígh, I can do only what I can do."

"And that is, uncle?" asked Gerrans, who had been listening in silence all this while, mouth well agape.

"To keep Keltia while the Ard-rían goes on quest for all our lives. No more, but also no less." Arthur laughed suddenly. "Gwennach kept it well enough for me when I went off reiving, Talyn, as you will recall; now it is my turn, and Goddess only grant I do as fine a job."

With that, we seemed to be finished for the night. I was weary past all imaginings; Gerrans too, from his wound and his exertions—even Arthur seemed drained, though that was no surprise, considering the magical work he had done that day. Yet of that we had not even spoken, nor of Morgan; and she was the one who had been general of all which this day had seen. But I felt her presence now, as indeed I had felt it all through my days in Oeth-Anoeth, though I had been too deeply ensorcelled by Marguessan's evil tricks to know it save in dreams; and as I snuggled down into my furs and groundleathers I let her image form before my eyes against the banked fire. . .

"Oh, Talyn," came Arthur's sleepy voice from the other side of the flames, "I was forgetting. . . Gwyn left somewhat for you in Gweniver's keeping: things that belonged to your mother. You left Dún Aengus in such haste he had no time to give you them, and they are very precious, and you should have them—"

I had sat up again, sleep and even Morgan momentarily forgotten. "*That* is what I could not puzzle out! In the cell at Oeth-Anoeth you spoke my mother's name to me— Cathelin—you even knew she was of Earth. But I only learned that myself at Dún Aengus! I had not yet reached Caerdroia to tell you; how could you know?"

"Truly," said Arthur, and wonder was back in his voice.

"Gwyn told us himself, when he came to Turusachan and gave us your message, and gave Gweniver your mother's gear; and Birogue confirmed it. It is a mighty thing, not so? To know that your own mother came from Earth, was a Terran lady by her bloodline and her birth. . ."

I was silent again. Truth be told, I had always envied Arthur a little the glamor of his parentage: to be the child of the Lady Ygrawn and the Prince Amris Pendreic. Indeed, I had often thought it a little like being the offspring of gods, or at least of the Shining Ones. Now it seemed that I myself had a parentage equally glamorous: My father, Gwyddno, had gone to Earth seeking help for Keltia, and had come away, not with that sought help, for Earth had desperations of her own just then, but with a bride—that fair brave lady, who went with him for love and who would one day give birth to me among stars she never dreamed of. . .

"She left you *books,* athra!" That was Gerrans, a thrill in his voice that I had not heard there since he was a little lad given a garron for his birthday. But he had ever been mad for books. . . "We have not looked, but Gwyn said there were all her writings—songs, poems, journals from Earth— and she my own grandmother!"

"And you shall read them and share all her legacy, amhic," I promised; though as bard I was myself scarce less thrilled than as Cathelin's son, or indeed than my own. "We shall read them together, you and your mother and I, and we shall know—"

But precisely what we would know must wait its proper time; just now, sleep was the only knowing, or rather unknowing, I wished for. I turned over again and settled down; but something dug sharply into my ribs, and with a swart oath—was I *never* going to get any sleep this night?—I fossicked through the folds of saddlecloth and sleeping-fur until I found the offending point.

It was protruding from the mouth of the green leather pouch I had so hastily snatched up from the floor of my cell in Oeth-Anoeth and had as swiftly forgotten. In the heat of our escape I had not paused to examine the bag's contents, and due to my mindclouding I had never even noticed it while still captive. But I had surely noted it now.

I did not break the seal on the drawstrings, but pulled on the pointy thing until it came out into my hand, and gasped aloud. Arthur and Gerrans, better warriors than I, both surged upright, full awake and weapons drawn, at my cry.

"Talyn?" and "Father?" came in the same breath, and I shook my head in sheepish denial of danger.

"What is it?" asked Arthur, sheathing Llacharn once more and peering at me keenly over the top of the grieshoch.

"A gift I did not know I had been given," I said with a strange note in my voice. Nay, no more did Marguessan know either, it seemed, else she had never have let it remain with me. . . I held it out for them to see: a bronze dagger, forged all of a piece haft and blade, gold-bronze on the blade-edges and the rounded bosswork ornament, black-gold in feathering watery streaks all elsewhere. It was double-edged, with a cutout for the thumb, and quite surprisingly heavy for its size and slimness, with a presence and a heft to it that had naught whatever to do with weight.

"It is a blade of the Shining Folk," said Arthur reverently. "They do not use steel; or indeed cold iron of any sort, save for that thunderbolt-iron we do sometimes see applied. . . Did Gwyn give you this, under the hill, or the Lady Birogue?"

"Under the hill, aye," I said with certainty, and with a kind of awe also. "But not, I think, from either of them."

I could tell by the weight and irregular contours of the leather pouch that other things were contained therein, doubtless with significance of their own, but by now I was too weary to care. *My sorrow,* I apologized to the unknown tokens, *but you must wait a bit.* . . I kept the seal intact, and tucked the pouch into the compartment for carrying valuables or secret things that was cunningly built into the high square pommel of my saddle. But the bronze dagger I kept beside me, and fell asleep with it clasped in my hand.

For any gift from Merlynn Llwyd was sure to have purpose indeed; and, over and above this day's events, I was taking no more chances with dán.

CHAPTER 5

Arthur and Gerrans, naturally enough, had been wild to bring me home in triumphant splendor to Morgan and Caerdroia, indeed in full sight of all Keltia; and when I would have none of it, were considerably deflated.

Though Gerrans, in filial feeling, or perhaps simply prudence, soon gave over the pressure when he saw how it stood with me, Arthur went right on cajoling without letup, or even shame.

"The folk long very much to see you safe home again, Tal-bachgen, I do not think you know how they do feel about you, they have missed their Pen-bardd sorely. . .", that sort of softsauder, you know by now how Arthur was wont to do to get his own way; though you would think that long years as my fostern would have been long enough to teach him better, at least where I was concerned. . .

"Missed me sore, have they?" I was remembering well by now how little it sometimes had taken for Arthur to exasperate me to snapping point. "Well, they can manage to go on missing me a day or two longer. All that their Pen-bardd wishes in the way of triumphal welcome home is the arms of his lady, and maybe some quiet words after with his methryn and his Queen."

Arthur sulked and muttered a while longer, like a little black cloud over on the other side of the campment fire, but gave in at last; most like for that he knew full well I was quite capable of leaving him and Gerrans right there and finding my own way home without them. . . So we departed Gwynedd in secrecy aboard an unmarked ship of the Royal Flight, and came again to Tara half a day later.

It was late summer here in the north of the Throneworld, and we flew into weather as soon as we came to atmosphere in our small shuttle. My old fear of flight had by no means been diminished by my stint of forgetfulness in Oeth-Anoeth, and it was beside me like a brother as we fell toward the clouds. But even in my disquiet I found wondrous the sight that met my eyes: We were descending toward a massive slow-moving thunderstorm that was blundering its way through Pass of the Arrows just south of the Loom. We were already a mere ten miles up, moving through a clear starry dark-blue night just above the tops of the towering, moon-silvered clouds. It was magical, in all senses of the word: no thunder, only the explosions of blue flame, the sullen shuddering bursts of the lightning—great silent concussions of cloudfire, all aimed downward. Here above the cloudroof we were safe; we were as gods, hurling down the levin on the cowering world beneath.

Suddenly we were deep into the storm, for a few very unpleasant tossing moments, and as suddenly out from under it, gliding in to land quietly at Mardale Port in the soft rain. From here it was but twelve miles to Turusachan on its hill-crown above the City, I would be with my Morgan again in a matter of minutes. . . I looked eagerly for the usual aircar transport, but Arthur had other plans, and to that end directed my attention to the horses and Fian escort that waited patiently off to one side.

I protested long and bitterly and most blistering eloquent—sometimes, as Gweniver often put it, it can well repay one to have a tongue that was trained to kill—but Arthur ignored me; and, though it near killed *me* to admit it, we had not ridden two lai in the cool rainy darkness before I knew that he had been right. This was a way for me to temper down, to decompress as a ship must after travelling the overheaven; I had long time been as stressed as any metal—two years at Oeth-Anoeth under ensorcelment, the high drama of my liberation, the gnawing urgency of my message that had gone so long undischarged—and I was after all not findruinna but mere flesh. . . So I lifted my face to the rain and threw back my hood and breathed deep of the air of my home, letting the wind and the water and the smell of the rain on trees in heavy leaf cleanse my heart of any lingering trace of Marguessan's evil miasms.

We entered Caerdroia not through the great main Wolf Gate, but passed on and came instead to the smaller Seagate, little used save by those going down to the empty shoreland by the mouths of the Avon Dia. The Seagate opened on a broad paved way leading past government buildings and town maenors straight up to Turusachan, and when the gate had swung wide we saw that three cloaked figures were there to meet us, on horseback, under torches in the deep shelter of the arch. By their stance and seat and stature I would have known them anywhere, save of course in Oeth-Anoeth where I did not: Morgan, Ygrawn and Gweniver the Queen.

You may well be thinking that Morgan and I did fling ourselves upon each other right then, kissing madly; but that was not how we did things, my Guenna and I, and if you think a little further you will most likely agree that you yourself would not have done so either, not just then. . . But Morgan came forward, reaching one hand to me and the other to Gerrans who rode on my right. I cannot speak what was on her face or in her eyes. She said no word to either of us, her mate and her son, and I knew she had not truly thought to see either of us again in this life. But she only looked, as we on her, and then she turned to her brother who sat his horse on my other side, watching the byplay approvingly but with most of his looks for his Queen.

"Well, Arthur," said Morgan then—even in this moment of all moments forbearing to address him as did all the world else, almost never was the High King 'Artos' to the younger of his two sisters—and Arthur bowed his head, one deep nod of acknowledgment, but made no other reply.

I pulled Morgan out of her saddle and caught her up before me into my own; my arms held her fast, but they shook, and my face was but inches from her rain-damp hair.

But still we did not speak aloud. . . Ygrawn and Gweniver, who had watched all this with somber relief—well, that is what it looked like to me just then, in truth they were too wrought to allow of a reaction—now turned their horses' heads uphill, Morgan's mount following unled after, and we went clattering up through the empty, windswept, rain-shining, sea-scented streets, up to Turusachan which flamed with lights on its high ridge above the dark sleeping City.

So I came again home.

For all that Morgan and I wished naught more than to be as alone as we could get, just as quickly as we could get so, other matters were more pressing; and though we did manage a brief few minutes to, if no more, simply stand and *look* at each other, with sight and Sight, we were still royal, we still knew how to stand by and let duty prevail. . .

Once we were all dry and warm inside Turusachan, Gweniver had greeted me rapturously, as beloved friend as well as her son's godfather (though young Arawn Amris Taliesin Gorlas was well asleep; I would have to wait till the morrow for my first sight of Keltia's new prince). As for Ygrawn, she had contented herself with looking silently upon me and touching slim cool fingers to my cheek. But in those greetings I saw all the pain and fear and dull throb of loss that my two years' absence had cost them, and I knew that now was perhaps not the best and proper time to inform them I had not remembered either one of them only a day or two since. . .

But none of us had forgotten that great evil was afoot, and the sooner we addressed it the better for all. To that end, Gweniver had called a small council of friends to meet the instant we came to the palace; but Arthur had some moments ago drawn her aside and whispered somewhat, and she had nodded and smiled and altered her order.

So that now I was following docilely along—Ygrawn had taken me by the sleeve, like the lad I would ever be to her in her mother's heart—down palace hallways to a tower I did not recall ever having visited.

"Come," said Ygrawn. Nothing loath, I passed the door, and stopped dead.

It was a spacious chamber in the oldest part of the palace, its proportions the perfect double cube of felicitous design. Many feet above my head there was a vaulted glass-work ceiling, through the stained panels of which, on sunny days, the light must blaze in glory. Even now, more than a century after, the scene still glows in my mind as if freshly painted: the warm ruddy stone of the walls, the jewel rich-ness of the wovencloths upon them, with their depictings of figures from Keltic history. I recognized Athyn of the Storms with Morric Fireheart her mate, and their beloved companions and dire foes alike; Saint Mirren; Siriol the great ally of Brendan; the Battle of the Angabharna; King Cadivor and Juthahelo his fell enemy; the Grey Graham and the Lion of Badenoch at Caranagreisha; and more whom I did not know or recollect—all was red and blue and green and ivory and shaded gold, figures of arrowstitch and feath-erstitch and sheafstitch.

The chamber the tapestries lighted was not empty but full of folk, I saw with another shock; after my long solitude it was hard suddenly to be back among people again, and especially those who were so full of gladness at my return, who wished only to embrace and kiss and hold and pound on. . . Morgan's hand slipped into mine when she felt me shivering under my cloak; and though I did not turn to look at her I felt her thought, like a deep calm river to bear me past the moment, and I took a steadying breath as we moved forward together.

Well—now that I looked more closely, the room was not entirely packed with folk as I had thought; perhaps three dozen. But it was full of another thing: a great table of carved ironoak that went clear round the walls, a table in shape of a wain-wheel, its center hollow like a ring, spoke-less, hubless; upon its outer rim were set high-backed chairs in spaced lines, and at each place stood one of my friends, though not all the places were filled.

"The Hall of the Table," said Arthur behind me as I stared. "This is Gwahanlen, the Veil of the Temple. Be wel-come to Rhodaur, the board of the Companions, you who

were first among equals, and first at my side; who should
have been first to sit here."

I remember moving blindly into the room—blindly for
the tears that burned in my eyes—sensing the loving familiar
presences all around me, tears on their faces as well. Dimly
I saw Morgan and Gerrans and Gweniver and Ygrawn taking places around the table's rim in no particular order or
rank; felt Arthur lead me halfway round to where an empty
chair stood with its back to the great tapestry of Athyn and
Morric above.

"Cader Taliesin," he said. "The Seat Gwencathra, the
White Stanchion of Truth; whoso is chaired here can speak
naught save what is so. It has been vacant for you all this
time, for none other was ever meant to occupy it. Not than
any would have dared try, even in *this* company—"

From her own seat across the hollow space between,
many feet away, Daronwy smiled and brushed tears from
her cheeks. Which troubled more than almost anything else,
for never before in all our time could I recall having seen
Ronwyn weep. . .

"It is the only designated seat at all this table, Talynno,"
she said, and love and humor went together in her voice.
"And if any had been so ill-advised as to *try* to fill your seat,
dear Tal-bach, be very sure it had been the *last* seat they
had had in this life. . . Indeed, I am not at all sure Morgan
did not hallow it about, so that whoever might presume to
sit in your place would vanish in thunder and flame."

But Morgan only smiled, and said nothing, and raised
eloquent brows.

I smiled at Ronwyn, gestured vaguely, but it was no
good; my tears overflowed, pouring down like silver, and I
leaned my head against Arthur who still stood beside me
and wept and wept and wept. It was too much joy, too
much wonder, too much lovingness, to be safe home again:
all my dearest ones, all the best and bravest in Keltia, the
innermost Company from of old—faces from Daars, from
Coldgates, from Llwynarth, from the Taran campaigns,
from the outfrenne reivings, from the wars following that
had earned us the Protectorates (of which more later), that
had earned Arthur the shining new title of Imperator,

Emperor of the West. . . All the loved faces thought lost
until my next life: Betwyr, Alannagh, Daronwy, Roric,
Tarian, Grehan, Ferdia, Elenna, Tryffin, Ysild, Keils, my
sister Tegau. . .

I put my face in my hands, felt Arthur's grip upon my
shoulder, the care and anxiety in it.

"Talyn?"

I shook my head and presently took my hands away.
"Nay—but it is *most* well with me, I tell you."

Reassured, he took the chair beside mine, though I knew
that was not his 'customed place; at this Table, all were of a
ranking, and when this Company was summoned to
Rhodaur, sat wherever a place was empty. But I was glad
this night that Arthur was beside me. . .

"No business before the Table tonight, Talyn," said
Gweniver from her place a few yards down to my left.
"This is just by way of welcoming home, to see Gwencathra
filled at last—but know that your message is long since
brought, your charge well discharged."

"I would speak it here even so, Ard-rían." I rose
unsteadily to my feet; Arthur looked up with sharp attention
but allowed me to do so unassisted. And it mattered much
to me that I did so; and, as bard, spoke so—for symmetry's
sake, and history, and for honor, in payment of duty and
debt of my own. . .

So, standing in my rightful place, before my destined
seat of Gwencathra, called for me Cader Taliesin, I gave
Gwyn's words of warning to the Table of Companions in
the chamber Gwahanlen. I need not tell you; it has become
a moment much commemorated in the decades since, in
song and story and picture. I also think I need not tell you
that most of those who so commemorate it get it wrong. It
is so very often the case, my sorrow to say; that those who
came later and never knew always seem to delude themselves that they know better and truer than the ones who
were in fact there.

The truth was staggering enough: Gwyn's naming of
Marguessan as the secret enemy of Keltia, betrayer of her
kin, hidden pupil of Edeyrn Marbh-draoi; her filching of the
sacred Pair, Cam-Corainn, the Cup of Wonder, the great

Graal of the Mysteries without which there is no healing, not of body nor of soul. And worse even than that, though that was ill enough, the tidings that Marguessan sought to create a Black Graal, a blasphemous Cup of Terror to set against the Goddess's rightful Cauldron. . .

I spoke no news here, of course; as Gwen had said, all this was long since known to the Company and to very many not here present, all by grace of Gwyn's coming to Caerdroia when I failed to do so. But by and large, the common folk of Caerdroia did not know the half of it; which was well for them that they did not. Too recently had they succeeded in reaching a state of fragile peace and freedom and healing from the wounds Edeyrn had gouged in all our souls; to spring upon them now a nightmare such as this would be to ask more of them than they were just now capable of giving, and not yet would we ask it.

"When then to ask?" repeated Morgan, as we went at long last to our own rooms, the greetings over and the Companions dispersed to their own beds. "Maybe soon; maybe never. Much will depend on Gweniver and on you."

"On *me*?!" I felt faint. "What in the name of the Mother can *I* do? I have only just recalled my own name, the fact that I am bard, had a message to deliver. . . And we all saw how mighty I proved against Marguessan, back there in—"

But I could not say the name, not yet; I trembled in spite of myself, and though I did not shame to do so, not in front of my beloved lady, still I would rather she did not see me do so. But Morguenna Pendreic ac Glyndour ever saw all.

"No matter. Listen cariad o'nghariad, croi o mo chroi, Gwyn son of Nudd has already pronounced: You and Gweniver are to be the soul of this Questing. You will choose the Questers, make up the companies, determine the search, ride out yourselves upon the sacred Hunt. And you shall find the Cup; for all find what they truly seek."

I stopped to look at her. "Do they? Do they, truly?"

"Aye. Truly. Have you ever—truly—doubted?"

I sighed. "Nay, not even when I forgot to remember. . . But such a quest, a Hunt of Dark and Light—"

"A plain hunt. No more, also no less." Morgan snugged against me, closer than before, her arm round my waist in back, and after another hesitation I put my own arm round her shoulders and pulled her closer still, and so entangled with each other we went on down the hall.

Later still, once again in our huge carved bed, its wood as golden with newness as it had been the first night we ever spent here together, I sprawled on my back and stared up at the ceiling. Beside me, Morgan lay quietly weeping; not for sorrow or failure in love, but for the desperation and joyful perfection we had found here tonight. *It seemed not possible*, I thought vaguely, and no doubt such transcendence of union merely portended fresh hells we could not even begin to think on. . . I ran my thumb over my marriage ring, just visible in the light that reflected in through the windows from the moon on the sea below. Two gold serpents, intertwined, ruby-eyed; the ring my lady had set upon my finger at our handfasting—and Gwyn had honored that too. How came it that I had forgotten, in Oeth-Anoeth?

Because the ring had been taken from me, I reminded myself; and that somehow seemed more a violation than even the violation of my mind's citadel. Morgan had slipped it on my finger once more, when we were alone in bed at last, telling me that it had been found in my saddlebag when my horses were discovered wandering by Drum Wood edge. But I was still troubled by the thought that it had been taken from my hand; and I knew why Morgan wept.

The morning dawned bright-cloudy, with a wind to shake the grasses on the plains below the City walls. In the first instant of my awakening, the light seemed the same as that in Oeth-Anoeth. . . In Morgan's arms last night, I had finally found the courage and the words to speak of my prisonment at her sister's hands. At the end of the telling (and you may be sure I told it full measure, I being bard and all), when Gerrans rode up like the Young Lord himself and unhelmed, and all else vanished away, Morgan had said no word, but had turned and taken my face between her hands in the faint moonlight and had kissed me gently and sorcerously, to take away all my fear and pain. I reached out now in panic renewed, but my hand brushed Morgan's bare hip beside me, and I remembered where I was, and with whom, and what had befallen. . .

After love and a quick plunge in the adjacent pool-bath and a few bites of bread dipped in ale and a mouthful or two of cold beef by way of breakfast, we clad ourselves to endure in comfort what promised to be a long, *long* Council meeting, and were away downstairs before the bell in the Salt Tower struck ten. (That is *early!* I know what you are thinking, but as a rule Kelts do not do mornings well, and if left to our natural rhythm, naught in Keltia would begin until high twelve, or, even better, an hour or two past. . .)

Today's meeting was to be held not in the Hall of the Table but in the usual Council chamber; and as I entered with Morgan and Ferdia, whom we had picked up on the way, the remembered immediacy of this place came back to me with a stunning rush. I knew this room! How fine that I remembered!

I looked around at the other Councillors even now taking their seats. Although in title and rank all Councillors were equal alike, in practice this had sifted itself a bit more finely than that. The Great Officers of State—the Taoiseach or the First Lord of War or the Lord Extern who governed dealings with outfrenne worlds—were more equal, so to speak, than such as Morgan or I, who for all our royal rank were more on the order of common-or-garden Councillors, private advisors to our monarchs. So we tended to sit on the outskirts of the room, which I for one preferred, as it gave me rather more liberty to employ a skeptic observing eye; and the Great Officers tended to seat themselves at the actual Council table, presided over by Arthur at the window end and Gweniver at the end nearest the door. (I go into this tedious seating detail for good reason; bear with me.)

Over on the far side of the long dark gray basalt table, the new Archdruid, Ultagh Casnar, was talking to Grehan Aoibhell. I shifted in my seat, and Morgan laid a calming hand upon my knee. I misliked more than I can tell you the thought of anyone, however worthy he might be as man and magician both, sitting in—*usurping*—the chair that by right should have been Merlynn Llwyd's. But that was not my only problem with the Order to which I belonged.

Up until the Battle of Ratherne—Nandruidion—we of
the Counterinsurgency, and especially those of us who were
Druids, had looked with awe not far off reverence for
Merlynn to bring back to its true Path the Order that
Edeyrn had perverted and disgraced. Oh, to be sure, there
were very many Druids who had rejected Edeyrn's dark
dogmas, utterly and with horror, and who had held steadfastly to their honor and the Light. Not all of them had been
of, or had been known to, the Counterinsurgency, even; it
was quite possible for true Druids to have escaped our
notice, down all those years when we did battle every instant
for Keltia's life and our own. Bastions of orthodoxy, like
Bargodion, where Arthur and I had learned Druidry, had
become embattled sanctuaries, keeping the Druids' way alive
in Edeyrn's despite—he who once had been its highest
exemplar, Ro-sai, the Great Teacher, and who had then
turned into the darkness all of Druidry that he could grasp,
and much of the rest of Keltia too.

It was therefore Merlynn—Ailithir of my childhood and
Arthur's—to whom we had looked for salvation and restoral;
and he would have done so, had he. . . had he not. . . I
forced myself to face it: had he not been destroyed at
Nandruidion. Well, not destroyed, perhaps, just so, as I
alone of all Kelts yet knew; but taken from us in a way even
I did not yet understand.

The Order itself had limped along in the years of Arthur's
absences on reivings—Gweniver, though full Domina of the
Ban-draoi, had no jurisdiction over her Druid counterparts
save as Ard-rían only, and would not have presumed to exert
any rule even if she could have claimed some. Before we had
gone out reiving, a new Archdruid, one Comyn Duchray, had
been appointed on an interim basis by a council of Druid
elders, until such time as an election could be held. But there
arose faction wars, and purges of tainted Theocracy pawns,
and Duchray had ended up holding the post of Archdruid for
almost two decades. Last year, however, while I was
ensconced in Oeth-Anoeth, an election had finally been held,
and the one chosen was this Ultagh—another native of
Gwynedd's Old North, as Duchray had been, from the clann
lands of Marguessan's lord, Irian Locryn.

So you may well imagine how 'ware and wary I was just now, as I watched, jealousy on my Merlynn's behalf hot in my heart, this new Archdruid turn to that place which had been of old the seat of the Druid masters at the Council table of Keltia... But, to my astonishment, he passed it by, and went on to take a seat not at the table proper, but in the humble row along the wall, and I tell you my eyes were on sticks to see it.

"When he became Archdruid last year, he requested in the name of Merlynn Llwyd—not in his own name, Talyn—that Gweniver remove the Archdruidship from all precedence in Council, and make the place of the Archdruid the lowest of all at the Council table, give him the last and least vote in counting." Morgan's voice was conversational, and I could glean no clue as to her attitude to all this. Then: "No fear, cariad! Our Merlynn has been neither forgotten nor usurped..."

I was incredulous. "Asked *he* so? This Ultagh?"

"Aye, asked that it be kept so forever, as undying reminder of Edeyrn and fitting homage to Merlynn, and Arthur and Gwennach both confirmed it. All this was while you were gone from here..."

Again I was silent. This grand gesture on Casnar's part showed a certain humility at first looking; but was it true humility, or merely a kind of humble arrogance, a fozing sham of the real soul-grace? I looked at him, and all at once he sensed my attention, and looked up to meet my gaze before I could turn away. He seemed to sense my thought as well, for he made me a small bow before taking his seat; needless to tell you, he had not been in Gwahanlen the previous night, being no member of the Company.

On my other side from Morgan, Betwyr—Druid also, of my own year at Bargodion, and Councillor like us—caught my need for reassurance.

"All those who carried any taint of the Marbh-draoi's ways and workings were stripped of their powers, as you well know. A fearful undertaking, you will recall; but it was done. The Order slowly cleansed its way, cleaned its own House; perhaps it was best for us, that the thing was slow in the achieving."

But I was still looking at Ultagh Casnar. "Think you it *has* been achieved?"

Neither Betwyr nor Morgan replied to that one; and with an effort I shut from my mind that secret sight of Merlynn I had been granted in that place I did not wish to name here, not even in my thought. Indeed, only to Arthur and Morgan had I spoken of it yet at all. . . True, there had been little time, but I could have told quite a number of folk, and had not, for reasons I could not quite put into words. But I had learned to trust my instincts; and it came to me, also, that the Old North, long a stronghold of Edeyrn, is a place where change comes slower than most elsewhere. . .

But Arthur and Gweniver had entered the Council chamber, and we all rose to our feet. As I watched them take their chairs at either end of the table, High King and High Queen so practiced now in rule, I felt a stab of pride for my own part in all this.

Morgan seemed to feel it also, for she found my hand and squeezed it. Only Betwyr and I heard her whisper.

"Now we shall see some proper deeds."

CHAPTER 6

> *"Here begins the Book of the Graal.*
> *Here begin the terrors.*
> *Here begin the wonders.*
> *Listen. Hear."*

That is how it is written. But I shall tell you how it was.

For of course it was *nothing* like to the way folk have come to think of it in the years since, or will think, centuries on; I must accept that, though I hate it more than I can tell you. But also I must do what I can to change it: As I said earlier on, it has ever been a source to me of amazement and rage that those who know best are often worst attended to.

The sorcerers have long had a maxim: 'Those who know least talk most; those who know most talk least.' Perhaps I have, out of love and honor and a desire for dignity and reserve, too long taken this for personal creed; the upshot being that I, who know more about Arthur the man than perhaps anyone else who ever breathed, should be so often discounted by the come-too-latelies and the never-were-theres

and the boneheads with invented wish-tales that they deem
better than the truth. My stature as bard seems to have little
if aught to do with it.

Sometimes I think I might have done better service by all
of us had I taken a leaf in action from Queen Athyn's book:
Now *she*, when evil folk spoke lies and betrayals upon her
and her beloved mate, hunted them down one by one; and
when she found them she explained to each with great courtesy and clarity of expression (Athyn was ever renowned for
both) precisely what offense of theirs had caused her to take
such course. And then she had killed them. Sometimes quite
inventively. As she herself did put it, with no small irony,
they died for the truth—or rather for their lack of respect
therefor—and it was their dán and their lessoning that they
should do so.

But Athyn, greatly as I admire her, sometimes frightens
me—although I must confess her methods have a certain
undeniable appeal. Arthur, as I have said elsewhere, all but
worshipped her as a goddess, an earthly aspect of the Mor-
rían Herself, and took her as his model for the greatness at
which he himself did aim. I am cast from lesser mold; but
even I have learned a few things from Athyn's way with
truth and with those who choose to defile it. . .

Any road, you shall hear the truths of the Graal hunt, of
this time and of these folk, from one who was there for all
of it. If you choose still to believe otherwise, that is your
privilege (and stupidity); but only thank the Goddess that
Athyn Anfa is not still here to show you the error of your
ways. . .

Gweniver called the Council to order that day, as was her
habit more than Arthur's, and she did so with no ceremony
and less patience than I have ever seen her use.

"Two years have been lost to us already," she said with
no preamble. "Here today we plan the hunt for the Pair."

Arthur stirred in his chair. "Gwyn has told us, and
Taliesin ap Gwyddno confirms it; no need to delay longer."

I sensed attention shift my way and back again, but kept
my eyes on Gweniver as Tarian spoke.

"Gwyn's word was that women, and men of art, should be the chief seekers."

"Indeed," said Gweniver. "And he said also that I myself, with Taliesin, should be the chief architects of that questing, and that the Ard-rígh must perforce stand away. As the Ard-rígh will doubtless remember?"

That last was a shot whang between the joints of the armor, and I hid a smile.

"He did, and he does," said Arthur, annoyance and resignation both plain in his voice; he wanted so very dearly to be part of this, and it was denied him. "But he said too that warriors in some number would also be needed—if not perhaps the Ard-rígh—as the Ard-rían will doubtless recall?"

My smile grew broader, and I hid it behind a judicious cough. Arthur recalled perfectly well what Gwyn had said; I had spent a few minutes before this meeting watching viewtapes of the historic scene of Gwyn and his companions at Turusachan, and the faerie Prince had spelled it out for Arthur in no uncertain terms. Clearly, the Sidhe knew their man. . .

"No matter," said Gweniver, and glanced up at Morgan before rising to face the room. "It has been determined. There shall be seven companies of seven to be sent forth upon this questing."

She glanced now at me—though certainly we had much to discuss between us, this seemed fine to me, no reason for me to interrupt or change her order, at least not in open Council—but she spoke to be obeyed. Beside her, Tarian began quietly to take notes in her own hand, in addition to the crystal recording made of all such meetings, and the chamber stilled to silence.

"There shall be Companions sent upon this errand; some of those in this very room. For the rest, as Gwyn ap Nudd has bidden, there shall be bards and Druids, Ban-draoi and Fians, brehons and lieges and peers: folk of all clanns and ranks and trades and kindreds. All Keltia shall be represented in this, for it is a matter that concerns all Kelts. I myself shall lead a company, and will have with me Morguenna Pendreic, and Daronwy of Endellion with Roric Davacho her mate, and Taliesin ap Gwyddno now restored to us."

I felt relief so keen I all but fainted. I knew, of course, that I should be named to one of the companies, but had feared lest Morgan and I should be separated. No doubt I could have argued against it, but still, better that the problem had not arisen. Then in the next breath I feared and wondered anew: Why had we *not* been separated? Would not the quest perhaps be better served, might not it be a better balance for Gweniver to lead one company and Morgan another and I yet a third? Did this mean then—

But Gweniver was speaking again; or began to, before Arthur rather pettishly interrupted her.

"That is but five of your seven, Ard-rían."

"My thanks to the High King to be so well reminded." But she smiled at her husband as she said it. "For six, then, Loherin of Kernow, son of Tryffin and Ysild who are Duke and Duchess of that same; and lastly—" Gweniver paused, deliberately stared straight down the length of the table at her co-ruler and her mate, her gray eyes suddenly as hard as the basalt the table was cut from, and spoke the seventh name. "—Donah, Heir of Aojun."

Tumult without peer. Even I was stunned. As for Arthur, he looked as if he had been gralloched; and half the room, I could see, was wondering immediately and loudly if he would permit this at all. For Donah, you will remember, was Arthur's firstborn; his adored daughter by the Jamadarin of the Yamazai, Queen Majanah of Aojun. I tried to recall if Donah was still in Keltia: I had not seen nor heard word of her in the few hours of my return, but that meant little. Before my enforced absence, she had been very much present at her father's court; Majanah had left her here a while, so that she might come to know and love the Keltic half of her high heritage, before being called back to Aojun to begin to learn queenship from her formidable mother.

But would that formidable mother even hear of such a thing?

"She is too young, surely," said Betwyr aside to Morgan. "And Janjan will never allow it."

"She is older than Gerrans," returned Morgan equably. "And he too goes upon this quest. And none knows duty better than Majanah."

I suddenly felt much as Arthur had looked. "Oh, does he now? There may be a thing or two to be said about that, lady—"

Morgan shook her head. "There will not, then. I know your fears, cariad, but they are *meant* to go, both of them, though that may be small comfort. But listen."

"The Jamadarin of Aojun has seen and recognized the necessity," Gweniver was saying, her voice cutting clear above the murmurs. "And has consented full willing; indeed, she it was who first spoke to me on the matter, for it seems that they have had magical tidings of this on Aojun also. . . Though it will be for Taliesin and me to make up the rest of the companies, I shall name now two questers more, and they are Geraint Pendreic ac Glyndour, and with him his cousin. . . Gwain Pendreic ac Locryn, youngest child of the Princess Marguessan."

Well! Trust Gwennach to end on such a hai atton—if she had flung a thousand gauntlets in their faces she could not have given greater challenge. With perfect timing, she nodded to Tarian to close the meeting, bowed to Arthur and to the room at large, and was out the doors before anyone else could even think to stir. But Morgan, as usual, seemed to know all about it, and she was tugging at my sleeve to follow before Arthur was full out of his chair.

"What then?" I snapped at her, for I was vexed and feared together. It seemed to me rashness beyond even the bound of daring to allow three young members of the blood royal to go on such a venturing as this. "Are you pleased that Gerrans and Donah should go on this errand? Not to mention Gwain, of whom I know little; but he *is* your sister's son, and of *her* we know much—" And all of it evil, though I did not need to say so; I was too lately escaped from Marguessan's hospitality to wish even to think of her.

Morgan was pulling me along the corridors of the palace at a quick pace, and I realized from our surroundings that we were headed again for Gwahanlen, the chamber of the Table. Probably Gwennach was there by now, and Arthur and the rest would not be far behind us. . .

"Not pleased exactly, nay, Talynno; but like Janjan I know the necessity of this. It is ordained that they should go, and there's an end on it. We cannot forever keep them coddled in tree-wool against all haps or harms of the world. Thus, and they do not learn; and if they do not learn they do not grow; and if they do not grow they will die."

I shivered once, for her words were hard; but if hard they were also most correct. As parents, our overriding instinct is to protect; but our equally compelling duty is to push our cherished chicks from the nest. It is up to them to fly; but we must adequately fledge them first. I felt distantly comforted; this I knew we had done for Gerrans, and done well if I may say so—and for witness I had only to glance back a few days to Oeth-Anoeth. Donah too: another fine flying hawk, well-managed and well-made by her mother and Arthur, who had made her between them in the first place. . . As I had said to Morgan, Gwain I did not know at all; and what Marguessan and Irian may have made of him was yet to be seen.

"Is there not some risk in naming Gwain?" I asked as we took our places at the Table, I in the Seat Gwencathra and Morgan beside me (though this she would not make a practice of down the years). "Will Marguessan not be able to read our plans and actions through his very presence, and alter her own to thwart us in our search?"

"She may think so," said Morgan grimly, "but I myself think my sister will be surprised to find what she shall find. . . More than that, I have not been given to See."

I sank down into the depths of my chair, and watched the rest of the Table fill up. There was room at Rhodaur for twelve times twelve Companions, but we did not make up anything near those numbers, not after the years of Edeyrn and the outfrenne reivings and the fighting for the Protectorates those reivings had unexpectedly won us; so many had been lost, too many. And so when Arthur called the Table to order there were perhaps seventy souls in the tapestried chamber. I knew and loved them all; but I worried, and I wondered.

"As the need is clearly paramount and the nature already determined," Arthur was saying, "I put it to Gweniver and

Taliesin, who are tarq-hijarun of this riding, that they let us
have their plan and listing in no more than three days' time.
There is much to put in order before so great a quantity of
the best blood of Keltia rides off on this search."

Tarq-hijar. . . That was a Yamazai word, an old term for the
leader of a hunting party; Arthur must have picked it up
from Donah. I glanced up and caught Arthur's eye, and
spoke to the chamber.

"If the Ard-rían is ready, I say we begin now. More
delay in choosing means more delay in setting forth."

Gweniver nodded, and for the next four days, with the
help of the Companions, she and I hammered out upon the
Table a list of seekers; drawn, as Gwyn had bidden, from all
ranks of Keltic society. All talents were included, and no
clann (save only the rígh-domhna) seemed overrepresented.
When Elen Llydaw raised this very point—for besides three
royal offspring, there were Gweniver, Morgan and myself,
not to mention Loherin who was kin by cousinage, his
father being nephew to the Queen-dowager Ygrawn—it was
Arthur himself who dismissed her doubtings.

"Whether it be so or no," he said with some asperity, "it
is also dán. I will explain to the folk, if indeed explanations
are warranted."

So we arrived at our forty-nine names—no fear that any
would decline our asking, and so we had chosen no alter-
nates—and messages were sent to those who dwelled away
from Caerdroia, that they should come with all speed to
Turusachan, and come prepared for an absence of unknown
duration. They were given a fortnight's grace to set their
personal affairs in order, and told to bring no weapon with
them, according to the instruction received from Gwyn.

That, as you may well imagine, did not sit well with
many, least of all with Arthur, and he visibly chafed under
it. "I like it not at all," he complained later, when the Table
had largely dispersed and our inner circle of Companions
was lounging casually around the board. "Who knows what
you may not encounter—"

Morgan shaded her eyes with one hand, spoke in a weary
patient voice. "As we were told, so we tell you: Only those
who are lawful Fians, or who have been given other license,

may go weaponed upon this quest. That is why Gwennach
and Talyn have included at least one Fian in each seven;
also a sorcerer and a bard. All possibilities are thus provided
for."

I thought about this for perhaps the thousandth time.
Though according to Gwyn's instruction we had relied
chiefly on women and men of art—aes dána, ollaves, masters of the work—our own group seemed perhaps over-
heavy with sorcerers. Morgan and Gweniver were both
Ban-draoi Dominas (and Morgan greater even than that), I
was Druid as well as bard, and Roric, Daronwy's mate, was
a sorcerer among his own folk, if a warrior also. Loherin,
though untested as knight, was yet Fian, and Daronwy, of
course, was Fian and Companion from the earliest days. My
concerns were more for those who seemed not so well
trained or gifted in magical art: Donah for one, though at
least with us she would be as safe as we were allowed to
keep her; and Gerrans and Gwain in a company led by a
Ban-draoi I did not know.

And others of our friends, too, had young kin upon this
quest: Betwyr's niece Keira; Shane and Síoda, children of
Tarian Douglas. . . But for the most part the chosen Seekers
were unknown to us, had been revealed through various
magical means, and we had to trust that the magic knew
what it was doing. I am the last one to give short shrift to
sorcery; but all the same I wondered if we had chosen correctly. . .

"We cannot know that until the thing is done with; either
achieved or failed," said Morgan later, when we had at long
last quitted Gwahanlen, the Quest settled, and retired to our
rooms.

That seemed reasonable; still—Suddenly Morgan went
rigid beside me.

"Donah and Gwain and Loherin," she said in a drowned
voice, and I looked keenly at her, for Sight had taken her far
from me just now. "They shall be of those who achieve the
Cup—"

"And us?" I asked, scarce daring even to breathe, though
it seemed the height of vainglory to wish what I now was
wishing.

"We shall be with it. But we shall not be of it. . ." Morgan gave a little gasp, and seemed to sag all over. "Oh Talyn—do you think. . ."

I drew her into bed beside me, cuddling her against me, and kissed her neck and breasts and shoulders, more by way of calming and comforting than as prelude to lovemaking, for it was afternoon after all, and we were expected for the nightmeal in Mi-cuarta in a few hours, though this was our first real chance for quiet privacy since my return. Also I was thinking furiously, and not of love. . .

"When I was in Oeth-Anoeth—" I began, then halted.

"Aye?" murmured Morgan.

"Something I saw—something I remember—" I stopped, confused, angry that I could not bring it to focus.

"Another time," said Morgan. "Another seeing. Let it be."

We awoke stupid and dazed from our nap—I have never understood those who seem to find short untimely sleeps restful, to me they merely clog the brain and throw the day off track—and only barely in time for the nightmeal. Plans had altered while we so fitfully slept, and now we would dine not in Mi-cuarta (thankfully! I was not yet ready, not yet 'back' enough for that) but in the Queen Ygrawn's small private hall, just the family and a few close friends—some of our soul-kin as we call it, those who if not of blood bound are bound of love, more than friends and more even perhaps than most blood-kin.

Before we dined I was introduced at last to the new Tanist of Keltia, Arawn, a well-grown faunt of just over one year, with the most alarming look of amused intelligence to him. He looked unnervingly as if he already knew all about us that he needed to know, and more than we should like. . . Apart from that, he greatly resembled Gweniver, save that he had Arthur's hair and fine peat-dark eyes—Amris's eyes, Ygrawn said, with a faraway look in her own. He was a fine fearless lad too, for he fussed not at all when I lifted him from his little ffridd, but peered round so as not to miss anything. I kissed the damp hair—how amazingly warm and alive he was—and sang him a soft song in the suantraí mode, calculated to charm sleep into him. Gweniver laughed to hear it.

"It takes more than a sleep-strain, Pen-bardd, to put my son out when he would stay up with company! Have you forgotten how it was with Gerrans?"

I smiled and set the young prince, not in the least bit sleep-charmed, down again in the well-padded ffridd.

"Long time indeed since I have held a babe. . . He is a fine lad, my dears."

Arthur reached out for his wife's hand, and I nearly wept with joy to see this; so long, too long, it had not been so.

"If we can do as well by him as you and Guenna with Gerrans," he said gravely, "we shall have done well indeed."

Now it was my turn to take my lady's hand. "Did not Uthyr say it best: The more bearing branches of the House of Dôn, the better rooted the stem— But what of that branch we have never dared trust our weight to?"

Gweniver looked distasteful and chagrined all in one. "Since your return from Gwynedd we have had no word of Marguessan or Mordryth. Irian remains at his seat of Lleyn, as he seems ever to do, and I think Galeron is with him. Gwain was off in training with the Fianna, and is now on his way to join us here. To Marguessan's great annoyance, I am sure."

Ygrawn entered just then from her solar, and I turned to greet her gladly. She and I had shared a tender reunion the day before, but in the hours since we had had no chance for private speech, and I had keenly felt the lack. Ygrawn Tregaron, onetime lady of Prince Amris Pendreic, latterly Queen of Keltia when wed to his brother Uthyr, was the only mother I had ever known. My true mother had died when I was an infant, and her grave was with the Shining Folk; my father's wife, Medeni, who had given birth to my six half-sibs and who had loved me as her own, had followed her two years later. Only Ygrawn, whose foster-son I had become at the advanced age of not yet six years, and who had reared me equal in love and law with her only son Arthur, had ever been to me the mother dán had denied. She had not been a *usual* sort of mother, right enough, but she was to my mind perfect in all ways, and I loved her dearly. Just as well, perhaps, as she was also my matemother, and even in Keltia *that* relationship has not yet been worked out to the joy of all. . .

It was with more than surprise that I noticed she had aged somewhat in the two years of my absence; not so much as a stranger might have seen, but there was a definite silvering in the blue-black hair, a small tightness around the violet eyes, a first faintest creasing across the high forehead. Now we have ways in Keltia to avoid such things that are eventualities on outfrenne worlds; even those among our midst who achieve the double century seldom, if they so choose, need appear older than latter mid-age. But Ygrawn, I might have known, would disdain such methods just yet, if indeed she ever took them up. We take no shame to don our years, to let them wear us in plain view, for among us age is prized for wisdom and insight that youth cannot match, and our elders are valued as highly as our young folk. We do not scorn the marks the acquiring of wisdom puts upon us; like marks of the sword, they are reminders of victories and defeats, and they are needed. But the first reminders can often come as a surprise; more so, perhaps, to our nearest than to ourselves.

As usual, Ygrawn wasted no time cutting to the heart of it. "No matter they," she said, curtly dismissing her daughter and that daughter's mate and get. "What *I* wonder is where may be Malgan Rheged ap Owein?"

A tight tense little hush fell over us all at the name: Artos, Gwen, Morgan, myself, Grehan, Tarian, Roric and Daronwy, Gerrans, Donah, Tryffin and Ysild in with Loherin from Kernow. I took advantage of the silence to glance round but saw naught of import, smiling when my glance crossed Donah's, who was doing the same. She had not been among the others last night when I came home, and so far today there had been no time for private talk; only a tearful rapturous hug, utter gladness that her uncle was safely home. In the months before my prisonment, she and I had found again the special close bond we had shared in her childhood on Aojun, and she had become to Morgan and to me the lass-child we had never had. She had grown in the two years I had been gone more beautiful even than her mother; but when Ygrawn spoke Malgan's name I all at once remembered. . .

There was a school of thought in Keltia, not very discreet nor yet very well concealed, that held, despite all claims and evidence to the contrary, that Malgan Rheged ap Owein (as he was properly styled), the son of Arthur's first and utterly unlamented wife, the late vile Gwenwynbar, was not Owein Rheged's son at all but Arthur's. Gwenwynbar, having dissolved her brehon marriage with Arthur in circumstances I have explained elsewhere, took up immediately with Owein, at that time master of Gwynedd and heir of the Marbh-draoi Edeyrn, like the faithless trull she was.

And she had borne Malgan a scant seven months later. . . Gwenwynbar had ever maintained that the boy was Owein's come-o'-will, two moons aforetime, and Owein had apparently believed her; more to the point, Edeyrn had made Malgan his heir after Owein—though that might have been read two ways, now I thought on it. If Malgan *were* Arthur's, and Edeyrn knew it, what better and more final vengeance than this could there be on the House of Dôn, to adopt and twist one of its own seedlings to his own black will. . .

And Donah. . . Otherwise her father's firstborn, she had a lawful claim to Keltia that none could gainsay; but as heir to Aojun, future queen of the Yamazai, Jamadarin to follow her mother, her future was already assured. And now too there was Arawn, already named as Tanist— But still the question of Malgan's true paternity had never been settled to anyone's satisfaction, no matter who benefited therefrom. Of course there were many ways in which this could be done, medical as well as magical; but it had never been put to the test, chiefly, I presumed, because Arthur himself wished it so. Still, it would have to be tried one day. . . Though not this night.

Ygrawn's question had gone unanswered all this while, and now Arthur seemed to shake himself.

"Malgan is a man grown," he said, his voice carrying no inflection whatsoever. "He goes where he will; but last word we had of him, he was at Saltcoats on Gwynedd, and he was there alone."

Saltcoats! Now *that* brought up memories, and not a one of them good: The streppoch Gwenwynbar had ostentatiously set up court and household of her own there, in the most royal of state, during Malgan's childhood. He had spent much of his youth there, before going into hiding with his mother once Arthur openly challenged Edeyrn and Gwynedd was taken by the Counterinsurgency. On Gwenwynbar's death (at the fair hand of Ysild tonight here present; and far too merciful a death it had been, to my way of thinking), Arthur had brought the boy to Court as a royal ward, and he had made his quiet way among us. I came to know and like him; but he never seemed at ease here, and I could well understand his present retreat to a place of happier memory.

But I knew too why Ygrawn was worried. "Think you he has thrown in with Marguessan and Mordryth?" I asked quietly, and was rewarded by the familiar dark purple glint in the violet eyes.

"Nothing would surprise me less," she replied; and Arthur sighed deeply, but said no word, and after a moment Tarian adroitly shifted the topic.

But the seed was sown.

Little more to tell of our time of preparation: That same fortnight we had given to those we had chosen for this questing was filled for us at Turusachan with the like cares and frantic doings. Gweniver had suddenly realized she would be apart from Arawn for perhaps months, if not longer, and was full of haverings and heartscaldings so that one would think Arthur could not care in her absence for their son, or even had had aught to do with him in the first place. Morgan, who though she loved Gerrans dearly had turned him over to his milk-mother and then to his fosterers with scarcely a backward glance, found this tiresome in the extreme, and was rather less patient than was her wont.

For the rest of us, it was, past the initial flurry and clamor, a quiet time, where we began to reflect on and to realize the huge import of the task we were about to undertake, and to prepare our spirits as well as our bodies to face it.

We were on point of setting out to reclaim one of the chief Treasures of our race, the lack of which bore greatly upon our physical well-being as well as on the peace of the Keltic world-spirit. Without the Pair, all healing would vanish utterly from Keltia, and that Seeing I had had so long since, in the wake of Cadarachta so long ago, come at last to be: the land laid waste, made waste; the dead land—and the dead King.

So I reflected; and came to see that I needed something more by way of making ready for this endeavor than the others seemed to need. Before dawn one morning, therefore, I rode quietly out of Caerdroia down to Mardale the spaceport, where I had ordered a small ship of the Royal Flight to be made ready for me; and dismissing the pilot I took the controls myself—and if you think that was not a hero's feat you do not know how bone-deep went my fear of heights—and headed east like an arrow in the dark.

By the time I reached Mount Keltia the sun had still not yet tipped the peak's double horns; but I knew my hours even so ran short. So, greatly daring, I breathed a prayer against the possible sacrilege of the thing and set the ship down on the very plateau that cupped Caer-na-gael, a safe distance away from the sacred stones.

The air struck clear and chill as I stepped from the ship; the grass—it was early autumn, after all—was brown and crisp with frost under my boots. I reached the dolmen gateway, and laying a hand upon the deosil pillar I cast my othersense about me. No need, even, for so much as that: The one I had come here to meet already awaited me at the circle's heart.

Gwyn ap Nudd watched me gravely as I came toward him barefoot over the frozen turf. He said no word; and when I halted and made the reverence I ever made him when we did meet, I too was silent. He was Prince of the Sidhe; the first word was his to speak. And presently he spoke it.

"You are wondering why we did naught to keep you from falling into Marguessan's hands, when you left

Glenshee all those months since. And I think you are blaming us—me, even—for that we did not protect you our guest. Talyn?"

Now I would never in all my lifetimes, yet to be or past and done with, have laid the least littlest feather of blame upon the Shining Folk. They are not to be held to mortal standard, though sometimes I have thought that they, for reasons of their own, hold us to theirs. . . But Gwyn had just now named a thing I had indeed felt in my heart's core, that I had not dared to name or admit even to myself, and he merited the truth in answer.

I rose from my reverence and looked him straight in the eye; and that too was a thing we were warned against. . . "Aye, lord," I said after a moment. "And aye again. My sorrow for it, but it is what I have felt, perhaps, sometimes. I have not spoken of it to any, not even Guenna. It seemed—not correct; either to speak so or to feel so."

Gwyn laughed, and though the sun had still not touched the circle I felt suddenly flooded by light and warmth together.

"And in despite of that you came here to seek me. . . We called this place Turusachan ourselves, once, you know, long time since."

I started violently at that small, seemingly offhand remark, though well I knew that the Sidhe did nothing offhand. Turusachan—the name Brendan had given to the palace hill that rises above Caerdroia—means simply 'place of gathering, pilgrimage's end.' Even on Earth we had had sites named so, though not very many. Though the word had become ours by usage and linguistic shift, I knew from my bardic studies that it had not been Keltic in origin; but none even among the ollaves knew from what tongue it had come to us of old.

Yet though in the common tongue Turusachan signifies completion, in the bardic speech the word means 'The First Place.' Not journey's end, but place of beginnings; first, not last. A paradox? Perhaps; but a unity also.

Gwyn saw my surprise, but he offered no further elucidation, and for my part I had more pressing concerns than a word gloss, however much I was intrigued (and I was), and asked for none. But he touched my arm, startling me even more, and began to walk with me toward the circle's center.

"Of all those chosen to go on hunt for the Pair," he began, "you are the only one who thought to come here before setting forth. Morguenna and Gweniver are ranking sorceresses among their sisters, and others there are who might be—no insult—better expected to set a seal of the spirit upon the questing by making pilgrimage here. Yet you are the one who came; and I am not surprised."

"Nay, well, it seemed the thing to do," I muttered. "Although I did not think to find *you* here, lord—"

"Did you not? Was it not to find me here that you came at all?"

I glanced sidewise, but his eyes were on the great recumbent stone at the heart of Caer-na-gael. Yr Allawr Goch, the Red Altar; none knew why it was named so, as it was neither a proper altar nor red in color. . . Saint Brendan himself was barrowed beneath it.

"He it was who brought the Pair to Keltia," said Gwyn, following my thought as easily as ever Arthur did. "And all else besides—Kelts, Treasures, all."

"And you? Did he bring the Shining Folk with him also?" That was a question to which I had long wished an answer—I and every other Kelt who ever was.

"It may be," said Gwyn, but the deep voice was veiled, and the eyes still would not meet mine. Abruptly he turned to face me. "Taliesin. This quest that you go on for the Pair concerns my folk as well as yours, for it was out of our keeping that Marguessan caused it to be lost."

I closed my eyes briefly and drew in a deep breath. "No fault to you or your folk, Lord."

Gwyn gave a short gentle laugh. "Not fault, but dán; and we love not the part we have been made to play in it. Yet things of dán can be altered, as you have come to know—" He fell silent a while. "It is not given to us to aid your search, at least not openly. But I may tell you you will have help unexpected on your way."

"And I too have a word for you." Birogue of the Mountain's clear sweet voice came from behind us, and I turned at the sound. She smiled at me and came forward, as

I gave her the bent knee due a queen, though she did not hold that rank among her folk.

"I had a thought you might be here, lady," I said. "Yet why me to come, and not my Guenna?"

"All messages are not meant for general messengers," said Birogue. "This one, as it falls out, is for you. Morguenna shall hear what she needs to hear in good time."

I was beginning to sense that vertiginous dazzle with which the Shining Folk were wont to take leave of mortals, building up around us all three like the dyster, the coriolis-driven storm that scours the Timpaun, the great plain of the Drumhead on Erinna.

"The sword broken must be reforged," said Gwyn, and already he was almost an echo of himself, iridescent as the sun now beginning to touch the peaks above our heads. "That too is part of the quest for the Graal—for any graal."

"Taliesin," came Birogue's voice out of a sparkling woman-shaped cloud, "evil came never out of the east. Remember that. We cannot be with you, but we shall be among you. Remember that too."

Then the Gates of the Sun blazed open to the dawning day, and they were gone, and I was alone in the circle, cold and sad and strangely exalted. I had the blessing I had come for, the benediction of the Sidhe upon the quest. But something else was needed—and turning back to the Red Altar I knelt briefly, and spoke to him who lay beneath, whose spirit was all about me; spoke and asked his help and blessing, he who had set it all in motion long ago. I wish I could tell you I had some great, some tremendous revelation, some towering assurance, some touch of Brendan's hand, or Nia his mother's, to take with me upon our hunt. Not that the grace and words given me by Gwyn and Birogue were insufficient to their purpose; but only for that it would round something off within me, give to this moment that feel one has when a magical action has been full and well completed. You stand in the circle, and you—*know*.

I sighed, and rose stiffly from my knees. Perhaps it had been too much, after all, to ask for. But then, as I began to turn away, I caught something of that feeling of certainty I had prayed for. Who was it, then, if not Brendan, who had brought me here together with Birogue and Gwyn in the first place? As Gwyn himself had said, this was, truly, the *first place*, and had been named so, by his own folk, long since.

And so I took my answers with me, back to Caerdroia, and then out upon the quest.

BOOK TWO:

Neartraí

CHAPTER 7

It was a dark and stormy night, with rain, a wind, no moon. I was alone; those with whom I had set out upon the questing had been separated from me several days since, and I could only dread what might have befallen them. As to what might befall me, I had no clue either; I but rode wherever my horse was minded to carry me, and prayed that he at least could choose a likelier path than I had so far managed.

I huddled my cloak tighter around me, but the rain was sluicing down my neck with what seemed a special viciousness: It was raining on *me*, on me personally, only on me, all others abroad this night had fair skies. . . I shook myself, and rain flew from the ends of my beard and draggled hair. All at once I sat up sharp in my rain-slick saddle, for I had seen something in the middle distance, or at least I thought I had seen. . . My horse in the same moment quickened his hoofworn plod, and not just for that I had shifted weight upon his back; he had seen too.

There was a crossroads up ahead, and in the angle between west and north stood a small annat. Nothing grand or lavish, merely a roadside shrine, such as might be visited by wayfarers or by local folk, if any resided roundabouts. Usually such places were consecrated to a deity with ties to the vicinity—perhaps some miracle of some goddess or god

had been performed nearby, or some transformation had
taken place, or a deity had dwelled here at one time long
ago. I ran my mind over the possible divine connections,
but since I did not know precisely where I was, I was not
likely to find any answers. Or perhaps it was merely an
annat to Aengus, the god of travellers, whom passers-by
would be wise to honor if they wished fair roads and journey's safe end; or one of the shrines to the Goddess and the
God that are found all over Keltia— But my horse had
come to a shivering halt before the shrine's door, and I
leaped from his back.

Leading him round to the lee side, out of the wind, I was
surprised to find a small shelter, obviously designed for the
comfort of any beasts belonging to those who would stop
here; it was snug and dry and warm, and to my astonishment there was even hay laid by—not perfectly fresh, but
still sweet and edible, no more than a week old. So I took it
as gods' grace, and gave thanks, and untacked my weary
horse and made him comfortable.

All this took time; and then I thought to attend to
myself somewhat, some dry boots and warmer garb and a
meatroll or two could do no harm. . . But something, or
Someone, said not yet, and with no thought of disobeying
I set down my change of clothing and put my food-satchel
carefully out of reach of any chance thieving animal, and
going outside again into the storm I hurried round to the
annat's small porch.

The door was unlocked, of course, as was custom in all
such places. Pushing it carefully open, I peered inside for
the light I had seen from the road. There was a glimmer at
the western end, but that would not seem to account for the
brilliance that had caught my eye, and presumably my
horse's as well.

The air was cold but stuffy, as if the door had not been
opened for a long time nor the windows unsashed. Yet the
floor was swept and clean, its stone slabs ringing faintly
under my boot-heels as I walked cautiously toward the faint
light.

I came to the altar set a few paces out from the western
wall, and looked for a dedication, but there was nothing;

only the plain unadorned bluestone slab. Then suddenly the sky outside was split by a blue-white seam of lightning, and in time with the concussion of the thunder a light to match the skyfire blazed inside the shrine.

I reeled back, surprised at the abrupt coruscation but terrified witless by the thunder without. When I lowered my arm that had been flung across my face, the light still filled the annat, but fell down almost at once to a glow like an altar-flame, or one of the vigil lights we set out for rituals or holy days in places such as this.

I was all at once suffused by that sense of joyful expectation that so often a ritual will impart, though I had done nothing here with any remotest sort of ritual intent. So I assumed an appropriate attitude, and then I found myself entranced. . .

I was back at Caerdroia; we were just about to set out upon the search for the Graal that all Keltia so desperately sought. I saw myself, looking exalted, sitting my new gray stallion with the black mane and tail and stockings: Feldore, the very same draggled beast who now was hanging his once-proud head in the shelter outside. Saw Morgan, Gweniver, Gerrans, all the milling others who would ride upon this quest. Saw Arthur bless us, bid us go. . .

Then the scene changed, and it was as if I lived it all over again. . .

We had taken ship to sail round by the huge headland of the Dragon's Spine, intending to begin our search in the southern latitudes of the Throneworld. Others of the seven companies had taken ship indeed: off-planet, to Gwynedd and to Scota and to Kernow, to Vannin and Erinna and Arvor—one company to a world. Later, as the plan went, those companies who found no sign of the Graal's presence would join the companies who had not yet found any sign either aye or nay, and so augment the search's numbers. In the end, again as the plan went, if the Graal had still not yet been found, all the companies would be searching one planet; we thought this might be Tara, but there was no guarantee. Some held the Cup would be found on Kernow, some said Gwynedd or Erinna. . . no one had had clear Sight, not even Morgan.

Any road, as I say, we had been sailing, far past the Kyles of Ra, when Donah, who was standing in the bow, suddenly straightened and lifted her head. I was close by, busy with charts and maps, but sensed her sudden alertness.

"Donayah? What is it?"

She pointed ahead and slightly to starboard. "A mouth in the sea."

I looked and was chilled from top to toe. Indeed, a mouth in the sea, a foaming gaping maw that looked all too capable of swallowing down our little craft in one snapping gulp. . .

Morgan had come up beside us. "Do not alarm the others just yet," she said quietly. "That is Corryochren, the Hungry Spiral, the great whirlpool that lies between the two isles Kedria and Carbria. Many ships has it taken down into itself, with all aboard them, and naught left upon the water for any to find after."

Donah flinched just a little. "Shall we sail round then, modryn?"

Her aunt put a gentle hand on the young woman's shoulder, gave a little shake to her. "Nay, lass; we must sail through."

I would have been glad of a comforting hand myself just then. "Let me guess: It is part of the Rule of Seeking?"

Morgan watched me calmly, and though she gave me no answer I did not truly need one, for I knew. . . Before we left Caerdroia, she and Gweniver and I had held a taghairm to learn, if we could, what geisa might be upon this quest. And what we had out of that trance was this Rule of Seeking I spoke of so disrespectfully just now; though in truth I respected it as well as any, and better than most. I had more reason to do so.

But Gweniver had now joined us in the bow, and after one quick glance at what lay ahead she deliberately turned her back on it.

"You had best call the others forward as well, Talyn," she said. "They will see it soon enough."

So I did as she bade me; and when Loherin, Daronwy

and Roric had joined us, Morgan turned from her contemplation of the approaching horror and spoke.

"You see what is played out," she said evenly. "Now the Rule of Seeking has told us we may not turn away or aside from any encounter of this quest, be it boon or peril, but face all fairly; that is the way by which we shall come to the presence of the Pair. Therefore we sail ahead—through that."

I must say, they all took it calmly; but then, we had faced worse in our years together. The ones I was most feared for were Donah and Loherin; as the youngest of us by many years, of ages to be our children (and *were* our children, more or less), they had neither the experience nor the assurance we ourselves had earned and learned—usually the hard way. Now it seemed that their education had begun in grim earnest. . .

I glanced over at Loherin, Tryffin and Ysild's boy. Of an age with our Gerrans (Donah was a few years older), he was as unlike his own parents as Gerrans was unlike Morgan and me. Tall like his mother, he had dark blond hair and gray eyes, and was built slight and lithe; more for the glaive than the claymore, as the Fianna put it. More than that, though: Loherin may well have been the fairest creature I had ever seen, on our worlds or any other. Indeed, he seemed too fair for the haps and harms of daily life. Yet he was clever like his father, wise beyond his years; though with a certain sadness about him that rose from no known spring. We call such a one 'fey,' an ancient Gaeloch word for someone who can sense what the dull rest of us cannot; and who is often fated to a dán very different from all other dooms that can be set down. Looking on Loherin, loving his parents as I did, I sent up a fervent prayer that this was not the case; but then I saw Morgan watching him too, and I knew. . .

But later of that. For the moment (and you will recall I was still in my trance, there in the dark annat in the storm), we had the Hungry Spiral to deal with— Following Morgan's orders, then, we made all secure aboard our little craft (well, not that little; it held the seven of us, plus our horses, and all the supplies for our journey), then lashed ourselves to each other with long lengths of silk rope and secured ourselves on deck. Why we had chosen this form of safety measure, I had no idea—if one were lost, all would be—but Morgan commanded, and we obeyed.

We had not long to wait. We heard the thing roaring long before we drew near to see it clearly; the mist drifting out of it began to settle on our faces. But it grew swiftly, and now just peering over the gunwales I could see it plain.

Truly a mouth in the sea, as Donah had called it; and a hungry one too. . . Corryochren was lipped with gray-yellow foamscud, its walls smooth bubbled green glass going down into the depths of Ocean. Though I tried to keep my mind from it, my bard's fancy would insist on picturing the broken bones of ships down below, the drowned carcasses flung from the wrecks like sodden poppets. And always there was the *sound* of the thing, the throb and howl, high and low together, deafening, shivering our bones, making our ribcages vibrate like timpauns. . .

In less time than any of us liked, we were upon it. The roar was beyond believing now, as dense as the mist and as palpable. Then the little ship gave a lurch from fore to aft, and immediately following a much sharper one to starboard. We had crossed the outer lip of the maelstrom, and had entered upon the heaving swirling waters that seemed more than ready to gulp us down.

I closed my eyes and considered. Tried I never so hard, I could not see us all perishing here in Corryochren; there was no logic or reason as foundation for this feeling, but I had no feeling of imminent destruction all the same. Glancing through the sheets of water now falling like iron veils upon our heads, I saw that the others, for the most part, did not share my certainty. Even Morgan seemed unsure; only Loherin, of all our seven, appeared confident of survival.

It did not go on very long; perhaps half an hour we heaved and tossed upon the cross-currents, spinning all the while to deosil, borne upon the spiral. Then the tide shifted, for I could feel through the hull the grip of the waters slacken upon us; we rolled violently, took an enormous wave bow-on and all at once were sailing serenely onwards, Corryochren howling empty behind us.

I lifted up Donah and Morgan, and raced astern to watch. Already a lai or so behind us, the Hungry Spiral seemed to have fallen in upon itself; it was now a broad furious patch of wild water, white and gray and thrashing. But when the tide turned again, the mouth in the sea would gape once more, and the next who sailed by might not fare so lucky. . .

All at once I was back in the annat, briefly aware once again of my surroundings, before the vision shifted, and took me with it—

—and I found myself struggling to come to land through rolling surf that broke upon green bright machairs. I looked around, but could see none of my companions, only my horse floundering strongly after me and coming to stand upright upon the shingle.

We had survived Corryochren, but the shoals that extended like a spiny shellback along that part of the coast had claimed our little vessel. There had been just enough time to abandon ship, with our beasts and a few packs of food and clothing, before the shoals ripped the craft to pieces. In the tumult I had tried to stay close beside Morgan and Donah, but the strong seas that had been running counter to the coast soon pulled us apart. The others of our company I had not seen at all.

So I stood shivering on the dry sand as my horse came up to me and nuzzled my shoulder; he seemed as glad as I of the company, and presently I gathered up what remnants of my packs I could find and sought a hollow out of the wind, to light a fire and dry my clothes and maybe eat a little.

I must have slept a little as well, for when I woke it was late afternoon of a bright day, warm sunlight making my grassy hollow a comfortable nest. I glanced around for my horse, and saw him placidly cropping the seagrass a few yards away, near where a little stream cut through the machair and ran over the sand to enter the surf.

I shook off the grass and sand and considered. I had not the faintest idea where I was; not specifically, at least. We had been standing off the coast near to where Drum Wood crept southward to end in a line of downs and dunes; but the current could well have carried us many miles in any direction. This was a most remote corner of the Northwest Continent, some of it unnamed and unexplored, almost all of it empty and unpeopled.

No help then, or very little. . . Still, if I headed east, sooner or later I was bound to strike the Rhinns of Kells—unless of course I was east of there already, and in such case I was deeply lost—and folk lived there, though not in great numbers. The other way lay Drum Wood, even vaster and denser and wilder than Corva Wood on Gwynedd, and with evil associations for me; in any case, naught there to fend Feldore and me. So after washing in the stream, and tending to my gray's needs, I mounted and we set out at last in earnest upon our quest, heading east and a little north.

Again my sight spun through darkness—

—and I was in my saddle, straining to see ahead as Feldore cautiously picked his way through a marsh as gray as his own coat. The good tidings were that I knew now where we were: not many miles from the strand where we had come ashore, on the fringes of the great marshlands called Siennega, or by some the Marai. The ill tidings were that we were well east of the Rhinns of Kells, and beyond the help of mortal Kelts, for no one lived in the lands past there, and certainly none dwelled in this Marai.

I pulled Feldore to a halt and stood in my irons, trying to see as far as I might into the featureless misty wastes. It was not all swampish: There were expanses of bright green grass spangled with tiny flowers, where it seemed a traveller might let down for a rest. He would be resting his last who rested so, I knew, for that shouting green color betokened danger. Below the interwoven cushiony mat lay a sort of earth soup of water and gravel and mud, and it was hungrier even than Corryochren.

But paths had been laid by someone in white stones across the treacherous green, and around the standing waters; and putting all my trust in Feldore's instinct (not for naught was he named 'Water-wolf'), I kneed him forward into the marsh.

While the light lasted I had not feared, or not much; now, though, with dusk beginning to shut down over the Marai, I was growing, oh, the tiniest bit uneasy. How simple to lose our way if we kept on; how fatal, possibly, even to lie down. . . A bad place, truly.

To this day I cannot tell you where he came from: the tall white-bearded man of years, dressed in gray and brown and russet like the swamp in which he dwelled. But all at once he was there, standing beside my off knee, one hand on Feldore's blue leather bridle.

"You will perish yourselves completely do you keep on so," he said in a tone of mild asperity. "Let me lead you in."

Without waiting for my assent, or consent, he tugged gently on the rein, and Feldore ruckled eagerly and moved willingly to follow—

It was that ruckling which brought me back briefly to the annat; more than ruckling, for I heard Feldore squealing and snorting in the shelter outside. The storm raged, though more wind now than rain, and I guessed the beast was merely lonely and frightened, and sensing my presence had decided to try to get my attention. I would have comforted him if I could; but—

"Who are you?" I ventured to ask, after the remains of a very excellent supper had been cleared away, and my bene-factor was fussing with bedding for his unexpected guest in the culist behind the free-standing hearth. But no answer came.

I sighed and bit my lip and looked around instead. The steading to which Feldore and I had been conducted was more than a steading; it was in fact a small keep tower, its battlemented roof rising up out of the marshland like a ghost in stone. And stone-built, that said much right there; for no such blocks came from any quarry closer by than a hundred lai. . . Yet whoever had raised this place had not been troubled, apparently, for either labor or expense; but why?

"Inisguidrin," said my host's voice, close beside me, and I started violently, upsetting my mether.

"My sorrow," I muttered; the stone floor was awash in ale, and I sorrowed more than he knew. . .

"No matter," he said courteously, and sopped up the drink with a cloth. When that was done, he sat down across from me and fixed me with a penetrating blue gaze.

"Inisguidrin," he said again. "The name of this place."

"White Island?" I had given the name's meaning in the bardic speech; strange if so, for it was neither an island nor white.

He nodded, and continued to regard me. I began to grow most discomfortable beneath that gaze, and more than once cut my own gaze longingly toward the door. He was tall and spare enough, but he was closer to the double century than the single, as we said; I could most like outrun him to my horse, but after that, how could we manage in the Marai without a guide—even such a one as this?

He seemed to know all my thought, for presently the blue gaze took on a warmer, amused glint, and all at once he smiled.

"Well. No more mystery, my kinsman. . . Taliesin son of Gwyddno, mate of Morguenna, I am called Avallac'h. I am the son of Cador, third child and youngest son of Alawn Last-king, and by my reckoning, that makes me the son of your wife's great-great-great-uncle. A far cousinage; but I am here."

A far cousinage indeed. To say that I was staggered would be to put it far too lightly; what is more, my bard's mind had instantly computed. . .

"Yet if that is so, lord"—I had instinctively given him his royal due, for he was a prince and the son of a prince— "you should be. . . the heirship of Keltia. . . "

He smiled again. "That is long gone by me, Glyndour. Shall I tell you how and why, and how I came here?"

I nodded, for by now I was past speech. This changed everything; or did it? I shivered a little, even so near the fire, and leaned forward for his answer—

* * *

—and found myself sprawling prone on the cold stone floor of the annat. This time I was not drawn back at once into the vision, and I thought I knew why.

For I could sense it all around me now, a creeping pervasive evil that seeped along the floor like the boot-high mist that comes off river-lands at night. Doubtless this was what Feldore had earlier sensed and had been protesting; or warning me of, more like. . .

But the light was still there overshadowing the altar, and the light was good, the light was safe, the light was protecting—I moved closer, by instinct as well as inclination. Despite my entrancements, not more than an hour had gone by in real time of the world; and I guessed I was being shown all the steps and paths that had brought me to this place for some reason I did not yet know.

So I circled myself about with all the protections I could muster, and threw my awareness into the light, and followed after—

—Avallac'h was speaking to me, Avallac'h ap Cador, and I forced myself to concentrate upon his words.

"You will know from the histories that Edeyrn Marbh-draoi slew all kin and connections of Alawn Ard-rígh," he said, in a voice at once eager to share a long-kept truth and reluctant to be forced at last to speak.

I nodded, for every child in Keltia knew this: how Edeyrn, having turned against his King and friend, had hunted down and murdered every member of Alawn's kindred. Even to foster-kin, marriage-kin, and kin of those kin—none was spared.

"None escaped save Seirith, Alawn's youngest; or so it was commonly held."

The chamber was suddenly silent, as if itself did listen to what this ancient scion of a lost house should say.

"Not even my aunt Seirith, Ard-rían that she then became, did know," said Avallac'h at length. "But I survived. And I did so because I had betrayed my own kindred into Edeyrn's hands."

Silence absolute. Even the marsh without seemed aghast,

all the little sounds of night-creatures suddenly ceased. I dared not move, still less speak. . .

"Not a betrayal of choice," he went on after a while. "That would have merited death on the instant, and Seirith—rightly—would not have held her hand from it. But a betrayal out of over-trustingness and shameful stupidity. I wonder now that I could ever have believed what he did promise me, to have bought so blindly on his word—"

"No shame there," I said softly but very firmly. "I met him. I know how it might have been. The guilt was not yours."

He seemed hardly to hear me. "The guilt, perhaps not. But the lack of wit, oh aye. Any road, I betrayed them into his hands—my own aunt and uncle, Athonwy and Brahan, and Athonwy's two children Farrand and Keira. They died because of me."

"They died because of Edeyrn!" I said in a voice of stone. "They would have died had you been duped or no, for it was his intent."

Avallac'h waved a hand. "Perhaps so. But I did not see it quite that kindly, and so I went to one I knew, a sorcerer of great might and repute whom some whispered was even of the Sidhe-blood—"

"Merlynn." The whisper was like tearing silk in the silence. After a moment I realized it had been I who had whispered.

He looked surprised. "Aye, he! Though he called himself Maglaras when I knew him—"

"And Ailithir when he came to be known to me," I said, still softly. "He comes yet again into the tale, it seems."

"Nor is he yet gone out of it," answered Avallac'h gravely. "But I went to him, and he absolved me of what I held to be my guilt and my sin and my failing. But I asked him for more: I asked him to set me a task, and that I might survive until that task be done did it take never so long. He was hard to persuade, but in the end he agreed, and so it was that I came here to Inisguidrin, to wait until the time and task came round for which I had craved indulgence. And now it is here. It is why you have come; why the rest will come."

"You know about the quest then?" I gasped. "That the Cup goes missing?"

"And that Marguessan my far-cousin has been trying to work great evil against it. Aye. I know it all."

He broke off to drink sparingly from a gold goblet at his elbow, and I took the moment to reflect. Suddenly something came to mind—

"At supper—you fed me of the best beef, yet you yourself—"

"Yet I myself ate only bread and drank only wine and water," said Avallac'h with a smile. "Aye so. It is part of the bargain I made with Merlynn and with magic and with dán: that so long as I did insist on remaining part of this weave, I should partake of naught else. For the measure of all grain is wheat, and of all metals gold, and of all creatures man. Wine is the gift of the Goddess, and in water is a quality endowed with blessing. Had I wearied of the bargain and the waiting, I had only to break my fast with any unsanctified fare and the thing would have been over. But I did not weary; and now the time is come, and you with it."

I closed my eyes briefly. "I am not the one," I said honestly. "Morgan herself said so; said we should See it but not be of it. . . "

"And she spoke correctly, for all it grieves you. . . But if you are not the one you are the forerunner, and the herald; and I know by your coming that the time of my abiding is drawing swiftly to its end. When he comes, I shall know him."

"But to me? I am parted these many days from my companions who sailed on quest with me. How shall I find them again? And how do they do?"

Avallac'h seemed to be fading into himself; the fine skin had become almost translucent, as white as hair and beard.

"The River of Blood, the Mountain that Walks—pass and put them behind you. The Wood of Tiaquin—seek the laughing flower that is guarded by a corrigaun with a flaming sword. The woman and the white stag and the hound. The Wood of Seeming and the Wood of Shapes, Shadow Valley and Joyful Valley. The apple and the tree, the snake-maned lion—nay, not for you. For another, then."

He had fallen into a kind of trance as he spoke these signs, or whatever they were—and let me tell you how not pleased I was at the sound of them—but now his eyes blazed open again, and he seemed to grow larger as he sat there in his chair beside the fire, and his voice was no dotard's.

"Taliesin. The Cup's danger is now, and will be settled. Tell them of the danger to the Sword."

"To Fragarach?" I asked, puzzled, and more than a little surprised. I had always thought, along with the rest of Keltia, that that great Treasure, known also as Retaliator and the Answerer and forged by Gavida himself, was beyond peril; had been given to Keltia to defend *us* from dangers. That the Sword itself could be endangered was a new and distinctly alarming thought.

"The Sword will never break save in the Peril of the World," said Avallac'h. "And only Gavida and Kelu know when, and what, and if, that shall be. More than that I cannot say. But the Sword has always meant sharpness, separation, correctness, definition, clearness, achievement of goals."

"And the other Treasures?" I asked.

"The Cup's meanings are what you now ride in search of; it will be for those who achieve the Cup to tell of them. The Spear is aim, direction, intent, impact, velocity, awareness of goals; and the Stone is beingness, endurance, rootedness, absorption, reception, acceptance of goals."

"I know," I said softly, "for so we have long been instructed."

"So. But, Taliesin, the Sword also means cleanness and death. Instruct them of that too." Avallac'h leaned back in his chair, seeming spent; but presently he raised a long pale hand. "Leave me now, my son. There will be provisions in your pack in the morning, and provender for your good beast. The road will be before you straight across Siennega; you have already come east of the Rhinns of Kells, and your road will lie easter still. East of east. Greet my kindred well from me."

He smiled and fell asleep, and I prepared to go and do the same, in the culist where my bed had been made up for me. But before I went in to my couch, I knelt and gently took Avallac'h's hand and kissed it; in part as a liege to a prince (for had he not set himself out of the succession and time alike, he would quite possibly have reigned himself, and the story I am telling would have been most different), but more as a younger kinsman to a revered elder of his line. Morgan, I knew, would have done so herself had she been here.

In the morning grayness, little different here in the Marai from the afternoon grayness, I looked for my host; but he was nowhere to be found. So I mounted Feldore, all brushed and shiny and rounded with apples and hay, and rode again east, and the way was before us all along—

—until *here*. Again I was flung onto the floor, and as I scrabbled to my knees yet once more I stopped and dared not move. The light was changing, somehow; was not as it had been. . .

And I saw why. From a crack in the stone slabbing beneath and in front of the altar, something was groping its way upwards. It moved in a blind yet somehow knowing way that filled me with utter terror and dread; outside, I could hear Feldore give that high thin terrible horse-scream. But I could do nothing for him; I did not know even if I could save myself.

For now the thing raised itself up out of the gap in the stone. It was a black hand and arm, all black, as if gloved and sleeved in darkness. It groped, flailed, pulled back— then reached eagerly forward, its fingers seeming to close to a fist.

And the light was extinguished. There came a horrible wailing sound from the direction of the crack at the altar's foot, and no more. Or no more that I waited to hear, at least. At the instant of the light going out, I found my legs beneath me, and I take no shame to tell you I turned and ran like the hounds of Arawn for the door behind me.

For *this* is what I remembered from Oeth-Anoeth, the half-memory that had tugged and teased at my waking mind and my sleeping mind alike, that I had come nearest to remembering when I lay beside Morgan the day after my return from my captivity. And I would for no sake remember any more about it. . . So I ran.

The rain had stopped, and stars were beginning to show through ragged flying clouds. I grabbed up my gear, slung it onto Feldore's saddle, followed it up and we were gone, the horse no less eager than I to put as many miles as we could between us and this uncanny crossroads place. I do not recollect where we slept that night, but there were seven running streams that lay behind us before we felt it safe to rest. And even then neither of us passed an easy night.

CHAPTER 8

In the days—I know not how many there were, truly; time seemed strangely altered—between leaving Inisguidrin and coming by night to the haunted annat, I came to face a few of those terrors Avallac'h had warned of: Feldore and I at the River of Blood; giving wide skirt to Ben Shulow, the Mountain that Walks (and not soon did *that* horror leave us; for nights thereafter I woke with pounding heart from dreams of that gray monster, shedding stones like raindrops—hence its name—pursuing me like some great stalking beast); some minor portents and menaces here and there, easily countered.

But I knew well that the real questing was barely begun. What the others were doing, either here on Tara or off on the other worlds, I did not know. In my familial concern I hoped weal and luck to Gerrans my son and Loherin my wife's cousin, but the forefront of my thought was full of three only: Morgan, Gweniver and Donah. We had been separated in the aftermath of Corryochren, and not all my magical seeking could find them. They were as hid from me as was the Cup itself, and I liked it no more than I liked that first loss.

So it was with no high expectations that I rode into a wood in which I had been told was a fountain, called Venton Race, where very often things happened; though the

countryman who confided this to me could be no more
forthcoming than that. Still, it seemed a thing to be looked
into, and I had turned Feldore's head off the highroad with
vague hopes stirring.

The wood was larger than it had appeared from across
the valley, and it was aflame with all the colors of the
autumn, so that it was lighter within than it would have
been in high summer. Feldore found his own way among
the trees, his hoofs silent on the yellow leaf-carpet, and
barely troubled to allow clearance for my booted leg on
either side as he ambled between treetrunks, or for my
height above his back as he went under the bright branches.

I had fallen into a kind of waking dream, an ashling of
sorts, so that when Feldore snorted and half-reared and
bounced back to earth again I was myself all but bounced
from the saddle. But he was chuffing and ruckling with
eagerness, not with fear, and I hauled myself back upright
behind the pommel and peered forward into the clearing
ahead, which was the clearing of the fountain, Venton
Race—Fyntenras or Fount of Grace—and seemed overhung
by a veiling blue mist.

And I all but flew from the saddle, for before us in the
clearing by the fountain one stood attending to the lamed
off fore of a splendid bronze chestnut mare. I was hugging
Donah before she was even full aware of who it was
embraced her; but she was as joyful to see me as I to see
her, and it was many moments before either of us calmed
sufficiently to give coherent account of our doings and
whereabouts since that unceremonious and nearly fatal
beaching off the southern coasts.

"It was much the same for me as it was for you, my
uncle," she said, companionably linking her arm in mine
and leading me over to where she had deposited her gear
and made a small cookfire. "I have been thinking perhaps it
is part of our search, to go alone for a time and consider?"

"Maybe so, but it is hard on the goers—and I was so
feared for you and Guenna and the Queen that I had little
time to ponder quest-mysteries."

Donah grinned, and I saw her father stamped upon her
face, like a doubled impression upon a silver coin.

"Not to make light of it; but I am sure they are as well as we have found ourselves. . . Are you hungry? I have made shakla, and there is some cold beef we could grill again over the fire—"

During the impromptu meal I listened to Donah recount her own recent adventures, and truth to tell they were even stranger than my own. . .

"When the ship broke up, I found myself in the sea," she began, her voice and face reflective, and reflecting of wonder, "and though I felt about to go under for that the waves and tiderippets were too much for me, suddenly I felt myself pushed and lifted and carried through the breaking surf to shore."

"Silkies?" I asked with interest, remembering well a time when the gentle seal-folk had done as much, and more, for me. "Or was it the Moruadha—the merrows? They favor that coast from of old."

"Neither of those folk. It was sun-sharks; indeed, I saw them help others as well, though none of us came to land together. They even helped my mare—I saw them press against her flank, to guide and steer her just as my leg would have done had I been in the saddle. . . Any road"—the Keltic idiom sat delightfully upon her—"I set out inland rather than along the coast; it seemed best at first, but I did not meet any of the others whom I had thought to come up with."

"It is a wide and empty land throughabouts. Perhaps the others hauled out farther along the shore, or rode west rather than north or east." I gave her shoulder a small swift shake. "We will find them now, do not doubt it! But you found nothing to the quest's purpose?"

For the first time Donah seemed ill at ease, and when she spoke again, there was new hesitancy in her voice.

"Not found. But I did See."

She fell silent again, and I did not press her. But I did watch her with a new attention, not as an anxious uncle to a cherished niece but as a sorcerer to one afflicted, one who has encountered things with which she is not fit or trained to cope. Perhaps Gweniver had done ill, to choose Arthur's daughter to ride as one who sought the Graal. . . But then I

looked at Donah again, and suddenly saw that which
Gwennach had seen, to make her choose so: For, in all the
royal houses of Keltia from of old, there have always been
those of the blood to tend the Treasures; usually not the
monarch or the heir, but one of the line and Name. And
sometimes even to some of these a greater calling was given,
a higher consecration: to be Sword-Prince or Graal Princess,
Stonelord or Spearhand.

Not always was there one of this special, holier calling to
serve one or another of the Hallows; but when one was
called, the vocation must be served out. For such tasks did
not always last forever; and afterwards the one so chosen
was free to go about as before. But the Hallow must be
served, there was never any choice about that; and the one
chosen as servant very often did not know of his or her
choosing until the moment was come for which the choosing had been made.

So I looked now at Arthur's daughter, Majanah of
Aojun's daughter, who was a niece to me in law and love,
and saw not Donah the Jamadarin that would be but the
present Graal Princess of the Kelts. And was pleased in
what I saw: She had grown tall and fair and quick of mind
and speech; I knew well her skill with sword and with the
bow that was the chief weapon among her own people.
Morgan had trained her not as a Ban-draoi, for magics on
Aojun are not as magics in Keltia, but in the way of the
Ban-draoi with sorcery; she was well able to withstand all
but the mightiest of cast spells, and could defend herself
with active returning if so she chose.

Yet as I watched her and was so pleased, it came to me
also that there was another young princess of the House of
Dôn: Galeron, whose mother, Marguessan, was the author of
all this dark unblest web. And if Marguessan sought to make
herself a Black Graal, a Cup of Darkness, might she not also
seek to raise up a dark princess to serve that Cup as Donah
must serve the true Graal?

Not a pleasant or an easy thought; and immediately I had
thought it I knew it for truth. Whether Marguessan had as
yet acted upon it, I could not sense: But it was not far off;
might even, indeed, be upon us.

But before I could voice my fears, Donah began to speak, in a low hushed hurried voice, and all my worst fears were turned to fact.

"When once I had come to land," she said, "as I just now told you, I set out away from the water, following the line of a small river running northwards. After a day or two, the river brought me to the foot of a great ben, which a woman I met on the road did tell me was called the Cobbler."

The Cobbler! Now we were getting somewhere. . . . I pulled out my well-worn and much scrawled-upon map of the Northwest Continent, stabbed an area far in the southeast known as the Hand, fingers of land running through the sea.

"Over here, that is where you were. And you came all this way back."

Donah nodded, studying the map closely. "Aye, and you were here, and rode as far again eastwards. But see: Where this river went by the Cobbler, there was a ford of white stones, and by it stood a man in black, who spoke my name and said he was the ford's keeper, and I must ask his leave to pass."

"This has a strangely familiar ring to it—and did you ask, then?"

"Oh aye! And he was nothing loath to allow me, but said I must take him up behind me on my horse, so that he might the more easily point the way across. Well, that did not altogether gladden my heart, and I said so. But he said there was no other ford and that if I would cross—and cross I must—it must needs be as he had said. So I did as he bade me, though with no great liking."

She was silent again, and I did not press her. "Well, it was strange," she said after a while. "He was most mannerly and full of all courtesy, that is the simple truth. And he did guide my horse's way across the ford."

"But?"

"But it was not a ford at all! Somehow it had become a bridge of glass, so solid that it bore up under all our weight, but so clear that I could see the water running beneath as I

looked down through it. When my horse's hoofs beat once
more upon the earth, he—this fordkeeper—leaped down and
took the bridle, to lead us forward into the wood that was
there."

I poured us both another mether of the shakla that had
been warming over the fire, and did not let on by an eye-
lash's flicker how alarming I in truth did find all this coil.
That man in black I knew of old, or thought I did; and
though there was no evil in him, still I wondered. What did
Fionn the Young at the White Ford, and did he represent
the will of the High Dânu toward the Graal Princess, and
the quest? But Donah was speaking again.

"He did not lead us far into the trees, but stopped by a
huge-grown hazel. Its leaves were already turning, and yet
the ground about its roots was thick with shed nuts."

"Not so strange, that."

"That is not the strange part." She smiled, but I could
see that fear and awe were still upon her. "There was a
child standing in the branches, whether lass or lad I could
not tell; very fair of hair and face, and robed in red. But the
tree, uncle—"

"Aye?" I asked gently, when she did not at once go on.

"The tree was feyn—alive and aware. And its branches—
they were full of tiny lights."

Her voice had fallen to a whisper, but it was not this that
had sent the grue shivering down my spine, and I said the
first words that came to my tongue.

"The black hand—"

Donah looked at me with astonishment. "The hand in
the annat—the child spoke of it, and, I know not how, I *saw*
it. Or rather Saw it. . . Any road, the child then bade me
take an apple from a tree I would find, and that tree would
be guarded by a snake-maned lion. But I was not to fear,
for only one who has taken a throne unlawfully can be
harmed by such a lion; and I must give the apple to the
Keeper when it was asked for."

I shivered again in spite of myself. "You saw Avallac'h."

Again her face went bright and blank with amazement.
"Aye, but not yet a while—how did you know?" Then,
answering her own query: "Oh aye, he said one had been—

you then, of course, it would be. . . Well, after the tree and
the child, the man in black having somehow vanished, I
rode on alone, and I came to the apple tree the child had
spoken of. And at its foot, curled up asleep like any sunning
cat, was the greatest lion I have ever heard of. He was tall at
the shoulder as my mare here, and his mane as black as
Feldore's, and his coat deep dark gold. And his mane was
naught but snakes, hissing."

"Did he speak to you?"

She nodded slowly. "To say that only the usurper need
fear him. I said with some sharpness that I was the heir of a
king and a queen both, and no usurper, and then—it is
strange to tell of—it seemed that the lion bowed to me."

"And you took the apple as bidden."

"Indeed, I dared not otherwise!" she said laughing.
"From there I must near have crossed paths with you,
uncle, for I came to the swamp of the Marai, and found the
path of white stones, and came to Inisguidrin in the dusk.
Gerrans was there before me, and after him came Loherin
of Kernow, and—and one other."

I had a sudden sharp flash of an-da-shalla. "Gwain son
of Marguessan."

Her face was white and strained. "Aye. It seemed—not
correct. That he should be there with us, or at all, or even
on the riding for the Cup to begin with. Oh, do not mistake
me, he was friendly and courteous, greeted me as cousin,
seemed cheerful and honest enough. . . I do not wish to lay
upon his shoulders a mantle he does not merit, but—well, is
he not a spy for his mother?"

"Very like," I said. "Then again, as likely not. We do not
know. When Gweniver chose him to be one of the seekers,
she herself admitted she did not know why she chose him. But
she also said she was not the one who did the choosing. . .
What came to pass, then, at Inisguidrin?"

Donah smiled, the smile of one who sees a wonder in
memory's eye. "We spoke to him! To Avallac'h—he told us
of his kinship in the House of Pendreic to which we four
belonged; and how he had come to be there, in the White
Island; reminded us that we were all cousins, bound by
blood and by dán to do as we must. And then he looked

straight at me, and asked if I had such a thing about me as an apple."

I had tears in my eyes, thinking of that ancient noble soul, kept so long past his release by his own honor and a crime not his to atone for.

"I gave it him, of course," said Donah, after another long silence. "He received it from my hand as if it had been the Cup itself."

"For him it was," I said softly. "It was his deliverance, his key of freedom. He had kept well his faith and vigil. . . Did he go well?"

"The gentlest going I have ever seen," said the girl gravely. "He ate the apple, down to the very nub, then smiled at me—at us all—and he was simply. . . gone. Sunlight was in the room, and a wind out of summer; and when those had gone, so had he, not even his body left behind. And yet I could not feel that a death had been. Strange."

"And Gerrans, the others?" I asked presently. "What did they then?"

"Not much," said Donah reflectively. "We honored his going, then we ourselves rode all our separate ways. When I looked back, I saw that the tower Inisguidrin had crumbled away, and stood now a ruin."

As if in five minutes all the centuries of its lord's enduring had caught up with it. . . I was silent again, seeing before me that ancient gentle face, hearing the wise words. And I wondered anew, feeling as Donah did, if this were truly the end for Avallac'h. It seemed that there was deep work yet undone; for had not Avallac'h said to me that the Graal Server would come to him before the end, and he would know him when he came?

"Well, did he?" asked Donah, and I realized I had spoken my thought aloud.

"You must tell *me* that, I think," I said, for I had a thought I dared not speak, about one of the royal cousins. . . "Did Avallac'h say aught that might point to one or another of you?"

"Not that I recall, though he did bless each of us just before he went. But he did say one thing to me that struck strange. . . He said that one can only be called if one is free and prepared to obey the calling; if one is not able to be called, one will not be. Does that make any sense to you, uncle?"

I murmured something meant to be reassuring, but otherwise took care to conceal from her my true feeling. She was too young yet for such a truth to find any fitting-place in her soul, though I understood why Avallac'h had held it out to her—to them all, come to it.

By now it was full dark, and we were both weary, so after seeing to Feldore and Donah's lovely chestnut Khamis, we settled in on either side of the fire and went to sleep. Though not before I had drawn, once Donah was safely slumbering, a triply-sealed protective circle round us all, and set runes of might and terror at each of the Airts, for good measure. . . *For you never know,* I thought, as I lay down at last, *and all too much can be abroad at night in such a place as this, where folk say things happen.*

And folk, as usual, were right.

I woke to hear a woman calling me from a long way off. At first, naturally, I thought Morgan, but that did not seem right; nor did it seem to be Ygrawn or Gweniver, or even Majanah, concerned about her child. I knew I slept, for I could feel my sleeping body heavy about me, but my mind was bright and waking, and it seemed that I stood on a ledge behind my eyes to peer out at. . . what? Or whom?

The woman's face I saw shining in the firelight was no face I had ever seen in waking life, and yet I knew I knew her. When she smiled at me and held out her hands, I smiled back and spoke her name.

"Mamaith."

"My son." Her voice was of medium pitch, clear and light, and her accent not of Keltia, nor of any other out-frenne world whose accents I knew. I threw out my arm like some small earthly graffit, to keep me linked with myself though I was all asea.

"How come you here, mathra?"

"No matter that. I have words for you, Taliesin, if

naught else, and little time to speak them. So hear me. You must leave this place before high twelve tomorrow, and go on from here alone."

"But Donayah—"

A glimmer of impatience flashed over the smile. "—will be well on her own way. I think you will find when she awakens that she too has had instruction this night; and any road the young of the duck soon learn to swim. But listen now, amhic—here is one who would speak to you of weightier matters even than a mother's love."

The vision pulled back, another figure fading forward through its radiance. And I sat up with a gasp, for this was Merlynn Llwyd himself, my beloved teacher.

And clearly I was still beloved of him, for he smiled at me every bit as warmly and protectively as my mother had done.

"I have as little time as the Lady Cathelin, lad, so listen well, and having heard remember: Bid Arthur take with him, when he goes out in Prydwen from Keltia, the Treasures from beneath the hill, and Fragarach with them."

"But how can that be, as we have not yet found the Pair!" I cried out in my desperation. "And what going-out is this you speak of, why would Artos and the rest of us be doing so?"

Merlynn waved a hand in impatience, as so often he had done in time past, and in spite of myself I gave a snort of laughter: How little do things, and people, change on the other side!

"All in good time; as I was bidden tell you, so I have told you. No more, no less." He seemed as amused as I; but suddenly, through his shimmering light-form, I glimpsed Donah's man in black, and knew Fionn the Young had hand in this as well. Other shapes there were, too; gods and goddesses both, but them I could not discern so clear. . . for this was the Wood of Shapes.

Then my mother came back. "Talyn, cariadol, one thing more. The sword must be reforged before the end; see you do not forget. Return it as you did find it, to the place in which it lay. . . Farewell, amhic, for this time!"

Now where had I heard that cautioning before, to be

'ware that a sword (which, whose?) needed reforging. . . But she was fading out now with Merlynn—Fionn had swirled his black cloak to usher them away—and I felt a last wave of love and warmth so strong it felt like a blow, so that I doubled over and wept as it ebbed and eddied round me. When I could see again, they were gone, the clearing stark in moonlight, and I looked in anxious haste for Donah.

The girl was lying on her back as if asleep, but her eyes were wide open, moonlight trembling in them, tears upon her cheeks. When I scrambled over to her, she gave a great start, as if some spell had been broken, and clung weeping to me as if we had been back on Aojun again, and she a child of three.

"Was it real, uncle?" she whispered, still in tears, looking up at me.

I smoothed back the hair from her face, with a sudden pang that I had so seldom done this for Gerrans, and never for a daughter of my own. "Oh, aye, lass, most real! True, too; which is not always the case. Can you tell me what, or whom, you did see?"

Donah looked at me as if I were some aged doddering relative whose last remaining wit had just been vanished away.

"Why, *him*, of course. I saw him. The King that was. Uthyr. And the King that should have been." When I still looked my question: "My grandsir. Amris."

Well! After that, as you can imagine, sleep was right out of the question for the remainder of the night; which, thank gods, was not much, and so we sat up again, utterly awake, drinking new-brewed shakla and rehearsing over and over the import of the visions we had been given to see.

"Well," said Donah at last, looking around consideringly, "that ban-a-tigh did say that this was a place where things happened! But to see them so, all of them! Was she wise and lovely, your mother?"

The question caught me off guard; but after a moment I nodded. "Aye. Aye, she was; and is. I did not know her in life, you know. And in the haste of our leaving on this quest,

I did not even have a chance to see those belongings of her that came from beneath the hill. . . Nor did I have the chance even to visit the splendid new castle Morgan built for me when I was in Marguessan's prison."

"Tair Rhandir, modryn called it," said Donah complacently. "For that your old lost home was Tair Rhamant. We have all been there; it is most fair. But, uncle"—she twisted a little where she sat, as if to better focus herself—"what does it mean, what we have seen tonight? Why did they come to us?"

I curved my hands carefully around my mether, taking heart and comfort from the warmth of the steaming liquid therein. How best to tell her. . . well, as she herself had said earlier, she was the child of two monarchs, I would guess straight out would be the best for all.

"In the Graal Kinship, for a woman it is her fathers that signify most; for a man, his mothers. Plainly put, in this thing, it matters more that you are your father's daughter, not your mother's; even more so, that you are your grandfather's granddaughter."

"The Prince Amris was never king." She was looking less feared—only minutes ago, she had seemed taut as a harp-string about to break—indeed, seemed eager to hear and learn.

"No more he was. But he should have been king, and would have been if Darowen his mother had not knocked dán awry by her pigheaded refusal to accept Ygrawn as her son's choice of mate."

"Who could refuse the Lady Ygrawn?"

I gave a short laugh. "You did not know your dama-wyn. Be grateful! The High Queen Darowen had many ideas that did not march with wit, or even common sense. . ."

"And my great-uncle Uthyr?"

"Ah, he." Suddenly I could not speak for the tears that blinded me, the tightness that had closed my throat. . . "Forgive me," I said presently. "I love Uthyr-maeth still, as my own father; would that he had come to me as well as to you, though I do not grudge my own niece her vision of him. . . And after all, it was given to me to see my mother, and Merlynn who was mother and father both to me, in those terrible days after Gwaelod—"

"Aye," said Donah doubtfully. "But was it only that they came to hearten us—which is no small thing, and I am most grateful!—or did what they say have meaning?"

"Meaning? No question," I said. "But *what* meaning—that, I think, may take some time to sort out."

We fell silent then, each of us busy with our own thoughts, our own speculations. When I opened my eyes it was full day, perhaps an hour past sunrise; I had fallen asleep without even noticing.

And another thing I had not noticed until now: Donah was gone. But she had left for me a message, and I smiled in spite of myself even as I read it. *Morgan has been teaching her well, no matter all her disclaims of magical gifts. . .*

For Donah's brief note to me hung sparkling in the air above the ground where she had been sleeping: *Lord uncle, I go as my grandsir bids me.* And as I read the words, they vanished clean away in the brightening air of dawn. I drew water from Venton Race for Feldore, filled the water-keeves either side of my saddle and rode out of the wood, strangely contented.

CHAPTER 9

So I was alone again, but feeling much less disheartened. It seemed to me that, though we had little solid news of the Pair we sought, the quest on the whole was progressing well.

For the undertext of the quest—to speak like a bard yet again—was far more than the regaining of the Cup. Though the recovery of the Hallow was of course most paramount, and did we fail all Keltia failed with us, still there was more to it than that. And Avallac'h had had the right of it, when he spoke to Donah of the timeliness of the Calling.

True it is, that long we never so dearly, we cannot be called upon any Path until we are free to be called so. We may still choose, of course, to refuse the call once it comes to us—and not be blamed for so doing—but unless we are at liberty to accept, we will not hear the call to begin with. And if you think about it, you will see it must be so. No matter her own wants and wishes, how could a ruler be called away from her realm, or a man be called from his family who need his strength? They might well wish to follow such calling, or even imagine they have one; but the lords of dán will never send a clear summons save to those who can freely answer.

Now this should have comforted me, when I in my rabbity fears and frets did agonize over having chosen Gerrans for the quest, or Gwain, or Donah. But it came to me that I had not chosen; they had. The lords of dán had spoken their names, and therefore it was correct for them to be on the search, and that should have been enough for me. But I did not seem to be able to let it rest, and now I began to worry it all over again.

Only by degrees did I become aware that Feldore, far from his usual responsiveness, was steadily ignoring even the minimal commands I gave him, and choosing his own way. I sat up and began to ride more actively; but the stallion would neither turn aside nor halt to let me dismount. When I tried to rein him one way or another, he began to rear and kick and goat-jump with all four feet together; and when at last in desperation I cut him a good one behind the girth with my belt as an improvised whip, he bent his neck round and tried to bite my knee above the riding boot.

I yelped aloud and gave him my heel across his muzzle, and he turned his head to the front again and kept right on cantering. I did not try again to jar him from his chosen course, and he seemed tireless in his long rolling gait.

As dusk shut down, I noticed that we were making, apparently, for where a light showed in the valley cleft between two distant hills. Not a light of steading or township, but a light as from some great outdoor lowe, a festival-fire, perhaps, though today was no feast-day I knew of. . . Feldore continued on, but even after full night had fallen I saw with some misgiving that the light between the two hills had drawn no nearer.

By midnight we were no closer still, and I had begun to panic. Feldore kept on in gait unchanged, and this seemed most unnatural, no beast could go on so, cantering untired hour after hour, not with a man and full pack upon him. All unbidden, tales of my childhood leapt to my rattled brain: stories of were-horses, water-horses, creatures of dwimmer-craft that would take on the form of honest beasts, to lure the unsuspecting riders to destruction. . .

I shook myself. *This was I, this was Feldore, nothing of dark making here.* . . Looking ahead between the black-tipped ears still pointing toward the hills, I saw with a tiny shock that we had arrived. The edge of the light was just before us now, and I could see that it was a great stone circle, a nemeton, with a huge fire blazing in the center. Indeed, it seemed most like a feast.

And the folk who greeted me merrily and ran forward to lead Feldore by the bridle, welcoming us to Shadow Valley, seemed most like festival-goers, dressed as they were in fine attire. And the ale in great keeves, and the many cookfires with savory roasts and stews on each, and the music from many harps and pipes and borrauns, and the flying feet of the laughing dancers. . . it all seemed most well.

They all seemed to know me—sometimes being wedded to the King's sister can be a help as much as a hindrance—and there was joy in their greeting. They helped me dismount from Feldore, who was steaming as if he had just come off a racecourse, and led him away to be cooled down and brushed and given his fill of oats and mash and water.

Me they treated similarly, talking all the while, soothing me, sympathizing with me for all my hardships and difficulties of the road, stuffing food into me, pouring drink after it, helping me out of my stiff travel-stained clothing and into soft clean fine new garb. A beautiful new green cloak, cut full and hooded just as I like my cloaks cut, was laid upon my shoulders and its great bronze brooch clasped at my throat. I was led by my new friends, or guides, or whatever they were, to a place on the edge of the circle, from which I might watch in comfort all that went on, and I take no shame to tell you that I proceeded to enjoy myself greatly.

And why not? I had been through much over the past weeks; I was still deeply worried for Morgan and Gweniver and Gerrans, if now less so for Donah (and that only because I had had earnest of those who were looking out for her from the other side); why should I not take this chance to forget my woes and the quest itself for a time?

I cannot say just when the change began to become apparent: The music was no less merry and loud, the dancers no less enthusiastic, the food and ale no less abundant or less freely supplied. But a change there was, for after a while I noticed that the revellers were all watching me. And not the usual attention to which, as bard and prince, I had long been accustomed to receive—that was part of my job, to be looked at, and I had accepted it, though without much relish. Nay, this was a different sort of note I was occasioning, and then I began to hear what they were whispering to one another in apparent dismay.

"Gods, who is that? It is not he! It is not he!"

Now what did *that* mean? I endured it for as long as seemed prudent or polite; then I cast back the fine new cloak and rose to my feet. And was struck dumb, for in the instant of my rising all folk save I myself had vanished away. I had been drawing breath to address the nearest dancer; now my mouth hung dumbly agape and my chest went down in one bewildered puff, and I began to tremble a little, for I was confused, and alarmed, and very, very frightened indeed.

Now that the press of whirling dancers was gone, I could see clear across the nemeton, to where in the usual place in the north an altar stood near the border of the ring of stones. Two torches had been set in the ground, one on either side of this altar, and though all other light in the circle had vanished with the people, these still burned. I located Feldore tethered over to my right—he was munching hay, and seemed perfectly content—then I went across the well-trodden turf to the circle's far side, where the altarstone stood dark between its torches.

As I approached, I began to make out something laid upon the altar, what seemed a huddled length of rags: some clootie offering, perhaps—a bundle of torn strips of cloth often left by country people at a sacred spring or well, as symbolic gift to the tutelary spirit dwelling therein. But the nearer I got, the less the mysterious thing could be so featly explained away: It was far too regular and neat of aspect, for one thing, and for no reason I could put into words, then or later, my heart began to pound.

As it turned out, with most good reason: For as I halted before the waist-high bluestone slab, and looked down on what lay there, I went as frozen and moveless as the stone itself. . . A dead body, arrayed as for Fian burial, lay upon the altarstone: a bearded man, his hands folded over the hilt of his leaf-bladed sword, the scadarc crystal set upon his breast, all according to custom. But as I forced my gaze yet

once more to his face, seeking dreading confirmation of
what I knew to be true, I felt such a terror as I had not
known even in Oeth-Anoeth, that place of death and bones.

For the face of the dead man who awaited Fian speeding
was a face I knew well. Indeed, how not. . . The face was
mine.

I cannot tell how long it took me to come back to myself
from *that*; moments only, or just as easily days. All I know is
that when I was 'ware of myself again, *as* myself, I Taliesin,
it was dawn, and, still cloaked in the fine green mantle they
had given me, I was standing over the empty altarstone,
clutching with both shaking hands the hilt of the heavy little
bronze dagger I had found in my belt-pouch after Oeth-
Anoeth; and the bluestone altar-top bore scores and flaking
gashes where I had stabbed it over and over again. Whether
that act had broken the illusion (if illusion it had been) or
scotched the vision (if vision it was), I know not; but surely
it had done *some*thing.

I felt all at once unspeakably tired and depressed as I
stared first at the stone and then at the bronze dagger. In
truth, I had forgotten I even had the little knife with me; and
I had still to learn whence it had had origin, for I did not
recall coming by it in Glenshee. . . But that was the least of
my frets just now; and presently I shed the green cloak as if it
were aflame, put the dagger into its soft leather belt-sheath
and ran my hands over my face.

Feldore had come up behind me, and now thrust his
muzzle into my oxter, the vigorous insistence of which
nudge moved me several feet sidewise. But I agreed with my
dear horse's impulse and wisdom.

"You are quite right. Time to go. Let us do so."

Perhaps the sgian had some special power about it, or some
remnant of the magic of Fyntenras still clung to me even
after this false corvaen, for no sooner did we return to the
main valley track than we were loudly hailed by one
approaching at a gallop from behind.

I turned Feldore about, half hopeful, half fearing, my
hand not far from the dagger-hilt; I was otherwise without
weapon, for you will recall only Fians had been permitted to
go armed upon the search. But in a moment or two I saw
there was no need to fear, and was pleased beyond measure
to see ride up to me Loherin, Ysild and Tryffin's lad, and
he for his part seemed as glad to encounter me.

I knew him chiefly through his cousinly friendship with
my son Gerrans; the two had trained at the Fian academy
Arthur himself had not long ago established in the Arvon
hills near Daars (and had reluctantly allowed to be named
for him; Caer Artos it was from the day he had gone to
Gwynedd and blessed its founding). As has been pointed
out, Pendreic and Tregaron cousins were not thick on the
ground, and given the alternatives available, no surprise that
these two should have grown friends beyond mere kinship.

After we had exchanged warm familial greetings, Loherin
turned his horse in beside Feldore and we rode on knee to
knee. Almost the first news he gave me was of an addition to
that cousinage.

"—so now I have a sister, at my advanced age too!" His
delight was apparent through the mock bemusement. "My
parents have called her Ydain, for an aunt of my mother's;
they have longed for a daughter, but not as much as I have
wished for a sister—"

He babbled on amiably, then became suddenly somber as
he began to recount his own adventures since Corryochren.
His tale was much the same as Donah's and my own,
though one large piece of news set me thinking.

"Aye," he said, gravely, when I asked him to repeat it.
"The search is centered here on Tara now; most of the
seekers have returned from the other worlds, and even of
those many have left the hunt."

I thought about that for a moment or two. "Is there a
reason—some direction or vision—to call the hunters here?"

The untidy blond hair bobbed as Loherin nodded. "The
King himself had a Seeing: His own father—the Prince
Amris—came to him, and instructed him to bring the
searchers from the other worlds, that the Cup would not be
found thereon."

"Therefore it will be found on Tara?"

Again the glib swung, in denial this time. "Not so featly," said the lad with some reluctance. "But that if it *were* found, it would be on Tara that one found it."

We rode in silence a while. "I was forgetting," said Loherin suddenly, "there is news of Morgan and the Queen."

I near unseated myself turning round to face him, and he shrugged, smiling with all his father's charm. "My sorrow," he said ruefully, "but I did not see them myself, only heard of them from one I encountered in the Marshes of the Siennega—"

Again I stared and startled. "Avallac'h! You met Avallac'h—"

"Prince Avallac'h," he corrected courteously. "It seems many of those who seek the Cup have come to meet him, one way or another. But though he did not say overmuch, this he did tell me: that Queen Gweniver and Morgan had both been there, only days before me."

"Therefore after my own stay." First I myself, then Donah and the Pendreic cousins, now Guenna and Gwen. . . It seemed that Avallac'h played a larger part far than the one I had so blithely assigned him in this. I tried not to hear the tiny voice that asked mockingly far inside, *And what part more ere the ending?*

Loherin and I rode together all that day, then parted as mysteriously as we had earlier met: Riding through a narrow valley, Feldore leading, I turned in the saddle to say somewhat to my young kinsman and found he was no longer in the defile behind me. I rode back a ways in search of him, but there was neither track nor trace, and after a while I rode on again, reflecting on how strangely folk seemed to come and go upon this quest.

But at the least, I comforted myself, I had had certain word of my Morgan and my Queen. Not that I had *feared*, you understand; but it was good to be told for fact. Loherin, now. . . As I said, I did not know him as well as, say, I knew Malgan, even; although he was of my cliamhan kindred.

And as I have also said, he was one of the fairest folk, apart the Sidhe, that ever I have laid eyes on, combining as he did the best features of two far from uncomely parents with a grace all his own.

And it was that very beauty, somehow, and the fact that he had been of those who had met Avallac'h, that set me thinking. Had not the ancient prince said that he would know the Graal Servant when he came? And that he was not far off? But there were two who served the Cup, man and woman; and also those who would see it but be not of it. . . We had all come to Inisguidrin; or had we? Perhaps, still, there was one yet to come, some unknown quester.

Yet suddenly I knew as surely as if the Pair itself had told me: Loherin was that one for whom Avallac'h had waited, that one of the blood of Dôn (through Ygrawn's mother Keresen) to serve the Graal. And what that might mean—to Keltia, to Arthur and the rest of us, to Loherin himself—I had not the smallest idea. But I found myself thinking it was as well, perhaps, that Ysild and Tryffin had got themselves this young Ydain.

I slept that night with Avallac'h's words ringing in my fuddled brain; so that when I woke to full awareness, as if someone had called my name, it was no surprise—or at least not the surprise it might otherwise have been—to see what I did see.

A woman stood not ten feet away, facing me; and as soon as I perceived the faint glow that clung round her, the same glow that I had sometimes beheld round the Sidhe-folk in their high places (well, do you think they are called the Shining Folk for mere compliment's sake?), I was on my feet before her, bowing as to a queen.

She smiled but said no word, and I am sorry to tell you that I stared, plain and simple. Tall she was, and slim, though I cannot call to mind the color of her hair or eyes; and she was swathed from neck to toe in a sweeping white mantle embroidered with scarlet stars. At her left hand was a great black hound, of the breed we keep to course the wild deer of the uplands; on her other side. . . I ran a hand over my face, closed my eyes in brief incredulity—was there to be no *end* to the strangeness of this quest—but the image did not change. A huge-antlered white stag stood statue-still, only the moonlight glittering upon the mighty rack he bore, and on the collar of gold belted round his curving neck.

"Taliesin," said the woman then, musically. And, "Gwion." And again, "Mabon Dialedd." There was the touch of a smile even in the names, but she did not mean to mock me, and I gave her a deep slow nod in return.

"Lady," I said, putting on the word just the tiniest edge of question. As for the rest, they were all my names, or had been. . . "You may speak of me as Bhan-reann-ruadh," she said in a light, bright voice. "It will serve well enough for now."

Red Star Woman. . . Well enough indeed: I had remembered by now that Avallac'h, yet again he, had spoken of such a one. "The woman and the white stag and the hound," he had said, part of a long list of tests and things and folk I might expect to meet along my way; but he had said no more than that.

"Arthur knows better perhaps of blue stars," she said then, and at that I startled even more, if that were possible. For you may recall I spoke earlier of the Protectorates that Keltia had come to over the years of Arthur and Gweniver's reign. . .

Hardly by policy, I promise you; but petition and the wish for alliance and the greater, very natural wish for the protection of Keltia's sword against mutual enemies had won for us an empire of sorts. Though Gwen and Artos never permitted it to be called so, it *was* an empire, in all ways save the subjugation of its component worlds. These came freely to us, glad to huddle near for warmth in the howling storm among the stars; we deprived them of no rights, made no demands they could not brook, stayed well away from their internal governance. Yet among these worlds Arthur and Gweniver, and those who would come after them as rulers of Keltia, bore imperial titles and sway. And one of the outward tokens of that sway, worn only on presidings of state on some Protectorate world or other, never in Keltia itself, was a great blue cloak, embroidered about with stars.

"As Amheraudr, Emperor of the West," I said slowly, giving him the title that those very worlds had bestowed upon him, "surely he would. But if I may ask, lady, what is that to you—or to yours?" And I glanced as I spoke at the hound and the stag.

She smiled again. "More than you may think. See, Taliesin; there is little time for telling."

Before I could divine her intent, she flung a fold of the starry mantle between us, and the clearing in which we stood vanished away. All at once I could see Caerdroia before me in the misty darkness, very small and clear and far, unutterably dear. That pang was scarce gone before I was pierced by another: I saw Arthur, in his solar, the round room overlooking the rose garden, where he was accustomed to do his private work. Saw him seated in his high-backed chair, saw the disconsolate air about him, the way he rubbed his brow and then ran the same hand into his tousled hair. I inhaled unevenly, tried to call to him, but he too was gone, and in his place came a volley of images: things I myself had Seen in times past and things I somehow knew I would come to in life, or lives, yet to be. I saw Gwyddno; I saw my father. Saw Amris, Uthyr, Merlynn, Gorlas. . .

"For men, the Quest can be to do with fathers also," said the Bhan-reann-ruadh softly, and all at once I was back in that midnight clearing, the mystic woman before me, the hound and stag watching out of wise deep eyes. "But Arthur shall not have the Cup, though he might be the better for a glimpse of it."

"That is a hard saying, lady," I remarked presently, for I was trembling from head to foot at those quick—too quick—sightings, would have had longer to look upon them. *Ah tasyk. . .* My hand crept to my hawk's feather, then fell away. "How stands it with the Quest, then?" I asked, giving the word the special emphasis she herself had laid just now upon it.

Her answer was as surprising as her simple presence. "Better than you have been thinking. But there are perils yet before you. Do not forget the laughing flower, and the corrigaun with the flaming sword."

"Avallac'h told me—"

"And I tell you again. And also I tell you this: There shall be struck a blow of which such sorrow shall come in Keltia that only the Cup itself can heal. As for you, Taliesin: You must steal my hound and hunt my stag."

"I will do neither!" I cried vehemently. "Not the one nor yet the other, and I wonder that you do ask it of me."

There was a subtle change in the glimmering light that enfolded her like a second cloak, and I thought for an instant that I saw tears sparkle upon her cheek.

"I cannot command," she said then. "I may but ask and advise. In the name of that for which you have gone questing, then: Steal my hound, hunt my stag."

"And then?" I was still violently set against her words, and she saw it.

"And then you must do as you are bidden. Not easy for you, I know."

"If I do not?"

She ignored my truculence, even as she reached out a translucent white hand to me as in appeal. "Then again there will be sorrow in Keltia, and this time the Cup itself will weep."

She swirled her cloak again, and in the following darkness I saw float through the air a vision of the Hallow we so desperately sought. It was not as it had appeared the other two times I had been privileged to behold it; never the same vision twice of the holy things. Always there was some slight difference each time one was given the grace.

"That is not because the Cup is different." The Bhanreann-ruadh's voice seemed to come ringing from the place of her ruddy stars. "It is because you yourself are different, each time you see it—or have need to."

She spoke truly. The great Hallow appeared just now as the Cauldron of Kerridwen Rhên, worked all in heavy bronze, bronze both dark as iron and polished to the brightness of a flame. There were blue stones inlaid of the color of a summer sky over Kernow, a portrait on one curving side of Queen Kerridwen Herself among Her sacred beasts, on the other of the Cabarfeidh, the Antlered Lord who is Her royal consort. And this was a true seeing, undoubtedly the Cup had this aspect; and I yearned toward it with all my spirit, for I knew I would not see it so again. . .

Then it passed on in brightness and was gone, and I cried out in sorrow, so lovely and so sustaining had been the sight of it, and sank back onto my heels in my sudden bleak dole. Greedy to lament the briefness of my vision, how many millions were there in Keltia who had never been vouchsafed even so much as this? And even in my despair of the moment I knew I had no cause, that I should see the Cup again, and soon.

I turned to the Bhan-reann-ruadh, meaning to thank her and offer an apology, for it seemed I understood a little better now. But no one stood there between the fire and me, and no print of foot or paw or hoof marked the soft damp turf.

CHAPTER 10

And now all the ill haps that had been so long and so often foretold for me began to make themselves felt upon my Path, all the geisa I could have thought of, for others and for me. . .

You will remember, I had no idea, or very little of one, as to how my companions on this quest might be faring. True, I had encountered both Donah and Loherin, the two for whom I had most concern (and if you think there was aught of chance in *those* two meetings, well, there is a nice parcel of swampland hard by the Siennega that we might speak of. . .); the others in my own riding—Morgan and Gweniver, Roric and Daronwy—were too skilled and tough and cunning to have come to any great or lasting harm, though of course I feared for them as well. Of the rest, I knew nothing save what I had gleaned from both those meetings and from the visions that seemed to be so thick in the air these days. Of Gerrans, my son, no word; of Gwain, Marguessan's son, no word; none likewise of Tarian's two heirs, Síoda and Shane, nor of Betwyr's niece Keira—far less the dozens of those not known to us before this quest, who had ridden out into peril to bring the Cup back again to Keltia and to Kelts. . .

In the westering light, it was not hard to call up before my vision an image of that Cup I had seen last middlenight, in its aspect as Pair Dadeni, the Cauldron of the Mother of the World. But with that image came again the words of warning I had had of the Bhan-reann-ruadh (and just who was *she* when she was at home, so to speak? I wondered greatly, let me tell you, though I had my suspicions): the Dolorous Blow she spoke of, the Sorrowful Striking. And the other thing, the terrible commands she had laid upon me; that I should, indeed, must, steal her hound and hunt her stag. . .

I had been Druid long enough to know that very often on such quests as this, searches of the spirit, embarked upon for no reason of material gain or glory, one may well be given orders that in other time might be deemed evil or treasonous or simply cruel. And, if one is wise enough to know that such commands are not ever as they seem, will not have the same outcome as that same command given in ordinary time—well then, one may very likely find success at the quest's ending, for oneself as well as for one's errand. For a quest—any quest—is not always, or even entirely, about finding; sometimes it is the seeking that can matter even more.

By now I had lost all track of days. I tried to tell my time by the sun and stars and Tara's two moons—their hours of setting and rising, their places in the skydance; or even by the leaves and their colors upon the trees, or their falling therefrom. It had almost immediately become plain, however, that time for those of us who rode questing was not as it was for those whom we had left behind in the day-to-day world. Day or night was all we ever knew for sure—though even that not always, as we have seen—be it morn or afternoon or even, dawn or dusk. Otherwise, the heavenly bodies were either obscured by cloud or simply made invisible, and even when they could be clearly seen they did not appear to move, in outrageous violation of all laws of nature. As for the leaves, on whom I had pinned my small hopes, well, sometimes they were red with autumn, sometimes brown and dead beneath their trees, and sometimes full deep green with high summer. There was no telling. It was as if the

land itself and the heavens above did conspire to keep us
moving to a measure of time we did not know or understand, and that too was part of our search.

But at bottom it was graver even than that: The power of
the Cup was waning, I could feel it as I rode; and there ran
one time that even I could tell—the hour was gruesome late.

What happened next I am not proud of. All I can say in my
defense is that I did not know and acted only to save myself.
Still, I had been warned; and that alone should have made
me 'ware. But—it did not, and I was not, and so you shall
hear. . .

I do not even well remember where I was that day of
days: somewhere near Windred, I think, past Armoy and its
cold blue lakes, well into the Plains of Listellian with their
wondrous herds of blue-eyed white bison. The search had
led me farther east than ever I had been before on Tara:
These were empty lands for the most part, in this remote
southeastern corner of the Northwest Continent, and I wondered idly what would happen if I came to the last beaches
and was ordered onwards nonetheless. Take ship and sail to
the Easter Isles? What lay east of *that* east?

I was therefore paying no attention to the road or how
we went—Feldore seemed to have that well in hand, or
rather hoof—and so when the dark-cloaked horseman galloped out of some fold in the air (for I swear I never saw
nor heard him until he was all but upon us), it seemed that
he planned to ride me down a-purpose, and I hastened to
act.

Even then, though, I tried to hail him, warn him off; but
he *would* come at me. More to the point, he was armed, as I
could see, and I was not; and though he bore the badge of
the Cup upon his tunic, as all questers did, his intent was
plainly counter to that which the Cup embodied. I was on a
sudden angered and incensed past 'custom—I am not usually a wrathful person—at his hostile indifference and apparent murderous bent, and in my anger I resolved combat.

Now you will know from having read these chronicles
thus far that I am by no means a warrior, at least not by

comparison with such kin as Artos or Gerrans, or such Companions as Tarian or Roric or Daronwy or Betwyr or any of half a hundred others. Oh, to be sure, I had had a usual simple childhood training and familiarity with arms, such as every lass and lad in Keltia are given; and later, with the Counterinsurgency, I was given what more I might stand in need of to keep myself alive in my endeavors against the Marbh-draoi. So had we all been. But my vocation was not that of the warrior, and the Heroes' Way not a road I travelled by choice.

Yet, though we love peace well enough in Keltia, we are not slow to use the strong arm where it is called for; and most especially not when a mounted sword-pointing stranger is bearing down upon us. So I called upon my old training (not so rusty, after all, though even in my spydays I had had little reason to summon it up) and met him full on.

Now, even though he was armed and I was not (I had only my little bronze dagger, as I have said), still there were ways, as the Fianna had taught me—even I, their unlikeliest and unhandiest pupil. And for all his fearsome aspect and approach, he must not have been so skilled after all, or else he was merely exceptionally unlucky; for on his second pass I levered him out of his saddle in the way I had been taught, and followed him down into the grassy verge. It looked for all the world (that bard's brain, forever thinking of ways to put things into song—often when those things were still in progress) as if he had simply galloped up, lurched out of his saddle, flung himself upon the ground and handed me his sword.

No matter how it looked, it was over very quickly; and when he was safely slain I pulled off his leather helmet to see who it might be that had been mad enough or bad enough to attack without cause or warning, and while on quest too, a fellow quester. *What maggot in the brain can have caused him to—*

And as I stood there with the helmet dangling unregarded now in my strengthless fingers, I began to shake, for around the fallen warrior's neck, on a short leather cord half-hidden by his gorget, was a medallion whose aspect I knew well. Indeed, I should know it: For I had seen its like almost every day of my life, in the halls of Turusachan, in the caves at Coldgates, even on the other side of my own marriage bed. And what it meant to see it *here*—

I knelt down and took it between my bloodied fingers. A small gold disk it was, enamelled on one side—like Morgan's, like Gweniver's, like Arthur's, like Uthyr's—with the Red Dragon of the Pendreics on a white field; on the other with—I forced myself to blazon it out—on the other with the white stag of the House of Dôn impaling the blue boar of Lleyn, and those last differenced by the cadency label of a youngest child.

I held it in my hand and stared, hope gone. I had slain Gwain Pendreic, Marguessan's second son. I had slaughtered Arthur's nephew—and my own.

I cannot tell you how long I knelt there shivering in the deepening dusk, praying, whimpering, vainly striving to believe (if I were even capable at that moment of anything so ordered or coherent) that this could not be so, that it *was* not so. . . But so it was; and when at last that incontrovertible, unarguable truth sank home, I threw back my head and howled protest and anguish and disbelief to the darkening sky.

How could it be? How could it happen? *Why* could it be? Why *was* it? Who had allowed it, or could have allowed it? What reason could there be for it? But I had no answers, and none was sent me; so presently I dragged myself to my feet and began dully to consider what I must do next.

Without question, above all the decent and respectful disposition of my kinsman's mortal form; after that, I must quit the search for the Cup, which clearly I had irretrievably dishonored by my actions here. I was no longer fit for the questing, had stained it by this sorrowful blow. Too, I must go at once to the High King at Caerdroia—strange that I did not think of him in this moment as Artos, nor yet as the boy's uncle—and confess my deed and accept my punishment according to the brehon code. It dawned but slowly upon me, that though I could claim the title of uncle as well, I was but cliamhan, marriage kin; Arthur was Gwain's uncle by blood, as the little gold pendant so devastatingly declared—and even more devastating to me, by blood was my Morguenna Gwain's aunt, his mother's sister, and of the one birth. . .

But I could not think of that now, for that way lay only madness, I would run howling like a dog. It took longer than I had expected, but at last I contrived to set Gwain's body astride his nervous charger, lying as if asleep along the bay's powerful neck, and lash him into the high-cantled war saddle. I caught Feldore, who had wandered off to eat the grass once he and I had parted company in the fight, and mounting I picked up the leading-rein I had snapped to the other horse's bridle.

I gave one last despairing look around the scene, as if I could find even now some explanation, something by which the fact might be altered—where *had* he come from? *Why* had he attacked without warning or provocation, not even naming himself?—but I had no answer, neither then nor formerly. I clucked to the horses and rode slowly northward, in the hope of finding some town, even if only a street-town, where a lord or bard or brehon or sorcerer could accept my submission and my guilt, and where Gwain Pendreic ac Locryn could be given the rites of speeding. Though I myself was a priest, I was too besmirched and dishonored to do this; I was kinslayer now. Not for me to speed one whom I myself had slaughtered.

Though my map had showed a settlement of some size not many miles to the north, it seemed to me as I rode that I must have come to it hours since. True, I was hardly in a fit state for observing reliably the passing landscape, but I did think I should by now have come to at least an outlying steading or townland. Yet there had been nothing; indeed, the lands were growing wilder and lonelier the norther I went. My guilt and confession and punishment could wait, but not so Gwain; and so at last I gave up and gave in to whatever, or whoever, was ruling me this night. I could go no farther, and for Gwain's sake whom I had murdered I must without delay do something I felt I no longer had any right to do. But it must be so; Gwain's needs, of body and soul both, were paramount, and perhaps there would be some éraic in this for me as well. . .

So I made a small camp in a grove of old trees, well off the road, though not so far as any chance passing traveller might not spy the fire and come over to offer aid, and I made ready to act as Druid, perhaps for the last time in this life.

First I set a spell of staying over Gwain's mortal remains; it would not last forever (other spells can be set that do), but it would maintain him as he was for many days yet, and by then I should be back at Caerdroia where other folk could do better for him than I. But now, here, ritual was needed also: And so I began with a most unsteady voice and mind and spirit to chaunt the Last Prayers for my kinsman. He deserved much more, but also no less, even if I his slayer were the one to send him on—in more ways than one.

When I had finished my priest's task, I sank down beside the fire and stared dumbly into the flames. This had happened. This was real. I had killed my wife's sister's son. In my despair, my bardic training began to spill lore pertinent to such an act into my banjaxed brain: the honor-price attendant upon kinslaughter, the strictures, the public atonements and clearances, the possible defenses and mitigations for a slaying of this sort (not unknown in Keltia, my sorrow to say, and all contingencies are provided for under brehon law).

I went over this and over this in my mind, as a tongue will seek out and push against a sore tooth, until I knew every inch and word of it by heart a hundred times over, until I could replay the encounter in my mind as sharp and clear and vivid as a viewtape. But still I could find no reason for it. Why had Gwain come at me as he did? He was on quest even as I was, he bore the badge of the endeavor still upon his tunic; true, he had been full armed, but Gweniver and I ourselves had decreed the ban—only Fians and other warranted warriors to bring swords upon the search for the holy Cup.

When I got to Gweniver and the ban on arms, something seemed to sit up in my screaming brain and tap smartly on the inside of my skull, right where the throbbing was most painful. Weaponed, with neither cause nor warning, Gwain had heedlessly attacked a stranger while on quest; and weaponless, I had defended myself against a nameless attacking stranger while on quest. I had against all right odds managed to kill him—unarmed as I was—upon which he turns out to be my nephew by marriage. Something was not right here, was very much wrong here. . .

"I am no warrior," I said aloud. "And who was it spoke of the Dolorous Blow—"

"Who indeed," came a voice from out the darkness on the other side of the firelit circle. I looked up quick as a flash, but did not move nor attempt to defend myself. Whoever it was that had come so close undetected could surely manage to slay me with little further trouble; and perhaps all the better did they so, for it would save Arthur the pain later on.

They came forward into the light, two of them, a woman and a maid. I did not know the lass by sight, but the woman—

Marguessan Pendreic halted on the far side of the fire and stood gazing down at me where I crouched dumbly and all but out of my wits. For I tell you, even in that moment I still did not tumble to it. Nay, it seemed to me quite natural that the murdered youth's mother should turn up by my campfire after nightfall, in this region hundreds of leagues from anywhere at all, with her young daughter by her side.

Well, dazed I might have been; but *this*— Nay, this was beyond all reason, and its very madness shocked me back to my senses. This was the Wood of Seeming: All at once my mind cleared, and I struggled to my feet, seizing a burning branch from the fire as I rose. Without a second's hesitance I thrust the blazing stick right at Marguessan's eyes, and was not surprised to see it pass straight through her face.

"A taish, then." This was but a sending, a bloodless projection; I remained on my feet, hastily drawing my wits and the remnants of my power round me like a mantle of protection. But my wits were dull and poor just now, that cloak of power ragged and torn; and not even in the best and

strongest of times would either have been proof against the
living darkness that stood on the other side of the flames.
She had become as her teacher Edeyrn had been, a gate into
the Dark.

Marguessan smiled. "Do you not welcome us, Taliesin?
Since your most incontinent leavetaking from Oeth-Anoeth,
my castle has gone guestless. So I thought to seek you out
this night; you were so entertaining a guest. . ."

I never took my eyes from hers. "It was you, not so? *You*
who set Gwain on to attack me all unknowing, you who
caused me to strike him down. You, out of—" I could not
go on, the words froze in my throat. Whether Marguessan
claimed or denied it, it was truth all the same. She had killed
her own son, had used me as the weapon to cut him down;
and had cut me down as well in so doing.

I found my voice again past my gorge rising. "A crime
against the Cup, Marguessan; nay, but then you stole it in
the first place, another crime against it would be as nothing
to you. Against your own son, then. Against your kin.
Against the Light—"

She laughed, a sound I remembered well from Oeth-
Anoeth; crime and denial seemed alike in her eyes, and the
last thing on her mind.

"He had joined your side, Taliesin. He rode with you
against me, to find the Pair and bring it back; and after I
had gone to such pains and trouble to fetch it away, too. He
stood with my brother against me, and he was no son of
mine."

"Nay," I said savagely, "I bear witness for his soul that
he was not. . ." I glanced aside at Galeron, who stood silent
and calm beside her mother. "So—though he was not your
son, is she your daughter? Where stands Galeron nighean
Irian in all this?"

Marguessan laid a possessive hand on the girl's thin
shoulder, and I was startled and alarmed to see both their
faces change expression. Just what that expression might
mean or be, I could not tell, nor much wished to; indeed, I
think my high self stepped in just then to shield me from it,
lest I run screaming away, or perish simply from looking
upon it. . . After a moment I mastered myself and studied

the girl. She was older than Donah and Gerrans, though not by more than a year or two, and in looks favored her father, with long curling black hair and eyes of an astonishing shade of green. Fair to look on, if only outerly: She was her mother's creature, body and soul, spirit and heart.

"She is the Dark Princess," I said, coldly, suddenly sure, and Marguessan gave me the supreme satisfaction of seeing her confounded. I was grimly glad to know I had guessed aright; but it was after all not so great a shot in blindness. Had not Gwyn himself spoken of his father's fears of a Black Graal, a Cup of the Dark? Then it followed that so blasphemous a thing would need one to serve it, one consecrated to Unlight; and who would make a better handmaiden than one Marguessan had raised up to it, one bound to her by blood and love? For I could see there *was* love here between mother and daughter, a sort of love, if I may use so clean a word in so noisome a context. . .

I pressed my advantage. "So it comes to this, Marguessan of the House of Pendreic," I said, in the tone bards reserve for rightful cursing and the doom of anathema, and despite her art and arrogance I saw her shiver as she recognized that which was now in my voice.

And I spread my arms to either side, as I felt the power of Arawn, that one of the High Dânu who is Doomsman and Prolocutor of all that is made and moves, and I spoke with his voice to enumerate Marguessan's offenses.

"You stole the Cup of the World, or caused it to go missing from its rightful guardians. You brought unhealth and loss of healing upon the land and the folk. You used unwholesome arts you acquired unlawfully from the darkest lord of magic Keltia has ever seen—you were his disciple!—and committed therewith other acts of evil I have neither time nor stomach to enumerate. And today you have killed your own son by causing him to attack his uncle, each unknown to the other, and caused me to kill him in defending myself. The Marbh-draoi is doubtless proud of such a slate of deeds, wherever he is just now. Oh, aye, he trained you most well!"

During my denunciation, Marguessan's face—fetch-sending though it was—had registered a run of emotions for all

she struggled to control it: pride, satisfaction, pleasure, a
kind of urgent hungry need. Fear and guilt, if they were
there, were well hid. And though I had ended on a note of
such bard-honed, Druid-trained, god-inspired avengement
as could by its righteous wrath have flayed a palug,
Marguessan seemed still whole-skinned. But I found to my
surprise that I was not yet done.

"And now you lead your daughter to follow after you—
to keep alive the ways of the Marbh-draoi, to keep the Dark
in Keltia. . . Marguessan, in the Goddess's name, why?
How came you to take such a dark road?"

Everything I had, I put into that cry and question: every
ounce of bardery in me, every rann I had as Druid, every
scrap of strength of spirit and kinship. Arthur was in that
cry, and Ygrawn who had given birth to this monstrousness,
and Morgan who had shared the womb with her, who could
be closer to her than that? And almost, almost it turned her.
I say it without pride and without shame of failure. I felt it,
saw it. It almost turned her. Without question it reached
her; touched her, even. But turned her? Nay. That it could
not. I think now that by then nothing could have.

So I saw her face change, blur; saw the dark thing at the
back of her eyes lift and blaze and shiver, saw for one last
instant more the charming child I had known at Coldgates,
before the blackness had coiled inside her. I saw what toll
her evil had taken of her, and what more it would demand
of her before the end; saw how in guise of mother's love she
had passed the darkness on to the girl at her side; saw with
certainty, truly Saw, that the battle joined so long ago was
moving now upon the third generation. With Edeyrn had it
begun; his children—in spirit if not in flesh—had been
Owein Rheged, Gwenwynbar and Marguessan the greatest
of the three. Now Edeyrn's last living heir was passing her
legacy on: Galeron, dark princess of the Black Graal, would
be Donah's adversary and opposite, and there was naught
anyone could do now to stop it.

And I knew that as well as Marguessan. . . "For it is not
over yet, is it, Marguessan, not yet done?" I asked, and now
my voice had narrowed and chilled and sharpened, cold and
thin and silky had it become, the cursing-voice of the bards

I had never yet employed in all my life; had prayed, indeed, I would never be called upon to use in any life. What power it might have against such as this, I did not know, nor could my tutors have imagined; but I owed it to them, to all Keltia, at the least to try.

To my eternal surprise it rocked her as a blow to her body must have done; the curling tendril of steel-cold magic was finding chinks in her armor of unlight. But my own lorica was the Light. . .

"The Black Cup, the blasphemy, the obscenity you seek to bring through into the world? Leave it, Marguessan. Leave it where it is, on the other side, in its destined home. It is not for here, for us, for you. You have not the strength. Power, aye. Strength, nay. It will destroy you, and your daughter with you. Your son it has already destroyed."

Somewhere cold and far she laughed, and I nearly fainted before I could draw myself back. "Well enough, harper, so long as it destroys my halfbrother and his cousin-wife and their get and the rest of you as it does so. You it has already touched. For you see"—she jerked her chin at Gwain's mantled form, over on the edge of the clearing—"it is even now at work. And when I am done—"

Her face was drawn and terrible to look upon, her hands raised with palms facing, shoulder-high, her mouth working to shape some dire rann. But though I lifted my head to face my doom as proudly as I might, it never came. All at once, she was gone, as if some mighty wind had blasted her away, and I was fallen retching to my knees in her aftermath. But she was gone, and Galeron with her; and I knew it had been no power or virtue of my own here demonstrated that had hunted her off. Nay; it had taken an art and power greater far than mine. Not Morgan's, even; but whose it had been, I did not care even to guess.

And in my boundless relief I had an utterly irrational hope that all had changed, that all had been made different, and I turned eagerly to Gwain, fully expecting to see him battling off his shrouding cloak and getting to his feet, smiling and jesting all the while with his uncle. But nay; he lay there still, and stiller; and after a while I sat down again as near the fire as I could get, shivering, my back against a tree. In my hand now was the bronze dagger that I had received under the hill; though it would have been of no use in the fight that had just now been waged here, all the same it gave me comfort to hold it now, and I turned it over and over in fingers that seemed made of water, watching the firelight flare along the thick blade that was not sharp.

I felt—well, 'better' would not be the word, but it was the only word that I knew. Gwain was still dead, and I had still killed him. And though I now knew Marguessan to be the real murderer, it did little to requite me for what I saw to be my guilt. Never in a hundred lifetimes would I have imagined that Marguessan could slay her own son; though now she had done it I had no difficulty whatsoever in believing it, mind; it was just that I would not have thought so to start off with, not even of her. . .

I must have fallen asleep—for I was exhausted beyond imaginings in body and soul—because I woke with a start moments later, and proceeded to erect a circle and proper defensive wardings against any more such visitors, and by the time I was done even Marguessan would have hesitated to break through my shields. Gwain and the horses were included in the compass; who knew what might happen if they were not?

And at last I settled down again, still shaken to my soul, but feeling somehow lighter, clearer. The enemy had a true face now, in a way that even my forced sojourn at Oeth-Anoeth had not provided. Now I saw, as for the first time, how far Marguessan had travelled into the kingdom of the Dark; and how far she planned to pull the rest of Keltia in after her. Even her own children, seemingly, were expendable in her evil quest: Gwain she had given over to death; Galeron was become some kind of dark handmaiden; and Mordryth—well, since his combat with Gerrans at Oeth-Anoeth, we had had no word of the eldest of Lleyn. Though, I doubted not, we surely would. . .

But now was not the time to counter any of this. On the morrow I should go to Arthur, as swiftly as I might, and he would hear me and believe; things would be done. Just now, I would sleep; I had strained every fiber of my being in my struggle with Marguessan, had done violence and had had violence done me—and here I had thought earlier this day that I had used all my strength and resource to cope with the slaying of Gwain.

Ah Goddess. How wrong we souls can be.

CHAPTER 11

When morning broke, unseasonably warm and clammy, I ate a little, then attended to the two horses, placed Gwain's body in the saddle as before and rode out without looking back.

I made no pretense now: I was lost, had not the faintest idea of my whereabouts nor yet where I was hopefully headed. After some thought, I decided to keep to the way north. There were few roads of any sort in this part of Tara, and sooner or later, this one I was on must lead me to a town; why else had it been made?

Comforted with this doubtful logic, I kept on steadily until the early dusk of autumn began to throw long shadows across the wide-mouthed valleys through which I was now passing. Still no settled lands, much less a town of any size. Then, coming through a small wood, following a strong bubbling stream of whose clear waters I intended later on to make good use, I drew rein sharply. Feldore nickered curiously, not alarmed, and Gwain's bay mare joined him.

A pavilion stood by the banks of the stream where it ran through green-cut turf swards over white gravel. Willows overhung the brook and edged the clearing, and the rather grand tent—blood-red silk walls and white roof, with gold cording and silver-tipped lances for poles—had been pitched directly beneath one of the largest trees, which trailed its yellow feathery foliage onto the tent's high domed roof.

I hailed the owner as courteously and carryingly as bards can do, but no reply came; indeed, no one seemed near-abouts, no horse even, or any trace of either. Dismounting, wary and watchful, I tethered my two beasts (leaving Gwain's body, for the moment, as it was), and then stepped up to peer into the pavilion's dim interior.

Though there was no smallest sign of anyone's presence, nor even a sign that anyone had ever been there at all, the tent was lavishly and luxuriously appointed. A rich feast of meats and bread and wine and sweets was spread out in silver dishes upon a board draped in oréadach; there was a wide bed in the corner laid with silk and linen, its pallet thick to the height of my hip with the down of wild geese, furs of wolf and fox and mink piled deep upon it. A gold harp stood in another corner, and my fingers, deprived of Frame of Harmony (I could scarce have taken my beloved harp on quest, though I had made a rough road-harp or two to pass the time as I went), itched at sight of it; there were books bound in red leather, and a fidchell game standing, its counters of rock crystal and mahogany obsidian poised on an ivory and ebony board. All about me spoke of rich comforts and simple pleasures well merited and freely offered, did I so choose to avail myself.

Then as I turned to glance behind me at a fancied sound from outside, I saw it and froze: A black hound, tall at the shoulder as a yearling foal, lay stretched across the threshold, nose on paws. It glanced briefly up at me when I cried out in my startlement—well, yelled, is more the word, for surely it had not been there when I entered, and you cannot blame me for being surprised—but it made no move either friendly or not, seeming to wait upon what I myself would do.

My immediate impulse—all thought of feast and couch had fled—was to try to make it past and get to the horses, but I dismissed that at once. That was a coursing deerhound lying there: However negligent it might look, it could well afford to give me a morning's start and still run me down before the noonmeal. Only the great wolfhounds of Erinna, and Lord Arawn's own hounds, could outpace this one. . .

And then it all came back to me, though doubtless you are before me. But in the sheer horror of yesterday's assaults, the episode with Gwain and the nightmare of Marguessan to follow, I had clean forgot: Yet surely this was the giant hound that had accompanied Red Star Woman, the Bhan-reann-ruadh, when she came to me I do not even know how many nights since.

I looked at the hound again, but it lordlily ignored me. Now the Bhan-reann-ruadh had told me that I must steal this hound, and then hunt her stag, the great white roebuck that had accompanied her. Presumably I would have the help of the hound in my pursuit, but I did not know that for fact, and the hound was plainly not about to show me a sign one way or the other. It was here; it was waiting for me to act; that was its part for now. The rest was up to me.

Now I must tell you, since we have nothing hid 'twixt bard and hearer, I was far more taken by the thought of the luscious feast and even more luscious bed than by the idea of reiving away a certainly magical hound to hunt a just as assuredly magical stag. Kelts have a long if regrettable history of lifting and reiving—cattle and mates, usually, at least judging by our sagas and songs—so that theft in itself troubled me not so much as it might have; and besides, I would more or less be stealing under orders. Surely under geis. . . It was just that I had been through so much since beginning the quest for the Cup, and especially in the past few days, and a little earthly comfort is not a terrible thing, is it; nay, nor is one a mean ignoble person for desiring to come by some, however strangely. . .

I sighed, and drew myself up. I had forgotten or disobeyed instructions before now upon this search, and see what had come of it. True, I had earned everything I had gotten, and had gotten only that which I had been warned I would get; but it was grief and sin and sorrow all the same. Though rewards were seemingly offered here, it might be that I had not fairly won them just yet, and perhaps I was the only one who could so determine. Well, now I would obey: I would do as I had been bidden, just so, no more. I would reject the proffered hospitality (even though my battered body and starved spirit wailed at having to do so), and

I would outrage all tenets of honest guestship and I would
steal from my absent host. It seemed all throughother: But
keeping to rules for more ordinary times had brought woe.
Now I would conform agreeably to these rules of
strangeness that the Bhan-reann-ruadh had set down for
me, and trust on a better outcome.

I stepped forward, holding out my hand to the black
hound and rubbing my fingertips together, making the
hopeful encouraging noises that seem to be a universal signal to coax a reluctant beast. After a long considering
moment, the great hound flexed its mighty forequarters in
one slow prodigious stretch, then rose as slowly to all four
feet and looked up at me alertly, the tail beginning to swing
behind it. I looked to be sure: a bitch, and most extraordi-
narily tall and powerful for one of her sex, even dog deer-
hounds as a rule did not grow so large and strong. . .

I yelped aloud and looked down in amazement and dismay: The hound had given a sharp nip to the edge of my
hand where it hung by my side. I said a swart word or two in
protest, but the creature looked up at me again with gold
glowing eyes, and I said no more. I had never seen such eyes
in any beast; not even the recently late Cabal, clever and all but
human as he had often seemed, had had eyes like these. They
pierced through me, seeming to see even unto the end of my
days; but it was only a hound! Or—

A thought had come into my head: I had been nipped
directly I had made that impolite visual inquiry into the gender of this animal I had been all but commanded to steal,
that I was already well convinced was rather more than
mere beast. Could it be that my thought, no less than my
admittedly rude scrutiny, had *offended* the creature, so that
the nip she had given me—not a very grave one, though it
damned well hurt, and was just now even beginning to bead
a few droplets of blood—was by way of being a *rebuke?*
Could it be that—

But the hound had vanished out the pavilion door, and
after a moment I thrust back the white silken doorflap and
went after, closing it behind me. Though the thought did
cross my mind just then: Precisely who was stealing whom
here?

Who and whom became most immediately inconsequential as soon as I got outside: Gwain Pendreic's body was no longer in the saddle of his bay charger.

I must say I was not very much surprised by this development; it seemed as if something like to this had been about due to happen, and here it had come, ah, dead on time. I looked for tracks, of course, but of course there were none but my own, you know how these things go. . . After some thought I gathered up the soft leather thongs and cords that had held Gwain fast upon his mount—noting as I did so that every single knot was still fastened, and, again, unsurprised that they should be so—and began to transfer some of my gear from Feldore's saddle panniers to those of the bay, and took some more thought alongwhile as to what I must, or should, do next.

But all that was already determined: As I stood irresolute by Feldore's stirrup, I suddenly felt a cold nose in my palm, and startled to recall the black deerhound bitch.

Yet there she was, looking up at me with those alarming golden eyes, pushing her nose into my hand—my bitten hand—just as a true dog would do. Temporarily mad, I went to one knee and began to scruffle her under the chin, just as a true dog would enjoy. She bore it with equanimity, even some reluctant enjoyment, for a few moments, then began to growl so softly that it was more a purr. I took the hint.

"Well enough! We are going." I vaulted into Feldore's saddle, leaned over to catch the bay's rein and followed the black hound back over the stream and back to the road.

The hound led me at a fair pace through country wilder than anything I had so far seen on quest. We skirted harsh blue mountain ranges at a distance; crossed stony plains where I was hard put to find water for us all, still less grass for the two horses; heading always eastward now. Once we encountered a herd of the blue-eyed bison, their eyes startling sky-color beneath their white shaggy matted forelocks, on their way south from their summer feeding range in the Litherlands. But the beasts, though cranky just now with the rut, merely moved placidly aside for us to thread our way through their midst.

At last we came to wooded lands again, and I stared about me with wonder. No one I knew or had heard tell of had ever been in this region before; if any had dwelled hereabouts, they were long gone. Not even stones remained to mark where their housen had stood, nor fence that had bounded their fields; and the woods, once cleared and battled back, had encroached again on that which they had held of old. Indeed, some of these woods had never felt an axe since Kelts first came to Tara: Oaks the thickness of a small cottage, beeches whose smooth silver trunks stood like pillars in the Hall of Heroes, apple trees as wide in branchspread as any roof of thatch—all were here, and all somehow aware of me.

Still, I followed on after the black hound, as she trotted before me untiring, glancing back every now and again as if to be sure I still came after. I laughed shortly; as if I had any choice in the thing! But I must say it was pleasant to be led for a change. At least I knew I was being drawn to some purpose—to hunt the stag. And at that I grew again unsettled. Why would the Bhan-reann-ruadh insist upon an action so contrary to my spirit? Oh, I was no stranger to the chase, enjoyed a good winter morning's coursing as well as the next Kelt: Though these days we hunted only when the local population of beasts of venery needed thinning, in the first days of Keltia we had hunted simply to eat, as we had on Earth. In all honesty, what I liked most about the hunt was simply the thrilling gallop across country on a good horse; the rest was not my cup of ale.

Which was why I wondered yet again, why me? Why had Red Star Woman insisted? So now I had stolen her hound—or it had stolen me, was more like—and was at present, apparently, in pursuit of her stag. What then?

I was all but pitched from the saddle as Feldore surged eagerly forward, and in the same instant saw why. Heard why, rather: Far ahead, the black hound had given tongue on quarry sighted, and Feldore, by no means reluctant in the chase, had responded. We were cantering now, and I redistributed myself 'twixt pommel and cantle, checking over my shoulder to see that Gwain's bay came along at speed. Not to fret: Horses are gregarious creatures, and will do what they must to stay in company with their friends. With that we flashed beneath the eaves of the wood.

In the cool dimness—it was a fir-wood, this one, green-roofed when all other woods lay bare—I peered ahead as far as I could see. The gloom was all but palpable, and so thick did the needles lie upon the forest floor that I could scarce hear the sound of our own passage. But the hound's voice kept us on the track, and presently her note changed to that of a hound that has brought its quarry to bay.

Feldore thudded through into a small glade, and I hauled on the rein. Before me, the hound stood by a vast green-leafed bush, and whatever it had run down had gone to ground in this thorny thicket. I glanced round warily, then dismounted and tied both horses to the nearest tree. I had no weapons, of course, so dispatching the quarry was out of the question (and, before you ask, nay, I had not yet addressed the problem of how I was to deal with the magic stag when I caught it); but I approached with caution all the same.

"This is the Wood of Tiaquin. Who breaks our peace within it?"

I whirled round at the sound of the voice, which had seemed to come from behind and below, somehow. At first I could see nothing; then one of the tree boles shifted and moved and came toward me, and I saw that it was no tree piece but a corrigaun, one of the dwarrows, the halfling faerie folk. Not so fair nor yet so tall as the Sidhe, the magic being before me was of a race seldom encountered in Keltia and even more seldom spoken of, far less understood. Some think the corrigauns are no folk at all, but merely aspects the Sidhe themselves put on when they wish to go unrecognized; others think not, that the corrigauns are like to the Sidhe but lesser, more apt to mischief or even malice, where the lordly Shining Folk are creatures of the Light and do not deign to mere tricksiness. But we had been taught, when I was back there in Druid school, that the corrigauns are not evil (and indeed this is borne out by history; no tale of harm to mortal Kelt by a corrigaun has ever been heard in all our centuries), merely not so evolved upon the Path of Being as their elder brothers, more of the earth than is the race of Gwyn.

I stopped where I stood, and the corrigaun and I studied one another for what seemed a long while. I know not how he perceived me; but I saw a sturdy, well-built creature, about half the height of a tall man, black-haired and black-bearded, broad of shoulder, his arms and legs massively muscled, gnarled and iron-tough as apple boughs. He was not uncomely to look upon, if by no means so fair as one of the Sidhe, and his eyes were both dark and bright together—and keen as the unsheathed sword he held in his right hand. And at sight of that sword I started, and wondered greatly, for the blade of it was not naked steel but soft golden flame.

Though the flame licked and flickered, the corrigaun did not seem to fear it, or even feel its heat. Yet where the swordpoint touched the damp earth tiny gray wisps of smoke were curling upwards. . . But he had addressed me, and deserved the courtesy of a reply.

I bowed slightly—I was, after all, a prince of the realm by my marriage, and though he might well be a prince himself among his folk, I was the visitor here, and so had precedence over him—and spoke in the bard-voice.

"Your pardon, my master. I am Taliesin Glyndour ap Gwyddno, ollave of the Bardic Colleges, Druid, mate to the Princess Morguenna Pendreic and fostern to Arthur the King. I mean no trespass, but was led here by my guide."

I nodded to indicate the black deerhound, who sat now on her haunches, tongue lolling, looking much pleased with herself. She tensed her slim frame a little, in that way that dogs will do when they know you are speaking of them, and gave the small eager whimper that goes with that movement, but otherwise did nothing.

The corrigaun glanced briefly at the hound, then back at me. He had raised the point of the flame-sword as I had spoken, and it was now levelled at my chest. I deemed it best not to move, and to answer all questions.

"Why have you come to the Wood?" the being asked.

I opened my mouth, about to repeat the only reason I had, the one I had already given: that the hound had led me, and further, that I had not the faintest idea whyfor and that he would in such case do better to ask the beast himself. Then I thought flashingly of Avallac'h, and the things he had told me, indeed, the geisa he had spoken. What in the Mother's name had he said—oh aye, that the apple must be taken from the tree guarded by the snake-maned lion, and that of course had been quite awful enough, even if not meant for me, but then, but then he had said— I harrowed my brain, coming up with white fords and glass bridges from here to the Hither Hereafter, but— I had it!

Triumphantly: "I have been bidden seek the laughing flower, and take it from its guardian, who will be a corrigaun with a flaming sword. I take it that would be you?"

The dwarrow's shoulders heaved mightily, and I tensed, thinking that he was readying himself to swing that fiery blade; but then I saw with what I think was relief that he was silently laughing.

"It might well be, lord prince Druid, Pen-bardd, princess's mate and king's fostern. But what use have you for such a blossom?"

I was treading warily now, for the ritual questions were as thick on this ground as the pine needles, and needed careful answering.

"I have not yet been told it. But the Prince Avallac'h, he who dwelled until lately at Inisguidrin, bade me seek it and take it when I found it. If there is a use for it, be sure I will fill it as I am so given to do."

"No doubt." The corrigaun was silent for a moment, his eyes on me; then his glance shifted twice, first to the hound, then to the briarbrae behind him. "That which you seek is within. Go and fetch it out, and it is yours. Not yours, but yours. Do you take my meaning?"

"Aye," I said shortly, too annoyed to be ritualistically diplomatic—if we once began to bandy hidden meanings about, we should be here until the snows flew—and any road, he was laughing again, no doubt at me.

He saw this, and shook his head. "Nay, take no offense! You have done more than well to have found your way here at all. To pass the Siennega of ill repute; to speak with the Keeper, who shall not be named here again; to come by Shadow Valley and the false corvaen; to have withstood the temptation of Joyful Valley and to have countered the dark power who goes before you into the east, and all haps of the questing—"

But I was a bit behind him. "The dark power? You mean Marguessan? Came *she* here?"

The corrigaun nodded, eyes now like black flints. "Came, aye, but came away empty-handed. Now, seek what you—and she—did come for." He gestured into the depths of the brae with a royal courtesy, as if he ushered me into a hall of the presence. "In there. I will wait upon your return."

He seemed as he spoke to fade from my view, though with my sidesight I could still see him, standing motionless off to one side of the clearing. Then I turned my full attention to the thicket before me.

I could see no way in. It was more than a thicket: a mass of briars, woody vines crossed and woven together like our famous Keltic knotwork, and every crossing was bossed with a thorn the length of my thumb, dull bronze in color and sharp as a brooch-point.

I drew a deep calming breath in the way I had been taught, resigning myself to death by shredding, when again I felt the cold touch of a hound's nose in my palm. I looked down—so tall was the beast that I met her grave golden gaze somewhere around my waist—and then flinched uncontrollably, as she bared her gleaming fangs. But this time she only mouthed my hand in the great jaws, as delicately as if she were carrying a puppy by its scruff, and tugged so that I must move forward with her into the brae.

And where the hound led me, the briars gave way for us to pass by unshredded. Not so much as one thorn-hook snagged on my tunic or scratched the deerhound's wiry black coat; as for the vines themselves, they had become of a sudden as pliant as ivy tendrils in spring.

I do not know how deep in we went, the magic hound and I; it had been dark beneath the trees, and was darker still amid the briarbrush. But all at once, in the thickest, thorniest heart of the tangle, something gleamed before me like a ruby, like a drop of blood in sunlight, and I saw that it was a flower.

Why 'laughing'?, I heard myself wondering far away, and not for the first time; for there was naught mirthful about this bloom. Very fair it was, a perfect wild rose, its petals opening out but its secret heart still tightly furled. I looked at it, then searched carefully around, lest there should be some other flower and I in my haste pluck the wrong one. But nay; there was only the one, and I reached out a hand for it. . .

. . .and was instantly nipped on the other hand yet again by the hound at my side. I opened my mouth to roar a protest—what in all the hells had I done to merit *that?*—but my jaw remained well agape as out of the close air words came to my ears.

"Ask first, and thank it."

I stared wildly in all possible directions, but saw no one who might have uttered so much as a syllable that I could have heard here deep inside the briars. Then, as the words were repeated, a little impatient snap to them now, I suddenly understood. It was the hound who had spoken.

Well, my methryn did not raise a stupid Tal-bach; slow I might be at times, but on the whole it did not take a house to fall on me. . . And also I recognized at once the rightness of the command I had been so strangely given.

So I bowed to the flower, and did not feel the least littlest bit embarrassed to do so; I begged its aid in my quest as gravely as if it had been some armed champion I besought to fight for me—and perhaps in its own way it was just that. I thanked it for allowing itself to be employed in such wise; and then gently, very gently, I broke its stem from the thorned branch where it had grown and waited who could tell how long. I dared not look at the hound.

At once the darkness lifted, and sunlight streamed down upon me as I stood there stupid as an owl with the rose in my fingers. The briars grew on a sudden lush and thick with a flush of green, supple as willow-wands, and rose blooms were thick on all sides. Roses without thorns. . .

A path stood open back to the clearing, and the hound

was already loping down it. I followed after more decorously, for I was a bit dazed by now, as you might well expect, and in a few moments came again to where the corrigaun had stood. But he too was changed.

The flaming sword was gone now, and he was no dwarrow more but a flame himself, white and gold and tall as a spear. For one glad moment I thought that it was Gwyn come to me, Gwyn son of Nudd whom I dare to call my friend; but when I lifted my dazzled eyes to his face I saw that he was not. *Though surely of my friend's folk*... Tall he was, dark gold of hair and sea-gray of eye.

"I am Allyn son of Midna," said the Sidhe lord then, and I could see through the silver light that mantled him that he was smiling. "Gwyn who shall be king did set me here to guard the Rose. He had a thought it would be you, Penbardd, who would win it, and wished to have a friend, even if one only by remove, here to greet you and see all was done properly."

I bowed deeply and made some courteous speech of reply, but I was in truth no more than one enormous manyaspected question, and I felt that much was owed me (felt rightly or no, is not the point), and so I scrupled no whit in asking.

"But why, lord? What shall I do with it? Where must I take it? Why is it named the *laughing* flower, to me it seems nothing to smile about? What purpose to it? And that stag I must hunt, and what of the others—"

He raised a hand in protest, laughing now. "Peace, peace! All in very good time, I promise you. But I will say this: As to what you must now do, with the precious thing you bear, you must bring it with you to the Castle of the Cup, Caervanogue where it stands upon the Dragonsea, and there you shall give it into the Keeper's own hands. Its nature shall there be made clear, and its name explained, and its purpose fulfilled—to your personal joy. And as to the White Hart of the Mountain, you already have your guide." He nodded at the black hound, who was sitting a few feet off looking very proud of herself.

I still had goleor of questions to be asked, but Allyn son of Midna did not seem one to be pressed; and as I watched

he drew himself into himself—it is a hard thing to explain—
and I yearned toward him in protest.

"Ah, nay, do not go, not yet! It is true, then, that the
corrigauns are but the Sidhe-folk in other garb? Tell me that
only, of your courtesy, before you leave!"

The light that had cloaked him—Allyn son of Midna—
was beginning to grow blinding bright from within itself, as
a cloud will when the sun that has run behind it is about to
break from the veiling mist.

"For that you are friend to my folk, aye," said the brightness, and even now I could hear the smile. "The answer is
aye and nay both. It might be so, but it might also be that
we choose to put on dwarrow-shape, as you might choose
between leinne according as to your whim on such and such
a day. But whether that makes us one or the other—you
must tell us."

With that Allyn mhic Midna was gone. *Typical!*, I
reflected with no small bitterness; well was it said 'Seek not
the Sidhe for plain speaking'! Whoever had first said so—
probably in as fierce a frustration then as I now—did not
know the half of it. . . and, I conceded with even more rue,
no more did I.

But it seemed that Allyn had not yet gone altogether, for
as I stood there thinking these hard thoughts I heard his
voice ring clear, from the place where he had been.

"Taliesin. Go now. Bring the flower east. He Who Frees
the Waters shall have a need for it. Go."

Then the light was gone for truth, and the wind with it,
and the sun ran back behind the blue hills beyond the fir-
wood. I stood a moment longer, then carefully folded the
rose into a small soft leather pouch, tucked the pouch
beneath my leinna, where the gold hawk's feather held the
true plume within, and went to find my horses.

CHAPTER 12

Now begins the most difficult part to tell of, after, that was of all my questing; and the most glorious also.

I was riding hard, following the black hound through wide rolling desolate upland valleys forested sparsely with oak and beech and birch. We were hunting the white hart of the Bhan-reann-ruadh, the ghostly stag; and, let me tell you, my mind was no whit easier on that than formerly, for all Allyn of the Sidhe's words of heartening. True, now that I *had* those words, could add their weight to Red Star Woman's geisa—and had I not already partly fulfilled those, by stealing of the hound that ran before me?—it seemed somehow more correct. And any road, it was not as if I did this thing unbidden, or out of mere whim: Allyn had companioned Gwyn and Birogue to Caerdroia, to bring the word of the Cup's loss to Gwen and Artos, when I myself had failed to bring that word from Glenshee. Nay; Allyn Midna's son was part of this coil as surely as was I or any other quester, and the road we went was a right one.

Well, for the most part. I glanced back at Gwain's bay mare following contentedly after; but the thought of her dead and vanished master was never far from my mind. I faced forward again with a sigh. With the Cup's finding, maybe, that wrong too could be righted. . . But the remembering of Gwyn and Birogue comforted me a somewhatly; always those two of the Shining Folk seemed to turn up at my life's most crucial moments. Oh aye, they came at good times too, of course: It was they had wedded me to my beloved Guenna, and when our Gerrans was born they had come to his saining, honoring him and us and the rite with their presence and blessings, bringing rich gifts from under the hill, to stand as faerie godsparents to our son.

But that thought led also, inevitably, to thought of Merlynn Llwyd, and how I had last beheld him. If we hoped for any help beyond our own in this thing, save that of the Goddess Herself, surely it was Merlynn's that we had all longed for in our hearts, though we knew in our cold clear brains, well enough, that we should never have it; at least, not just now. For that promised future, when my much-loved teacher should be among us again, was far distant, but our need was here, and hard upon us.

I made camp that night on the edge of a nameless plain bordered with trees. The weather was turning colder as the year turned; even for those of us who rode on quest, the seasons could not be slowed altogether. Tonight there was a blue mist rising above the rowans and wych-elms that formed a straggling line against the wind. The Moon Wolf was out on white Argialla, that ring of glittering ice round the moon that heralds hard weather, though Tara's other satellite, red Bellendain, was not yet up; and from the trees behind me I could hear the high anxious call of the gabhairin-reo, the little goat of the frost, as she gathered her new-fledged family to fly south before the snows.

Nothing happened in the night, save that I bolted awake once under my sheepskins to hear what seemed a flight of spears passing overhead—sshháa! isshháa!—but when I looked up there was nothing and no one between me and the cold majesty of the autumn stars. There strode Caomai, the Armed King, over the western horizon, with the Ellwand, the six stars of his baldric, glowing their astonishing bitter blue; above my head trailed misty gold Llenaur, the Lady of Heaven's Mantle. Over in their pickets, my horses dozed peacefully on their feet, both Feldore and Gwain's bay mare, whom (not knowing her right name) I had taken to calling Rylan, after a horse Gweniver had loved in her girlhood. In the dim light from the shuttered quartz-hearth, I could see the black hound's eyes gleam red.

In the early morning I rose and made some shakla to take off the chill, and while waiting for it to heat I looked out over the lands around. It was almost a desert place I saw before me: but a cold desert, a basalt plain that rolled for twenty miles or more to the foot of a gigantic mountain rising from the valley floor like a dark crenelated wall, a towering rampart flinging itself skyward, perhaps seven thousand feet straight up.

But our way did not lead there, for no sooner was I in the saddle when the black hound, having accepted her share of breakfast fare as little more than her right and proper due, bounded ahead of me, ever to the east, across the sea of bare basalt.

Toward noon we came to one of the few landmarks in all that featureless trackless waste: a small cairn of rough-hewn stones that marked a well, with a bent branch atop it for bucket-winch. And I gazed at it in wonder, for I knew it to be Saint Clears's Well, a sacred spring called up out of the stone desert by a holy hermit of old. Most folk in Keltia thought it to be a faery-story only, holding that there never was such a place, or even such a saint. But as Druid I knew better on both counts: Not only had there *been* the holy Clears, but he had called *two* springs bubbling up in the Goddess's name. Red and white they were: the white clean and cold and pure, for simple slaking of thirst; and the red, tinted to its startling ruddiness by (it was said) the saint's own blood, for healing. Wondrous powers of the miraculous were attributed to the rust-colored water; but too many folk these days thought such a marvel could not be true—as if truth and miracle could not exist side by side in the same thing.

As I say, I had been better taught, though even I had never thought to see the well of Saint Clears with my own eyes. For the double spring was believed to mark the farthest northeastward anyone had ever gone in the uncharted reaches of the Northwest Continent. Even Edeyrn and his Ravens had never come this way in their unclean pillagings; even Athyn on her Long Hunt, Raighne in her wanderings, Brendan in his explorations, none of these had been this way. And yet here a great scholar and saint had chosen to spend his days, none knew why; it was still a mystery.

I drew of the white delicious water enough to drench my horses and myself, then filled up all the waterbags, then had another long drink of the cold spring. I knew by my very arrival here that my way lay easter still, still onward. *And the others?* I wondered. *What of their road? Had they come this way? Or was this easting mine alone?*

But I could not pass so sanctified a place without a pause for prayer—a prayer for Arthur back at Caerdroia as much as for us who rode on quest—and to speak to the spirit of the well's guardian, and to fill a small crystal bottle with the ruby water that was held to have such healing powers, aye, even in the teeth of death itself. Or so at least Saint Clears promised, to any who took from his fountain in the proper spirit. . . So I drank yet again, a libation from the Fionn-uisge, Phoenix, the White Spring; and took of the waters of Uisge-ruadh, Iscaroe, the Red Spring. Thinking all the while of Gwain my kinsman, and of how perhaps it was still not too late to restore him, could I only find his body, and how thereby I might yet have forgiveness for my sin of kinslaying.

So I spoke there in the cold desert silence to the saint of the spring, and to the Powers he had so well served, giving thanks for the twin benisons of the waters, speaking his name to the Goddess; and rode on ever east.

That night toward sunset I had for the first time a glimpse of the quarry we hunted. All the west was aflame behind me, and all the east a huge blue bowl before, when suddenly fled across the middle distance the great white stag, the hart with the collar of gold about his throat. He shone like a flame himself in the flying light, blue-white against the oncoming dusk, and moved like a footless ghost over the darkling plain. As he crossed before us, he slowed and halted, one strong slim foreleg slightly raised in an attitude of heraldic grace, and turned his head to us.

Across the darkening distance the stag and I looked long upon each other, and I saw for the first time that he bore a great clear jewel between his mighty spread of antlers, a jewel that caught the sunset light and broke it into a million sparkling flashes and flung them all back at me, so that I blinked helplessly; and when I opened my dazzled eyes again the hart was gone.

The black deerhound gave a small eager whine from where she stood by Rylan's forelegs; she was not looking after her declared quarry but up at me, and her golden eyes gleaming in the dusk so unmanned me in that instant that Feldore actually leaped sidewise his own length, as if in battle, so sudden and so hard was the jerk of my leg against his girth. *Mighty Mother! That is no dog!* I avowed fervently and silently, behind deep shields. What she was, I knew not—not yet, any road—but if she proved in the end to be a mere hound with rather oddly colored eyes, hear me Hornèd Lord, I would eat my own toes. . .

We had sight of the stag again at dawn the next morning— he was poised on the edge of a small pinewood, precisely as if he well intended to be seen, ghostly and visible against the dark trunks of the trees—and then we lost his track all the long chilly day. I was nodding in the saddle, huddling inside my sheepskin cloak, a little dull with fatigue and the cold. It had turned blustery, though the sky stayed clear and bright, and the fallen leaves were seething along the ground like the seidean-sidhe, the faerie whirlwind that comes when the Sidhe do ride among mortal woods and fields.

And then he was there, the white hart in his splendor, his gold collar shining in the first rays of the sunset, the jewel alight amid his giant rack. I cried aloud to see him, and he whisked himself about and ran before us, heading toward a thick oakwood that lay far down the narrow empty valley. Feldore needed no urging but surged into the hunting gallop, Rylan close behind, and already the black deerhound was streaking ahead of us, levelled out in a long dark arching blur parallel with the ground.

We covered the distance to the oakwood in what seemed mere seconds, though surely it was many minutes. Before I had time to reflect on how strangely similar all this felt to that wood where I had found the magical flower (still carefully tucked away against my breast, in its leathern pouch), Feldore was standing stiff-legged in the center of a broad clearing and shaking in every limb, and Rylan with him. The stag was before us, and he was tremendous, much bigger than he had seemed heretofore; and the black hound was crouched low before the stag, ready to spring.

I dismounted as if I moved in dreams, not even troubling to tether the horses, and walked slowly forward until I stood beside the hound. Seen close to, the stag seemed right enough a beast of this world, save for his color and his collar and his jewel and his size. He was massively muscled, furry with his winter coat coming in; his heavy horns were thick at their base as a man's arm, their twelve tines sharp as spearpoints, and his breathing was that of a beast run hard and hunted close many miles over rough country. Then his eyes met mine, and I could not recall why I had *ever* thought, for the least tiniest moment, that he had seemed a natural hart. . .

The huge deep dark eyes held a light that was only in part reflected from the flaming skies above; the rest of the piercing luminescence came from some other place, and I was not at all sure I wished to learn where that other place might be. His coat too had begun to glow, blue-white, fearfully distinct in the clearing's darkness. I stepped back a pace, involuntarily, with a half-formed thought that even at this late hour, perhaps I might yet turn away. . . But it seemed I had no choice in the matter; not here, not now. Indeed, I doubt me now that I had ever had one.

Then the stag spoke. His muzzle moved, his velvet nose twitched and from his mouth, the mouth of a beast, came human words in a human voice—a deep voice, that vibrated through every bone in my body; grave, and yet also mysteriously gay, as if the creature rejoiced in his own capture, was glad of the fact that I was the hunter who had brought him to bay at last.

And what he said to me was terrible.

"Kill me," came the calm deep merry voice. "Kill me, and nail my head to the greatest of the oaks. This is Ashnadarragh, the Place of the Oak, the Gateplace, the hinge upon which all doors turn. It must be done, and done now."

I quite think I lost my mind just then, at least for a moment or two, for when I was 'ware of myself again I found that I had fallen to my knees, hands blindly in front of me pushing against the turf, my head shaking in mute unseeing unreasoning denial.

"Nay," I said when I found my voice at last. "Nay. I cannot. Not—not that. Do not ask it of me."

The royal stag said nothing for a few moments, but gazed upon me in silence, and I could not *endure* it, could not bear the sadness, the eternal, the inexhaustible patience in that glance. It was as if he—never once in all my pursuit had I thought of him as 'it'—could not bring himself to chide me, or berate me, or bully me, even; but knew so well that I was only wasting his time and my own with my feeble futile outcries and denyings of what I and he both knew well must be done. Then he spoke again, still gently, but this time with a steel sternness beneath the velvet. *Like his horns. . .*

"Taliesin. Do it. Trust it. Trust *us*. It is yours to do."

"What—what will come of it?" I managed to gasp, in a croaking uneven shuddering voice that no bard living had ever used till now.

"What must come. What shall come. Trust. Do it now. The hour is here. Take it."

I stared wildly about me, but there was no help anywhere in the dark wood, no help for perhaps a thousand miles. Even the black hound gave no sign but lay in the grass flat on her belly, her nose on her paws, and would not look at me.

And in my stark desperation, my lastmost extremity, my despairing finalmost relinquishment of hope and thought and horror, just as I felt myself slipping over the edge into true madness and knew that in an instant now I would no longer know even that I *was* mad, in that moment came over me a feeling, I say, such as I had never felt before. It was not unlike to the Awen, that hushed immensity that comes down upon one like a mighty hand from heaven, and that raises one to the hugeness of itself. Not unlike; but it *was* different, and I knew in my deepest soul that, like the Awen, it must be obeyed. There was not even the choice to *not* obey. . .

So in the end I did as I had been bidden, though I could scarce see my ghastly work for the tears that blinded my eyes and streamed scalding ceaseless down my cheeks, and perhaps that was much the best for me. Oh, it was a right action that I performed here, and no mistake; but sometimes a right action can be clean contrary to our hearts' inclination, can seem so *not*-right. But we must aye perform it all the same.

For tool I used the small bronze dagger that had come from beneath the faerie hill, had been Merlynn's own gift to me. I would not have thought such a weapon could have accomplished such a deed, but it found the heart of the great white stag as if it had been forged only to that purpose. Perhaps it had been. I do not know.

Nor do I know where the silver nails came from, with which I fixed the majestic head to the trunk of the vast oak in the center of the clearing, nor yet the golden hammer I used to drive home the silver spikes. They were simply there for me to employ in this purpose, and I did not question how they came there, or where they went, after.

When I had finished, I stepped back, still weeping helplessly, angrily, and surveyed my grisly deed: the antlered head upon the oak, the headless body upon the bloody grass. And in that moment I hated the stag, and the Bhanreann-ruadh, and the black hound, and the quest, and Arthur, and Keltia, and myself; and I howled then, a great keening lament, my whole body and spirit throbbing in sorrow and protest and fury. But the stag was still dead.

Spent at last in every part, I threw myself face down in the cool damp grass, then leaped up again, fired with a sudden resolve. This was one hart that would not be gralloched by any chance hunter who came after I had gone. . . I whirled round with all the force of my grief and rage and caught up a stout branch that lay on the ground nearby, and, with a single blast of druidry, such as I had never used once since my student days at Bargodion, I set the branch ablaze. I would burn the stag's body, give him the clean honor of sending by the flame. This at least I could do for him, for the pointlessness of his sacrifice. . .

But as I turned to set the torch to the dry leaves and branches around the body, a voice came from behind me, and I stopped where I stood, as rigid on the instant as if some unseen bowman had put an arrow in my back. A blaze of silver light came softly welling over my shoulders, a cool gentle cloak that seemed to heal my anger and my sorrow alike; and I trembled from head to foot, in great shaking spasms, more terrified of that light and that voice than I have ever been in all my days; nay, not even the Marbh-draoi himself had filled me with more fear than now I felt. For the voice from behind me spoke my name.

I think it was the bravest thing I have ever done in my life, to turn into the unknown and face full on whoever it might be that had spoken—for bravery, as you doubtless know by now, is not the being fearless in face of peril but the willing oneself to act against the fear the peril causes, and then so acting. So I turned, so slowly, turned as if my body were suddenly no longer flesh and blood and bone as ever but fashioned now of ice-crystals, had become flesh of diamond, blood of silver, bone of the cold that lies between the stars. . . And yet I knew that I *must* turn, that I longed, even, to do so, and the burning branch was extinguished by a sudden wind.

The silver light came from the jewel between the stag's great horns, welling up like the white water of Clears's spring, spilling over the dead bloody muzzle and poll and neck, glittering upon the gold collar still buckled fast where it had been. The oak brand dropped unheeded from my suddenly strengthless fingers; and though I had turned, bravely or arrogantly or despairingly I will never know, to face that unknown, I could not move, could not stir nor hand nor foot, could not I think even comprehend what I saw now before me. My mind seemed to shut down, allowing only so much of this reality to enter in, protecting me

against something it had no place to receive or accept. But if
my mind could not comprehend what was here before me,
something wiser or deeper or other could. . .

The stag's head was no longer nailed to the oak, the
stag's dead body no longer lay upon the short dry grass.
The stag was going, drawing together and changing in a
way I shall never be able to explain, and in his place— I bit
my lip until the blood came, bit it against the tears, against
the disbelief, against the feeling that burst through me now;
and I flung back my head, lifting my face to the sapphire
sky, and let the feeling take me. Whatever this feeling was:
joy, power, love, rightness—even for a bard there come
times when words are not enough. I was exultant, I was
exploding, I was soaring out of myself and within myself all
in one, rising up through all my selves and bringing my
body with me, rigid with joyousness; it felt like the triumph
of lovemaking and the victory of dying and the paroxysm of
birth all together.

Aye, truly, even for a bard words sometimes do not suffice. For He Who stood before me now, His back to the
oak, was greater than them all.

And I saw Him! For an instant, all my mortal frame
could bear or my mortal mind endure, He was there, the
Cabarfeidh, that one of many names, He, the Goddess's
mate. Lord of the Wood, we call Him in the sacred Litany,
and other names beside: He was before me, the Winter
King, and in the glory of His nature I could dimly discern
still the antler crown rising up from the dark hair that fell
past His mighty shoulders. But that appearance was His
grace to me: His presence made easier for me. In His true
guise He stands with Her before Kelu's throne, Their faces
ever turned in love to Their creation; through Them both we
come to the One. He is the Salmon of Knowledge and the
Bull of Battle, the Wolf of Rannoch and the King-horse of
Pride, the Hunter in the Dawn and the Master of the Hunt. I
spread my hands and lifted them in the attitude of prayer,
unaware that I chanted aloud, and did worship.

"Helm of the Gael. . .Lord of Lightnings. . .Dragon
War-shout. . .Red Dragon of the Rock. . .Fire on Brega. . .
Armor of Bards. . .Chief of Chiefs. . .Dún of Justice. . .Rider

upon Storms. . . Fort of Eagles. . .Light of the
Encompassing of Gwynfyd! Thou Who art the Heroes' Way
and the Road That Is Hidden, the Face That Teaches and
the Hand That Reaches—"

And as the power rose up around me as I prayed, I
passed it on to Him as I had been taught, to Him from
Whom it had origin; and at the peak of prayer and power
both I called Him by His truename, and He smiled, and
before I died altogether of the beauty and the perfection He
changed—

—and Fionn the Young stood before me, clad in black,
the blazing jewel bound upon his brow, the Young Lord,
Fionn who was both God and god alike, who could move
between the higher and lower worlds as he did please; Fionn
who was here a vestment the God had donned, a lesser raiment, an aspect that mortals could the more easily and comfortably comprehend. We are not built to bear too much
pure divinity; we are not yet ready for it, it is what we are
here to learn. But the smile was the same.

"Taliesin," came the deep voice, so beautiful; the voice
of the stag, of the God. "We have put you through some
harsh paces."

I bent my knee before Him then, bowed my head until
my forehead all but touched the grasses, but did not speak; I
did not trust my voice just yet. And then I was glad I had
said no word, for another voice spoke instead, and when I
turned from Fionn (only partway, to be sure, not done to
turn one's back upon Deity), I saw that it was the black
deerhound who had spoken.

"And well he trod them out. . ."

But she too was changing, and I watched with calm joy,
not surprised in the least; I had long had my suspicions
about that hound, good it was to be proved right at the
last. . .

Though She had not chosen to reveal Herself to me in
Her completeness, as Her mate had done before putting on
Fionn's aspect (perhaps had I been Morgan, or any woman,
She might have done so; but I was a man, and the Lady
does as pleases Her best), still I was given to see somewhat
of Her true, full nature, as a veil or coron-solais round the

slim lithe form that stood now where the black hound had crouched. Not tall, long-muscled like a runner or a swordswoman, Rhian, the Maiden, the Young Goddess, shook out her streaming unbound brown hair and took her place beside the Young Lord, beneath the sacred oak.

Though They in Their divine kindness had assumed these shapes for my peace and easiness, still I could scarce bring myself to gaze upon Them. It was too much for me: All my life I had yearned—vaingloriously or impiously, as you please to call it—to be granted the grace of such a visitation as this, and now that it was vouchsafed me I felt suddenly shamed. *Surely there are many souls in Keltia who merit this blessing far more than do I. . .*

"Well, maybe not *so* many, but if you insist, Talyn, we will go and visit them instead," came Rhian's voice, full of loving, teasing laughter. "But first there is a small matter of a vow I mind me of—"

I made reverence to her as I had done to Fionn, and rose again in a sort of fit of boot-scuffing modesty that, truly, ill became me.

"Well enough, but, Lady, my sorrow, I do not recall—"

"Ah, the memory of bards!" said Fionn, and he too was smiling. "*I* recall well enough, at the least, to the tune of how if that hound were *only* a hound, one here present would make a meal of his own toes—is not that much how it went?"

I had the grace to blush and the wit to laugh. "Aye, Lord, something very much like! Well, if your honors both insist, I would be pleased to—"

"Nay, nay!" came a rippling voice from behind the oak. "There will be no faring on footlings here!"

The Bhan-reann-ruadh came round to us, drifting like mist through the forest dark, her starry mantle glowing about her. She made a graceful curtsy to Fionn and to Rhian, and they bowed their heads gravely in return.

I was pretty much past surprise now, and so when she too began to shimmer and alter aspect I merely watched and was not of any amazement; and when Dâna stood in her form before the two gods and my mortal self, I bowed to her, though not so deeply as I had done reverence to the

others. For though the Aes Dânu are gods—indeed, had not
the God Himself put on the aspect of Fionn just now?—or
at the least closer to the Gods than we mortals are, and
though Dâna should be queen among them, still these two
here were above her, as she herself had shown.

"Rían na Reanna. . ." I said, giving her one of her titles.

"Pen-bardd," she said in reply. "And Knight of the
Graal that shall be. . . Indeed you have stood well to your
tests."

I bent my head. "Not all the tests," I muttered, for honor
compelled me, and I thought of Gwain.

Fionn smiled. "That too," he said, and said no more of it.

"And the others?" I asked after a moment.

"All testing now is done with," said Rhian. "All roads
lead now to the Castle of the Graal. The Cup will come
home to Keltia. And you shall be of those who see its
return."

"And its leaving again also," said Fionn. "But you will
hear that word in full at Caervanogue."

"Where—"

"All in good time," said Dâna, and she did not smile. "It
goes back a farther way than you can know. For the King
received from the poisoned spear a wound that did not
heal."

"Uthyr," I said with certainty.

"Uthyr, aye; but not Uthyr alone. He was not first to be
touched by the wrongness. . . For the Lords of Dán had so
ordered it, that a certain maiden should come to the world
to wed and rule with a certain king, for she was his destined
mate and he was hers. But though they met and loved and
had union, they failed at their test. They did not wed or
reign as had been meant, and so failure came upon them
and the land alike."

"Amris," I said wonderingly. "And the maiden was
Ygrawn, who should have been the Graal Princess, as he the
Sacred King, the Graal Server. Yet Arthur was gotten
between them all the same."

"Aye," said Fionn somberly. "And so the failure was not
complete, and the land survived, if barely. As for their dán,
it will weigh out accordingly. But mark: Neither was it the

web that had been woven for these two, the dán that had
been spun for each and both upon the Wheel. And *this*,
Talyn, is why the sorrow came upon Keltia—why the
Marbh-draoi reigned past his own dán's time, why
Marguessan was able to steal away the Cup, though it avails
her not, even though she in her traha seeks to make herself
the Sacred Queen. And so we sent the Quest."

"But Arthur—"

"Arthur too failed at the Wheel's turning," said Rhian.
"What does the name Gwenwynbar mean in the bardic
speech?"

And I flinched as if she had struck me; for the name of
Artos's first wife, you may recall, meant in the metaphor of
bards the Poisoned Spear. . .

"When he wedded Gwenwynbar, she became the
Poisoned Spear that wounded him, that had wounded all the
land before, all the kings—Amris, Leowyn, Uthyr. . . Only
when Arthur and Gweniver did wed was dán set right. But
not entirely; and evil still shall come." Rhian lifted her white
arm, stretched it out above me. "Taliesin. Evil came never
out of the east."

And that was the second time I had been given that word
of warning. . .

"But is not all set right now?" I asked humbly. "The
Cup, you have said, will return; there is an heir now for
Keltia doubly of the blood of Dôn Rhên; is the flaw not
mended?"

But none of the three made answer to that. Presently
Fionn spoke again.

"Taliesin. Seek until you find, and then be astonished.
Neglect no part of this equation."

I nodded once, but said nothing. Then Rhian:

"Taliesin Morguenna's mate. Live in the Light, by all
means, but do not lose your shadow-vision. Do not forget
how to see in the Dark."

Again I bent my head, and Dâna's clear voice rippled out
above me.

"Taliesin Cathelin's son. It is the Lance that kills, and
the Cup that brings to life. You live the gods' death, they
live yours. Take care to love the highest when you see it;

and mind well you mistake it not, for men are wont to do so more than women. Go then to the Graal."

I looked up in purest panic, for that had been valedictory; and indeed the three figures were beginning to blaze like king-torches, changing back into their natural states, leaving form behind them, cast off, the forms that had been their gift to my mortal sensibilities, for in their own kingdom they have no need of such. . . A pang of sorrow and loss lanced through me then, so sharp and piercing that I looked down full expecting to see an arrow in my heart; but the shaft was no less real, I think, for being of a different and unearthly fletching. This, then, is why the High Ones do not more often appear to mortals; they cannot bear the grief they cause us when they withdraw from us as they must, the grief that is by its very vehemence a measure of the joy we shall have when we join them beyond the misty hedge. Caer Coronach is but the name we give that place, in our sorrow; when we dwell therein it shall have another name.

All this flashed through my mind in the briefest of moments. But apart from my grief at the gods' departure, and my natural selfish wish to go with them, there was something more. . .

But Dâna was still before me, she who had never failed her folk and never would, and she spoke from the gathering splendor the words she knew I needed to hear.

"The Castle of the Graal, Taliesin! Caervanogue. The road to Fairlight, upon the western edge of the Dragonsea, east of east."

The brightness blazed and bloomed; it seemed as if a gate opened, a door swung somewhere outward—and they were gone.

I collapsed upon the cold ground, my bones gone to water, and pulled from my heart, as it were, the transfixing spear of grief. For a moment, indeed, I actually wondered if I could possibly bear it, the absence of what I had not known until mere minutes before could even be. . . Then I got a grasp of myself, dragging my spirit back, inch by protesting inch, from the place where the gods and I had met and spoken. It took a time for me to feel at home in my own body again, and all the while no coherent thought ran in my head but one exultant refrain: *I have seen Rhian! I have seen Fionn! Dâna the Queen came to bespeak me!*

Their names echoed like far trumpets, and I felt flow back to me a tiny touch of their loving presence, a reminder that they were not gone utterly nor indeed for always. And, true to my bard's instincts, I was actually already beginning to frame the whole thing in song. But for myself only, not to be sung for others, save perhaps Guenna and Arthur alone. . .

Then in another perfect panic I leapt to my feet, frantic lest I had already forgotten Dâna's words of guiding to our goal. But to my unspeakable relief, there it was, just where she had placed it, in my mind and heart and instincts. So much so that I would need no map to find it: Fairlight, east of east. There would come the others also, and that which we had sought so long and so hard. High time I took the road again; they would be waiting for me.

CHAPTER 13

It was as if some great invisible barrier that had been before me all this while, before all of us most like, hindering, baffling, turning us aside into woeful byways, had been suddenly lifted out of our path. I rode swiftly and happily eastward, singing 'Hob y deri dan do!' and other such as I rode, and I doubt not the others did the same. For the first time since our quest began, I could sense their presences, as all of us began to draw near to Fairlight, upon the Dragonsea.

This was truly east of east: The Dragonsea is a wide, shallow, warm-watered bay, which laps the empty shores of the Northwest Continent on its western side and has for its other selvedge the rocky crags and tiny seaplots that are called the Easter Isles. Fairlight itself is no town, nor village even, though there are the ruins of an ancient castle, long thrown down—some say by Keian, though other some say rather Raighne (and in truth everyone in Keltia knows perfectly well that neither of those two great queens of might and legend ever set so much as a foot here. Or so at least is thought).

But from the shore at Fairlight runs out in the Dragonsea a road of white stones and crushed shells, that becomes a huge-blocked marble causeway where it disappears beneath the green waters of high tide. Twice a day this causey is uncovered by the tides that go out a league or so eastward, and then one can fare dry-shod all the way to the small single-peaked islet of Beckery that dominates the entire bay. But you had best have a good swift pace on you: The tides here are fierce and fast, come foaming in quicker than a man or even a horse can outrun them. It is well to take care, and to mark how the waves are breaking, before venturing across in anything that does not float. Being stranded upon Beckery would be the most pleasant of the fates that can befall the unwary walker upon the sands.

Not that just anyone can cross to Beckery; I have a thought that no one ventures over save that he or she has been summoned there. For upon the central crag that comprises just about the entire island stands a castle that, unlike its neighbor on the mainland, is *not* a ruin: Caervanogue, long uninhabited yet mysteriously not derelict, whose name has never been satisfactorily translated but which in the bardic tongue means Castle Rising. Once, long ago, the island of which this is the center and crown lay beneath the restless waters of the Dragonsea. Then the land rose in great seismic heavings, and for many centuries the island was thrown high out of the water, to become part of the mainland coast. When the earthshakes came again and let the waters back, it became an island once more; and perhaps its tale will end as it began, long centuries hence, when it sinks again beneath the waves.

I knew all this well, of course, when I arrived at last on the shore at Fairlight, and sought eagerly for the castle of my destination and my dán, as I had been told. But looked I never so closely, I could ascertain no trace of it: not the castle of Caervanogue, nor the island of Beckery, nor even the causey that led across—only an unbroken sealine all the way out to the nearest of the Easter Isles, dim and blue ten miles away. This was not the expected end to my quest, and I stood there staring a long time, baffled and, aye, I confess to it, angry with those who had sent me here.

Had it all been mockery, then? It did not feel so, nor had it seemed so, and I had the proofs to hand—the magic rose in my breast, the empty saddle of Gwain's horse. More than that: the memory of Avallac'h, the words of my mother as she had come to me, the bottle of rust-colored water from the sacred spring. Nay, it had been real enough. But as I stared out in vain searching over the blank dazzling water, I came to a bleak conclusion.

Perhaps this was as far as I was permitted to come. Indeed, had not Morgan said in some dream or Seeing or some such that we should not be of the Cup? True it was that the finding was not the sole end of any quest; the seeking could be just as important to the seeker, if not to that which was being sought. . . Hard thoughts, these; but if I were not meant to come to the Cup after all, then that was dán too. Perhaps what I had done to get here had put the holy Cup forever beyond my attaining. . . I did not know.

But I knew even as I thought it that if it were so, then so must I accept it. If I were unworthy, then so must it be; I could content myself and my soul with the quest, and with the knowledge that sometimes one must cast a circle for the power to be raised otherwise. . .

So I got back on my horse, and gave one last look and salute and farewell to the quest and the quested-for, and turned Feldore's head again westward, back along the road we had come.

And then all at once it was there, across the bay, perhaps a mile offshore from where I now so abruptly drew rein. All of it—Beckery, with its craggy hill and the machairs around its feet, and Caervanogue upon that crag, with its towers and courts and open gates, white-gold in the sunlight. But every part of a castle shines. . . It was as if—well, no as-if about it, really—the act of humbly turning away had called it into existence, the humility of acknowledging the possibility of failure was the final test to prove I did not deserve to fail. . . I do not know why, not truly. But I was glad.

The tide was out farther than ever I had seen tide withdraw itself. There was only clean packed sand on either side of the huge white marble blocks that formed the causeway leading to Beckery, no water even in the finely fitted joinings between blocks. I judged it still safe to ride across; and Feldore, Rylan and I were perhaps two-thirds of the way there when I noted with some alarm that broad silver stripes of water had crept in unnoticed across the sand, gray and smooth and shining, with fine dry sand, hard-packed, between each stripe. Even as I watched, the tide began to pour back in earnest, the stripes widening and rippling as they joined together on the flood, making one seamless gleaming skin of water that overlay the sand beneath to a depth of a few inches.

I kneed Feldore, clucked to Rylan, so that our pace quickened considerably, even as did the returning tide. We were safe on shore on Beckery perhaps ten minutes before the water began to rush with frightening speed at the causey sides, leaping up in little crashing fountains with its own force; and shortly thereafter there was nothing but unbroken water betwixt the mainland and ourselves.

I turned my attention to our present location. I had seen no sign of the others as yet, but now I could sense their presence. They were all here, and I the last to join them. . . So I left the horses in the machair-meadows, noting as I did so the fresh hoofprints of many other beasts tracking round the point, and began to climb as the others had obviously done, afoot to the castle above me.

As I drew near a buried memory came at me with a rush: Oeth-Anoeth. It had looked quite astonishingly like this very place, I saw with sudden swamping doubt and dismay. One castle can look very much like another, that is true enough, but the likeness was too great to dismiss as chance. Had Edeyrn built Oeth-Anoeth so a-purpose, and had Marguessan kept me there for a darker reason than I had known?

Then all such doubts and fears were for the moment dispelled, as I came to the castle gate and Morgan came running through, straight into my arms, the very first person I saw. Well, not saw, to be strictly accurate about it; I never saw her coming until she had flung herself upon me. But I did not complain.

"Anwyl, anwylyd," I said raggedly, when we had stopped hugging and kissing and weeping and laughing long enough for speech, "how is it with you, oh gods, where have you been, what doing, why have we—"

She kissed me again. "Later," she whispered fiercely against my cheek. "Enough now to know that we are

together and here. We have other business just now. It is
what we have come for."

"I know that," I muttered in mild protest, but she slipped
her arm through mine and dragged me through the faha and
around the other side of the castle and down upon a great
wide grassy place set over the sea. And then I saw them, all
the rest, arrayed in half-circle ranks and all facing eastward.
Donah, Gerrans (and my heart nearly failed me with sheer
relief to see him there), Gweniver my friend and Queen,
Loherin whom I had met upon the road. . . indeed, of the
seven sevens that had been sent out, twenty-six souls had
won through to Caervanogue; twice thirteen would witness
the coming home of the Cup.

We all went down upon the strand that lay below the
lawns, a wide white beach that stretched the length of the
little island, facing the Easter Isles. I noticed that the horses
too had come along—saw my two faithful friends among
them—and smiled to see them. Well, and why should they
not be here? Had they not quested and served as surely and
as bravely and as devotedly as the rest of us? They were
questers as much as we were, and should have their part in
the quest's happy resolution.

"This is Garanwynion," said Morgan then, gesturing to
the white rocky sands before us.

"And?"

"Not long now. We wait."

Indeed, not long. He came out of the eastern sun, so that
none of us who awaited him saw his coming, quiet and simple: A path shone in the waters and then he was there, his
presence a wonder of dán.

And I stared and smiled to see him, Avallac'h, the prince
of my wife's line, who had bought his freedom, and ours too
maybe, with his service. He stood tall and straight before us,
robed in green, and it seemed that he looked on each of us
in turn, and knew us all—as later converse with my fellow
seekers was to prove he did; each of us had passed our night
in Inisguidrin with the Keeper of the Graal. He had fulfilled
his self-chosen atonement in every particular, had paid his

honor-price to the Cup and was free to move on. Yet here
he was, and I drew a silent shivering breath, for I thought I
knew why.

Before any word was spoken—and I saw Morgan and
Gweniver moving near to him, intent on address—a sudden
shadow came over us all. The sun seemed run behind a
cloud, and all around was bleached of color, livid, as the
world will look when you open your eyes wide on a hot
summer day after they have been a long time closed. A
fever-chill seemed to have taken us all, and I looked wildly
around me, suddenly sure, for I knew that presence, had felt
it myself not all that long since, in a silent grove at night,
alone with a slain kinsman's body. . . Looked round, and
saw Marguessan Pendreic gliding like a nathair down the
castle steps. Galeron, her daughter, was with her, as in the
sending in the forest clearing, and on her other side—

I reeled, for the world seemed awry and unmade. On her
other side was—*Avallac'h?* I whipped my outraged gaze
back to the figure in green who stood before me on my left,
his back still to the sea and his own gaze fixed calmly on the
newcomers; then again to the one beside Marguessan. There
was not a pin's worth of difference between them, not an
inch, not a crossic, not a cantlet, not a flitter. They were the
same; how could this be. . . Even Morgan appeared for the
moment discountenanced; as for the others, they looked as
frightened and unsure as I was just now feeling.

And yet, and yet. . . Something there was that I was not
remembering, and that was most needful I remember, for its
hour was come.

For her part, Marguessan looked her old self. She had
not glanced aside even at her own sister, but kept her gaze
trained on Avallac'h, or he whom we had thought was
Avallac'h. She did cut her glance furtively once to Gweniver
and once to Loherin, but she would not look at Morgan and
she would not look at me. Which suited me fine enough,
especially after that last encounter of ours, when she had
brazenly vaunted her hand in the death of her own son; and
of course there was still between us that small matter of two
years of my life in Oeth-Anoeth. . . But Morgan beside me
seemed now untroubled, as if she too waited for something.

"Keeper," said Marguessan then, and though her voice was clear and carrying it was also threaded with the least tiniest uncertainty. Which meant she was very unsure indeed, for she had not let even that much show, given the choice. I harrowed my brain to recall what still eluded me; but the false-Avallac'h beside Marguessan stepped forward to face his mirror image ten yards away, and when he spoke it was in that voice I well remembered from my night in the marshes of Siennega.

"The Cup returns," he said, "and its Keeper has come to receive it."

The true-Avallac'h smiled. "Nay," he said courteously, in the very same voice as the other, "though the Cup returns, it will have a new Keeper from now. A new Server has come among us. Not thou, Avagddu, Aviach, Avarwyn. Not the living Graal for thee."

The false-Avallac'h made no response, but it seemed to us gathered breathless upon the foreshore that he—*darkened* somehow. And I suddenly wondered how he and Galeron and Marguessan had even come here in the first place, how they had even been suffered to set foot upon the isle of Beckery. Unless, of course, they had been called as we had been called? But to what purpose? And by whom? My musings were cut off by Marguessan.

"Who speaks so?" she said softly, and such was the sweet poisonous power of her voice that some of the less seasoned sorcerers among our company visibly flinched. I moved to steady Donah as she swayed a little on her feet, but she smiled tremulous thanks and gently shook me off, and Loherin on Morgan's other side stood like a rock in the sea, like Rocabarra itself. Gerrans, as ever, was impassive, though the eye he bent on his aunt glittered darkly.

"Whose the word in the great glade?" said Marguessan then. "Stand aside, falseling, that the true Cup may come to its true Server."

Then, to my great and everlasting astonishment, I felt something roll over within my being and come surging to the fore; I felt myself moving forward, my hand delving under my leinna to bring something out into the light. For I *remembered;* and, remembering, I rejoiced.

I halted halfway between the two Avallac'hs. The one looked serenely upon me, unafraid, untroubled; the other glowered and bridled, started to speak. But I lifted my hand in an attitude of power, and he fell silent. I did not look at Marguessan.

But I looked at the first Avallac'h, the true Graalkeeper, and I smiled.

"Evil came never out of the east," I said, and I spoke to be heard not only by all that company, but by the island, and the Dragonsea, and the Cup itself, wherever it might be, wherever Marguessan's evil workings had sent it. And as I spoke I held out upon my open palm that which had lain in my breast, all the long road from the hidden wood.

The rose was as fresh and supple-petalled as it had been when still it clung to its stemlet; its color was clear true ruby in the sunlight, its fragrance clean and sweet and strong even over the wild sea-smell rising from the waves. And I remembered very well indeed the instruction I had been given concerning it: to give it into the Keeper's hands, at the Castle of the Graal. *Aye,* I thought desperately, *but* which *Keeper?*

I swung instinctively toward the first Avallac'h, who seemed to have wrapped himself in calm expectation like a mantle, boundless as the sea behind him; and, cupping my hands carefully around the Rose, I lifted the flower to his stern lined face, so that he must inhale of the bloom's perfume. He bent his head to it, drew in a deep long breath of the fragrance, then lifted his head again, eyes closed. When at last he opened them, he smiled.

I bowed, and turning I did likewise for the other Avallac'h, aware every instant of Marguessan's eyes in my back like needles of ice, like fingers of fire. *She knew, she knew. . .* Now this Avallac'h fought for the same high calm as the other had so effortlessly attained to, and almost he reached it, or an appearance thereof; but all present could see the strain it cost him to do so. With a certain grim satisfaction I raised the Rose inexorably toward his face, in the end all but shoving it against his nostrils, so that he must perforce breathe of it or not breathe at all.

And he breathed; oh aye, he breathed it in. And as he

did so the simulacrum of Avallac'h, the counterfeit of the true Keeper that had walked by Marguessan's side down to the strand of Garanwynion, shivered and shimmered and faded; it cracked and crazed like a faulty pot-glaze in a firing-kiln. And then it was gone, and the man behind it was fallen to his knees upon the shore, and he was Mordryth, son of Marguessan.

I gasped with the others; but, truth to tell, I was more shocked than surprised, and even that not very. And Morgan, I saw at once, was not even that. . . She had known all along, as her sister had known, how this must end (though I wondered greatly just *how* she had known, and resolved to speak at length with her as soon as this coil was run out), and now she stepped forward to face her twin.

"Sleights cannot prevail in the place of the Cup," she said, and though her voice was unemphatic and carried no overt threat, Marguessan quivered as if she had been struck in the face. "No false Keeper"—Morgan cut her glance to Mordryth, who still sprawled upon the sands, breathing hard, as if he too had taken a great buffet—"shall bring the Graal home. Your workings will not avail you, Uthyr's daughter."

Marguessan moved uncontrollably at that, and she seemed to my othersight a snarling, surging darkness, her words confirming.

"Say you so—Uthyr's daughter? Of all here you best know my work and my strength—ask your mate if memory lacks—do you think I will be so easily stayed?"

Morgan drew breath to answer, but before she could speak, the true Avallac'h lifted both his hands to the heavens, and it seemed that not only all the isle of Beckery but all Keltia fell silent. Even Marguessan held her peace, and on her face was a look of fear that even Morgan could not have put there.

"Your work *is* known, Inion Durracha, Merch Dhu. It is known also into what tides of iniquity you have cast your own children—" He gestured with both his upraised hands, a beckoning gesture, and above us the castle doors were thrown wide, and a procession paced slowly through. A funeral procession of eight bearers, the points of whose

upright spears transfixed a red cloak that served as bier; and
upon that taut crimson mantle lay the body of Gwain
Pendreic.

I choked back a cry of despairing guilt as they came
slowly past me, dared not raise my eyes to Avallac'h out of
purest agony of shame. But he made no sign of blame or
accusation, and the bearers set their burden down upon the
strand a few yards off. No one, not even Marguessan, said a
word.

I forced myself to look upon the face of the young man I
had been cozened into slaying. Gwain looked but deep
asleep, not dead at all: His long brown hair fell clean and
curling upon his shoulders; his face, though pale, was calm
and unmarked. He was clad in black, and the small gold
medallion of his House lay in the hollow of his collarbone.

I dared a glance aside. Gwain's sister and brother were,
for once, plainly, visibly fearful. Mordryth had picked himself up off the ground and was standing now beside
Galeron, both of them wearing an expression compounded
of equal parts terror and furtive cunning. Not only were
they feared of their dead sib, I saw at once, but of their own
mother, who stood now a little way away from them. Even
more so were they feared of Marguessan, in plain fact; yet
even in their fear of her they could not be free of her. . .

Marguessan, without turning her head, hissed a command at her daughter, and Galeron came forward obediently as a hound at the touch of the huntsman's lash. She
gave Gwain a swift guilty glance out of slitted eyes, then
turned to face the rest of us. After a tense silent moment,
Morgan too whispered somewhat, though in no wise so
peremptory a fashion, and Donah—to my instant protesting
astonishment—moved to face Galeron down near the edge
of the surf.

Feared as I was for my godsdaughter, I was still wondering about her cousin Mordryth. We had seen, on the whole,
almost nothing of him since that night at Turusachan, when
he struck Gweniver and the Cup came among us all; though
of course Arthur and Gerrans and I had seen rather more of
him, later, at Oeth-Anoeth. I studied him closely now, noting that he had grown to favor Irian, his cipher father, in

physical appearance; ah, but his soul was his mother's, right enough, to do with as she would. She had tried here to pass him off as Graalkeeper, using him as her pawn to secure for her what her own magic could apparently not do—as Keeper in Avallac'h's place, Mordryth could of course call in the Cup as its rightful servant would have done, and could then turn it over to his mother, since she had not been able to come by it through her black workings.

But she had been foiled here at Garanwynion—and again I wondered at how the thing was being played out. I glanced down at the rose I still held between my fingers: She had been balked not by grace of mine, but by a high purpose and a vast Design; and that was well. Yet it seemed, for so great a sorceress as she vaunted herself, she had made but a poor effort; surely she could have managed something less easily thwarted. Which meant she had not yet made her great move, had something else in mind for her true effort, something greater and darker, to which this coil with Mordryth-Avallac'h had been but a testing-spell. . .

Galeron and Donah faced off against each other now, darkness and dawn; against the Graal Princess was set the Maiden of the Cup of Darkness. A wind was rising, and out to sea over the Easter Isles great racks of cloud were building and massing slowly in slate-blue ranks. And now Avallac'h had turned his back on us to face east, over the wild waters, his arms flung out to either side; and I knew that the Cup was preparing itself to return home, to come back from where it had withdrawn itself in safety against Marguessan's blasphemous theft; knew also that Galeron at her mother's bidding would try to steal it away again, to divert it to a destination—Oeth-Anoeth?—of her own choosing, so that Marguessan's nightmare vision of a black Graal could be made real at last.

Though the foreshore of Garanwynion was thick with sorcerers, there was naught any of us could do now; the thing was well out of our hands, after all our questing. Little enough even to see, save perhaps for Morgan and Marguessan, whose younger aspects the two maidens had now become. Avallac'h's entire being was concentrated on the approaching Graal, on the pathway he must open for it;

he had no scrap of strength to spare even to defend it from its enemies, those who sought only to plunder it. I sensed too, as all the others surely did, that we would not be permitted to interfere; Those who ordered this struggle were implacable on that. It must play itself out: This was a battle between Queens and Princesses, Morgan and Donah on the one side, Marguessan and Galeron on the other. . .

I met Gweniver's eyes, and she looked as drowned in despair as I had ever seen her look; or had ever imagined she could look, it was not a mood that the Ard-rían of Keltia often entertained in herself. Yet I myself could not feel so; I seemed possessed of some joyous upwelling certainty that we would prevail here. Oh, this feeling had no root in anything I could name, I assure you, there were no grounds whatsoever for anything of the kind. Yet sometimes we know better than our selves what is real and true; and I have learned down the years to go with that feeling when it chooses to grace me with its presence. . . But things were happening now, and I could not look away.

Avallac'h still stood, tall and motionless against the clouds and sea. Then from the east came a sudden bloom of pale golden light, a soundless explosion of incandescence that dazzled us yet did not pain our sight, and I knew that the Portal had been opened by the true Keeper, so that the Cup might come through to the world again.

But if this were our joyful moment it was our moment of most peril also. For as one with the light came a—not a darkness, just so, but an *anti*-light, if you can conceive such abomination, such an offense against the laws of men and gods. A nullity, an inexistence, that yet had substance of a sort. . . It was frightful beyond all imaginings; it sickened us, it maddened the horses, it seemed to turn the waves backward from the shore—and it was Galeron, as Marguessan's instrument, who was calling it down upon us, chanting this nonbeing into being. This was Marguessan's great work of which she had boasted, and I of all folk knew how long her heart had been set upon it, for I had seen its pattern in her eyes when she had been a child of ten. All this was her doing, in which she rejoiced, this dark halo that heralded the coming of the Black Graal.

For that was what Galeron was calling, in place of the true Cup that Avallac'h besought and we had fought to bring home again. Mother and daughter, they worked as one, to capture the true Graal and to bring their own dark Cup into reality. And we could do nothing to stop it, we had done all we could by coming here; our quest had served to summon the Cup home again, and that was its dán and ours. But evil too has dán, and its dán is not always to lose to good.

Yet even as the' dark Graal trembled on the verge of accomplishment, it was forced back, by cleanness and true Light, by the only one who could do so. I saw Donah, rooted in the power of the world, gleaming like sunlight shooting out of the stormclouds. Saw Morgan's might behind her, and our own force behind that, and the strength of the folk behind that again—back and back and back, in a seemingly endless chain, boundlessly strong, linked together to bring back to us one of the Elements of the Keltic soul, without which we could not live. And overshadowing even Donah—if light can be said to shadow—was the bright image of One I knew, as a veil over Donah's humanity, a phasma, an indwelling presentment; and I bowed my head to Rhian, the Young Goddess, who had set Her hand above my brother's child. . .

Though contested, the outcome could scarcely be in doubt; yet it came to the balance of a hair, and surely Marguessan had confidently expected it to be other wise. Perfectly matched, light and dark strove together, while Avallac'h all the while stood above the fray; then the balance shifted. With a cry of bitter pain, Galeron fell to the sands as her brother earlier had done; but, unlike Mordryth, she lay still and small and did not move again. Donah, who also had gone to her knees with the strain and its sudden releasing, rose triumphant as an arrow in the gold, breathing hard but otherwise composed; and she stared down, her face unreadable, at the crumpled form of her cousin.

"Is Galeron slain?" I whispered to Morgan, forgetting in my distress to use mindvoice, and she nodded once. "Did Donah—"

Morgan shook her head, but her eyes were on Marguessan,

not on either of her nieces, and she chose to speak with
voice rather than with mind, so that others than I might
hear the explanation she chose to give us, and not fear.

"Nay; Galeron was her own executioner. The power
of the dark Graal overcame her as she tried to bring it
through. True it is her mother had commanded her to do
so, set her to it; but in the end she chose for herself the
dark road, and so fell, for it is easy to stumble in the
dark. . . The black Cup was her killer, not Donayah.
Slaying is not permitted upon the Island of the Graal—at
least not of the sort we are sadly 'customed to—and any
road the Keeper would never have allowed it. But to freely
choose self-slaughter—that does not fall under the ban.
And all this Galeron has now learned for herself, and she
will be better instructed elsewhere for a time. As to her
mother—who can say?"

I followed her glance—colder and brighter than I had
ever seen it, it was the gray of sword-metal, of battle
armor—to Marguessan, who still stood unmoving with
Mordryth crouched now at her feet. Galeron's body lay as
she had fallen, and Gwain's robed reposeful form was only
yards beyond. *Two dead children, Marguessan,* I thought, not
entirely without pity, aye, even for her, *Is your vengeance
against your brother worth so much? And what of the one chick
you have left to you?*

Marguessan stirred then, as if she had caught the wind of
my thought brushing by her, but it was not at me she
turned to stare but Morgan beside me. And I was staggered
at the expression my matesister bore upon her countenance:
Not the look of a woman with two of her three children
lying dead on the ground beside her, but the flickering
banefires of Uffern itself clung to Marguessan's features. If I
had thought her the living exponent of evil before, I had no
words now for what she had become, right before our eyes.
And if ever there had been a moment when Marguessan
could have been turned, when her first self could have been
reclaimed from the wrecked edifice that was her present
soul, that moment was gone for good; had died with Gwain,
with Galeron, perhaps even with Uthyr. She looked as the
Gwrach y Rhibyn, wasted with the fires of hate, all her

beauty gone, her features corded and fissured, her doom upon her.

So that is how it looks when dán is turned rightfully back upon one. . . . I had known that tenet of our faith from my childhood; but never before had I seen it drawn so plainly upon a human face. My eyes went to Morgan, who stood as unmoving as her sister, and I quailed within, seeing what was in her face. What was it like, to watch your wombmate destroy herself, and not be able to halt or help her? They were not identically twinned, and therefore no closer, in theory, than any other sibs; but yet it *was* different for them, for they had been born of the one birth, had spent those months of forming in a closeness unparalleled even by that of husband and wife—how must my Guenna feel? Then I looked again at my mate's face, and I knew.

"Sister," she said in a voice of command and compassion both, and Marguessan looked dumbly back at her across the width of all the seven hells. "Go now. Take your eldest, and be gone from here. It will be better for you both if you do go now."

Marguessan seemed to come back into herself at that— perhaps the command compelled her, or the compassion stung—and with a gesture at once protective and impatient she dragged Mordryth up beside her by a clawed hand on his collar.

"Go?" she said softly. "Aye, we shall go. I have no wish to see what comes here, and it surely does not wish to see me. . . But the work is not yet done, sister; not yours, not mine. Tell our brother and mother so, from us both."

She raked blazing eyes over me, Gweniver, Donah, Gerrans, Loherin; spun on her heel to blast Avallac'h (who lifted a hand slightly from his side, in warning or in farewell I could not decide); and then she was gone, and Mordryth with her. Galeron's body too; Gwain's lay unheeded behind her on the sand. I drew a long shuddering breath, let it out carefully, in soft measured puffs; but she was still gone. As each of us began to turn to one another, whether in joy or triumph or relief or fear we did not know just yet, Avallac'h called us back to business.

He clapped his hands twice, struck his bare right heel

hard upon the shingle of Garanwynion that bore us all upon its breast, and spoke to be heard not by us merely.

"Let that which is lost find a way," he said. "Let that which has been gone come again home."

And we all of us knew he did not speak of the Cup alone.

CHAPTER 14

From that moment I have no right judgment of time passing, as regards what happened next. Though I remember it all, to be sure—not hard, for the events of that day are graven with a pen of diamond into the palimpsest of my soul—sometimes it seems in memory's eye that all those things happened in one merest instant, one brief snap of time's fingers; while other times it seems that centuries were passed there on the strand Garanwynion. For the time in which the Cup, or the other Hallows, operates and has being is by no means the same time in which we mortals move and live and have existence; and when the two structures impinge so near upon each other, as now, a certain temporal dishevelment is bound to arise. Whichever it was, a span or a spasm, the great thing is that it truly *was*. . .

So Marguessan was gone, and in wrath too (though, as Gweniver remarked to me later, she had brought it on herself, and Gwen was right to say so; and too, as Gerrans said, there was no pleasing everyone, and he also was correct). But her departure, though surely it promised only worse to come from her hand what time we would be least expecting it, meant now that we were free to devote ourselves to our quest's rightful conclusion—though to my way of thinking, it was more the Graal that had found us than we who had found the Graal. Still, we were here, and it was about to be here, and that was what it and we both alike had come for.

Exalted by the moment (though perhaps 'giddy' would be a truer word), I looked around me at the faces of my fellow seekers, and they were alight even as my own. And mostly unknown to me as well: For all the whingeing complaints when the quest began, of how the companies of seekers were so heavily weighted to the rígh-domhna and the high nobility (a complaint not entirely without merit, mind), the twenty-six seekers who had won through, who had earned the right to be here this day, were as level a mix as you were like to find in all Keltia. True, the Pendreics were perhaps over-represented; but, quite apart from merely being royal, each of us here present was here for a reason in which our royalty played no part—and even the most fervent antimonarchist could not long argue that.

But the others, as I say, were strangers: folk of all ranks and trades and crafts and callings, from each of our Six Nations; men and women, youths and maidens, all equal here in the Place of the Graal.

I roused suddenly from my musings, and hoped I had looked rapt rather than merely daft, to find Avallac'h standing patiently before me. A smile touched the corners of his mouth, and he raised silver brows and made the smallest of interrogatory expressions. I had not a clue, of course; and must have shown it plain, for at that he laughed aloud.

"He charged with bringing the ale to the feast must broach the keeve ere any can drink—I think you have somewhat to our need, Pen-bardd?"

And then of course I remembered, and blushing ruefully I drew out the magical rose again from beneath my leinna, and laid it gently in his hand; for so, of course, had I been bidden. Avallac'h smiled again, and bowed to me, and turning once again to the sea he crumpled the flower in his right hand at arm's length, until the bloom was but petals and scraps.

"Not the Laughing Flower, but the flower that restores laughter," he said. "I give you the Rose that brings back Joy." He flung the petals from him into the sea, where the foam caught them, and the swift unseen tiderips spun the red shredlets out past the breaker line in a long bright string, and we all stared after them, and him.

For a path was forming in the sea along the line of the red petals, a path coming in the waters along the bright broad track the sun laid down: a road in the sea for the Cup to come in on, to follow home from the regions it had of late inhabited, protecting itself against the sacrilege Marguessan would have wrought upon it.

And now out of the heart of eastern light came a new brightness, boundlessly bright, blessedly bright, a brightness that cast no shadow and pained no eye. It came, as I say, from the east; but it seemed also to come equally from the other airts as well: For the direction from which it truly came had naught to do with our twelve earthly quarters, and that which the light heralded had *all* to do with mortal order. . .

"When first the Hallows came to the Kelts," said Avallac'h, all but invisible himself in the soft lucent glory, "that was the Opening of the tale. They came, and they went away again; now they are come once more, and this is the First Continuation. And they shall go again—for things have dán even as people do—and come again, brought back to Keltia by one whose dán it will be to do so; and that shall be the Second Continuation."

"And the Third?" asked Morgan beside me, very softly.

"That shall be at the end of all. Some of you here may see it, though you will be wearing other forms than those you inhabit just now. But the Cup shall know you even then. And now let us bring it home for this time."

He stepped down from the uneven ledge of dark-green, cream-veined marble upon which he had been standing, and bowed profoundly to the empty sea. But even as he did so we saw that the sea, and the air above it, and the shore beside it, was no longer empty: With joy and wonder I beheld grave tall spirits pacing the wave-crests, and the white horses of Manaan frolicking upon their wide salt plain like springtime colts; upon the sands fat little portunes ran between the legs of our own horses, who looked amiably on; and in the air soared feathered flames, crowned

and wingèd hearts, and other heralds of the Hallow that
now drew near.

The light rose to a pitch of purity that, had it been sound
instead of light, would have been well-nigh unbearable; it
seemed to sink through our skin, soak into our bones, filling
us, lifting us. . . And then quite suddenly, quite quietly, it
was there with us, among us, the Graal, the Cup, Pair
Dadeni that had been gone from the world and now was
restored.

I do not know how the others saw it—very few of us
cared to speak of it after, or perhaps it was that we *could*
scarce speak of it, out of a love and reverence and awe so
deep and holy that even I can hardly bear to write of it,
even here, even now. But you must know. . . For me, then,
it was much as I had beheld it before: the great Cauldron of
the Queen of the World, the Pair of Kerridwen Rhên, its
spirals and symbols trembling as if alive.

And it *was* alive, this Graal: Cam-Corainn it was, and An
Cuach, and so many other names beside, so many other
forms and appearances. For the Cup is different for each
soul that comes to it; each person who seeks the Graal has
different needs of it, different reasons—it is only right that
each should achieve a different Graal in the end. And the
Graal requires different things of each seeker, too: The Cup
also has its own needs and reasons, and never asks the same
thing of any two who have sought it. This is why we seek it
at all, so long, so dearly; and why, of course, it seeks us.

I do not know how long we stood there, upon the strand
Garanwynion, living the Cup as the Cup lived us. I mind
me that we bowed to it, deeper than we would do reverence
to any mortal king or queen, or to any ruler of the Sidhe,
even; our horses too knelt at its coming, touching their muz-
zles to the sand, forelegs bent in homage.

And then suddenly the Cup was as it was, as it had been
in the hall beneath the hill at Sychan, as it had appeared in
the air above our heads at Mi-cuarta. It had put on mortal-
ity again, a kind of everyday dress—for even kings do not
go about their daily work in crown and robe and court
cloak. Once more it was the fair silver quaich of use that
Brendan and Nia had brought to Keltia in the carved

ironoak chest that Nudd kept so close; and as such, it was meant to *be* used. . .

Donah and Loherin had come forward hand in hand, and they came with high intent, as if they now fulfilled a part and task they had known long since they would be called upon to perform. Indeed, even as I had foreseen, even I with my meager Sight. . . Graal Princess and Graal Server, they bowed unsmiling to the Cup, and to Avallac'h, and to each other, and to the rest of us. Then Donah, still grave-faced, turned to me expectantly, and though she said no word, I knew well what she required.

I opened the leather pouch at my belt and removed the small crystal bottle that rested therein. The tiny flask was still filled with the rust-red water of Saint Clears's Well: the spring Iscaroe, that was said to be proof against death itself. I handed the flask silently to Donah; I had begun to tremble, for I knew what was about to be done here, and I was glad and fearful both.

She took the vial, unstoppering it of its silver cap, and emptied the contents into the Cup that was itself proof against death. The red water filled the silver bowl halfway to the pearled rim, and lifting the Graal in both hands, Donah saluted the Four Airts, then turned to face Loherin.

"He Who Frees the Waters," she said, and saluted him with the Cup.

He bowed and took the Cup from her. "She Who Binds the Lands," he responded as solemnly, and raised the Cup alike to her in turn.

Donah reclaimed the great Graal into her own keeping; then, after the tiniest of pauses, a deep breath to center herself, she crossed to where Gwain Pendreic, who was cousin to them both, still lay upon his bier of cloak and spears. Kneeling beside his motionless form, she balanced the Cup against his lips, tilting it just so much, so that a tiny sip of the blood-colored water trickled into his mouth.

And then—I cannot report of this so lucidly as I would other time have done, for tears were scalding my eyes and streaming down my face, and yet even so my head was flung back with the joy and wonder of it (and is again just now, as I write these words)—Gwain whom the Dolorous

Blow had struck down, Gwain whom his own mother had magicked into needless and all unmerited death, Gwain whom I had killed, stirred, and opened his eyes, and sat up upon his bier.

The hush into which he awakened to life again was profound—even the waves seemed to quiet themselves—so that of all of us Gwain himself seemed alone of an everyday demeanor. He looked around him, a small puzzled frown and smile together inhabiting his so recently reinhabited countenance, then catching sight of Gwen and Morgan and me he flashed us a cheerful grin. But before he could hail us or scramble eagerly to his feet, as he was so plainly on point of doing, Avallac'h's shadow fell across him, and he looked up, startled now, as the awe came upon him.

"Welcome back, kinsman," said Avallac'h then, and reached down a hand to pull Gwain to his feet. "Be thou reborn, by the Cup's grace."

Gwain, as well he might, looked astounded; he went from white to red to white again, and would have fallen back upon the cloak from which he had just arisen had not Donah moved quickly to support him.

"I was dead," he said wonderingly, to all of us and none of us. "I was dead—I *remember*. . ." His gaze sought me out, and he looked at me with an expression of compassion and comprehension both together. "It was not you, my uncle," he said, shaking his head in the knowledge. "Not ever you. . ." And then it all came flooding back to him, we saw it come as a tide upon him; and he raked his glance over the company, searching for the one whom it *had* been, fury blazing in his face to kindle the air around.

Morgan came swiftly forward, and courteously but firmly moved Donah aside.

"She is gone, amhic," she said gently, and I heard the calm-tones in her voice; the suantraí, but raised to the pitch and power almost of a rann. And so he desperately needed just now, else he had gone mad entirely. . . "She is gone from here, and your sister with her." She touched his brow, and he shivered once, closing his eyes.

I watched Morgan beckon to Gerrans and Cristant, a young Ban-draoi priestess who had led one of the other companies; they came to Gwain and gently led him away, and I was frankly glad it had not fallen to me to comfort my restored nephew. After all, it had been I who had slain him in the first place; and though I was joyful and grateful beyond all earthly measure that he had been returned to life by the Cup, still I should not like to have to tell him that not only had his mother arranged his murder by his uncle but his only sister had herself perished in further darkworking against the Cup. . .

Avallac'h spoke to their retreating backs. "Though this was well and rightly done," he said, a warning tone now in his voice, "and only what dán required, not wise to do so commonly. In such pass even Athyn hesitated, and in the end had sorrow as well as joy from a like use, though it too was fated and correct. Be warned."

No fear!, I thought fervently. Life and death were never meant to be too often overset, either way; though Gwain's restoral was an unimpeachable righting of a wrong done to him and to the Cup itself, and surely would never have been permitted had it been sin or misuse, still, to bring someone back from Arawn's kingdom was an undertaking beyond all imagining, and only one in all our days in Keltia had ever imagined to achieve it. We would *not* be making a custom of it. . .

Avallac'h seemed to have heard my thought. "For that was Marguessan's intent and purpose," he said, nodding. "To wield that power over the folk for vainglory and tyranny, and to pervert the Cup to that end. . . Now she has failed in that hope, but has constructed for herself a dark Graal to set against Cam-Corainn; but the first sup of *that* Cup will be far the bitterest, while the last will be past fatal. She has already drunk too deep, indeed, of that draught which she has brewed for herself, and she is poisoned thereby." His voice and face, which had been hard as stone and deep as thunder, cleared now, and he gestured to Donah and Loherin who had stood quietly by. "Now let the land be cleansed."

Donah went at once to the rough marble slab upon

which Avallac'h had stood, and poured out onto the
sparkling stone half the remaining contents of the Cup. The
green rock took the red water into it, seeming to shimmer
and expand as it did so; and far out over the sea, between
us and the Easter Isles, a storm rose up and began to move
swiftly toward the land.

A storm unlike to all others: It did not drench us, though
from its dark boiling clouds blue lightnings lanced the sea
and islands over which it passed, and the wind of its coming
flung our hair back from our faces and our cloaks from our
shoulders. It moved over Beckery, its torn skirts so low they
all but scraped the castle's towers, and then it was advanc-
ing on Fairlight and the Dragonsea's western edges.

"It will renew the lands," breathed Morgan, watching the
storm's shoulders broadening as it came upon the shore.
"All Tara, and all Keltia, shall get good of it."

We still stood beneath the storm's shadow—it had grown
vaster than any storm of earth—and in the roar of
Garanwynion and the blue-litten seas beyond Avallac'h
stood tall against the wind. High he held above his head
now the Cup, which blazed with more than reflected lightnings, and he poured out the remnant of the sacred waters
into the sea.

As the holy vintage of Iscaroe, ruby in the stormy light,
mingled with the waters of the First Ocean, linking sea to
land, suddenly the clouds split above Caervanogue and a
shaft of light shot through, to seize upon the Cup and make
it blaze to outshine the levinfire. Avallac'h towered up amid
the ruins of the storm, and the light grew, and with it a joyous certainty, and I knew the Cup was come truly home to
Keltia.

Avallac'h spoke to us then, long and long, most gravely
and lovingly out of his centuries of guardianship. He gave
the guardianship into our hands now, all of us here, made
us knights of Cam-Corainn, investing us with the charge of
the Cup and its fellow Hallows, giving us to drink of the
Graal's bounty. And though the touch of the Cup did not
confer upon us any kind of immortality or invulnerability,
still were we changed thereby; and with the bronze dagger
Merlynn Llwyd had given me beneath the hill, Avallac'h,

prince of Keltia and Keeper of the Graal, laid the accolade upon our shoulders, left, then right, then upon the crown of our heads, to helm us with the Light.

So there in the golden morning we made peace with hand on Cup, there on the shingle of Garanwynion. The waves washed the tails of our horses, who had knelt when the Cup returned; and all had from the Cup that which they best loved to eat and drink, Donah and Loherin serving us, their beauty in that hour such that few could gaze long upon them.

But at last the feast and revel were done, and the mood changed as Avallac'h spoke to us yet again. And this time we of the quest were not the only ones present on Beckery: The sprites and fetches that had welcomed the Cup's return now drew nigh to hear his words also—spirits of each element rooted in each, water-spirits to the sea, air-beings in the lift, earth-feys upon the sands and fire-fetches upon the stones. And then, with a leap of my heart that moved my body forward in a sudden uncontrollable surge of gladness, I saw Gwyn ap Nudd and Birogue of the Mountain riding toward us over the sea.

Not they alone, though it had needed only they to make this day's joy complete: Overshadowing their forms were other aspects, other Presences and Powers I had come to know, a little, on this quest—Rhian the Young Goddess and Fionn the Young Lord. And the wonder was that not only did Their overshadowing lay upon Birogue and Gwyn but upon Donah and Loherin also, the fiala, the bright veil of Their divine presences, cloaking the two young mortals with a visible sheen.

And I knew by that veiling, by the coming of the gods and the Sidhe, what was to happen next. . .

First, though, Avallac'h would speak: He gathered us all in around him, mortal and unmortal and Immortal alike— for all are the Cup's creatures and children, first to last.

"I said earlier that the Graal would go and come again, as its dán commanded. But that is not all the truth. . . You have all wondered, I know, how the Cup came to be stolen in first instance: Nudd kept it, and its fellow Hallows, safe and close beneath the hill; how could it be that Marguessan Pendreic

winkled it out? The truth is that the Cup itself *chose* to be
reived away, for that Keltia had become too bound up with
things of the world and needed to lose in order to learn.
And you yourselves have been the docents: If created things
are allowed too much, all creation suffers for lack of that
which is past creation. And so undoubtedly the Cup will go
again, though next time its healing graces shall not depart
with it. But for the Cup itself, and more beside, a different
dán is laid down, and far from here."

"But not to be gone from us forever?" That was
Gweniver, sounding more shaken than I had ever heard her
sound; and, judging by the almost annihilating compassion
in the glance Avallac'h bent now upon her, she knew more
of this than she was just now prepared to share with the rest
of us. "That would be too cruel, surely—"

"Aye so, and therefore has Kerridwen Rhên Herself
decreed otherwise. But though the Cup be gone for a thousand years, until that one I spoke of be born to fetch it
home, the Cup's Server shall here remain, to guard the
Gates and welcome it when it comes again at Keltia's need."

A breath of awe touched me like a cold finger upon my
nape; and again it was as if Avallac'h read my thought.

"Nay, that Server shall not be I," he said, with the breath
of a laugh in his voice. "My covenant with the Cup has
been redeemed, my stand here at Caervanogue is relieved. I
have served as the choice was given me, and my freedom is
at hand. I shall go now, and the charge I have borne is now
offered to another—though he too has that choice I was
given, the choice to freely accept or freely set aside. I give
him that choice now, does he care to make it."

But Loherin was already striding across the strand to
him, such a light of eagerness and joy upon him, transfiguring mere beauty into sacred, that I dropped my eyes before
him. But then I raised my head to gaze steadfastly upon my
young kinsman, to do honor to him and to the unimaginable
task he took upon him. Of the actual moment, when the
Keepership of the Graal was passed between the old lord
and the new, when Avallac'h relinquished his holy charge
and his magical existence, conferring both upon Loherin the
fair, I know not; I did not see. Such sacredness is not for us

to behold, however consecrated we ourselves might be to the same high ideal.

All I saw for sure was a brightness that enveloped both of them, all I heard was Avallac'h's voice from the heart of the splendor as he spoke to us.

"You who have sought and found: Your task here is achieved, and with honor. Tell Arthur Ard-rígh so, the King in the Light; and tell him too that his own task also is well achieved. Naught more difficult than to wait in patience: Arthur's severest test in this matter was not to seek, as you have done—that had been an easy task for *his* questing spirit—but to possess his soul in patience, and that is the thing he finds hardest of all to do."

Loherin's voice came, glad and young, already somehow subtly changed. "Arthur the King had no need to seek because he has already found; what seeking he yet must do shall come later, and in the end he himself shall be a quest—to be sought and found again."

Well! It was all getting just a scrap too fraught with dán for me, if you take my meaning; still, since it was. . . Greatly daring, I took my chance, to speak the thought and hope of my heart, and risk the answer I might get.

"And Merlynn Llwyd? What of him?"

Avallac'h again: "So it is with hunting birds, son of Glyndour, as you well know, you who bear the gray hawk's plume against your breast; for sparhawk chick or she-eagle, they cannot do other. . . Merlynn sleeps now in his esplumeor, that bright cage-place where hunting birds in the moult are kept while they renew themselves. Feathers must needs be shed and regrown, worn-out pinions be replaced by strong new growth, to support the flight of new deeds and new demands."

"Yet surely this is what a soul does betwixt lives, as we are taught," said the young priestess Cristant, doubt in her clear voice. "Is not Merlynn Llwyd then dead as we thought?"

I dared a quick glance at Birogue—Merlynn's mate, though as yet that was a secret only I, and perhaps Morgan, was privy to—but her countenance revealed nothing; indeed, a snow-glazed stone at the winter solstice would have been more forthcoming. But that was the way of the Shining Folk.

"Aye and nay," said Loherin, though how he came to know I could *not* tell you. "Dead in this world, but not in the greater; dead to this life, but not to living. He is taken out of time awhile; Taliesin knows, for he has seen this"—I fingered the gold case that held my gray feather, and nodded once—"though the rest have not. Not dead, then, but renewing; not alive, but transforming. And Merlynn must be protected from the world, and the world from him, until this state of peril and glory shall be completed, and he return at need."

"So he comes again!" cried one of the young members of the company, a dark Kymro I did not know.

"Oh aye," said Avallac'h, and now I could hear the centuries of exhaustion in his voice, and closed my eyes for pity of it. "He comes again, right enough, and not he alone. I say again: The Graal will not remain among you. It has a quest of its own to go on, and the other Hallows with it. For things have their dán even as do people, and the dán of the Treasures is this: that they must go from here, in the proper time of going, until the time is on them to return. They themselves shall set in motion the means by which they will be restored, and one shall be sent to the world whose dán is to bring them back. There shall be great need in that time, but though desperate it will not be the true need; for that Merlynn must awaken, and counsel be taken of the Graal Keeper. My charge to you, Pen-bardd"—I startled at his use of my title—"is to keep them all alive. Sing, then; sing of them all until that day comes. Sing of the Treasures, and Merlynn, and Arthur the King, and all of us, until the future hears your song."

He was growing weary now; but Gweniver too had somewhat she must ask.

"And are there no more words, then?"

"For the Ard-rían of Keltia, peace after pain"— Gweniver's mouth tightened briefly, but she did not speak— "and for the daughter of the Yamazai, a daughter of her line to help that one who brings the holy Quaternity back to Keltia."

Donah looked thunderstruck, but exalted also. "*My* daughter? But Prince, I am far from even troth-plight—"

It seemed as if the pillar of brightness that was Avallac'h and Loherin together smiled benevolently upon her.

"True enough, but the daughter shall be of your House, not of your immediate bearing. So let the name Fionnabhair be given now and again to lasses of your line to come; she shall have need of that name to help her in her task."

Donah bowed but found no words; and I startled yet again as the brightness seemed to bend itself upon me. The words confirmed it.

"Pen-bardd"—and now it seemed Loherin who spoke— "one word more. Let the sword be reforged, and returned to its homeplace. Let the sword flash downward in the stroke, and be sure it is well reforged ere that day of need is come."

And, ah, that bard's brain was already translating this into songspeech deep and far within me, music already blowing through my awareness like mists in autumn. . . But now Gwyn and Birogue had come forward, and they were near as bright as Avallac'h and Loherin; and again I saw Fionn and Rhian upon them and through them and beyond them.

"We will take the Cup back beneath the hill, to lie with its comrades, until such time as they must go upon their *immram*." Birogue spoke for the first time here, and those of the company whose first encounter with the Sidhe this was caught their breath at the sound of her voice. But not all were too awed to speak up.

"Then what does Loherin remain to guard?" called one young Druid, a friend of Gerrans. "If the Cup does not even rest here—"

"The Cup will ever be here," said Gwyn, before any other could answer. And if they had shivered at Birogue's power of voice, they positively shook at Gwyn's. . . "Its physical self goes with us back to our own place. But its reality remains here at Caervanogue, and this is where it must be defended. Thus Loherin is Guardian, in the Castle of the Graal, until the need of him is ended—however long by your count of years that may take. And so now"—he

moved forward and took the Graal from the brightness that
had been Avallac'h and was now Loherin—"we bring them
away. Farewell in Nudd's name, all you who have sought so
well and found so fairly. Taliesin Pen-bardd, brother to my
folk, we shall meet soon again."

"'Soon'!" I said, startled into speech and discourtesy
alike. "By whose counting?"

But the seidean-sidhe was swirling round us now—
though, strange to tell, not a grain of sand rose with it—and
though I heard Gwyn's laughing farewell to me over the
rush of air and unseen troops or wings ("Soon, Talyn! No
more! Be content!"), when I could open my eyes again
against the light and wind, Gwyn and Birogue were gone,
and the Cup with them.

And Avallac'h too was gone: The light that had been was
vanished, and Loherin stood as he had been, the son of
Tryffin of Kernow and Ysild the valorous of Arrochar, in
plain light and ordinary guise. He looked to the outer eye
much his usual self, but we knew so much better now. . .

Again a shiver of awe rippled over me. From this hour
on, Loherin would never again be as other Kelts; indeed,
was already not so. He might age, slightly and slowly, but
even that was doubtful; more like, he would stay even as he
now was, young and fair and unchanging in the world, until
that long day came of which Avallac'h had spoken, and that
one should come to seek his counsel, and to waken Merlynn
my beloved teacher from his long sleep.

I was momentarily blinded by dán—quite literally
blinded; the sight was taken from me for a few seconds, all I
saw was blank brightness—and when I could see again, I
wondered what it was that had gone by me. Certain sure it
concerned me or mine most nearly; otherwise I had been
permitted to see. And a tiny secret thought crept somewhere
far within, full of traha and humility both together: Could it
be true, as one or other of the principals here had implied—
that I myself should be at hand, in the body, reborn when
all these things should come to pass that my songs would
serve to keep alive until that day? Hu Mawr! In what guise,
whose form, which name?

But in Her mercy the Goddess does not usually give us

to know of our incarnations and lives to come, any more than She permits us to keep more than a shadowy inkling memory of lives gone by. Either way, that knowledge would destroy us more surely than a sword: We would never *do*, but spend all our time in watching ourselves; we would not grow, and dán would not be served.

Thoroughly frightened now—bards, who so readily can calm or fright others, do a *masterful* job of daunting themselves—I pulled Morgan to me and held her close, to take of her what comfort I could. I felt older than Avallac'h, and every bit as weary; I longed now only to go home, as swiftly as I might, with my dear ones and companions riding beside me, to bring the news to Arthur the King that the Graal had been found, and that dán had been both met and set.

I looked at Loherin, who was speaking quietly and gravely to Gweniver Ard-rían. Even in his everyday existence Loherin of Kernow had been the fairest of mortal Kelts; now his beauty had become like to that of the Sidhe themselves, raised by high purpose and the hand of the gods to the measure of the task he had so joyfully accepted. And I felt a sudden stab of envy for the nobleness of the task, and also for the knowledge of what Loherin would come to see, down the centuries of his duty, with those very same eyes with which he now studied Morgan. . .

I came to myself with a start, to find Loherin's eyes warm and kind on me in my turn. I did not need to explain a thing to him.

"Nay, cousin, do not grieve for me," he said quietly. "Nor yet covet the task. Yours will be greater still, I promise. All is as it will be, Talynno. Go now. We shall meet again." And he kissed me, and embraced me, and we parted for this life.

He made his farewells to the others of his kin and friendship—a long and deep converse with Donah, which none overheard, words to several of us to be given to his parents—and then he was gone from among us, suddenly, silently, just as Avallac'h had come and the Graal itself had come, and gone as he had gone. Only, above us, the great seaward gates of Caervanogue swung slowly closed, and no hand was seen to shut them fast. . .

. . . and we found ourselves standing upon the farther
shore of the Dragonsea, at Fairlight, our horses with us (and
they not best pleased at the sudden alarming change of
scene). I believe we all shouted, in terror or amazement or
surprise or sorrow according to our feeling and nature, and
turned as one to the island whence we had so precipitately
arrived here.

Beckery was vanishing even as we watched: It went shimmering, back once more behind its shields and veils of magic,
safe in the power of a new Graalkeeper, the white pennon
upon Caervanogue's highest turret the last to disappear; and
then it was gone, and the white causeway even, too, and the
sea stretched seamlessly green from our boots at its western
fringe to the shores of the Easter Isles.

"Well," said Gweniver, Ard-rían of Keltia, and she spoke
for all of us, "that is that."

And she was so right to say it.

BOOK THREE:
Suantraí

CHAPTER 15

Arthur was in the gate to meet us, as we had rather
thought he might be. Although no advertisement had
been made of our coming home, he had known even so of
our midnight arrival—perhaps Morgan had bespoken him,
mind to mind, or perhaps he had just, well, *known*—for here
he was, come hastily as it seemed, clad only in boots and
trews and a thin silkwool cloak flung round him against the
October chill.

"You might have dressed for the occasion," I remarked as
I swung stiffly out of my saddle and into his bear-hold of an
embrace. We held each other a moment or two, scarce long
enough, then turned as one to help Gweniver and Morgan
down from their own mounts. A passionate embrace for his
wife and Queen, another for his sister; then Arthur was moving like the seidean-sidhe down the line of riders to Donah—
who was nodding in her saddle, poor weary lass, with
Gerrans watching carefully lest she topple over.

We had ridden home to Caerdroia straight and swiftly,
bidding farewell along our way to the others of the Graal's
Company whose own homes lay elsewhere on Tara; had
even seen a good few off-planet at Mardale, the spaceport
that served the Crown City, twelve miles to the east in one
of the Loom's broader vales. Now the Caerdroians had all
come home together from the great quest.

Arthur shepherded us all inside Turusachan, as if he had been a particularly assiduous sheepdog and we excessively strayed lambs of the flock. Pendreics, friends, kindred, neighbors, even those we had not known before the quest began—all were chivvyed alike into the palace by the High King, who seemed to have assumed for the moment the duties of eager doorward.

Though my most overriding emotion just then was plain simple childlike gladness to be *home,* I did manage to be glad to see how Arthur received his long-absent Gwen—they had flung themselves upon one another with a will—and all the more so because I myself had been parted from my own mate until that last day at Caervanogue and knew well how it felt. But here we all were, safe home, and though I was longing very much by now for naught but my own wide soft familiar comfortable bed, the news had to be imparted to the High King and his chief ministers—just Tarian, Grehan and Ygrawn, for now—before any slumber be selfishly thought of.

So Arthur solicitously ordered us fed and drenched, most heavily and unsuitably for the time of night and the state of our bodies. To my everlasting surprise, we all revived with the onslaught of food and drink rather than collapsed beneath it; revived sufficiently to give lucid account of our questing before sleepwalking off to bed (and the nightmares our overeating would soon cost us). Even Donah, who had more cause than most for weariness, woke up to tell her father all her adventure (Arthur threw me a deeply grateful thoughtsmile when it came to her telling of my small part in her quest). As for the rest of us, we acquitted ourselves respectably and gave good enough accounting of events, for now at least; fuller details, and a complement of recorder-bards to hear them, must wait till the morning, or some morning. . .

Then we all went to our beds and slept like the slain. Sounder. I did not even recollect Morgan beside me, and was in fact quite surprised to find her there when I wakened a day and a night and a day again after.

* * *

On the morning of the day after that, I was slept out, and up betimes to watch the day break over the City and the valley of the Avon Dia spread out below me.

I stood on the topmost tower of the Keep, the great square-built tower at the heart of Turusachan. Raised by Brendan's master-builder Gradlon of Ys—he who had engineered the Nantosvelta—the Keep was the first structure to rise on the level small plateau between the Lower City and the Loom behind. Indeed, it set its granite back against the hill itself; Eryri, Mount Eagle, made the fourth wall of Brendan's tower.

I had long time since discovered a high rampart overlooking the fifty-mile view, where I could see and not myself be seen, and had come there often. So now that I was home at last from my captivity—there had been so little time between escaping Marguessan and leaving on quest that I did not trouble even to count it—this refuge was the first place I sought. And I was not the only one to seek it.

"I knew you would be here," said Arthur, looking pleased with himself. He came through the door in the tower behind me, latching it so that none else could intrude, and settled himself into one of the merlon nooks, levered out from the battlements, five hundred feet above the Great Square.

"I *wish* you would not sit so," I snapped, as my guts seemed to plummet like a stone down through my feet and right straight through the embrasure where he was so comfortably lodged.

He laughed, but did not move; and throwing him an evil look, I retreated to the curve of the tower wall, planting my back firmly and solidly against the ruddy eternal granite of the ashlar that formed it. *Some things never change. . .*

When no word came from Arthur's vicinity for more minutes than usual, I glanced curiously up at him. He was not looking at me but out over the million-acre vista, as I had earlier done myself, and I schooled myself to study him, as the King, as a bard and a stranger might see him.

And, tell you the truth, I found it unexpectedly difficult: I had known this soul, this Artos, all this life, and, no doubt, many lives before it. Scarce a memory I had that did not have him somewhere within it, or near: I knew his face better than I knew my own, his moods likewise, his weaknesses and his strengths. I knew him in many, many aspects: When I looked at him I saw the High King of Keltia and the little runabout lad with whom I had taken the vows of fosterance before I was six years old. Saw my wife's brother, my foster-mother's child; Gweniver's wedded lord and Majanah's onetime mate; Arawn's father, Amris's son.

"Sometimes you are hard to find, Artos," I said aloud, "in the midst of yourself."

A smile touched the mouth in the silvering beard, but still he did not turn to me.

"So Gwennach said the night you all returned. . . But I am here, Talyn; indeed, I never left."

"Do you mind?" I asked presently. "Avallac'h said it was your dán to remain, and that it would be harder for you to wait than for us to ride on quest."

At that he did laugh, and shot me the old sparkling glance full of amused chagrined admission I knew so well.

"And how right he was to say so. . . Nay, I do not mind, not truly; yet still—it would have been a fine thing to ride with you, to have made a twenty-seventh in your company. And to see the Cup so!" He was silent a moment, and I knew he was remembering as I was that day beneath the hill, when Nudd ap Llyr had tested us and then rewarded us with the proffer of the Treasures. Arthur had accepted only Fragarach, the great Sword of Light that never let itself be drawn in evil cause; the other sacred things he had left in the Sidhe's keeping. And it was from that keeping that the Cup had been snatched away by Marguessan and her dwimmer-workings. . .

"Aye," said Arthur, nodding, for he saw what I saw. "What *are* we to do about her?"

"She is your sister," I said to remind him, and let a tiny note of reproof edge my voice. He shrugged angrily, and I tried another tack. "Have you had word of her since the Graal came back?"

Arthur shook his head. "Only that she is thought to have left Tara, after—Galeron's death."

"And Gwain's reviving," I said sternly, and he nodded.

"What *is* it with Marguessan!" he suddenly exploded. "Tell me, Bard of Keltia, how is it that from the one birthing can come two souls so utterly opposed as Morgan and Marguessan?"

"I know not," I said. "It is almost as if—"

"As if what?" When I did not at once reply: "Speak, Glyndour! Speak your mind to your Ard-rígh!"

"As if they had but one dán and soul between them," I said slowly, "and it was halved, the part of the Light being Morgan's and the Dark—"

"And the Dark for Marguessan's portion," he finished for me. "Aye, well, naught new there, that has been said many times before. Only now, with this matter of the Cup—"

"Artos," I said, suddenly sure, "what is the trouble? It is not your sister's devilry, not this time. What is on you?"

Arthur threw me another of those looks. "You truly are a tiresome man, do you know that. . . Well then, two things. Three."

"Never mind how many; only tell them. This is I here, Talyn; none else is near to listen."

"Melwas of Fomor is coming to Keltia," he said then, no preamble, and smiled grimly as I gaped. "You do remember Melwas?"

"Oh aye," I said slowly. "I recall the Prince of Fomor's heir very well."

"No heir more, nor yet Prince himself but King now," said Arthur, pleased to have confounded me. "And it seems that that seed we put down of friendship has come to flower at last: He comes with an embassy to make a formal treaty of friendship and trade with us, enlarging on that pact we made on Ganaster."

I thought for a while, recalling the circumstances. "Friendship is well and good, but trade is done on Clero. Is that not why we have a trading planet in the first place?"

"It is," conceded Arthur. "But I have called some of our merchant chiefs home from Clero to negotiate with the Fomori trader lords. All of them will arrive before the winter Sunstanding, and will remain at least until Brighnasa."

I thought some more, about the prospect of being shut in for the solstice revels with Fomori and gods knew what other folk. . .

"There will be spies in the delegation," I said after a while, and was rewarded to see the look of complete eye-rolling exasperation on Arthur's face.

"Well of *course* there will be spies! And never fear, we shall have our own spies' knees under *their* table! I have spoken to the Queen about it, and she agrees, if not gladly; and of course I did not take the decision alone, to have them come—Tari and Grehan and Keils and our mother approve of the course."

I brightened. "Ah well then, if methryn approves—" Little chance Ygrawn Tregaron would consent to any plan, even one of her son's, if she had not gone over it most minutely and found it to Keltia's weal.

Arthur raised his brows and quirked his mouth, but said nothing.

"You said there were three things," I prompted him after a while. "Melwas; and—?"

He looked a touch cast down. "I have had word from Majanah. She wishes Donah to be sent home to her after the solstice season is done. I did not know how much I had come to count on the lass's being here."

"Well, Artos," I said, trying to comfort, and also feeling strangely and suddenly forlorn myself, "we knew Janjan would not let her stay here forever. Time it is for her to begin to learn how to rule her own world, as one day she must. And you have Arawn now, it is not as if Donayah is your one chick, or could inherit Keltia after you."

"All very true. Still, I shall miss her so much."

"As will all of us here. But we shall have her back again soon, and maybe even Janjan with her." I paused again; gods, it was like pulling teeth with him sometimes. . . "And the third thing?"

"Ah, that." Arthur leaped up, caring nothing for the stab of vertigo that shot through me from my breast to my boots. "I do not know how to speak of it."

"Artos. Speak."

"Well then, it is Malgan Rheged." When I said no word

but only stared: "Surely you recall *him?* At least as well as, say, Melwas?"

I glared at the sarcastic edge he had put on it. "Rather better, I would say. . . What is it with him?"

For the first time in all our talk Arthur let his uneasiness be seen upon his face.

"That is just it, Talyn. I do not know. No one knows. He went from Court not so long after you were taken by Marguessan, as I think I told you when you were rescued, and established himself at Saltcoats. I gave my permission for him to do so, of course, though Gwen was not best pleased to see it. But she never liked the lad."

I was silent, thinking furiously. Of all those closest to Arthur, I alone—and later, perhaps not so surprisingly, Ygrawn—had not assigned to Malgan Rheged the manifold sins and offenses of Owein his late father. Or *alleged* father, I reminded myself yet again: All that could be said with certainty of Malgan's parentage was that Gwenwynbar, Arthur's first wife, had been Malgan's mother. The other side of the pedigree had yet to be filled in to Keltia's satisfaction.

"Is he working some treason or miscontent?" I asked then.

"Not to my knowledge."

"Has he spoken out against you or Gweniver?"

"I have not heard that he has."

"Has he refused any due or obligation you as King have set him?"

"Discharged all with great correctness."

"Well then!" I threw back my head. "What is your problem? Or, nay, wait, I know—it is the same problem there has been from of old with Malgan, not so?"

Arthur's sullen silence confirmed it; and, truth be told, I could not blame him for it. I do not think Arthur had ever managed in all these years since his first marriage ended to convince himself that his wife's son was not of his own begetting. True, Malgan had been born a mere seven months or so after Gwenwynbar had ended the marriage and run off to attach herself to Owein; but Owein—and more telling to my way of thinking, the Marbh-draoi Edeyrn himself, whose adopted heir Owein was—had never (at least publicly) shown the smallest sign that *he* was convinced the lad was not of *his* own begetting, if born a trifle early.

But if Malgan *were* Arthur's son, gotten in lawful brehon marriage (if perhaps not born so), then according to all laws ever made he was the right heir to Keltia.

Which put him into crowded company. . . I reflected on the current field of claimants both subtle and plain. Arawn, of course, was as child of Gweniver and Arthur the front-runner and lawful Tanist; but there rose up here all that old coil of the correctness of Arthur's *own* claim to the Copper Crown, and curst Marguessan of Lleyn still held to her stubborn belief that as eldest daughter of the restored King Uthyr, *she* should be High Queen, and her son Mordryth to rule after her. Not to mention Donah's claim; and who knew if Avallac'h the recent Graalkeeper had not a line of his own hidden away somewhere, senior to the stem of Pendreic that now ruled?

It was all most 'scruciating complicated, and it was making my head hurt. . . In the end we both went down from the Keep in silence. But the doubt was real.

In the two years of my enforced absence Morgan had busied herself with a number of matters so that she did not go mad entirely, and one of the most successful of these was the building of a castle of our own. We had dwelled, since the war ended, at Caerdroia, in the palace; but it had never been home to us, and even before that, in the long years of our hunted and hiding existence on Gwynedd, we had built skycastles to ease our hearts, thinking of a time when we might have a true place that was ours only.

So Morgan, in part as fulfillment of those dreams of ours, had had built a place for us on Gwynedd, not all that far from my own lost Gwaelod. She had called it Tair Rhandir, in honor of Tair Rhamant of my boyhood; but that was where the likeness ended. Rhamant had been the simple castle of a rather minor and far from wealthy local chieftain, lord of a poor province; Rhandir had been raised by a princess for a mate she feared was lost to her.

Its white walls were visible thirty miles away; faced with

quartzite, they gleamed in daylight and flamed at dawn and dusk. Four huge towers stood at the airts, concentric walls made it a most defensible place: But the chief charm of Tair Rhandir was its lightness of heart. If ever gaiety and young love had been made manifest in stone, it was here; Morgan had made Tair Rhandir a tale of ourselves.

So now for the first time I came to the home my lady had built us; Gerrans was with us, and Donah, and Gweniver and Arthur and Arawn, my sister Tegau and her lord Eidier from their own place not many miles distant—a family holiday after the stresses of the Graal quest and before the arrival of the Fomori king. Morgan had invited some guests also, and for the first time ever Tair Rhandir welcomed me as lord.

I needed the time it gave me, and badly; my imprisonment had left me unsettled, edgy, unwilling to be alone, and the quest had hardly helped cure that. It was better than I can tell you, to be here, in this house of love my mate had made for me, with all my dearest kin and friends about me; it was just what I needed right about now, and I blessed Morgan's wisdom, doubly, for bringing me here and for building it to begin with.

Good it was, too, to spend time with my son. Gerrans had had as eventful a quest as the rest of us—for the most part he had travelled with Loherin, or with Gwain before the incident of the Sorrowful Stroke—and though he too would not admit to it, this holiday came at a good time. He had brought a guest with him, a young Ban-draoi priestess whom I had met at Caervanogue, and who had seemed even then to be rather more to Geraint ap Taliesin than just another Graal companion. Her name was Cristant, a close connection of the Aoibhells of Thomond; Morgan spoke well of her as sorceress, but more than that I did not know.

Tryffin and Ysild were here too, though their infant daughter Ydain had been left at home on Kernow. I had not seen either of my old friends since the end of the quest and the translation of their only son—Arthur and Gweniver together had gone to Kernow to tell them of Loherin's calling, and that he would not be coming again home—and I was saddened at the change I saw in them.

"Well, it is hardly to be otherwise," said Morgan when I spoke of it. "They adored him—as did all who knew him— and though the grandeur and glory of his task are honor enough, still and all they have lost their son. A hard thing for any parent."

"And to lose him so strangely—" I was caught up in it all over again: could smell the sea-tang at Beckery, could see the beauty of Loherin and the ancient wisdom of Avallac'h. . . "But to know that he will live with the life of the Cup, and for it, centuries uncounted—surely that must be worth all? Do you think?"

"Oh aye, and they do so, but still it is hard. Thank the Goddess they have this new Ydain to help them, and to be Duchess of Kernow one day to follow her father. . ."

"'Princess' it may be by then," I remarked. "Artos has thoughts of elevating the Dukedom, so that the ruler of Kernow would be a planetary prince to rank with those we have from of old: Gwynedd and Dyved and Caledon and the rest."

"Tryff cares little enough even to be Duke," Morgan said smiling. "Nor yet Ysild, though knowing her as I do I doubt me she would turn down the coronet! Great scout to Marc'h's ghost, though; he must writhe in Annwn to know that Tryff, whom he so despised, should be prince where he was not."

"Never mind Marc'h," I said hurriedly, for I minded me of how it had come about that Marc'h *was* a ghost, and of how it had worked on me in the process. . . "We have pleasanter things far to think on, at least until the Fomori arrive. I would not waste the time."

But it seemed that none of us could distance ourselves just yet from the quest, and seemed also that talking about it was the only way to try. . .

"I wonder does Loherin get to sleep for a thousand years," I speculated aloud, as I soaked luxuriously in the huge pool-bath of Morgan's own design; she was in it with me, as were also Donah and Gweniver and Gerrans and young Arawn, who squealed with delight and splashed water

at me from where Gerrans carefully held him half-sub-
merged.

"Or at least until such time as Merlynn wakes and he
himself is needed, as Gwyn told us," I continued, carefully
avoiding Arawn's very good aim. "Tell you all, I would not
mind that so very much myself."

"Ahé! For my part, I would rather spend the centuries in
such a bath as this," said Gweniver. "One long warm
soak—" She sank down until only her eyes showed, her dark
hair spreading out like seagrass, and floated over to tease her
giggling son.

"And think how you would look when you came out,"
said Morgan.

"I would be at the table, I think," put in Donah. When
the rest of us shouted with laughter and scudded water at
her, she bridled, but grinned. "Nay, truly! I am no usual
watchpot, as you well know; but I say I could do great
deeds in Mi-cuarta for the outside of a sevennight just now!
Little enough faring we had of it on quest."

"All part of the trial and testing," said Morgan, ducking
the girl under and smiling when Donah came up laughing
and sputtering. "A fine easy time! No sleep, baths in freez-
ing streams, talking beasts, walking mountains, rivers of
blood, prodigies from morn to middlenight. . . Not a dull
moment in it—and what sort of a quest would have been
otherwise? They are not built for the comfort of those who
go on them."

"Aye so, but the Graal?" asked Gerrans. He had been
more subdued than was his wont these few days we had
been here at Rhandir. Part of it was plain reaction to the
quest's rigors—as it was with us all—and part of it was due
to another cause entirely, and I thought I knew what that
might be, and resolved to speak of it to my son's mother
directly we exited the bath. But Gerrans spoke again, a
plaintive note to his voice.

"If the Graal is gone, or not real, whatever it was my
lord Gwyn said it was, how then can my cousin Loherin be
its Guardian, and why is *he* gone?"

"When we see the Cup," said his mother gravely, all at
once the mighty sorceress she was, "it is *in* the created world,

but it is not *of* it. And so did I say to your father, before the quest began. And when we do not see it, it is *of* the world, but not *in* it." She laughed at the blank stunned faces peering at her through the steam as uncomprehendingly as cows. "No fear! We have done our part. Well, for now, any road."

"For now?" repeated Arthur darkly, as he stripped off tunic and trews and joined us in the pool. "Well, no matter that 'now'. . . I have other news, which you may like still less than that," he added, turning to Donah who was disporting herself noisily and very wetly indeed with her delighted infant brother a few yards off.

She saw the look on his face, and divined instantly his news. "Ah nay, tasyk! Not yet—not *now*—"

Arthur nodded, shrugged helplessly with it. "Your mother calls you home, lass, before the solstice—nay, it will be only for a brief while!" he added hastily, to forestall the mutinous protest he saw building like a thundercloud upon his daughter's fine high brow. "I shall be sending Daronwy and Roric with you, as it happens, and back you all shall come in a year or maybe two."

Donah sent some water his way, but her heart plainly was no longer in it; and as it turned out it would be longer than Arthur had promised before she would come again to her father's realm. . .

So Donah left for Aojun in the week before the winter Sunstanding, happy enough, in the event, to see her mother again and her homeworld. As Arthur had ordered, Daronwy and Roric accompanied her, with their son Harodin, who was a year or two her junior, and a tail of suitable size and composition as to be fit for a princess of the reigning Houses of Keltia and Aojun both. All this time had it been Donah ferch Arthur—Duanagh Pendreic in the Gaeloch, or Penarvon as she styled herself, following her father's stubborn preference. Now once again it was Jai Donah, daughter of the Jamadarin Majanah, of the Clan Manchéden of the Yamazai: You could see it come upon her; indeed, she put it on like a long-unworn cloak, wrapping it around her, comfortable inside it.

Roric also was glad of the chance to go home for a time. Though since Ronwyn had chosen him for mate he had become more Keltic than the Kelts, as our saying goes, still and all he remained a lord of Aojun, had not been born one of us—though this he seemed to forget even as did we. As for Daronwy, she was well pleased to accompany Donah as a sort of foster-aunt; she loved the girl dearly, for her sake as well as for Arthur's, and she had remained dear friends with Majanah and other Aojunese down the years since our time there. Too, she wished to present her son to his kindred as Yamazai law and custom dictated—so it worked out very well for all.

Just as they were departing Keltia on the first stage of their voyage, Melwas the King of Fomor was arriving. Indeed, I fancied their ships passing each other in the space beyond the Criosanna, could picture Melwas and Donah gazing all unknowing at one another's ships across the starry dark. I wish I could also tell you I had a stab of Sight then, a bolt of an-da-shalla, so that what would happen years along might never have taken place; but I would be lying if I did so. . .

Any road, I stood proudly near my King and my Queen as they welcomed for the first time in peace a Fomori to Keltia. Melwas had become a finely grown young man from the spirited, gifted lad I remembered; he had only recently come to his throne, upon the death of his father Tisaran. Nanteos his grandfather, with whom Arthur had played so dangerous a bout of fidchell, all our lives as pawns, had died not long after our one encounter, not much mourned.

I could see too that Melwas had lost none of his youthful hero-worship for Arthur Penarvon. Indeed, I daresay that that admiration, the shining memory of Arthur's fair dealings and kindness to a young hostage prince, was the chief cause and reason why this breathtakingly delicate new treaty was even being signed. . .

All the same, it was surprisingly straightforward for so momentous a document. Not ones to leave aught to chance, both Arthur and Melwas had taken care to import jurisconsults from Ganaster, to have them in attendance for both sides during the treaty negotiations, as utterly impartial witnesses who could attest before all challengers to the strict legality of the thing; and, as matters were later to prove, it was as well the lawdogs had been there.

It was Arthur who handled the diplomatic treaty; with his superior knowledge of and acquaintance with his Fomori counterpart, it made sense he should do so. But Gwen it was who arranged the other part of the business, the trading contracts; and that was rather less speedily hammered out. Oh, not for any lack of good will on either side; but, though it sounds strange to say so, the trade agreements were of vastly greater complexity than the political ones, and so took more time and care.

She did not act in vacuum: Some of our own merchant chiefs had been ordered home from our trading planet of Clero for the negotiations, and they brought with them certain agents (Melwas too had his own experts), and I noted these with more interest than I had shown for the rest of the admittedly complex proceedings. Some of our agents were Kelts, resident on Clero to do our tradework with the other worlds; some part-blooded; others not Keltic at all but of other species entirely, who had thrown in with our interests on Clero for pure profit's sake.

Of those last, half a dozen caught my eye and notice: first among them one Tembrual Phadaptë, Coranian, a plausible sleekit streppoch whom I loathed upon sight and instinctively shrank from, as from some noisome clinging muck one might step in by ill hap and clean off grimacing from one's boot. She had with her hangers-on to do her bidding: several half-Kelts, by name Phayle Redshield, Kiar mac Ffreswm (especially maukit) and Rannick of Lissard; another Coranian, Sleir Venoto, a smooth smiling chiel with the look of a liar about him; and oddest of all, a creature of some simian race I did not know, a smallish long-armed bony hairy thing with sly light-colored eyes, called Granúmas, who was cleverer with the crossics than all the rest. Less ethical too, though never so that one could charge him outright with fraud. Yet our merchant chiefs seemed to rely on them, and Melwas showed them marked favor.

In the end, saving my misgiving, I had no reason to distrust them either; indeed, they fulfilled their parts perfectly, and Gweniver herself acknowledged their contributions. Melwas left Caerdroia after the Brighnasa feast with a treaty both sides could happily live with, and the trade envoys returned to Clero with fat contracts all round; and all seemed most well.

As if to crown all our endeavors, Majanah sent word from Aojun that Donah and her party had arrived safe and sain. Arthur sulked around the palace for a time—a talpa could see that he yearned to be there himself—and even Gwennach could not forbear a sigh or two; despite black expectations (or secret hopes?), she and Arthur's outfrenne ban-charach had grown to be dear friends, and she would have greatly liked to visit Aojun herself, to see Majanah in her own realm and sphere of rule. But it was not to be.

Things slowly settled back to normal, or what passed for normal: Peace was upon us all now, the Cup's return had seen to that. Healing had been restored to the land, and if Marguessan still nursed her dark hopes of queenship and a black Graal to empower her, she nursed them in secret and alone. Or as near as makes no matter: Mordryth she doubtless held still to her side, but Galeron her daughter was slain; and Gwain her youngest had publicly repudiated her, declaring himself quit of her in formal ceremony, like to a divorce but between child and parent. Arthur had received his kin-fealty, and had taken him as a sort of foster-son, so that Gwain's royal blood remained so and his kinship was not lost to us.

As for me, I returned to my 'customed duties and tasks: serving Artos and Gwen as they had need of me; performing my bardic chores at the grand new star-shaped hall Arthur was building for my order across the Great Square from Turusachan. Seren Beirdd it was to be called, 'Star of the Bards,' a fine graceful edifice of cream-colored stone to replace the somewhat shabby hall that had stood there.

And I travelled on errands of state, and otherwise simply spent time with my wife and my son, as so seldom before I had had the chance. It was as well I took the time when I did; for like all very good things it did not last as long as any of us might have liked.

CHAPTER 16

It was on a cold quiet sunny winter afternoon at Turusachan that I opened a chest in my bedchamber, and quite without warning came across something I had, utterly, unaccountably, forgotten. Though just how I could have done so. . . well, you shall hear.

Rummaging through assorted presses and cupboards and coffers, looking for something I cannot now for all the life of me recall what, I touched what seemed an ungainly bundle of oddments wrapped in a velvet cloth. As I had thought I knew, more or less, what possessions of mine were here present, and could not place this parcel among them, I found my attention instantly diverted.

What I drew out from under the untidy welter of harp-music and spare strings and other bardic rubble was a small package, quite heavy for its size, around which was neatly folded a swath of somewhat threadbare brown velvet cloth. Within the velvet folds was a small chest of figured metal, and within that was a pouch of dark green leather, its corded strings doubly knotted closed upon its contents and fastened with a crested lead seal. No more; but at sight of this my heart began a slow pounding—for this I most assuredly *did* recall. Indeed, how not, for I myself had snatched it up from the floor of my cell in Oeth-Anoeth, just before Arthur had magicked us away to freedom and safety out of Marguessan's hands.

And, incredibly—though truly the time 'twixt then and now had been not only short but crammed with far more pressing matters—in all the months since, I had not been moved to determine what the pouch did hold. Perhaps I was simply afraid, perhaps— Well, any road, aside from the bronze dagger I had extracted (not even breaking the seal) that night Artos and Gerrans and I lay by the fireside in rough camp on Gwynedd, I had neither removed aught nor looked within. Nor even, consciously at least, remembered it at all.

Well, better now than never. . . Slowly I untied the draw-strings, and, all in one quick motion, before I could change my mind again, spilled the contents out onto the fox-fur coverlet of the great fourposted bed I shared with Morgan. The things glittered in the low afternoon sunlight that flooded the room through uncurtained windows: mostly jewels, as I had surmised that night in camp, judging from the weight and the sharp irregular outlines; but other things too.

And I stared at the little heap through stinging hot tears, for these assorted tokens were treasures of my mother's; some of them plainly Keltic in origin, others of them so foreign in look and technique of working that surely they had come from Earth, cherished heirlooms she had brought away with her—but all of them the dower property of the Lady Cathelin of Gwaelod, and hence, now, mine.

After a while I reached out a tentative hand to touch the jewels, marvelling at their beauty and strangeness. There was an elaborate heavy necklace worked in silver and beautiful blue matrixy turquoise, skystone, and a ring to match it of one huge turquoise slice the size of a child's palm; a pendant of watery gray rose-cut diamonds in shape of a heart, a silky blue sapphire at its center; a big square emerald set as a ring in some glowing hard white unknown metal; a heart-shaped ruby as big as my eye, framed in tiny diamonds; a fabulous necklace of seastones and those same rose diamonds, fashioned as a collar delicate as lace; oh, and much more besides, it was a hoard that would have disgraced neither a queen nor a dragon—and I knew, plain as if I had been told, that most of these fair things had been my father's gifts of love to the woman he had reived away from Earth.

And that she had received them, and had worn them, as lovingly as they had been given, could not be doubted. . . I ran my fingers again through the gleaming tangle, thinking that I must show Arthur the Terran pieces particularly. We had nothing in Keltia to rival some of this work—the turquoise necklace in especial, which had a ritual feel to it— and Artos with his own great gift for goldcrafting would appreciate the artistry. Morgan too; she should wear all these, I had a sure and certain feeling that Cathelin who was her matemother would wish it so. . .

At the very bottom of the tumbled glorious heap something gleamed and vanished again amid the glitter of the more lavish pieces. I sifted the tangle of gems and pearls and chains, searching for what I thought I had glimpsed; and caught my breath, stared at it unseeing, when I found it.

Stared not so much for its value or uniqueness as for its utter startling familiarity: I had seen tiny silver pendants such as this one a thousand times, at the throats of Bandraoi throughout Keltia—a crescent and V-rod, adorned with the spirals sacred to the Mother. And upon the same fine gold chain, a suncross in the same rose gold: the suncross, bossed and equal-armed within a circle, that is the universal symbol in Keltia of our ancient faith.

I turned the two small pieces over, to make certain of what I already somehow knew, and saw without surprise the alien hallmarks of the Terran goldsmith who had fabricated these tokens long years since—perhaps even in a corner of Earth that had once been Keltic, had seen the great immrama, even, centuries ago. That my late mother should have worn such tokens came as no surprise—half Keltia did so— but that they had come with her from Earth, as part of her personal dower, was more than surprise: It was shock.

And it raised more questions than I could just now compass: Had my mother, a Terran, yet been of the faith—a Terran Ban-draoi, if such could be? Was that how Gwyddno had met her, and why he had loved her, and fetched her away with him? I would give much to know, I suddenly realized; and then all but stag-leaped off the bed in surprise, as I glanced up to see someone standing quietly in the doorway.

"I knocked," said Gweniver apologetically, "but you were a million star-miles away."

"Nay, further still, I think," I said, recovering myself though my heart still raced. "But see, Gwen! See what my mother has left me."

The Queen came and sat beside me cross-legged on the coverlet, and we yearned over the jewels like eager children dazzled by a faerie hoard, touching them with reverent hands, exclaiming at the strangeness of the Terran pieces, admiring the skill of the metalworkers.

"After all this time—" she breathed. "Oh Tal-bach, I *am* glad. . ." She reached behind her for the thing she had been carrying when she entered, which I had noticed but not *noticed*, if you take my meaning. It was an ancient leather satchel, unmistakably Keltic in design, its worn brown leather studded with rock crystals and garnets and chunky amethysts in hammered silver bezels. We use such things— tiachán in the Gaeloch—to house even more elaborate book-shrines, in which are protected rare or valuable volumes, kept as they deserve.

"Gwyn ap Nudd gave this me," Gweniver was saying, "what time he came to Caerdroia when you were in Oeth-Anoeth. He bade me hold it safe for you against your return; but, tell you the truth, I did not think of it when first you came home, and after that there was too much else to think on. My sorrow for the delay."

Aye so; and how uncannily Gwen had just echoed my own thoughts of scarce a half-hour since. . . This seeming coincidence was no chance hap at all. I reached out and took the thing from her, sliding it over the coverlet. It was quite astoundingly heavy—she had held it in both arms when first she came in—and I stroked the smooth brown leather, shiny with age and long careful polishing.

Oh, I remembered *everything* now, right enough: how when I had stood before the crystal tomb of Merlynn beneath the hollow hill, Birogue herself had given the leather pouch of jewels into my hands. I could see her in memory's eye, taking it from the niche in the stone in which it had been carefully kept until what time I had arrived to receive it. And my surprise had flared and faded, for I had by then seen my mother's grave in the halls of the Sidhe, had heard Seli the queen of the Shining Folk and Birogue my Morgan's tutor in magic tell me how my mother, their friend, had died among them and they could not save her. They had passed on to me, as legacy from her, her jewels and her truth; and Marguessan's final, greatest cruelty in my two years' captivity was that she had taken the memory of all this from me, while yet leaving me the mere possession of the jewels themselves to torment me.

But now the whole of my heritage had come to me at last. . . Gweniver was watching me with close concern, her gaze shifting from the satchel to me and back again.

"Well, Talynno, there it is. I did not know about those"— she gestured to the gems sparkling on the coverlet—"and had I done so perhaps I might have delayed bringing you what Gwyn had consigned to me. Perhaps too much *is* too much, and now is not the time to open the tiachán. But I will tell you what Gwyn told me: It holds your mother's writings, her journals and chapbooks and such, both here in Keltia and in her home on Earth. I do not know, I have not looked within—no one has, the seal is intact—but it seems to me that there is some great reason for the timing here. You remembering the jewels, I remembering the satchel—something more than memory seems to be moving here. Surely it cannot be chance." The ghost of a smile as she nodded at the gems again. "Neither of us believes in that."

When I did not answer, she smiled a real smile, dropped a quick kiss on my cheek and was gone. I looked sidewise at the tiachán as it sat there, glared evilly upon it as if it had been some coiled nathair; then took grip of myself. How could aught be here to hurt or harm me? This was of my mother; and perhaps here in that satchel were answers to those questions I had been asking myself ever since the jewels spilled out onto the bed. . . With a gesture half resolve, half resignation, I pulled the tiachán over to me and broke the seal—the seal that matched the one upon the pouch-strings, the seal of Merlynn Llwyd himself, who had been mover and guardian of so much.

Within the four leather flaps that formed the satchel was a thing of piercing beauty. I had in the course of my bardic studies seen a goodly number of these book-shrines, but never had I beheld one so fair as this. . .

It was like a little house of silver, an oak box shaped like a high-roofed cottage completely covered with shining silver plates. Rope-edged with twisted gold and copper wire, it was studded with all manner of gemstones and enamelled in bright clear colors with armorial devices. Among those I marked my own House's wave-embattled tower (how ghastly prophetic *that* had proved!), and side by side with Gwyddno my father's particular arms, there was a lovely rendering in opalescent greens and blues of a sea-gryphon, surely my mother's own device. . .

But all this splendor was mere shrouding to what was within: Neatly packed within the silver shrine were perhaps ten or twelve leather-bound volumes, in two tiers, all with bone-stiffened covers and interleaved with butter-soft suede squares to cushion each against the next. The books themselves were small, thick, filled with tough tissue-thin paper of the sort our bookbinders call crystalskin; most perdurable. Whoever had made these had made them to last.

Also there were four books the like of which had never been bound or made or even seen in Keltia. . . I touched one of them, gently, breathlessly. *So foreign*— Like those certain jewels, this book and its three fellows had been fashioned on Earth, had been written in by my mother upon her native world, long before ever she *was* my mother, before she had met Gwyddno, before Earth itself, even, had made the least tentative sortie out of itself and into space.

All at once I was shamed throughly of my fear and hesitance. My mother had died leaving these to me; it had been all she could do for me, all she could give me save life itself. Surely it was little enough to give back, that I should read her words; did I not owe it to her, and to my father, to do so? I settled down against the pillows; and with a feeling of a vast journey about to be embarked upon, in a kind of peace and a sort of triumph I opened the most ancient of the journals from Earth—dated on the flyleaf, in a delicate hand using blue ink, '1935'—and began to read.

* * *

Morgan found me there, hours later, curled up in the semi-darkness, a book still open and unregarded beside me. I had skimmed through all the volumes, right straight through to the last, written beneath the faerie hill when the author knew her end was upon her; then I had gone back to the first and begun to read slowly, savoringly, with care and attention and the bard's sense for language alive and alight.

For all my familiarity with Englic—the tongue my mother had spoken on Earth, and one with which the bardic colleges were well conversant—still I found parts very tiring going, the idiom hard to interpret and shade. But throughout the journals I could sense the flair my mother had had for words, the flair she had gifted over to me—this for her, like music for me, was how the Awen had worked in her—and she had even filled the margins and blank leaves with vivid, humorous, enchanting sketches. She had been an artist, and I was glad to learn it; had learned, too, why she had worn the medallions. . .

Morgan said no word, but slipped in behind me and put her arms around me, letting her cheek rest against my shoulder; and after a moment I reached a hand up to touch her face.

Her lips brushed my fingers. "Gwennach told me," she said quietly. "I did not know if you wanted anyone, but— Do you care to speak of it now?"

I opened my mouth to say Aye of course, but instead to my great surprise heard myself saying something quite other.

"Nay, I think not. Not yet. Not now." I gestured helplessly to the scattered books and jewels. "She was—I do not—I need to be *with* her a while, I think, cariad, before I can speak of her, even to you. Do you mind? I do not mean to put you off—look, she has even given me her jewels, for my wife to wear after her. She would like you."

Though I could not see her face, I knew that Morgan smiled. "Nay, love!" she said, tightening her arms around me. "This is the first time you and your mother have spoken, heart to heart; small wonder you need time to take it to you. Besides," she added, and I heard the smile now in her voice, "no woman who calls herself wise ever intrudes between her mate and his mother! But you have had enough for one day; let it be a while. Speak to *my* mother, if you like; hear her wisdom on this. As for these, we shall read them together, one day, if it is your will; aye, and Gerrans too, to learn of his Terran grandmother. But now"—all at once her voice was of an everyday note—"it is time for supper, and Artos and Gwennach are waiting on us to go down with them."

I felt a short sharp flare of utterly unreasonable annoyance. Supper! Please! I wished only to go on reading all night, all next day, *that* was the only hunger I needed to feed just now. I longed to revel in my mother's wit and words and insights, to learn what she knew and how she felt, to hear of her thoughts and hopes and fears, her life on Earth so strange to me, the grim account she had given (which I had only skimmed) of the great war that had come upon all Terra's civilized nations, out of which dark days Gwyddno had borne her away. . .

But I also knew my wife was right, as usual. It *was* too much, all at once; I would do better to ration this out to myself. Anything more was a kind of soul gluttony that served no one and that would only make me sick, and do no respect to reader and writer alike.

So we went down to Mi-cuarta for the nightmeal, which Artos and Gweniver had made their pleasant custom that they and all others who dwelt or worked in Turusachan should share. It made for an easy and calming end to the day, and ofttimes was the only hour or two when friends and kin could be together. As now, for instance. . .

As Morgan and I took our usual seats at the high board, I saw Gerrans come in, and as usual these days he was not alone. Cristant Kendalc'hen was with him, the young Bandraoi priestess who had ridden back with us from Caervanogue, as one who had achieved the Graal. She was a tall silent pantherine creature with the red hair of the Aoibhells of Thomond, to whom she was closely connected.

Morgan and I had given her hospitality many times before, at Tair Rhandir, as the guest of our son; but we were as yet clueless whether or not a romance was toward—they seemed to prefer the dueling-hall to the trysting-bower—and since they seemed perfectly content we offered no prying parental word. Though we *thought* much. . .

It would displease no one if they did *choose to make a match of it,* I thought privately, watching them together. Indeed, Cristant seemed with Gerrans different than her usual grave capable self, and was by no means as silent as most folk thought her, and as I myself could attest. I had heard her speak her mind to Gerrans when she thought no one was about—and nay, I was *not* eavesdropping, merely too close *not* to hear—and she was not slow to do so, her words neither scant nor off the mark. Gerrans called her Crissa, though none else was permitted to tamper so with her name, or, knowing her, would even dare. . .

Morgan, as usual, had had no trouble following either my gaze or my thought.

"Someone full fit to wear the Lady Cathelin's jewels after me, I think," she murmured, and to my astonishment I found that the thought did not jar me in the slightest; indeed, I very much liked the prospect.

"Aye, well, any lass the Cup thinks worthy is worthy enough in my book," I said, and meant it. "And Artos and Gwen seem to like her well—"

This last was a not unimportant consideration, since the Crown must give consent to all marriages of the ríghdomhna; and in this instance, both Arthur and Gweniver, as High King and High Queen, must approve. Even more importantly here, as Gerrans (and any future children of his) could well end up heir-presumptive to the Copper Crown after young Arawn. Of the other young royals, Donah was ineligible, as half-galláin and being destined in any case for the crown of Aojun; while Mordryth was most like to be declared unfit for the succession, after his actions at Caervanogue, for which Marguessan his mother was already banned. Gwain, the only other firstcousin surviving, was older than Gerrans, but would give him precedence. Of course Gwen and Artos might well produce further offspring, and by grace of the gods Arawn would succeed safely in good time; but the chance was there all the same.

Matters came to the point even more swiftly than we had thought: Only a fortnight later, Gerrans came to Morgan and me, most formal, terribly nervous, to ask our blessing and grace to wed Cristant at the stones. By that time, we had taken pains to ken her, to speak with her on every possible occasion—I blush to admit I had also verified her pedigree in the bardic libraries, and had had several long cozy ale-chats with my old friend Therrian, the Ban-draoi Reverend Mother who had taught Cristant at Scartanore on Erinna—and we were well satisfied with the report of the lass, and with what we ourselves had learned. She was a most skilled sorceress—her preceptresses spoke naught but praise of her—which would make her right at home among the Pendreic kindred; a competent warrior too, and came of a blotless family line. Oddly, and endearingly, she was also a champion lacemaker and a very able smith.

So Morgan and I gladly gave our consent and approval, and Gerrans made his asking, and was of course accepted; and after that the thing became a matter for the marriage brehons and family jurisconsults to hammer out among them—contracts and tinnscra portions and titles and settlements and dowers on both sides. When it was finally arranged to everyone's liking, Gerrans and Cristant together, with Morgan and me standing proudly behind them next to her own parents, knelt before the Ard-rían and Ard-rígh in aireachtas presiding, and formally petitioned them for permission to wed.

And Their Keltic Majesties most graciously and joyously consenting to the marriage of their trusty and well-beloved cousin—as the traditional wording of the public announcement had it—the Lord Geraint Pendreic ac Glyndour ap Taliesin and Mistress Cristant Kendalc'hen nighean Dahal were wedded at Ni-maen the royal nemeton, on the last day of the Otter-moon, at the end of a famously hot summer. Grehan Aoibhell, the bride's cousin, gave his clann's leave for Cristant to marry, and Arthur himself gave ours for Gerrans. The rite was conducted, as was fitting for a royal wedding, by the Mathr'achtaran Therrian and the Archdruid Ultagh

Casnar, which last we were not best pleased with, as he was still Irian Locryn's loyal liegeman (and hence Marguessan's); but there was no help for it, the man *was* Archdruid. . . Gerrans had, with stupendous if perhaps unconscious irony, chosen his cousin Gwain for groomsman, while Cristant had her sister Lorrha as her brideswoman. For tinnól, she gave her new-wed mate a huge sapphire, and hers from him was an emerald roughly the size of Erinna. A year later were born to them twin sons, like as two castauns, Sgilti and Anghaud; two years after that came a daughter, whom they named to my everlasting joy Cathelin.

They were young for the cares of a family; but perhaps they already sensed there was need of haste.

CHAPTER 17

The next years were for us the peace that comes after pain, the calm coasts after the wildness of the open ocean; and we had well merited what we now received.

Arthur and Gweniver had settled down in earnest to their reforms; so long hampered by dramatic detours, they were free now to work out their vision for Keltia as they had yearned to do. And they began to work it in their own inimitable style.

The treaty with Fomor was but the first step, but it would prove to be the most fated. Our trade, never robust since the days of Edeyrn, had blossomed almost overnight since the signing of the trade contracts; our agents on Clero were well pleased, and the wealth that came flooding into the Keltic treasury was put to good and imaginative use across the realm.

During the Theocracy, the fabric of Keltia itself, as well as that of Keltic society, had been allowed to grow sorely threadbare. Edeyrn had not troubled himself with such mundane (and benevolent) matters as road repairs or healing-houses or the stocking of granaries against lean times to come—his bent had been for the training of yet more Ravens to further crush the Counterinsurgency, which of course responded by refusing to be crushed, necessitating more Ravens still, you know how it goes. And so there was, even all these years after our final victory at Nandruidion, much to be done to improve things for the folk.

Schools needed to be built and re-established, and the trained bards to staff them must be found; various institutions needed reforming, the Druid Order not least of those (and we were still encountering, every now and again, the odd unregenerate spoiled Druid still loyal to his Marbhdraoi); a standing army needed to be built up against the ever-present threat of alien invasion (we were weak just now, vulnerable from the outside), and for that we needed loyal Fians to do the training. The planetary governing bodies which had been among the first agencies to be restored needed continuing guidance and support, as did the Senate, Assembly and House of Peers. In short, just about every corner of Keltic life that had been left unswept and unattended for the last two hundred years. . .

Gweniver and Arthur worked like gaurans, and they were neither slow nor shy to press the kindred and the Companions into like service. We were glad to help, to be sure, if only to lessen the burden those two must carry; and at the table Rhodaur in the chamber of Gwahanlen, the talk these days was less of high matters of the spirit and more of such humbler topics as the price of grain stocks and what could be done with available monies to improve the bruidean system on Erinna and Powys.

It made for a shift of focus, right enough; but as the years went on, and things grew first a bit better and then very much better, soon a new complaint began to be muttered in the market squares and drapers' shops and victuallers'. And it was this: that Keltia, in pursuit of improved and easeful living, had begun to lose its soul.

According to this fell thought, which crept like some swamp-miasm, never seen, only sensed, too much effort and energy and resource had been spent on reform and rebuilding, and not enough attention paid to restoring the edifices of the Keltic spirit. This line of thinking, I need not point out, conveniently ignored the entire Graal search—which had been about nothing *but* the Keltic spirit—not to mention the great endeavors of the Ban-draoi and the true Druids both during the wars and in all the years since.

Yet those who spread this sort of rot, as well as those who lapped it up unthinking, could never be pinned down as to precisely what, if aught, they would alter or have done in other wise. Nay, they could not *tell* you, it was all more a *feeling* they had, or a word they had heard, something someone had said. . . very like you know the phenomenon well.

But I found myself deeply troubled, and I thought long about it, and at last one night I took it to the Table; and what I found there was even more troubling than I had thought.

"They are saying *WHAT?*" For one brief blinding moment of white and purest rage, I could not believe, simply, what I had just heard Alannagh Ruthven tell us.

"It is the sort of muck that is being spread about," said Alannagh quietly. "I cannot say if it is being believed."

"And if it is?" snapped Betwyr. "And if so, what are we here to do about it? The Companions, if anyone, must move to scotch this before it spews itself more widely than it has; say you not so?"

A murmur of agreement went round Gwahanlen like summer thunder, but I could see that many of my fellow Companions were having difficulties with problem and solution all alike.

I myself was one of them, to some extent, despite my initial fury. Although we had no formal plan for these fortnightly assemblies, the usual way of them was this: The Companions would gather in Gwahanlen at the new and full of the moon Argialla, for addressing of any matter any one of us found good or ill or needing of attention. Arthur or Gweniver would preside, which of them depending on the press of other matters upon them; and in the rare instance neither could be spared from other duties, some one of the old-line Companions—Daronwy or Tanwen or Ferdia or Betwyr or Tryffin when he came in from Kernow—would run the meeting along such sketchy lines as we were wont to follow.

Tonight, I was presiding from my chair of Gwencathra, over a turnout not over-large but extremely contentious

even for us. And this night we had good and grave cause to
be. For no matter my own misgivings as to the general temper of the realm, what Alannagh had just reported to us
struck harder and deeper than all: that rumor whispered that
Arthur the King had not only married his cousin but had
slept with his sister.

"It is but the names, do you see," said my old teacher
Elphin Carannoc, his bard-voice rising above the general
stour, but his tone one of uttermost disgust. "Gweniver,
Guenna, Gwenar for Gwenwynbar—it must be that the general run of folk are too stupid or too slovenly of pronouncing to trouble themselves in distinguishing among them."

"Too stupid to live, you mean!" snarled Tarian Douglas.
"If they cannot tell the differ after all these years between
three very differing people—"

I hid an undiplomatic grin. Nay, twenty-odd years as
Keltia's Taoiseach had mellowed Tari not one jot; still she
did not only not suffer fools gladly, but did not suffer them
at all. But she had seen my mouth twitch, and turned on me.

"Well, Talyn, what then is *your* thought on this? Since it
is your wife and your matebrother who are being slandered
here—what do *you* recommend?"

I sighed and sank back into the depths of my chair.
"There is no way to counter this sort of lie, as all you know
very well. The more energy you give to it, the more the liars
feed on you and the stronger it grows. Best to ignore it, and
so let it starve. It is hard to do, but it is best. Besides," I
added, stretching casually, "I already know what source it
springs from."

Consternation and shock. I watched carefully, noting
how the currents of both did run, for I had said that quite
deliberately, and I did indeed know the source of the poison.
What I wished to see here and now was how many minds
even among our own Companions—and my heart broke to
think there were some—believed the lying tale, or shared my
knowledge of its origin. My sorrow to say, I was disap-
pointed on neither count. . .

"Well then," said Tarian in a deadly quiet voice which I
knew well from of old (and she was *not* one of those I had been
watching for), "if you know, Talyn, best it were you tell us."

I closed my eyes and leaned my head back, not wishing to see any more, and said a single word.

"Marguessan."

Over the years since the return of the Cup and the apparent thwarting of her aims and plans at Beckery, Marguessan Pendreic had kept a very low sail against the skies. Indeed, for quite a long time we had not even known for sure of her whereabouts; she had not slunk back to Oeth-Anoeth, for constant watch was kept on it, nor had she gone to ground in her old familiar earths elsewhere. Irian Locryn, her dullard lord, denied all knowledge of her comings and goings, and claimed he had had no complicity in any of her actions. What he thought of the death of his daughter Galeron, or the near-death of his son Gwain, could only be guessed at.

So when the rumors and sly snipings and contumely began to crawl round Keltia like nasty animalcula out from under stones, I did not need a house to fall on me to let me to know whence the horridness had origin. But even now in my anger and revulsion I found crossing my mind the possibly significant thought that no one in all her life had ever thought to give Marguessan a shortname or byname, either out of affection or out of hatred. Arthur was universally Artos; Gweniver was Gwennach or Gwennol or Gweni or Gwen, at least to those who loved her; I had ever been Tal, Talyn, Talynno; while Morgan had been Morgan so long and so exclusively that nearly everyone was surprised to be reminded from time to time that she had been born Morguenna. Yet Marguessan had remained Marguessan, defiantly and aridly unshortened. . .

But there was a problem here, and not only the one Alannagh had pointed out to the Table. I sat up and raked the room with my eyes, and there was sudden quiet.

"This is not to come to the ears of either Gwen or Artos, do you hear me? True enough it is that all are equal around the Table, and no Companion gives orders to any, save the High King or the High Queen alone. But I give this order tonight, and I will be obeyed in this."

There was general profession of obedience and acceptance, for nearly all who sat at Rhodaur were of my mind

and heart, and would spare our rulers whatever they might.
Yet, gods, there is always *someone* who cannot resist being a
stone in the boot. . .

"Well enough," came the mocking voice from across the
room. "But since what time do bards think they may call all
tunes, not merely the ones they harp to? And since what
time more are commands given in Gwahanlen?"

I found myself considering quite another use for that
metaphorical boot I had just now thought of, for I knew the
voice. One Morholt, a comparatively recent addition to the
Company's ranks, who loved naught more than to flaunt his
standing in the faces of his seniors, the tiresome little pest. . .
But though I heard the civilized little breath-catches round
the room that are the polite person's disguise for a horrified
gasp, I would not play to my cue, and a long moment passed
before I spoke in answer.

"Since tonight, when the bard is a prince who outranks
all here," I said, and I edged my voice with the word-whip
as a reminder. Bards can kill with words, have they a mind
and a cause to—and, aye, I have done so in my time, if you
must know—but worse still to some ways of thinking, they
can blotch faces and reputations alike with well-placed aers
of satire. And I knew enough about Morholt to raise a fine
crop of blotches indeed.

He took the point, and had blotched himself a dull ugly
stain of red before I spoke again, soothers in my voice now,
to give him the grace of escape.

"And also, more so, when the bard is a man who would
protect his wife and his foster-brother; none here, I think,
can find fault with that?"

Morholt had the wit to shake his head, and said no word
more. Tarian, after a glance at first me and then him, stood
up and tallied Gwahanlen with her eyes, as if she had been
at a Council meeting.

"We are agreed, then?"

Murmurous assent, even from Morholt. But Alannagh
held back, still troubled.

"Agreed, aye, to be sure," she said, shooting me a long
unhappy unquiet glance. "But, Talyn, who—"

I raised a hand to cut her off, but tempered it with a

smile, for she was a dearly loved friend; it had cost her something, moreover, to raise this issue here at the Table tonight, and I was grateful she had found it in her to do so.

"No fear, Lann-fach. It will be attended to. You shall see. All of us shall see."

And we did. The nasty mouthings went on a brief while longer, and then suddenly they were gone, to be heard no more, the lascivious perversions blown away as if by a great clean scouring wind.

"No lasting harm done, I think," I said hopefully to Morgan, who had not been present that night in Gwahanlen only by sheerest chance. Just as well, too, for never in all our life together had I seen Morguenna Pendreic possessed of such an anger as that which had, well, possessed her the moment she learned that rumor was saying she had slept with her halfbrother.

But she had cooled enough by now to content herself with a grim laugh. "Nay? They have no idea how near they came to the lasting harm *I* had dealt them. . ."

The hazel eyes still flickered pure green behind, and I reflected *very* privately that the cooling had gone not so very deep after all. And indeed, why not? If I, a mere bard, had been provoked to none-too-subtle reminders of what I could do by power of my words given cause, what greater cause did not Morgan have, who had been lied about in so loathsome and frustratingly unfightable a way? What terror might not she have struck even round our own Table, had the Companions seen her eyes as I saw them now—let alone the muckmongers themselves, to be on the receiving end of that emerald-lasra stare?

Well, I had been wed long enough by now to know when to speak and when to be silent. . . After a while Morgan's familiar elbow found its place among my ribs, and I squirmed out of digging distance and turned on the pillows to face her.

"It is not my sister only, is it?" she asked quietly, and I goggled in my startlement before I could master myself. She laughed in my face. "Well, cariad, you may have been able to pull the hoods over the others' eyes, but only recollect that I know your little ways rather better. Now. Tell me."

"It is Marguessan, right enough," I said, a trifle sullenly. "But also it is Mordryth. And more than that, it is Malgan Rheged ap Owein as well. So."

"Ah." She mused on that awhile, and I was myself surprised to see how little surprised she was to hear those names I had thought would shock her. "Well," she said at last, "we have long expected *that* union, have we not?"

"Nay, *cariad*, no more we have!" I said, honestly angry now. "What but weal have any of us ever done to Malgan Rheged, that he should so repay us in such wise?"

"We killed his mother. You were there. I was there. Arthur was there."

"And richly she deserved it! My sorrow, but that is no excuse! Nay, Guenna, by the gods it is not!"

"Then why did you not tell the Table? I have spoken to Tari; she says you never said aught to them of Mordryth, nor yet of Malgan, in it; that you said my sister and my sister only, and the Table bought it unquestioned."

"Aye, well, I had my reasons." I lay down again beside her, stared up at the underside of the bed canopy, thinking it was too plain, we must put some proper ornamentation up there to look at. . . "Any road," I said then, "Marguessan was doubtless far from displeased at the currency those evil tales gained among the folk. I do not think folk truly believe them, but you know as well as anyone how people like to think ill when they are given the chance. And hard it is to root it from their minds when once it has lodged there."

"What they are pleased to call their minds." She was silent again. "Well, the damage, if damage there is, is done now. What we must decide is what to do about it."

"Naught. It is generally best."

"Do we tell Gwen and Artos?"

"If they already know, they have not spoken of it to us, and that means they do not wish to 'know' it; and we must honor that wish. If they do not know, then I say we keep it so."

"And if they tax us with it later, that we knew and did not say?"

"Then we will worry about that when and if we must.

Any road," I added hopefully, and not at all convincingly even to myself, "if ill *were* to come, it would have happened by now."

It had, of course; but we were not to know it for quite a while to come.

You may recall that when Melwas of Fomor made his historic visit to Keltia some while back, he had suggested to Arthur and Gweniver that one or both of them should repay the courtesy, and come to his own homeworld on a state visit. There had been a general sort of agreement that this was a good and acceptable idea, likely of fulfillment, and then it had been promptly forgotten, at least among ourselves.

But a couple of years following the rumor-spate came a formal diptych from Tory—bound in the correct silver covers, sealed with the regulation gold wafer—that reminded the rulers of Keltia of the invitation, and set a tentative date, even, for it to be taken up.

"Well, Artos," said Tarian, tossing the diptych into the middle of the Council table, "you know you must go. Either one of you. Not both. We have done too well out of the Fomorian connection and the trade links it has given us to risk insulting Melwas now. My agents on Clero advise me so, and I agree with them. And any road, you liked him, did you not?"

"Very much," said Arthur. "But I do not much wish to return to Fomor. Gwen, you shall go. It is your turn for some travel."

"A generous offer, Ard-rígh," said Gweniver mockingly, but her face was wreathed in laughter. "But nay, I think I must stay here a while yet."

"Aye so, but you are always lamenting that you are never given to go anywhere," said Arthur, and all the coaxing plausible smoothness he could put into his voice was there now, and working hard. "You could even stop and visit Aojun on the way; time it is that Daronwy and Roric were back here, they have been gone too long altogether this time. And perhaps Majanah would let Donah come back again for another visit.

It has been too long since her last couple of times here, and Janjan might be the more easily persuaded if she knew the lass could travel with you."

"A masterful try, cariad, but a failed one," Gweniver told him, and he shrugged comically. "But why do not you yourself do just that, Artos? Make the visit to Melwas, then go on to see Janjan yourself and bring Donayah back here. Or, better, stop at Aojun first and take Donah to Fomor. She would be thrilled to be with you, and Fomor and Aojun are on terms just now. Besides, there is a most excellent reason for me to stay." She paused, her face bright with her unspoken reason, and raised questioning brows. When Arthur grinned and nodded, she faced the rest of the Council. "Well then, my reason is that very shortly there is to be another Pendreic to make wretched all your lives."

She laughed at our astonishment, and Arthur joined her.

"Aye, an eightmonth you have to live in peace," he said. "Then shall be among us Arwenna, Princess of the Name. So that Donayah and Arawn shall have a sister in their old age—"

"—and perhaps Malgan Rheged too shall have one in his age yet older."

The words dropped into the chamber like flaming spears. I shot my glance round the Council chamber to see who it was had spoken, but everyone else there was doing likewise. It seemed that no one had spoken, or that the offensive words had come out of the air itself, or from the moons; and after an extremely tense and twangling few moments Arthur dismissed the Council with the customary phrase of royal thanks.

But Morgan and I lagged behind a little, the better (or so we hoped) to study the faces and postures and lowered voices of the departing Councillors. And two things there were that we both noticed. Today, for the first time in years (though he had never left nor been dismissed from the Council), Keils Rathen, Gweniver's old lover and Arthur's— and Uthyr's—trusted warlord, had attended a Council meeting. And Ultagh Casnar, the Archdruid, who had never missed a Council meeting in near as many years, had today left smiling.

* * *

In the end, things were done as Gweniver wished them.
Arthur went to Fomor on his state visit, complaining bitterly
until the moment he lifted off from Mardale in his beautiful
ship Prydwen; and Gwen herself had stayed home delighted
in the excuse of her condition.

"I thought you *wanted* to go to Aojun," I said peevishly
to her as we returned from seeing off the King. "You are
always going on about how since you are Ard-rían you
never get to go anywhere. . ."

"Oh aye, and I do still wish to," she explained kindly. "But
not if Aojun is the carrot for the stick that is Fomor."

"Sometimes I should like to smack *you* with that stick," I
told her, still annoyed, and she laughed. "You are scarcely
with child at all, that you could not have gone; and Janjan
would have dearly loved to make great fuss over you."

"It would have been pleasant," agreed Gweniver,
diverted somewhat. "But, Talyn, there is still that matter we
both know of, and I judged it best that Artos not be the one
to deal with it. While he is gone I hope to settle it. And you
and Guenna will help me."

"Indeed aye, Ard-rían, if you ask it." But I was not so
sure. I knew well what Gweniver meant: that little matter of
Malgan's name so featly popping up in Council a few weeks
back. Perhaps she was right: Perhaps it was time at last for
that to be settled once for all. The only reason it had sur-
faced again after all these years was that spate of rumor a
year or two ago, those noisome petty sewer-ravings spread
by Mordryth and Marguessan. And, so it appeared, Malgan
himself, as a means of casting muddy doubt onto Arthur's
character; so that when he finally declared himself openly to
be Arthur's firstborn, as plainly he was working up to do,
the folk might be less like to believe Arthur's denials and
more disposed to accept Malgan at his word.

I shifted uncomfortably next to Gweniver in the big well-
upholstered closed chariot. Somehow that did not make
sense: All Arthur would have to do would be to submit to
certain tests, and the thing would be proved one way or the
other. These tests were not medical in nature, not all of

them; and though one or two might prove inconclusive, their very variety gave ironclad evidence as to the validity of any claim of blood.

And what of Ultagh Casnar? Morgan and Grehan and Betwyr and I had had long converse as to his part—or possible part—in all this. And in the end had come to no agreement among us.

"I know you have never trusted nor liked him, Talyn," Grehan had said, "not since you returned from Oeth-Anoeth and found him sitting in Merlynn's chair at Council."

"*Not* Merlynn's chair," I muttered pettishly. "He took great pains to ensure he never sat there—perhaps he feared it might emulate Gwencathra, and open up to gulp him down to hell. False modesty, no more."

"Whether that be so or no," Betwyr had concluded reluctantly, "we have naught of evidence to impeach him, or even to offer as suspicion to Artos or to Gwen. Only the monarch may choose to remove the head of an Order."

I was thinking how from time to time in Keltia the monarch had chosen to remove the *head* of the head of an Order, and how very much I should like to see that happen here. . . But Morgan had read me as she ever did.

"We have no proof. We must bide the issue. Whoever it may be, they will set a foot wrong soon enough. And then—"

"And then?" I had prompted.

Morgan's countenance had taken on a look I was more 'customed to see upon her brother's.

"And then they are ours."

Oh, they set more wrong than a foot only. . . And they moved swiftly, when once they began to move. I wish I could tell you that we were ready for them; and aye, to a certain point, we were. But they had planned longer and better and more desperately than we, and the hand they raised against us had many fingers, and weapons from an armory we never once suspected.

CHAPTER 18

Keils Rathen had exiled himself from Court many years since, when first Arthur returned from his own stay on Aojun. There was no need for him to have done so—his rank as First Lord of War dated from the reign-in-exile of Uthyr Ard-rígh, and his status as Gweniver's lennaun was known by all and approved of by most—but as Arthur and Gweniver began to pull in double harness, as Ard-rígh and Ard-rían according to the terms of their marriage contract, Keils seemed to be prescient, to have had an-da-shalla of the outcome. And by the time Gwen and Artos finally fell in love with each other, Keils had quietly pulled away from all royal involvements and attendance.

He could easily have stayed on as First Lord—indeed, Arthur himself begged him to do so—but chose not to be swayed. And long before my immurement in Oeth-Anoeth, Keils had retired and returned to Gwynedd with his new lady, Meloran. It was lost on no one that she bore a rather startling resemblance to Gweniver the Queen.

And there he had lived in semi-exile, all these years. Arthur had gifted him with a dúchas and the title of Earl of Sulven, in token of his many services to Uthyr and to Arthur in the fight for Gwynedd, and he had also been granted the governorship of the rich province of Sarre, to provide him revenues and keep in political fighting trim. But

though as I have said he never gave up his seat on the
Council, in all those years Keils never came once to court,
and saw his onetime beloved and her mate only when they
chanced to visit Gwynedd on progress every year or two.

His behavior on such occasions had never been anything
but scrupulously correct. He had received Artos and Gwen
at his splendid new seat of Archdale, the Lady Meloran by
his side, and had fulfilled in all particulars his duty as liegeman. I myself had been on several of these progresses, and
had also made a point of visiting Keils when Morgan and I
were in residence at Tair Rhandir. And he had been the
same Keils I had known and loved and admired from of old.
We had refought old battles, old defeats as well as old victories—Keils still rolled his eyes every time he minded himself
of the notorious escape from Talgarth—and had refound
our old friendship and old Companionship as strong as
ever.

And yet I never dreamed of asking him his reasons for
staying away. Perhaps I was afraid to hear them. So when
all unheralded and unannounced Keils simply arrived one
gray wet morning at Turusachan, throwing the palace rechtair into a state unparalleled as he rushed to find suitable
lodgings for the great Keils Rathen, I was not alone in wondering what had brought him back at such a time.

And when on the very day he had attended his first
Council meeting in more than, what, twenty-five years?, and
the name of Malgan Rheged so coincidentally dropped into
the midst of it, again I was not alone in wondering how
Keils of the Battles, as he was known to ballad-bards, figured in it.

"No great mystery," said Keils in the old deep voice I
remembered. "My lady died last year"—he waved away my
protestations (sincere ones, to be sure) of sympathy—"and I
had been considering returning to Court for some months.
So I left the governance of Sarre in the hands of my son—
oh aye, did you not know? Meloran and I could have none
of our own, and so adopted Brennic five years after we left
Tara. He was orphaned in the fighting on Gwynedd, and we

fell in love with him as soon as we found him. Any road,"
he resumed, "he protested my resigning the office, but I
think he was pleased in the end to have real work to do.
And I came back."

"To find Gwen alone, and Artos gone to Fomor."

Keils's eyes glinted. "Not quite—I was here a full fortnight first. We even dined together once or twice."

"I did not know."

"Nay, well, no matter. Talyn"—he turned and looked me
full in the face, that old straight sword-look of his—"I heard
things on Gwynedd, things that troubled me sore, and that
is why I have come."

"Have you told that to Artos?" I asked, keeping my eyes
fixed on his; I would know it at once if he lied. "Or to
Gwen?"

"I have not," he said steadily, and I knew he spoke truth.
"And maybe I should have come sooner, but Meloran—
Well, now I am free to be here, and I should like to do what
I can, or may."

"What do you think that might be?"

He stood up and began to pace the room, just as of old
he had paced the command-tents when we campaigned on
Gwynedd. I watched him covertly: He had changed little in
all the decades; though he was some few scores of years
older than Arthur and Gweniver and I, who had all been
born in the same year more years ago than I quite cared
to remember, he was a powerful man still, one I should
not wish to have to meet either in challenge-ring or on
the field.

But Keils was speaking in a low rapid voice. "These
rumors of some time back, that muck about Artos and—"

"—and Morgan," I said calmly. "We heard it here too,
you know."

"Well then, you must know also that not every Kelt there
is found it wholly impossible of belief."

"So I have heard," I said, still evenly. "Given who had
begun the lying tales, I suppose I cannot wholly blame
them. But I do."

"Truly. But we cannot kill them all, Talyn." The old
wolf-grin flashed, and I answered it, for well I knew that

catchline of his from the Llwynarth days, when he had employed it to comfort Arthur in his dubhachas every now and again over some colossal blunder or error or betrayal or stupidity.

And all at once I found myself *missing* Keils sorely, though he stood before me. . . It was gone in a moment; but, I say, I missed him.

"I cannot say why I came, Talyn," said Keils then. "And if Morgan or Tari or Grehan finds me suspect for that, my sorrow. But Gwennach may have need of an old friend, and I would that I were here should that need come upon her."

It was upon us all almost as soon as he had said it.

It came as a double blow, so close together and so hard upon each other that it fell as one. But such a one. . .

The first we heard was a frantic message from Majanah, sent across the many star-miles to inform and apprise. When her face came upon the transcom screen, a private transmission, only Gwen, Morgan, Tari, Grehan and myself there to hear it, we all felt the same ghastly cold shock at what we saw there. She wasted no time on greetings.

"Donah is kidnapped," she said in such a voice as I had never heard before in all my life. "And Artho has gone after her. I will join him as soon as we have finished speaking."

I opened my mouth, but nothing came out. Gweniver was more successful at commanding her response.

"How? *Who?* Who would dare take the Heir of Aojun and a daughter of Keltia?"

Majanah smiled, and I saw Grehan step back a pace. "Melwas of Fomor. The *late* King of Fomor." Seeing the question: "Nay, he is not dead. Not yet is he dead. But he will wish himself dead a thousand times over when Artho comes up with him; unless I find him myself first, and then he will wish it still more. . ."

All at once she became again a mother wild with terror for her only child, and I closed my eyes briefly. When I opened them she was once more the warrior queen, and almost I could find it in my heart to pity Melwas. Almost.

"Do you wish our help, Janjan?" That was Tari, and the

quiet inexorable question somehow shocked us all back to our old working mode. This was something we could do. . .

"Whatever you could spare would be helpful," said Majanah carefully; you could see how she hated to ask even in such straits.

"It is on the way." Tarian turned to another transcom, spoke swift sharp orders in battle language, turned back to Majanah. "Done, Jamadarin. Tell us more, if you will. How was Donah taken?"

The forcing herself to tell the account seemed to help Majanah deal with it, for she looked less dazed and more centered as she told us. It seemed that Arthur had visited Aojun first on his way to Fomor, and had brought Donah with him to Melwas's court. Where apparently she had been a great social success—the heir of a prosperous and thriving planet, and a very beautiful young woman, how could she not be?

It seemed that Melwas of Fomor thought so too, so much so that upon the conclusion of Arthur's visit he had requested a private audience and had formally besought Arthur—and by proxy Majanah—for Donah's hand, to wed her as his queen.

"Artho put him off," continued Majanah calmly, "but when Melwas pressed him Artho rightly refused, in my name as well as his. Also Donayah much misliked the Fomorian king, and would for no sake have considered such a match. But Melwas would not accept the refusal, though he gave most plausible appearances of having done so; and when Artho and Donah set out from Fomor to return to Keltia, stopping at Clero your tradeworld on the way, Melwas organized an abduction."

"He must have had help from Clero, then, his own agents or hired ones," said Grehan instantly, to cover the moment, for Majanah appeared on the edge of breaking. "We can begin with our own spies there; I will contact them at once. And, Talyn—?"

I nodded unhesitating agreement. Though we do not like to make too public a thing of it, bards are among the best spies in Keltia. There is for one thing that convenient little law that makes sacred the lives of bards, and so we carry a protection with us into dubious situations that your more ordinary sort of spy could not command nor hope for. But as a rule we do not like to resort too often to the pressing of bards into spycraft. Only when no other course will serve. . . But Grehan, I knew well, was asking me not only for my help as Pen-bardd, but for my personal help as onetime spy. And, no question, I was going to give it, for this was my niece in peril here; besides, I had spied before for lesser cause, and now I would again.

"Shall I go to Clero, then?"

Tarian and Gweniver shook their heads as one. "Nay," said Gweniver, "I have a thought there is more to be found out here. Perhaps Melwas has agents or friends among us we know naught of; renegade Kelts, or galláin who have been smuggled in—"

"Marguessan?" That was Morgan, and her sister's name the first word she had spoken since Janjan had shattered us with her tidings—shattering us anew, so seldom did she speak it.

"Naught likelier," said Grehan, and turned as the door blew open and Keils came through, the Fian doorwards snapping to the salute for their onetime commander.

"I called Keils in," said Tarian quickly, to forestall the surprise she saw just about to be writ plain upon our faces. "When I bespoke the Fian commandery just now— We could have no better help. I do not need to remind this company of that."

"Not for my part," said the High Queen Gweniver, and gripped Keils's forearm in the Companions' old straight-armed salute. Keils said no word, but covered her hand with his own other hand, and took a seat by Grehan.

"I thank you, lord," said Majanah's ghostly image. "The name of Keils Rathen is not unknown on Aojun, either. . . My consort, Brone, will rule here while I am gone, and Roric and Daron will sail with me to join Artho."

"A war fleet is on its way at all speed to you even now," said Tarian, after another side-converse with the Fian command. "Only let you tell us what is your plan, and Arthur's, so that I may give orders more to your need."

"The plan is to get back my daughter," said Majanah,

faintly surprised. "Artho will attack Fomor itself, if he must; though I trust he will not have need of such a measure. Does he stand alone, or will the rest of Keltia stand beside him?"

"No question," said Gweniver swiftly, before any other could speak. "We will do what we must."

"And our treaty with Fomor?" murmured Tarian.

"They themselves put paid to that when they took Donayah," snapped Gweniver. "Artos will get her back."

"And then?" asked Keils.

The queen of the Yamazai and the Ard-rían of Keltia looked long at one another across the long, long star-miles between.

"And then Fomor will pay," said both at once. Gweniver added, "Dearly."

But others, as it turned out, were to pay more dearly still, and that accounting came rather sooner.

Keltia must be one of the few—perhaps the only—realms in the known settled galaxy where even the monarch can be compelled to stand forth to a challenge from a private person. We call it the fíor-comlainn, the truth-of-combat, and it may be either military or magical in nature, according as to how the challenging party (not the challenged, you will note) does choose.

Though our brehon system of justice is rightly renowned for its compassion and its sheer breadth of scope, still there are times when even brehon wisdom does not or will not or cannot suffice. And in such cases, the aggrieved Kelt, of whatever social station, has the right to seek justice through fíor-comlainn. Even against a clann chieftain or overlord; even against the High King or High Queen. And the challenged party must give satisfaction. Not necessarily in person: Champions may be sent in to settle the thing, if there is good or sufficient excuse (not simply lack of skill with sword or spell, either) for the challenged to step back from the contest. The one who seeks this justice must always, of course, fight for himself or herself; no hired strength here.

This has been our way from our time on Earth. Brendan

in his wisdom brought it with the first ships, and it was among the earliest established codices of justice declared for the new worlds of Keltia. It has worked out most well, all in all; oh, to be sure, you will have the odd frivolous suit now and again, but you would be surprised how quickly frivolity fades away like Beltane dew, once the frivoler realizes that true life-peril comes into it.

For though these days fíor-comlainn is mostly settled when first blood is drawn, in the old days it was just as often to the death—and sometimes still is, or can be demanded to be. . .

We were not expecting it, I can say confidently. So intent were we all on this matter of Donah, and Arthur after her, and Majanah and both Keltic and Aojunni fleets after him, that we were not looking closer to home for any more trouble. And, of course, that is ever *exactly* when you get it. . .

The challenge was delivered to Gweniver in aireachtas the morning after we had heard about the abduction. In Arthur's absence, I was presiding with her in the hearing-court—another excellent institution Brendan brought from Earth—and we had been having a rather dull morning of it, the usual disputes about inheritances or land-rights or quit-claims that these courts were intended to resolve.

We had been dispensing royal justice for the better part of an hour when the doors opened to admit a litigant not on the day's roster. Gweniver scowled and quietly questioned her secretary in an undertone, but Tammas seemed as surprised as she. Or indeed as I. . .

None of us—Gwennach, myself, the secretaries and jurisconsults and recorder-bards in attendance, a Councillor or two—knew the man who now approached us. Averagely tall, strongly built, by coloring Scotan or perhaps Erinnach, he was clad plainly and bore no sword nor badge of rank nor clann token nor even personal arms—in short, no clue to who he might be, nor his affiliations or loyalties, nor yet his errand here.

Coming to the high seats whence Gweniver and I watched him, he bowed, straightened, then flung down upon the steps of the low dais a sgian with a parchment impaled upon its short sharp blade. At a nod from Gwen, Tammas retrieved it and handed it up to her, and she read the contents attentively, with no change of expression.

"Ard-rían?" I murmured, when she did not appear at once disposed to share her newly acquired information with the rest of us there present.

But she spoke in the same instant. "The Ard-rían is well pleased to accept," she said, and the man bowed again but did not withdraw, clearly waiting for some other word or action which Gweniver had not yet given. And I felt sudden cold touch the back of my neck, for those words were the words of formal acceptance to the fíor-comlainn.

Gweniver did not leave us in any more suspense. "Let it be recorded," she said in her most royal voice, and the scribes and bards and legists leaped to obey, "that by this document, I, Gweniver Pendreic ac Penarvon, High Queen of Kelts, am challenged to fíor-comlainn by—" She consulted the parchment ostentatiously, an outrageously insulting provocation which was by no means lost on the incomer, whom I saw flush darkly and shift his weight from side to side. "—Errian of Kerveldin, commoner, of the planet Arvor."

I was surprised at least as much by that last as by the declaration on the whole, for I would never have taken this man for an Arvorican, and I flattered myself that I had a good eye for origins (bards need to; but that is another tale). But Gweniver was reading on.

"The ground of the challenge is—" And here she fell silent, staring at the paper in her hands, as if the enormity of what was there set down (which she already knew, having read it silently only moments earlier) rendered her scarce capable of forcing her lips to form the words aloud. But again she went on.

"—is that the High Queen of Keltia failed to cause to cease the shameful 'haviors of Arthur Penarvon ac Pendreic High King of Keltia with Morguenna Pendreic ac Glyndour, Duchess of Ys, his halfsister in the blood; or, sith that there was no such misconducting, that the High Queen failed to cause to cease the *appearance* of such, which did occasion much scandal among the folk and loss of face to the Crown, that being a crime of no less standing by the brehon code."

Her voice rang out coldly as she read out the formal wording, as if it had naught to do with her or Arthur or anyone else, and when she had finished she passed the paper to me to verify what she had read.

I scanned it quickly, committing it to memory in bardic fashion, then passed it on in my turn to the senior Crown legist, who took as if it had been some noisome dead thing found squashed on the highroad. I turned back to Gweniver, intending to advise her to put this complainant off for the moment with some words about Arthur and Donah and the more pressing business just now at hand, but she was already beyond advising.

Gweniver stood up in her place, tall and all at once very much the High Queen. In her hands was the sgian upon which the challenge had been impaled; a usual way of delivering a challenge, if not much used in these degenerate days. She looked at it a moment, then with unerring aim threw it so that it stuck quivering in the ironoak table directly before which Errian was standing. Challenge accepted; I slumped in my chair and shaded my eyes with one hand, not caring how this might be interpreted by anyone.

Through a pounding headache, a river roaring through my ears, I heard the legists discussing with Errian's second, whom I only just now noticed, the details for the fior-comlainn itself: place, time, weapons, seconds. And all at once, even through my headache, I knew what I must do.

"The Ard-rían has the right to a champion," I heard myself saying, and had the intense satisfaction of seeing everyone jerk to a surprised halt, as if I had hauled hard on all their reins at once.

"Talyn—" That was Gweniver, but I was past caring or commanding.

"The law says," I went on in a silky voice, "that the challenged party may choose a champion, magical or military according to the challenge given; or may serve as his or her own champion. Not so?"

"True, my prince," said the senior legist, all but yammering in his relief, and in chagrin that he had not remembered to put this forth before I did.

I was beginning to find a grim enjoyment in this. "And the law says also that no reason need be given for such a champion to be chosen."

"True again, lord."

"But I shall give a reason all the same," I said, and I spoke now in the bard-voice that took all the air from the room and filled my lungs to sound. "The High Queen is with child, a daughter who shall be Princess of the Name, second heir to Keltia after the Tanist Arawn. Therefore she will not take up this challenge in her own person, but some suitable champion shall be found, to fight in her cause and her name. So say I, Taliesin Glyndour ac Pendreic, Prince of Keltia, Duke of Ys, called Pen-bardd."

I sat down again, well pleased to behold the dropped jaws and glazed eyes all round, and would have given this Errian a frump to his face had I dared. As it was, he saw it in my face, and that sufficed us both. Even Gweniver seemed taken aback, and as I watched Errian of Kerveldin gather his badly scattered forces, I suddenly caught sight or sense of something more, something else, something behind that which he had brought into the chamber. And I thought I knew it from of old. . .

"It is not he," I said at once, when Errian and his second had taken huffy departure. "He is not the originator of this challenge."

"But he must be," said Alwyn Harlech—the senior legist—bewildered and most unhappy at the sudden horrific turn of events. "The law says—"

"The law!" Suddenly I was angry, for it seemed I saw the whole thing laid out before me, like a war-map, all arrows and blocks and strategy. . . "Think you all that the *law* has aught to do with any of this? Nay; he is but a tool, and the hand on the moving end is Marguessan's." I brushed off their babble. "Do not trouble yourselves, I am correct in this. . . Now!" I said, turning to Gweniver, who sat very still and pale in her chair. "We have bought us some little time. Upon whom can we call for champion?"

She seemed not to have heard me. I spoke her name and

title, rather sharply, and she came back into her face, started and turned to me.

"I am here. I am here. What next?"

I rose, grabbing her hand and pulling her with me. "Let the lawdogs send what answers will win us most time. For now, we must take this to the Table." And I dragged her from the dais and out of the chamber.

Gwahanlen was no more than half full—all Companions were not in Caerdroia just now, and indeed many who might have proved most helpful had already left Keltia on their errand to rescue Donah—but such Companions as could be assembled were there in their seats within the hour after my summoning went out. I did not tell them what was the cause and reason, but the fiosaoicht, that shared super-knowing common to all close-bound groups united by purpose and consecrated by action, seemed to have let them to know something grave was toward, for the faces that turned to me and Gweniver were wary and fraught.

They do not yet know the half of it. . . When I adjudged that as many as were going to be here had arrived, I rose at my seat of Gwencathra. This was *my* assembling, they would hear *me*. . . As I recounted the events that had put paid to today's hearing-court (the cases we had been giving judgment on should have to wait another day), I watched the reactions most carefully, and I had already had mind-speech with Morgan and one or two others, so that they should be looking-past, in the way of sorcerers, for hidden meaning and guilty knowledge imperfectly concealed.

"And it is my thought," I said in conclusion, "that these two things are by no means unconnected. The taking of Donah, so that Arthur must hare off, and rightly, to rescue her, taking strength from here and Aojun both to do so; and the challenge to Gweniver, in Arthur's absence, he not being here to answer the charge for himself, so that his Queen and wife must do so for him. It was only by grace of the Goddess that whoever set this Errian on to make the challenge—and I believe with all my life and dán and lives to come that that one is Marguessan—did not know that

Gwennach is with child, and may not risk an heir to Keltia so—though any woman else in a like state may fight or not as she shall choose. Therefore have we bought ourselves some small sword-room. The question now is, Who shall be found to champion our Queen who is a Companion of this Table. The rest may all be dealt with later."

I sat down, suddenly weary beyond all words. Why could not someone just stick a handy sword or other through whatever vital part of Marguessan was reachable, and end this endless blood-feud once for all. . .

But my words had let loose hornets, it seemed; hornets of dissent and discord and blame, that buzzed and snarled and stung indiscriminately and promiscuously wherever targets presented. Gweniver appeared to be taking no part in the discussion, if you could call it that; and Morgan too seemed oddly withdrawn, though I thought I knew the reason for *her* detachment.

And as I scanned the Table I slowly began to see, to my horror and utter disbelief, that no champion was going to stand forth for the High Queen here. The black tides Marguessan had sent coursing through Keltia of lies and evil had washed up on even these shores, it seemed; had left wavemarks even in Gwahanlen of the Table. . . This could not be; *would* not be. I rose to my feet again, and was drawing breath and bard-power in alike, to blast them as only a bard can blast, when the chamber doors swung open once more and Keils Rathen strode in.

"Give me leave to speak here, my Companions," he said at once. "For though I am still a member of this board and Company, I have not taken my place among you for long enough that I feel I needs must ask."

Unerringly, he had picked me out as the presider here tonight—and I had not summoned him here, for I thought him busy with the fleets on their way to meet Majanah—and I bowed to him at once.

"Keils Rathen onetime First Lord of War has ever leave to speak at the Table to his brothers and sisters of the Companions. The Earl of Sulven too may speak." And I took my seat again to see what would happen next.

Keils bowed to me, or to Gweniver who sat beside me,

and went to an empty place halfway round the Table's rim
before he spoke. His words were no surprise.

"I will stand as champion to the Ard-rían in this challenge," he said to a silent chamber. "I know not why none
other has offered sword to the High Queen here tonight,
and nor do I wish to know. But if she will have me, I will
serve. That is all."

He sat down and stared at the wood of the table before
him. I wish I could report that every sword in Gwahanlen
was offered on the instant to the defense of Gweniver; but
I would be lying if I said so. No one made offer, as no
one had made offer before Keils's arrival. And if I felt disgraced and dishonored by my own Companions—though I
must also say that the true, old Companions were not present, Tari, Grehan, Tryffin, Betwyr, Ferdia, Alannagh, all
were occupied elsewhere on matters just as crucial; and
had they been present Gweniver would not for an instant
have gone unchampioned—how much more so must
Gwen be feeling it! She was High Queen; that alone
should have been enough to have commanded every
sword-arm here to rise in her cause. That none had done
so spoke volumes for the pervasive power of Marguessan's
poisonous workings: To have corrupted the Companions,
to have breached the unity of the Table was no small
accomplishment. Something would be done about it—I
had still to put on my mantle of spy, much might be
gleaned when I did so—but right here, right now, the danger was apparent. The Table was not broken; but it had
been sorely cracked. Now, however, was not the time for
repairs. . .

As no one else appeared wishful of speaking, I rose
again, and this time I let the word-whip take my voice to
strike. I do not recollect what I said, but I know I flayed
them, lacerated their souls with their own dishonor; and
hoped that the poison had been lanced clean.

At last I turned to face Keils, and bowed deeply. He too
rose, and at my side Gweniver stirred and slowly came to
her feet also. I drew breath to speak, intending to accept
Keils's offer and thank him for the generosity of spirit that
had made it, but Gwen was there before me.

"My lord," she said, and she looked at no one but Keils as she said it, "my thanks."

"You *have* thought, of course, that this is how Marguessan intended it to play out?" Morgan, readying for bed after the Table had dispersed, was pacing the floor of our bedchamber like a she-wolf caged, shedding garments as she went. I picked them up as she did let them fall, and let her speak.

"Does it not strike you—nay, it must! How not?—as just the tiniest cantlet *too* perfect, the timing of all this? The return of Keils, but *only* after his wife had died, *only* after he had heard those noxious lying tales about Arthur and me; the kidnapping of Donah, so that not only Arthur but a not insignificant part of our fleet strength must be gone from home just now, and our firm ally Aojun must respond likewise; the issuing of the challenge to Gwen, knowing that she would have no recourse but to accept. Even the knowledge that no one of the Companions would defend her, and that Keils out of past love and eternal chivalry would not fail to do so. . . The only miscalculation, if indeed it be that, is that Keils *will* defend her, that she will not herself fight out the challenge because of her condition."

I watched her pace, let her talk; and by and by she quietened, and sat at her dressing table in her shift to brush out her hair—something that calmed her as not even a sleeping-drench could, I could see her grow visibly more tranquil with every stroke of the silver-backed brush on the still-golden tresses.

At last she set down the brush, stared unseeing at her reflection in the mirror, and sighed once, slipping off her shift and coming naked into the bed beside me. But love was not on her mind as she fitted herself against me, her head on my chest and my arms round her as ever.

"Do you think Arthur has found Donah yet?" she asked in a small voice, and I knew she was thinking of Gerrans now, who had gone on the embassy with his uncle the King.

"If he has not, be very sure he will." I kissed the top of her head, and stared up at the new constellations that had

254   *Patricia Kennealy-Morrison*

recently been installed on the underside of the bed
canopy. Diamonds for white stars, sapphires for blue
ones, rubies for red giants, topazes for yellow dwarfs. . .
all most correct. I stared at the biggish gold diamond that I
knew represented Fomor's sun; and then I shot upright,
shaking all over. Morgan surged up beside me, put her arms
round me.

"Beloved, what? What is it? Have you Seen?"

Oh, I had Seen, right enough; and could not believe what
I thought I Saw. . . Slowly I allowed her to draw me down
beside her, to cradle my head against her breasts. But I still
clutched at her arms like a terrified child, and indeed I still
felt like one. . .

"When first we heard from Janjan that Donayah had been
taken," I began hesitantly, still striving to See my way
through the tangle, and not liking at all what I Saw, "you
remember how surprised we were that Melwas, of all folk,
would choose to do so?"

"Truly," she agreed at once. "We had made that treaty
with him, for one thing, and you yourself have often told
me how long he has been an admirer of Arthur—from that
time all you yourselves kidnapped him away from his grandfather. . ." Her voice trailed off. "Oh Goddess—Kerridwen
Rhên ferch Hu—nay, oh Talyn, tell me this is not so. . ."

"I cannot," I said. "For it is true."

"But why would he feign to be friend, all these years,
and only *now* choose to take revenge for that? Besides, it
was a reiving, not an abduction; even Nanteos had grudging
admiration for the action."

"Again true," I said. "And therefore—"

"Therefore something, or someone, else."

We were both silent, but the same name was ringing like
a great bell in both our souls. Marguessan. Again. Or still.

"But how?" breathed Morgan at last. "How could she
have turned Melwas against Arthur? And whyfor?"

"How is easy," I said bitterly. "No doubt but that he was
indeed smitten with Donah, and would have wished to
wed—and perhaps Marguessan had hand in that as well, a
small pishogue or love-cantrip, naught easier for her to cast
from afar. Or from close to, for that matter; she has long

been difficult of finding, as you will recall. Maybe she was farther away than any of us ever thought to think."

"And the whyfor?"

I gave a short laugh. "I think we have long since had the answer to that. But as soon as the fíor-comlainn is done with, I shall go and find out for myself. Perhaps I can learn something that may be of use."

I was wrong and right, as we most always are. The why-for was not as I had thought, and what I learned was of more use than I could have imagined.

CHAPTER 19

The fíor-comlainn to settle the charges of Errian of Kerveldin against Gweniver Pendreic was set for noon three days hence, at Turusachan, in the Fian compall behind the commandery; it would be public, as such things are required by law to be, but minimally so—the compall stands could seat only a few hundred at best, and most of those places would be filled by the royal family and kindred and Councillors, and by the Fian command. Few ordinary Kelts would witness the defense of Gweniver against what was now thought by all to be the malice of Marguessan—and which I intended to prove so the earliest chance I had.

Errian's chief second, one Rannick of Lissard, whose name struck me for some reason as not unfamiliar, made loud objections to the arrangements out of sheer bloody-mindedness, mouthing irately that it was by no means a neutral site as law prescribed, and suchlike, but really now. Gweniver was High Queen of Keltia; did the little toad hope to find a neutral site he would have to take this trial to some other galaxy. . .

By default as well as by unanimous decision of the Council Arthur would know naught about any of this until it was over. Ygrawn and others had wished him recalled at once, but Gweniver would not hear of it, saying Donah's safety was paramount claim here and she herself was well defended already, and she had bullied the Council into so voting. It would have been impossible in any case, as none in Keltia or Aojun, either, knew just now where Arthur and Majanah were. He would learn the outcome soon enough, Gwen had argued; for the moment let him have no other concern but the safe recovery of his daughter. We did not like it much, but, as with so much of late, we had no choice in the matter.

Keils had spent the time in hard practice in the Fianna's dueling-halls. Errian had elected to use claymores to settle the trial, which seemed to me and others more than a little vainglorious, but the choice was his to make. And as I watched Keils now from the viewing balcony of the hall, even to my far from expert eye the onetime warlord still looked to be one of the finest warriors ever to lift a blade. *Mighty Mother*, I thought, *he will have to be. . .*

"How comes it that this unheard-of Errian thinks to prevail against Keils of the Battles?" demanded Ferdia indignantly. He was watching with me as below Keils cut and blocked and parried with what seemed languid ease, and I was glad of the company. We had not seen so much of late of our old Feradach; he had come into his lordship of Valtinglas on Erinna some years since, and the dúchas being a demanding one and difficult to run, he had spent less time on Tara among us than he or we might have wished. But on the instant he had heard of the challenge he had come racing to Caerdroia, full of fury at the monstrous wrong done Gweniver by her own Companions, swearing to beat them senseless one by one when all this was over, vowing that had only he been there sooner Keils should have been *his* second, instead of, as was now the case, Ferdia being Keils's. He studied his principal now, critical but approving.

"Well, he thought not that Keils would be the one to fight him," I said reasonably. "He challenged Gwennach, remember, and had no reason to think that she would not champion herself. It was a gamble on his part, but one he thought to win. He did not know about—"

"—about the bairn to come," said Ferdia, nodding. "Aye, aye, just so. Ah, look, that old parry, so sweet he makes it look, so easy he takes the blade— Even so," he said, returning

to his original line, "Gwen is no feather-arm! She is a better
general than a sworder, right enough, but we all of us have
seen her put steel to good account. I mind me of that time
at Glenanaar—"

And we were off, trying to lose a little of the terrifying
present in the long glow of our shared past. Even if
Glenanaar was perhaps not the piece of the past I would
myself have chosen to be minded of just this minute—

Below, the match ended, with Keils victorious—as he had
been in every single one of the seven back-to-back bouts he
had just now fought, the best swordmasters in the Fianna
having been his practice partners—and not one of them had
tossed the Queen's champion any charity touches, to be sure.
Nor would Keils have wished or expected any: For him, it
had ever been no quarter asked and no quarter given, and
injustice was to him the greatest evil there could be. Which
creed played no small part in this matter: that, and the utter
unswervable loyalty to the Crown that had marked his service
to Uthyr as well as to Uthyr's two co-successors. And the
other thing? What of that? Had Keils's well-known loyalty
to the Crown been surpassed here by his equally well-known
loyalty to his Queen—to the woman who had long time
been his beloved? And was that a good thing or no?

I went down with Ferdia to the practice floor below,
where Keils was stripping off the dueling plastron and trews
he had worn for the session. He greeted us cheerfully, and
motioned us to follow him to the adjoining pool-baths,
where he plunged into the steaming waters to ease his muscles and stop them stiffening. We did not converse much;
little needed be said.

He had seemed to take in good part the marriage of state
that had been at first between Gweniver and Arthur, and it had
certainly not altered his own relationship to either. For royal
personages, no less than common folk, have had lennauns, or
céile-charach, or co-mates, even, for all the years of Keltia: Our
marriage laws allow for any number of humane combinations
of lawful union, and for quite a few outside the law as well.
And indeed, Gweniver and Keils remained for many years a
devoted loving pair, as they had been for even longer before;
Arthur, who for his part wished to lose neither wife nor

friend, Queen nor warlord, was troubled not in the least by
their continuing union, and himself found love with
Majanah of the Yamazai.

But then Arthur and Gweniver had suddenly seen each
other plain, and had fallen in love, simply, suddenly; coming
at last to that union of heart and mind, soul and dán, that
Uthyr and Merlynn and Ygrawn and so many others had
foreseen for them. And Keils had borne himself with grace
and honor, even as had they. He had by then found
Meloran, and left with her soon after for the estates Arthur
had granted him on Gwynedd. But who knew what he felt
in his heart, or spoke to the winds, alone on the battlements
of his castle, in the dark Gwyneddan midnights? And who
knew how Gweniver herself felt now, about this knight of
hers returning to fight her cause once more, this time to
such deadly and final purpose. . .

I started as Ferdia waved a hand in front of my face.
"*Miles* away," he was saying cheerfully. "Star-leagues, probably—"

"My sorrow, Ferad." I put an arm round his shoulders
and, bidding farewell until later to Keils and the small knot
of Fians with him in the pool, left the commandery with
Ferdia and walked back across the Great Square.

Halfway to the palace I changed my mind. "I have just
remembered a thing I need to do in Seren Beirdd," I told
him. "But do you go and talk to Gwennach, cheer her up. I
think she and Morgan are finished by now with the day's
hearing-court."

Ferdia shook his head. "How can she think about little
pismire grazing rights disputes on Kernow, when all *this* is
on her?"

A good question, and one more folk than he were asking.
For Errian of Kerveldin had followed another old tradition
besides that of the sgian through the challenge-parchment:
He had chosen that this fíor-comlainn should be to the
death.

And so it would be: Keils was nothing loath to rid the
realm of "this slinter"—one of the more repeatable terms he
had for his opponent—and he was still less loath to hazard
his own life in the combat. But did he lose, Gwen's life was

forfeit along with his, and that was not to be thought of—
though should it fall .out so, the sentence upon her would
not be carried out until her child was safely born. But Keils
would not permit it even to be spoken of, and we were with
him on that. Still, it must be thought of, and there had been
several very secret Council sessions on it already. . .

"She thinks about those things *because* of all this which is
on her," I said, answering Ferdia at last. "If anything can
help her through these few days—"

I bade him distracted farewell, and turned my steps away
from the palace, past the House of Peers and Senate and
Assembly buildings, past the house of the Ban-draoi, to
Seren Beirdd, which rose complete now in shining newness
on the middle part of the palace plateau, hard by the
entrance to the Way of Souls. And tried not to think of
where that way led—up to the royal barrowing-ground at
Ni-maen.

Star of the Bards was a fair house, for music and for words.
Built of the lovely gold-veined creamy granite from the
quarries of the Dragon's Spine, it stood eight-rayed and
many-towered around a central grassy court. Cloisters and
smaller quadrangles filled out its interior, and at night its
lantern windows could be seen from most quarters of the
City.

I loved the place—indeed, I had had no light hand in its
designing, for who knew better than bards themselves what
bards might need by way of working precincts?—and spent
more time there than my other duties did strictly allow. But
I did not go there now to play musical truant, pleasant
thought though that was. Nay: I had business, terrible business, with the head of the Order—business that bore on the
two desperate situations in which Keltia now found itself.
And I had found help here, before, when I came to Seren
Beirdd in need.

Perhaps I should clear up one minor matter, before you
in your rightful confusion begin calling hard on me for mis-
leading you: I was not, neither at this time nor any time
past or to come, the leader of the Bardic Order. Oh, to be

sure, sometimes, often, I was called Chief Bard in popular nomenclature, and Pen-bardd by those who would honor or flatter; but in strictest truth I held no title in my Order grander than that of ollave. And that was by any way of weighing quite grand enough for anyone.

No more did I covet such rank: To be head of the Order of Bards was like herding cats. It was to be more the chieftain of an unruly fractious clann, to be more jurisconsult or administrator or politician than practicing bard; not my idea of a good time, or even a desirable one. 'Chief Bard' was a title used for any ollave in these days—the actual, presiding head of the order was known as the Blue Bard; or Derwydd, meaning Trunk of the Oak; or Cath-Awen even, Head of the Holy Inspiration—and was by no means the codified title given to the chief of the order that it would later become. Just so you know.

Any road, I went in at the hall's west door, stopping even in my haste and preoccupation to marvel yet again at the wonder of the carvings upon it—a great frieze-fan of saints and kings and gods and bards and queens—and then headed to a wing of the huge brugh where only the most very senior masters were given leave to go. For I was planning my spying stint to come, and I had need of expert advice.

My advisor, indeed, was awaiting me. I apologized for my tardiness as if I had been a lad back at school, even as I made him the reverence due to a great teacher from his pupil—for so he was, and so I had been. Elphin Carannoc had been the first one ever to see in me the spark that, properly fanned and fed, could grow to bardship's flame. He had been my teacher at Daars, set to instruct me by my foster-father Gorlas Penarvon, who was that time wedded to Ygrawn; he had been my companion in the days before there were Companions, with me on the roads of Gwynedd, spying for the Counterinsurgency against the Marbh-draoi; he had brought me to Tinnavardan, the secret hidden bard-school, and there had spoken for me to masters whose names rang like harps themselves down the halls of years.

I loved Elphin most dearly. Since Merlynn's strange going, and Gorlas's death decades since and Scathach

Aodann's only last year—she who had been the first true
Fian Arthur and I had ever known, who had taught us both
in the warrior's way, Arthur of course far more successfully
than I—Elphin was the one surviving mentor of my youth.
And though I was called Pen-bardd, and he himself had
been first of all Kelts to call me so, for my invention of the
Hanes in my student days, I knew there were things he yet
could teach me. For he was now Cath-Awen, and so I had
come to him today.

He seemed to be quite fully informed of all the momentous
happenings of the last couple of days; in the end, I had to
apprise him of very little.

"Ah well," said Elphin complacently when I remarked on
this. "Good it is to be king. . ."

"Maybe not so much, not these days, not for Artos," I
said, and the smile went out like a snuffed candle from his
face and from his eyes.

"Nay; maybe not so much. Well, Talyn, I do not know
how I can help you. It seems a thing you alone can do, and
you have it well lined out."

I sat back in my chair, much eased in mind. "That is all,
really, I wished you to tell me. We are all asea here: Artos
being gone, and Donah taken, and now this terrible thing
come upon Gwennach—I did not know what else to do,
how to help."

Elphin was silent a while. "How does the Lady Ygrawn?"
he asked then, and I glanced swiftly at him in surprised
gratitude. In the press of other fears and concerns, few
indeed had thought to inquire as to the state of mind in
which Arthur's mother and Gweniver's aunt-by-marriage
now found herself, and I found myself remembering how
close Ygrawn and Elphin had been in the days of Daars and
Coldgates.

"Well enough," I said. "Though when one has a reputa-
tion for strength unwearied and peace of mind untroubled,
sometimes it is hard for folk to realize that strength and
peace are acts of will, and can fail one when they are most
needed. . ."

"It was ever so with Ygrawn," he agreed, smiling that smile which comes from memory's heart. "Never did she receive the support that should have been hers; no one ever thought she needed it. . . And truth to tell, Talyn, you and I know well she has ever preferred it so! She will come through this, as will we all."

"Be it so to that." And for a short stolen time we spoke of other, lighter things, to cheer ourselves and ease our hearts awhile. But always, always, behind all else the dark clouds were rising; and how pitifully little we had as weapon against that night.

The day of the fíor-comlainn dawned bright and cold. I was with Keils as he armed himself in the vesting-room just off the compall ground; Ferdia, as chief second, Betwyr, Alannagh, Tryffin and Ysild—Tarian and Grehan, as officers of state, could not join us, but sat with the judges in the ring without—all our oldest fellow Companions, together again, for comfort and for assurance of victory to come.

Keils himself seemed confident and calm, though with that necessary edge of sky-high 'wareness he would need if he were to triumph here—as triumph he must. For though he was by far the more skilled warrior in this match, anything could happen in the fíor-comlainn; and though we had, as was our right, studied Errian in practice-session as hard as he had studied Keils, still and all we knew but little of his true skill and resource in the ring. But I kept my fears firmly hidden, and knew well that every other soul here was doing just the same.

At last Keils was accoutered to his satisfaction, and the moment was upon him and all of us. He embraced each of us Companions, with a quiet word to each and from each in turn, then looked at me and knelt for my Druid's blessing.

And a strange, not altogether unexpected thing happened then: As I laid my hands upon Keils's bent dark head, and called upon those gods who might best be expected to lend their strength to such a task as his, and to the rightness of our cause, I was all at once aware of some Other present, who worked with me, and through me, who enveloped my body and being like an invisible mantle. And I gave myself up with joy and faith to it, and to him: For Fionn the Young, it seemed, had business here this day as well. . .

Outside in the compall, Keils went with Ferdia, who carried the three claymores the law allowed, to the center of the ring where Errian and Rannick already awaited them. The rest of us took our places in the first tier of seats, and I cast an anxious glance over at Gweniver, where she sat under heavy guard, and not a Fian there but who plainly and visibly hated the duty. She looked a touch paler than usual, her hair loose in a dark cloud, and she was clad in the unadorned royal blue of the House of Dôn—a statement if ever there was one. She was completely composed; but she never once took her eyes from Keils where he stood below, and he for his part had never once raised his own glance to her.

Reassured, if that is the word I want, I scanned the tiered galleries to ascertain the mood of the watchers. As expected, few of the plain citizenry of Keltia were here to witness this world-shattering event, though of course the time and place were known to everyone, and crowds had gathered—kept to a prudent distance—in the Great Square outside.

Most of the faces turned to the ring like flowers to the sun were faces well known to me, therefore—and well disposed at least to Keils, if perhaps not entirely so to his cause. For I saw with a sinking heart that Marguessan's poison had been at work even here in the place where truth had come to be tested. . . and for the first time I began truly to fear that test.

Below us, the pre-bout formalities were being scrupulously observed, for no one wished to be held accountable later—whichever way this thing went—for lapses in lawfulness. The combat judges had entered (though not introduced to the combatants, and they had been approved by both sides for their neutrality); last-minute ministrations of water and advice to the fighters were being given, and now the Taoiseach of Keltia rose in her place to read aloud the scroll of charges.

Tarian Douglas had perhaps never in all her years as First Minister to the Crown had so difficult a task as this. But only those who knew her best could see her anger and her pain; the rest saw only the calm countenance, heard only the clear, even, expressionless tones. Gweniver's face did not change in the least degree during the reading-out of the charges and sentence, though when Tarian finished and bowed pointedly to her—the loving act of a longtime friend here, a declaration of public and private support, by no means part of the usual order of this sort of thing—she gave the Taoiseach the flash of an expression too small to be called a smile, the hint of something like the thought of a nod.

Now Keils and Errian stood forth to hear the chief judge's brief as to the rules of the combat; being as this fight was to the death, there were no rules to speak of. Nor were the fighters armored, save for studded leather vambraces on their forearms and a sort of half-glove with a patch of mail across the back of the hand and a stout, though flexible, leather palm-piece. These they now pulled off, and clasped forearms in the traditional gesture, then chose each a sword from the *other's* armory of three, the preferred length and weight and reach having been supplied beforehand to the seconds. This choosing was in fact an ancient safeguard against treachery: You are not likely to poison the blade you know your opponent is going to be using against you. And putting aside all those intolerable possibilities of bluff and antidote—against which chance a drench was administered to each fighter that would negate any immunity to poison— so were these contests kept honest. Any road, the list of suspects in event of treachery would be an extremely short one.

The claymore is an impressive and difficult weapon: Almost as tall as its wielder, bearing cross-hilts like steel wings and a blade that could cleanly cleave an oak sapling without losing its edge, this great sword is seldom chosen for such contests, the simple reason being that few indeed can wield it to effect. In battle it is different; but in fior-comlainn the usual aim is first blood or disablement, not slaughter.

But not so today. Errian's choice of the death-fight had

made strategy all but irrelevant: The two in the ring would
be observing no niceties of swordcraft but would be bent
each from the first exchange on the utter destruction of the
other. So as Keils and Errian took their prescribed stances
either side of the dueling line, I drew in one exceedingly
deep breath, let it out all at once, closed my eyes and did
not open them again until I heard the fight begin. And then,
of course, I could not look away.

In claymore fighting, unlike most other sword disciplines, you
have little strategy but wish to go straight for whatever will
soonest disable your opponent at least cost to yourself: torso
blows from the start, but if the defense is too good for you
to get through often enough, or at all, then you go for arm
and leg blows, to disable and handicap before you get your
chance to kill. It is not a particularly subtle form of combat;
in essence, you try for whatever you think you can hit, and
the bouts are quite short by comparison with other forms—
twenty minutes at the outside. Longer innings are simply
too exhausting: At the end of a half-hour combat, the two
wielding claymores would be too weary to drag their sword-
points up out of the dust of the ring.

Also a secondary weapon is customary, and today Errian
and Keils, should the fight get so far as that, would be using
curtal-axes, the deadly little short-axe or tuagh, which each
carried upon his belt at the back. There would be no
respite, neither for water nor for wounds; as Ferdia put it,
what would be the point? This thing was to the death.

It became very apparent very quickly that we had rather
underestimated Errian of Kerveldin as a sworder. Plainly he
had downplayed his abilities in all those practice sessions
over the last three days, to throw us off our guard; but I
consoled myself with the thought that even if he had done
so, Keils had done so still more. Besides, they had not called
him Keils of the Battles for mere flattery's sake.

And it was also plain that Keils had lost none of that skill
over the years of peace. I leaned forward, spellbound,
almost forgetting the desperate gravity of the thing, caught
up instead in its terrible beauty. There can be a kind of

THE HEDGE OF MIST

bardery in steel, a music in the way of the sword: timing, pace, tempo, phrasing even, the strokes set up as clean and neatly delivered as the notes of a tune. Keils seemed to move to a music he alone could hear; was it the sword that moved him, or he the sword?

All the same, it was Errian drew first blood. The crowd gasped as if itself had felt the blow, though Gweniver remained impassive; gods alone knew what it cost her to do so. Keils took the wound calmly enough, altering his patterns to fight around it, drawing Errian's defensive returns all to one side, then coming in hard from the other without warning.

They had been fighting perhaps ten minutes now, and bled on both sides. Errian's strokes were coming wilder and more uncontrolled, and that was one kind of danger, while Keils's were ever smaller and sparer and more economical, and that was another kind. To my eye it looked just about even, and that seemed to me good; but the look on the faces of better fighters than I—Alannagh, Betwyr, Ferdia—suggested that they saw something very much other, and that it was not to our joy.

Even I could tell that they were fighting much more slowly now than at the bout's outset, in an irregular rhythm that spoke volumes for their endurance as well as for their pain: cut, breathe breathe breathe, step back for purchase and leverage, breathe, swing and cut again, take the shock of the parry, breathe breathe, cut cut cut. . . It was all edgework with the claymores, all arm-and-backwork for the fighters. Though Keils's strokes were mightier, and appeared to be having greater impact, Errian's looked to be better planned and placed; more of a pattern to his blows, where Keils strung single strokes together, each effective but each apart from the last and the next. And even I knew that it was not thus that duels are won.

They were both badly cut about by now; Errian had taken more hits but Keils's wounds were the graver, his tunic dyed with blood. Yet still they fought on, as though none of it mattered in the slightest, and I knew we were seeing something out of which legends would be spun in after times.

Then, as Keils landed a fearful swipe, Errian parried strongly; something changed in mid-blow, and Keils staggered a little as he put a nick into the leading edge of his blade perhaps halfway down its length. A groan went up from the crowd, and Errian seized the advantage, laying in another blow at once in just the same place, and this time Keils's claymore broke cleanly and finally across, two feet below the quillons.

The watchers in the galleries gasped as one—even Gweniver's iron composure slipped, and all her anguish showed an instant on her face before the mask was back in place—but just then Keils Rathen proved before all Keltia what had won him his name and fame in battle.

To me, staring, not daring to breathe, it seemed that it all happened in slow-time, years even, though well I knew it was a matter of mere seconds. But as Errian began to swing what he clearly intended should be the deathblow, Keils coolly put up his left arm to block it as it fell. The tiniest miscalculation of angle or force and the huge blade would have sheared straight through his shoulder and not have stopped until it reached his ribs: But Keils had timed his move to martial perfection, had used his metal-studded leather vambrace to make the parry, turning his arm so that Errian's blade slid along the bit of armor. The edge sliced through leather and flesh alike, but the blow was turned; and with his other hand Keils flung the hilt-shard of his claymore straight into Errian's face. His left hand moved past the parry, and, protected only by the leather of the palm-piece, closed upon the langets of his opponent's sword and ripped it from Errian's grasp.

A move worthy of Cuchulainn, of Fionn himself, worthy of a song on any battlefield—Alannagh and Betwyr were thumping each other in their jubilation—and one that bought Keils just enough time to reach calmly round his back and pull his curtal-axe from its belt loop.

Faced with an axe-armed adversary and an unretrievable claymore, Errian did the same, and now the whole tenor of the fight changed. I for one could not believe they were still on their feet. . . But no more long sweeping graceful strokes; now it was short savage swipes, hack and slash, no style or finesse about it. They were fighting now as they would have fought in battle, and anyone watching could see that it would all be over very soon now, and I began to armor myself up against the worst.

For, unbelievably, *again* the luck turned to Errian: Hooking the tip of his axe under Keils's cutting edge, he jerked hard just when Keils was resetting his grip on the shaft. The axe flew through the air, to land a few yards away, and now Keils was weaponless altogether.

He did the only thing you can do in such case: He went straight for Errian, under the wicked flashing edge of the axe, taking a frightful slice all down his left shoulderblade, but getting his hands on the haft, just above Errian's own.

They stood toe to toe, breast to breast, face to face, and the axe between them, their fingers fighting for purchase on the blood-slick wood of the handle. A moment so; then Keils was swinging the tuagh in one last two-handed arc. I did not watch the deathblow; I was watching Gweniver instead.

Her face crumpled like a child's, and in a rare moment of unbridled emotion she closed her eyes and raised a hand to her mouth. But her relief was all for Keils, not for herself; he had won her acquittal, but what mattered most to the High Queen of Keltia was that her champion yet lived.

Though only just: Keils raised the curtal-axe about an inch in token of victory—all he could manage—and the judges signalled their acceptance of his triumph. With that we were free to dash down to him where he stood upon the field, too weary and bewildered to move. Ferdia was first, then the rest of us, and then Gweniver came, weeping as I had never seen her weep before, or since either, for that matter. And we had brought healers, and bore Keils from the ring; though I stayed behind with Tarian and Grehan to make sure that the verdict was down and Gweniver cleared along with Arthur and Morgan.

"All charges against all named parties are dismissed," said Tarian, her glass-blond hair disarrayed where Grehan and I had mussed it in our delight. "Keils is—well enough?"

"The healers say aye," I said, unable to conceal my own reaction. "Only he could have done it, I think—"

"No 'think' about it," said Grehan fervently. "I have never seen nor heard of such a contest. But—"

"Aye," I said with a grimness. "But."

Grehan's 'but' was no more than what we all had known must come next should Keils succeed (in our terror, we had not very much considered what should be if he had failed): the tracking to its lair of the source of Errian's actions. We were all agreed it was Marguessan; what we were not yet sure of was how to go about proving it, or for that matter what she had had in mind by going after Gweniver and Keils. Hence, my upcoming spy turn; and there was still no word from Arthur or Majanah or our own fleet as to the rescuing of Donah.

"Ah Goddess! One calamity at a time!" cried Gweniver at supper that night. But she laughed as she said it, and we laughed to hear her.

Keils had been attended to first of all, brought from the field to Turusachan and surrounded by the best healers in Keltia. "I wish Elenna had not gone with Arthur," lamented Tarian. "For so great a general, she is still the finest healer the Companions have ever had, and who better than our own for our own?"

Still, the unCompanion healers did well indeed, though they were more dour than most of their kind, grudgingly allowing as to how Keils would most likely live as long as anyone might be expected to do who had been sliced about as badly as he. Keils himself, when Gweniver and I sneaked in to visit him for a quick moment, seemed cheerful and much more confident than those who attended him, and laughed at us for fearing as we had. But Gwen spoke to him a few moments more, alone, her head bent close to his, whispering into his ear as he drifted off again, and I had to turn away lest I learn too much for my own peace of mind.

But now that we knew the hero of the day was comfortably settled, and the mending process well begun, we could surely allow ourselves a small celebration supper, a bit of sheer relief before turning sword in hand again to confront

the next set of troubles forming to crash against our battered battle line. So we gathered in Ygrawn's private feast-
chamber—just the kindred, blood-kin and soul-kin
alike—and had vowed in usqua that no word of any woe,
past, present or to come, should pass any of our lips at the
table tonight. Tomorrow's dán to tomorrow; this night, at
least, we could be happy.

I wonder, had we known what was about to come upon
us all, if we would have done aught differently. Or was it
just that dán, having thrown so much, took pity on us a little before throwing so very much more. . . Whichever, we
were grateful for that night, after. It was the last night of
things as they had been, before things changed forever.

CHAPTER 20

For one who had come so close under the shadow of the sword, Gweniver seemed surprisingly forgiving, if that is the word, of the Companions (now throughly shamefaced) who had so signally failed to stand up for her in her ordeal. I am not as a rule a violent man, but I would have been knee-deep in their bloody bones by now had they done to me as they did to her. But she planned no revenge; not even to disband the Company, or banish them from it or from Keltia.

"'Forgiving'!" she repeated with a grim incredulous laugh. "Nay, no fear! I will never forgive them until our next lives, and very like not even then. But what would you, Tal? They may be weak, or fearful, they may have fallen prey to Marguessan's slanders, they may even be stupider than ever we thought them, or could have wished them; but they *are* still the Companions, and there will be other needs for them not too far off now. I did not break my toys when a lass no matter how they did displease me, and I do not chuck out my tools now however much they have betrayed me. Toys or tools, they are all I have. They will get their payback from dán; do not doubt it. I will not have to lift a finger; they will do it all themselves. And I can live with that."

I was glad to hear she planned no wholesale reprisals; and also sorry to learn she now classed as mere implements those who had been of the Company through so much.

"It is their own fault," said Morgan stone-faced. "They brought it on themselves, and I will have not hand nor heart nor part in it. Go away." She would say no more no matter how I pushed, and at last, disconsolate, I wandered off. Some time later I found myself outside the chamber Gwahanlen; I dithered a little, then pushed open the tall doors that were never locked and went in.

It seemed unchanged; and yet all had changed. . . It was somehow sad. I slouched down in the nearest chair and stared across the room at my own seat Gwencathra. What would I see when next I sat there, the Table in session? Would there even *be* a next time? Would I see a dead or disbanded Company? A broken Table? A pack of misbegotten cowardly creevies?

I shifted uncomfortably. And what would *Artos* think, when he got back and found out what had nearly happened in his absence? What would he *do?* I put my head on my hands and laid it down on the Table. Because of the Company itself, the Company that had held together since Cadarachta and Coldgates, through the first and second Llwynarths—because of the Company and what it had failed to do, Keltia had come within a touch of killing its High Queen on a lying trumped-up charge. Only Keils's courage and sense of high justice had saved Gwen and us together—and what would Artos have to say about *that?* Presumably he had not yet been informed of the fior-comlainn and all that went with it, but one never knew exactly just what Arthur did or did not know and it was never wise to assume one way or the other. And we still had had no word from him as to Donah's safety.

The one thing that *had* been decided since two days ago was that I should leave on my spy tour as soon as might be arranged; and after discussing it with Morgan, I had myself decided to leave the very next night. Delay seemed not to our interest: If Marguessan were up to something more, or new, best we learned of it soonest. For a delicious idle moment I contemplated just what it would cost to rid Keltia forever of my matesister: We would have to take out Mordryth also, most like—did we leave him alive he would only start down another tiresome road of revenge—and probably Irian, though Marguessan's lord had ever seemed incidental to any of her machinations, or to anything else, come to it. . .

My ashling of a Marguessan-free Keltia was broken by Morgan's entrance into Gwahanlen. She took a seat a little ways away from me, but said no word; and after a while I glanced up at the tapestries that hung round the walls. And was heartened thereby: Strange days and trying ones had been in Keltia before now, and doubtless would be again—if any of the various prophecies I had been hearing since the Graal quest had truth in them, and I doubted not for the smallest instant that they did—and Keltia had survived; thrived, even.

And we had so much now: We had the Treasures back, the Cup again safe among us, and the promise that even if they went, their benisons would remain with us, and they also would return even so. . .

"You are planning to leave," said Morgan, and I startled to hear her, for truly I had forgot she was even there. "Where away?"

"No name springs straight to mind," I admitted. "This is not the time of the Counterinsurgency, where as a rule I could come by information of *some* kind no matter where I put myself in the way of it—but I have a sort of idea that Gwynedd would not prove entirely barren a ground."

Morgan smiled. "I have ordered our rechtair at Tair Rhandir to be ready to receive us," she said in a pleased tone. "And Gerrans and Cristant and the children are thrilled we are coming."

So we went.

Almost it was like the old days. Nay, I can hear you jeering at me across the pages: Very well then, it was *exactly* like the old days, and I was glad of it; does that content you?

I had left Morgan at Tair Rhandir, according to plan, and I had set out on foot across Gwynedd. I did not look like myself, thanks to my lady's magic, and when I contemplated myself in a mirror after Morgan had finished her work on me to her satisfaction, even I was hard put to think that Marguessan would recognize me. I had true-change put on me, not a mere fith-fath or a glamourie that Marguessan, with skills of Seeing the Marbh-draoi had honed, would have no trouble piercing at a glance. Nay; this was other, a change that *was* change.

So I looked into the gold-framed mirror, and another man looked back at me. I could not decide: Sometimes he seemed older than myself, other times younger. He was lighter of hair and darker of eye, with the ruddy clear skin of a countryman and the build of a fistfighter. We had agreed that for me to go in guise of a travelling bard would be too obvious, and had settled instead on the profession of itinerant bootmaker—I even had a well-stocked pack-pannier for each of my three baggage-horses, full of beautiful hides of suede and leather, and the tools of my new trade.

So I bade farewell to Morgan and Gerrans and Cristant, and to the young Cathelin—the twins being away in fosterage on Erinna—and set out eastwards. I had arranged with Morgan to contact her each evening for exchange of news, but apart from that I should be very much on my own. Plans had been put in place for me to be able to go for help to certain of our loyal lieges, should help become necessary; yet even this seemed fraught with risk. Better I should stay apart from any possible link with Tara, or with the truth of my masquerading. . .

And as yet I still had no idea where I should go. The Old North, Irian's lordship, his family's lands since the High King Elrick's reign, was the logical choice; but to go there first, blatantly, seemed not only unsubtle but unsafe. And there was not overmuch time, either, to learn all I desperately needed to know. . .

And so, of course, in spite of my better judgment, I turned my steps in that direction, a little north of east.

The Old North of Gwynedd, strictly speaking, is neither very far north nor even particularly old. But it had been among the very first settled regions, centuries since, when Brendan's dear friend Conn Kittagh had come here alone to found his dúchas, and it was much the norther of any other townland on the planet for centuries to come.

Even still it was: Coldgates, and Tair Rhamant when there was still such a province as Gwaelod, a few other places, were more to the north of Lleyn; but not many more than that. And I wondered as I rode through the Mains of Gwynedd, passing Agned, sighting Glora, had Conn chosen a-purpose to dwell in so lonely a spot; and did the kindred of Locryn, no kin to him, choose for purpose of their own to dwell there now? ~

Any road, the country was lovely, all rolling plains rising to the Lleyn foothills and then real mountains that rimmed the Sea of Glora on its western edge. Collimare was norther still, I remembered, and I wondered if Morgan would find time during our stay to visit her old school-haunt—or if Birogue herself ever came there these days. . .

But the small villages and maenors and townlands through which I travelled held custom quite sufficient for a fraudulent travelling bootmaker; I was kept busy enough at my hastily assumed trade, and thanked the gods that I had of necessity learned the basics of this honorable calling during my days at Tinnavardan, when besides bardery would-be bards were obliged to set their hand to anything that needed making or mending. I found to my surprise that I had chosen a disguise better and more effective than I knew: Not only were folk well disposed and eager to recount local gossip to me as I measured their legs or stitched up torn boot-shafts, but the *making* aspect of the craft satisfied my own need to make—bardery being pretty much denied me on this jaunt, since though Morgan might put change on my countenance, never could even she have disguised my art against detection. . .

I learned more than you might think. They knew the Locryn kindred well in that region; had little good to say of Irian save that he was seldom seen or heard of, no good whatsoever to say of Marguessan. On Galeron and Gwain they were silent—apparently there were wounds not yet healed even among the folk—and on Mordryth, surprisingly, they were deep divided. Some chaunted his praises, other some used bad little words that as a bard I found professionally interesting, and had not heard before but filed away for future use.

One of the two most interesting things I learned, though, was that a small trading enclave originally established on Powys, for the convenience of outfrenne traders needing more immediate access to Keltic sources than our merchant planet Clero allowed, had recently been moved to Caer Dathyl at Irian's petitioning. I minded me vaguely of Gwen or Arthur speaking of it, and had given it no more thought than that; but when a talkative lordling (who must have been more than usually hard on boot leather, for he brought me four pair to mend and gave order for four more) informed me gaily that aye indeed, there were galláin in Caer Dathyl, and thick as wax they were with Mordryth of Lleyn too, I began to think perhaps the capital city of Gwynedd might be better harvested than the grounds of the Old North.

Besides, it was a damn sight too near to Oeth-Anoeth for my comfort, this region, and the sooner I was quit of it the better I would feel. So I bespoke Morgan that night, as we had arranged, and I informed her whither I now was bound. She did not like it much; but, well, she was not here to like it, was she. I did not like it much more myself.

So I came to Caer Dathyl, still in my bootmaker's guise—I would be able to find custom even in so large a place as that—and took humble rooms at a bruidean just at the foot of the castle's massive outcrop.

I had friends and contacts here—well, Taliesin Pen-bardd did, and so also Prince Taliesin—and went to seek them out, to hear what I might hear. I wound up giving them more news than I got, particularly about the fíor-comlainn and Donah's kidnapping (or what I could tell them, at least), but they had things to tell me as well. For one thing, that trading enclave just relocated from Powys; for all it was strictly supervised, those dwelling within being most carefully watched and regulated in their comings and goings, it was commonly held by just about everyone who lived in Caer Dathyl to be a nest of spies.

And not just any spies, either, but Coranian and Fomori

and Fir Bolg spies. And blame my evil suspicious devious
bard's mind if you must, but no sooner had I heard that
than I knew very well where had been Marguessan Pendreic
all these times when she could not be found in Keltia; and
what Mordryth—and maybe even Malgan—was keeping
busy with of late. . .

Of the galláin present just now in Caer Dathyl, five or six
interested me most particularly. Not chiefly for their planetary origins—some were galláin, some half-Kelt—but for
their previous job of work and place of location before coming here to Keltia to play merchant aide.

All of them—the slot-faced Coranian Tembrual
Phadaptë, that other of her ilk calling himself Sleir Venoto,
the pair of cooperative (or co-opted) half-Kelts by name
Phayle Redshield and Kiar mac Ffreswm—had been to
some extent or other involved in the trade treaty made
between Melwas of Fomor and ourselves some years since.
And all of them had come here from Clero.

Now it seemed to me passing strange that they should
have all just *happened* to turn up together again in Caer
Dathyl, a happy chance indeed; and when further investigation made by my contacts let me to know that working hand
in paw with these four were Granúmas, the simian-being of
the race of the Voritians, from the planet Uxellos, and
Rannick of Lissard—aye, aye, that same very Rannick who
had been so helpful to the late Errian of Kerveldin—I felt
my senses quicken.

"Aye, it sounds most likely, but you would think they
had covered their tracks better than that," said Morgan
when we spoke mind to mind through our link that evening.
In the light marana trance in which this sort of communica-
tion was conducted, I could see her face before me as
clearly as if she had been in the room with me. Her expression too: And the thing most clearly stated there was doubt.

"True, they might have done better to have taken on
other identities," I agreed. "But they have no cause just yet
to be suspicious, and perhaps they fondly imagine
Marguessan's protection to be enough, or to be there

always. Little knowing how quicker than knife she would
fling them to hungry tigers if by doing so she could save
herself some trouble. Any road, though they seem wary
enough, I do not think they know themselves twigged."

"Well, nor have they been, not yet," said Morgan tartly.
"We have still only circumstance and threadwork to go on. . .
Any news of my sister's likely whereabouts?" she asked,
changing the topic rather abruptly, and even in the mind-link
I could not forbear a snort: For almost never did Morgan
refer to Marguessan by name. Always it was 'my sister' or
'your matesister' or 'my mother's other daughter' or even 'the
Duchess of Eildon.' As if she so much misliked framing the
name that she would not have even the touch of it upon her
tongue. . .

"Aye!" I hastily responded, for Morgan had asked again,
rather more testily this time too. "And you will never guess
where—"

No more did she: For this was the second of those interesting snibbets of information I had culled from that tattle-
tongued boot lover in Lleyn, and had not imparted to
Morgan until I knew for fact it was true, for if true it was
devastating.

And it *was* true, true beyond all doubting: Marguessan
Pendreic, when she deigned to dwell at all on Gwynedd
these days, lodged not with her lord Irian in his ancestral
maenor but some long ways to the south—at Gwenwynbar's
old haunt of Saltcoats.

"And well we know who has dwelled there himself these
last years," said Morgan bleakly when I told her.

Well we knew indeed. Malgan Rheged.

It was all beginning to fit itself together very neatly and very
swiftly now, but still I could not return to Tara without
some more crucial chunk of the central puzzle-picture completed. Gweniver—and more especially Arthur, given that he
was returned by now from Fomor or wherever, the which
we still had not heard—would never act against a princess of
the blood without something very much more definite and
very much more damning by way of evidence than that

which we could just now offer. However much the Ard-rían,
or Ard-rígh for that matter, might share (and oh, they did
share) our own certainty of Marguessan's guilt, the link to
spies and hostile outfrenne powers had yet to be proved.
Nay; I should have to bring to Artos and Gwen something
substantial, and I should have to be most careful about how
I got it. For venturing to Saltcoats—and I minded me of the
last times I had been there, and those not happy memories—would be like to putting my hand into the very mouths
of those hungry tigers I spoke of earlier, and I thought long
and hard on how it could be done and I myself still get safe
away with my proofs.

Then, considering blackly, all at once I smiled. I was still
clad, as if in armor, in Morgan's magic of change; why
should not my original plan now serve at Saltcoats as I had
intended it to serve at Lleyn? I leaned back on my bed-pil-
lows and smiled again. Perhaps Marguessan, too, had need
of a new pair of boots. . .

As I crossed the Saltney Marshes on the coast road from
Caer Dathyl, I saw on the morning of the fourth day the
castle from which marshlands it had taken its name, rising
up across the wide curving calm-watered bay. And though
I knew I was well disguised and equally well defended, still
I could not forbear a shiver or two, for Saltcoats held for
me many memories, and just about all of them greatly
unpleasant.

The castle itself had changed not at all from
Gwenwynbar's day, and as I rode into the outer faha I could
only think that Malgan himself had kept it so, for his
mother's memory, and his own too, who had been a little
lad here. It had ever been a fair place—I grudgingly gave
Gwenwynbar marks for that, and for preferring its isolation
to the splendors of Caer Dathyl, though if truth be told
Gwenwynbar had made herself a court here of queenly
scope and style—and it was still.

For all my misliking of the place, I had in truth been
here only twice or thrice. When I was in bard-service to
Owein Rheged, spying for the Counterinsurgency under the

somewhat pretentious falsename of Mabon Dialedd, and
when Gwenwynbar was mistress here as consort to Owein, I
did my best to avoid being commanded here, for obvious
reasons. And so only a few flying errands, message journeys
for Owein, had seen me visitor to Saltcoats. I had never
gone within; and I resolved me, staring up at the outer walls
of the great keep and feeling Marguessan's presence like a
coiling dank darkness, that I would not for any sake go
within now. Nay, the new mistress of Saltcoats—and a fit
successor to the last—must needs come out to me. And I
thought I saw a way to make her do so.

I had customers before even my packs were unloaded from
my patient beasts. Perhaps travelling crafters were scarce on
Gwynedd these days; or more like such as there were did
not much care to come to Saltcoats. Whatever, folk longing
for new boots came clustering round, and I accepted all
their orders and did my best to humor their requests; and
before very long, as I had hoped, word came down from the
keep that the Princess Marguessan had seen some of the
very fine work this sir bootmaker had been doing, and
would do him the honor of allowing him to craft a pair for
her.

I grovelled quite satisfactorily to the rather arrogant cow
of a lady-in-waiting that Marguessan had sent, and presently
certain foot measurements were forthcoming—the which,
being the same as Morgan her twin's, I already knew well,
and had done some work beforehand to prepare. I humbly
inquired as to her highness's choice of leather and ornamentation, and when provided so I ran up a fine pair of boots of
Kernish leather, with turn-down cuffs for riding. They were
by no means cheap, and the lady-in-waiting, impressed with
the looks of them, paid me at once and took the boots into
Saltcoats.

The next morning she was back, looking more like a
goat than a cow, and complained that the boots had not fit
her mistress, they were too loose in the shaft and too short
in the foot. I need not return the payment, but another pair
would be required. I apologized profusely, and set aside all

other commissions to make another pair of gilded leather
boots, and was paid accordingly.

Back again next morning came the lady-in-waiting, and I
found myself hard put to think just what animal she was
resembling today. Her speech was a good deal sharper, and
simpler also, as if she was beginning to think she spoke to a
lackwit, no matter how skilled he was with leather. Well, and
plainly not all *that* skilled either, she immediately informed
me, for the second pair of boots had been rejected also by the
Princess, who had found them too big in the foot and too
tight in the shaft, and besides that the cuffs were mismatched.
Again, I might keep the crossics, but yet another pair must be
made, and this time there was no mention of payment.

"Well," I said at last, sighing hugely and throwing down
someone else's rather humbler piece of footwear, "I shall
make no more boots until the Princess comes down herself
and permits me to take her measure. Royalty perhaps have
feet unlike common folk, for never have I had such difficulty making boots for anyone as I have had these past days
in making these for her. Tell her I have said so."

The courtier flounced away—I had it! A cross, deeply
offended, long-legged storkish bird of some kind—and I settled comfortably back to await Marguessan's coming. For
that she would come to me I had no doubts: I had seen the
gleam of her covetousness in her servitor's face. She craved
the boots with the gleam of their own in the leather, and she
would condescend right gladly even to an itinerant cord-
wainer if that was what she must do to have them.

She came sooner than I had thought; almost *too* soon, for
I was not quite ready for her. One of the reasons I had
sought to entice her to come out to me was that I deemed
Saltcoats too well warded (also Morgan had ordered me not
to go within), and that did I venture inside its walls not only
would my magical protection be violate but perhaps I should
be cut off from outside sensing (and help, if needed). As it
turned out, I did right to fear so.

"Well, bootmaker," came the voice from without, unnervingly like my Morgan's, so that I startled to hear (even

though I had been braced for just that happening), and
whanged my thumb with the little tapper.

Marguessan had paused outside the door of the open-
sided work-shed where for the past three days I had
ensconced myself. I did not look up from the boot I was
carefully renailing; but I could sense her suspicion, and
retreated at once into the eidolon of Rhobat the humble
cobbler, built it up with bardic skill, sent myself very far
from Taliesin Glyndour. . .

"Highness!" I said, bowing deeply and awkwardly, hand
on heart, not as one who was 'customed to such gestures,
praying it would pass. "An honor—so sorry for the inade-
quacies—my fault utterly—pray come in—" She swept by
me, and I kept up the chatter, glad of my nervousness, for it
made me sound natural.

"Your boots are lovely," she said, sitting down in the fitting-chair, "though you seem to have had some difficulty in
following my measure."

"My sorrow for it," I said, as I took her foot in my hand
and began to use the taperule on it. "But now your highness
is here I am sure I can do better."

Now I did not for one instant think that Marguessan
would of a sudden begin spilling out her treasonous soul to
a perhaps incompetent bootmaker, but the direct physical
contact somehow seemed enough to verify that this was a
woman with great and terrible secrets. And as I worked and
measured and talked humbly, in my construct of a role, I
sensed it more and more; and when I glanced up from my
work, out at the faha, and saw Tembrual Phadaptë just then
dismounting from a lathered bay gelding, I was hard put to
it indeed to keep the joy and dismay off my face and out of
my voice.

But Marguessan seemed not to notice. She was pleasant
enough, if coolly distant—in all ways unlike her twin sister,
who treated cobblers as kings and kings as kings, all alike
and all equally honorable—and after a few more exchanges,
and more apologies from me, she went out from the shed
and back into the palace.

I sat down hard in the fitting-chair Marguessan had
vacated and blew out my breath in one explosive sigh of

relief. But I was not relieved entirely; I had still to find out that which I had come here to learn, and even though I was now certain beyond all doubt that Marguessan was plotting treason with offworlders—and had the evidence of Tembrual's presence to back that up—I had yet to obtain proof concrete.

But I curled up and slept that night, in a corner of the work-shed, with more confidence and less fear than I had felt for some time.

I never learn.

CHAPTER 21

Next noontide I was commanded to the presence of the Princess Marguessan, and bidden bring the—correctly fitting—boots with me. And although I feared to my bones to go within Saltcoats, I dared not decline. To a humble travelling cobbler, would it not be the crowning moment of his life and profession alike, to be summoned into a castle at a princess's command, to deliver to her in her own person the boots he had made for her at her behest? Indeed it would be; and that was why I could not refuse the bidding. There was not even any time to warn Morgan; I would have to rely on my wits and wariness alone. So I dashed some water on my face, scrubbed clean my hands of leather stain, pulled on my own boots—far less wonderful than the ones I bore with me for Marguessan's approval—and with a terrible presentiment of disaster about to come rolling over me like the wave over Gwaelod I followed the servitor within.

Inside, Saltcoats was spacious and beautiful as a keep of this particular style and vintage seldom is. As a rule defensive structures do not lend themselves over-well to grace of design—and no more should they, for their purpose is to keep their folk safe, not to delight the gaze—but somehow Saltcoats managed to fulfill both functions. Whether this was of its current occupant's doing, or of her predecessor's, I neither knew nor cared. And where was Malgan Rheged?

In all the days of my trade-plying here, I had heard his name mentioned perhaps thrice; all the talk had been rather of Marguessan—and of her offworld visitors.

For not only had Tembrual Phadaptë put in an appearance, but she had been joined this very morning by some of the others on my list for watching as well: the half-Kelts Phayle Redshield and Kiar mac Ffreswm. And I felt something brewing like a thunderstorm in the air, and I liked it not.

Marguessan did not keep me waiting. I had been prepared to hang about many hours in the servitors' hall to be favored finally with a ten-second audience and the offer of her hand to kiss before being shuffled off again to the worksheds. But nay; I was ushered at once into a lovely chamber that must have been her private hall—not the Great Hall, but a lesser, more comfortable one—and she swept in at once to greet me.

"Welcome, ollave!" she said with a smile, holding out her hand.

I bent over it dutifully, taking care not to kiss but only to bow, hoping desperately to cover the start of alarm I had given when she addressed me by my title. Although I minded almost at once that 'ollave' was a title of mastership in a craft, by no means exclusive to bards, and that she meant only to honor my skill, it had been a nasty little moment, and I prayed that Marguessan had not noticed my break.

Which apparently she had not: She graciously accepted the boots—or rather she allowed a maid to do so—and then, quite astonishingly, offered me a cup of wine and a seat across from her by the fireside. I took the cup and tried not to stare down into its contents—all my instincts were screaming Do not drink!—then glancing up I caught Marguessan watching me with the expression more customarily worn by a mousing cat or a heron poised to spear a fish. Well, this time the prey saw it coming—but for all of me I could not work out why I was suddenly suspect. Then Rannick of Lissard joined us in the hall, and I began to see things a little more clearly.

But still I clung to my concealment. They could only have doubts as to the blameless innocence of one who claimed to be naught but a travelling cobbler; it did not seem possible that they knew me for who I was in truth, so perhaps all was not lost just yet, and would not be, provided I kept my wits about me. The worst case was that Rannick had seen me in Caer Dathyl or had heard of me asking questions in Lleyn, and now was distrustful to find me turned up at Saltcoats. Well; could be allayed, it seemed, with a plausible story, and when Rannick began artfully to sound me out as to my recent adventures in the boot trade, I did my best to appear as artless as I might.

"Oh aye, my lord, Lleyn to be sure—your highness's lands, I know well—and aye, Caer Dathyl—not so much business, not there, nay, better in the provinces—" I rabbited on, even drank some of the wine, and prayed I sounded more a harmless gormless minkler than a clever spy; not hard, for 'clever' was about the last thing I was just now feeling.

And, bit by bit, I began to get the terrible, the sinking panic-clawing feeling that they were not believing me, not one littlest word. I did all in my power to sway them back to me; I did everything but juggle with the winecups, growing more desperate with each little tale or anecdote.

At last, beaten, I lapsed into uncertain silence, looking helplessly around at the expressionless faces of Marguessan, Rannick and Tembrual Phadaptë who had come in whilst I was floundering, whispered briefly to Marguessan and taken a seat to one side. Finally Marguessan, who had been sending out little fingerlings of magic toward me, creeping and patting and prying, trying to dislodge she still had no idea what, lifted her head and looked straight at me.

"Enough of this. You are no cobbler, though the boots could not disprove you. Will you tell us of your will, or shall we have the truth of you in other ways? It will not be pleasant, do we resort to that."

I met her look for look, wondering if she knew more than she said, feeling my disguise falling from me like a cracking glaze, like ashlar shedding from a weathered front. In a very few moments now I should stand bare-face before them all;

we had underestimated Marguessan's power in her own hall, and what she would do when she saw me there. . .

I said aloud, "I will admit to it. But not before these out-frenne lieges. Let them be sent from here, and your highness shall know all."

Rannick made an angry surging movement, but Marguessan stayed him with one uplifted hand.

"Nay—I am well able to defend myself in my own place against such as this. Go. Both you. But come again when I do call."

Tembrual, who had raised an eyebrow at my demand but made no other sign, rose to her feet and moved rather ungainly to the door, Rannick reluctantly following after. When they had gone, and the heavy oak doors closed behind them, Marguessan looked at me.

"Well, Taliesin," she said. "Shall we speak face to face, do you think?"

Silence for a long, long moment. Far away I could hear a piper, the notes rising silver into the afternoon air, and it troubled me that I could not place the tune. . .

"Aye or nay?"

I closed my eyes. It seemed to be one of Adoran Tudur's, slower than a march, but swifter than a marúnad or coronach: stately, soaring, so beautiful. . .

"Taliesin."

I opened my eyes and smiled into Marguessan's. "Oh that," I said, and let the mask fall away.

I do not think, looking back on it from the vantage of years and thought, that Marguessan truly had ever expected me to yield. It was as if an enemy had suddenly handed her a sword upon the battlefield, hilt first in token of surrender, and she did not know how it should be taken, or what should be done after she had received it. But this was her victory; I was not about to help her. Yielding was all I would do for her.

"How did you know?" I asked then. "The magic—"

She seemed to startle back to herself. "Oh, nay, the magic was good enough, though coming into Saltcoats were your downfall. My sister's webs are strong outside, but here I am the spinner, and soon or late you would have been ravelled out. Nay, a simpler thing entirely, and a strange one. Look at your hand."

"My *hand*—" But I looked as I had been bidden, and felt a shock as of icemelt thrown in my face. The spell Morgan had cast on me had been proof against almost all magics—I did not fault her for that she did not prevail entirely against her sister—but this was something that had naught to do with magic, and, all unthinking, I had brought my discovery on myself.

For glinting on the smallfinger of my left hand was the marriage ring Morgan had set there—the match to her own, the two serpents enknowed of each other, their eyes rubies, their scales clearly cut in old dark gold—the ring I had left there as of habit so old it was beyond habit.

"It is part of my hand," I said, still looking upon it. "I did not even know I had it on; but then, I never take it off." I looked up at her, and small knives came in my eyes. "Save that once, in Oeth-Anoeth, but then I was not the one who removed it. And you remembered."

"And I remembered." Marguessan's face, not very like her twin's but almost as fair, bore now an extraordinary expression that I could not unskein. Envy seemed part of it, and pity, and hatred, and a strange crabbèd kind of love, and sadness; but those were not the whole of it, nor even the main. What that was I did not know. But in that moment I think Marguessan and I were closer than ever in all our lives we had been, true sibs, and not just through Morgan alone. . .

But it passed. "Fitting that your marriage ring should so betray you, Talyn," she said then, and that was the old Marguessan we had known and loathed all these years.

Outside, the pipes had been joined by drums and horns; the sound had surely reached the edge of space by now, so high it soared. I let myself rise with it, then pulled myself down again to the moment.

"Fitting that my marriage ring should so sustain me, Marguessan," I said gently, with the tiniest bard-weight laid on the 'my,' "that you should fear it enough to take it from me in Oeth-Anoeth. Think you to do likewise here in Saltcoats? Or just take the hand with it? Your choice."

She flushed dull red under the insult to her own wedded state, then was white again, whiter than before. But I was yet getting started. . .

"So why do you not just tell me what are your plans, and we will go on from there," I suggested in the most reasonable voice in all the worlds. "You already know why I am here; do me the like courtesy in return."

She stared me down, then all at once she began to laugh. "Why not, why not after all?" she said, still smiling. "Though I doubt not but that you and my sister have already guessed the main of it, and by now my cousin-brother and his mate also. . . Well, my plans then are these, Taliesin Pen-bardd: to overthrow the double throne and set a single one in its place, and I the one to sit upon it."

"No news there," I said in a bored voice, to bait her, and it did.

"Not? Well then, hear this: I it was who set Melwas of Fomor on to reive away the little highness of Aojun, my brother's halfblood lamb."

"Knowing that Artos would of course go after her." *And so had we all suspected. . .*

"Counting that he would." Her eyes did what in another person and another moment would have been called dancing with merriment; but not her, and not here. "And I did so rouse the spirit of avengement for sullied Keltia in the breast of Errian of Kerveldin that he declared fior-comlainn against his own Queen. Came close to winning, too."

"Closer than you know," I said calmly. "Keils was all but struck down when he turned it from defeat to triumph. He lived, and he won."

Marguessan smiled outright. "He won, but does he live?" At my sudden sharp intake of breath: "Nay, do not even think it! Besides, you cannot. Try."

I felt that far too familiar sinking feeling come again upon me, but leaned cautiously forward in my seat, until I felt the edges of an invisible net begin to cut against me, and I sat back again.

"I have had it round you since you took your seat there

an hour since," Marguessan kindly informed me. "Do not move of a sudden, either, thinking to defeat it; it will tighten on you the closer the more you struggle against it."

"Neat, but not gaudy." I forced myself to calmness, pulling in away from the unseen net. "But this that you have said of Keils—"

"Keils is nothing!" she hissed, standing up and beginning to pace the chamber, her skirts frothing, whipping over the leather boots she wore which were none of my making. "Arthur, Gweniver, all nothing! I shall be High Queen, my son Mordryth Tanist to follow me; and I have the allies to make it so." Her glance went to the closed oak doors at the far end of the room, and mine went with it.

"*Them?* They are your—"

"They are my trusted and honored agents." She laughed again. "Well, not so, not quite. They are my bought dogs, my hirelings. I have paid them as befits a princess, and in turn they will do for me what must be done to make me Queen."

"Ah, the same old things, Marguessan," I said, shaking my head in mock sorrow and disappointment. "Never anything new under the suns. Always the old frayed plans that you recycle and hope to make into shining new ones. But to do that you needs must put something new into the mix."

"But I *have* something new," she said, and I heard the note of triumph in her voice. "Several things new, what is more; and one of which you will remember well—from Caervanogue?"

And the room went black before my eyes. I learned later that it had done so chiefly because I had surged forward uncontrollably against the unseen net that held me fast—snaoim-draoi, it was called, the druid's knot—and it had cut off the blood to my brain. But as I reeled back sick and dizzy in my chair, I knew it was for a different reason that the light had fled: The new thing Marguessan spoke of—or one of them—was in fact that very old thing of joyless bane and utter damnation, the Black Graal.

"Not *that* old thing," I muttered, when I was again able to speak.

Marguessan laughed knowingly and with scorn at my

vaunting attempt to deprecate it, for she knew well how we
had all dreaded such a resurgent chancing.

"Aye, you all prayed and hoped and trusted that it was
gone, you hapless hopeless children—you cling to the Light
as babes to your methryn's skirts." She paused, looked down
at me. "Well, Glyndour, I tell you, it takes more than a
pretty-lad Guardian to keep the Gates against the one who
taught me how to break them—but that for later. Just now,
there are matters more of the world with which I must deal."

"And you purchased yourself some suitable outworlders
to help you."

"Some, aye, are outfrenne. Other some are Kelt, or
rather part-Kelt—barred or banished by my brother or his
mate. Denied, they made their way to Clero, changing their
names and histories as seemed good to them, and prospered
in becoming useful. They will prove even more so—both
useful and prosperous—in the end."

But I was back a few thoughts. "And Keils—"

"—most like is dead by now," she snapped. "I arranged
things most well, do you not think so? That Gweniver's
onetime lover—or perhaps not so onetime as that, not so
former as folk thought?—must come back to defend her,
because *I* had arranged such doubt in folk's minds that
none else would do so. It was a perfect plan perfectly executed, save of course that Keils himself was not executed,
there in the ring. An oversight merely, which I trust is set
right by now, seen to by my helpers on Tara. Oh, and also
it has been so worked that Arthur himself will be blamed
for Keils's death—a jealous husband, returning home unexpectedly, coming upon his wife's long-gone lover conveniently returned. . . Well, you are a bard; you know how
those tragical balladries go."

Keils dead? I could not credit it, could not feel it. And yet
Marguessan's voice carried the unmistakable note of truth;
and this, remember, was a woman had not scrupled nor
hesitated to sacrifice two of her own children to advance her
dark cause. She would not lie to me about Keils; but thinking of him slain had brought me round to what I had some
time since accepted: that Marguessan would not in a thousand thousand lifetimes let me leave Saltcoats alive.

And, truth to tell, I was not much disturbed at the prospect. Events seemed now to be woven in some vast tapestry to encompass all the worlds, not Keltia alone; my own life and death and life (or lives) again were but a tiny strandlet in that great and everlasting fabric. If, it were to be hoped, a goodly gleaming one. . . But I grieved just now more for Keils than for my own apparently quite imminent demise.

Marguessan was watching me quietly, and out of nowhere I asked her a question to which I had long desired an answer.

"Why do you and Morgan never speak the other's name? I have noted it with you here today, and with her ever: Neither will allow the other one's right name to cross her lips. It is always 'my sister' or 'my twin' or some such. No great matter; but I have always wondered."

She stared at me, her face so white it bore blue under-tones, her expression one of pure terror. I stared back aghast, wondering now not about names or their unspeaking but why she looked so frighted at such a harmless question. Well! Therefore it must not be quite so harmless as I had thought; though *why*—

Marguessan had regained a little of her color by now, but still she had not answered me; and just as I was about to follow up my query to see if another innocent inquiry could produce the same 'stonishing result, the doors opened at the far end of the chamber and Malgan Rheged entered alone.

He was a man of full age now, and as he approached us I felt the blood leaving my own face, draining away as swiftly as it had done from Marguessan's. For the man who approached me where I sat bound in my chair by unseen restraints looked more like Arthur Penarvon than Arthur himself had looked at that age. Which meant, of course—

Malgan halted by Marguessan's chair, looked across at me with an expression not altogether that of an enemy. The which he had never been to me, I reflected, nor I to him; perhaps now we should see if he recollected that as well and as clearly as did I.

It seemed that he did, for he nodded to me, his mouth

tightening for a moment in what might have been a smile had it had a better reason.

"My sorrow to see you so, Prince Taliesin," he said. The voice at least was not Arthur's, but lighter, and the eyes were the eyes I remembered from the latter days at Turusachan, before he left for Gwynedd, when he was lodged in the palace as a royal ward after his mother's death. We had grown friends then, he and I. . .

"My sorrow to be so seen, Lord Malgan," I returned politely, and now the quirk was a smile.

But a fleeting one. "I say truly, Talyn," he said, dropping down into a chair across from both Marguessan and me, "when I say it is sorrow to me that you are caught up in this. But it will be; it is going to happen. You nor any can stop it now."

"Oh aye?" I asked with unfeigned interest. "What then is this I cannot stop?"

"Only but what I have told you," interposed Marguessan sharply. "My rightful claiming of the Throne of Scone from the usurping kindred who stole it from me and my line, what time my father Uthyr Ard-rígh was let to die."

I cut my eyes over to her, and she must have read their flash aright, for she flinched a little and looked away.

"The High King my foster-father and matefather was by no means 'let to die' by any," I said, and my voice sounded dangerous even in my own ears. "He spent his last strength in battle, on his feet as a warrior, and died of that unholy magicked wound dealt him by Owein Rheged in the tent below Agned, after the battle of Cadarachta. A wound dealt with Edeyrn Marbh-draoi's hand behind it; but the hand was Owein's, and it was raised not only against Uthyr but against—Malgan's father."

Malgan flushed. "I see you have come at last to the knowledge that has long time been denied me. But aye—I am not, it seems, ap Owein after all, but ap Arthur. The evidence is incontrovertible, there is proof now of what folk long have thought and mouthed behind their hands. I am as much a Pendreic as any here. And as royal."

"Ah well," I said comfortably, "I am but a Pendreic by my marriage's grace, royal only by courtesy; not to be

included in such company as this." But my bantering tone
covered something much deeper: Though I had long
believed—and the main of Keltia with me—that Malgan was
indeed Arthur's son by Gwenwynbar, not Owein's who had
claimed him, still it came as a levin-bolt from clear skies, a
tailstar slamming into the planet, to hear it confirmed at last;
and I strove to cover my staggerment with jest. And then
the past rose blindly up to choke me. "Malgan—"

It was all I could say. I was remembering. Remembering
Arthur with Gwenar at Llwynarth; before that, even, when I
had stood by him at their brehon bridals in Gerwin's hall; or
later, when Gwenwynbar had shouted down the Bear's
Grove and fled before dawn, ending the marriage by declaration and heading straight for Caer Dathyl and Owein
Rheged. We did not know she left us carrying a child.
Perhaps she herself had not known, or told herself she did
not. And when later on four of us saw her with Owein, that
dramatic night of dinner with the Marbh-draoi, and heard
of the boy's birth some while later, still we did not *know*,
and did not care to try.

But to think that he had been Arthur's son all along, and
did not know it, though doubtless he suspected even as did
we—what he may have wished one way or another we never
knew—nay, that was hard. I was sorry for the lad he had
been and the man he now was, sorry for us that we had not
known him for who and what he was; but sorriest of all for
Artos, who had been denied his firstborn for these many
years.

Nor was the screaming irony of it lost on me: Arthur had
done to Malgan just exactly what had been done to him. He
himself had not known himself to be Amris's son until he
was half-grown; now he had visited the same anguish and
uncertainty and doubt upon his own son, though Malgan
had had to wait many years more than Arthur before learn-
ing the truth of his parentage. And I, who had been with
Arthur the night he heard that truth, remembered well how
it had worked upon him, and pitied Malgan anew.

But then that little bardic voice—the one I ignored at my
peril—came whispering inside me: *If firstborn of Arthur, then
surely Arthur's heir. . .* I sat up very straight, and stared at

Malgan, and my jaw may have dropped just the smallest tiniest bit.

He read my thought; well, it would not have been hard just then, would it. . . "Aye, that too," he said equably. "But I am not out to displace Arawn; not for myself, any road. The High Kingship is not what I have longed for down the years, nor even in the short time since I have known for true whose son I am. And that is part of the reason I am here."

Now I had been wondering just that for some days: What could Malgan ap Owein, as we all still thought him, be doing here in the same castle with Marguessan? But now it seemed both clearer and muddier at once: Sith that he *was* Arthur's son, gotten in lawful brehon marriage if not born so, that gave Malgan unassailable claim upon the Crown. And that being the case, would not he, or any with such a claim, be the uttermost *last* person in all the settled galaxy that Marguessan would even allow to live, much less sit down beside in amity? What was in all this for her?

"Ah, that is the rest of it, Talyn my brother," said Marguessan archly, who had followed my line of reasoning as easily as ever her sister had. "But as my new nephew has just now said, he does not, truly, covet my aims and goals, at least not for himself. And he has graciously—and wisely—seen his way to back my own claim upon the Crown, setting his aside."

I was neither impressed nor surprised; well, not very much. "What claim? What right?" I said scornfully. "You know the law of succession as well as I, *sister* Marguessan. Probably rather better."

"When my father died—" began Marguessan, stung.

"When your father died," I interrupted, riding over her words with the ease of my training, "you were never for one least little snippet of time the rightful Queen, nor yet heir whilst he still lived. Nay, let me: The Prince Amris Pendreic, far-charach of the Lady Ygrawn Tregaron, was heir to his mother Darowen Ard-rían. He had by his consort a son, Arthur, and died before becoming High King, much lamented. According to our longtime and excellent well-thought-out law which rules such events, his son, still a minor, was set aside for the moment, and Leowyn, Amris's next brother, was proclaimed the next Ard-rígh to be. When he succeeded and died in turn, leaving his daughter Gweniver, she too was set aside as her cousin had been, and the last of the brothers, Uthyr, became Ard-rígh. Now the difficulty here is—"

"—is that Arthur, set aside on Amris's death, should have become High King on Leowyn's," said Malgan impatiently, and I gave him an approving little nod.

"Just so; but Arthur was still a minor, and besides that, he had been hidden away by Merlynn Llwyd and by Ygrawn, so that none even knew he existed at all. When Leowyn died, Gweniver herself yet a minor, Uthyr took the throne-in-exile as you have said. But when *he* died, according again to law—"

"—Arthur, set aside on Amris's death, should have been named High King in his own right." That was Malgan again. "He was senior heir."

"And that is the foundation of your claim—my sorrow, I mean your *non*-claim—to the throne." I was enjoying myself now, in some most perverse way I could not begin to puzzle out. "But the weight of the law on both Arthur's side and Gweniver's was found to be so exactly equal to so far a calculation that none could decide one claim above the other. And so Uthyr's wish and wisdom were honored in the end: to have them succeed him jointly, to rule as co-monarchs, High Queen and High King together. And so the problem was solved."

"Not *quite* solved!" That was Marguessan, more heated than before even. "Their rule, whether shared or single, meant that I was set aside upon my father's death. *I* was Uthyr's eldest child, his heir, and should have become High Queen to succeed him." When I began to remind her, gently still, of what she had pigheadedly ignored all these years: "Nay, Taliesin, none of your tiresome brehon rules! The law is outmoded, and should have been changed long since!"

I opened my mouth to reply, then changed my mind and closed it again, and she went on.

"The thing was simple, and should have been seen so. A king dies, and his heir succeeds. No more; but also no less."

It was hopeless, and useless; she would never see it. "And now?" I asked after a while.

"And now I make right that—error."

"And Malgan?" I asked, still quietly, still unclear as to where he fit into Marguessan's grand picture.

"Ah," said Malgan, and rose from his chair to pace, and I was stabbed to the heart at his likeness to his father in that moment, just so did Artos pace the bridge, or the Council chamber—

"I have never had any wish to be High King," he said presently. "Though surely I did have the wish to know my father, and to be known in turn as his true son. . . and perhaps to have some small thing of my own to control—something like, perhaps, Gwynedd. Therefore I chose to throw my name and such power as I can command to the side of the Princess Marguessan's claim. Her claim will be made the stronger thereby, one more contestant will stand away from the succession fight, and my childhood friend Mordryth will be Tanist, and King thereafter."

"And you get Gwynedd."

"And I get Gwynedd."

"And also you get revenge upon your father?" I asked, and felt a small grim satisfaction to see him flinch.

"Perhaps," he said evenly, but he did not look at me.

I leaned back in my prison-chair and smiled pleasantly at both of them, who were just now watching me lynx-eyed for I knew not what.

"So then," I said, and I smiled even more as I said it, "I think I do understand very well now. You have both made it all most clear, and for that I thank you." I turned my gaze on Malgan, and I looked at him for a long time before I spoke again. "So you are yet another of Marguessan's 'new things,' then. Deny your father, renounce your rightful heritance and claim, and support hers in all its lunatic dubiety, and you will be tossed a planet for sop. Gwynedd shall not be your dúchas, Malgan Pendreic ap Arthur, but the price of your soul."

He turned as white as had Marguessan earlier, at the name I gave him and the doom I pronounced. But I had chosen to do both quite deliberately, to see what he would do, how he might take it. And now I had seen in his eyes and face, as well as in his sudden bloodlessness, how he felt about it in his inmost heart. *Well then,* I thought behind my deepest shields, *this one may yet be saved*; and glad I was to know it. *But for* her, *nay; no help or hope for it, she is past saving, lost to us forever now. . .*

Which may seem to you a strange thing for me to be thinking, I who was just now on the very verge of being lost—or at the very least shoved unwilling into my next life—myself. And doubly strange of me to think thus of Marguessan, whom nearly all Keltia had held to be beyond redemption for these many years now. Still. . .

But Marguessan had stood up, an air of triumph and expectation about her, and Malgan with her, a sense of angry reluctance clinging to him. She gestured to me to rise also, and I did, tentatively at first, to find that the snaoim-draoi which had held me fast was gone. I looked full into Marguessan's face as the hall doors opened once more to admit Rannick of Lissard, followed by a band of eight sworded guards, and I gathered my time was run out.

"Will you go with these, Taliesin, or must they take you?" she asked.

"Oh, go, by all means," I said, agreeably and at once. "I would for no sake—least of all mine, and surely not yours— choose to die under this roof. Without will serve me well enough."

"Be it so then." She nodded, and forestalling Rannick's rough grab I strolled forward to take my place among the guards. Then, as I turned away with my escort: "Only remember, Talyn. I sent you back your ring, back there in Drum Wood."

"So you did," I said after the briefest of pauses, but I did not turn round to look at her, and I walked out steadily with the guards, out to the faha where my death presumably awaited.

But I never got there, and whether the guards and Rannick did or no I cannot say. For no sooner had I set boot without the castle gate, on green turf under bright skies, than something unseen came down from clear heaven and snatched me clean away. I was as surprised as I daresay

were they: It seemed like a hand, then more like a whirlwind, then like some bubble of time or place that had of a
sudden swooped me into it, and it was utterly unexpected,
by me no less than any. I saw Rannick and the cohort
blown and scattered like October leaves, tumbling over and
over each other, helpless and doubtless furious. Though
surely not so much as Marguessan, watching from her window, must have been. . .

And then I was gone from Saltcoats, and knew no more,
until I opened my eyes against a great warm soft ruddy light.
Was I dead, then? I could see nothing in the warm red
glow; but if I *were* dead, should not someone be here by now
to fetch me away? A dear kinsman or kinswoman—Uthyr,
say, or Gorlas, or one of my sibs—or a significant mentor
of the spirit or venerated hero from out the past: These are
the usual guides sent to greet one who has just passed into
the 'next room' of the time between life and lives to come.

But though I waited in expectation, no one showed up,
though the light remained all round me, steady and red-
gold. Could they have *forgotten* me? Was there a great crush
just now in the Hither Hereafter, so that souls must wait
their turn for guiding? The Guardians of the Door must
surely know I was here? I would not have to find my own
way to Caer Coronach, would I? I had merited better than
that, had I not. . . And slowly I began to fear.

Then a hand came strong and white and slim and shining out of the red light, and I clutched it, and it tightened
on mine, and I pulled, and the hand pulled, and I came up
from somewhere into Morgan's arms.

I fell heavily against her, holding her hand—her saving
hand—in both of mine; we were both weeping, and she held
me for a long time before I felt any wish to sit up and
demand of her an explanation. When I did, we began to
weep all over again between kisses, and this went on for
quite a while longer before we seemed to have ourselves in
hand once more.

"I thought I was dead," I said, in a voice which conveyed
how pleased I was to find it not so.

"Almost," came Morgan's voice from above my head,
which was by then safely cuddled in her lap. "You never *listen,*

and you a bard. . . Did I not tell you again and again not to venture within Saltcoats? I did; and do you never hear me? You do not. Why else do you think we fashioned that little charade of the misfitting boots? All to keep you outside the walls of the castle and to winkle my sister out from behind them; and what do you do? You troop obediently within the instant someone invites you. You might just as well have thrown yourself at my sister's feet and set one of those boots you made her upon your throat with your own hand. Bonehead." And she swatted me.

"And that is another thing," I began, diverted at once, to the point of ignoring the swat, by the non-mention yet again of Marguessan's name. But Morgan put her fingertips across my mouth, silencing me gently, and I could tell by the touch the change of her mood.

"I did not think I would be able to lift you out of there in time," she said, and her voice trembled.

"And that is another thing again," I said, indignant all over. "You might have taken the trouble to inform me that you were going to use magic like some great cloudhook on me. I did not know *what* in all hells was toward. And *then* I thought I was *dead!* Perhaps I never listen, Guenna, but then *you* never tell me aught to begin with, so there it is."

I could hardly believe we were quarreling at such a moment, and all at once we both of us began to laugh.

"Ah me," said Morgan, wiping the tears from her eyes, tears of laughter and relief from terror both. "Never shall we do things like other folk, you and I. . . But I think you have brought no mirthful news with you from Saltcoats?"

"Aye so. That sister of yours, whose name you will not speak and who for her part will no more mention yours—"

"Just so. But you shall tell me now."

She lay down beside me on the bed (which I had only now discovered I was comfortably stretched out upon, in our own chamber at Tair Rhandir) and put an arm across my chest in her usual fashion, her cheek against my shoulder.

So I told her, told her all of it, and she harkened gravely and carefully to all I had to tell: Marguessan, Malgan, the outfrenne paid lackeys, the whole of it. When I was done, she shivered a little, then reached herself up and kissed me lightly upon the lips.

"Imagine," I said dreamily, for I was by now come to that toppling edge of slumber, having forgotten for the past little while that I was utterly exhausted. My body was falling asleep around me, though my brain was still wide awake—with good cause to be. "Imagine Malgan all his life not knowing whose son he truly was."

Morgan was silent a long while. "Nay," she said then, and with her next words the last pieces of the puzzle came crashing into place. "Imagine Edeyrn Marbh-draoi not knowing whose son Malgan truly was."

And that, of course, I could *not* imagine.

CHAPTER 22

"Well, *surely* he knew! Edeyrn may have been evil unspeakable and incarnate, but stupid he most assuredly was *not!*"

Gweniver rolled her eyes at no one in particular and flung herself into a chair. "Why else did he choose to make Owein his heir?" she continued in a voice of elaborate patience, as if she spoke to furniture not folk. "Only because he knew Owein's heir was Malgan, and knew also that Malgan was Arthur's son, not Owein's at all. And the idea of his worst enemy's son as his eventual heir, a Pendreic to be suborned and perverted and given to the Dark, a son of Dôn to succeed the Marbh-draoi, was too tempting for Edeyrn's twisted humor to resist. So he did not."

Morgan and Arthur and Ygrawn and I studiously avoided one another's glances, but we all knew Gwen had the right of it. We were together again in Turusachan, home from our various voyagings, some of us with more success than others—as Arthur, for one, who had come back from Fomor with Donah, both of them safe and sain, and all those who went in Prydwen. And that, of course, was something. Much.

But the return had been to a Keltia uneasy, unsettled, fraught with troublous rumor and cry: the news I had brought from Gwynedd; the news with which Gweniver had greeted Morgan and me on our arrival, that Keils Rathen was indeed slain, and by treachery too; and, perhaps worst and direst of all, the news Arthur bore home, when he came to Tara only hours after we ourselves had landed.

We had trooped right back to Mardale to meet him, just Gwen, Morgan and me; even our closest Companions had been bidden stay behind at the palace until we returned. Prydwen was just coming in to land as we got there, settling down like a dark-green feather upon the field, still in the grip of the mighty motiving force by which it sailed the stars. I for one never tired of watching it: Since Arthur had had it built for him at the very start of his reign, Prydwen had become well known by sight to the star-navies of many worlds, and usually for excellent cause. But for all its deadly power, it was beautiful withal: long and lean of line, not so big as many battle craft, but able to carry a score score of warriors with ease. And never did I look on Prydwen without minding me of that first great reiving we had had in it; for on that sailing we had met the Yamazai, and of that meeting Arthur and Majanah had met. . .

And *that* meeting had produced the tall, rosehoney-haired young woman who was even now running at us from across the field. Donah threw herself upon the three of us all together, laughing and weeping, and we were doing the same back to her; but when the man who had followed her out of Prydwen came up behind her, we felt our laughter freeze on our faces at sight of him.

Arthur looked to have aged ten years in not even so many weeks, and he did not spare us any cushion of time to prepare for the blow but dealt it hard and swift, as was his wont; and perhaps that was best.

"Aojun is at war with Fomor for this," he said, "and Keltia will not be far or long laggard in joining her."

Now, as we sat in Ygrawn's solar, just the five of us, all the news had been heard and told. I had had for my sins the task of giving Arthur the certain tidings of Malgan, and I must say he received them with the calm that befit a great king. But then he had always believed in his heart that Gwenwynbar had lied about the lad's parentage, lied to him even as she had lied to all Keltia and to Owein himself; and, give him the praise, Arthur had ever conducted himself to Malgan, if not quite as a father, then as a watchful and compassionate guardian.

"And you would have thought *that* had carried some weight with him!" complained Gweniver bitterly. "Never did you behave to him, Artos, with aught save grace and kindness; and see how he does now."

Arthur and I exchanged glances, but neither of us spoke. Still, for all its mighty reverberation within the Clann Pendreic, this of Malgan was nonetheless the least evil of the many tidings that had come our way this day. For one thing, Arthur was most interested to hear of Marguessan's doings, and before I had quite finished telling him had already dispatched Fians to Gwynedd to round up whatever outworlders they could find, in especial her particular several tools. I myself much doubted the Fians would find any galláin on Gwynedd, let alone Marguessan's outfrenne lackeys; they had surely been warned and gone long since. All the same. . .

And Keils Rathen was dead; that was true as Marguessan had told me. He had been found in a deserted street of the Stonerows, and judging by his wounds and the signs of struggle and the blood not his own, he had not made it easy for his slayers. Still, it was not the end he might have Seen, or any of us could have wished; and when word began to run like the Solas Sidhe that the shortsword that had killed him carried the High King's personal device upon its hilt, you may well imagine the stour that followed. Arthur, in his grief for Keils, dismissed this angrily, saying, and rightly, that the most languid swordsmith in the land could forge such a hilt and fit a blade to it and claim that it belonged to the Ard-rígh; and that of course was true, but the whispers grew apace to surly rumblings, and something would have to be done to put cease.

But none of this could help Keils, nor could have saved him either; and in the midst of the turmoil we were angered all the more because we were denied time even to grieve properly for him, could not mourn our dear friend and Companion as he had merited of us, though of course his

murder was being investigated most throughly at Arthur's
own command. Nay; we could not have saved Keils, cogged
we never so well: His doom had been appointed from the
moment he entered Gwahanlen to stand up as champion for
Gwen, and though he had won that fight he had died for his
Queen all the same. I think he would not have been displeased.

Arthur was watching me, knowing my thought. "Later,
braud," he murmured. "We will honor him after, as is right
and fitting. Just now we have other matters to think on. He
will understand."

And I knew, of course, that Keils of the Battles would
understand indeed—and did. But still it was hard.

Everything had seemed to have happened in the last few
days, when I was myself on Gwynedd being toyed with like
a captive mouse by Marguessan and her creatures. Arthur,
raging out of Keltia after Donah, had come first to Aojun
and found Majanah cold and wrathful, her world already
armed for war.

Together, they had sailed in pursuit of Melwas, who had
fled with all speed to his own homeworld. Not the cleverest
of actions—some hidden sanctuary world would have been
by far the better choice—but he was harried and distracted
and his common sense overridden by Marguessan's workings; and instinctively as a hunted coney he had bolted
home.

It had then gone thusly: Aojun's forces, already raised,
had joined the fleet Arthur had led out with Prydwen, and
together they came upon Fomor. Melwas had put up resistance at first, but he was no match for Majanah and Arthur
united, and when enough bases and crucial stations had
been blown into space-sparks, and when threat incontrovertible had been at last posed to his capital city of Tory,
Melwas had finally given in and relinquished Donah to her
avenging parents.

"Though even then with great and strange reluctance,"
said Arthur. "Aye, not though Janjan vowed to leave his
planet a cold clinkered ball of slag lurching through the void

of space. And she would have done as much, too, and I
would have been with her in it, had harm befallen
Donayah." He smiled at his daughter, who had come from
her enforced nap and joined us, and was now lying on her
stomach on the hearth-furs, barefoot and quite at her ease.

"Not before I had cut him into tiny pieces and fed him
to the geese," she said happily. "What is more, he knew I
would, and I think he even *liked* the knowing. But he never
harmed me in the least smallest way, unless you count being
near bored to death with dreadful poetry as torture."

"And I for one well might," I said smiling. "But we are
only glad and grateful to have you back, lass."

"My mother thought it best that I come here while the
war is on," said Donah. "Though I did not wish to leave
her and Brone to deal with this without me—" All at once
she looked as a child fighting to keep back tears, and she
was. Ygrawn, who was nearest, reached down a hand, and
Donah took it and clung to it.

"What now?" That was Morgan. "Marguessan has in her
traha brabbled most of her plan to Talyn, so that we can
prepare against at least that. But I cannot help but think that
there is more."

What more, we could never in all our lives have imagined.

The next morning, we awakened to the news that the
Archdruid, Ultagh Casnar, had crowned Marguessan
Pendreic Queen of Kelts, and Mordryth Tanist. The thing
was done on Gwynedd, in Oeth-Anoeth of baneful memory,
in the presence of the kindred of Locryn (much diminished
since the death of Galeron and the defection of Gwain, who
was with us this day in Turusachan), some malcontent
Companions who had seen fit to take Marguessan's part—
including that Morholt who had helped begin it—and quite
a number of trimmers who set their sails to fit the wind that
blew; also Marguessan's outfrenne abettors, whom many
held responsible for the death of Keils.

Arthur had summoned us to the Council chamber:
Morgan, Gweniver, me, Ygrawn, Gwain, Gerrans who was
in from Gwynedd, Roric and Daronwy back from Aojun,

the true Companions. And there he told us of what had befallen, and looking round the chamber I saw that no one was surprised.

He gave us the news in a quick, clipped voice—the bare facts, little more was just yet known, though indeed those were ill enough.

"The Archdruid gives as his reason the certain knowledge that the monarchy is corrupt, witnessed by the fior-comlainn to defend the Queen—plainly rigged, for clearly she was guilty and her champion should not have triumphed so featly against the truth—and the subsequent murder by the Crown of that champion, as equally plainly he knew the truth, had been bought off and must have his mouth stopped before he talked."

Elen Llydaw, newly returned from Fomor with Arthur, looked ill with anger and disgust, but spoke with all her customary force.

"Artos, we must isolate Gwynedd as it were the seat of infection. Do we cut Marguessan off from any outside help, we can contain the revolt, limit the danger and the damage to one world."

Arthur shook his head. "The danger is spread, Elenna, and the damage is done. We must call up all our forces, and prepare not only for civil risings against us but against invasion from outside as well."

"This Marguessan has promised," I said, over the denials and protests. "We were fools indeed to ignore aught she may tell us, and I was there to hear her say it. I do not think she lies."

"And for certainty we have war with Fomor," Gweniver reminded us. "Aojun has already declared, and we as Aojun's ally—and fellow aggrieved party—will soon do the same."

"And what of the Protectorates?" That was Ruard Darnaway, who was Lord Extern, responsible for the administering of Keltia's commonwealth worlds—several dozen systems by now, all looking to Keltia for a shield against the peril that can come from far stars.

"A good question," said Arthur. "But quickly answered: They are not in this. We will not withdraw from them any patrolling ships or forces, but nor shall we be able to send them any more than is already there. They must make do with what they have."

"And so must we," said Tarian grimly. "We shall be hard put to it even so, Artos. Fighting outfrenne invaders—Fomori certainly, and who knows what others Marguessan has contracted for—and quelling civil disturbances at one and the same time. . ." Her voice trailed off, and that was not like her.

"Can it be done, Tari?" asked Gweniver quietly.

"It must be done, Ard-rían," answered the Taoiseach.

"And so it shall." Arthur had leaped up and begun to pace, and I had a sneaking suspicion—shared, I could tell, by a number of the others present—that Arthur was not entirely displeased or even very much daunted by these developments.

No surprise, not for one who had known him as long as I had; Arthur was ever at his best when his forces were out-numbered and his back was to the wall. Desperate odds seemed to lift him to a next higher plane of being, a redoubled fervor of action and thought; this we all knew well. But then he had never before come to such a strait and struggle. . .

Gweniver had been mostly silent, but you could sense it was white silence, the strains building, until at last she gave vent to her feelings with a sound that might have been made by a she-wolf fettered, and stood up.

"The idea of Marguessan crowned Ard-rían," she explained to the staring faces turned her way. "It—grates me. That is all. But what do we do now? Grehan?"

Grehan Aoibhell, who had been this long time busy with star-maps and holomaps of Keltia and many notes, looked up from his computations.

"As First Lord of War it is my duty to see us ready to meet this threat, and as of this moment we are not. But we shall be, and that soon." He rose, and addressed Gweniver and Arthur. "If I may have your permission to leave, and to take Elenna, Betwyr and Daronwy with me? We can more readily plan our course at the Fian commandery."

Arthur nodded, Gweniver lifted a hand, and they were

gone. The room seemed somehow to close up behind them, as water cut by a knife. Arthur stared unseeing a while at the table, then shook himself all over and stood up.

"Well. Do the rest of you go where you are needed, also. But I must speak with Talyn and with Guenna."

When the room had emptied, I turned in my chair to inquire with my eyebrows of my foster-brother. The chamber seemed colder and darker now with only ourselves in it—Ygrawn too had been bidden stay behind—and I had a terrible feeling something I would like not at all was on its way. . .

And I was so right to think it. Once the doors were shut and we were all gathered round Arthur's end of the long basalt table, he looked at Gweniver, who nodded, and then looked at us.

"Talyn, you and I have a thing to do ere this begins in earnest," he said in a low hesitant voice. "I have Seen it some time since, and I have spoken of it with the Ard-rían, and now I would speak of it with you three who are most dear and near to us both." He paused, then went on. "You and I, Tal-bach, have another errand to Glenshee, and this time it will be the last."

I caught my breath back into my chest, but in all truth I had been half-expecting something of the sort. How not, when all such encounters for the past three decades and more had been every one of them pointing the way to this? And I called deliberately to mind the great visions that had been vouchsafed me during the quest for the Cup: what, and who, I had seen in that time; what they had said to me; what they had told me I would and should be. . .

And I heard myself answering Arthur as in a dream. "Last, and, I think, greatest. When are we away?"

"At first light," said Arthur. "There is much to settle here before then, and no time to delay past. We will take an aircar as close as we dare come, and walk the rest of the way in." He closed his eyes, sighed deeply and ran both his hands over the center of his face, speaking through his fingers. "Much shall perish in this bitter harvest tide."

For it was Lughnasa here on Tara, and August had been held since our time on Earth as one of the months of sacrifice. And as I left the Council chamber with Morgan silent beside me, I turned my mind in terror from the thought of what—or whom—might not be asked in offering so that Keltia should go on.

Morgan and I went early to bed, for sheer weariness of spirit and body both. It had been a long and mortally taxing day, and we were far forspent, I even more than Morgan.

With good cause, I might add: I had been all but executed at Saltcoats, then snatched away to Tair Rhandir thinking I was dead, and then discovering that I was, in fact, not; travelling home to Tara only to learn of Keils's murder; last of all Arthur's own return, with such dark tidings as made it seem that Annwn itself had been loosed upon our worlds and lives. A busy enough day right there; and now according to Arthur, he and I had another call to pay upon the Shining Folk in Glenshee.

Oddly enough, that prospect which would have frighted most Kelts else gladdened my heart—a good thing too, since naught else this terrible day had done so, save of course Donayah's rescue—and as I tumbled bonelessly onto the piled pillows I found myself eager for the dawn journey to the north and east.

"To see Gwyn again—" I said, half-asleep. "And Birogue, and my mother's grave, now that I know all her story—"

"And Merlynn Llwyd," said Morgan softly. "You are called to this tryst beneath the hill, trygariad, for high purpose's sake; and it is in my mind that it is Merlynn himself who calls you, and his great purpose which you and Arthur shall work. Else is all in vain."

I sighed deeply and pulled the coverlets up to my chin. "I know. I mind me of things I Saw—as a lad, on the quest—and now it is come upon us."

"Of my sister's doing." She lay silent beside me a while, then began to speak in a hushed voice, scarce audible even to me on the pillow beside her own. "I never answered that

asking of yours, Talyn, back in Tair Rhandir, as to why she
and I do never speak the other's name, sith that it cannot be
avoided. Well, there is good reason for that."

"I'll bet there is," I muttered grimly. "When I asked her
in Saltcoats that very question, she went white as, well, salt
on the instant. But she would not tell me why."

"Nay. She would not. And in more conformable times
no more would I. But these times are very much other, and
so I will let you to know, because you may have need of the
knowledge before the end."

Again she paused, as if she must forge the words deep
within herself before bringing them out into speech. "Well
then," she continued, "there is an oath we have among the
High Ban-draoi, and they have it too among the Pheryllt. It
is the sorcerer's oath with dán, and it cannot be broken. Not
even broken with consequences or punishments. Nay; once
taken, it cannot *be* broken. And that is what is at work,
between my sister and me."

I was shivering a little by now, no matter the coverlets,
quite certain that I did not wish to hear another word, sorry
to my bones that ever I had asked. But I must hear, and she
must tell me. . .

For the oath of which she spoke, the Tynghed, was
dreaded more than even death itself, for it bound more
surely on both sides of the Door; I had heard only dimly of
this terrible swearing, all Kelts had, but I had surely never
thought to encounter it side by side with me in bed. But
Morgan was speaking again, and with an effort almost physical I forced my head incline to her, to better hear her
words.

When they came, they were terrible indeed; and long it
was before I could close my eyes after. . .

I stole away in the darkness before dawnlight without
waking Morgan; rose and clad myself in the dark—no arms
taken, one did not go with earthly weapons into the faerie
halls—dropped a gentle kiss on Morgan's bare shoulder
where it glowed like a pearl above the dark sleeping-furs,
and went to join Arthur for the journey.

He was already awaiting me, at the small landing-place
between the palace proper and the great Keep where he was

accustomed to keep an aircar standing ready, and when he saw me he thrust his gauntlets into his belt, nodded, and swung into the small ship. I glanced back up over my shoulder, though I knew perfectly well that the windows of the chamber where I had left Morgan asleep did not overlook this faha but faced on to the sea, and followed him inside.

We touched down in the Hollow Mountains just after dawn had broken, leaving the aircar on the far side of the last ridge before Glenshee began. It was as close as we could come to the Hill of Fare, beneath which lay our destination, Dún Aengus, behind the great waterforce and stone passage known as Sychan, the Dry River. We would have a bit of a hike, I reflected, but it could not be helped, and with luck and a good strong pace we should come to Sychan by midday at the earliest.

As usual, I had reckoned without thinking that the Sidhe might have ideas of their own; and as soon as Arthur and I had set foot over the ridge's backbone into the lovely valley beyond, we were reminded of that in no uncertain fashion. . .

We stood there a moment with all the vale spread out before us. Here, well north of Caerdroia, it was already autumn, and I looked in wonder at the spectacular fall tapestry that lay unrolled at my feet: red, yellow, gold, the shine-purple of sumacs, brown oak, with the bone-white of trees already bare veining themselves like ghost rivers out of the flaming colored map of the forest wall.

And a moment, quite literally, was all we had to behold it, for of a sudden came in the air around us a white light and a subtle vibration, and before I could cry out to Arthur we were taken up and set down again a few blank moments later before the great silver gates I well remembered.

"I hate it when they do that," muttered Arthur, straightening his cloak and his shoulders under them.

"Aye, well, it saves on boot leather, and it was a long walk from the ship." I was suddenly, unaccountably happy, with a joy that came from everywhere at once and nowhere at all, all but buckling my knees with the force of it. And when the gates swung open soundlessly, and I saw who stood on the other side to welcome us beneath the hill, I was not a whit surprised.

Gwyn son of Nudd, prince of the Sidhe, bent his head to his guests and raised it again smiling.

"It seemed best not to make you walk all that way," he said, in the voice I knew and yet could never keep in my head, between times of our meeting.

"And we are both grateful for it," I said, with a swift sidewise glance at Arthur. "We thought there might be need of haste, that you did so."

"There is indeed, and much to be done, for now all times run short until the end." He gestured us to follow him, and we passed the gates into the Dún.

This time, unlike my last visit or even my first, the halls were full of the folk of the Dún; perhaps they had been present both those other times also, but my mortal eyes had not been permitted to behold them. I did not know. But we passed through halls and corridors that seemed not unfamiliar to me, then a chamber I knew I knew, and another and another—

"We are going to Merlynn Llwyd," I said suddenly, and certainly.

Gwyn smiled. "Ah, the memory of a bard," he said. "Take care to keep it bright and sharp, Tal-bach; it shall be needed sorely, and that soon."

With which ominous words he left us standing alone before a blank gray wall of solid granite. I glanced wildly about me, but we were alone in that place; no sense even of the Sidhe who were doubtless watching us unseen came to me, and I took a deep breath and turned back to the inconversable stone.

"It is a test," I said helpfully. "With the Sidhe, there are always tests for mortals."

"Well, you are bard," said Arthur, and for the first time in our lives I heard his voice shake just a little. "And you have been here oftener than I. Chaunt something."

Slowly I unslung Frame of Harmony, which of course

had accompanied me here, listening all the while for an unspoken word of bidding or forbidding. I cast out again with othersense to learn if it were even lawful for me to play here—though I had done so once before, among the Sidhe the rules change often and unaccountably. When I received no sign one way or the other, I sighed, and took the silence for assent, and began, as strongly as I could, to sing.

   "'Bard am I full fraught
       With aptness not to be compelled.
       Be not perverse in the court of thy ruler;
       But as to the name of the verse
       and the name of the vaunting
       and the name of the sphere
       and the name of the substance
       and the name of the speech
       and the name of the sayer,
       Let those above and those below ask in stillness,
       and receive what may be said.'"

Not perhaps my best making; but in the circumstances, quite the best that I could manage, and it served us well enough, for no sooner had the last echoes of the harp-chords died away than the stone wall became transparent before us, and then it was gone.

And behind it was that same cavern-*annat* I had visited once before, the fane where Merlynn Llwyd lay in the crystal tree that was not quite his tomb. I moved confidently forward, and Arthur followed more warily.

In the niche at the rear of the fane, all was as it had been when last I had stood in this place. Merlynn was unchanged, still entranced, or asleep, or removed, not dead if surely not alive as we are 'customed to think of it, within the prism-prison that Edeyrn Marbh-draoi had set about him. Arthur, who had not until now beheld this admittedly unnerving sight (though by leave of the Sidhe I had recounted all to him, after my rescue from Oeth-Anoeth), was as staggered as I myself had been, and every bit as deeply moved. Merlynn had been *his* teacher and protector too, not mine alone; had guarded us our first five years of life, apart, and then the next fifty together; he was part of the fabric of our very souls.

"Nay, touch not the tree," I murmured softly, as Arthur, seemingly in a trance, reached out a trembling hand to the cloudy ice of the crystal. He hesitated, then closed his fingers slowly, slowly, into a fist, and pulled his hand away.

"Not so," came a low clear voice I knew well, not Gwyn's, and both of us turned as one. Birogue of the Mountain came forward, and we bowed deeply to her as she entered the fane and looked upon her lord and mate.

"This time you are bidden set your hands to it," she said, still smiling. "For rules *do* change beneath the hill—" She gave me a wicked amused cat-look, sidewise out of astonishing silver-green eyes, and I blushed and laughed.

But she grew grave again at once. "There are things you must hear, and know, and do. And only he"—she nodded once at Merlynn's unchanged, unchanging form—"can let you to know what they might be."

Arthur's face was one great enormous question-hook, but he controlled himself nobly, and said not a syllable as Birogue took our hands by the wrists, Arthur's right and my left, harp-hand and sword-hand, and with an air of consecration and holy purpose that I had seen before, and been awed by, in the Sidhe-folk, set our hands upon the crystal tree that entombed Merlynn Llwyd.

CHAPTER 23

It was as if we had been plunged of a sudden into ard-na-spéire, the overheaven that is hyperspace. There was the same thick furry darkness, the levin-blue lightlines that netted and fretted the stars, the sourceless opalescent glow that could never be seen by straight vision, only by sidesight (and then, from out the corners of your eyes, it filled the world). But we were still beneath the hill, fast in earth, on earth, of earth. . . or so at least I presumed, for I had become utterly unaware of my body, even of my hand that seemed frozen to the crystal tree of Edeyrn's making and Merlynn's inhabiting. It seemed that we were no longer in Dún Aengus nor yet Glenshee, but in something, somewhere, more akin perhaps to a thought, a construct, a postulatum; then suddenly to anchor me I heard Arthur's voice speaking nearby, in a sort of dreamish drone.

"A time that is not a time, a place that is not a place. . . Who is it brings us here? Edeyrn or Merlynn, Dark or Light—"

The note was not strange to me of hope and disbelief in his voice rising toward terror; how not, for I had heard it sound just so in my own ears, back there in the Wood of Shapes, and in plenty of other places before and since. I did the only thing I could for both of us: I reached blindly out to my side with my free hand, to find Arthur's own, and

when I found it I grasped it and I held on hard, as he and I
had done from time to time as frighted children, back in
Daars. And neither of us took shame of the comfort; not
then, and not now.

Our joined hands must somehow have sealed the circle,
for the curtain of spark-shotten darkness seemed to turn to
silver brightness and then roll back before us; and Merlynn
Llwyd was there. Partly he stood on his feet a couple of
paces in front of us, awake, alert, all-seeing as he had ever
been in life; and partly he still lay in his enchanted sleep
within the crystal coffer (or coffin—I could not make up my
mind how to think of it). The one image of his reality, if
such it was, seemed to change and pulse and shift through
the other, like a thing seen doubly through water or a diamond or blowing smoke.

But the voice was all unchanged; nor, it seemed, was the
inhabiting spirit any the less for its strange sojourn.

"Ard-rígh, Pen-bardd—" Then, warmer: "Artos, Talyn,
do not be afraid! Only keep your hands upon the crystal,
and in each other's, so that I may continue to speak, and
you to hear."

"Athro?" That was Arthur, hesitant, wanting desperately to
believe, yet fearing that to believe were a joy beyond all hope
even of wishing, much less of attaining. "Is it you, truly?"

"Who else?" came the well-remembered testy flash, and
in spite of my awe I laughed aloud, for just so had the
vision-Merlynn spoken to me on quest in that nighttime
wood, beside the fountain where things happened; and I
reflected yet again that some things are in one's essential
nature and change no whit upon the other shore; well, at
least not straightway. And this I found rather more comforting than not. But Merlynn was speaking again.

"I have leave to speak here but little time," he said. "So
let us not squander that which has been allotted us. Aye, it
is I, and aye again, it is you—both of you—and so let us
take the thing as read. Now. Arthur, hear me."

And Arthur leaned forward, though his booted feet did
not move upon the stone; more a yearning forward, a moving into his arm that still stretched rigid between the crystal
and himself.

"When last you were here," said Merlynn, in an utterly familiar (and tiresome) tone of didactical reminder, "you were offered certain things by Nudd who is king beneath the hill. And of those Treasures you took only the one, to aid you in the fight against the Marbh-draoi."

"Aye," said Arthur. "Fragarach I took, the Answerer, the great sword of divine forging; and left the other Hallows here. It did not seem their time to come away. And then the Cup was stolen by my sister, and I have wished often that I had accepted that at least when offered it, so that the theft could have been prevented."

"Nothing and no one could have prevented it," said Merlynn. "Let your mind be at ease on that account. And a greater good came of your declining. . . But as Talyn and the others learned at Caervanogue, the Hallows have dán of their own even as souls do, a quest of their own to fulfill. Today you must take them from here, and when you leave Keltia, as you are very soon now about to do, you must take them with you."

He must have seen, or sensed, the instant incredulous refusal in Arthur's face—for surely I sensed it in Arthur's hand—for he shook his head and smiled.

"Nay, I speak correctly"—and that was purest Merlynn—"and I will not be doubted. It is dán, as I have told you. They came to Keltia, the Treasures, with Brendan and Nia, as did the Kelts themselves. And now it is their time to go from Keltia, with you and your Companions upon your last venturing."

" 'Last'?" echoed Arthur after a rather packed silence. But he did not seem surprised, nor even much distressed; seemed somehow to have known this was someday to come, and now it had. It was not even a matter for his acceptance; you might as easily say that *it* had accepted *him*. . .

Merlynn read our doubts; never had there been any hiding things from our Ailithir. "They shall return to Keltia one day, right enough. Brought back by one whose own dán shall be to do so. . . But for you yourself, and those who sail with you, no returning. Seven alone shall return from Caer Sidi."

And as he spoke those words I felt with a great inner

gasp and shiver the wings of the Holy Awen brush against
my soul, those mighty pinions beating upon a chill wind out
of an unimaginable future; felt a great work being seeded
somewhere far within me, as a child takes root in a woman's
womb, to be born in its own good time or ill. And that too
was dán.

"It is all part of the same seeking, the same quest," said
Merlynn, "this sailing that shall be, and the return that shall
come of it. And even that shall not be the end of it. You
have Seen it yourselves, long since."

At that my knees gave way all but entirely, for I minded
me well of that long-ago Seeing, and of what each of us had
Seen. . . Apparently Arthur remembered also, for he had
startled likewise, his hand suddenly spasming, clutching
mine, until I felt the stab and pinch of the seal ring he wore,
the great emerald Athyn Cahanagh had had of Morric
Douglas cutting into my flesh.

"In Daars," said Arthur, in a drowned voice. "Talyn and
I, in our little schoolroom—we had hoped and begged and
badgered to see magic, and you lessoned us well by showing
us some we wished we had never clapped eyes upon. You
remember, Talynno." It was not a question, and he did not
pause for my assent, seeming to sense it through my
crushed fingers. "A dry harsh plain on an outfrenne world,
a red sky; and out of that sky a dark-green ship, a starship,
falling like an arrow straight into the flaming throat of a firemount."

He was silent a long moment, then raised his head and
brought his glance across Merlynn's like a blade.
"Prydwen," said Arthur. "My ship. My dán. Is that then the
end?"

Merlynn smiled, the old smile of Ailithir whom we loved.
"Certainly it is not! There is no end to such matters as
these—have I taught you nothing at all, and have you
learned less even than that?"

"But of us, athro?" I asked humbly. "*Our* end?
Ourselves?"

"Not in a thousand thousand lifetimes," came the cool
clear voice of Birogue, whom we had not known was still
present in this—whatever this was, vision or ashling or

marana. She moved forward to take her place beside
Merlynn who was her mate, and I blinked to clear my sight,
for—as in the Wood of Seeming, as in Ashnadarragh which
was the Place of the Oak, as upon the strand
Garanwynion—there came a wavering and a shimmering,
and I Saw upon those two I loved and revered as soulpar-
ents the duality of the fiala come down, in likenesses of Two
I loved and worshipped as Makers. . .

"It goes on, Pen-bardd," said Birogue, knowing what I
Saw; and making a gesture of showing with her hand; with
Her hand.

And as I had in that schoolroom, as I had at
Cadarachta, as I had once here in this very Dún, I Saw-
past, oh, far, far into the future, down along the track of
years. Saw again, as I had Seen at Nandruidion, that one of
whom Merlynn had just now spoken, the one to come
whose certain dán would be to return to Keltia the Hallows
that our dán in Keltia was yet to have us bear away; saw
her come to them in their distant longtime home, out of her
own desperate need—and knew, awed afresh, that I would
be the one to send her after them, so that she might fetch
them back. Again I saw her face, a look of Grehan about
her, and of Tarian, and of Arthur and Morgan and
Gweniver and myself and even of Majanah; and above all
the look of a queen and a sorceress. . .

I drew back shaking all over, almost severing the link; but
throughout my Seeing I had kept my hand fixed upon the
crystal treetrunk as if nailed there, and I kept it there now.

"I charge you both," said Merlynn then, "none must
know where the Treasures are bestowed when once they
come there; none save we three here, and Gweniver and
Morgan and Ygrawn, and Gwyn Prince of the Sidhe. This
great secret must be kept, so that she who must redeem
them shall come to them as dán decrees—hers and theirs
and yours alike."

"But how shall she know where she must go to find
them, if the place be secret-kept?" asked Arthur, and his
voice seemed stronger than before, stronger than it had been
since this whole strange encounter had begun.

"Gwyn shall give her the word of them," said Birogue

simply. "The word that he shall receive of you, Talyn. We do not forget."

And again I shivered as under a cold blast out of Northplain with the awe that was upon me, and turning I met Arthur's eyes, which were just now as wide dark pools in the paleness of his face. Each knew what the other was thinking: Not only would word of what we did be passed to this longtime-descended queen, but Gwyn would give her that word himself, in his own person to her in her own person. He, who had been our friend in our time, would be hers in her own, so long-lived were the Folk of the Shining, and so young was he yet in the counting of their years.

"He will be king himself by that age," said Merlynn, who had been watching our faces. "Even kings of the Sidhe do come at last to their reigns' ending, as Nudd shall do—aye, and Gwyn after him."

"And you, athro?" I burst out, suddenly unable to bear another instant of this, it was too much for me, *too* fraught with dán. "Will you be there too for her, or them?"

But for the first time since I had known him, Merlynn Llwyd evaded a direct question. Oh, to be sure, plenty of times he had not-answered my askings, in that little way of his, but always he had done so with an answer of sorts. Not this asking; and that was yet another thing to puzzle at. . .

"Even shall I dwell in this house of glass," he said, "and the Thirteen Treasures be taken from here; even shall Arthur sleep in the island Afallinn, with his Companions round him, until such time as he comes again; and even shall seven alone return from Caer Rigor."

Caer Sidi, Caer Rigor—again I felt the Awen moving somewhere far away, felt a mighty sandal set on stone; but I had suddenly minded me of another thing, a different thing, a thing I had read of and wondered on greatly—

"Athro, when you and my mother came to me that night, in my vision in the Wood of Shapes," I began, halting-voiced, "I had not yet learned what true-treasure she had left for me. Oh, not the jewels and trinkets, though they are most fair, and knowing that she wore them and loved them means much to me; but rather the books and words and writings. For she too, it seems, was bard: Some of those writings were her own, but other some had been of others' making, that she had written down for their truth or their beauty or their wisdom. And in these last was—was Arthur spoken of, and all we beside."

I half-heard Arthur's gasp beside me, felt the startled pull of his hand in mine, saw Birogue's slow lovely smile; but I pressed on, for this matter had troubled me long and greatly, and I knew well that this might be the only chance I should ever have in all my lives to learn the truth of it. I had never before even dared speak of it; had not shown those particular writings to Morgan or Gerrans, even, much less to Artos or to Gwen or to Ygrawn. Yet were they all written down therein; it was a mystery, and I would have it solved now and here.

"She—my mother said most carefully that they were but tales she recounted," I went on, after a moment. "Others had made them, she wrote, but she so loved them that she would record them to read again to herself in her new home of Keltia, lest they be forgot. They were tales of the folk, and bards' work too, some of them; but all had the common thread: that they spoke of Arthur as King, by name, as if all men did know that name. Spoke of you, Merlynn the great sorcerer; and Gweniver, and Morgan—even of me!"

I paused again, for my voice had begun to tremble, and however understandable that may have been for Taliesin, not so for a bard and Pen-bardd.

"So I ask you now," I continued after a while, "how came the Lady Cathelin to know these things, to know of *us*—she who came to Keltia long before most of us were even born, much less named or crowned or chaired as bard or wizard? How came Earth to have tales of us here in Keltia centuries before we ever even *were*? Athro?"

The living, speaking Merlynn faded briefly, and the sleeping Merlynn shone strongly through, as a pulse-star will do far in its corner of space; then they were once more as they had been.

"Those tales your mother loved so on Earth and brought with her to Keltia," said Merlynn, and I all but died at the gentleness in his voice, "were not tales of things as they had been but things as they would be."

His face had taken on a look I had seldom seen upon it since my childhood, as if he would reach out to comfort me, hold me safe in his embrace; as sometimes, indeed, he had done—as my parents had not lived long enough to do. But he was speaking again, and I strained to follow, desperate to learn.

"The stories your mother copied down into her books were stories only to the main of the folk of Earth, and remained so; but to those whose knowing went deeper they were a *prophecy*. A prophecy Seen by one of us, just before that time when Brendan led out Gael and Danaan together from Earth in search of a place he was not sure existed. And that prophecy was spun into tales and fireside legends and nursery-lore by those—and not Kelts only—who lingered behind when the immrama began. Therefore are the names the same, and the titles, and the deeds: a story on Earth, but a prophecy for Keltia. And, as prophecies are wont to do, in the course of dán some things did change as the years and folks' choices worked upon them. Lies were told, truths bent out of plumb, facts altered. But always the basic fabric remained intact and untorn, for the weave was true and the loom was Kelu's."

"And then the Lady Cathelin came here," said Birogue, in the same soft voice that Merlynn had used, "and she it was by whom the prophecy was set into motion. And so we came to stand here today; there is no Uncaused Cause but the One. All things else, aye, even of the Goddess and the God Who work Kelu's will through Their own, are made. Take comfort in that, both you, here and when you go out from here; as soon you must."

I closed my eyes, dropped my head back upon my neck and took a long, precisely drawn breath that seemed to reach down to my toes. Now I had not known, I admit, *quite* what to expect when I had asked my question of Merlynn Llwyd; but I do know, certain sure, that I had not been expecting anything even remotely like this for answer. And yet I did not doubt—nor, I could see, did Arthur—not for the least littlest instant. The ring of truth was in it all: I heard it in my old teacher's voice, and in Birogue's, and above all I knew I had heard it in my mother's words.

"Dán's hand is over many worlds," said Birogue, still softly. "To bring the Lady Cathelin together with the Lord Gwyddno, when she met him on that desperate brave journey of his to Earth; to cause them to love; to move her to follow him here to Keltia, to be his ban-charach and to give birth to you; to link with the dán that was unfolding here for so many others, Amris and Ygrawn and Uthyr and Leowyn and Gweniver and all the rest, and the Marbh-draoi being a prime worker of that dán even as was Cathelin of the other strand of the story—and all the long rolling tale set into motion, as it has been centuries past. And now it sends you from Keltia, as it brought Cathelin to Keltia: sends you to Afallinn, many to perish, seven to return—and one to go and return again long ages hence. In that you may rest secure."

"A tomb that is not a tomb," said Merlynn, his voice seeming to chime with his lady's. "An isle that is not an isle. . . Powers shall sleep and not sleep; you and I, Arthur, shall both wake, though not wake alike. And in the Mysteries there shall be not breach nor break. The Graal will be served again; indeed, it will never cease to be served."

As he spoke I could see another fiala coming upon him, and for an instant his countenance was the countenance of Loherin, Graalkeeper, Guardian of the Gates; and then the face of Avallac'h his predecessor; and then in swift succession the faces of others I did not know, man and woman alike, all keepers and guardians of Caervanogue in time past or ages yet to be. And then he was once more Merlynn, and by his smile I knew our time together was all but run.

"Nay, do not think of it so!" he said, knowing the weight, the staggering weight, of the sorrow that was suddenly on us. "We shall meet many times more, doubt it not. And even when you doubt it, for doubt you will, even then do you believe."

Merlynn raised his hands, palms facing out to us, then reached out from the crystal, or across it, to touch our heads in blessing, his left hand upon Arthur's, his right upon mine. And yet he still lay within the crystal treetrunk as Edeyrn had ensorcelled him, all those years ago at Nandruidion, when the Boar had been hunted by Gwyn himself. . .

And then he was gone, and we were fallen to our knees with the speed and surprise and grief of it; and standing beside Birogue, who was now behind us as earlier she had been, was that Hunter, that prince.

Gwyn ap Nudd smiled, and coming forward lifted us both from where we sprawled dazed as children upon the stone floor of the fane.

"Come, m'charai," he said, in that viol-voice of deep beauty which bards could only envy. "We have much yet to do before you go out from the hill."

And so we went to do it. First of all we were conducted to the great throne-room we so well remembered from our first visit to this Dún, silver-walled and golden-roofed. The crystal throne of Nudd the King stood empty at the far end, no faerie courtier attended upon it or us; but Gwyn and Birogue gave sanction to our errand here, and together we took from its curtained niche aside the throne that ancient carved wood chest which held the Hallows; all save Fragarach, and that would we collect when we were once more at Caerdroia. Even the Cup was here, and I gave it a hard suspicious eyeing before I closed the lid upon it, half-thinking to see it fly up in the air for another such antic as it had put on once before.

I do not recall how we bore the chest away with us, through the halls and corridors of the Dún; but suddenly I found us all standing without that chamber wherein lay my mother's grave, and with no words, eyes only, I sought permission of Gwyn and Birogue to visit her restplace one last time.

Pacing round the broad pool of mirror-silver water, I halted before the polished plate of stone that had been let into the cavern's natural rock, the marker she had, behind which she lay, or all that was mortal of her lay.

And standing there, staring at the simple carven slab, touching with trembling fingers the letters of her name, I suddenly thought how better it was for her that she should lie here, far removed from all earthly visitors. Even with the best will in the world, they would have made a pollution and a circus-place of her grave, had she been laid to rest in more usual surrounds. Because of the singularity that was her own, her tomb would have been a curiosity for ape-mouthed strangers to stand round and leer and gape at, or worse; her peace, and that of her loving kindred, and above all others' that of her beloved, would have been shattered beyond all bearing.

Nay—this solitude was cleaner, better, higher; this peace was alone what she deserved. And any road she was not here—not the Cathelin who mattered, the Cathelin who was real, the woman who had lived and loved and risked and died.

And suddenly I wished to leave something of mine here, something I loved, to be with her always and never to be taken away. After a moment's puzzling, I smiled with certainty and lifted from around my neck the gold chain Arthur had crafted for me so long ago, and the gold locket that depended from it: the case that held the gray hawk's feather which had been my mother's first gift to me of all the gifts to come, save life alone.

I held the gold case clenched a moment in my fist, willing into it all my love and loss and blessing, then raised it to my lips and kissed it. And then I hooked the chain upon the corners of the slab of stone that bore my mother's name, so that the gold locket in hawk-feather shape hung just below that name chiselled a finger-length deep into the rock: Cathelin. Ban-charach of Gwyddno Glyndour; Lady of Gwaelod; mother to Taliesin, matemother to Morguenna, dama-wyn to Geraint; a woman of Earth, and of Keltia also.

When I looked aside at Arthur, who had followed me in a few moments since, his face was streaming with tears, though his features were as iron.

"It is well bestowed," he said gently. "My honor, to have crafted it to find so fitting a lodgement."

"It is a good place," I agreed, suddenly lighter of heart than I had felt for many, many years.

"And here it shall remain," said Gwyn, who stood now with Birogue behind Arthur, on the ledge beside the pool. "For as long as our folk do dwell beneath this roof and hill."

He waited courteously with Birogue until I had finished

my last farewells (Arthur too did reverence to this woman he had never known, who had played even in her absence so vast a part in all our story), and then led the way out of the chamber, so that I was last to leave. Never would I, or any other mortal, return here; and I for one was glad of that.

The rest of our duties were quickly accomplished: We bade greeting and farewell alike to Nudd himself and Seli his queen—not in the throne-room, but in a smaller hall, and alone—and to Allyn son of Midna, whom I had met in the Wood of Tiaquin and who (an-da-shalla told me) would have part in the coil to come; and now we stood with Gwyn and Birogue and the Hallows in their chest before the silver gates that led back to the world.

"The stream of dán is running swift now," said Birogue. "Taliesin, we shall meet again ere you launch your curragh from it. Arthur, not again in this life." She held out her hand, and Arthur went to one knee and kissed it, and she laid her other hand upon his bent dark head in blessing.

He rose, his countenance unreadable, and we turned as one to Gwyn.

"Have no fear for these," he said, nodding once at the chest which held the Treasures. "I shall be here to send their seeker on their track, and shall greet them and her with them when she brings them again home. I shall be with her, after, in the time of her great need and testing, and when he who sleeps below has awakened again to the worlds. She will be their savior, and they shall be hers. Be comforted, King in the Light; after loss and bitter pain, great joy."

"My days as King are drawing to a close," said Arthur without a trace of self-pity, merely as simple statement of fact. "And yours are yet to begin; shall our reigns never be destined to run in pace?"

"You shall never not rule as King of Kelts," said Gwyn. "For all reigns to come, monarchs in Keltia shall take their thrones in your name, make their laws in your name, fight their wars in your name. King once, king ever, king that shall be."

He gave Arthur the straight-armed salute of the Fianna,

hand to shoulder; and as his hand came down upon
Arthur's cloak the familiar spin and dazzle came with it, and
we found ourselves outside in the gray dawnlight of what
day we did not know. The little aircar in which we had
flown from Caerdroia was close by, and the Hallows were
safe in their chest at our feet.

We lifted the chest into the cabin, sealed the door after
one last look back at the blank gray flank of the Hill of Fare,
and headed west ahead of the rising sun. Neither of us ever
saw Dún Aengus again.

CHAPTER 24

The very first thing Arthur did upon our arriving back in Turusachan was to place the Hallows, still within their gold-bound ironoak coffer and now joined by the Sword Fragarach, into a place of safe hiding, a niche where he could feel reasonably certain that they would remain concealed and undisturbed, until such time as they must depart with us; as had been so frequently and so wearisomely told us. The niche where he bestowed them was behind the Throne of Scone, in the findruinna-gated vestibule where the Nantosvelta debouched into the Hall of Heroes; belike the safest place in all Keltia.

And he might have thought more than once or twice about joining them there until that much-mentioned departure, for the second thing Arthur did upon returning to Turusachan was to formally declare Malgan Rheged his son.

Oh, strictly speaking, he did not have to trouble himself even so much as that: As soon as Malgan's proofs had been submitted to those whose task it is to judge in such matters, the thing would have been done anyway, and Arthur need not have lifted a finger. But Arthur had never been one to shirk the truth or brook a lie, and I think this matter of Malgan's delayed recognition had weighed heavily upon him all these years, so that he hastened now to make what amends he might.

But though the reaction of the realm varied from outrage to yawns, one there was from whom Arthur might have done well to hide himself along with the Hallows in the Nantosvelta: Gweniver. He told her first in private, of course, and what went on behind closed doors between those two in that moment is something none of us shall ever know. But her public reaction, and even her private display of feeling to her kin and friends, was a matter of record: Gweniver was incandescent with fury, at least at first. But when cooler and more disinterested souls pointed out to her that mere acknowledgment of fatherhood did not of necessity constitute any alteration in the Tanistry, and that in fact Malgan himself had disavowed all wish to displace his young halfbrother Arawn in the succession, Gwen seemed to grow rather less angered than resigned. But of course she might have been fozing us all; although that had never been Gweniver's way.

Whatever Arthur had hoped to accomplish with this declaration, though, it cannot have been achieved; for, scarce a fortnight later, Malgan joined Marguessan and Mordryth in a declaration of their own: civil war.

"And not civil merely," Tarian was saying to a hastily assembled meeting of the inner Company, "but she has hired outfrenne mercenaries to fight for her, as did Edeyrn Marbh-draoi aforetimes."

"Doubtless contracted through those offworlders you saw, Talyn, at Caer Dathyl and Saltcoats," put in Grehan. "They are not now so shy of showing themselves with her, and boast brazenly of how they will be well rewarded for their actions."

"All in a day's labor for folk of that sort. They are trash, and lower than pig-offal in the great plan of dán," said Ysild of Kernow, who had been here visiting at Tara when the strife broke out on Gwynedd. "We have before now crumbled better than they like crackers into soup; we can deal with these out of hand, surely."

"All most true." I rose in my place, for I had certain information that none here yet knew, not even Tari or

Grehan, and I had been instructed by Gweniver—not present but closeted with Arthur and Ygrawn—to impart it to the Companions. I looked across the chamber Gwahanlen to the tapestry of King Cadivor and Juthahelo, and drew a deep breath.

"There is word received from our trading planet of Clero, and I am bidden by the Ard-rían tell you all: Raids have been made on our settlements there, and prisoners taken; and it is the Fomori and the Fir Bolg who do so." I lifted a hand for silence against the excited angry babble that ensued, and it died away like a stream drying up in the hills in drought-time. "And there is worse: Marguessan has brought the Coranians into this. They it is who will be coming against us here."

I did not have to ask for silence now: The chamber was of a sudden still as a burrow of coneys with a weasel coming up the run. For the Coranians were, past all doubt, the paramount king-stoats of the known galaxy. We were well acquent with them of old, of course: In truth, the Coranians (or Telchines, as they were then) were the chiefest reason for the Kelts (or Danaans, as we were then) leaving Earth. So far back, indeed, did the long enmity have its roots in bloody ground. . .

For myself, I was only surprised that they had waited so long before moving against us. Plenty of occasion, in all the years of Arthur's and Gweniver's reign, for them to have struck at less cost to themselves. . . And even Edeyrn, who had not scrupled to hire any buyable race he could offer coin to, had balked at purchasing the services of the Coraniaid—or perhaps they had merely scorned to take coin for a thing they would sooner do for sheer joy's sake. Therefore had they not been—unlike the Fir Bolg and Fomori and so many more—on Arthur's roster of races to be chastised, when we went out in that first great reiving in Prydwen, so long ago.

But it seemed they were come against us now, right enough, and Marguessan it was who had invited them to do so. . .

And they would be formidable enemies when they came; but that would not be for a while yet. Our most immediately

pressing problem was the uprising on Gwynedd that
Marguessan had launched last night. All at once I was
struck by the killing irony, and glancing at Morgan I saw the
same thought on her also: Once, *we* were the ones who had
launched rebellion and civil strife on Gwynedd, to strike
against the master of Keltia; we had done against the
Marbh-draoi, and now we were being done against as we
had done ourselves.

But there the resemblance ended: The Marbh-draoi had
been Keltia's great enemy, and the Counterinsurgency had
been indisputably correct to have vowed to bring him
down. This thing with my matesister and my fostern's son
was cloth of a whole other weaving; and even now
Gweniver and Arthur were forging the shears to cut it to
their pattern.

"At least they have not gone against the Protectorates,"
Tarian was saying. "For that we can be thankful, if for little
else; and here is where we shall most miss Keils."
Murmured sorrow and agreement. "For more needs than
one. . . But here is how I see it—"

Swiftly she outlined her plans for our assault on
Gwynedd—strange just *how* swiftly the sophisticated, diplo-
matist Taoiseach of decades' service fell back into the gait
and garb of catteran warlord—and just so smoothly did
Grehan Aoibhell move to her side, as they had done so oft
of old.

I was less sanguine and inspired, I am nothing loath to
tell you. It seemed to me that we had earned better than this
over the years; this outfall and upshot were naught that we
had merited of the lords of dán, for all that we had done we
deserved better in return. I was by no means alone in so
thinking; but it is never good and rarely profitable to blame
dán—see that you follow not my deplorable lead—and any
road sulking in my tent was no answer.

Certainly no answer Arthur wanted: He sat now across
the table Rhodaur from me, having just joined us from his
private session with Ygrawn and Gwennach, and I could tell
by his silence and his countenance he knew just exactly
what I was thinking, and loved it not at all. *How then?* I sent
to him sullenly. *Would you rather I seemed to be having a fine*

time of it here? Are you? But no answer came back to me by
any form of speech.

Tari and Grehan had finished their detailing of the pre-
liminary strategy for our riposte to Marguessan—local
forces first to contain, then an expedition in strength to
crush; nothing gaudy—and had paused to look expectantly
at Arthur where he sat with his chin in his hand and his
elbow on the arm of his chair. He was staring at the huge
holomap that shimmered in the center of the hollow space
in the table's ring; then he stirred and seemed to come back
to himself, rising to speak as if this were merely one of a
thousand dull Council sessions down the years.

"In the old days, our wisdom held it best that when con-
fronted with two enemies of unequal strength we should attack
the stronger first," he began. "Well, we were younger then"—
comfortable chuckles ran round at the shared memories—
"and perhaps our *traha* served us better than we knew. But to
do the same here and now is, I deem, little better than self-
slaughter." No chuckles now; Arthur shivered head to foot,
and went on at once. "So. We go first against Marguessan on
Gwynedd, to clear our rear ere we venture out; then meet the
Coranians as they sail in, if they still choose to do so. After,
if there is need and we yet may, on to Fomor and Kaireden
of the Fir Bolg." The druid-power he so seldom used flared
out now, to touch with fire an area of Gwynedd I remembered well from my bardic spy-jaunts. "Here. First. The
ridge of Kellanvore is where we shall engage my sister and
her forces. And Elen Llydawc shall command."

Elen Llydawc, Elen of the Hosts. . . I looked where the
map was glowing brightest: a place called Barrendown.
Then looked round the table Rhodaur, and was struck chill
to the heart, remembering. We here had shared and survived the end of the beginning, when we fought Edeyrn and
won; now we had come at last to the beginning of the end,
where we must fight Edeyrn's last and greatest pupil. And
what then? I denied, of course; but I already knew.

Morgan was more than usually subdued as we went to bed
that night; more than usually loving, also, as we found com-

fort each in the other—perhaps the last time we would lie together for many days to come. When she still would not speak, I shook her playfully, but she could not be chaffed nor coaxed from her mood.

"What is it?" I asked presently. "You know we shall be returning here to Tara, once Marguessan and her offworld vermin are swept into the great midden of dán and defeat. We shall not go out against the Coranians and the rest without first seeing our dear ones here before we go. What is on you? Is it your sister? Cariad o'nghariad, we all of us knew this day would come some time to be faced, and fairly faced too. . ."

"Aye," she said, after a very long, very troubled silence, "but perhaps not *as* it has come." She shivered a little against my side, moved deeper into the curve of my arm. "Barrendown," she said then, and I could tell by her tone that Sight had taken her far from our warm firelit bedchamber. "Dragon shall fight dragon, not for the first time nor yet the last. Ships in a dead sea. . . Two parts of my life have gone, and two parts of your own. Have you news from the Gate?"

With that she went small and lash against me, and did not stir. After a while, to make sure she was deep asleep, I lifted her gently onto her own pillows and pulled the coverlets up around her bare shoulders, settling back again on my own side of the great bed. But I courted sleep no whit just yet.

In her usual fashion of saying little more than nothing, Morgan had given me just now much to think on. Barrendown. It was the name I had seen on the map in Gwahanlen—the hill by the mountain ridge Kellanvore, where Artos had pronounced we should face Marguessan; no surprise there. Yet what had Morgan Seen, to pronounce of her own so direly? I did not like at all the sound of that saying of how two parts of our lives had gone; and nor was the rest of much greater cheer. And what that Gate was I did not even dare to think.

And, not-thinking, I fell asleep at last; and in the morning Morgan was herself, no sign of having ever been aught other. She would not have shown it even had it been so, for we were all but ready now to sail to Gwynedd, and by her own request she was to stay behind with Gweniver. And that was a thing so at variance with what all who knew her had expected as to cause dire mouthings and frettings among the folk.

Even Arthur had been surprised, though he had instantly granted her asking, only glad to have her with Gwen and Ygrawn to hold Tara against any chance comers. But none of us, I think, guessed her real reasons; not even I, my shame and everlasting sorrow to say. Had we known, had I but guessed—perhaps what was later to come of it had been averted. But that was only hindsight; we all of us see like eagles when that is the eye we look through. . .

No matter how many times I ventured into space, never, it seemed, would I ever grow 'customed to the sight of my worlds when they could be seen *as* worlds: fantastic spheres hanging brilliant and astonishing in the dark spangled void. Or even going in, diving down into atmosphere: seeing the red rolling deserts of southern Gwynedd where none had ever dwelled; farther north, the forested uplands with trees strewn like dark sand along the hill-edges; clouds like towers reaching up to us, like great ships with all sails set, sails of silver and hulls of dark blue iron; so lovely.

Arthur made some small noncommittal grunt when I spoke of this: All *his* attention was already focused not on the beauty of the lands beneath but on their suitability for a fight; and so it should be. These were lands we both knew well, that all our force knew well: Most of those on the ships of the fleet behind Prydwen were old Companions and aux-iliars of the campaigns, or Gwyneddans themselves; they did not need to be told twice of Marguessan's likely dispositions. They had fought this ground before, and please Goddess, would be spared to fight it again if so it must be.

I was for my part a little surprised, and unpleasantly so, to see just how impressive a force Marguessan had already assembled. The lines of her leaguer, clearly visible from space, were extensive and at the same time compact; she had had good advice, then, for she was naught of a soldier

of herself, and Irian her lord was less a warrior even than
she. Someone, though, had experience of these lands. . .

"Malgan," said Arthur, looking at me as at a dotty old
grandsir who needed to be reminded of his own name.
"Who else? He grew up here with Gwenar and Owein, and
I doubt me he stayed tucked away at Saltcoats all that
time."

"But those are galláin troops she works with!"

"So? What of it? Any trooper, even a gall, can learn with
speed a new ground, sith that he is paid enough to make it
worth his time, or cares enough to look after his own life.
My sister"—now he sounded just like Morgan, and I startled to hear it—"has never been ungenerous to those she
thinks she can do her better or greater service than she does
them. Besides, you yourself told me she had outfrenne
help."

"I did." I was silent, thinking of that 'help.' Those outworlders I had seen at Caer Dathyl and at Saltcoats, and
before: that scranbag of feiching sharnclouts, Tembrual and
Rannick, Granúmas and—what was his foul-fared name—
Redshield, Sleir Venoto and the gricemite mac Ffreswm.
There were goleor more, very like, who had aided
Marguessan, who did so still; but these six were the ones I
most longed to gralloch. I am not known for a man of wrath,
as having read thus far you will no doubt attest; yet I say to
you, and you will believe my saying it, that these and a few
more I could cheerfully have filleted with a dull fork and fed
to the hogs, save that such an end would have been both too
swift and too merciful, and such a diet like to have put the
hogs off their feed forevermore. I brightened: Perhaps justice
might not altogether be denied me; for who could say, after
all, how the fight to come might not play out? Malen Ruadh,
goddess of war and lawful avenging, might yet smile her
favor upon me. . .

We landed at Kellanvore, the great mountain wall running
up to the Havren range that divides the empty provinces of
Sarre and Pontrilas, northeast of Caer Dathyl. We had seldom fought so far east in the campaign for Gwynedd

against Owein Rheged—well, we of the Company, any road;
it had been others' lot to fight in the eastern shires, while
Artos was making himself master in Arvon—and the country was less familiar than we liked.

The onetime master of Arvon paid it no mind. Though
Arthur had valiantly studied to keep his countenance grave
and cryptical of what thoughts and feelings did lie behind,
twice or thrice now I had surprised upon his face that look I
knew so well of old: the look that had gotten us into
Glenanaar and out of Talgarth, the look that had won
Cadarachta and willed Caerdroia. Truth to tell, I was not
sorry to see it—it might well be that look alone which would
triumph for us here—but all the same it filled me with a certain, all-too-familiar dread.

Others too: Tarian, who had accompanied us, spoke to
me privily of her own like misgivings; Alannagh Ruthven,
as well, had a narrow look in her astonishing green-blue
eyes; and goleor more of the Companions who had seen in
Arthur what we had seen, the which we all had rather noted
than liked. But when I spoke hesitantly of it to Arthur, I
found him unexpectedly loquent withal.

"Well, it *is* like old times," he said, and there was naught
of defensiveness in his voice, but only surprise that I should
be so wary. "But Talyn, do not you or the others ever forget: I am fighting my own sister here. Aye, and her son, and
my son. . . That I should wish to get through this as best I
might should come as no surprise to any who have ridden
with me as long as you lot have done."

"Nay, Artos," I began, abashed and heartsore for him.
"We are not *surprised,* just so—it is only that we are, well,
somewhat feared for you. And feared too for what is coming."

"Who is coming, you mean," said Arthur darkly. "And
well you might be. No matter, Talyn. I have a trick or two
prepared against them. But—"

"But?" I echoed in sudden terror, and he smiled a true
smile this time.

"We both know, I think, what is to come of this," he said
quietly and with a certain calm joy. "We have been told so
often enough, by tellers who speak only truth. Nor is it so ill a

way to take our leave, after all we have seen and done and
been and had. Is it?"

"Nay," I said after a while, to my great surprise, for I
found that as usual Arthur had the right of it; and besides I
too had heard those tellings he spoke of. "It is not. Nor will
it be, when it comes. But not, I think, here."

"Nay," he agreed after a pause of his own. "Not here. Not
for us."

The Battle of Barrendown, as it came to be known in the
war-lists, was joined two mornings after our landing by
Kellanvore. Thanks to Marguessan's hasty wholesale
importings of mercenary talent, our forces met on almost
equal footing; well, at least as far as mere numbers went.
Also, sad to relate, some few—blessedly few—of the
Companions and auxiliars we had trained and ridden with
and fought beside had chosen for reasons of their own to
sell their swords to Marguessan. Had acknowledged her as
Ard-rían, even, and Mordryth as Tanist and Malgan as
Prince of the Name; and that bit deeper than all. But the
greater part remained loyal to Gweniver and Arthur. To
their Ard-rígh, aye; but still more, and always, to their
Artos.

And it told in the fight, indeed and truly. Even so, the
battle raged for four days and nights together; and many
fell. Chiefly outfrenne fighters, I am pleased to report; the
bought dogs of Marguessan stood against the Companions
no better than Edeyrn's Ravens had stood when it came to
it, and for the most part very much worse. Still, we suffered
losses too; if none of name or note that you would recognize
and grieve for, yet they were ours, and we could ill spare
them, and we lamented.

It was on the morning of the fourth day of fighting that I
got my heart's wish of that strife: Leading a small party of
heavy horse in support of Elen's war-chariots—even more
than Tarian had Elen Llydaw authored this battle, and
already out of it, as Arthur before them, they had begun to
call her Elen Llydawc, Elen of the Hosts—I came quite by
chance upon a small company of galláin, led, I was so

happy to see, by none other than Tembrual Phadaptë and Phayle Redshield. And nor were their comrades in iniquity very far distant; certainly not too distant to feel the weight of my arm. . . And for one of the very few times in all my life as a warrior—and you will of your grace remember that, circumstances aside, the life of the blade was never my calling—I was seized by the battle-fury, the gae catha, the Red Mist of Doing that comes over one on the instant and can only be lifted by blood.

So I sought some, the blood to ease my heart, galláin blood, traitors' blood, vermin's blood. Alannagh, who rode as my lieutenant, told me afterwards that she had actually halted in her own tracks to stare with wonder and horror equally at what I then did; but I do not recall the act, only the results. The Red Mist of Doing was upon me; and when at last it no longer veiled my sight and ruled my deeds, and I could gaze, uncomprehending and stupid as a noontide owl, at what I had wrought, I could scarce believe it, any more than could Alannagh or the others in our riding.

I do remember slaying Tembrual, perhaps because she was the one who had galled me (pun intended) the most. Seeing our oncoming, she had turned to flee like the coward she was—bullies never stand up to a fair fight, that is what makes them bullies in the first place—but in my gae I had no compunction and less pity (and would have had none even in cold blood), and I cut her down from behind as she deserved, so all would know her for coward by her wounds. Scarce was her head rolling amidst the horses' flashing hoofs than I was riding grimly on to deal likewise with Phayle, then with Rannick, then with. . . One by one, Marguessan's six outfrenne henchmen fell beneath my dripping bright blade where it bit; and it bit often, and deeply, and redly, and where it bit it killed.

When I had at last been forsaken by the gae, or it had moved on to find another so hospitable to its indwelling as I had just now been, I leaned on my sword for support and stared satisfied upon my handiwork. It had been too easy: spearing fish in a weir. In the end, none of them had put up the least sort of proper fight, which told you right there what sort of creature they were—as if there had ever been doubt. Indeed, Kiar mac Ffreswm had whined like a hedgepig for his sorry little life, before I let it out for him; and the slorach Sleir Venoto had loosed his guts in his terror, soiling his breeks, before my sword separated him and his innards from further activity. The little ape-thing, Granúmas, I had neatly and simply quartered; his hairy scrawny limbs lay strewn across the field, you could track his coward's flight by how they had fallen.

You may perhaps think me harsh and cruel and vengeful for this; evil, even. But I will not accept that judgment. They had brought their ends upon themselves, with their lying ways and their betrayals and their easy simple lust for gold and power. Heedless of honor, willfully perverting the truth, of their own will and choice they would not learn. So I, of *my* own will and choice, had merely sent them along, expeditiously, to another, higher schoolroom; and there they *would* learn, will they or nill they. I am not sorry for my action, save that I did not so sooner. But, I must tell you, nor am I glad of it, beyond a certain undeniable satisfaction.

Slaying—even in battle, even for cause—is an alteration in dán unlike all others, for slayer and slain alike. Though it can like other alterings be lawfully made, it sets up a vibration, a resonance that will sound in the end through both. Unlike the Christom, we are not commanded by our gods 'Thou shalt not kill,' but rather 'Thou shalt not kill without some very excellent reasons, and thou hadst better be prepared to explain to us just what those are.' Our gods leave it to us to decide if those reasons of ours are indeed excellent enough; and we know that we ourselves shall be called to answer for it if they are not so excellent as we thought them, and we must be willing and 'ware, to accept the dán we may incur. We think this a good and fair system; but if you do not, peace to your bones.

Though I must admit, after Barrendown I surely understood Athyn Cahanagh ac Douglas far better than ever I had done before. . .

In all this flurry of busyness it came about that I did not see Arthur for quite some time, and when at last I caught up

with him I regretted that I had spent my time even so use-
fully and pleasantly as I had, and wished passionately that I
had remained close beside him as was my wont.

He was kneeling in the middle of the field—the press of
the fighting had moved on, and few were nearby—and
across his knees he held a fallen warrior. My heart in my
mouth, I spurred forward, flung myself off Feldore's back
and pounded up to Arthur, each footfall on the torn red-
dened ground jarring a name of one I loved: *Tarian?
Alannagh? Betwyr? Ferdia? Roric? Ronwyn?*

Then I came up beside him, and I saw the man's face
whom Arthur was cradling so carefully. It was Malgan, and
he was dying. His gaze moved past Arthur to rest on me; he
knew me, and he smiled faintly.

"A song before I go, Pen-bardd, to ease my passing," he
said in a clear voice. "You sang long for my father—"

"Aye," I said, rocked considerably by the play on words,
which, though there have been better sallies of wit, in the
circumstances was past all praise. And true with it: For
though I had been bard five years to Owein, Malgan's father
of record up until last week, all my life I had been bard to
his true father, and still was, and would be. . .

I dropped to my knees in the blood and mud, near his
head. "I will make a song for you, Malgan Pendreic," I
promised, and tears stood in my eyes, and I could say no
more.

"I learned too late," he said then, and I saw his spirit
begin to pull back within him, so that it might have
draught to set sail. "I was hurt and angry—she offered balm
for that—I took it. Too far, too long—athra—I am sorry."
And spoke no more this side.

Arthur did not stir, only remained kneeling there, holding
him; and I remained beside Arthur.

"He told me all before you came, Talyn," said Arthur at
last. "Of Marguessan—she has fled rather than face me
here—and of her plans and wiles and treasons. Sought my
forgiveness for having out of that hurt and pain he spoke of
sided with her against me; and I freely gave it him. He has
found his peace along with his name; perhaps it was meant
to be so all along." He was silent a long time, and I dared

not even think for fear I would overhear his thought. "What of the others who aided Marguessan?" he asked presently. "Her outfrenne jackals?"

"Dead and killed and slain," I said complacently. "A little small thing it was, I was only happy to have been of some assistance. . . Have we won here, do you think?" I added, glancing round; it was hard to tell by looking.

"Oh aye, if you can call it that. Marguessan and Mordryth are both escaped, my sorrow to say; they showed no reluctance to leave Malgan to take the éraic upon him. It was Mordryth and two of the galláin who cut him down, I saw it happen; two of those ones you slew, Talyn, well done."

"Indeed." I signalled across the field to some of Arthur's guard, who raised their swords in token of having understood and came at a run. "We will bring him back to Tara with us?"

Arthur shook his head. "Nay; let him be borne in state to Saltcoats, to be laid there to rest. It was all the home he ever had, and he was happy there, if he was happy anywhere." He eased Malgan's form to the ground, and I slung off my cloak and draped it across Arthur's shoulders; his own cloak already did service to shroud the dead.

Presently Arthur spoke again. "He said before he went that Marguessan has not yet given up on her—work."

I felt a shock as if Malgan's dead hand had suddenly grasped my wrist. "Her *work?* That can but be—"

"Aye. The Black Graal, all over again. Apparently she no longer needs the true Cup to be perverted to her ends; she has chosen instead to try once more to bring the Cup's dark opposite through the Gate. Well, and she must be prevented! Morgan must—" But he could not go on, bent his head to Malgan's still form and was silent.

I rose to stiff joints and aching bleeding cuts I had not known I had taken, and looked down on Arthur as he knelt over his dead son. A great fear was rising in me like a wind from Annwn, and all I could hear, innerly, was Morgan's voice in bed not a sevennight since: 'Dragon shall fight dragon'—and where had I heard *that* before?—and, more dreadful still, 'Have you news from the Gate?' What news,

then, had it been that she did ask of; and of whom? And
when were we to know it?

But some had arrived at last to relieve the High King of
his burden; well, of Malgan's mortal form. The rest was a
burden of which none could ever relieve him; nor would he
be relieved, even if he could.

The rest of that day was spent in the usual aftermath of battle: tending the hurt, speeding the dead, tracking the bolters
who had chosen to flee rather than fight. I stayed close
beside Arthur all that time as he went his customary rounds
of the healers' tents, paused by each of the captains' standards to speak at length with his weary commanders, halted
to hearten almost every kern or galloglass he passed as we
walked. This had been our custom from the first battles he
and I had ever seen, and neither of us saw cause to change
the practice at this late date.

Or hour, even—it was near middlenight when Arthur
finally withdrew to the tent he shared with me, to eat a pastai or two, sip some shakla, try for a few hours of fitful sleep
before the morning's duties would be close upon us.

I watched him as he paced the tent's length and width,
restless as a flame and plainly far from sleep. Once or twice
his gaze went to a corner of the tent or the place under the
field-desk where Cabal had been wont to curl up, near his
master but safely out of treading-upon range; but Cabal had
not been there for many years now, and Arthur had never
managed to bring himself to acquire another hound to take
his place.

We spoke briefly, sparingly, every now and again; and
at last I exercised my rights as fostern and matebrother, and
all but forced him at swordpoint to his couch. I rolled
myself in my own cloak and lay down upon the other pallet—the stray memory crossed my mind of that lavish tent
by the stream I had found on quest, and the wonderful
featherdown couch prepared for my temptation within—and
was asleep almost at once.

But I came awake suddenly to blackness, though I had
left one torch alight; or perhaps I was awake on some other

level. I was still in the tent, and Arthur still asleep a few yards off, but something else was here, someone— I had set wards round the tent before lacing the door-flap behind us, and had left word with the Fians on guard outside, so that they should not try to enter through the circle of protection and do themselves harm thereby; belike it would not be one of them here now. But who could, or who would, dare try to breach a Druid's wards? And then, of course, I knew.

But either I had suddenly become very much better at warding, or she had been weakened by the battle or overuse of her powers, for Marguessan (for it was she) could not bring herself through into the tent. I sensed her, saw a vague indistinct blue-glowing form pulsing, but more than that she could not, seemingly, accomplish.

I watched the writhing light for what seemed a very long time. After my first start of fear and surprise, I had known she could not come at us, and so I watched with a certain interested detachment to see what she might do, and for how long. Was she trying to reach Arthur, or me, to tell us something, to do us harm while we slept—the harm she had failed to work on us in battle? Was she cross, as seemed likely, at my dispatching of her six offworld toadies this day, and was this nighttide visit to take their éraic of me for my deed?

We have an éraic to take of you, *Marguessan,* I thought, and was grimly pleased to see the blue light flicker violently as in a sudden wind-gust. So, she could hear me, if naught else. . . I carefully framed some very particular thoughts and fired them like lasra flains straight from my inner being, into the heart of the wavering blue light. It jerked and swayed and then it was gone; Marguessan's failed taish had, plainly, gotten my message.

I watched and waited a while longer, to see if she should try once more; but the tent felt right to me, its unnatural darkness gone, again the low dim torchlight I had set out for comfort. So I slept again, and without fear and without dreams.

But in the morning, when I woke before Arthur to the faint far sound of the dawn drums and the piper's flourish to the Royal Standard, I saw upon the tent floor where the blue lightshape had bloomed a ring of faint dark discoloring; and once again I blessed the wards, and Morgan, and Malen Ruadh Rhên who had delivered us the victory, and anyone else I could think of. And before Arthur stirred upon his couch I had taken salt and water and the smoke of herb averin to cleanse the place ere he could see or sense it.

I was barely done with my smudging before he woke. But beyond a brief morning-greeting he spoke no word, merely splashed some water on his face and neck and hands, clad himself in the lorica he had worn in the fighting and, nodding at me to follow, went outside.

The day was fresh and brilliant, a lovely dawn of middle spring. The Havren Mountains were so close in the clear air it seemed but a moment's journey to reach them, while the huge blue wall of Kellanvore loomed over us like a breaking wave, and the hill for which this fight would evermore be called, Barrendown, was clean and bare of yesterday's ghastly detritus.

Arthur gave quiet orders: We should ourselves go on to Caer Dathyl and Tair Rhandir before returning to Tara; several of the old Companions should remain to attend to any mopping-up that might have been missed; scouts should be sent out to try to track Mordryth and Marguessan and any others who had slipped through our nets. Then, orders given and taken, he gazed out once more over the field below Barrendown, torn and quiet as it was in this morning. He said no word; but I knew he was seeing (for I saw it myself) the past four days spread out before him like a tiny living moving tapestry, a picture in small of all that had befallen, every terrible detail plain to his mind's eye.

"Barrendown," he said at last, not turning to me but still looking out across the plain. "Cadarachta below Agned, the first; this below Kellanvore, the last. Nay, not last. The last in Keltia, then." And then he did look at me, and I wished with all my soul that he had not. "We," he said. "Us."

And he took my arm through his, and drew me away down the hill to where Prydwen had come in to fetch us; and so did Arthur ap Amris and I leave our Gwynedd together for the last time.

CHAPTER 25

Word of our victory had reached Caerdroia long since, but Gweniver had expressly forbidden any sort of triumph celebrations, saying that we were in posture of war, both civil and outfrenne, and could ill afford such frivolities to take our minds from our tasks and duties.

Not that folk were all that wishful, I think, to rejoice: The shock and outrage of Marguessan's proclaiming herself Ardrían, sole monarch over Keltia, far outstripped any martial revelry that might have been thought of, and the mood in the City was rather one of grim contentment in resolve. If the Caerdroians had aught to say in it, Marguessan should already have paid the éraic for her offenses; and they would do all they could to see she did.

I must say I was pleased to note this; and to note further that all the unpopularity and animosity that had swirled and eddied round Gweniver and Artos of late had vanished like taisher at cockcrow. All the vile suspicion and gossip of Marguessan's sowings had been blasted away, as when the Solas Sidhe runs along the ground and cleanses it of old sere leaves and withered grasses.

But that was below-text: Keltia was in arms against invaders for the first time in centuries; now we should see how well Arthur and Gweniver had built and rebuilt. It was the first real test there had been of our work since the over-

throw of Edeyrn; and I was not alone in praying that we
had done our work to last.

Donah came to meet her father at Mardale, and what they
said each to the other I know not, nor wished to. Doubtless
he consoled her on the loss of a brother she had ever
admired unknowing of their kinship, and she in turn con-
doled with him on the death of his firstborn at the order of
his sister. (I promise you, family life in Keltia should *not* be
judged by the tangled affairs of the Pendreics and
Tregarons! We do not make a habit of slaughtering our
kin—well, not that often, any road. . .) She greeted me in
my turn sweetly and soberly, and we all went back to
Turusachan, where we were awaited.

I had had a feeling a visitor of that ilk would come to us
before the end. Oh, we had made our farewells to those
beneath the hill, though I held in my heart the promise of
meetings yet to come; but Arthur, I knew, had truly believed
he had had his last sight in this life of the Shining Folk.

Wrong again! I sent cheerfully, and saw his fleeting grin
before he mastered himself to graveness, as befitted a High
King embayed with mortal and ancient enemies who greeted
now an equally ancient friend.

"Welcome to Caerdroia, Allyn son of Midna," he said,
and the tall red-clad Sidhe lord bowed in return courtesy.

"Glad am I to see you once more, King of Kelts," said
Allyn, and gave me the grace of a sidewise glance and small
slow smile. I bowed in my own turn, the memory of
Tiaquin with me as with him.

Gweniver stirred where she sat. We were in the chamber
Gwahanlen, somewhat to my surprise—I knew that on their
last visit, the Sidhe had declined to venture withindoors—
and Ygrawn, Morgan and Donah were the only others present.

"My lord Allyn is come on the bidding of Nudd who is
king beneath the hill," she said expressionlessly. "There are
tokens he brings us, if you would see."

Now I saw for the first time the wooden coffer that stood
before Allyn upon the table Rhodaur: naught fancy, merely

a plain joined box in dark wood. Presumably the other three knew all about its contents, for their expressions, or rather lack thereof, matched their Queen's; and not a one of them seemed unhappy or displeased. *What, then?* I privately queried Ygrawn, as likeliest to tell me, but my foster-mother gazed back at me out of remote amethyst eyes and told me naught.

After a glance at his wife, Arthur crossed the open space within the Table's ring, so that he and Allyn faced each other over Rhodaur's width, and, holding the Sidhe lord's eyes—a *very* chancy thing to do, as I who had been in Tiaquin and Ashnadarragh could have told him—lifted the coffer's lid.

The four sides of the chest fell away like an opening flower, and revealed within were— I took a deep uneven breath to steady myself, shot a venomous glance at Morgan, who *might* have warned me, and looked upon the severed heads of Irian Locryn, Marguessan's lord, and Ultagh Casnar, Archdruid of Keltia.

Now before you start calling hard upon me for a nithart and a quease, recall of your grace that at Barrendown I had had no difficulty whatever in interposing my sword-blade 'twixt head and neck of those six loathly slinters. Nay; it was but the surprise of it, that and the fact of these heads being whose they were. That they were here, not so much: We have taken heads in battle since before our time on Earth; and that the Sidhe too would do so—Well, a line from an old ballad rang in my ears, that praised the Shining Folk for their fierceness in war: 'Good they are at manslaying.'

"You have foreseen our wish as well as our will," said Arthur calmly, and Allyn bowed again.

"They thought to invade Glenshee," he said with the tiniest hint of a smile grazing his mouth. "It pleases us that your need marched with our own: and we have long known that this one"—his glance fell upon Ultagh—"had plotted against you with the other's mate."

I looked up at him with interest: Even the Sidhe, it seemed, did not care to spoil their mouths with Marguessan's name. But the folk beneath the hill had done us yet another service, for we had not known the where-

abouts of either Ultagh or Irian. The latter counted for little—as ever, he but obeyed his wife's bidding—but Ultagh
was a different case, and could have worked much ill had he
been free to do so. But the Sidhe had altered his case, and
ours as well. . .

With a start I came out of my reverie to find Allyn looking at me; then I realized it was not myself but that which
was above my head that his glance was bent upon—the
great tapestry of Athyn and Morric, and those who had
been their friends and their foes. I dared not turn to look,
but in my mind I could see it plain. And I straightened in
my seat, for I had not before thought—

Allyn was smiling now, gazing at me direct. "Aye,
Taliesin," he said, "just so."

I twisted to look, just to be sure, and the others looked
right along with me. There in the tapestry's fine-worked
portraiture was the very image I saw across the room: the
same red cloak, the same dark-gold hair and proud carriage,
even the same bronze stallion that now stood awaiting his
faerie master in the Great Square without. . . Allyn mhic
Midna stood before us as he had stood beside Athyn; and I
think all of us felt the cold feather-touch of awe brush past.

Then Allyn smiled again, and it was gone. "To them in
their time," he said, and his voice was warm with memory,
"and to you in yours."

"And to whom in future time?" asked Donah, greatly
daring, though her voice was small.

He looked upon her for a moment before he replied.
"That is the province of greater far than I," he said smiling.
"But we shall see."

Gweniver rose and came to join Arthur where he stood.
"Our thanks, lord," she said. "To Nudd who is king beneath
the hill, and to those whose arms did strike these blows for
both our weals."

"We are Kelts also, Lady," he said somberly, giving
Gwen her title as Ard-rían. "In all matters such as bear
upon Keltia's need, we are as true lieges of the Copper
Crown as any other dweller on any Keltic world."

"And in other matters?" asked Ygrawn, speaking for the
first time.

"There we are true liege also," said Allyn, and such a light came in his eyes then that forbade any further query.

"You know we have been bidden depart from Keltia to fight the invaders," said Arthur then, and Allyn nodded once. "Is there aught other word you bring us from Glenshee, or from any who dwell there?"

"Naught but that which you have heard many times before now," replied Allyn after a moment's pause. "And of which you need not be minded. But I do have a word for Taliesin Pen-bardd," he added, turning again to me, and I rose to stand at my place of Gwencathra to hear his words. "Seven alone returned from Caer Vediwid," he said, in the bardic intonation, and I caught my breath, remembering. . .

"And for thee," he said then, turning to Morgan and speaking in the High Gaeloch that the Sidhe commonly used amongst themselves, "a word from thy teacher: that thou shalt have the wish of thy heart for thy folk, and all thy work be lasting work."

What that wish might be, that work, he did not say; but Morgan plainly knew very well what was meant, for she heard his words and took them in with—not a smile, more a sort of shining acceptance that seemed to make her larger than herself.

And that appeared to conclude Allyn mhic Midna's embassage to Turusachan, for he made his farewells to Arthur and Gweniver and Ygrawn (with a special one for Donah, and greeting given to her to take home to Majanah as well), as to those he should not meet again. To Morgan and to me, a different sort of parting-word, and I for one took comfort in the unspoken promise of another encounter more before the last: But then he was gone, in that way the Sidhe do have; even, it seems, among mortal folk in a mortal city.

Arthur shook himself all over, as a hound will who has just come in from the rain. "Overmuch is sometimes too much," he muttered to himself, then turned to the rest of us, the ghastly coffer still gaping behind him on the board. "My lord Allyn speaks truly," he said then. "Time is soon that we were gone from here."

Gweniver made a swift small movement of protest, instantly caught and halted before Arthur could see it, and I knew she was thinking of the daughter she had within her, knowing perhaps even now that Arwenna Pendreic would never meet her father in this life's round. But this she would not have him see, nor the rest of us.

"Then let you come with us to the Council and see how we have done while you were doing on Gwynedd," she said lightly, slipping her arm through his. We followed after, a silent threesome, Ygrawn and Donah and myself; and I think all our thoughts were in that moment the same. But we would not have this seen either.

Things moved swiftly from then on; as indeed they must, for we had word from the outpost worlds that a great fleet was drawing near to Keltia, sailing straight. They could have come in through hyperspace, and been at Tara all the quicker; but perhaps they feared the unknown overheaven in our vicinity, and dared not to try it.

With good prudence, I must say, that became them well: We had mined ard-na-spéire between all Keltic worlds, mined it near as thick with fearful ship-traps as space-normal is thick with stars. And we had mined that too. . . But it was never Arthur's wont to wait when he might venture out to meet his enemy, and choose his own ground. As I have said elsewhere in these chronicles, his eye for ground to his own advantage was all but faultless. Two times only did he choose awry, the first being at Moytura, when our line was set on sand. The second— well, you shall hear.

But first came the preparing and the departing. Much had to be done, and though Gweniver had performed hero-ics of governance in Arthur's absence on Gwynedd that were full the equal of his feats in the field, much remained to be attended to. There were forms of succession to be set up should the worst befall, and not just for the Ard-tiarnas alone but for any who were of dúchas standing and had aught to leave to heirs. Since both Morgan and Geraint had been ordered by their High King to remain, this consideration troubled me not so much. But one part of it troubled me more than I could quite credit—

"They are not going, and there's an end to it!" I stared angrily at my son and his mate, and Gerrans and Cristant looked serenely back. "What can you be thinking?" I asked in a calmer tone. "They are but lads; to take them on such a venture—"

"What 'them'?" asked Gweniver, coming in on the heels of my outburst.

I threw her a black look. "Gerrans and Cristant have just informed me, Ard-rían, that Sgilti and Anghaud are to accompany us on Prydwen."

"So Artos tells me. So then?"

I ran a hand over my beard, which was probably gone gray altogether in the space of the past quarter-hour.

"Oh then, perhaps it is *I* who am the lackwit here, failing to see why two lads barely out of fosterage should go to war against the Coranians? Do you think? Am I so?"

Morgan spoke from the corner of the chamber, where she had been placidly observing the debate in silence heretofore.

"That's as may be, Talyn. . . But why do you object? They have been on training missions before now, as Fian candidates."

I exploded all over again. "Training missions! Oh Goddess help us! They are our grandsons, lady! Would you have them go, Guenna, while even Gerrans remains behind, and he a Fian captain?"

"Gerrans remains for that Artos and I have commanded him," said Gweniver sharply. "We shall have need of him here—*I* shall have need of him. So many of the old Companions have sought to go with Artos that I would keep whomsoever I might to help me when you go—and after. As for the twins, they are older now than was I when I first saw battle—or you yourself, for that matter, Talynno. Or have you forgot?"

I glared at her, but she returned my glance equably. "I have *not* forgot, Lady," I said after a while. "But what did we fight so to win for our children, if not the surety that they themselves might never have to know what we were forced to learn at so young an age?"

"Indeed," said Gweniver. "But the case has altered, I think; any road, the lads shall go with their grandsir and their great-uncle, and there's an end to it."

"Truly, athra-chéile," put in Cristant adroitly, using the formal address to me, 'mate-father,' "it will be most well for them. They can be no safer than with you and the Companions as protectors."

In spite of myself, I snorted with laughter. "'Safe' and 'Companions' have never been two words that ran together, at least not in *my* remembering. And they would be safer still did they stay behind."

"Enough," said Gweniver, rising from the chair where she had bestowed herself, and I could see from the way she stood that she was weary beyond wisdom for one in her condition, and I was suddenly contrite. "It is decided. Let be, Talyn. There are graver things we must decide than that. The succession, for one."

I looked sharply at her. "What need be decided there? You are Ard-rían. Should Arthur fall, you are still Ard-rían, only then sole monarch over Keltia. In due time, Arawn inherits; or, if not he, then this Arwenna yet to be. What is the difficulty?"

"Oh, only that Marguessan yet maintains *she* is Ard-rían, by lawful right from Uthyr Ard-rígh her father."

"She has ever maintained that," said Morgan quietly. "The folk for the most part have never upheld her in her claim."

"Not until now." Gweniver's words fell like small dark heavy stones on slate. "You remember that there was great support for Errian of Kerveldin when he made accusation against me—of Marguessan's doing. And when the Archdruid Ultagh, late by grace of the Sidhe, did proclaim Marguessan rightful High Queen, with Mordryth her Tanist, there were more who approved and swore allegiance than we could have liked—or even imagined."

This was true, unfortunately, and great was our shame and anger for it. We had over the past years underestimated the current of resentment and hatred that had run like an ice-freshet just below the surface of contentment the folk had, mask-like, worn. There was no real cause for this,

mind: Artos and Gwen had done naught but good for Keltia
in all the years of their reign, and the people in strictest justice could not complain of their rule, far less claim they had
suffered for it.

Nay: The malcontent lay deeper than that; ran in plain
truth all the way back to Amris son of Darowen.
Marguessan had merely drawn upon their vague discord
and chafing, tapping it as one might tap an aquifer to water
one's fields. And her fields had borne full, fell crop.

"Well," I said at length, "I do not think the folk will balk
to follow you, Ard-rían, should it come to it that you must
lead us alone, and may a merciful Goddess prevent it." I
halted abruptly, for I had caught a swift fleeting othersense
of where her real disquiet lay. . . But if she chose not to
share it with us her kin just yet, that was the High Queen's
choice; I would for no sake ask of her aught she was not yet
prepared to give. There would be enough and too much of
that yet to come.

It was not so surprising how swiftly we mobilized: One of
the greatest reforms Gwen and Artos had made was that
Keltia should never be without a standing army. Never
again, they had promised us, should we be caught unawares
by an enemy—whether that foe was from within, as Edeyrn,
or outfrenne as now we faced.

And with that standing army, a mighty star-navy, and a
goodly sea-fleet as well. No possibility had been neglected,
no cost spared; and yet all had been so well managed by
those whose task it was that, now, all these years after the
Marbh-draoi's downfall, Keltia was not only an armed
power but a wealthy one as well—even an empire of sorts,
if you count in the Protectorates. Hence the attack that was
provocation, with Donah's abduction, to this very war: on
our trading world of Clero, by the Fomori under the
deluded Melwas. Well, we would deal with him, and them,
soon enough. Just now the more pressing problem was
coming at us from their ancient homeworld of Alphor, and
to be honest with you—as I have been throughout these
chronicles—I did not know if we could stop them.

However, I confided my fears to Morgan alone, when we went down the night before departure to fetch the Hallows, from their hiding place in the Hall of Heroes, and to set them aboard Prydwen as Arthur and I were bidden.

She was not unsympathetic to my fears, but she was perhaps a touch more dismissive than I liked, or needed just then for her to be, and I am sorry to say I snapped at her as seldom I had ever done. But it was her own fault.

I stood back as Arthur, with Gweniver and Morgan, parted the heavy curtains behind the empty Throne of Scone—still with its two high seats before it, as had been the custom all these years—and watched as first the plain stone wall and then the great findruinna gates rolled back, to reveal the open dark mouth of the Nantosvelta, like a huge stone throat beneath the mountains.

Morgan's hand crept into mine, and I was glad of her touch even as I was shamed for my earlier impatience. I knew she was remembering, as was I, that first time of all times we had stood in this place, and had seen that tall throne of cloud-white granite. She was trembling now, as she had then, and I soothed her with thoughtspeech as I had done before; but the reason this time was a different reason, and I myself was shivering as I watched Arthur and Gweniver lift out the familiar chest, bound with magic equally as with dull dark gold. Then it had been the beginning, and beginnings are ever a time for fear, the fear caused by uncertainty and high hopes. Now it was the end, and the fear at the end of things is the fear of certainty, and of hopes relinquished.

We did not look inside the chest; but closing off again the way to the Nantosvelta, we bore our burden out into the faha where an aircar waited to bear us all to Mardale, where Prydwen lay in skydock being readied for battle. Ferdia was at the field to meet us and see that all went well, and he and Arthur carried the chest aboard, puffing a little at the unexpected (or so they said) heaviness of the thing. But for my part I think the weight of it was largely in their own minds—though I suppose thirteen assorted magical objects might well have a reasonable heft to them. Nay; it was the weight of the power in them that Artos and Feradach were feeling; and that, at least, was *not* unexpected.

They carried it aft and to deosil in the ship—that would be to the rear and on the right-hand side as you face front, for those of you unused to ships, with sails or without—and into a chamber that opened off a short alcove, a little set apart from the rest. This was Arthur's own cabin when aboard Prydwen, and mine was right across from it. Though all the cabins on Prydwen were commodious by warship standards, these two were somewhat larger than the rest; and Arthur's, quite properly, largest of all—perhaps twoscore feet to each of its square sides, and with a ceiling of quilted silver metal ten or twelve feet above the black solenized floor. Spacious indeed for a ship of war; but, having myself sailed in Prydwen for *years* at a time, I can tell you plain that sometimes it had been that extra cabinspace alone that kept us sane, and our hands off one another's throats.

The furnishings were by no means kingly—that was never Arthur's style—but they were handsome and comfortable enough: a wide low bed with a dark fur coverlet, an upholstered chair or two, a carved desk, books and statuary, a little wall-shrine with the small figures of the Goddess and the God known as lamh-dhia, not so much more. Ferdia and Arthur set the chest with the Hallows at the bedfoot, and stood back to survey their placement.

"That feels right," said Ferdia, and Arthur nodded abstractedly, as one who is listening on more than one level at once.

"It will serve," he said, and rather abruptly hustled us all out of the cabin and sealed the door-stud behind him. "The kerns and officers have still much to do to make the ship ready for tomorrow's sailing," he explained, sensing our surprise. "I made them all leave whilst we put the Hallows aboard—none but ourselves must know, and a few other of the oldest Companions, where they are bestowed—and now they must finish their chores."

He suited action to words by signalling to a bored-looking officer who waited at the far end of the skydock, and then we found ourselves back in the aircar returning to Turusachan.

As we drew near Arthur suddenly sent us soaring high above the Loom in a great banking circle, and I knew what he was doing: taking what might well be—nay, be honest about it, what *would* be—his last look at Caerdroia by night.

It was a sight that was well worth the looking: The lights of the City lay upon the dark lands round like a huge carpet of furry golden moss; then, as we dropped closer in, the moss broke apart into tiny shining spires and squares, with little veins of light running up into the black folds of the hills behind. And above it all was Turusachan, crown of the Crown City, lifting itself against the darkness of the Loom one side and the sea on the other.

No word was spoken. We knew one another too well to need words, and none would have sufficed, any road, not in that place, that moment. But as Arthur made one last sweeping circle out over the sea and mountains and the flat plain below the walls, and then came arrowing in again, I saw in the reflected light of the City that tears glittered upon his cheeks.

And was no whit surprised, for my own face was wet likewise, and I would wager that of all those present. But what surprised me—and in some incalculable way made my spirit sing—was that Arthur was also smiling.

In the night, in our chamber above the sea, Morgan and I loved long and fierce and often. But at length even passion was not enough for us—not close enough, not *something*— and we simply held each other, found refuge in each other's arms as we had so many hundreds and thousands of times before. We talked, now and again, but to what purpose? We already knew each thought in the other's mind and heart and spirit; no need to speak aloud, for all was spoken already. Yet at last, as the sky to the east began to begin to lighten, we did sleep; but when Morgan's chamberer came to wake us, that we might bathe and dress and break our fast in good time to meet the King and Queen below, we were already awake, lying there side by side in the creeping dawnlight, staring up at the jewel-stars on the underside of the bed canopy.

Everything seemed now to be as if we moved in dreams; or nightmare more like, there was no choice about any of this, no more than there would be in an execution, say, or a surgery. Will we or nill we, the thing was happening, and we had no choice in it at all. I cannot *tell* you how I hated that.

So we went down to the Hall of Heroes, where were met for this leavetaking most of those who dwelled in Turusachan; not to mention high officers of state, Councillors, Fian commanders, the heads of the various orders and *their* high officers and councillors. . . In the rather subdued throng that all but filled the Hall I saw Elphin Carannoc, who nodded twice but vouchsafed me no other comment, and over against him was an old friend and teacher of ours from our Druid days in Bargodion: Alein Lysaght, who had just been named Archdruid. Named by Arthur himself, moreover, who had exercised an ancient and little-used right of the High King, as Chief of Chiefs (and, technically, High Priest of all high priests), and superseded the Pheryllt whose equally ancient right it was to choose the Archdruid. And sullen angry hornets they were about it, to be sure. But Arthur had wished no repetition of the Ultagh Casnar error, especially whilst we were gone off to war; and so, over many objections both bitter and loud, he had named his own choice.

I thought about it as we waited for Gwen and Arthur to come in. Oh, it was not that Alein was disliked or distrusted by the Pheryllt, nor yet by the rank and file. Nay, the master-Druids were but peeved and cross that Artos had overruled them. Well, they would get over it, no doubt. . . And then I forgot my musings and misgivings alike, for Arthur and Gweniver had come to the huge beaten copper doors, and pausing a moment as royalty should, they began the long ceremonial stately pacing that would bring them, in about three minutes' time, to the two thrones that stood below the Throne of Scone.

As I waited with the rest I wondered if this elaborate and time-consuming ritual of leavetaking had been really necessary. It was uncharacteristic also—neither Gwen nor Artos favored this sort of thing at the best of times. But as I

looked around at the exalted faces, I began to understand
why Artos had insisted; and when they stood at their places,
and the whole vast Hall filled with the solemn soaring
anthem sung by all of us together, thousands of voices many
of whom would soon be silenced forever, my own perhaps
among them, I knew he had been right to so insist.

Arthur had never been one for speeches. Though in his
time he had delivered some few that would live forever even
in the annals of a folk renowned for wingèd words, he did
not love having to speak to order, as it were, and last night
in our small family gathering before retiring had fretted endlessly that he would not today be up to the mark. He need
not have worried.

"My friends," he began, and the Hall went silent as snow
on the instant, "this may perhaps be the last time I shall
come to speak to you so, or that you shall come so to hear
my words. Therefore let you listen and let me say what I
would."

It was a speech that stood with the one he had given us
from the bridge of Carnwen, what time we had made our
crossing from Gwynedd to Tara, bringing war against the
Marbh-draoi on the very world he claimed as his. Arthur
had then still been but our King to be, and the theme he
had sounded had been like to the opening movement of a
great piece of ceól mór, the Great Music, where all the
themes to come are laid out in small. Now he *was* our King,
and perhaps soon would be our King that had been; and his
statement now was a coda, a final movement, the themes of
his kingship all recapitulated with variations and resolutions,
played full out one last time more ere the great shouting
final chord was sounded.

What he said mattered little, though the words were fine
and high and fair. How he said them mattered more than
all. And he said them well indeed; as well as he had said
those first public words of his, still a lad, barely fourteen,
back at Coldgates, when for the first time he claimed his
birthright as Amris Pendreic's only heir, and vowed to his
awed hearers, and to all Keltia, that mystic compact a prince
makes with his people, and they with him.

Today, here, he made that compact with them yet again,

and they swore it as fervently back to him. As I listened, tears scalding my eyes (for I would *not* weep, not in front of the entire kingdom, and then I saw that everyone else was weeping, and I was too by then in any case), I felt again that eerie far-off touch of the Awen upon my soul. *This too, then. . .*

But Arthur was coming to the end of his brief text—in his years as High King he had learned to edit his natural eloquence, for which we were all most grateful—and I set myself to hear him as a bard would, to hear and to remember, though the moment was recorded by many means and there was, strictly speaking, no real need, save the need I felt in my soul. For I had share in this, I had come all this way with Arthur, this moment was mine as much as his; aye, as it was Gwen's, and Ygrawn's (ah Goddess, Ygrawn!), and Morgan's, and Donah's and Arawn's and Tarian's and Grehan's and oh, all the rest beside.

"Tide what may betide," he was saying, in a clear and joyous voice, "we know what we have done here. Keltia is Keltia again because of what we did together, none of us of more worth or import than another. You are my folk, I am your High King, Gweniver your High Queen. And I say to you that no matter the victory or the loss we go from here to find, that shall never change, not in the memory of the world. Never shall I cease to be your Ard-rígh, for so long as it is in my power to be so. That is why I wished to speak to you all, here, now today: so that I may say to you now, as I said once before, 'Lean thusa orm!'" He paused for one electric instant. "Follow thou me!"

It was the old ros-catha he had cried us on with to land on Tara; Caerdroia itself had heard it shouted from the Stonerows to Turusachan, and in the long years since, it had been heard—and feared—on many worlds. Now as Arthur cried it here, to those whom he would almost momentarily be leading out against the Coranians, it seemed to resonate through the Hall and back through the very mountains behind us. And we shouted it back at him, ten thousand voices all as one, "Lean thusa orm!"

But he did not respond with the battle-exultance that had for so long been his trademark, only stretched out his arms

above the crowd as the priest we often forgot he was, and in
the sudden hush after the great tumult spoke the Beannacht
to us, the blessing of the gods and man; and we received it
solemnly and humbly. Then Alein the new Archdruid and
Therrian who was still the Ban-draoi Mathr'achtaran came
forward, and Arthur received their blessing as we had taken
his.

With that, he became all business, and issued crisp
orders to his chief commanders; the great mass began to
disperse and in surprisingly few minutes the Hall of Heroes
was empty save for the true Kindred: blood-kin and soul-
kin, the royal family and the Companions who were also
family.

This was the moment I had feared and dreaded above all
else, the farewell we all must make to one another, in front
of one another. But as I glanced round on these faces I had
known for the better part of a lifetime, I suddenly saw there
was naught here to dread or to fear, for there was naught
here but love.

And so no need to linger: After all our partings were
made, those who were to remain behind went up to the top
of the Keep, so that they might watch Prydwen and her
escort as they rose to join the fleet that waited for them out
past the Criosanna. Ygrawn, Gerrans, Donah, Grehan who
had been ordered to stay to help with the home defense
should any be needed, and with the remnants of the civil
strife if not, a few more: and with them, leading them,
Gweniver Pendreic ac Penarvon ferch Leowyn gân Arthur,
Ard-rían, High Queen of Kelts.

The rest of us took swift way by aircar to Mardale, and
went each to our assigned craft. Most of our contingent
was already aboard Prydwen, bursting with pride for being
ordered to the flagship; many were soldiers we had fought
beside for years, many more were newer, younger. And the
leaven in all this was the core of Companions: Betwyr,
Ferdia, Tanwen Farrach, Alannagh Ruthven; Daronwy and
Roric (who had begged to be allowed to join us on this
reiving, swearing that he was more Kelt by now than
Aojunni); even my old teacher Elphin Carannoc, though
his coming left us Chief Bard-less; my sister Tegau

Goldbreast and her lord Eidier; Elenna, our Elen of the
Hosts, who was in command second only to Artos himself;
my young grandsons Anghaud and Sgilti, who if not
Companions precisely were surely of the Company; even
Tarian, who had signed over her Taoiseach's office to
Grehan Aoibhell, so that she might come with us. Oh, and
many more beside, who had been with us in Coldgates or
Daars or Llwynarth or Tinnavardan or so many of the old
cherished lost places. It was not a crew merely, but a living memory. . . A great freight of Fairface were we that
went with Arthur; and I could not help but wonder, as
Prydwen rose beneath us and the techs on the field
snapped to honoring attention as the ship took the air,
how many of that freight would still be filling Prydwen
when she came again home.

For that she would, I had no doubts; that had been
promised too many times. For the rest of it, nay; there was
no certainty, and I knew already some of the dán that was
beginning to make itself felt here. Would that I did not; but
I had no choice in that, and in that choicelessness there
could be found a certain peace and freedom, something like
a stone wall against which one could set one's back. And
sometimes, when your back was to such a wall, you fought
your best. . .

So I mused to myself, as I stood beside my King and
brother upon the bridge, and watched him watching Tara
fall away aft. For myself, I did not wish to look. If my dán
held for me as I had been given to believe, I should be seeing it soon enough again, and therefore did not need to look
now, for it would only cause me pain. If my dán worked out
other wise, then I should not be seeing it again until my
next life, and a last look now should only cause me more
pain; and so again I would not watch.

And in the end I did not watch Arthur either, not until
Tara was a full bright sphere behind us and we had passed
the Criosanna and red Bellendain—Argialla was just now on
the other side of the planet—and even the tiny shepherd
moons that rim the Criosanna's outer edge and, some say,
keep the rings from straying.

I did not watch him until he had given the signal to

send Prydwen into the ard-na-spéire like an unleashed wolfhound on the chase, when he lifted his hand and let it fall in accordance with some inner timing of which only he was aware. And with the dropped hand he spoke another word he had spoken once before: "Ymlaen!"

Which signifies in the Kymric, "Forward!"

BOOK FOUR:
Diachtraí

CHAPTER 26

We met them as we could have wished to do. Arthur had his own choice of battleground, which was of course as he ever preferred it; and though you might think that one place in space is much the same as any other, you would find yourself wrong to think so.

The place Arthur chose for our stand against the Coranian and Fomori and Fir Bolg invaders was called Camlann; or rather, that was the name of the nearest planetary body, a small uninhabited planetoid. And according to ancient military custom it went down so in the histories: the Battle of the Roads of Camlann. And it was eternally and forever the wrong place to choose; the second, last and greatest of Arthur's wrong battlefield choices—more wrong even than Moytura. "Two only!" I said to him later. "You might have gone for three; no bard will ever be able to make a triad out of this!" I said so to twit him, but the within-thought was to take some of the gravity from the moment, to ease his desperate pain at having so chosen, his blaming of himself; and to his credit for all time he laughed on both counts. But that was later.

We were a full three hundred on Prydwen this faring. Not a single Companion but had not begged fervently and eloquently to be included in this sluagh; but Arthur had ordered many of the best to remain at home with Gweniver and Morgan, in the very real case of war breaking out behind us in absence. All the same, it was a massive fleet we led to Camlann. Commanded by Elen Llydaw and Arthur himself, it was an array the like of which had not been seen in Keltia since Athyn's day, or the Grey Graham's, or maybe even Raighne's or Brendan's.

We had a while to wait: We could sail straight or take the road of the overheaven as we so chose, but the invaders had to come in through mined space, and also the Morimaruse, the great Dead Sea of the stars not so far from Keltia's outmost borders, was a daunting obstacle to folk who had not previously encountered it. It would take a while to sail round, and all the while they sailed was time for us to fling ourselves like a deadly cloak across the stars.

But all too soon—it is so in every battle, even the ones for whose commencing you think you have waited ages long—they were upon us. The enemy had come.

And none other to lead them than Marguessan Pendreic. She announced her presence on a swift and deadly Coranian dreadnought—not the flagship, which was a mighty thing called the Marro—and Arthur chose at once to speak to her.

Well—if you could call it that. He remained many moments silent, looking at his sister's face as it filled the viewscreens—mocking, brutal, angry, pleased—and then on a sudden came a cold deadly rain of speech, a great hearkening-wind and following storm of words all sharp and fierce and stinging, as when An-Lasca flings its sleety freight against the walls of Caerdroia. Arthur—he who was known on worlds litten by strange stars for the honor and princely courtesy of his tongue—now spoke words like a storm of arrows, like the tip-whip hurling its savage little lash to hook it deep in flesh. Arthur was speaking to his sister Marguessan, who had dared to call and crown herself Ardrían of Keltia. I will not repeat his words.

She went very white and very still, and when he was done spoke not one syllable in answer, but threw her chin up a little and vanished from the screen; and, all around, the Coranian (for so I shall call them, though there were others with them) battle lines began to shift the smallest tiniest bit. Not Marguessan's command, then; I wondered briefly who it was that did lead here—the captain or war-admiral aboard the Marro, was my guess—and then had no leisure more for wonder, for the fight was joined.

"Shall we force them to fight as we do wish, then, Artos?" I asked, a little hesitant at the sheer volume of ships out there that must be overcome.

"We will pound their bones for them if they do not," answered Arthur cheerfully, and turned to the screens to watch his fight unfold.

There are surprisingly few rules for fleet battle in space. We—I speak here of the Kelts, and, latterly, the Yamazai (who of course had been trained up alike, under the goad of Artho Kendrion)—were 'customed to apply the principles of chariot warfare (at which we were acknowledged masters) to starship warfare. There is not so much difference as you might think, between a small, fast, supremely maneuverable war-chariot and a similarly small, fast and even more maneuverable (in three dimensions, not a paltry two) spacecraft. Whether one is fighting on the plain below Caerdroia or below the plane of the solar ecliptic, the rules are the same, and we did now as we have ever done: Lead them after you with speed, then turn hard and fast and hit them harder and faster, while they are still coming up to you and helpless to alter course, so that they are struck not only with all the strength and force of your movement but with theirs as well. It worked surpassing fine with chariots, as many worlds could tell you; and, as Arthur and Elen employed it, finer still with chariots of the stars.

So began the Battle of the Roads of Camlann, fought in bitterness and silence and utter mercilessness; not a long fight as such things go, but one that changed forever the fates of more realms than our own, or even the Coranians'.

The difficulty of ground, if I may call it that for mere convenience's sake, was made apparent early on. We had thought that the uninhabited condition of the nearby planetoid would provide perfect shelter for us, as a small hillock or rise will often do on an earthly battlefield—a place to go for momentary respite and regrouping. And, at first, this

purpose it served, the small planetoid Camlann. But as the
battle wore on, more and more of the enemy ships began
making use of it themselves for shield, luring our craft in
behind and blowing them to dust once they tore by in pursuit.

This had happened often enough for Arthur to give
orders that our ships were not to dodge behind Camlann,
however crippled or temptingly slow the enemy targets
feigned. Worse, the tiny planet's gravitational field was out
of all proper proportion for a body so small, and began to
play hob with the navigation systems on our smaller craft.
Larger craft could compensate; not so the little dart-fighters,
whose very advantage lay in their smallness and blazing
speed. Coranian cutters gobbled them up like great calm
salmon gulping down minnows at the bottom of a dark loch;
and we could ill afford to lose even the least minnow of our
schools.

So Elen, after consultation with Arthur, ordered a great
flanking maneuver, such as might have been employed with
stateliness and terrible grace on some snow-covered battlefield below, in the churned wake of which the snow would
be red indeed. She made a monstrous scythe of our middle-
rank craft, the cruisers and barques and destroyers, a giant
curving wall of deadly ships; bladed the scythe with the
swift biting smallships; and for the weight that swung it, the
huge galliasses and dreadnoughts and carracks, the ships
that anchored the line.

All this Elen flung out from Camlann, the planetoid as its
fulcrum and the scythe poised to swing. And for the
moment, she held it there; held it and looked to Arthur for
the word, and he stared out at the great glittering array and
did not give it.

For good reason: That word, once said, could not be
called back again, and this for all intents was all the strength
we had. There were fleets and divisions protecting the seven
settled homeworlds, to be sure, but we would sooner perish
utterly than call on those, for they might be meeting sore
need of their own soon enough.

And yet to delay too long were also a hazard. Very soon
the formation would begin to break up as the Coranians

dove and bit and worried it, and then the Fomori and Fir
Bolg would bring their lesser, slower ships up for the kill.

"I like not this pack-dog strategy of theirs," Daronwy
remarked to me in an undertone. She glanced across the
bridge at where my two young grandsons, Anghaud and
Sgilti, were watching wide-eyed from a shielded viewport.
"Do you think they are best kept up here?" she asked quietly. "I know they have been useful, Talyn—the communications bards have been singing their praises all day—but
should aught go awry they might be safer below."

I made some noncommittal face, quirked mouth, raised
brows, a sort of shrug above the neck. But it had occurred
to me before now to wonder as to what was best for my
son's sons—especially should aught truly disastrous befall.
Every warrior in Keltia knew what the Fian way was at such
times—and if you could not manage your own sword to
your own best interest it was fair to ask another to help
you—but Anghaud and Sgilti were barely out of childhood,
still more lads than youths. Would it fall to me, in such evil
case, to have to slay my own grandsons to keep them from
falling prey to the Coranians?

I knew in my heart that I could do so, if I must; knew
too that Gerrans and Cristant and Morgan would not blame
me for it—or blame my ghost, more like, since if I were
forced to such act on my grandsons' behalf I should not be
far behind in doing the same service for myself. But if it
came to that—I resolutely veered away, then my bard's resolution brought me back to it again—could I, truly? On
them? On, say, Daronwy or my other dearest friends? On—
Arthur?

I did not know, and prayed I would not have to find out;
for just then Arthur gave the order for the scythe to swing.
And Elen did so with a will.

It was a staggering thing to see, that huge arc of fire
and findruinna, starlight washing over the ships' hulls
impartially with enemy lasra bolts, beginning to move with
awful majesty upon the Coranians. It seemed as if our ships
were some immense seine being drawn tight upon a suddenly panicked shoal of sgian-fish, who responded by snapping indiscriminately at foe and friend alike, so that in the

end they themselves accomplished much of the destruction we had willed to work on them.

But suddenly Prydwen lurched violently, first to starboard, then to port. Arthur righted himself, then seized the helm himself to do likewise for his beloved ship. Roric, over at the main bridge, saw what had happened before it dawned on the rest of us, and was already trying to get us out of it. But it was too late: In our concentration on the vast bulk of the enemy fleet, we had spared less attention than we should have done for the actions of the enemy flagship. Now the Marro, while all eyes were on the great scything maneuver, had done some maneuvering of its own, and we were caught up in its jaws.

However, Prydwen was no minnow to be swallowed whole, but a fighting salmon itself; and Elen being still busied with the direction of our own fleet, Arthur took her place at the war-helm and began to use his ship as he would have used his blade in fior-comlainn.

For that is what it now was, between Prydwen and the Marro, between Arthur and the unknown warrior who was master aboard the enemy flagship. Our scythe seemed to have cleared most of the ships like stubble in its path—even as I watched I saw it destroy one of the Coranian frigates, and heard Betwyr say expressionlessly to Arthur, "That was Mordryth's command ship."

"Pity it was not Marguessan's," muttered Tanwen, who stood by. She was of the Coldgates vintage amongst the Companions, from that same year that brought me to the Company from my bardic training, and Daronwy from her father's liegedom of Endellion, and Ferdia from Erinna. Now she was Countess of Dyonas in her own right, having inherited from her mother; yet she had chosen to throw all that to the airts and go with Arthur.

And as I thought that, something in the rhythm of the words caught and tugged at my bardic sense, at that part of me—I know not how to call it—that knows a right phrase or a tune or a title when it hears it, and sits up and pricks its ears and hopes to hear more. . .

No time now for poems and making: We were still locked mortally with the Marro, and though Mordryth's ship, with Mordryth aboard it, had been blown to flinders, Marguessan's vessel had been seen to make a hasty and undoubted withdrawal well before the death-edge of the scythe of ships cut anywhere near her. She would be back, also undoubted; but just now we could not concern ourselves with that.

And then the scythe cut through, and what paltry few ships survived its swing were taking the same line as Marguessan, and racing for home wherever home might be, so long as it was away from Keltia. We raised an exultant glad shout to see this, and bent all our efforts yet again to our own problem.

We had been battered badly by the Marro—and done some battering of our own in return—yet as the minutes became hours and there was no perceptible easing of the choke-hold the Marro had on us, we began to despair. There were not so very many choices, and looking at Arthur I could see that he had measured them out each by each long since. . . We were badly damaged, but not unto our destruction; not yet. We could remain as we were, holding the Marro off from our throats until help arrived; but there was no guarantee that their help would not arrive timelier than did our own. We could try to flee, as so many of the enemy had done, but there were populated worlds not all that far away and the Marro would not let us go so easily; an escape that dragged the enemy flagship with it into habited Keltia were no escape at all. Or—we could destroy ourselves by our own hand, knowing that we should surely take the Marro with us; the great difficulty with that one was that we would have to go ourselves.

"Well," said Arthur at last, "there be two cross-days each moon when whatever is begun shall never see completion, and this day I feel quite sure is one of those. . ."

"What shall we do, then?" I asked, humbly—and fearingly, though my fear was not for myself: Sgilti and Anghaud still huddled in a corner of the bridge.

Arthur did not answer straightway, but his dark eyes went to one of the screens on the console before him. I followed his glance, and went cold to my boots; for upon that screen was a view of the Morimaruse, and knowing my

fostern as I did, I perceived instantly what he had in mind
to do.

"Get me a clear link to the Marro," said the High King
of Keltia. "I will speak with whomever commands therein."

The Marro's captain must have had much the same
idea in the same moment, for a transcom link opened up
between the two bridges as if by, well, magic. And all of
us on Prydwen stopped and stared at the image on the
screen.

He was tall, this Coranian; he had golden eyes and
golden skin with it, and I was reminded sharply of Majanah.
But there the resemblance ended: His hair was the black-
black of space outside, his face was strong of bone and
pleasant of expression—or would have been were this a
mere courtesy call between war-admirals. Behind him, the
Marro's bridge looked much the same as ours: smashed
equipment, injured personnel, the uninjured moving with a
kind of frantic smoothness to do the work of the fallen. Yet
this foreign captain did not look at all defeated or even
much daunted, and when he saw Arthur standing there
looking back at him he turned a fearsomely intelligent eye
on his opposite and smiled.

"King of Kelts," he said correctly, and gave the precisely
proper nod due under the circumstances from an admiral to
the king of an adversary power in posture of war. I for one
found this greatly impressive; but he was speaking.

"I am Jaun-Zuria, Lord of Vidassos on the Imperial
Throneworld of Alphor, Master of War to His Majesty
Hasparren Lacho, the Cabiri Emperor, captain of the
Imperial ship Marro. I salute a worthy opponent."

"And I return that salute," said Arthur, giving a nod in
his turn, calibrated with even greater nicety—he was after all
a king. "I, Arthur Penarvon ac Pendreic, Ard-righ of Keltia,
captain in this ship Prydwen— We seem to be in posture of
stall-mate: Neither one of us may break the lock."

The captain Jaun-Zuria looked briefly doubtful, then
gave a short unamused laugh. "It would seem so," he
admitted, to the obvious shock of his bridge officers, who
muttered protest and dissuasional advice behind him. He
cut them off with a swift chopping gesture of his hand held

low and a warning half-glance to either side, then returned his attention to Arthur.

"We are bound never to yield," he said then, spreading his hands in a gesture as infinitely sad as it was warning. "No more, I think, are you."

He spoke excellent Gaeloch, I noticed suddenly, and found myself surprised that he had chosen not to use the variant of his own Hastaic tongue that was at this time an unofficial galactic common language. Wondered too where he had learned his Gaeloch, and who had been his teacher. . .

"Nay," agreed Arthur, his own manner every bit as bleak and menacing. "Again, stall-mate."

Jaun-Zuria was silent a moment. "If we both agreed on oath to withdraw and break the lock?" he asked then. "As two fighters do in"—he used a word in his own tongue, which almost certainly meant something like fior-comlainn— "to break off and draw back and begin again. . ."

Arthur smiled. "A goodly solution," he said. "But oaths in battle are meant for breaking, and we have here no judge of the bout to see that all is observed and done aright."

The Coranian's golden-skinned face suffused with anger to a dark bronze, even as he nodded wry agreement with Arthur's observation. "Then what do you suggest, lord?" he asked, and reached out a hand to the transcom button, preparatory to breaking the link.

Arthur's smile barely grazed the edges of his beard, and I almost fainted where I stood, for I knew that wolf-smile well of old. . .

"This," said Arthur Pendreic—Penarvon—and sent Prydwen into the overheaven.

To go into hyperspace from a standing (as it were) start is a move beyond foolhardiness; the texts of the Fianna, and those of every other starfleet college in the galaxy, are filled with dire cautionary accounts of the misguided, and invariably late, individuals who thought to try it. It is not by definition perilous to sail the overheaven, but all the same there are certain conventions one must respect if one is to do so

safely and live to tell of it after; just as one who would sail a
birlinn on Glora must have knowledge of wind and tide and
current.

And to achieve the ard-na-spéire it is least hard on everyone if the ship has a moving start, for any of a dozen different reasons all turning on unbudgeable points of interstellar
physics. All of which Arthur had chosen to ignore, here,
now. . .

The jar as Prydwen leaped out of space-normal was
indescribable. I do not think a single person on board kept
his seat, and many of us were trying, indeed, to keep our
gorges where they belonged. But at least we seemed to be all
alive, and that alone was starfleet history. . . When I could
see again, past the burst blood-vessels in my eyes and the
red-hot sgians poking at my skull from the inside out (sudden entry into hyperspace will do that to you, and often
worse), I blinked away the bloody tears and stared out the
viewport in disbelief.

Oh, we were in the ard-na-spéire, no doubt about it;
what was so amazing was that the Marro had come too. Its
jaws locked on our flanks as ours upon its own had not lost
their grip, and now it tumbled with us over and over, top-
for-toe, through the blue fretfire of hyperspace. Well, this
was certainly a novel solution to what had been our problem, and as certainly it got the danger of the Marro away
from Keltia; but unfortunately it gave us a whole new set of
problems, and I had the surest and most terrible feeling that
Arthur was not yet done with his solving. . .

It is no joy always to be right, though I say so in all modesty and only where Arthur is concerned; and nor did it take
much cleverness on my part, to read him so closely and correctly. I had known him since we were five years old; and
though I could generally predict with a fair degree of certainty what he would or would not think or do in a particular situation, still after all these years I could never predict
how; which is why what came next came as a surprise even
to me.

What came next has become legend even in the few brief
years since it all took place; indeed, I think it leaped into
legend even as it was happening, even as we ourselves went

into legend along with it. . . But as Arthur had been speaking fair to Jaun-Zuria, he had also been privily busy coding certain sequences, the first of which had scooped us into the ard-na-spéire; and now as we were hurtling toward the place in which his subsequent codings were meant to put us, he was also sending. Arthur was speaking to Keltia, sending a message back to our own people; and what he said now in this moment was simple and tremendous.

First he bid farewell, for himself and for all the rest of us on Prydwen; gave details of the fight at Camlann, lest stray enemy ships turn up in unguarded regions thinking to work harm; placed rule absolute and sole and uncontested into Gweniver's hands, and Arawn's after her. He asked that Keltia should not forget us, as we should not forget Keltia so long as memory remained.

And then he said the banner-words, the sword-words, the words imperishable, the words that have never died and never shall, not in the memory of any world.

"I will come back to you. When Keltia has need of me, I shall come again. I have not gone. So say I, Arthur King of Kelts, hear me gods."

That was all! And yet, as I heard those words pronounced on Prydwen's hushed and war-wrecked bridge, as I felt them in my heart and saw them blaze like the Solas Sidhe on the faces of my comrades and Companions, as they assuredly blazed on the countenances and in the hearts of all aboard this ship and all in Keltia behind us, I knew, somehow, that Arthur spoke truth. He would not be forsworn. He would come again. I did not know how, or when, or to what purpose; but I knew it would be so.

And then his hand moved again, and, responsive as any biddable mettlesome mount, Prydwen gaited down beneath us, and when we burst from the ard-na-spéire back into space-normal, we found ourselves in a strange place indeed, the place Arthur had contrived to bring us. We were in the heart of the Morimaruse, and the Marro was there with us.

CHAPTER 27

Was once that mapmakers whose certain cartographical knowledge ran short or otherwise failed them would make up their lack with the cryptic caution, 'Here be dragons.' Well, like anything else, sometimes there were and other times there were not; but the warning served a purpose either way.

There was something of that same here-be-dragons sensibility clung to the Morimaruse. It was not a place we Kelts were strangers to—indeed, it had been one of the final spacemarks by which Brendan knew he was drawing near at last to the home we had been seeking—but we had ever maintained a healthy respect for it and all its little ways. It was not known as a galactic graveyard for naught. . .

Such places were by no means uncommon in the great interstellar reaches, though few were either so violent or so vast as this one. It was an electromagnetic derangement, an ionized hell twenty light-years across, spinning in the darkness of space like some huge malevolent Corryochren of the stars, its giant rolling clouds of spacedust shot through by fireflaws that could have swallowed suns. Donah had called Corryochren a mouth in the sea; well, the Morimaruse was a maw among the stars, and those whom it gulped down were gone for aye.

And now we were tossed upon its currents, all our systems

blinded by the atomic chaos, the stars by which we might have steered hidden from even our direct sight by the roiling flashing clouds. But there was more to the Morimaruse than that, a kind of evil chill; it cared nothing for us or our little problems, never even noticed us at all, so intent was it upon its own business of hell and tumult and birthing stars.

I found that I could not look out the viewports at the thing, not without becoming deathly ill; something there was about this Dead Sea of Space that outraged perceptions and unbalanced inner equilibrium. So I looked at Arthur instead, as he stood there at the helm, and found to my astonishment that he was smiling.

"This is part of your plan, then?" I said snappishly. "We remove ourselves from Camlann and end up here—what difference, a sword through the throat or a spear through the heart? The end is the same either way."

Arthur's smile vanished, and he was silent a moment, so that I had full leisure to wish I had not spoken at all.

"The end would have been the same in any case," he said quietly, so quietly that none but I heard him. "You knew that, Talyn, from Dún Aengus and otherwhere. . . It might have come at any time for any or for all of us; but it comes now, and this is how it shall come. At least we have left behind us victory, and glory, and a mystery for the ages. That is not such a bad bargain, surely."

"Nay," I muttered, sorry and chastened. "I know— It is just that we of the Companions have ridden long roads together, and it is one thing for us, and quite another for— others."

"Your grandsons," said Arthur. "And my great-nephews, I remind you. . . But do not fear for them, Tal-bach. Indeed, do not fear for any of us."

He turned his attention back to the screens as Prydwen rocked under fire from the Marro, and signalled to Elenna that we should return fire as she pleased. It seemed that we had still a battle on our hands, strange as that was to think on: and I attended to my own soldierly duties at my own post.

I was cheered somewhat by the enemy flagship's apparent condition: We were in bad case, right enough, but they were in worse; and though it seemed all too likely that Prydwen should never come out of the Morimaruse, it was all but certain that the Marro should not do so. We were as two mortally wounded fighters in the fior-comlainn ring; the victory was ours, but we should be as perished as our defeated opponent in the winning of it.

Still, as Artos says, not so bad a bargain. . . Presently Arthur indicated that I might have my turn of duty-respite off the bridge, and I thankfully took myself away amidships. In the common-room aft which the Companions of the inner, old circle had more or less claimed for their own I found Daronwy and Roric deep in talk with Betwyr, and had scarce sat down to join them when Alannagh and Grehan Aoibhell's cousin Tarsuinn came in.

Beyond the barest of greeting we did not speak for long and long; so well did we know the tenor of one another's thought that it seemed but wasted effort to comment upon it. But though the silence was unstrained and companionable as ever, at length Daronwy broke it.

"Not so ill," she said, uncannily echoing Arthur's own words. "It will sound most high and gallant in the history-texts by the time your little bardic friends are done with it, Talynno—how Artos and his Companions came to find their fate, and took the pride of the Coranian fleet with them for escort. . ."

"You speak as if all were settled," I said, my earlier annoyance suddenly back full force. "Must we give up just yet?"

Daronwy turned that old amused wry look of hers on me. "Have you troubled to look out the ports in the last few hours?" she asked, smiling with a certain pointedness. "If not settled just yet, it is not so far from it; and I for one would like to order my last hours, and my bones, as neatly as I might. Who knows but that someone will not find us here a thousand years from now? And if they do, I would like it to be seen that we did all correctly right to the last."

I deflated suddenly. "Oh, I know. . . and I am with you on that last, and this is an end I would have chosen—to be with all you, and with Artos, what end could be better found than this? When I think of the many, *many* times we thought our end was on us, and it turned out other wise—"

"And now it is upon us, and we feel that it is not," said Roric composedly. "Nothing strange there, my brother. . ." He put his arm round his mate's shoulders, and Daronwy leaned into his side. "We are all glad to be together in this."

Save for the ones we left behind. . . But that was the unspoken thought in all hearts, and I forced myself to examine it in mine a little closer. I had never thought to die apart from Morgan, I realized, chagrined; when I had thought on it at all, I had confidently expected to lie down beside her one day and drift off to our next lives together, our arms round each other. Failing that, I had hoped, selfishly, that I might go first, that I would never have to bear the loss of her, the grief of her absence in my life; and now I was, and would not, and was glad. And I was 'ware of a sudden envy of Roric and Daronwy, who at least were together here and would go out together when the time came. . .

And thinking this, I was conscious also of a sudden flood of what felt, astonishingly, like well-being, a sunny tide of warmth and joyousness that lapped me round and that seemed to come out of the air. This, then, was dán's fulfillment, and I no longer worried or fretted for any of it. Even my two young grandsons seemed to have share in this beautiful new certainty; and whether it was certainty of death or life made no differ, for either road it was the same, and my fears for them were gone. . .

Abruptly I excused myself to my friends and went alone to my cabin aft, across from Arthur's own. Once there, I went straight to the chest against the wall and took out Frame of Harmony, as if I had been under some geis to do so, some rann of compulsion. Bards will know whereof I speak: Sometimes the urge to make is a physical thing, a force that drives one to harp or pen or brush as surely as desire may drive one to a lover's body, or hunger to food, or weariness to the pillow. And it cannot be mistaken, and it cannot be resisted. . . All you can do is obey; it is greater than you are, and when it chooses you out to work its will in the world, give thanks to all gods, and do its bidding. To deny it is sin of the highest order.

So I did not deny it now, though as yet I knew not what it would of me, and the tunes I sketched were but forerunners to what I knew was on its way: marked them down, and set them aside. They would speak to me in their time, not in mine. But already it seemed that their work was well advanced, for I found as I loosened the strings and set Frame of Harmony back into its satchel that I was at ease now with our circumstance, stood in my soul where Artos and Daronwy and the others stood; and if the song whose first faint notes had here been heard could only be sounded in full on the other side, then that too was well. I was bard; I would go where I must to find my music.

One time, long ago on a planet whose name escapes me, where we had gone with strong force in defense of our new-born Protectorates, I saw a bear-baiting, a vile spectacle long since outlawed on civilized worlds. And now, as I stared out at the Marro from my place on the bridge again, I minded me of the bear-dogs in that baiting, and how their jaws had locked upon their prey and could not be pried open even in death.

So it seemed now, for Prydwen and the Marro; they were each of them baited bear and baiting dog together, their grip not to be broken even as the life went out of them. We had been battered sorely, and had battered as sorely back again; and now both ships were all but derelict in the currents of the vortex.

Arthur still stood unwearied at the helm, the kingly oak to which Merlynn had once likened him, straight and unbending in this last gale. He sensed my attention and gave me a quick sidewise half-glance.

"Not long now, Talyn," he murmured. "We will know when it is time." Before he had quite finished speaking, a tremendous explosion rocked the ship, knocking us off our feet and darkening the bridge. *Nearer than you knew, braud,* I sent silently, but as I hauled myself upright once more I saw with astonishment that the explosion had not been on Prydwen, but on the Marro, and that that mighty craft was dead in space.

"What happened there?" I gasped, and Arthur shook his head.

"Some delayed hit of ours," he said. "We fired into their drive, and it seems the bolts found a target after all. . ."

Not only that, Elenna informed us from her post, but the two ships had been thrown from their death-lock by the blast. We were free of the Marro; but the Marro was not free of us. . .

Arthur took a deep breath, as if to compose himself, then asked for a link to the Coranian captain. It took a moment or two to establish this time, and when Jaun-Zuria appeared at last upon the screen, his face, no less than the destruction behind him, told all the tale.

"King of Kelts," he said, giving Arthur the deep bowing of the head a vanquished opponent in the combat-ring will give the victor. "As you see, we are yours. Though you yourselves may not find it so easy to escape from here. . ."

"Perhaps not," agreed Arthur gravely. "You gave most painful account of yourselves. What would you ask, Jaun-Zuria, that we may now give?"

The Coranian smiled. "I think you know that already, lord," he said evenly. "In your tongue it is called the ergyd; in ours the katxa-raika. I have heard, and have seen, that Kelts are a folk to whom battle-courtesy matters much. You will not deny us this last."

I caught my breath: What the Coranian warlord was asking of us was the deathblow, the coup, the final mercy a victor could of martial pity accord a mortally wounded foe. It in no way diminished either party: In truth, there was nobility in both the giving and receiving of such a stroke, and had our cases been reversed we would surely have now been asking of Jaun-Zuria the selfsame grace.

So I looked expectantly at Arthur, thinking to hear his willing assent to this, and was instead astounded afresh to see the vivid bleak refusal stamped upon that countenance I could read so well. Nay, this could not be! How in honor could he deny a brave enemy what had been in honor asked? Heartsick, I reached out to catch at my fostern's sleeve; but he was speaking, and the pain in his voice caught at my soul.

"We would do so full willing if only we could," said Arthur, and all over the bridge heads snapped round to stare at him in shocked surprise no less than my own. "But my first duty, and my last also, is to my own folk; and if there yet be a chance by which I can bring them out of this place, I must conserve that chance as long as I may. And while there is still some strength in Prydwen to strive to leave the Morimaruse, I cannot spare aught of it for other purpose. Not even for the blessing of the ergyd for you and your folk and your ship."

Jaun-Zuria heard this as seemingly untroubled as if he had asked for a cup of water and been refused for lack of a suitable vessel.

"Well," he said lightly. "If it must be so, then it shall be so, and we will find for ourselves another way home. Belike a swifter one. No dishonor to you, King of Kelts," he added, and I closed my eyes briefly at the courage of him in that moment. "I know you would grant my asking could it be done without harm to your folk and your chance. It is you, after all, are victor here."

Arthur flinched as if he had been struck upon an open wound, a solitary jerk from head to foot, as if someone had twitched all his muscles at once, some unseen puppeteer.

"My sorrow, lord," he said then, recovering. "If ever we find our own way from this place, I shall send messages to your homeworld and all nearby stations, so that a rescue may yet be yours. I can do no more than that; but that, I promise you, shall be done."

Jaun-Zuria bowed, more deeply than before; already he seemed remote from us, as if his inner being had even now turned to commence its journey.

"My thanks for that at least," he said. "And if it be not irony past words to say so or feel so, I wish you gods'-speed, Arthur of Arvon. I shall leave word of you and of this day for whomever may chance to find us here. Whatever else you may have been, you have been a worthy enemy. Go now to find your own fate, and leave us to ours. Speak of us to the gods."

He saluted Arthur in the graceful manner of Alphor, then the screen went dark and empty. Glancing out the viewport,

I saw the Marro, listing badly, turn and begin to drift; and I prayed devoutly, not only as Jaun-Zuria had begged for his folk and himself who had deserved better of us, but that Arthur should remove us from soul-proximity, now, before Jaun-Zuria took his folk home by the only road now left open.

For obvious reasons, that was one leavetaking I did not wish to be witness to; and venturing a glance at Arthur I saw that he was, as usual, of more than one mind in the matter. Plainly he shared my own feeling—this would be too huge and too painful to endure—but just as plainly he thought this was a thing he must witness fairly, as something he himself had caused to be; that he must thole the Coranians' self-slaughter because it was he who had denied them the honor of eacht-grásta, the mercy-blow.

And that was all very fine and noble for him to be thinking, but there were other considerations here, and I was opening my mouth to persuade him of them when, visibly, his mind shifted. And upon his face, in the bearing of his body, I read the outcome of his inner struggle: However he himself might feel, this was not a thing he could rightly or reasonably ask his people to endure. In battle's heart and heat it is different; death is all around, and the ever-present possibility of one's own somehow insulates each warrior from the mass of the violence, from the sheer press of souls taking flight.

Not so here: We should not of course be able to ignore the backwash, as it were, when the Coranians chose to take their lives in their own hands and by their own hands move on; mere distance would have no effect on that. But there were in the event certain preparations we ourselves could make: not to diminish the impact we should feel, but to encompass it, and to draw out of it some measure of comfort for our enemies to speed them on their way, as well as some measure of resolution for ourselves.

So Arthur thought, as he gave order to Elen to take Prydwen off on a new heading, out past one of the Morimaruse's spiral arms. But he remained standing there at the war-helm, watching the one screen that showed the Marro falling away behind us, drifting now into a great clear lacuna that shone like a giant eye in the midst of the dust-storms. And as the clouds began to swirl between to veil even that poor view, the eye began to close, I moved to stand just behind him, and so was near enough to hear him say a few words in the tone of a prayer and a farewell and a salute all three, and none but I upon that bridge heard him speak them.

"Bydd i ti ddychwelyd," said Arthur to Jaun-Zuria, and left the bridge alone.

I gave him an hour or two, then went in search of him, finding him where I had thought he would be. He was in his own cabin, sprawled sitting on his spine in one of the low armchairs, and he was staring at the chest at the bed-foot that held the Hallows, and his eyes were haunted.

"Did you see him, Talyn?" he asked without preamble. "Did you see my honored foe?"

"Aye, Artos," I said quietly. "All the time."

"I could not even grant what was asked of me," he went on, ignoring my reply and even my presence. "I have dis-honored myself forever, and well may dán do to me as I have done to them."

"They have not yet gone," I pointed out. "Perhaps they will delay as long as their supplies and air and power hold out, and perhaps by that time we shall have escaped from the Morimaruse, and can send a message to a rescue ship to come for them. It may yet happen."

"And, indeed, pigs may sing," he muttered. "I do not deserve to have these"—he jerked his chin at the Treasures in their coffer—"even *near* me, far less in my care and keeping. I do not know why they are with us, or what we are to do with them. And I do not know how, or even if, we ourselves shall ever find a way home. Upon my soul, I do not think it."

Now there were two ways I had traditionally used to deal with Artos in such a mood and mode: One was to jest him out of it, even (especially) if the jest were at his expense, and the other was to join him in the mire of his own cre-ation and wallow until we both grew bored. This time I chose neither, but simply and soberly agreed.

He did not even notice my departure from policy. "We are badly damaged, Talyn, as you have seen," he said. "Many have been hurt, some beyond our power to heal, at least while we stay shipbound. And there is yet an errand for us to accomplish, before we may hope for home. . ."

Arthur was thinking aloud now, and was not to be questioned while he did so, as I knew very well from long years' familiarity. So as much as I wished to know about this errand—of which this was the first I or anyone else, to my knowledge, had heard—I held my peace. Arthur went on staring at nothing a while longer, muttering and nodding every now and again; then at last he seemed to reinhabit his own body once more, and saw me still sitting patiently in the other chair. He gave me that spacious grin he so seldom chose to employ—and a pity too, for it was quite the most irresistible thing imaginable and made him look fourteen again—and was about to say something when both of us froze into immobility, suddenly hit with a wave of presentiment.

I cannot speak for Arthur, but I found myself flung back nine decades in a single instant, once more a frightened five-year-old waking up in a strange bed, knowing that my father was dead at Edeyrn's hand and that my whole province was drowned behind me. This feeling now had much of that same nightmare coinage about it, but seemed also to be less immediate to *me*, wider somehow yet also more diffuse; and I stared gape-jawed at Arthur.

He recovered first. "It is the Marro," he whispered. "They have gone." He rose and pressed a button on the wallscreen; instantly the image formed of the Coranian flagship, far behind us now, drifting through the giant clear eye in the dust-clouds.

"They are like caers, those great clear places," said Arthur then. "Fortresses in the vortex, where things may rest for aye. . . The ship will be there centuries from now, belike; long after they have been honorably reborn—"

I had risen to my own feet; it seemed the respectful thing to do at a death, and so many deaths. . . And now as I cast round me with othersense, I could feel the altered mood aboard Prydwen, as realization came to the rest of those who went with Arthur. I said the Last Prayer for Jaun-Zuria and his folk with my outer 'wareness; but, true to form, that inner Taliesin was busy even now putting music and words together, somewhere way within. Something I had just remembered, something Gwyn had said, or Merlynn, or Arthur just now, something I could *use*. . . I shook my head angrily. This was no time for bardery: Hundreds of souls had just made their crossing, and we had not helped them to it, and I was *songmaking*?! What was the matter with me? And then I thought, *Nay, not so; it is the perfect time for songmaking, it is just such times as these that bardery was born for.*

So as I looked with Arthur upon the once-lovely Coranian flagship tumbling far astern upon the wild currents of the Morimaruse, I thought of those for whom she was now cairn and tomb and barrow, and it seemed to me that song was the last and truest honor I could offer. *You will not be forgotten,* I said to Jaun-Zuria as he went, *I promise you shall be remembered,* and I think perhaps he heard me.

But Arthur still stared bleakly and blankly at the screen. After a while I touched his shoulder gently, and he started.

"They should not have had to shift so for themselves," he said in a low voice.

"We could not do for them," I said, my own voice pitched to carry reminder and absolution, as it seemed to me he needed both just now. "Not and yet do our best for our own. . . That is no dishonor, Arthur Penarvon, but duty, and dán. Let be. Come away."

He allowed himself to be drawn over to the couch, where he flung himself down atop the coverlets still booted and clad, and was instantly asleep. I pulled up a corner of the coverlet over him, and sat by to watch a while. Elenna answered my mental summons when her own duties spared her—as healer to the Companions since the Llwynarth days she knew best what each of us needed in such times, and she would do better for Artos than I or any other might—and I left her to minister to him in peace. A sprayshot of some tranquilizing herb, a deep dreamless sleep, and he would be himself again when he awakened.

Or would he? I glanced one last time at the screen and the drifting Marro as I left the cabin. Indeed, would any of us. . .

When I stepped onto the bridge for my next turn of watch, Arthur was there before me. I took a hard, if covert, scan of him as I came up to my post beside him: Elenna's herbs had plainly done him a power of good, for he looked his old self, vital and alert and alive, and I saluted him with a smile and hidden relief.

"Well, Ard-rígh."

He cut his glance sidewise and smiled, looking straight ahead. "Well, Pen-bardd," he replied, and all at once the most frightful suspicions leaped into my bosom.

"Artos," I said after a while, "where are we headed? Yesterday you spoke of an errand—?"

I had edged my voice with curiosity and just the tiniest touch of warning; he heard both, and laughed. My alarm-sense went into a sort of hyperspace, and I put a hand on the console behind me for anchorage.

"An errand indeed," said Arthur, and now he was very much the High King. "You will recall that Melwas of Fomor had made a raid on our tradeworld of Clero, and had made hostages of those of our folk there residing whom he did not slay."

"Aye, I remember," I answered, though my head was beginning to pound.

"We are going to rescue them," said Arthur calmly.

"But—"

"Oh, aye, I know all, we are in no case even to think of raiding, we should be bending all our efforts to come safe home again— But we are going to do this, Talyn, and do it now. There were some six hundred souls taken when Melwas made his raid, and I shall not leave them to the mercies of the Fomori."

I was busy calculating. "That is twice as many again as are in Prydwen this moment—can we carry so many?"

Arthur gave me that wolf-grin, and I moaned inwardly to see it. "Prydwen can carry thrice her freight with ease." As I startled, he added in graver mood, "It is only her destination that is in doubt; if it be Keltia, home, that is well. If it be that same port where Jaun-Zuria has by now entered harbor, that too is well. But we *will* liberate them from Melwas."

To what? I thought, but did not say. Presently I spoke again. "And where must we go to liberate them?"

Arthur nodded at the viewports ahead. "Where they are," he said then. "On Fomor."

CHAPTER 28

"Fomor."

I repeated the word for perhaps the twentieth time, hoping against all hope and logic that it might have somehow changed or altered in the saying of it; but nay. There it was, and there was Arthur who had said it first; and that was the time that counts, and naught any of us could do for it.

We were in the common-room, a handful of the Companions and I, a few hours after Arthur had made his stunning announcement. Under any other circumstances it would have been perhaps not quite so stunning as it, in fact, was. But this time out we had already been in a decisive space battle, one for the histories, and had been victorious too, had repulsed the combined galláin fleets that Marguessan had invited in for our destruction; had rewritten the texts on the ard-na-spéire and how to achieve it; and had bested a superior adversary in a way that felt like no victory we cared to have—though we were grateful to take it all the same.

And now we were ordered to a raid on Fomor, despite our current state of battle-readiness—which was to say not ready at all. . . Was it any great wonder we sat sullen and silent here, why folk muttered behind Arthur's back all through Prydwen?

Well, there was no joy here, and no light cast on any of this either; so after another long and most discomfortable silence I quitted the common-room and went to my chamber. Halfway there I changed my mind, and turned instead to a cabin not far from my own. Inside, my two grandsons, Anghaud the elder and Sgilti his twin, sat as silent as any of the Companions; but the difference here was their silence sprang from fear, and I for all my bardery and all my mastery and all my years with Arthur could not allay it.

Anghaud looked up at me out of Morgan's eyes, and suddenly I saw behind that longtime-seen resemblance another, more distant one. . .

"You look like your great-grandmother, lad," I heard myself saying, to my own surprise.

And his also, it seemed. "The Rían-dhuair Ygrawn?" he asked with a tentative tone to his voice—and even in that moment I could not fail the professional assessment: baritone with some tenor reach, good resonance. . .

"Nay," I said, collecting myself, "your other great-grand-dam. The Lady Cathelin."

Sgilti gave me a sharp look—they both knew very well I had never seen my mother in remembering life—but said no word. He was the print of Gerrans his father; for all the two lads were twins, they shared little outward resemblance, though it was very much otherwise with their inner selves. Sgilti was taller and blither like his father, while Anghaud was, save for his eyes, the picture of his mother Cristant, and had her vivid nature as well. They were staunch and charming young men, courteous and principled, and not too biddable—*a goodly mix,* I found myself thinking privately, *Gerrans and Cristant have done well by them.* . .

"Is it true what we have heard, syra-wyn?" asked Sgilti presently. "That the Ard-rígh has ordered the ship to Fomor?"

"True enough." I sank down into a chair and ran my hand over my face. How to get into, or indeed out of, this next. . . "There are many of our own folk held prisoner there, taken by the Fomori when they raided Clero, and the King would rescue them if we can."

"And can we?" said Anghaud quietly. "We were on the bridge during the fight with the Marro, we saw the damage—if we take on three times as many as this ship was built to carry, will not that end what chance we might have to get safe home again?"

I looked him straight in the eyes, then Sgilti likewise. "Aye, most like it will. But still there is the chance that it may not; would you leave them there to their fate, if they might be saved?"

Both youths flushed, and Anghaud shook his head. "Nay—of course I would not, and would hope that someone would do as much for us were we in such case. But after that?" His voice shook a little, and my heart bled.

I reached out and took his hand in mine, and Sgilti came to sit beside me, so that I put an arm round him, much as I had done with them when they were little lads and needed comforting.

"True it is that we will likely not return home," I said gently. "We must face that, as dán. You have been training as Fians, and I know your preceptors have instructed you in how this must be dealt with."

"Oh aye—" began Sgilti, then fell silent.

"But it is never easy, the waiting," I said. "There has been much of that, and will ever be more, where there is battle." I had one arm now round each of them, and tightened my hold for a moment. "You will do well. And if not, remember that I am here with you, and your great-uncle the High King, and your grandaunt Tegau, and many others who love you, and we are doing as well, or as ill, as you two are."

They laughed at that, as I had intended, and when I left them a while later seemed to be of better cheer, or at least better set now to hide what they were feeling. I headed for my cabin, where I had been going before I looked in on the lads, and flung myself down upon my couch. After a while I rolled over and pulled Frame of Harmony out of its nest among pillows on the floor beside the wall, and not bothering to tune it began to pick out little vague songlets of no known provenance or fame.

I had spoken to my grandsons as best I might, to hearten them against the ghastly probability, the all but certainty, that this sailing should see the end of us. For those of the

Companions, it made little differ: This was a thing we had been prepared for since first we went out against Edeyrn, back on Gwynedd, for the Counterinsurgency and for Artos. We had had long and happy lives since then, had seen our cause triumph, had crowned Arthur and Gweniver, had restored Keltia and won back the Graal; for us it was no great tragedy to perish on this rade.

It was different for the young ones, the ones of an age with Anghaud and Sgilti, or a little their elder; though they were doubtless as brave to face their fates as we ourselves had been at their age, still it was all but impossible, I knew, for them to believe. At their age, I too had found it impossible to believe, that I myself might die; we are all immortal when we are young, or so we think. It is only when we are older that we *know* we are immortal, though in rather a different way than we might have earlier believed.

I rippled my fingers down the strings, and Frame of Harmony responded with a shiver of silver sound, a minor-key shower like rain with a sundog behind. My lads would do well whatever they came to; and, as I had said, I and Artos and Tegau the other Companions would be with them, to help them thole whatever might come upon us. My thoughts now were far behind Prydwen's course across the stars: back in Keltia, with Morgan and Ygrawn and Gerrans and Cristant and all the others we had left there. But most of all my thoughts were with Gweniver, and with the child she carried: Arwenna, who most like would never know her father save by what she was told of him. It now seemed probable that I myself would never live to make songs which might help this coming niece to know her royal father; but I began to line out a chaunt or two all the same.

I woke with a start: Frame of Harmony had fallen and hit me on the chin, and it had fallen because Prydwen had changed course sharply. I paused briefly to stow the harp securely and then ran for the bridge, for a course change could mean one thing only: We were at Fomor, and we were under attack.

"Ah, Talyn," said Arthur without turning as I lunged for my post. "I was about to call you here. As you see—"

He waved a hand, and I saw only too well. We were coming in to Fomor, right enough, and we were by no means alone in the space between the planet and her moons. I watched for a moment, then made some calculations on my screens, and frowned.

"There are not—"

"Nay," said Arthur serenely. "There are not as many enemy craft to come against us as we might have expected."

"And that would be because—" I prompted.

"Because most of them were destroyed at Camlann," said Elenna, overhearing our discourse. "And those that survived were not undamaged, and are limping home full slowly. We got here before them."

"And a good thing." I was watching as we made our way closer in to the planet, past the darting craft launched from the surface who sought to bar our progress. "Have we a plan, Artos?" I asked presently. "Or do we but invent as we do go?"

Arthur grinned. "That would be no new thing for us. But aye, Talynno, there is a plan. . . We know where the prisoners from Clero are being kept, and we will go straight in to get them."

"Will not the Fomori be expecting just that?"

"Oh aye," said Elen, "but with so few ships they cannot prevent it. Though—" She hesitated.

"Aye? 'Though—'?"

"Though they may yet wound us too badly to come safe away."

"Oh, if *that* is all." I turned away, strangely comforted and confident, back to my screens and patterned trajectories. "Old dogs to hard roads."

Well, not quite; but close enough as to make little differ.

We landed on Fomor unhindered, though we sustained more damage to Prydwen's hull than Arthur liked to see there, and lost no time getting the prisoners from Clero out of their durance and into the ship. Most were wounded, and all were very weak—the Fomori do not always abide by the humane code Ganaster sets strictly out for the treatment of prisoners of war—but we managed to take them all aboard in swift time. Arthur himself set Anghaud and Sgilti to over-see the arrangements, to see that the rescued were cared for and made comfortable, or as much so as could be given the circumstances.

Once the liberated prisoners were safe on Prydwen, Arthur gave the order to head out as speedily as we might in the direction where lay least danger and fewest Fomori ships. We had done some damage of our own in the rescue, both to the harrying craft and to the planet itself—buildings and folk too, my sorrow to say. I comforted myself with remembering how Melwas, Fomor's king, had reived away Donayah, and thought his folk were lucky to come off so unscathed.

We were heading out to space again when it happened. To this day I do not recall seeing the moment, but there it was: Out of the ard-na-spéire, or merely out from the blind side of one of the many little Fomorian moons, came a ship that could have matched the Marro, and we were not ready for her.

She was a dreadnought, a giant ship of war, perhaps the last one left behind from the venture against Keltia to defend Fomor itself; we never learned her name, not then nor after. Then we were too busy, and after—well, you shall hear, but after we had not the heart to ask.

She came, I say, out of nowhere. There was no room to turn and not time enough to run, and we took her fire square on. I have sailed in Prydwen many star-miles, and I tell you that never did that ship of Arthur's building, that ship he loved as it might be his horse or his hound or his hawk, never did she take such a pounding as she did in that moment. So hard were we struck that Prydwen rolled full over, like a sun-shark at play or a piast lanced by a muirgha. It was bad enough on the bridge, but what it did down below was unimaginable, and I tried to keep my mind off it as Arthur and Elenna and the rest of us fought desperately to right the ship and get her the hells out of there.

It cannot have been longer than a quarter-hour, but it felt like centuries, and we under fire all the time from the Fomorian, who did to us what not even the whole Coranian fleet had managed to do; but we flashed beneath her and behind one of the smaller moons and got free of the gravity well long enough to leap blind into the ard-na-spéire. And never was I so glad and grateful to be there: But the cost was fearful.

Once safe in the overheaven where the Fomorian could not follow us, we allowed ourselves to breathe; a moment or two only, and then we fell to as desperately as we had just now fought, to heal Prydwen's hurts and those of the folk who sailed in her. The toll, we quickly found, was worst among the rescued of Clero; but the Companions were by no means unscathed, my great sorrow to tell. And gravest of all, Prydwen was losing air and power steadily, from a great wound bleeding away her substance all along her cithóg side. Arthur said no word, but his very silence said more than we wished to hear.

But later, alone with me in his cabin, he delivered himself of his fears and his hopes alike, and the first were many and the second all but gone, and I perceived why he did not wish to confide this just yet to the rest.

"In all the years we have fought together," he began, "this, or some end like to this, could have come upon us at any time. Yet it did not; and the farther we went down that road of triumphs the more I came to think it never would. This—this was what we did to others, to our enemies. I never truly thought it could ever be what they might one day do to us."

"And that is just precisely why it did not come upon us until now," I said, with a lightness I was far from feeling. "Soon or late, King of Kelts, it must come to us all. We had a fine hunt of it, the best and longest day's run of any, and now it is our turn for the blosc-báis to be sounded, the mort to be blown for us. We are all but quarry for Arawn's Hunt in the end."

Arthur unexpectedly roared with laughter. "Thou hast

comforted me marvellous much," he said at last in the High
Gaeloch, still grinning. "What a cheerful soul you are, and
how dull of me not to have noticed until now."

"Ah well," I said, "better late than never at all. But,
Artos—"

"Only one 'But, Artos' will I allow, Talynno." He ran a
hand over his beard in the old gesture, and it went to my
heart to see it. So many times in the past, in so many
moments such as this one. . .

"It is well enough for the Companions," I said after a
while. "But for my grandsons' sake, can we not make it as
swift as we might? For the hunt *is* up, not so?"

Arthur's eyes had gone bronze-dark, and he was silent
for a long time before he spoke.

"Perhaps not just yet," he said then. "There is a thing
we yet might try."

The thing Arthur had in mind to try was a planet called
Kholco, and when first we heard the details of his plan, and
what like was this planet and those who dwelled there, many
there were who were all for opening Prydwen up to space
right there.

"And give ourselves an ending that is even one with that of
Jaun-Zuria and the Marro," said Roric. "Not so bad a way to
take."

"If we try Artos's plan we might not have to think of
ending at all," I said, and glanced round at the faces of the
Companions who crowded the common-room, trying to
read their thought.

But truth to tell, I was not all so sure how I myself did
feel about Artos's plan. Kholco was a populated planet not
too far off from our present position; with care we should
be able to limp there even in our grievous state. And, as
Arthur had vigorously pointed out, Kholco had a history of
trade with the pre-Theocracy Keltia—rare earths and metals, mostly, which would with luck meet our desperate need,
and could be used to patch Prydwen's hide to sufficient
strength to get us home. Or so Arthur said. . .

"Provided the folk of Kholco will remember the old

trade-bond," said Daronwy. "Provided they are even willing to trade. Provided—"

"Oh, well, if we go into it *so!*" snapped Arthur back at her. "Is it not worth the trying? If we get no joy of them on Kholco we can take the way you would have us take now, and only a few days will have been wasted. But at least, Ronwynna, we shall have *tried*."

"What like are these Kholcans, Artos?" asked Betwyr. "And for that matter, what like is this world itself?"

For the first time I saw Arthur look just the tiniest bit distant, and that suddenly. But distance was not the whole of it: Evasion was there, and a kind of defiance, and a concealing cunning that all at once made me wonder just what it was he was trying to hide from us. But when he answered, he was so frank and open that I thought I must have mistaken him. . .

"It is a fire-world," he said. "A planet largely volcanic, and actively so; hence the metals and earths they have in good supply for trade."

"If it is so fierce a place," asked Alannagh Ruthven, "what folk can live there, as Betwyr asked?"

Again Arthur paused. "They are the Salamandri," he said then. "They are ophidians, saurinoids, evolved from lizards and other reptilian races. It is said that they can live in the flames of the firemounts, and come to no harm with it."

The room thought about that for a silent moment or so; and as they thought, I had the distinct feeling, caught as if by chance out of the air, that this whole scene was a thing rehearsed between Artos and the others. Not *all* the others—Daronwy and a few more seemed to share my ignorance—but there was something afoot, or so I sensed. . . And then it was gone again, and the Companions were discussing aloud what like these Salamandri might be.

"I know little more," Arthur was saying, "save that our trade with them was begun long since, under Raighne Ardrían, and continued until the days of Alawn Last-king. Beyond, even; but Edeyrn treated them as badly as he treated everyone else, and for that reason alone they may be glad to help us now. We can but try."

In the end, of course, he had his way, he always did; but I have wondered ever after if just this once, getting his own way was not in Arthur Penarvon's best interest after all.

We were in grave straits indeed by the time we made it to Kholco's system, where a fierce yellow-white sun and a huge dim red-giant star reigned over five most inhospitable planets. Many of our folk, both the rescued and the rescuers alike, were dead and dying, and few were without hurt of some sort. Even the hope of repair to ship and folk alike, as Arthur continued to hold out to us, was not enough to rally our spirits, but we went along with him out of custom and under that vivid infusing force of his we knew so well.

And as we drew near to Kholco, I myself even began to think that, perhaps, just maybe, it might be possible, and Arthur might yet pull this off; like the evasion after Talgarth, and the snow-march along the Loom, and so many other unexpected and unexpectedly successful feats. Hope began to bloom in me again as I watched Kholco grow larger in the screens; and that alone should have warned me, as it had not in the past. . .

Kholco was as Arthur had described it, an amazing-looking world, dull red for the most part—no green thing grew there, only a few hardy scrub plants that clung to meager soil in the lava cracks. We could see, from orbit, how the firemounts ruled this world: hundreds, thousands of active volcanoes; even from space we could see the black low land laced with ribbons of firegold, the rafts of dark clinkered rock sailing on pools of what looked like gold water or yellow rippling silk and was instead pure melted rock, heart's blood of the planet. The ground shook ever; and all along the fault lines that radiated out from the great craters were towering veils of sulphur curtains, punctuated by flung fire-festoons and fountains, and slow tongues of moving lava sending up hissing billows where they met the tiny remnant seas.

Yet there were settlements in the more stable cliffs, and some of them sizable ones. There was no weaponry on this world—the Salamandri prided themselves on their neutrality and peaceability—and very little technology, save that needed to extract, as cleanly and correctly as possible, the ores and earths and gases which the Salamandri sold for trade goods to worlds who had insufficient resources of their own.

We went into a middle orbit round the planet, while Arthur opened communications with the leaders of one particular region he had singled out as likeliest of approach. They governed an area near a great high plain called the Morann, according to the geocharts they sent up to us, and their city-cave, a settlement of some thirty or forty thousand, called the Ras of Salhi, was the capital of the empty lands roundabout.

But more awesome to behold were the two giant volcanoes, huger than any I had ever seen—not even the tremendous craters that form the Long Valley on Gwynedd were bigger than these—that faced each other across the plain of the Morann. Both were alight just now, in full and dramatic eruption, and even from our distance they made a most impressive spectacle: their sides stitched by scoriac rivers, their throats lined with flame, their heads crowned by pillars of glowing smoke that reached to the very edge of atmosphere. Staring at the screen closeups, I could even imagine I heard the sound of them as they spoke to each other: a huffing, snuffling sound like some great beast breathing, or a huge pot seething on the boil. . .

All at once I started back violently from the screen, my own breathing suddenly disevened. Alannagh, who was by, looked over curiously.

"Talyn? What is it?"

I shook my head, still staring blankly at the unchanged picture on the screen of the firemountains in their shouting glory.

"I know not—something I saw—or Saw—"

But I *had* Seen, Seen plain, though I did not understand: a hand, Arthur's hand—for I could see his face up along the length of his arm, though he seemed asleep—and upon his hand not the great green stone of Athyn's that he wore for Seal but a ring I did not know, had never seen him wear before. It was onyx and silver, massive, finely done, and

bore for device a wingèd unicorn, rearing and regardant, its
wings raised above its back; but I knew of no House in
Keltia that had such arms, and as bard I knew them all.

"Nay," I said aloud, to myself as much as to Alannagh.
"It was nothing. Be easy."

But I could not take my own advice.

We had been orbiting Kholco for perhaps five or six turns
when Arthur called me to his cabin. He was in merry mood,
and yet also somehow somber, and I could only think this
mismatch of feeling had origin in our plight: on the one
hand, the seemingly real chance of repair and return to
Keltia, on the other the undeniable losses we had suffered
amongst Prydwen's crew. But Arthur, though he talked for
many minutes of all sorts of things, made no mention of any
of this; and at last he told me that he had a task for me to
perform, and began to explain its nature.

"I had forgotten we had escape boats aboard," I said
honestly, for it was true on both counts: We had several
such sloops, and I had indeed forgotten. "But, Artos, will
they serve your purpose? Will they even launch at all?"

"Oh aye," he said, rather quickly. "Elenna has made
sure of it, but only one of the four is spaceworthy and also
capable of being launched. Any road, it is only a little outer
inspection I would have you make, and then to stay in orbit
on watch-station while we take Prydwen down to the planet
for repairs. It is all settled now with the Salamandri. . . But I
would not be left blind down below and have some Coranian
or Fomori marauder catch us on the ground. And the
Salamandri, as you know, have no weapons."

Well, that seemed a prudent enough plan, and straightforward with it, for once. . . "Shall I take the sloop out on
station alone?"

"Nay," said Arthur. "The boat can carry six besides its
pilot; as well to take the full count, you never know. I have
made a list—"

He walked his fingers slowly down the piece of paper
with which he had been toying, seeming to touch each name
as his fingers came to it, then pushed it over to me. I read

the names attentively: Daronwy, Ferdia, Elen, Tanwen, myself as pilot, and my two grandsons Sgilti and Anghaud, to make up the seven.

"A serviceable crew," I said with a grin, and never noticed that his own smile was a fraction slow off the mark in answer to my own.

"Truly," was all he said.

"And if we see trouble coming?"

"From an orbit this high you will be able to see trouble coming, if any comes, from far enough away to let us know in good time below, so that we may take space. You are to be lookouts, no more, do you hear me, Talyn; no hero-feats."

"Well, but the sloop is armed—"

"Aye, but confine yourselves to giving warning if such should be needed. We will do the fighting. But it is on me that fighting is done with, for us, here, now."

"And a very good thing too." I rose to leave. "Now, then?"

Arthur nodded slowly. "Now would be best."

All at once he came round the desk and embraced me, held me close and long, kissed me as a brother and a friend. I smiled a little quizzically, but even then, oh gods, I did not twig, did not sense aught but what he would have me sense: his love for me, and our long shared intertwined lives and histories, and the promise of the same to come, for aye.

So I gave him the same back, no whit reluctant or shamed or sorry to do so, but thinking perhaps this small brief parting were not worthy of so fraught a farewell. But I loved Arthur as I have loved no other being, not even my own mate or my own son; never would I have stinted to show my love for him, nor scorn to receive the same from him. . . As we drew back from our embrace but still held each other's forearms in the Fian way, I looked at him; truly *looked*. Still the same peat-dark eyes, keen and deep as ever; the same red-brown oakleaf hair, though with a vein of silver threading it here and there; the beard also; the same tallness and strength in the spare frame, most of the height of him in the legs. . . Nay, this was my brother, my Artos, my anama-chara, and no stranger to me; we would meet again soon, and together go home to Keltia. What tales we would have to tell Gwen and Morgan. . .

And as I left his cabin and headed down to where the sloop was decked, I caught never a mindwhisper nor a mouthword as to what was about to come upon us all. Perhaps it was best that way, as so many have since told me, hoping to comfort; but I have never ceased to wonder if it was not.

CHAPTER 29

Hard it will be to set down what comes next in the tale; but it must be set down, else all the tale foregoing were in vain. Hard it will be to read it as well; or so at least I trust—nowhere in the Bardic Code is it written that I as teller should spare you as hearer (it *is* written that I have a duty to set it all out for you; but the duty from there on is your own).

But the difficulty lies not only in the pain of it (and it was, and is, the greatest anguish I have ever known, of body or of soul; not even my Morgan's passing would be worse grief to me than this) but also in the fact that I myself was neither privy to nor present at much of what came to pass, for reasons that you shall learn. Much was concealed from me, and much I was required to piece together afterwards—even long afterwards.

But I shall recount it here as it happened, and as I knew it, as best I can, so that you may know. And if I have judged you aright—and I think I have, else you would not have read so far in these chronicles—you will be no gladder of the knowing than was I who knew it first.

I swung into the pilot's chair in the command cabin of the sloop—we call these partner craft such small names as 'sloop' or 'pinnace,' but in truth they are full starships, able to sail deep space for months at a stretch, and so this one was—with a cheerful greeting to the others who were there before me.

Daronwy occupied the second-command chair, to my right; while just behind us Ferdia had taken the astrogation helm and Elen the weapons array. Naught unusual in these dispositions: Each was longtime expert in the stations elected; and in the blastcouch alcove aft, Anghaud and Sgilti sat quietly, their eyes on sticks, as Morgan put it. Tanwen was with them.

We detached from Prydwen smoothly enough, though it seemed more that it was Prydwen detached from us, moving away and then beginning a long falling arc planetward while we held our position in orbit. I was admiring the lines of the graceful dark-green ship as I always did, thinking that though the battle damage sustained in the Morimaruse and at Fomor, plainly visible from this high angle, was very terrible indeed, still it might be possible of repair. Suddenly Daronwy, beside me, stiffened and straightened bolt upright in her chair.

"Ronwyn?"

She ignored me, was busy configuring a course, her fingers flashing over the boards, and I saw that the course was Prydwen's own down to Kholco. Or so I thought.

"Oh Goddess—"

Daronwy's whisper and the screens before each of us crackling into sudden life came in the same moment. And I stared at mine with rising dreading horror, as I knew the others did also, for before me on the screen was Arthur as he stood on the bridge of Prydwen. As soon as I saw his face I knew what was afoot; it all came clear to me in one terrible instant, and in that instant we each of us spoke the other's name.

"Artos—"

"Talyn." His voice was as it ever was, but his face— His face was changed utterly, so signally altered from the countenance I had not ten minutes since given a brotherly kiss in parting that almost I could not even say I still knew it for his. Yet it *was* his, was *him*. . . Only it was lifted now to

some higher sphere and power, a face perfected and refined
and raised, reflecting all that was perceivable by earthly
vision of a higher self and a greater reality. It was grief and
it was glory at the same time to behold; and yet still he was
our Artos. . . I was dimly 'ware of the muted protests
behind me as the others came to see what I was seeing, to
realize its import and implication: There was naught we
could do to alter this, this was dán and it was run.

I heard a voice speaking somewhere far and fast, but on
the screen Arthur's lips framed no words; and after a
moment I knew that it was I myself who babbled on in panic
and denying. . .

"Nay, Artos, not this way—you cannot—must not—"

He let me go on, very briefly, then gently cut me off with
a smile and an upraised hand.

"Peace. You remember, Tal-bach. We Saw it—or I did,
and told you after—our schoolroom in Daars? And
Merlynn, Ailithir, plagued into showing us something more
than pishogues. This is what he let me to See, and what
Gwyn spoke of, and Merlynn again later. And now it is here
at last, and it is well."

"Nay," I said, blindly putting out both my hands to the
screen, as if somehow I could reach through to touch him.
"Nay, Artos, it is *not!* Do not do this—Gweniver, and
Arawn, and Arwenna whom you will never now see. . . And
what in all the hells shall I tell our mother?"

The face on the screen was brilliantly alive, and also
somehow remote from me, drawing away, as if the decision
he and the others on Prydwen had already taken (and had
selfishly—or so I felt it—kept from me) had already
removed him from the world and its cares. But he reached
out to me as I had to him, so that our hands seemed to
clasp and hold across the miles of space.

"Tell her we went most well, for so I hope we shall," he
said. "Tell her—well, you will know what to tell her. As for
Gwennach, she has my heart; the children also. Majanah
and Donah— These lastwords are naught, all the rest is
naught. Save for those sacred things you know of, and those
are well bestowed. They, and we, shall be safe here; for have
we not been told what the end of it shall be? One of our

own shall come one day to find us, and to bring the Treasures home. That is enough for me and my peace." I knew what my face must have looked like by the way his own changed just then. "Talyn, it is the only road! We could never get home again, Betwyr and Alannagh tell me; you yourself see what case Prydwen is in. There is no repair even our own skydocks could do for her now. Would you have us die as the Marro did, choking and alone between here and home?"

"Nay, surely not!" I snapped, anger edging my voice to carry me through the pain and the tears that threatened to silence me. "But what of our own, our Companions? Are they too beyond repair?"

He smiled gently, and fresh terror struck me to the heart. "For the most part, they are, aye. Most of us are wounded sore, with no hope of healing; many are dying or dead already. I ask again, would you wish us to try to struggle home to Keltia, knowing that we should never last the voyage?"

"But not even to *try!* And what of us here?" Tears were streaming unheeded down my face by now; anger had been overborne by grief and an all but overmastering feeling of desertion. They were leaving us, leaving *me*, behind; *they* would all be together, crossing over, and we would be abandoned, *I* would be abandoned. . . And the thought overwhelmed me: For all my days Arthur had been the one value that had *never* abandoned me. I had hardly known a conscious life without him in it, he had been my armor against so many losses; and now this choice of his was forcing me to go unarmed on without him. He had been there for me always; now in the worst moment of all he would not be, and it was he himself who was causing that moment to be. . . I must watch his ending and witness it— stand witness for them all. And I did not think that I could bear it.

Arthur saw all this, and spoke in a tone of utmost gentleness, such as he had used to me that first night in Daars, and so often since.

"We could save only seven; that is all the sloops can carry, and there was only the one sloop we could get away.

We are glad to save even so many of us—better seven saved than all lost alike."

I was angry again. "And are you Arawn Doomsman, to decide for us who should be saved and who should not? We would all have far liefer stayed; shame to you, Arthur Penarvon, to presume to choose for us! You tricked us, where we would have chosen otherwise!"

He laughed. "And do you not think we knew that perfectly well? So we chose for you. Sgilti and Anghaud for their youth, they being much the youngest of all on board; there was no debate about their going. You, for that you are Penbardd of Keltia, and we all wish to be written of correctly. Besides, it needs a bard to tell of this, and to leave words after for those to follow who will. The rest were chosen purely by lots drawn—Tarian and I excepted ourselves, and did the drawing—and not a Companion has gainsaid or envied your choosing. We are glad that you are saved, Talyn, all of you; and glad also that we shall go."

"But we want to go with you!" The cry cut across the space that divided us like a sgian to the heart, and Arthur closed his eyes briefly, and I saw him draw a ragged breath. I was instantly sorry for my selfish outburst, to make it harder even than it already was on him and on the rest of them; but I was not sorry for feeling so. . . Yet when he looked again at me he was entirely the Ard-ríigh.

"I know. But you cannot, and you may not, and you shall not. This is not only farewell from your brother but the lastwords and final bidding of Arthur King of Kelts. And have I not promised Keltia that I shall come again when they have need of me? Go now. Do not stay for us to end it. Come again safe home."

In spite of my grief and terror I laughed. "Oh aye, Artos, think you your commands hold any weight with *me*? *Now?* Think again, braud! They scarcely did before. . . So I say we shall not leave you; I say we shall follow you and be with you, whether you will or nill."

"Nay, that you will not," said Arthur, patience and love in his voice, as he heard the others in the sloop muttering mutinous agreement with my defiance. "Talyn—this is the last thing you can do for me, for us. I know well that you are both brave enough and loving enough to do it. It is just that you must give me a hard time first. . . Well, be it so. But I am not the only one would speak to you."

He stepped aside, and Roric came on screen, to bid farewell to Daronwy his wife; who at once begged to be allowed to join him, and whom he gently and implacably denied; and we all turned away that they might have some poor privacy for this. After, Roric said a few words to each of the rest of us, and then one by one our oldest and dearest and best Companions spoke their farewells likewise: Betwyr, Tarian and her lord Graham Strathearn, Alannagh, Tegau and Eidier, Elphin Carannoc—oh, and more besides, each bidding us a loving parting and to meet soon again, as surely we would. And I knew it was so; but sometimes—ah Goddess!—it is so hard to *feel* it so. . .

When all the farewells had been made, Arthur came back on screen, and I gasped to see him, as did the six behind me. For his face was shining now so that I could scarce look upon it, his eagerness for this venture transfiguring him; and even in my bitterness of loss I could not but be glad for him in his going—glad for his gladness, and a little, nay, *greatly* envious also.

"Talyn," he said then, in the gentlest and most implacable and most loving voice in all the worlds, "take them home now. Tell Gwen and Janjan; tell Guenna and our mother. Tell my children, when they are old enough to understand; tell all Keltia. This is the charge I lay upon you, and it is harder by any measure than the one laid on me and those who go with me now. I know you have strength for it."

He raised his hand again to the screen, and I slowly lifted my own, so that it seemed our fingers touched, and we looked upon each other for the last time in this life. All our past was in that look, and all looks since the first we had ever given each other, on an autumn hillside across a little valley from a walled town.

I had no words, nothing was left me; but Arthur smiled and spoke.

"We will meet soon again. M'anama-chara. . . 'S é do bheatha, Taliesin Glyndour." And he was gone.

I lunged forward in a yearning desperate movement, my

mouth open to frame a protest, or at the least some of the
uncounted words I suddenly needed to say to him and now
never could in life; but the screen was dark and pitiless,
utterly black. Or perhaps it was my sight that had gone
black, at least for a moment, for the next thing I beheld was
Prydwen turning her nose slowly to the planet below. I
hastily recalibrated the scanners to follow her down as far as
they could; and when I saw the course she was taking, in
spite of myself I laughed aloud, through all my tears and
grief and protest, and shook my head. *Ah, my Artos! Trust
you, braud, for the dramatic end to it all.* . . But it was dán,
and he had had the right of it, as he had almost ever done:
We had Seen it all before.

For sharp and true as a spear, as *the* Spear that she bore
within her, Prydwen took aim at the great firemounts I had
earlier noted, that faced each other across the lava plain. And
as the distance grew shorter between falling ship and rising
ground, I saw that Prydwen was headed for the greater of
the two, the one which the Salamandri we had bespoken had
named the Firehorn. Arthur had chosen the Tântad for his
last road. . . and belike it was no bad choosing.

It is graven upon my mind's eye, forever, the way
Prydwen blazed out of the sky, so that 'falling' was not the
word. There is but one time in all times, of the ships that
carry souls, when the ship is free of a master's hand and may
herself be master. And that is when the last aboard falls and
the ship is free to choose. And so Prydwen went now, with
purpose and celerity, free to go as she pleased, and this the
course it pleased her to take. She went as by will of her own,
and was never a handspan out in all her going, as if she too
had chosen the same end as those who sailed in her.

Like an arrow to the gold she went, a dark arrow to the
gold heart of fire, a lance between the horns of light. And
whether it was by one last magic of Arthur's making or one
final grace of some pitying goddess or god, we in the little
sloop were suddenly permitted to see, or See, all; as if we
were beside them, with them, right to the last. . .

All throughout Prydwen they had bestowed themselves
like warriors in an ancient barrow, had laid themselves down
upon the couches in their cabins, or upon cloak-covered

pallets on the floor if there was no couch to take. Their hands were folded upon the hilts of their swords, they were clad in the arms and colors of their Houses, torcs gleamed bright about their necks. Those who were kin or friend or beloved lay together side by side and hand in hand; there was no look but peace on any face I beheld.

And I saw them all, my dearest ones, they were all there: Tarian with her glass-blond hair smooth as ever; Alannagh, the green-blue eyes closed now; Betwyr with the ship's log lying by him, as if he had just now finished entering the account of Prydwen's last sail; my sister Tegau Goldbreast, who had guarded Uthyr, now as guard for Arthur; my teacher Elphin Carannoc, chief of my order, with his harp cradled in his arms. . .

They were gone or ever the ship pierced the mountain's heart; they had taken Jaun-Zuria's way, or Arthur had chosen it for them as a last mercy, casting all into sleep before they fell together into a deeper slumber.

And though tears blinded my sight I Saw with other vision, Saw how it would be for them, how I myself could wish it. That deeper slumber would lead but to a bright awakening: They would open their eyes to find themselves lying on the floor of a fair pavilion by the shore of a highland tarn, with wild hills golden with morning autumn light across the sparkling water, white clouds running on a northwest wind across skies of impossible blue depth; and bending down to awaken each sleeper would be the one he or she loved best in all the worlds. Perhaps for Arthur it would be Amris, at last; or Gorlas, or even Athyn his hero and his guide—and for the others the one they would wish it to be. Or perhaps Fionn the Young would come for them, or Malen Ruadh Rhên, as they deserved, for they had gone out as warriors all—

And Arthur lay alone, King in the Light. The Hallows, the Treasures of Keltia, slept in their chest at the foot of his couch, waiting for the day when they themselves would waken. Two guards—one was Tegau—with bared swords in fisted hands sat outside his cabin door; the device of the Red Dragon blazed upon his breast. And it seemed to me in my Seeing that I drew near to him as he lay; I looked down upon him, as I had done so often when he slept and I waked watchful, and I marvelled at what I now saw upon that face I loved so well.

Strength was there, as ever, and resolution, and all the merry brightness of his youth and the wisdom of his years; and something else, something I could not at first put name to. Then it came to me that it was the look a maker will have as a made thing becomes itself, when the efforts of his hand have brought into being the vision of his mind and the desire of his heart. And it goes both ways, you know, the thing makes him as he makes it; the work does work of its own. . . It is a look I have seen often, on Morgan's face or Ygrawn's, a look that no doubt comes upon my own countenance when I have made correctly, when the words within become the song or poem without. And the look I saw now upon Arthur's face was that very look of completion, and achievement, and rightness; and it was a most fair thing to see.

And then Prydwen came to the Firehorn and stinted not but went straight within, cleanly, like a sword striking home into the scabbard, or the Blade into the Cup in the High Mysteries. Prydwen vanished into the mountain that would be her long home and the lastplace of those who sailed her, and it seemed that I vanished with them from myself. . .

When I came to my senses again I found myself in the little alcove aft that housed my blastcouch, with no recollection of how I had come there. Craning, I could see in the dim light that the others were all similarly disposed; indeed, they slept, or else feigned well thereof. And perhaps that was best for them, and I was suddenly exhausted, and thought to do the same.

But as I lay down I felt something round and hard between my pillow and my coverlet, and reaching my hand under I pulled it out to see. And stared, looking upon the thing that had lain there for me to find: the Seal of Keltia, the great emerald carved inghearrad with the knot of the Six Nations, the stone Morric had given Athyn at their handfasting, the flaw deep within it dancing like a far flame.

And I cast my mind back to the Seeing I had had, Saw again Arthur as he lay there upon his couch, and his hand

was bare. Then that other Seeing came to me, that I had
had just as we had come to Kholco: Arthur asleep, or dead,
and on his hand a ring I did not know. And I was comforted obscurely: This would be. This was meant. This was
going to happen; and again I felt, far and faint now but very
true, that lovely water-clear certainty like a swift-flowing
stream, and I smiled.

As I turned over in my own couch and prepared for
sleep, I chanced to glance down at the foot of the bed. And
was startled anew, aye, and much moved besides: There,
through a wrapping of cloaks and curtaghs and other such,
Frame of Harmony's unmistakable outlines jutted through,
like a ship through fog.

I remember very little of the sail that followed, at least up
until the Aojunese destroyer met us halfway home. I do
recall conducting a ritual of sending for Arthur and the others on Prydwen—as the only Druid for many star-miles it
was my obligation, and my joy also—but not much after.
The others told me later—a long while later—that I had
gone to my couch and remained there as one dead himself;
indeed, for a time they had thought me so. Perhaps I was: I
do know that I followed them out as far as I might, though
by no means as far as I would. I was turned back at my
strength's limit, though I would have gone on even then;
turned back gently but most firmly, and in that turning I
sensed Rhian's hand, the Young Goddess, and I obeyed.

But the voyage itself, nay, that I do *not* recall; nor even
the others, not so much. I had no wish to speak with them,
though they needed comforting as much as did I, and what
this was doing to Sgilti and Anghaud, even, I had no care. If
I were not dead, then at the least I must have been for the
moment out of my head with grief and loss and anger and
longing. But to me it seemed like neither death nor madness: My mind was filling with images and words and the
beginning strains of music. And though all my being was
one long denying shout, 'Croesawr i mi!', something else
was stirring and waking and walking here, drawing nearer to
the birth. But not yet was it come to term.

* * *

We were escorted by the Yamazai ship straight to Aojun, and Majanah herself was there to meet us when we landed. No formal ceremonial: She had eyes for none but me, and I for her, and she knew as soon as our glances met what was toward. But she said no word to any other, just put her arm through mine, said my name—"Talvosghen"—and drew me away from the rest.

We went away from the city, she and I, to a small oak-wood on the side of a mountain, where we could look down upon the fantastical roofs and towers of Mistissyn rising through the April dusk. We did not speak for long and long; then out of the speaking silence came a sudden sense of peace, and dán also, a kind of inevitability—what the Aojunni themselves call khazei'khar—and I knew then that it mattered not a whit what was said or thought or felt about any of this. The thing was sufficient to itself; the truth was the truth, and in the end would prevail.

So I told Majanah all that had passed. She harkened most intently to all my telling, and in the end asked one question only: "Did he have pain in the going?" And I was able to assure her that he had not, that there had been in death no hurt for him or for any of the others. She nodded, accepting this as a queen and warrior, and also as a woman who had greatly loved this man.

We stayed in Mistissyn some days while a proper ship was made ready for us—the journey back to Keltia would have taken months in the little sloop—and Majanah did not surprise us when she announced that she would accompany us. Donah, of course, was still on Tara, and as yet unaware of her father's death (though I myself was not so sure of that); and Gweniver would need all the friends she had to help her through not only the losing of her mate and King but the coming of her child.

Just now I was more concerned with Janjan. Of course she and Artos had long since ceased to be lovers—he had come to Gweniver, and she to her own consort Brone—but they had remained close and loving friends, and of course they had Donah to link them forever. But even in my own half-dead stupor of shock and grief, I saw that Majanah, though she tried to hide it and for the most part succeeded, was very near as lost as I. Yet her Yamazai soul, the findruinna core that lay at the heart of her, would not allow her to acknowledge it.

Part of this was because it had been decided en route from Kholco, among the seven of us who lived on, not to announce to the world that Arthur was dead. After all, we reasoned, none save ourselves had seen him die; and, strictly speaking, we had not seen even that. It was possible that Prydwen and her crew had survived the volcano; it might be, it could have happened so. . . And to keep his death secret was in chiming with his own lastwords to Keltia, that he should come again when there was need. Had we known, then, what this decision would mean, in full, perhaps we had not so decided; but we did not, and did.

Majanah, for her part, fell in with the fiction, though she ordered Court mourning as sign of respect, and the whole planet complied. For Aojun had not forgotten Artho Kendrion; the Young Lion would live forever on this world.

But her own grief could not be masked so featly; and so when one sunset she came to me in my chambers—the same I had had when I dwelled here so long ago—and said no word, but only looked at me out of haunted eyes and a face which though set as steel seemed about to crumple like a sorrowful child's, I knew what I must do. So I took out Frame of Harmony, and I began to harp for the Queen of Aojun; not the marúnad I had made earlier in hall but an older song, and one not of my own making: the song she wished, and needed, to hear.

> " 'My love in green came down the meadow
>   Let it follow, let it follow
>   My love in green came down the meadow
>   Long time ago. . .' "

CHAPTER 30

We left Aojun for Keltia a day or two later. Majanah had us sail on a warship in a martial convoy of six, for she had earlier told us two things we had assumed but did not know for fact: that the Fomori were still hotter than hornets over our raid to rescue the Clero captives and the damage we had done to Fomor in the rescuing; and that the remnant Coranian fleet was still skulking about, the Cabiri Emperor Hasparren Lacho as cross as two sticks that his great venture had been so spectacularly and finally crushed—not to mention the loss of the Marro. The little sloop we took in tow, as the last of Prydwen; it would be kept in Keltia in honor and remembrance, and perhaps, some time to come, one might find a further and equally high purpose for it. Until then let it rest.

We came home to Keltia this time on a befittingly leaden afternoon of cold rain and bitter wind. Word of what had befallen at Kholco had been kept utterly secret among the seven of us who had returned therefrom; on Aojun, only Majanah and Brone had been told, and the matriarch of Roric's kindred, and they had all vowed by their own gods to keep silence on the matter. The rest of the Aojunni had been fed the line we intended to feed not only the Kelts but all the galaxy as well, the line we had sworn mighty oaths to our lost ones and to each other that we should hold past death. Else all had been in vain, and that was not even to be imagined. . .

At Mardale, Gweniver was on the field to meet us despite the storm, and if she knew or guessed or sensed aught more than our bare and guarded transcom exchanges had told her, she gave no sign; nor would she have let anyone see it in any case. True, arriving home without Arthur, Prydwen or our crewmates might have given the clue; but there could have been any number of explanations for that—and we only prayed the folk would accept the one we were going to give them.

But Gweniver was a different case, and, like Majanah, she twigged instantly from our faces—from my face.

"Tell me not anything now," she whispered as we embraced in greeting. "I felt him go. . . felt all of them. I will hear. But not yet."

And not later either, not until she was alone with me in the chamber where she had chosen to hear the tidings she already knew in her heart. Not even Morgan or Ygrawn was with us; we were alone, the Ard-rían and the Pen-bardd, Gwennach and Talyn. About us, the great double cube of Gwahanlen was dim with rainlight filtering through the leaded glass of the ceiling, and the tapestries on the wall had lost all color in the gray gleam.

We sat anyhow at the table Rhodaur, a few places apart, our chairs angled to face each other across the empty seats between. As clearly and calmly and concisely as I might, a supreme bardic effort, I gave her the outlines of what had happened at Camlann and in the Morimaruse and at Fomor and on Kholco, all the details she did not know, telling the tale as a bard would tell any hero-tale of old—only so could I hope to get through the telling.

And perhaps only so could Gweniver have received it: It may be easier—though never easy—to hear of the death of one's King than the death of one's husband. That the two were in this instance one and the same mattered not; it was all in the telling and the hearing. So Gweniver Ard-rían heard of Arthur Ard-rígh's passing, and the passing of her

Companions, as she had heard of so many passings before; and at the end of my account, when I fell exhausted against the high back of my chair, she asked the same question Majanah had asked. One question only, as there had been but one question asked on Aojun, and the answer I gave now to this queen was the same answer I had given the other. Both had loved him, and still loved him, and that fear had haunted them. But I thanked all gods that I knew from my othersensing that it was the truth I gave them both.

At Gweniver's request, or maybe command, I left her there in Gwahanlen, and what she said then to Arthur I do not know. That she spoke to her departed mate I have no doubt, and that he was there with her I have also no doubt: I felt his presence, as I had so often since his going, and as I knew I was destined to do for the rest of my own span this-side. But I closed the doors behind me, and went on to my next ordeal—telling Ygrawn—and the details of that meeting I will keep between her and me forevermore. She was Ygrawn; that is enough.

And lastly I told Morgan, who had of course known before anyone and needed no telling at all. But she attended gravely to what I said, even as her cousin and her mother had done; and when I had finished this third recounting— the most terrible triad that ever I had known—she said no word but took my face between her slim cool hands and kissed me gently, and naught more needed to be said. Keltia could wait; we had our own loss to bear first.

But after, when we all came together in Ygrawn's solar and wept and laughed and raged as was fit and needed, the four of us agreed on one thing paramount: that the truth of Arthur's death be kept secret still. It would be given out to the folk and to history that Arthur Ard-rígh had vanished in battle, had gone away in Prydwen with his Companions around him and sent seven alone home to tell of it. After all, all Keltia had heard his message from the Roads of Camlann, when he had locked Prydwen's jaws on the Marro's flanks and taken them both into the ard-na-spéire and into legend. He had told the folk plain that he would come again; therefore let them continue to think so. And if

the days and months of their thinking and hoping stretched
into years and centuries and even millennia, what of it? The
secret of his death and the departure from Keltia of the
Hallows must be maintained; so that when that one who was
to find them again came at last to do so, naught would be
known save what I myself would leave for clue in song.

Not even all the surviving Companions would know the
truth of it, decreed Gweniver, and we concurred. Oh, the
old guard, the Coldgates leaven, to be sure: Grehan,
Tryffin, Ysild, the few others who had been commanded to
stay behind—and who were as shaken and comfortless and
heartsick and, aye, furious as we who had also stayed
behind, or been forced to do so.

But for the rest of it, we had done well: We had been
utterly victorious at Camlann, Grehan told us—hence the
pique of Alphor. When Arthur had removed the Marro
from the field, the other invading ships had lost heart as well
as direction, and our own fleet had picked them off like fish
in a keeve. True, these particular fish had shot back, and
aye, a few of the fishers had ended up in the enemy creel;
but it had availed them little in the end, and Ganaster had
already been contacted to begin the drawing up of truce
documents, all of the terms thereof being most favorable to
Keltia's interests. That, and the memory of the mailed fist,
should keep them away from our door for long time to
come; or so at least we hoped.

Morgan, listening to Grehan tell us seven all this, stirred
in her chair at the Council board.

"I should feel easier to know we had a greater safeguard
even than the assurances of the High Justiciary and the
weight of our own arm," she said darkly. "A year or two,
well enough. A decade, or two or three, and they will forget—the Coranians, the Fomori, the Fir Bolg. They always
do, as we have always seen, and they will try us on again.
And though we lie our faces black and direly swear to them
other wise, truth remains we have no Arthur left us to hold
them off again. It is on me that we must find another shield
as proof against our enemies as the power of Arthur's
name."

But what that shield might be, or where it might be

found, she would not say. Our need, though, was past disputing; as ever, Morgan had the right of it there.

So Gweniver announced to the folk that Arthur was gone from us, gone with his ship and his Companions; and though they were stunned and grieved to hear it, they accepted it at once as truth—and as fact also, which is not always the same thing. But it also somehow made their acceptance of Gweniver as sole ruler, Ard-rían alone, easier to encompass also, this mysterious vanishing of the King; as for Marguessan who claimed the title Ard-rían for herself, naught had been heard of her since her ship had basely fled from stricken Camlann, leaving her son's vessel to be destroyed behind her, with him still aboard.

"What else did we think would be?" I remarked bitterly to Morgan. "She comes and goes like some dark comet, an evil tailstar. A baleful influence and an erratic orbit and malisons raining down on all in her path, and then she is gone again."

"She will be back," said Morgan, and in her voice was mere statement of fact, pure comment; no emotion I could discern. "One time more; we may depend upon it."

And we did, and she was; but even the self-styling Ard-rían Marguessan was just now not in the forefront of our frets. In our traha and our grief and the momentary madness that comes with such stark sudden overwhelming loss as we had suffered, we had somehow neglected to remember that maintaining the fiction of Arthur's death, or undeath, would exact a soul-price on us who knew the truth.

And that toll of spirit, terrible enough already, grew heavier and harder to bear every day; even now, looking back, I do not know how we managed to find our way through to even outer peace. There were a million things that could have betrayed our secret, a million times one or all of us could have misspoken or said awry. All our thoughts must be watched and warded; even our grief must of force be secret. Gweniver had at once put on royal mourning, inflexible in her resolve, and none of us could persuade her against it; indeed, she had ordered the Court into mourning as well. Those of us in on the secret knew well why she did so, of course, but we did gently point out to her that this might be a rather notable and easily read signal to the truth. She would not be turned; and after meditating a little on the problem of the discrepancy—if Arthur was not dead, why was his wife wearing mourning?—had given out that she did so for those who perished at Camlann, as honor from their Ard-rían. If the Queen could not mourn openly for her dead King, Gwen might still grieve, privately in public, for her Artos. We did not press her.

And yet, you know, the secret held. Perhaps it was dán that it should remain unbroken; perhaps our terror of betraying the truth somehow shaped a new truth from concealment, as adamant is forged in the firemount's throat. Now whether one may rightly make truth from lies I do not know; as a bard, I would say under no circumstances should a lie come to stand for what happened otherwise, and perhaps even our good intentions did not excuse us. But I can tell you that for Keltia, Arthur lived on, and all his Companions with him, and the great ship Prydwen; and perhaps, in our grief, we came to believe this ourselves even, a little, sometimes, for comfort—though we knew well it was not so. And perhaps that was not so terrible a thing. But it troubled me to lie to the world, though most of the others seemed not to mind so much as I. Then again, they were not bards.

Majanah, who as I have said came with us from Aojun, had herself given her daughter Donah the news of her father's death, so I was spared at least one encounter I had purely and priorly dreaded. Hard enough had it been to tell Gwennach and Morgan and Ygrawn; to have to look into those young eyes so like my friend's, and speak to her of his ending, would have been more than my soul could have endured, and I was glad, if that is the word for it, that Janjan had drunk that cup herself.

As for Arawn Pendreic, the young Tanist of Keltia had been himself told by Gweniver his mother and Ygrawn his granddam, so again the task was spared me. Though I am bard and every lament and marúnad and coronach in Keltic letters is mine to know and to sing, I am not skilled at speaking of true grief in life, nor yet in imparting it to the bereaved. Perhaps no one is, mask it never so well; in telling of the death of others we are reminded that we ourselves may be called to face such loss.

But I could not avoid Donah forever, nor did I wish to. It was just that I had taken some hard, hard buffeting these past days, and I knew that did I see Donayah just now, the encounter would—literally as well as figuratively—send me to my knees. Knowing how Artos had loved his firstborn, loving the lass myself from an infant—I had attended her saining on Aojun, one of the proudest honors of my life, to have been named for the night to the ranks of women, so that I might attend a ritual of the Mother; I had held her when she was a scant hour old, and had gone on to make a bond with her of uncle and niece that, though I loved him dearly, so far I had not managed to make with Arawn my nephew—knowing all this, I could not think to find a way to comfort Donah on her loss, which was my loss as well. I never thought it might be she would end up consoling me instead. . .

She came to my music-room late in the day, the same day that Gweniver had announced the news to Keltia, giving birth to the myth. She wore the red of everyday Keltic mourning, in obedience to the Queen's command, but around her hair was the blue scarf, folded as a browband (and which would be exchanged in public for a blue faceveil; Yamazai men do so too), that on Aojun is the sign of one who mourns.

Donah said no word, but came in as if by right and sat in the window-seat she favored, that gave out over the view below: a corner of the City, the rose gardens of Turusachan and the great shining sweep of the bay. I continued with the piece on which I had been working on and off ever since Kholco; but it continued to defeat my every effort, or maybe it was just not ready to come to me, and finally I slammed it into my leather satchel with a fearful oath.

Glancing guiltily up as I belatedly called to mind Donah's presence, I saw her watching me with a half-smile.

She raised her brows and gave me a quizzing look that reminded me so much of her mother that I burst out laughing, and felt better at once.

"Ah well," I muttered, with a shamefaced shrug. "Some days you get it by the throat and show it who is master here, and other days it gets you so and shows you. . . It evens out in the end."

"Very like," she agreed, still smiling. "Else we would have no songs at all. . ." She drew a deep breath, then found somewhat of great interest in the coping of the stones round the window-ledge. "My mother has told me," she began in a low voice, "of what ending my father made on Kholco, and of how this must remain hidden forever."

"Aye."

She turned to me all in a rush, lest her courage should fail her. "But, uncle, you were there! You were with him! He spoke to you before he went—did he say—well, did he say aught of me?"

Her voice quivered on the question, and I almost broke on hearing it. I went over to her and put my arms round her where she sat.

"Oh cariadol, surely he did! Of you and your mother both—how not?"

"Then—will you tell me? How it was? How he died?"

And I, of course, could not refuse. It was not as if she were still a lassling, after all: She was a young woman of her majority now; should aught befall Majanah, which Goddess forfend, Donah could assume her rightful place as Jamadarin. Also she had been Graal Princess, and was still on the inner planes. But chiefly she was our Donayah, and also a lass who had lost her much-loved father; she had the right to hear.

And though I began this telling with as little joy as I had begun the others (though with as scrupulous accuracy also), by the time it was done I found to my own 'stonishment that I was feeling the tiniest scrappet less hurting about it, as if it had helped me to share no less than it had helped her that I should share. Not healed, nay, that should never be; not in this life, not in all the lives of all the worlds. . . But just for this moment, I could speak of Arthur and not weep,

or at least not overmuch. Telling Donah had been a way of
abreacting my own feelings of guilt, in a way that telling
Gwen and Morgan and Ygrawn and Janjan had not been.
Even my formal recounting, as Pen-bardd, for the historical
records, made to Grehan who had succeeded Tarian as
Taoiseach and to six recorder-bards, had not been so healing and restorative.

She was silent for a long while after my tale concluded,
and I did not press her into speech. Then she stirred, and
brushed back her bright hair in the gesture she had inherited
from her father; but her fingers touched the blue silk of the
hilyat-shaar, the mourning scarf, and she caught her breath
back a little at the physical reminder.

"It seems to me," she said carefully, "that tasyk made the
best choice he could make in such straits. Too, to go out in
flaming glory must not have displeased him, either. For my
part, I only wish I could have gone with him."

And hearing my own deepest wish and desperate regret
and gnawing guilty longing given voice by Arthur's daughter
turned a key then far within me: A door unbarred that I had
guarded, a gate swung open that I had locked, and all the
pent-up denied blame and grief and if-onlys and what-ifs
came flooding through and out at last. . .

"There now," said Donah solicitously, her hand patting
my shoulders that still heaved with the aftermath of my
weeping. "Is that not better, so?"

"You are a clever wicked girl," I said presently, tears still
streaming. "It must come to you from your mother, for
your father, who was devious enough when it suited him,
was devious in a different way that I would have known to
guard against."

"As you had been doing," she said with a certain complacency. "And that was just the problem. . . We all of us
thought it was long past time you dropped that mask and
wept. And though Gerrans put up a valiant case, I claimed
the errand as my own idea, and so I came."

"Aye, well, and here *I* thought to comfort *you*," I said.
"And I have done my share of weeping, you know; it was
just that I did not wish to do so before Gwen or Morgan or
the rest."

"Silliness," Donah rebuked me with great fondness. "They would have wept with you, any of us would have—and will yet. And it will be, not well, but better."

I began a reply, but suddenly found myself snatched away down a different trail altogether, utterly unvoluntary; and I knew that feeling. . .

"You must leave me now, alanna," I said abruptly, though not ungently. "I do not mean to be discourteous, but something is upon me that requires I pay heed—and I have learned long since that I ignore this sort of claim to my sorrow."

Donah smiled, dropped a kiss on my cheek and went out, well pleased with herself. I scarcely heard the door close behind her, so away was I already with whatever it was that had so commanded my attention. The words that had been niggling at the edges of my awareness, refusing to accommodate themselves to the music that had been echoing half-formed in my inmost ear, now came together, clear and plain and sure, innocently astonished, as if to say 'What, *us*?', as if there had never been any question or trouble about the fit. I began to write them down before they could change their mind.

It was not one of my best or even better efforts in the end—though I know the bard-historians will be annoyed about it, liking to date all work precisely in an ollave's creative life, I shall not tell you what song it was—but it served its purpose. It pulled me out of myself and my grief, it got me to write out the whole of it—the sorrow and the loss and the anger—and it performed that magical and notable antic that only one's art can do: to distance what is felt from what is made of that feeling.

Nor was it the great work that had long been presaged by Merlynn's words and Gwyn's; that one was yet to come. This now was only a forerunner, a trial-piece, as when one who carves that magnificent Keltic knotwork in silver and gold will try them first in bone. A humbler medium, before the hand is set to the greater: but not to be scorned for it. There is as much honor in forging a boot-nail as in forging a sword, and both are necessary to their purpose. I would forge my song-sword in its own good time.

All the same, though, I reflected as I read it over, I would not be presenting this boot-nail any time soon before my peers. But I was grateful to the trial-piece all the same.

The season following produced rather more than an indifferent chaunt: For one thing, it produced another Pendreic. Gweniver gave birth to Arthur's second daughter, Arwenna Seren Siedah Ygrawn, early in the Bear-moon—an omen not lost on those who were inclined to see such. Her father's name had indeed meant 'bear,' and surely Artos had comported himself like that creature on many occasions (too many perhaps, you might be thinking); but Arwenna was a most usual babe, a quiet pleased infant with her father's red-brown hair and her mother's cool gray eyes, endlessly interested in anything and anyone who came within her chub-fingered, acquisitive grasp. For all she resembled her parents, though, many there were among older Kelts who swore she was the image of her grandsir Amris; and not a few complained of the Yamazai birthname her goddessmother the Jamadarin of Aojun had bestowed upon her. But Gweniver curtly dismissed this, saying only that Artos would have wished it so, and doubtless she was right.

True to her given promise, that goddessmother stayed with Gweniver until the child was weaned, as did Donah also, thrilled with a new halfsister; and for her part Gweniver, whom those two and Morgan had assisted at the birth, took great comfort in their presence. Arawn, who had been away in fosterage with the Clann Chattan, had been recalled to Caerdroia's greater safety during the brief outfrenne war and its sequels; and now, after the birth of his fullsister, he was sent away again, this time to foster with the Ó Torridon at Rosyth on Caledon. Many wondered at this, thinking that surely the Ard-rían would wish to keep both her children close by her just now, as she strove to adjust to ruling alone. But then, they did not know their Ard-rían; and clearly they did not know our Gwen.

Nor, it turned out, did we, not so much; which is why, when at last Gweniver made that pronouncement at which all

Keltia would so soon shake in thunder, we were as taken by surprise as any.

"Resign!" I gasped. "Nay, Gwennach, you cannot—"

"I can, and I shall," said Gweniver calmly, not looking at me or anyone in the chamber. "I have not spoken of it sooner, because so soon after—well, afterwards we had many graver things to consider. But I determined on this that very hour wherein I knew my Artos was gone, and I will not be swayed nor gainsaid. Not by you, Talyn, not by any. This shall be."

Looking at her, I hardly felt inclined to do so; and the others she had dismissed along with me—Morgan, Ygrawn, Majanah, Ferdia, Grehan, Daronwy—seemingly shared my feeling full measure.

"How, then, will you go about this?" asked Ygrawn after a long and twangling silence. "Arawn is still far too young to take up rule—"

"Just so," said Gweniver. "Therefore upon my resignation as Ard-rían I shall set up a Regency for my son, and there shall be three Regents who shall rule for Arawn until he comes of age. I myself shall be one of the three."

"And the others?" asked Majanah, her face giving no clue to her feelings on this decision.

"The Rían-dhuair Ygrawn Tregaron ac Pendreic gân Amris," said Gweniver, deliberately giving her matemother not only the honorific of Queen-dowager and the surname of her marriage but the sponsal affix that she derived from her first pairing, the céile-charach union with a prince of Keltia that had produced Arthur for us all. Ygrawn's face did not change nor did her gaze shift or falter at this perhaps over-elaborated naming; but that with her was only usual.

"And the third?" said Grehan, unable to hide his annoyance; as Taoiseach he should certainly have been consulted before the Ard-rían took it into her head and hands to disarrange all Keltia, and I sympathized with his wrath, the more so considering Gwen's answer.

"The Princess Morguenna Pendreic, Duchess of Ys."

I started violently, but really I should have seen it coming from a very long way away; and reaching out to sense Morgan's feeling on the matter I found at once that she had certainly expected it. And, to my continuing surprise, was by no means reluctant for it. . . But Gweniver was not yet done with astonishments.

She paused a moment, her gray gaze touching on each of us in turn around the table.

"We three shall act as Regents for Arawn, as I have said. But one thing more. . . I have taken counsel of the Chief Brehon of Keltia and a panel of her ollave-legists, and I have found there is full lawful sanction for this I declare now to you, and tomorrow to the folk: that Arthur Penarvon, born Pendreic, Ard-rígh of Keltia of the House of Dôn, shall remain King of Kelts until such time as his death can be proved most uncontrovertible. And therefore all rulers after him, Ard-rían or Ard-rígh, shall hold their rank and rule by his grace and make their laws and judgments in his name. For did not Arthur say he would return? And shall his crown and Seal not be awaiting him when he does?"

The look of triumph on her face hit perfectly off the blank gaping astoundment she saw on ours, and glancing round at each of us again she laughed.

"Not often I manage to silence all you together! Has no one aught to say, then?"

I opened my mouth, drew breath to speak, then closed it again decisively. Let someone else talk against for once; I for my part was not venturing to touch this one with a lonna. . .

"It is on me we have more crops than one being sown here," said Grehan carefully. His earlier annoyance was gone, replaced by a wariness unparalleled; he would have continued, but by now Daronwy had recovered from her dumbfounded silence, and she had never been one long to remain speechless when events threatened.

"Are you *daft?* Ever was it Artos of whom I would so inquire, but, Lady, it seems you are taking up his mantle where he did cast it down. . . Gwennach—"

Now even Daronwy seldom spoke to her High Queen in such wise, and though she had almost constantly addressed

herself so to Arthur, generally it had been on points—war or
strategy or tactics—where she knew she stood on unassailable rock and he ankle-deep in a swamp. But this was different, and I thought I knew why: for that she had lost Roric
in Prydwen, her Aojunese lord of many years' pairing, and
this was a way of working through her grief.

But Gweniver only smiled at her, with the smile of a lifetime's friendship that understood, and shared. "No madness,
Ronwyn," she said quietly. "Indeed, it was you and Talyn
and Feradach and the others who returned that gave me
leave and license to declare so. . ." When we said naught but
only stared our question: "None of you saw my lord perish.
That is no fiction for the common hearing but plain truth.
Or is that too a lie?"

She challenged us with her eyes, and we could do naught
but shake our heads; she had the right of it. We had *not* seen
Arthur die; we had merely known it. Nor had we scrupled to
employ this useful fiction for our own purposes heretofore;
but now to find it employed on us in our turn, and by our
friend and our Queen—nay, that we could not have been
expected to foresee. Our lie was used against us: We had
been outfoxed and outfought, and the bout was over before
ever we had known it was fior-comlainn.

"And they all said you were not the strategist Artos
was—" I muttered, and Gweniver grinned.

"Ah well," she said lightly. "Down the years my lord
must have given me a hint or two. . . But you are not to
think yourselves outsworded here. That is not the issue."

Morgan, who had been silent all this while, suddenly cut
her glance up and over to her cousin.

"Then, Gwennach, tell us what is. I think we all know it;
but pray you tell us just the same."

The gray eyes of the Queen turned to findruinna-color.
"Then if you will have it so," said Gweniver evenly, "I have
never lost my anger at what this realm displayed to me, and
how it 'haved to me, and spoke of me, and thought of me,
what time I stood accused and challenged; and never have I
forgiven them for the slaying of Keils. They think I have
forgotten their perfidy, that I absolve them for believing the
lies they mouthed of me. Well, once you had a queen, and

fine she put it in like case; and as she said once so I say now: I do not forget and I do not forgive."

Now those words were Athyn's, and historically they had presaged retribution; and before more such words could be forthcoming (or indeed a sample of their intended sequel) I said hastily, "Not Keltia, Ard-rían; Marguessan only. More truly, her Coranian vermin, Tembrual and Granúmas and the rest, whom I slew at Barrendown. They were the ones—not Kelts, not entirely—who first planted those lies and saw them to ripeness; they also the ones who murdered Keils."

"And I thank you again for the dispatching of them." Gweniver made me a little bow from her chair. "And that may be so, but still it was Keltia, and Kelts, who believed the lying vomitous poison they spewed; indeed, I have no doubt some part of Keltia believes it still—many hateful folk love to think the worst in the teeth of truth to the contrary. Nay; the lies and spite and malevolences were what forced my need of a champion: because Kelts believed them, Kelts too stupid to live, who would be better sent to join the others of your outfrenne bag, a good day's hunting. Yet if only those stupidities had been rejected, if Keltia had kept its eyes and mind and heart open and its mingeing little mouth shut on what it did not know, Keils—aye, and my lord also—might still be with us."

The passion in her voice silenced us all; I had known Gwen held resentment for the ill treatment and lying gossip, and rightly, to my way of thinking; but I had not known it went so deep. What she had just now told us was a truth we had never wished to hear, had studied to dismiss and ignore because it was easier on us to do so. We had not thought of her.

But Gweniver was right to feel so. She had been betrayed by folk only too willing to think ill of her. All that she had done, for Keltia, for Artos, down the years, all that had been set aside, counted less than naught, so that stupid mean cruel folk could mouth obscene lies about something of which they stood in utter ignorance, set on by creatures who sought only to batten on it for profit to themselves.

Well—they had been paid now in their own bloody coinage, and I was pleased the payment had been made out

of my own pouch, as it might be. But Gweniver was owed a
debt that could never be made up to her, and she would
have scorned to accept their reparations even if offered. She
wanted vengeance, and justice, which in this case, as happens sometimes, were one and the same; and this she now
proposed—to remove herself from Keltia—was the only just
vengeance she could take: to refuse to continue giving them
a matchless gift that they did not deserve.

And she was right. She was right. It was insult unfor-
givable and unforgettable, and this was her éraic for it. Oh,
Artos's death had much to do with it too, make no mistake: It was grief as much as wrath that fueled this, and so
Grehan had meant when he said earlier that more crops
than one were in it. And I had to admire it all, we all did:
The thing had been brilliantly brought off. Artos himself
would be proud and amused to see it—as doubtless he
was. . .

Gweniver met my eyes then, and we looked at one
another as we had not done for long. No need for us two to
exchange words or even mindspeech: We had known each
other too long and too well for that. I knew her heart on
this, and she knew mine; and of all those at that Council
table, not saving even Ygrawn or Morgan, we two were the
ones whose hearts and knowing mattered most.

"Let it be so," I said aloud, and from the corner of my
eye saw the other faces turn to me in wonder, like pale surprised flowers. "Does any here need the judgment of the
Chief Brehon in this matter of the will of the Queen?" I
glanced round. "Nay, I thought not. . ." I rose in my place,
thinking with an inner pang of my seat Gwencathra at the
now all but empty Table. Gwencathra, White Stanchion of
Truth. But truth could be a stanchion here as well.

"Then so say I, Taliesin Glyndour ac Pendreic gân
Morguenna, Pen-bardd of Keltia: that the wish of the Ard-
rían be the will of the Council and the law of the land.
Arthur Ard-rígh is King of Kelts, once, now, for always. Let
it be so set down."

And so it was. The folk were bewildered at first, a little
frightened; many were throughly shamed by the Queen's
declaration of her reasons for renouncing the throne—

Gweniver, like another before her, was never one to hold
back an explanation. But in the end they came to accept her
will; indeed, there was little else they could do. Yet it was
wise of them; for had it fallen out other wise I think
Gweniver's actions in such event would have made even
Athyn seem a model of restraint.

So on the first observable-day of Arthur's passing—his
year's-mind, one full year gone (of which fact the folk yet
remained in ignorance, of course, as they should do forever;
or so at least I hope), for which somber anniversary
Majanah and Donah returned from far Aojun—Gweniver
Pendreic resigned the Ard-tiarnas of Keltia and the title of
Ard-rían, and became instead Regent, for Arawn her son,
with Morgan and Ygrawn.

After the fearful legal documents were all signed and
sealed and settled (for this was unprecedented in all our history; never before had a monarch resigned for a regency's
establishing, and the mechanics had all to be invented spe-
cially for this occasion), and the Councillors and brehons
and representatives of the various orders had gone, a knot of
the inner Companion-kindred remained. Gweniver, tired but
triumphant, had a smile and a word and an embrace for
each, until at last there were two only left in the Council
hall—Gweniver and myself. We looked at each other down
the length of the great basalt table, and then we smiled.

"You still have not heard my real reason, Talynno," she
said.

I nodded. "I know I have not. But it is for you to choose
the time of telling."

"Aye so? Yet I think you know already. . ."

My smile warmed and widened. "I think so too. But I
need to hear you speak it. I think you too need to hear
yourself speak it, and perhaps another also has need—"

At that Gweniver laughed in real amusement. "Oh, I
wager you he has known from the start! But though all those
other most sapient and mighty reasons I gave out just before
were true enough, the deep truth is other wise."

She paused, and her gaze went down the table, past me,
to the high-backed chair that Arthur had used to occupy in
Council; I watched her face closely, and presently she

smiled, though she spoke to the empty seat, it seemed, and not to me at all. And perhaps that seat was not so empty either. . .

"I did not wish to reign with him; but I did and I grew glad of it. And now I do not wish to reign without him; and I shall not and I am glad of that already. No more. But no less also."

I left my place and walked down the length of the room to her, took her hand and kissed it, raising it to my lips in the ancient gesture of fealty and honor.

"It is enough—Ard-rían."

And Gweniver gave me the gentlest of smiles, and as gently withdrew her hand.

That night saw a small, fiercely private ceremony up at Ni-maen, the royal nemeton tucked away high above and behind Caerdroia, in the tiny valley between the peaks of Eagle that is called Calon Eryri. Just family, in the truest and realest sense: the royal clann of Pendreic-Penarvon-Tregaron, now rather sadly lessened by events, augmented by the linked blood of Manchéden of Aojun; the few remaining original Companions, whom Arthur had bidden stay behind while he and the others sailed off into legend; the seven of us who had been denied that sailing; later friends and comrades—soul-kin all.

The sending ritual we did here, led by Gweniver and myself, who were both closest kin and ranking clergy, was by no means for Artos alone; nor was it the only one that had been performed. There had been an even smaller and more private one held immediately upon our return from Kholco, not to mention the one I had conducted aboard the sloop bound homeward. But this, tonight, this was the true sending: Even though they were long gone, and well gone, our dear ones, this would catch them up, like an errander riding hard after with tidings from those left behind.

As the rite progressed, I found myself drawing away within myself, separating into several various Taliesins: the bard, the priest, the prince, the brother. I had half thought to see others honoring this place and ritual: But cast round though I might, I had no othersense of the presences I sought. *Strange that the Sidhe who took to themselves the name of friend to Arthur have not troubled to ride to his sending. . .* But the Shining Folk did all things in their own way, and perhaps there was a reason I knew not, or would later learn. Still, I was hurt obscurely; though whether more on Arthur's behalf or my own I am sure I could not tell you.

Yet a stranger thing came out of that time than anyone could have guessed. . . Though Gwen was Ard-rían no more, the style of Queen still clung to her; and of course Ygrawn as Uthyr's widow had never ceased to be so addressed. Which was fine and good. But suddenly my Morgan, no queen ever in this life save queen of my being, now found herself being called so, and deferred to as such, by the vast run of folk.

There seemed no reason for this, and Morgan found it most distressing, and discouraged it all she could. But I thought I knew a reason all the same: We have ever loved triads in Keltia, and this one was too tempting to let pass— the Three Queens of Keltia's Regenting. The commonalty saw them so, and so did they become; for more, I think, than mere convenience's sake—if it be not blasphemous even to suggest it, that Triunity of the Mother Herself. . .

But I recalled a vision I had had, oh, long since: some battlefield Seeing or other, of three queens round a bier upon which lay a dead king. It came to me that never had I beheld the faces of the mourning queens, for they were veiled beneath their crowns; but the face of the king had been the face of Arthur.

How strange when Seeings become seen. And how sufficient also.

CHAPTER 31

And, it seemed, scarce breathing-time allowed, I went straight from that rite at Ni-maen into the blackest despair I had ever known.

It was not unexpected, nor yet unthought of, that it should come down upon me, so, now, after a full moonyear had passed and I had held clawing to my dignity and my masks through all haps and moods. I mourned, I grieved, I raged, I wept; for so do we all in time of bereavement. But I had not thought how much I would *miss* him, simply miss him, my brother and my friend; I ached with it sometimes, grew still and let the pain roll over me—for him, for all of them.

All the same, though, I had reserved myself from something, I know not what—life? Feeling? Admitting that this was real, that this had in truth happened? It is hard to explain. But I paid full price now, if grief was the coinage; and I did not know how to save myself from this accounting.

Most all else went well in Keltia. After a less than smooth start to it, the new Regency was working now most smoothly indeed; in fact, it had settled out rather predictably like the Ard-rían Gweniver running things as ever with the frequent assistance of the Queen-dowager Ygrawn, and the sometime opinions of the Duchess Morguenna of Ys. It seemed to suit them all three; and Keltia was prospering

again after the brief check and halt of the invasion and
rout.

Arthur was never forgotten, not for the smallest moment
of time; indeed, it sometimes seemed that he was more here,
more present, more beloved, in his mysterious vanishing
not-death, than ever he had been in his living self. That is
often so, with figures larger than life, as I have noticed down
the years. Alive, such persons are too strong and vital and,
well, alive for us; they have wills and wishes of their own,
they can thwart us and deny us and change on us. But dead
(or gone—we must keep up that lie now!), these folk
become fair game for admirers and detractors alike unfairly
to pursue with the intent of alteration. Their lives and reali-
ties are blithely ignored, so that needy admirers can bend
them to their own use; or half-truths are flung out like rot-
ten wheat, allowing envious cowardly detractors, who would
never in a thousand lifetimes have enough courage to live as
their victims had done, to raise crops of malice and spite.
And the ones they use for these evil practices cannot defend
themselves; and if those who know the truth are brave
enough or angry enough to speak out against all this, they
themselves are denounced, and the sham goes on.

So I had cause, then, for my despair. But elsewhere in
my life, things went well: Morgan, Gerrans and Cristant,
my two grandsons (who had recovered from their ordeal
at Kholco with all the resilience of youth, and, it must be
said, the not deeply imaginative). Even my granddaughter
Cathelin, now in fosterage with Tarian Douglas's own
grandchildren, gave no cause for fret.

So what then *was* it? And, more importantly, what could
I do to heal? The answer came in surprising fashion.

I was up in my music-room, that round room overlooking
the City and the sea. Over the past months I had begun
spending more and more time here—even going so far as to
have a shut-bed built in one corner, so that there were many
nights, perhaps too many, when Morgan slept alone.
Naught to do with her; it was all me, and now I had taken
to passing the days here as well, apart from everyone who

loved me, everyone I loved. It hurt abominably, it ached and
gnawed worse than I hope you ever know; but it was all I
wished to do, and by all gods I *would* do it. . .

I was lying disconsolate upon the shut-bed one afternoon
when of a sudden came in the air around me the sound of
bells. Seven small strikings upon a bell of silver, so small
and clear and fine of tone the notes.

I said unthinking, "Enter then and welcome," adding
hastily and prudently, "sith that you be of good intent."
Well, you never know, do you; and besides, Marguessan
was still roving round unleashed.

"Are you yet unwearied of your theme?" came a deep
and familiar voice out of the air. *Not Gwyn, but—*

I leaped from the bed, looked wildly around; the speaker
had not yet chosen that he should be seen, but there was in
the chamber no sense of evil, only benison, and my heart
began to slow its pounding.

"If you mean my grief at his going, I could harp upon
that theme from now to Nevermas, and perhaps I shall," I
said with the angry desperation of honesty that cares not
how the hearer may take it. "From now until Rocabarra
rises, until the Black Ox treads upon your toes. . . Whatever
futurity you like by way of metaphor. It is all one; and nay,
lord, I am *not* yet wearied. Not three years after, not three
hundred."

Allyn son of Midna was between me and the windows;
he seemed to have stepped out of the air or the shadows, or
perhaps he had been here all along and I had been too dull
or too doltish to perceive him.

"Then that is both well and ill," he said, in that Sidhe-
voice which is like to no mortal voice there ever was, and
smiled on me. "Well for that such resolution is needed for
the task you have ahead; ill—"

"Aye?" I asked in a challenging tone. Strange to say now,
but just then it astonished me not a whit that a lord of the
Shining Folk should have all at once turned up in my
music-room. What brought out the note of defiance was the
certain fearing dread that Allyn was here to make me *do*
something—a something that might mean letting go of my
sulks—or my sorrow—and I was by no means ready yet to

give over. And maybe I never would be, but that was *my* affair, it seemed to me, and no concern of his or any other's. . .

"Ill for that it has taken you off the path," said Allyn at last. "And all that you have gained till now be at risk unless you act to keep it. Taliesin—I know well that you blame my people for what befell Arthur and the others who went with him. And that is to be expected, though in this we are tools as much as you or he or any mortal—though I have no hope of your believing this. Nay," he said warningly, as he saw me gearing up for protest and denial, "it is so; nor need you blame yourself, call hard on yourself, for leaving them behind. You did not leave him, Talyn; he left you."

All the breath went out of me as if he had driven a spear-butt into my guts, and I stared at the fair face in white gaping astonishment.

"How did you know that?" I whispered at last, trembling as with a sudden chill. "I have told no one—*no one!*—of that fear, not even Morgan or Gwen. . . *How could you know?*"

"I admit you might have seen it coming," he temporized, passing over my question. "But Arthur was a master at such moves, and that you know very well. Nay; you were tricked by him, supremely, and now you are angry that you let him do so, to his death. Talyn, be easy: Never would it have been elseways. He would still have stayed, and you would still have gone. You but did his will as you had a thousand thousand times before; and as you shall again."

I was silent, and he did not press me. Then, to my utter amazement, I heard myself asking a question I had not known I needed answered.

"Why did not the Shining Folk honor Artos's rite of sending at Ni-maen?" I asked sullenly, and to my horror and annoyance I found myself fighting to hold back stinging tears. "Was he not so good a friend to you then? Did he not deserve such presence?"

The faerie lord's voice was veiled, and his eyes hooded. "It may be you left Ni-maen too soon that night you speak of," he said presently. "But I tell you we were there." His glance came up to mine and his voice rang and shifted. "Still, that is not why I have come here to bespeak you—"

Suddenly, all unwilled by me, my black mood, that high king of all dubhachas under which I had labored so long, as under a thick choking cloud, lifted and was gone; and I found myself expectant, full fain of hearing what was Allyn mhic Midna's errand to the Pen-bardd of Keltia.

"You and Morguenna both," he said. "Both of you have work to do ere the end. Morgan already knows what her task shall be, and how it shall be accomplished; now I tell you of yours." He smiled as he saw me lean forward the better to hear him, eager now as a hound for the chase. "Much of what has passed in Keltia of late—and I mean long before Arthur's going—has come about because of what I shall, for lack of truer word, call politics, though it is far more than that. Now my folk do not ordinarily concern themselves with such matters, believing them best left to mortal Kelts and tiresome in any case. But Nudd the King has bidden me come to you with a thought, which you may take or no as you shall please, and it is this: Keltia stands or falls by magic; but the magic that now prevails in Keltia stands or falls itself by political dominion and cause and the ascendancy of worldly claims. And this, we hold, should not be."

"It is pure truth," I said, interested in spite of myself. "Though we love to think it other wise, both magical orders in Keltia, Druids and Ban-draoi alike, have long time on certain levels worked more as a shadow Council—or Councils, since they hardly ever run in pace with each other—than as holy conventicles whose sole and high purpose is to do worship and teach that same to all."

"And many Ban-draoi and Druids do just that," agreed Allyn. "But some not so much, not of late; and therefore am I sent. Talyn, these are Nudd's words: A new Order is needed in Keltia, one that shall have for its heart and center the purity of pure magic, to whom shall be named and accepted only those men and women who are supreme in that one Gift. And if such a thing is ever to be at all, it must be now, and you are the one who must engender it."

Again my breath went out of me in one convulse: Whatever I had been thinking to hear him say, surely it had not been this! And though my heart yearned and leaped to it at once, my head said other. . .

"Why me?" I heard myself asking coolly. "Surely there are many others in Keltia far better suited to such a task than I. I am Pen-bardd, right enough, but only an indifferent Druid. Nudd might better have suggested one like Loherin, say, who now is Graalkeeper; someone of that same high exalted condition—a mystic and a sage, whether man or woman. A magician, not a musician."

"Nudd names you," said Allyn, smiling but dismissive of my modesty; not that he thought it false, for it was not and he knew it, but that he held it irrelevant. "And none asks Nudd whyfor. His reasons are his own, and if he himself is advised, we know not from what quarter such advice might come. Any road, this is no command nor prophecy, but suggestion only. Think on it. Speak of it to those you love and trust. And if in the end you elect against it, at the least it shall have been ventured in this age, and we shall know it was not to be."

"But what shall come to be if I decline?" I asked, suddenly, deeply fearing; I did not even know what this task might prove or demand, nor yet if I would take it up, yet already I despaired to lose it.

"That not even Nudd himself has been given to know," said Allyn, and even as the silver bells sounded again, crystal rain, the music of the Bell-branch, he was gone as silently and strangely as he had come.

I shook myself all over and glanced wildly around. Nay, surely this had not happened! I had been half-dreaming while nodding on the bed, that was it; the close warm air and sunlight streaming through the lancets had induced some doze-dream or fancy, an ashling at best. . . Then my eye caught something upon the table by the window, which had most definitely not been there before Allyn's visit, and I fell upon it and bore it back to bed.

Cross-legged upon the pillows, I examined it gingerly and avidly together. It was a small disk or medallion: a flattened ring of dull silver, very ancient, that enclosed the figure of a most elegant dragon. Silhouetted against open space, the creature struck a heraldic posture between passant and rampant, its wings elevated, its tail arranged in a graceful curve, one clawed foreleg reaching out, or holding

off. At the top of the ring was a little bail integral to the
piece, through which a cord of black leather had been
strung and knotted.

Without thinking I looped the cord about my neck, and
the silver dragon disk lay there upon my chest where once
my gold hawk's feather had lain, that now graced my
mother's grave beneath the Hill of Fare. My mind was full
of Allyn's words and Nudd's alike, and it seemed that the
medallion spoke to me also, or else it somehow enhanced
natural gifts of mindspeech and perhaps Sight also, were
one to be trained to it. . .

For as I touched the medallion to my lips, I Saw indeed:
a vast company of folk, reaching down the years like a river,
all of them robed in black and purple; and at each throat the
silver dragon gleamed. They seemed to me as a sword for
Keltia to wield where all other weapons broke and failed;
and now that the Sword was gone—for a time, for a time
only—they would stand forward to fill its place at need.

The vision faded, and I looked again at the little silver
disk. It minded me of that device Arthur had adopted for
himself and his House in the early years of his reign—the
Red Dragon, the which was already his byname on Fomor,
for his exploits there and otherwhere—though that dragon
was a fiercer far than this. And yet this wingèd silver beast
had strength and power of its own. . . All at once I leaped
from the bed where I had so long lain slothful and indul-
gent and despondent, and went by the inner corridors to a
wing of Turusachan I had not visited for too long.

When I entered Gwahanlen Morgan was there before me.
She turned to me with a smile; it seemed she knew all. And
yet as I began haltingly to tell her of Allyn's visit, and the
first delicate stirrings of a brand-new Order, it seemed she
knew nothing about it; for when I was done and she, shin-
ing-eyed, had added her voice to Nudd's and Allyn's urg-
ings—that this surely was a task with the name 'Taliesin
Glyndour' graven upon it—she began to tell me in her turn
of the task that bore her own.

"You will remember from Coldgates, Talyn," she said,

with an eagerness in her face that, though she did not know it, made her look a maid again, as young as she had looked at that same Coldgates. "How the pale cast round Sulven protected us all from discovery and destruction and even from the worst of the weather? Well then, I have mentioned to you on a time, or two or three, how if such a pale could be constructed to protect more than one mountain or one small ship? To protect all Keltia. . ."

"I remember," I said, surprised that I did. "Before Cadarachta, I think. We were talking of how such a thing might be done, and of what it might do, and of how it might work on Keltia once it was done. Oh aye, I remember very well."

Morgan smiled. "And liked it not so much, as *I* remember."

"Only for that I fear that to seal Keltia off from outworld contact, though it keep us safe, will also keep us same. To stand away so from the rest of the worlds— But I have argued so before."

"Indeed; and now it is on me that perhaps that may not be so bad a bargain: stagnation for safety. But I will not debate it with you, cariad."

"That is well," I said with a not-so-hidden air of relief. "For that you have always said you did not know how such a thing could be done?"

Morgan shook her head, and all my relieved air vanished like dew off the grass.

"Nay; because I know now how I might achieve it, and I intend to try."

Of the debate that raged through Turusachan over the next months, I shall spare you the grossest particulars; chiefly because I did not myself comprehend a tenth of the technical considerations that Morgan tossed off like the merest nurse-tales or counting-rhymes. Suffice it to say that she rolled right over all who stood in her path with a dispatch and celerity and inevitability that her brother would have cheered to the rafters. Sorcerer or scientist, it made no differ: All went down before her logic and magic as before a boulder coming down a mountainside; soon or late, they were hers.

She tried to explain it to me any number of times, though I always screamed and fled; she would talk about leys, electromagnetic tides and channels, and how the Morimaruse could be used to our advantage, as a line of defense—the idea was that the leys would shunt any invading or unauthorized ships away from our space and deposit them far on the other side of the Morimaruse—but I truly did not want to hear.

For, all comic reasons of my hatred for mathematicals aside, I knew that this pale Morgan was set to raise round Keltia—they were calling it the Curtain Wall, after an old and basic feature of defensive castle architecture—would be, literally, the death of her. And that not being something I was eager to rush to meet—well, you can imagine. But she knew what it held for her, too, of course; and though she would not have denied it if taxed with it, she did not speak of it to any, not even to me. Especially not to me.

But it was the task she had been set, perhaps even the one true task for which she had been born. She was afire with the idea, it consumed all her hours and thought and energy, waking or sleeping: endless huddled talks with Bandraoi Dominas or Druid masters or Fian astrogators and planetophysicists. The arguments continued unabated, in the Senate and Assembly, and in the House of Peers; among the folk also—and good strong ground and warrant did they have for it, either side. None of it seemed to matter a scrappet to Morgan: She would do what she would do, and that was the end of it. That it would also be, very like, the end of *her* made no bones.

Yet, even knowing that, incredibly, there were those who thwarted and denied her at every turn; and these were just the folk on whom she counted most heavily, who, one might be forgiven for thinking, would and should be her staunchest supporters.

They were the Pheryllt, the Druid supercollege of master sorcerers, from whose ranks in days past had come such as Merlynn Llwyd and Edeyrn Marbh-draoi himself. In the ranks of the Ban-draoi Morgan was the equal of any among them; but that was not why they now denied her the support she needed, nay. They denied it her because they were yet cross as two sticks that Arthur had gone above their heads and named an Archdruid in their despite, even the estimable Alein Lysaght.

The reason that he had done this was most good: Their last time on the field, they had chosen Ultagh Casnar, and just recall how *he* had turned out. No fault to Arthur for thinking that did they again have choice of naming their chief, they would do little better and very like worse; and he did not wish to leave behind him in Keltia another such success as Ultagh heading up the Druid Order. But they did not see it quite so, and now they were taking their vengeance for that choosing of Arthur's, and taking it out upon his sister.

But everyone in Turusachan these days seemed full of angry passion and spite. Gweniver and Ygrawn—Morgan was by now too taken up by her plans for the Wall to spare much time for her Regent's duties—were as one that the Wall should be raised; and of course to any right-thinking prudent person that should have ended the thing right there, for no one got the better of those two, particularly when they were allied with the third. But the debate burned on for months, oil on water, among the Councillors and officers of state, and would probably do so until the Wall was square in place.

The people seemed divided and uncertain as well. All Keltia, of course, was wishful of safety—over the past centuries the folk had had of alien invaders sufficient for several lifetimes—but still, few of those folk agreed on how this safety should be achieved. And the thought of a great magical barrier hanging in the dark of space, invisible yet impenetrable, hiding seven star systems from the galaxy without, was too much for them to grasp, and they felt stupid and afraid when they thought of it.

Well, I blamed them not at all; I felt stupid and afraid every time *I* thought of it too. But one night when I was feeling a little less feared and stupid than usual, I asked Morgan to explain it to me yet again.

She looked up from her work—the table in our bedchamber was chin-deep in paper and computer-crystals and arcane charts and plottings—and then gently set it all aside to come and sit by me.

"You make more of it than it is, cariad," she said smiling. "It is but a construct, you know, not a cosmology. A wall to be built like any other—like one in the rose garden below. Only bigger."

"Aye, well, it is *not* like any other! To begin with, it is staggeringly tremendous—"

"And so it has to be, to shut off seven stars and all their planets."

I blinked. "'Seven'? But there are in our declared space—"

"Twelve stars altogether; aye, I know. But why do you think we have never in almost two millennia settled any of those other systems?"

"I had not given it much thought."

"Nor does it need much. . . Well, we have never done so because those other five suns are variable and unstable, unable to support life; and their planets could never be made habitable by humans in any case, for many reasons. Too small, too big, too much gravity or not enough, one is a gas-giant, not enough breathable air, eccentric orbit, too swift a rotation. . . It makes a long list of why-nots. But they can still serve our need and purpose."

I was beginning to get a first faint glimmering of her plan, and already I could see why some folk liked it so little. But she was deep in her explanation.

"The Wall will of course need to be powered, and the power will need to last, if not forever, then at least a very long time indeed. It cannot be redone or renewed; we must get it right and running the first time or never at all. And to power something so vast, on such a scale, we need a like source."

"You would need a star," I observed unthinking, then stiffened.

"Aye. We would need a star. Five stars, to be precise; and every one of those hitherto useless planets. All of them must be exploded to give power to the Wall. This, then, is what I have been planning all these months. And, Talyn, it shall work."

I was silent; well, speechless, was more like. Oh, I had known Morgan was plotting out with the scientists and sorcerers something fairly, well, huge; but *this*. . . I could not even find a place for it in my mind, the thing was too enormous for me to grasp. Five stellar explosions—the stars Morgan spoke of were all sorts, red giants, yellow dwarrows, blue hobs—and gods knew how many smaller planetary ones, and they would not be small, nay, not by any measure. The scale of it was beyond me, and the thought that my wife, the mate of my heart, seemed to think it only slightly more complicated than masoning a wall in the rose garden was daunting in itself.

"What will it look like?" I surprised myself by asking. "Does it just hang there like an arras and cut off the stars we see?"

Morgan laughed. "Nay, nay! We shall not even see it, not even know by sight that it is there. Even from outside none will be able to see it; light will be bent through and around it—" She launched into another of her technical lectures—all the more daunting, for there was no proper Gaeloch for any of this, only techtalk—until she saw my eyes glazing over (it did not take long, I promise you!) and took pity.

"Well, then, think of a huge blue curtain of light, but you cannot see it, all round Keltia, in three dimensions—a great glowing sphere with us inside. We can see out, but no one can see in. We shall still be able to see the stars, but our stars will nevermore be seen beyond the Pale, beyond this Curtain Wall that we shall build. Our ships can cross it at will, but no outfrenne craft may pass within to the Bawn."

"The Bawn? But 'bawn' means the space within a castle-wall's defenses—ah."

"Strange how these ancient terms lend themselves so well to this new application," said Morgan blandly. "I would think that as a bard you would find that—intriguing."

I laughed dutifully. "Perhaps it is that I am rather more concerned about the workings of this thing. What happens, for instance, if a ship, Kelt or gall, *not* keyed to cross the Pale tries to do so?"

"That is where those leys I spoke of once to you come into play. The short explanation is that any ship to try such would not be destroyed, but would simply find itself many

star-miles away, across the Morimaruse; and I think you
yourself can say how effective a deterrent that would be."

"Truly." Any ship suddenly bounced, without explanation, from one corner of space to the far side of the
Morimaruse would hardly wish to sail back again for more
of the same. . . It was a brilliant plan, and it was being brilliantly executed. Save for that troublesome matter of the
Pheryllt.

"They will not help," said Morgan simply when I
inquired. "They say most fine and large that each Druid is
free to choose for himself after his own conscience, whether
he will help or no. But in practice—"

Just so. In practice very few Druids, save only the boldest
and mightiest (and those she had already), were prepared to
go against the stated wishes of their ruling body. I knew that
I would not, were I an ordinary Druid; but I was not, and
yet I still had not decided.

"Will folk know Keltia is still here? I should hate the out-
worlds to forget us."

"Some might think that a thing to be wished for—but
aye, they will know. That is, they will know *something* is
there, and they will know from their charts and rutairs that
the something is Keltia; but they will not be able to see it
and they will not be able to get into it. We shall be safe forever behind our Wall."

"Can it—could someone break through?"

Morgan's eyes shuttered. "Aye," she said quietly. "It is
always possible; no vault is thief-proof. But this vault will be
so constructed that to break in would take so stupendous an
effort, and require so powerful a sorcerer and so fell a rann,
that it is unlikely in the extreme. It is the least of my worries
just now. The Pheryllt are a greater."

I fell asleep that night with a greater understanding of the
work my Morgan was called to; and a greater fear than ever.
Not for the work; for her. For her alone. And so, of course,
for myself.

But I had a work of my own, and not bardic either. I had
told Morgan and Gweniver and Ygrawn of Allyn's visit, but

no others; and similarly only they knew of my efforts to bring to the birth that which Allyn had told me was Nudd's recommendation.

Heeding well Allyn's words, I had worked out a set of benchmarks by which candidates for this new Order might be chosen. No matter what they were othertimes—kern or duchess, bard or Fian, farmer or shopkeeper or tech—in this new company all would be equal before that which the Order served: And that was Magic. There would be no rankings, no titles, no hierarchy of officers: a chief and a summoner only, one to decide when assembly was needed, the other to call it. All and each would be equally valued, and the magic would be paramount. Each candidate would be required to demonstrate giftedness in at least one specialized magical discipline, and high proficiency in general.

I knew well enough that I would not find enough such candidates at first to make up the numbers I had in mind; nor did I think that even at full strength, the Order should exceed ten thousand souls in all. If qualified persons were not thick on the ground, we would make do with however many we had, and not admit any comers just to make up numbers. What was wanted here was Keltia's best; good-enough was not good enough.

Yet still the Order had no name. . . But I was toying one night with my dragon medallion, studying the workmanship of it—*surely of the Sidhe*, I thought, *or perhaps even of Earth?*—when suddenly a voice spoke far inside my head, very small but very clear, and I repeated aloud the words it spoke to me, in wonder and in rueful recognition. *Well* of course *this was the right and proper name, how not. . .*

"The Dragon Kinship," I said aloud, to the empty room, to myself, to Keltia. "Those whose Gift is magic supreme. They will be Kin to the Dragon. And to one another."

And so they were.

The Kinship when first formed was small indeed; pathetically so when compared to the ranks of the Companions. I had chosen for my own reasons to seat this new Order in Gwahanlen itself, and they looked all but lost in the reaches of that vast chamber. But Gwahanlen too had seemed all but lost these few years, never once used since the seven of us who had returned from Kholco spoke there to those who had remained behind. It felt right and correct that the Kinship, small though its numbers now were, should meet here.

To fill the twelve twelves of seats at Rhodaur, that once the inner circle of Companions had filled, I had so far mustered only seventy-one Dragons. Some of whom you know well from these pages—Daronwy, Tryffin, Cristant, Morgan herself—but the most part were strangers to our comradeship, and there would be more to come.

In those early days we did not trouble with robes and regalia, save that I had ordered made for each new Dragon one of the silver medallions to match my own; and these were worn proudly, if not yet always openly. For though the Kinship had been introduced to Keltia as gradually and as subtly as possible—the first new Order since the Bardic Association was founded in the year 347 Anno Brendani by Plenyth ap Alun, whose mantle of Pen-bardd had by common consent and usage fallen upon my own shoulders—still we thought it best prudence to keep as low a sail as possible against the sky, not to alarm the folk overmuch. They had endured enough these past years, and the blatant establishment of a new and potentially mighty order of sorcerers could very well appear to them as an arwydd, a portent according to the ancient prophecy: 'Where the true king has perished a thousand magicians shall appear in the land.' What then were the folk to think of a possible *ten* thousand magicians—for though they knew it not, the King *had* perished. . .

So we went softly on. Our first effort as a body was to declare unqualified and unconditional public support for Morgan in her labors on the Wall; and our act, though we had intended it to sway the shogglers, had surprising and far-reaching effect. For the Pheryllt, who so long had balked at blessing the work, suddenly found themselves shamed into that which they had been refusing all along, purely because of the Kinship's action.

I must say, it was pleasant to swing the scales, especially with the Pheryllt and the entire of Druidry in the one tray and only seventy-one Dragons to our own; and certainly it gave us an immediate prestige and weight that, all things considered, we were not entirely either comfortable or discomfortable carrying. But if it made things easier on and for Morgan, then we were content to have it so for us.

And so it seemed: With the capitulation of the Druids to assist the Wall's work, all sorcerers in Keltia were committed, and all sore needed to accomplish the task at hand. With everything now in place outwardly, Morgan went off alone on retreat for a few days to prepare herself inwardly as well, at a Ban-draoi place of solitude, an island llan far in the Kyles of Ra. For to direct so vast a magic one needed a strong place from which to act; and this magic had been long in the making.

You understand all this took years: By the time Morgan was ready to raise the Wall, and the Kinship was formed, Arthur had been near seven years gone. Soon Arawn would be of full age to rule alone; Gweniver's freedom would soon be upon her—all manner of things would change, and the price of that change was still to be set.

For myself, I knew in my heart that the raising of the Wall was going to cost me dearest of all; but even when Morgan returned from her retreat, her strong place built and all her armies massed, I could not speak of it.

But lying wakeful that last night before the work commenced, I could not but feel that she was gone from me already; though we loved and spoke and loved again, with all our old fervor and intensity, it carried more of a valedictory air than either of us cared to admit for fear of alarming the other. Which was loving and noble and all the rest of it, but laid a certain strain over this night, which well might be our last at Turusachan or indeed anywhere else this life round. Yet still we would not speak of it; but one thing came through even so. . .

Morgan, lying in my arms, her heavy hair flung across my throat in a silken cabled braid, stirred and moved closer, her arm moving up my chest so that she could brush her fingers over my beard.

"I have not told you enough, cariad o'nghariad, but I am beyond all words grateful for the support your Kinship has given to the work of the Wall. Even the Pheryllt had to bend to you at the last, and were they not cross to have to do so! But—my thanks."

I shrugged and kissed the top of her head where it lay just beneath my chin. "It was nothing, lady."

"Not so modest, Pendragon! Without the Kinship—" She went on with quantities of praise, but I did not hear, so caught was I by a word of hers; and after a moment or two I laid my fingers across her lips to halt her discourse.

"What was that you called me just now?"

"'Cariad o'nghariad', as ever I have called you, what else—"

"Nay, not that. The other name."

She was silent a few seconds, running back over her words in her mind.

"'Pendragon'?"

"Aye, that is the one. Whence came that? Never have you used to me such a title before."

"It is not mine to use, strictly speaking," she said, snugging closer. "It is what your own Dragons have taken to calling you, at least among themselves; and now the common run of folk have taken it up as well. But surely you have heard yourself called so before."

I shook my head. "Nay. I have not." And nor was I sure that I liked it overmuch. . .

Morgan seemed unaware of my uncertainties. "Oh, I can hardly believe *that!* They are calling you so all across Keltia. 'Dragon' for that you lead the Kinship, you are chief Dragon; and 'Pen', which means 'head' or 'chief', to echo your title of Pen-bardd—the which, if I may point out, never seemed to trouble you one way or other."

"Ah, so much *you* know, madam," I said with dignity, giving her the Yamazai title to twit her. "You were not exactly close by to see how ill it sat upon me, what time Elphin first named me so. . ."

Elphin—who had perished with Arthur on Kholco. . . I took a deep breath to stave off sudden tears. Morgan must have felt it, for she kissed my bare chest gently; I could see

her head move in the moonlight. Outside, the light of
Bellendain gave its faint ruby glow, like a Beltane fire seen
over the rim of a distant hill.

"It sat so ill on you only because Plenyth himself had
borne it; and your modesty, which well became you, disqui-
eted you, that such a name be given. But beloved, you have
well deserved it—and this new name also. Can you not content you?"

When she had fallen asleep against my shoulder, I lay
awake a while, watching the red-silver light change altogether to silver-blue, as Bellendain fled away westwards and
Argialla stood at the midheaven.

Pendragon. . . Well, if truth be told, I was secretly thrilled
to be called so, if openly honored; and even more for that I
had not boastfully claimed it for myself but had had it
bestowed upon me by my own. I had not even known they
had done so; surely modesty could live with that.

And also, amazingly, it even echoed my own ainm-pósta,
my gamonymic, the marriage-name of Pendreic I had
assumed according to our custom when Morgan and I were
wed. For 'Pendreic' was, incredibly, the very same name in
the Kymric as was 'Pendragon' in the general Gaeloch: Of
old, 'dreic' or 'dragon' had both been bardic usages for
'warrior,' and 'pen', as Morgan had remarked, had ever
meant 'chief' or 'lord'.

And that was as such not all so inappropriate, I thought
drowsily, *not even for me*. . . Any road, there was not a hope
of stopping it, not now. Pendragon I was, and would be, all
the rest of my days; and those who would come to lead the
Kinship after me, as first among equals, according to the
Rule of the Order that I myself had set down, would call
themselves likewise, or be called so by their fellows and their
folk. Perhaps that was not a thing to be too much modest
about, after all.

CHAPTER 32

I have said before now in these chronicles that words are sometimes not enough; that even bards—on occasion— can be failed by the tools of their craft. Not because the thing one seeks to tell of is imprecise, or invalid, or untrue— a feeling or thought too vague for describing. Nay; it is because the thing is *too* precise, too valid, too exact and rigorously itself, that there are no words near enough to it to name it rightly. . .

What comes next is neither pleasant nor easy to speak of, but it is a thing most precise and itself for all that; and I am in all ways glad and proud indeed that I may tell how it was. For Morguenna Pendreic, like her brother and her father and her uncles before her, had a blow to strike for her people, and the time of its striking was come at last.

We had done as much preparation as might be done and was demanded, for the raising of the Curtain Wall between us and the galaxy outside. And for a working that might seem to many so purely magical a task, it had proved surprisingly technical underneath; or perhaps it merely illustrates once again how magic and logic are not so distant cousins as we think.

To create this vast arras of unlight and concealment,

then, that Morgan had envisioned, four huge stations had
been built in deep space, out in the blackness between the
suns that light our worlds. They were positioned in such a
way as to cover each a quarter of our borders, with a generous overlap for safety's sake and a relay redundancy fac-
tor also, that one station might pick up the slack if another
faltered or failed for some reason. I admit it is a daunting
image, at least it was so for me—four wheels in space, caers
among the stars that could generate a shield for our entire
sector—and I found myself thinking of the stations as
maigen-stones, like the one I had encountered outside
Daars, on the road from Gwaelod. Markers for what lay
within; but these were more—they not only signalled the
protection, they *were* the protection.

What they were, of course, was far more complex: stations to collect and then disperse the vast amounts of energies that Morgan's great working was going to summon up;
and to maintain it so forever (or as near as makes no differ).
They would be charged by every sorcerer in Keltia and set
alight by the death of five stars and a score of planets; the
entire space of the Bawn would be scoured clean of any
stellar body that was not inhabited or otherwise useful. It
went hard with all of us to take this decision—Kelts as a
rule do not destroy the Mother's works so lightly—but we
did not do so lightly this time. The Wall needed to be
raised; the Wall needed power; there were five suns that
would destroy themselves in time anyway: The logic and the
need seemed to chime.

So the stations were built, constructed in the void; and
Morgan named them. Falias, Findias, Murias and Gorias
they were called, after the Four Sacred Cities of the Airts,
cities of the Danaans of old whence came the Treasures in
the beginning days of all. Some argued with heat and cause
that it was high blasphemy to name them so—I must confess I myself agreed at least somewhatly with this feeling—
but Morgan dismissed all such doubts with uncharacteristic
impatience.

"Those Cities protected our folk once and long time, you
know, Talyn; and then furnished us with the means of
doing similarly forever by giving us the Hallows, of which

present disposition we know. They will not take exception to having their names used so now, to denote these star-caers."

Well, she was master of this working, she would know if any did what was right and what blasphemy. And so the names were bestowed and the stations blessed and brought on line; upon each one now stood a full complement of sorcerers—Ban-draoi, Druids, even hedge-priests and village witches. Every sorcerer in Keltia had been summoned by Morgan to this great undertaking; we had need of every scrap of power we could find. All (once the petulance of the Pheryllt had been banished as it deserved) stepped forward gladly to serve; all stood ready to give to Keltia the service of their magic and their love. And perhaps, of some, more still would be required, for this kind of working was not without its own particular perils. Always a few—usually the very young or the very advanced in years, who were at risk for different reasons—would fall in the great push that sent the magic onwards, and not one of the hundreds of thousands involved shirked the task or shrank from the danger.

The last thing we did prior to the actual working was to make a sail of inspection out along what would soon become the Wall's perimeter, an irregular, meandering line through now-featureless interstellar space. It was strange to look out and think that very soon now, this line we were travelling would be alive with the power of stars and sorcery alike. . .

But Morgan had no time for such reflections. Over the past year or two, as the Wall became as real to the rest of Keltia as it had been in her mind ever since Coldgates, she had changed both subtly and plainly. Oh, not in any way that mattered; and certainly in no way that mattered to me, or that affected our love and bond. Still, there had been changes; and sometimes I wondered if some of Arthur's restless flame of a spirit had not passed from him as he went, and touched a like flame within Morgan that had not until now been kindled.

Watching her now as she quartered empty space like a questing hound drawing a starry covert, she reminded me so of her brother that almost I could not bear to watch her. But the job had to be done: These regions were soon going to be whelmed with washes and tides of energy such as had never been seen or imagined, in nature or in artifice; and, in any ritual, it is your life's and work's worth to know your sacred ground.

Which was, just so, why Morgan had chosen that particular ground upon which she herself would take stand to direct her working, directing the magic inward to herself and then outward to where those upon the stations waited to receive it and pass it on in their turn. In the end, all Keltia would be cloaked in a mantle of light that could not be seen but surely would make itself felt.

For Morgan had chosen once more to go to Caervanogue, to the island of the Graal, and I was going with her.

Well, not just we two, of course; some of the new Kinship came with us, and I had posted Kin to the Dragon on each of the four stations. But Morgan had summoned with us to Beckery those whose strength in battle she knew best and trusted most: Ygrawn, Daronwy, Grehan, Cristant, Alein Lysaght; other of our old Companions, comrades from the Graal seeking, fellow knights. Gweniver, who had been at our parting suddenly as remote as those starclouds in the southern skies we call the Veils of Aunya, remained at Caerdroia with Arawn and Gerrans and my two grandsons; Gwain, only other surviving cousin of that generation of Pendreic, came with us.

Which you might not have thought he would wish to, considering how his last visit to Beckery had gone: his mother denouncing her kin and folk and faith, his sister sacrificed to that same mother's dark aspirations. Not to mention the fact that he himself had arrived there dead, and been restored to life—a happy ending, if a strainful time for him. Still, we wondered at his decision. But he insisted.

So we left Gweniver and the others at home, bidding farewell to them in Gwahanlen itself, where they would themselves join in our endeavor, to be with us in more than spirit; and we took ship at Mardale, flying this time, to the regions east of east so long unvisited.

I looked down as we went, remembering my Quest: There lay Siennega, though the ruins of Inisguidrin were not visible from this height; over there was Ben Shulow; north stretched the Plains of Listellian—and I even spied a huge herd of the white and indifferent bison, many miles off to my left, moving imperceptibly over the green turf like a cloud come to rest. Far ahead, gleaming on the coast like a pearl, lay Fairlight.

We touched down upon the hither shore of the Dragonsea—we would walk to Beckery this time as pilgrims, not ride as questers—and gazed across at the mystic island. Today it lay plain upon the waters like a bossed shield; but there was wonder in our stares, and fear also, for just as plain there was no castle to be seen upon its hill.

"Where is it?" I asked at last. "Caervanogue—where Loherin keeps the Gates of the Graal—has it gone?"

Morgan shook her head. "Nay; but it has been taken away just for now, as what we must do there is not a thing it should behold."

"We do an honest work," said Ygrawn to no one in especial, though the edge-bite of reproof flicked us all.

Her youngest smiled. "Aye indeed, mamaith; but great works leave their echo behind them, and my cousin Loherin only takes prudent care that such an echo of such a working does not cling forevermore to the stones of Caervanogue. Nothing more."

She stepped then to the edge of the water—so clear and green it was, I can still see, a hue like peridots or spring grass—where it lapped against the white stony sand of the shingle, and shed her boots.

"The tide cannot be waited for," she said, as if in apology. "We must go now, as we can—"

And as if she set her foot upon that grass of spring, she set it now upon that emerald ocean, and did not sink. Stride after unhurried stride she took across the waves, stirring up no more water than if she walked along the edge of the tide-wash. Without turning she called to us to follow; and after a silent hesitation, we unshod ourselves, and did so.

Strange it was, walking upon the water as though it were the solid stone of the causeway that led to Beckery; the which, most disconcertingly, I could see, *through* the water on top of which I now so blithely strolled, gleaming whitely fathoms below my bare feet. I set my teeth and fixed my glance to the island shore, and walked on; what the others did I know not, but I am sure it was done for like reason.

We all arrived dry-foot upon the sands of Beckery, and I looked around in wonder. There was no sign that ever a castle had stood here, or foot had stepped here along the cobbled way that once I and the rest, or some of them, had walked. Beyond the narrow beach the sand gave way to low machair-grass and then to beautiful springy green turf that rolled unbroken up the island's single hill. On the hill's other side, I knew, was the strand Garanwynion, where the Graal had come back to us all those years ago; and I thought, as I know the others did, that that same strand was where Morgan would now lead us to begin the work.

But again she surprised us. We climbed the hill—Tribruit, it was called, no more than three hundred feet above the water at its highest—and when we had all gained the top she bade us halt.

"But—this is where Caervanogue should be, or was," said Gwain quietly, only his eyes moving as he cast covertly—and more than a little fearfully—all about him.

"And it is where Caervanogue *is*," said Morgan smiling. "And shall be again. . . No mistake, Gwalchmai. All is to our purposes."

She moved to the center of the hill-top, hands outstretched, fingers spread wide, as if she sensed her way before her in a dark room, and at irregular moments blue fire seemed to flicker from her spread fingers to the ground, and back again. It was as if she dowsed the ground of the magic, or the ground dowsed her. . . She had brought with her no gear of any kind, no magical implements or tools or trappings; no technological ones either. Yet as Morgan stood there barefoot upon the crown of Tribruit, she was also with Gweniver in Gwahanlen, and with the Fian scientists, led by our old Companion Elenna, on Arvor, and with the sorcerers on the four wards of the Wall that was to be, and with their fellows on every world of Keltia.

It was, as she had explained many times, not a complicated working, if a complex one; we were not trying for subtle here but massive—as the proverb puts it, not the laighen but the mataun. Our job was plain, if not simple: to raise as much power as we could; hers was to consecrate it to its purpose and to send it where it must go to act. As for the physical manifestations of the thing: We should not see the explosions of the five stars—they were too distant for that, and by the time their final light would have reached us, it would have been channeled instead into the Wall, and so never would have come to us in any case—but we should unquestionably sense them. The death of a star, or five stars, and planets also—all to raise something I was not sure even yet should be raised at all.

But I knew all the same, somewhere far within, that it must be; and knew too that I must exert greatest care not to let my uncertainty, and my fears for Morgan, color my work. But those fears were all but certainties now—and so they were no longer fears at all: Went the Wall as it might, the raising of it was going to part me from my mate for a long, long time to come. Not forever. Never that. But long.

She knew it too, of course; you do not grow to be so great a sorceress without being keenly 'ware of all such possibilities, nor to know when they leave off being possible and become what is. We had made our farewells, such as we could make them, last night; but in truth, we had been making those farewells all our lives together, and all our separate lives before that also. You do not meet before you are parting; and you are parting before you have ever met, and meeting after you have parted: It is all one. This now—well, it was much like the many battles we had gone into over the years, setting all thought of past and future aside, knowing that this very one might be the fight you would not come home from, or your mate or your child or your friend would not. . . I was prepared. But that is by no means the same thing as being ready.

To still all this, I looked out eastward, remembering. The Graal had come from that Airt, last time I was here on this isle, and its herald also. . . As I looked now there was only the open dark rough water of true ocean outside the huge calm bay, and strewn like landstars across the sea reaches were the tiny scraps of rock and earth that were the Easter Isles.

And standing there, my feet sinking deep in the warm green turf of the Graal island, I dared to let myself hope that what I feared, had feared from the first, might not come to pass even so. Morgan had brought us here last time to witness the triumph of life; it seemed unthinkable, if strangely fitting, that this time round and again in life's service, death should be the visitant instead. And yet I knew in my heart that it could be, and would be: whether for Morgan alone, or for us with her, or for other sorcerers on other worlds. That might well be the price Keltia paid for the Wall's raising.

Suddenly a memory lanced to the front of my mind: a paragraph in one of my mother's journals, where she described and commented on an ancient custom of our Keltic forebears on her Terran homeworld—how when they raised a defending wall, of a castle or some such, they would entomb in it a living thing, or more than one; immure it alive beneath the wall's footings, so that in death it might give its life-strength to the bulwark erected above it, and thus keep safe the folk.

And, my sorrow to report, all too often that living thing, in those times, had been no beast or bird (bad enough) but a human being. . . I could not keep the terrible picture and even more terrible comparison from my thought: Was that ancient and most barbarous custom about to be revived here? Would this Wall, too, require for its footings the strength—and the lives—of those it was intended to protect?

Morgan did not give us time and luxury to wait round and grow distracted or distressed by just such sleeveless queries as this. Working swiftly now, smoothly and serenely, she set us out into three circles atop the hill, each with a leader of its own to direct and link the working; and she herself took up her own position in the center of us all.

I had located myself carefully, so that from my own stance in the deosil circle I could watch Morgan where she now stood—Ygrawn, I saw, had done likewise, though Cristant and Gwain were so placed that they must keep their backs to their kinswoman—and as she lifted her arms to begin, I forced my attention to the work I had before me.

I felt it at once, the link, the chain Morgan had been quietly fashioning all during the journey here, and doubtless for a long while before that: the thread, finer than any silk, stronger than any findruinna, that connected each of us here to each and to all those on all worlds, and to those out among the stars. The timing was the same for all of us, the hour was long known; and we were eager for it, a hound pack held hard in before the hunt began, waiting on the Master's signal to course.

And—though as I have said no implement had been brought to the holy isle—it seemed to every soul in Keltia, in the magic or not, that a great horn sounded, a hunting-music, three long far cries that rode upon the wind and rang through every heart, a call to summon them all to the hunt. Even those who thought they had no magic in them, even children and the very old, even the beasts who shared our homes and hearths: All had their part in this. As never it had been before, and never would be again, Keltia was one: And that one was Morguenna Pendreic.

How she took it upon her I shall never know; even the spillover, the sparkling edge-currents and eddies of the power that the rest of us on Tribruit perceived, even those were staggering enough, and even to seasoned sorcerers. But Morgan drew it in, in calmness and in visible joy, knowing exactly what she did; held it, blessed it; and then sent it out again, to do her will.

And we felt it begin to build, felt the Wall begin to rise; and at the same time I felt the wall that was here on Beckery, the wall that was between us and Caervanogue where Loherin was master and Servant, begin to thin. And then, Morgan's will also being that we should see as she herself did, we began to see what our labors were creating.

It was very strange: Behind me I kept getting flashes of stone ashlar and long echoing corridors and rooms like

pools of peace—Caervanogue, beginning to come through—
but those were mingled with stunning glimpses of the space
far distant, where mighty things were in train. The first star
I saw die was a small and powerfully unstable blue hob,
tight and incandescent. It glowed fiercely, rippling the colors
of the sunbow; and then in a silent white dissilience, some
starflower pod of vast dimension bursting its hull, the sun
gave up its light. A thousand years, a million, who knows
how long its life should have gone on; but it would have
died in any case, and this way its end was no vain thing.
And yet I could not feel that it had died; indeed, I felt it was
glad so to sacrifice itself, glad as we ourselves would be.

Four times more this scene played out before our othersight; only the colors changed as the stars differed. Planets
added a different, earthier tone to the mix of colors, the
giant palette of energies unimaginable that Morgan was
about to put on her immensities of canvas.

And then, as the Gates behind us to Caervanogue
opened in the presence of the Power here resident and the
powers Morgan had called in, two things happened: Loherin
the Graalkeeper came forward. And Marguessan Pendreic
came forward too.

My first thoughts in that astounding moment were: *How
fair Loherin is, how his beauty reflects his soul and his task.*
And: *How at last her inside is revealed upon her outer self—
how the evil that found footing from the start, and bloomed
and blossomed under Edeyrn, is made plain in Marguessan at
last. . .*

No one, seeing her now, could ever have been blamed
for thinking her no relation in any degree to Morgan and
Ygrawn. Nor yet to Gwain, whose white face shone like the
moon Argialla out of the corner of my eye. Oh, her beauty
was still there, in a way; but now it looked as some fair tree
clutted with a noxious black devouring growth, its last
strength and goodness sucked out of it by the clinging para-
sitical leech.

And incredibly, I felt sorrow touch me for Marguessan
and her dán and her choices; for an instant only, faint and

far, but I felt it, and I knew I would remember it after, when
the coil had run out and things were as they would be.

But, as I say, it was a matter of an instant only; and then
I felt all those other things buzzing round me in an angry
cloud, the things that had always walked with me when
Marguessan was at hand. Chiefly, though, I felt fear: for
Morgan, for Loherin, for the work, for us all; since it was
very plain that Marguessan had *not* dropped by in a leisure
moment to help us with the raising of the Pale. And all the
while I felt the raised power checked in its rising, hanging
over us, still under the iron grip of Morgan's mastery but an
earthshake on a leash all the same—an earthshake that could
topple the stars.

There was naught any of us could do about it: We were
bound in our circles, unable even to cut ourselves a gateway
in the usual fashion and step out to aid Morgan. She had
designed the magic so a-purpose, so that if anything went
wrong with the shifting of power from her to the Wall we
would be protected from the worst backlash of it, and the
brunt of it come down upon her alone. Even Loherin, master though he was in this place, was barred from acting; and
any road he had his own concerns to look to and protect—
Caervanogue, and, overarchingly important, the Gates that
his predecessor Avallac'h had given into his care to guard,
the Gates that led from our reality into another, and which
could not be allowed to be breached.

That was it: As soon as I got to the breaching of the
Gates I knew. Marguessan was still up to her old and desperate tricks: She had come here to try yet again to bring
through her damned and damnable Black Graal, and she
thought to use the vast amounts of power raised here for the
building of the Wall, and Morgan's own power (vulnerable
at such a moment), to achieve her desire at last. Glancing at
my Morgan, in desperation of my own, I screamed out with
all the strength and clarity of my thought to warn her. But I
saw as I did so that she knew already, had come here
expecting it, even. Whether she was prepared for it: That I
did not know, nor was I eager to see proved.

Marguessan seemed eerily confident for one who was
also so plainly down to her last throw. Just for a moment I

allowed myself to wonder about all those years she had spent in exile and self-chosen banishment, after her theft of the Cup: the dreariness of it all, the futility of it, mumbling over her balked intent, alone in her dark little corner with her rags and bones of malice. But those rags and bones were many: the Cup, her killing of her own son and daughter, the first attempt on the Gates, the calling in of the outfrenne looters and the attempt on me at Saltcoats, her rising against her own brother and her self-coronation as Ard-rían. . . The slate ran heavy against her.

And I could see that she did not care, not in the slightest. She knew this was her ultimate effort, and for once she was ready to accept the consequences. But it inflamed me, the angry impotency of it, that I could not help my wife; until it came to me that this was her moment as much as Marguessan's, that high taut time when the buttons were off the foils and meaning came clear and roads that had been decades in the making drew together all at once like a sheaf of arrows, their points all aimed alike.

The two sisters approached each other; or rather, Marguessan came slowly over the turf while Morgan remained statue-still. Their likeness of countenance, never pronounced for all that they were twins, was suddenly more apparent than ever before: Each's features in the other's face had somehow sharpened and defined and focused, and they bore a greater resemblance to one another, now in this hour when their true resemblance and kinship and likeness could scarcely have been any the lesser, than at any time in all their lives before.

The moment seemed time-stopped, like something that had happened long ago, a scene from one of the great tapestries that hung in Gwahanlen. Even the sea below the hill had hushed its waves, and the wind that in those parts blew constant and fresh out of the east died away to a tense and bodeful calm.

Marguessan halted perhaps ten feet from her sister, her back to the sea. Their faces betrayed nothing but their stamped kinship; but they looked at one another then, with the click and jump of two magnets coming together, opposite poles aligned now. And as I beheld this I recalled a thing Arthur had said once to me, oh, years since. . . We had been atop Brendan's Keep at Turusachan, I cannot recall why or even when; and of a sudden he had cried out from his heart, wondering aloud and bleakly how one birthing could produce two such opposite souls.

And I recalled too that I had reluctantly opined, on his order to me as my Ard-rígh, that to me it seemed Morgan and Marguessan shared one dán and soul between them, had halved it, so that Morgan's portion was the Light and Marguessan's the Darkness. But now as I looked on them together I saw that it was by no means so simple an equation as that. Inheritance, then, was not merely a matter of worldly things only; but why it had sorted itself out so for these two, I could not say. They had been raised alike in all particulars, had had the love unstinted of their parents and their kin; yet Marguessan had for reasons that seemed good to her renounced the Light by which the rest of us lived, and Morguenna had not. (I realize that to the sorcerers among you reading this, such distinction of good and evil, bane and blessing, into Dark and Light, may be simplistic and even wrong-headed; but not all of you *are* sorcerers, and it is easier so, trust me.)

The thought went by in an eyeblinking instant; and in that instant many things happened. Morgan let the magic fly, releasing it as a hawk from her wrist; it roared out from Tribruit, a shout upon the hill to be heard among the stars. Marguessan reached out with both hands, as if she would catch it by the jesses and draw it to herself. Loherin stood before the opening Gates, and I knew that he would sooner destroy them than let Marguessan touch or taint them. And far off a black unclean unformed thing was howling—a loathsome echo of the shout that had set the magic free—and I sensed with horror shared by the others present that we were hearing the ravening cry of the Dark Graal as it clamored to be let through into our creation.

As the one magic went—and the tremendous burden thereof was lifted from Morgan, though the rest of us continued to carry our own share in it—it was replaced by another, as Morgan faced down Marguessan before the Gates of the Graal. And again there came into my mind an echo of the past, Morgan speaking to me in our bed one night, speaking from her Sight. *"Have you news from the Gate?"*. . . Well; and if we wished not that news to be of the blackest, we must break our hearts to keep the work in motion, so that those our fellows on the four star stations themselves be not struck down by the very work of protection they performed.

At first it did not seem that there should be any doubt of the outcome here: Morgan was Domina, one of the mightiest sorceresses Keltia had ever seen; perhaps the greatest ever, if this today succeeded and was measure of her stature. Marguessan had been denied by her own mother the Ban-draoi training she had craved—rightly denied, I might add—and so had sought a teacher of her own in Edeyrn Marbh-draoi, her kindred's greatest enemy. And Edeyrn, struck no doubt by the staggering irony of the thing, and seeing a chance to corrupt, had taught her such ranns as never are taught in honest schooling. If Birogue had given Morgan the secrets of the Sidhe in magic, Edeyrn himself was of the Sidhe, or half of them; and if the Shining Folk had a dark side not so shining, it would be certain that Edeyrn ap Seli ac Rhûn would have known how to use it—and would have taught it gladly to his star pupil.

And Loherin, who had now a magic taught him by Avallac'h and given him by the Cup itself, made the third line of this terrible triad, the Three Who Fought on Tribruit, a greater fight perhaps than any of Arthur's, not saving even his last. . .

They spoke in the same instant. "Marguessan."

"Morguenna."

And in that double naming lay the doom of the Tynghed that my beloved had explained to me long time since, the reason the two sisters never spoke the other's name. It was the Oath with Dán, that names and kills; invoked here, it meant that each should be the death of the other. And it meant too, I saw now, that each had named that part of the other in herself; a small part in each, to be sure, Light in Marguessan and Dark in Morgan. But however far each of us is inclined to the one or the other, rest assured both are present; else we could not live at all. It is as perilous to one's soul to deny the Shadow in one as it is to deny the Light.

It all happened, as I say, in what seemed one unbearably crowded and prolonged, eternal-feeling moment; doubtless it took real time in the world, but I have no idea. I myself was caught up in the Tynghed, as I had been ever since a ten-year-old princess with untidy blond braids, about to sail away in a magic silver-masted boat over an inland sea, tied a knot of remembrance into the cloak-fringe of a young bard. That knot had held me all my life, and would hold me past this moment, and for all my lives to come. . .

Marguessan went first. The Gates before which Loherin still stood, implacable and impassive as Maharrion Rhên, shimmered and shut; the dreadful keening that the Dark Graal had kept up all this time, rising and falling like some duergar-dirge, was suddenly raised to a shriek that seemed to come from all ends of the earth and all airts of the compass, hung there an instant and was cut off as if by the stroke of some mystic sword in the hands of a hero or a god.

And Marguessan was gone, or somewhatly: Something stood there before the Gates, something that may have been Marguessan as she truly was, or had become, or it may have been—well, something else. After the one brief glance I averted my eyes from it; whatever, or whoever, it might be, it was nothing I wished to imprint forever in myself. Know that it was ghastly, and it was enraged, and it was dangerous beyond anything I have ever known. It rose up in a choking black pillar, and yet also it stayed as it was. It is hard to explain in words; perhaps it is best so, lest your dreams be as haunted as mine.

But Morgan was changing too; and though I stretched out my hand to her, heartsick, from the depths of my sorrow to come and my love that would ever be, I would not for all my lives have hindered or made difficult her going, and I let my hand fall, and turned my strength to help her go. It was the hardest thing I have ever been called upon to do; but it was correct, and, more importantly, it was what she wanted.

For the Curtain Wall was fully charged now, the Pale

had been raised; it now needed only to be set alight, and for that Morgan herself, her self, was needed. She had known all along that it would be so, this last thing be required of her as it had been required of her brother. It was her task alone: None other could perform it, and without it all the rest was in vain.

She looked at me once, and smiled, and after that there was no need for us to look again. We had said all, now, then, before; and we would be saying it again. But just then the hill began to shake beneath our feet, and the magic circles shattered as if they had been glass, and looking eastward into a sudden looming shadow I felt my heart stop within me.

It had already obliterated the Easter Isles, the ones that had lain in its path. Twice the height of Tribruit, it was green-black as síodarainn; blue lightning laced the foam crown it wore, and already we could feel its salt wind as it roared to meet us.

And again everything seemed to happen at once, in one stretched moment: The Gates shone briefly out; then Loherin was among us, chivvying us within the solid stone walls of Caervanogue that suddenly stood behind us, rooted in more than earth, where nothing had stood before. I pushed Ygrawn and Cristant and Grehan before me into the open door of the Graal's castle, then was myself flung likewise inside by Loherin. Just as the towering wave hit Garanwynion below us, consuming the beach where the horses had knelt and portunes had danced, I saw Morgan move forward and embrace the writhing pillar of darkness that had been, or still was, her sister Marguessan.

What came next—well, again that is one of those moments I spoke of, when words are ridiculously not enough. What *seemed* to happen, what I myself saw happen (though the reality of it was doubtless very different; only Loherin saw that, and he was not saying), was that the wave somehow stripped away the darkness, leaving only light behind; and that that light, in the very same instant, went out from the hilltop like the rays of a crown, like one vast globe of splintered blue brilliance. It went in all directions, to all airts, and also it sank into the ground.

And still gifted with the Sight Morgan had lent us, I saw, and the others also, the Wall itself leap into existence, far off in space. Saw a blue curtain shimmering across the stars, just as my mate had promised. In that moment, too, we felt the whip that such working carries with it: Upon the star-stations and all across Keltia, sorcerers died for the Wall's making, and for the struggle with Marguessan also; they flickered and went out like pinched candles at day's end.

But they did not go unwilling and they did not go alone, nor did they go in vain; their power was added to Morgan's, to the Wall's own, to ours who remained. And never again would Kelts have to fear invasion from without; we were safe now, as Morgan had intended us to be. This end had come down the years to us, and would go down for thousands more: This that had had origin in an idle wondering— "How if a pale could be raised to protect all Keltia?"—had reality now in labor and in sacrifice. Our only peril now would come from within; or from one who scrupled as little as Marguessan, as Edeyrn, to use another such rann of the dark to break the Wall's light.

But if that was a peril to be faced, just now it lay far in the future, and others than ourselves must deal with it in their own time and turn. For now, there were other things to fear did we feel the need. . .though they would by comparison be small indeed next to that which we had seen here today.

Inside the Graal's walls—for Caervanogue *was* the Cup, in a way, and also it protected the Cup, in another way, and no doubt many other ways it had as well—we looked at one another in stupefaction and blind dumb terror. Then, just as we were getting worked up to it, the castle was gone again, and we were standing upon the bare hilltop. The turf was torn back with the wave's passing might, and all around us reeked of salt and coldness and the far depths of Ocean. A real wave; and yet not so. . . Sent by Manaan Sea-lord, perhaps; maybe even now his crystal ship rode above the heaving waters, conveying Morgan and Marguessan to Caer Coronach, whence their true journey would begin. Perhaps this had all been played out by a greater than Manaan; or perhaps even Arthur had come to give his sisters escort to the other side of that Sea. . .

For me, the one certain knowledge was that my Guenna was gone from me; and that was grief paramount, with which I would deal in time, or maybe it would deal with me. But it came to me too that at last I was free of Gwaelod; this wave that had come to cleanse had come to heal also. As I stood there, apart from the others, I sensed someone by me, and I turned to see Loherin.

He was himself, and more than himself; he had taken on that air Avallac'h had had, of sternness and serenity both, and was more beautiful than ever with what he now knew.

He was smiling, and after a moment I smiled back at him.

"Go to Caer-na-gael, Talyn," he said. "At the horns of the white moon. We shall meet again. But take them home now. It is done with. For now."

CHAPTER 33

So I took them all home, home to Caerdroia, where Gweniver the Regent, looking in that moment very like Gweniver the High Queen, met us in a mood that I had never seen before, a kind of grieving triumph. Ygrawn spoke somewhat in her ear, then went alone straight to her chambers; just now she was best left so, to grapple in her own way and time with the loss of the last of her children.

I myself was not quite ready to go to the rooms I had shared all these years with my wife, so I went instead to Gwahanlen, and I sat there alone until the leaded glass of the ceiling had grown dark with night and bright again with morning. I felt curiously light and detached from my body, not sad, and I wished to see no one, and to say nothing, and to do nothing, not for a long while yet. Perhaps not for a very long while.

It seemed that the others who dwelled in Turusachan understood my wishes and my need, or perhaps I had unconsciously been sending it to them, for not until evening of that second day began to draw in did one come to Gwahanlen to trouble my vigil.

The doors opened and closed. "Talyn," said Gweniver; no more.

I had known it was she before she set hand to latch; but still I sat on in silence. Then drawing a breath I lifted my head and looked her in the eyes, there in the dim blue-litten room. What I saw in her face then—well, even in so open a telling as this there are some things I must keep for myself, and that is among them. But it was real.

"They were not ours to keep," I said at length, and she held my gaze with a steadiness that was itself an acknowledgment.

"They are Keltia's to keep forever," she answered after a while. "And we, of course, are theirs."

I smiled in spite of myself. "Now that is a thing either, or both, of them would have said to us."

But still I could not speak of it any plainer; not of Morgan's going, not of Arthur's. Gweniver had had seven years to learn to live with her mate's absence; I had had a bare thirty hours, more or less. But in that seven-year span, Gweniver had spoken Arthur's name only when context demanded it; never once, to my knowledge, had she spoken of him of her free choice. And I knew it was not for lack of love or loss she did not speak so, but because both love and loss alike were for her too vast, too sacred, to share with others or to profane with speech. . . Too, neither of us had been granted the solace, even, of barrowing our dead: Artos lay on Kholco, Morgan only the Mother knew where. There would be a ritual for her, of course, and for the others who had also been taken by the backwash of Marguessan's final evil; and that would be a comfort, such things are. But not even to know where she was; or, more accurately, where her mortal form had gone to—that was harder than I had thought it would be to master. And aye, I know, it was only a body, only flesh and bone, she was not there; but I had loved that body, it had been the vehicle by which Morguenna Pendreic had manifested her soul in the world. And not to know where it lay—though I daresay she would have preferred it so—well, it was a heavy thing to bear.

But, widowed though I was, I was not the only one in Turusachan that night who had suffered loss; and in answer to Gwennach's unspoken question I rose from my place at Rhodaur and went out with her, to comfort in my comfortlessness.

* * *

Gerrans and Cristant were in their chambers in the Rose
Tower; Sgilti, Anghaud the eldest and the lass Cathelin were
with them. At my sudden entrance they raised stiff and still
white faces, and Cathelin ran to me for hugging. I did so,
looking across her at Gerrans, then gently released her and
went to my son. They had all been told by Gweniver and
Ygrawn what had happened there on Beckery, but they
needed to hear it from me; only that could make it real for
them. And to my everlasting surprise, I found that I needed
to tell it, to make it real for myself also. . .

Afterwards, the weeping and laughing done with (for at
such moments there are both), I went alone to the familiar
rooms in the small tower that overhung the sea; entered and
closed the heavy oak door behind me, leaning back against it
and staring at the chamber as if I had never seen it before. I
was not seeing the room just then; I was seeing Morgan in
that room, in many moods and all corners and every age of
our lives. She was not here—not even her presence, though
that would come later, and often—but it seemed even so
that she had been here, for lying upon the bed was something small that gleamed in the light from the windows;
something I knew very well had not been there when we set
out for the castle of the Graal.

Presently I went over to the bed and reached out, shivering, to pick it up in faltering fingers. Two disks shone gold
and silver on a fine gold chain: the suncross of our Keltic
faith and the sigil of the Ban-draoi that had been among my
mother's jewels passed on to me by Birogue.

Never since I had first clasped the chain around Morgan's
neck had she removed these tokens from her, and I knew
that, even as I knew I had seen them plain at her throat
when she stood upon Tribruit. . . My hand closed round
them, and I slowly toppled over onto the bed, lifting my fist
to my lips, pulling Morgan's pillows, still imprinted with her,
into my arms and curling up around them. . .

When I was done at last with weeping, or done for this
time, at least, it was dark again, or maybe still; I felt all at
once better, and took advantage of that by beginning to sort

haphazardly through Morgan's things. A mistake; and I did not get very much the farther before grief overtook me again, but I did manage to order some things—to sort through the writings on her desk, to set aside her jewels and my mother's to divide among Gwen and Ygrawn and Gerrans, Arawn and Arwenna, Janjan and Donah, and our closest friends also; to keep a few of the pieces she had loved best for myself a while yet.

But in the end I decided to alter nothing: I would continue to live in these rooms as I had lived in them with her, for so long as I continued to dwell in Turusachan. Nothing of hers would be changed or touched: Her cloak would hang on the back of the door where she had left it, her garb would stay in the chests and presses, things would remain as far as possible where she had set them. If that sounds perverse and strange to you, so be it; but should you come to such a place as I then stood in, perhaps you will do likewise, or at least comprehend my actions. It would be so for as long as I felt it necessary. After that—well, after that we should just have to see.

When the five stars were exploded to power the Pale, I could not feel that they had died; well, no more could I now feel that Morgan had died. I knew she had—at least my mind knew the fact had happened—but it seemed somehow not true. And though it may sound a strange and loveless thing to say of the death of one's own wife, I was oddly less distraught, less *angry*, at Morgan's going than I had been at Arthur's. Perhaps because I had, it seemed, always known how she would leave me, and his leaving was (to my way of seeing it) a surprise and a betrayal, however dán-ruled and well-intentioned. I could not help it, it was how I felt; but all the same I did not speak of it to the others.

The ritual of sending was held for Morgan *and* Marguessan—aye, truly! Even she must be given the grace of such a farewell—and for all the others who had died in the raising of the Pale, a few nights later at Ni-maen. I had of course already conducted a private ritual, for her and for me, in our chamber; and a sevennight later, I held another

for her, which closest kin and friends attended. The night
after that, I took ship alone and headed east to Mount
Keltia. It was the night of the first horns of Argialla, the
waxing of the white moon, and I had been ordered to Caer-
na-gael; and I thought I knew why.

The silver-blue crescent blazed in the southern skies,
looking astonishingly close, as if I could reach up and
touch it—the which I would not even if I could, for its tips
were sgian-sharp. I set the aircar down on the high plateau
below the great peak's own horns; a little way away, Caer-
na-gael stood ghostly in the meager light of the crescent and
the greater luminosity of the Criosanna's arching veils. I
unshod in the usual manner; and, pausing briefly as I passed
the entrance dolmens to right myself from the wave of pain
that washed over me—the first time I had ever come here
had suddenly been before me, more vividly than I could
bear—I went within.

At the heart of the circle lay as ever Yr Allawr Goch, the
Red Altar that was neither one nor other part of its name; but
this night something else lay there, half-shrouded in blue
shadow. Then, as my eyes adjusted to the light, and Argialla
helpfully mounted higher in the heavens, I saw what rested
upon the ground before the great bluestone slab, and my
world was unmade.

It was a hollowed-out oak-trunk, carved with skill and
care; within it, upon a cushioning of rich woven-stuffs, lay
Morgan my wife. She looked as if she but slept, no mark
upon her of her titanic struggle: Her face was white in the
moon, she was clad in her Ban-draoi robes of office; and
round her neck was the medallion of one who was Kin to
the Dragon.

I made not sound nor movement; only looked. And as I
did so, a voice came quietly from the shadows beyond, from
the great granite chair that had not been built to hold mortal
form.

"She felt no pain, Taliesin," said Gwyn ap Nudd, rising
from the throne and coming forward into the light. "The
Mother did not allow it; and we thought it right to bring her
here. Do you object?"

I shook my head, still gazing at Morgan where she lay.

"Nay. . . That she should be here—" Then I startled and looked up at him, as his meaning came clear. "You mean—to barrow her *here?* Here beside—" But I could not say more.

"Beside Brendan," said Birogue softly, from where she had stood beside Gwyn. "What could be fitter, Talyn, than that she should lie here for all time? To be a protection herself to Keltia, and to be herself protected—I can think of no better place for her, save maybe one, and this is more meet, truly. Also that other place shall be finding a fate of its own—"

"Collimare," I said. "Nay; that would of course be well, and she would like it, but this is better. She will be with Brendan, and what Kelt could ask better company than that?"

"Be it so," said Gwyn. He raised a hand; and suddenly, slowly, with a groan that seemed to find an echo in every other stone in that circle, the huge bluestone altar block began to pull itself out of the earth, and rose majestically into the air.

I shivered once, then started forward, for I knew I had little time. Going to my knees beside Morgan, I lifted her hand and kissed it, and it was neither cold nor stiff to the touch. Nor was her brow, nor yet her lips. . . With the bronze knife of the Sidhe, I cut a tress of her hair and tucked it inside my leinna, and cut likewise a lock of my own, to place it upon her breast; then, gently, I lifted the Dragon disk from my neck and exchanged it for Morgan's own, to hang beside the two medallions of hers and my mother's that were already there.

I took her hand again, and felt the ring upon it, the ring that matched my own—the marriage rings that the two Sidhe-folk now present had themselves once blessed, when they wedded us in this very place all those years since. At first I had thought to place my own upon her hand beside it; but it came to me that that would somehow be a declaration that the marriage was ended, that I no longer considered myself wedded, and that of course would never be. How could it, for we had taken vows that even death cannot break. . . Any road, the serpent ring had become part of my hand, grown to feel so natural upon my finger that I could sooner part with finger or hand than with the ring. Nay; I would wear it until I myself died, no matter where I should come to it.

So I placed another token with her instead, something I loved and which shall remain forever secret between her and me, and kissed her hand one last time. I rose and stood back, and nodded to Gwyn. Again the faerie prince lifted his hand, and now, just as the altar had risen, the oak-trunk of Morgan's coffin sealed itself over and moved slowly down into the vaulted dimness below, and the earth drew aside to receive it.

I watched stone-faced until I could see it no more—nor could I see any other casket there below, in the dark, nor wished to—and then the ground closed up like water, the immense bluestone slab settled once more into its accustomed place. There was no doubt now as to the weight of it; it thudded back into the earth a good three feet deep, looking as if it had never stirred one hand's-breadth since the day it first was set there.

"Well, Talyn," said Birogue, in a voice of such gentleness that I thought I would die of it where I stood. "What then to you?"

I laughed shakily, still seeing Morgan's calm face. "Oh, you know, the same as ever. There is Gwen to be helped, and Ygrawn, and the children; and of course there is my bardery. I shall do well enough."

"I do not doubt it," said Gwyn. "But listen to me, Talyn: Their going was of their own willing and choice; therefore is it a positive thing, a right action. They—Artos, Morgan, all those who went in Prydwen or who stood at the raising of the Pale—made a postponement of worldly joys and a submission to dán, to the will of the One, which was also their will. Merlynn made that choice, and you shall make it yourself in your time, and Gweniver in hers. And because of those choosings you shall be the eternal heroes of the world. Even those children's stories in your mother's books from Earth said as much; they were couched in child's language, and knew little of true prophecy, yet they prophesied true."

"You will be transformed, Talyn, as they have been," said Birogue. "You will die, but you shall never perish. Growing old then young again, when age finally comes

upon you, you will journey to the place of your heart and
await the renewing of your body and the next turn of the
Wheel."

I gasped, for she had named something I had told no
one, not even Morgan: a Seeing I had had. . . "To be
reborn on Earth?" I whispered, awed. "Apart from all my
dearest ones? I had sooner stay here, lady, and enjoy a less
lofty destiny. I would not come to my next life without
them."

"They will be with you," said Gwyn. "Always, ever. It
makes no differ where. Merlynn in his house of glass, Arthur
sleeping in his cave beneath the mountain with his warriors
about him—it is all the same. Had you not guessed it? And
when that one comes to find Arthur whose dán it is, and
takes on his powers, that too shall be part of it."

I was only half-hearing. "One thing I have always wondered at: Why did it take so long for me to be conceived of
my parents after my mother came here from Earth? Surely
it could not be for lack of love."

Birogue answered at once, with a full frank air I knew
marked her words as truth.

"For that in coming to and from Earth, your father and
the others who sailed with him crossed and recrossed time
itself. In those days only Edeyrn commanded the secrets of
travel in the ard-na-spéire, and your father and his comrades were obliged to use other, older means to go to Earth
and back again. When he brought your mother away with
him, she had to age anew, as it might be, to where she was
before they crossed time; you could not be born until she
had attained that same age here as she would have had she
stayed on Earth. No more."

"And Loherin? Since I am asking and being answered so
readily—"

"It is not yet the time he told you of," said Gwyn. "It
will not be for long and long; but it shall come. Let be."

I suddenly remembered something, a thing I had brought
with me, and I turned to lift it from the ground where I had
set it, holding it out to the two who stood before me.

"This should go back to your folk," I said quietly. "At
least for now—until you see fit to bestow it again." I flipped

back the soft leather and velvet swathings, and the cathbarr of Nia the Golden shot silver sparks to every corner of Caer-na-gael.

Gwyn took it gravely from my hands. "She wore it well, your lady," he said. "And you have the right of it; we shall keep it until such time as one is meant to wear it again."

They were beginning to withdraw now, that sparkle I knew so well by now beginning to form around them, though this time it would be they who departed and I who remained. But Birogue's voice came clear.

"One more task for you, Talyn, before the end. The sword Llacharn. Restore it to its home. Let it be reforged before the end."

I started violently, and reached out in protest and delaying. "Is *that* what has ever been meant by that?"

Her voice came now as from a great height. "That; and more. But bring it home."

They were gone now; only above Caer-na-gael I could see a broad shining road spiralling up and out and northeastward, a highroad of stars that aimed itself straight for Glenshee and the Hill of Fare. I heard a faint chime as of silver bells striking; then a brief wind, and they were gone.

I stood looking after them a while, until the path among the stars vanished; then I turned to look once more on the bluestone altar beneath which my beloved now rested, by the side of the first great Protector of our people. *Nay*, I thought through tears and a smile together, *it is* not *unfitting. I can leave her here, and not fear for her, and go. . .*

And so I did.

At Caerdroia, all gradually settled back into smooth running. The Wall, a continuing marvel, performed perfectly, just as Morgan had envisioned it. Indeed, as I went through her notes on its construction, I was startled to be reminded that it had been Keils Rathen, long ago at Llwynarth, who had first kindled her interest in the possibility of such a construct. I passed this on to Gweniver, knowing she would be glad to hear it, and she was.

"Keils was ever interested in such dream-forging," she

said with a smile that recalled old memories. "Trust it to be Guenna who made it reality. . . But it is good to know where the thought had origin. And speaking of such—now that there is an empty chair among the Regents. . ."

"Ah nay!" I said swiftly and with emphasis. "Not I to take Guenna's place! Surely you and Ygrawn between you—"

Well; suffice it to say that I was named Regent the next day to fill Morgan's duties as best I might. As Gwen pointed out to clinch the matter, it would be but for a few years; and in these new safe days that the Pale had given us, a mere sinecure, hardly worthy of the name. Though Gweniver's idea of a soft ride and my own were almost instantly proved vastly different, I found to my surprise that I enjoyed my new task and responsibilities, finding them none so onerous as I had feared.

And perhaps a great deal more beside: In my new busy life I had little leisure and less energy to sink into that slough of despair and grief I knew lay so near at hand. Easy it would have been to do so; but Morgan would not have cared to see it, and many times over the next few years she let me know it, in no uncertain ways. . .

But at length Arawn attained his majority, and needed Regents no longer; though he would gladly have kept us on, Gweniver held to the letter of her promise to Keltia and to herself, and dissolved the Regency on the day her son turned thirty-three. She would not have stayed even for his crowning had she not understood so well the demands of sovereignty and the need for continuity, and so watched with the rest of us as the Copper Crown was placed upon Arawn's head.

Strange it was, I can tell you, to see there in the Hall of Heroes only the Throne of Scone, where for so long had stood two chairs before it. . . But Arawn my nephew looked both grave and proud that day, and as I knelt before him and put my hands between his for the homage 'of hand and heart' that was required on this day and no other in all the days of a monarch's reign, I knew both his parents had come to attend this rite; and I was not the only one who knew it.

Gweniver stayed on a brief while more, to help Arawn

ease into his new duties; but we could see she longed to be gone, and one lovely cool summer morning, I stood with Ygrawn and Daronwy and Gerrans and a few others on the field at Mardale, and bid her farewell as she left at last for her refuge on Vannin.

"Glassary is not the ends of the galaxy!" she said smiling. "I shall expect visits from all of you, and I shall come here, too, as often as I may."

But I was still finding it difficult to encompass: We had been through so much, been together so long—of all those dearest in my life, only Arthur and Ygrawn had I known longer than I had known Gwen—how was it possible that we could be parting after all that?

She saw this on me, and drew me aside. "Ah, I know! But the Company is over, Talyn; its work is finished. And you have the Kinship to carry on in its place—I may no longer be Ard-rían, but I shall ever be a Dragon, and you Pendragon. The Work is still ours to do. But what shall you do now?"

"Stay here for a while," I said, still unsure of any of it. "The children have of course told me to come to them at Tair Rhandir; Ygrawn, I think, will do so eventually, and there are Tegau's brood too, near by. But we shall see."

"Arawn would be glad of your staying on," she said, glancing over at her tall auburn-haired son. "Arwenna also—they have few enough kin left to them as it is."

"Will not this be hard on her, your leaving?"

Gweniver shook her head. "Not so much. She is in fosterage now, and I shall make a long visit with her before going on to Glassary. Any road, she will soon be of an age to go to the Ban-draoi herself does she choose that way, or the Fians even. . . Nay, she will do well; and Arawn too, especially with his uncle Tal near to help out should he feel the need. And this is right for me, too, Talyn," she added in a lower voice. "I am shut of all this now as it is shut of me, and I have *not* forgotten, nor forgiven. . . But do not *you* forget me: Come visit when you will, and bring your harp. By then you may have new songs to sing us all."

And she was so right to say so. . . But as she kissed me farewell, she pressed somewhat into my hand and folded my fingers round it, and then kissing Arawn one last time she vanished into the ship. I did not look to see what it was, but watched the ship lift off and gazed after it, until it blinked into the overheaven out past the Criosanna. Only then did I open my fingers, and smiled, not really much surprised, to see what she had placed there: On my palm lay the sapphire seal ring Gweniver had worn in her years as Ard-rían. Arawn wore his father's huge flawed emerald now, that I had brought back from Kholco, and there was no real need for this in its intended function; it was Gwen's to dispose of as she chose.

And though she could have had the seal debruised, she knew well that I would not be using it to any unlawful purpose, and had left it as it was. I tossed the ring into the air, suddenly lighter of heart, and caught it up again, slipping it onto my right smallfinger. *I will give it to Arwenna in time,* I thought, *or to Arawn's daughter should he come to have one.* But in the meantime I would wear it for the thought behind it, and the memories, and the love, and for the reason Gweniver had given it me: For I too had been of the Ard-tiarnas of Keltia, and not only in my brief term as Regent.

CHAPTER 34

So things moved and changed and shifted, as things do down the road of years. Arawn, though younger at his accession than any monarch Keltia has ever had, proved a worthy successor to his great parents; and if sometimes he found himself daunted in his heart by the splendor of their memory and deeds, he did not show it—or only to those of us closest to him.

Unlike his father, Arawn had not that easy gift of drawing folk to him; his friends and advisors were not many, but they were of the finest, as fine as any Companion, and they were as loyal to him as we had been to his father. He would find his footing; and at the least the Pale would give him, and Keltia with him, breathing space and time to find it.

The rest of us went on as the days took us. Gerrans had upon his mother's death taken up her honors of the duchy of Ys, and had left Caerdroia for aye, residing now as Duke, with the Duchess Cristant, at Tair Rhandir. As Duke-dowager, I was of course welcome to dwell there also, and they had begged me to do so any number of times, but though I visited there often, still I clung to Caerdroia, still lived in the rooms where I had lived with my mate. For this or other reasons, it was not yet time for me to leave.

Ygrawn felt other wise, and she did go to Rhandir, where she lived contentedly among her grandchildren ten years more and died very quietly. We barrowed her beside Amris her lost prince, and set up a stone for them both, as parents of Arthur Ard-rígh.

And to round off the tale of the House of Pendreic (which is now lawfully Penarvon, as Arawn has declared for the choice his father had made so long ago), Gwain, sole inheriot of his branch of our kindred, duly and dutifully succeeded Marguessan his mother, and became Duke of Eildon, and went there to dwell. When Irian his father had been slain long since by the Sidhe, Gwain had let lapse the title of Lord of Lleyn, and never set foot there again; and who could cry him blame? He wedded in time, and had a daughter and a son who would come to Court in the service of their cousin the High King. He seems happy enough when I chance to meet him at Court functions, though both of us attend such rarely. But there is a shadow to him that I think will never lift; and nor do I think he wishes it to do so.

And, one by one, down the years, the Companions died also. Few of us indeed had been left when Gweniver took ship to Glassary; and since then, they have all gone to be with Arthur, gladly and I think with a great feeling of 'at last!' about it—and I cannot say I blame them, for I am envious that they shall see him before I shall.

Elenna, now known to all Keltdom as Elen Llydawc, Elen of the Hosts, for her great generalship at Camlann and before, died the year after Ygrawn; Tanwen and our old Ferdia and Grehan the Taoiseach were not long in following. On Kernow, one autumn afternoon, Tryffin and Ysild died within three hours of each other, as seemed only fitting for a pair who had shared so great a lovematch. Tryff went first, and I know that he waited for Ysild to join him, so that they might journey together; and what could be better than that? Two rosetrees were planted above their grave by their daughter Ydain, a white one and a red, red for love, white for loyalty; their branches intertwined, so that only by the color of the blooms could one tell which bough grew upon which tree.

And my dear Daronwy died on Caledon, joining her

Roric at last. I felt her loss perhaps more keenly than all the others; apart from Artos himself, Ronwyn had been my oldest and closest friend and truest comrade. She had been of the Companions since the very earliest days at Coldgates, even before the first Llwynarth. We had struck a friendship from the start, and she and I had often gone together 'raiding,' as we called it only half-humorously, among the folk of town and mains, to find things out for Arthur in the days of Edeyrn's rule. In the years since Arthur had gone, as one of the Seven, Daronwy had been a strength beyond strengths to Gweniver and Ygrawn, and she had never ceased to be my beloved friend. But she had longed endlessly to be with her Roric again, and with the others of our Company; and now she was. I would miss her.

But there was one I would miss as greatly, and more: At Glassary, very quietly and unheralded one Samhain morning, died Gweniver Queen of Kelts.

And with that last link snapping of the chain that had so firmly bound us all through so much for so very long, I felt somehow that all that was best of the Company had come down to vest itself in me; I had become their last heir, the last of us left to inherit the tasks the others had set by. It was mine to keep the name of Companion alight forever; why else had I been spared so long, and through so much, to be the last of the Companions of Arthur the King?

It was after Gweniver's splendid state funeral at Caerdroia—Arawn had commanded it and overseen it himself, knowing his mother's wishes did not run to a simple burial at Glassary, just one among many humble Reverend Mothers of the Ban-draoi, and I have to say he was quite right in that—that I knew the time had come at last for me to leave Turusachan.

I had thought of leaving, many times before now, and always somehow the time had not felt right. Whether it was that I could not bring myself to leave Morgan behind me, or Arthur, or all of it together, the life that I had known, had made for myself, all the way from Gwaelod, I do not know.

But just as before I had known surely that the time was not yet, I knew as surely now that it was; and a fortnight or two after Gweniver's barrowing at Ni-maen I went to my nephew the King to tell him of my decision.

Arawn protested long and fluently and sincerely. He had been hard hit by his mother's death, and I was the only kinsman of his parents' generation he had left. Indeed, for a while I thought he would not scruple to command me, as my Ard-rígh, to stay where I was; and he was mollified in the end only by the solemn assurance that I would not be vacating the immediate neighborhood.

In truth, I would be moving only across the street—or the square, rather; to Seren Beirdd, where the new Chief Bard, Bronwen Lanihorne, had felt it her personal privilege to offer me my beloved teacher Elphin's old rooms. He had been her immediate predecessor, and when he went with Arthur and came not home again she had kept his place empty for him, out of her respect. Which was surpassed, apparently, only by her respect for me; for now his rooms would be mine, and I was well pleased. But she had been a good student.

As for Gweniver: Well, there is little I can say that I have not said before. She and Arthur, Morgan and I, we had made a foursquare keep and had held it against all comers save death alone. Her death—and she was deeply mourned throughout Keltia—seemed to me simply to put the seal on the past. She was the last of the Companions save myself; I was alone now, and as if that had been the signal something had long been awaiting, as if some trackway or channel had been cleared within me, something came to me very soon thereafter that had been long on the way, and now was set free to run.

On my last night before beginning to move my things to Seren Beirdd—well, I had been living at the palace full fifty years or more, there *was* rather a lot to be shifted, and I had yet to decide the disposition of Morgan's things also—I felt those stirrings begin that I knew well.

Any maker knows them. You will be sitting doing some

chore or other, or nothing, and then coming in from nowhere will be a sort of insistent tugging that cannot be ignored, be you never so absorbed or so idle. And you will go to the instrument of your craft—harp or pen or brush or hammer—as a lover goes to the beloved. And then—the clearest and best I can put it is that you will be *used*. Something will take you up to do its will in just the same way as you do take up your instrument. You are a means, no more, to set down what needs, what wills, to take form; and which has done you the inestimable honor of choosing you to do it. This is no complaint; nay, I loved this! It is what artists pray for and hope for, and sometimes delude themselves and their following into believing has been granted them. But you—and your following should you be good enough and lucky enough to have one—will always know the difference.

It came, I say. And it came to *me*.

Twelve hours later, I seemed to be myself again, and looked around me, a little startled and dazed, and oddly sad. I was sprawled on the floor of my chamber, where I do not even recall resorting; my back ached miserably, my arms were numb from fingers to shoulders, I was famished and parched, shivering, cramped in every limb and cross as an ice-bear waked before the thaw. But I was also transported. I had a song. I had *the* song; or perhaps it had me. But it had a name, and a dán of its own, if Gwyn were to be believed, and there is no reason he should not be.

But it was here. I stared down at it, still staggered by the gift. This was not to be shown to anyone just yet—I felt a far-off pang as I remembered that there was no one living to whom I wished to show it; and as for the dead, they had seen it already, had perhaps even sent it—it was still a thing for itself and myself alone. But I looked hungrily and happily at what I had been given (and aye, it *is* a gift, but not *my* gift), and I felt that incomparably proud and humble thrill any maker feels, when he or she has correctly heard that which the Awen—and each craft and calling has an Awen of its own—has been saying, and correctly set it down.

I touched the paper again. "'Preithi Annuvin,'" I said

softly, as to a lover or a child. And spoke its name again, this time in the common Gaeloch.

"'The Spoils of Annwn.'"

I took it first to Arawn my nephew. Though at first we had not been so close as I was to his elder halfsister Donah, over the years we had changed that, and he for his part had come to look on me as a second father; which was good and fitting, since I was after all his godfather as well as his namesake. But he was also High King now.

He received me in Arthur's old solar overlooking the rose gardens, and as we stood back from our embrace I looked at him. And gave that laugh which is also a sob and a shake of the head, for so like was he to his father that for an instant I could not speak. He understood at once, and laughed himself.

"I do not see it, not so much," he confessed, smiling. "But so many say it who should know, so there it is."

"It sits well on you, Ard-rígh," I said ceremoniously, my use of the title a quite deliberate one, and he colored a little.

"What, my father's looks?"

"That; but the High Kingship." But the last thing I wished was to unsettle him; he was a sensitive and generous soul, and though he strove to hide it, the death of his mother, with whom he had ever had a close and loving bond, had deeply shaken him. I was the only senior member of the House of Dôn left—there was Gerrans, of course, and Gwain, and Donah and Majanah, but few others indeed—and I felt for Arthur's sake and Gwen's that I must stand as surrogate parent here; and Arawn himself seemed eager for the closeness.

"I have a thing to show you," I said then, drawing a small book forth from beneath my tunic. He took it from my hand, exclaiming over the fine blue leather binding stamped with Gwynedd's silver stag—he was his father's son there, keenly alive to craftsmanship of any sort—and riffled carefully through the thick parchment pages.

"It is most fair! What is it? Of your composing, I am sure—"

I stared at the pages for a moment before I replied. "The key to the future kingdom; the map to your father's return."

He looked sharply up at me—again that old glint of Arthur's—and went a shade paler.

"In what way, just so?" he asked carefully.

I smiled suddenly. "In this way." And I began to read.

It had not seemed in the writing as it did in the reading—any bard will tell you that—but more so even than usual, even more than honest modesty allowed, I felt as I rolled out the sonorous phrases that Taliesin Glyndour had had really very little to do with this chaunt after all. . .

"'Three times the fullness of Prydwen we went into it.
  Except seven, none returned from Caer Sidi.
  Am I not a candidate for fame, to be heard
      in the chaunting?
  In Caer Pedryvan four times revolving,
  The Shout above the Abyss, when was first it heard?
  Is this not the Cup of Kerridwen Rhên,
  Ridged round its edge with pearls?
  It gives no life to a coward, nor to one forsworn.
  A sword of light to a seeker shall be given,
  And before the portals of Uffern the horns of light
      shall burn.
  And when we went with Arthur in his
      splendid labors,
  Except seven, none returned from Caer Vediwid.

  Am I not a candidate for renown, to be heard
      in the singing?
  In Caer Pedryvan, in the Isle of the Strong Door,
  Where twilight and black dark come together,
  Is not bright blood the guest-drink offered?
  The point of the lance of battle lies lapped in
      fumes of sleep.
  When shall it waken?
  And the bronze lid of Fál's eye, when shall it
      loose its light?
  Three times the fullness of Prydwen were we that
      went on sea,
  What time we went with Arthur of glorious memory,

Except seven, none returned from Caer Rigor.
Am I not a candidate for peace, to be heard
    in the harping?

I give no praise to the lords of swords,
For beyond Caer Wydyr they saw not
    Arthur's might.
In gear of battle stood they upon the walls,
But hard it was to speak with their watchman,
Though their captain had fair words for ours.
Thrice the freight of Fairface were we that went
    with Arthur;
Save seven, none returned from Caer Coronach.'"

I glanced up at dwned's end, to see how this was falling
upon him, and hesitated in continuing: Arawn's face was
white and taut, and his long strong swordsman's fingers so
convulsively gripped the stem of the silver goblet he held
that I could see the metal bend before my eyes. But he
dragged his eyes back from whatever they had been behold-
ing, and nodded at me to go on.

"'Shall we not be candidates for rebirth,
    to be heard in the telling?
The Answerer answered, the blade reborn.
Complete shall be the prison of Gweir in Caer Sidi,
Through the spite of Pwyll and Pryderi.
Few before him went into it, the sea's blue chains
    to hold him fast.
Before the Spoils of Annwn shall he sing,
And until the end of time shall he be bard for it.
Three times the fullness of Prydwen we went into it;
Except seven, none returned from Caer Sidi.
Thrice the freight of Fairface were we that went
    with Arthur;
Seven alone returned from Caer Sidi.'"

I ceased my chaunt, and drew breath, and did not look at
Arawn. It seemed that the words had called all the light out
of the room, leaving us in a circle of faint brightness cast by
the crystals on the table between us. I dared a glance at my
nephew, but his face was in shadow, and he offered no
word.

"I have written it—or it chose to be written—in the high style of the ríogh-bardáin," I ventured. "So that its truths and secrets will be veiled to the casual reader, or one who reads out of mere curiosity. Only the trained mind and heart shall find the hidden guidewords; only a sorcerer shall know how to act upon them. And that one, we have the word of many, shall be the one whose dán it is to do so."

Across the table Arawn stirred and seemed to come back to himself, and as he leaned forward into the light, I reeled within myself. Like to Artos he had been before; just this instant he *was* Arthur. . . But he did not note, was intent on the meaning of what he had just heard.

"Uncle—" He spread his hands helplessly, and now he was Arawn again.

"I know," I said, to help him. "I felt the same. I did not make this, amhic; it made itself through me. But the tale is there, the tale you know—"

And I led him through it, line by line: told him how the sea of the poem was in truth the Morimaruse; how the caers were the places we had gone to in Prydwen's last sailing; how the horns of light, and Uffern, were but poetic bynames for the great firemount in which Prydwen had buried herself and those in her.

"But 'thrice the freight of Fairface'?" asked Arawn at last.

"When we raided Fomor—Caer Rigor and Caer Pedryvan—and we took off the prisoners of Clero," I said steadily, "they added twofold to our numbers, so Prydwen, which is 'Fairface' in the bardic speech, carried thrice her battle portage. Some nine hundred souls in all."

"And seven alone returned—from Caer Sidi."

"Again the Morimaruse," I said. "Spiral Castle—you have no idea what it looked like. . ."

"Nay," he said quietly. "But I see it in dreams anight, as did the Queen my mother." He reached across the table and took the little book from my hands. "And this last dwned? Who are these folk you speak of, Gweir and Pwyll and Pryderi? And why is Gweir their captive?"

I brightened a little at the question. "I have not the smallest idea. That is purest prophecy, and I do not argue nor ask small quibbling queries; I take it and set it down and am grateful."

Arawn smiled unwillingly, still paging and repaging through the volume. "Whence came this?" he asked suddenly. "If you only made the poem last night—"

Now it was my turn to smile. "Morgan had some dozens of these made for me, one birthday a while past. Blank books, bound with the arms of our House—I filled most of them with love poetry for her. But I had yet some left, and I spent the night in writing out fair copies of the poem into several of these. This one is for you; Arwenna shall have one, and Donah, and Gerrans and your cousins of Lleyn and Kernow, and the Bardic Library." I broke off, for Arawn's face showed the shining tracks of tears in the sconcelight.

"It made it real for me," he said presently, "in a way I had not previously felt it. But uncle"—here he leaned forward and grasped my hands, his eyes fixed on mine—"shall it be so? Will one come to find him? Can we be sure of it?"

I tightened my fingers on his. "As sure as we can be of aught dán sends us, amhic. But these were spoils—the Treasures—and Artos reived them from Annwn, and took them to Annwn; and from Annwn shall they be brought back when time is."

He nodded, and did not smile, only ran his finger lightly over the silver-stamped stag of Dôn. I felt a great wave of love and pity for him; he was so young to be High King, and to have come to it in such a way. . . And he had so few round him to help and share; where Arthur had had so many, and such as they had been—

"One thing more, Ard-rígh," I said aloud, and Arawn's head came up like a hound's who hears a stick snap on the path without. "I have planned to write histories of the Companions, and of Arthur and Gweniver, and in them I shall have to say somewhat of that which we all know to be truth—"

"You mean my father's death in Prydwen with the Companions," said Arawn calmly. "What more need we give out? You and the other six who returned to tell the few of us here—we have kept the secret safe all these years."

"And soon there will be none left to tell it, once you and Gerrans and Sgilti and Anghaud are gone," I agreed. "Even so, I think a touch on that web may be in order."

The King smiled. "What did you have in mind, Penbardd?"

"Oh, just a judicious clouding of the truth." I rose to leave. "But be not too surprised should you begin to hear tales of how Arthur the King sleeps in an island across far dark seas, with all his Companions round him; sleeps until they shall be awakened, when Keltia has need of them."

"I like it well," said Arawn softly. "Would that it were true—but you will tell me that it is."

"Aye so."

"Aye so." He was silent, running his thumb over the emerald of his seal ring. "And the name of this island? For surely you shall not be calling it by its right name—"

"Its name is Avilion," I said, though how I had known that name I could not tell you, any more than I could tell him. "In the Gaeloch, folk will turn it as Avallinn."

CHAPTER 35

So I moved to Seren Beirdd, where I settled swiftly and happily into Elphin Carannoc's old chambers, white-washed and airy, tucked into one of the turrets that made the points of the star that was Star of the Bards; and with a view scarcely inferior to my old one in the palace across the square.

And as I had told Arawn my nephew, I began to write. Not so much music, not these days, though I did enough duty on Frame of Harmony to keep the harper's calluses upon my fingertips. Nay; my task these days was history, and I did my best to chronicle it aright, as I did know it. Oh, to be sure, in time to come, ignorant folk who think they know better who in fact know naught at all will begin poking sgians into my accounts; but those are just the sort of folk who could not be told the truth from the truth's own living mouth, and who would not know it from a bull's backside to begin with. They are not the ones for whom I have written; they are not good enough.

But this particular chronicle, of which you are drawing near the end at last—and I salute you as fellow Companion, for you have been with us all our long road—will not, I fancy, be found for a good many years after I am gone. Decades, centuries, millennia; perhaps not even before I am come again as has been promised; and just to be the more

certain of that I shall take steps to ensure that it shall be
so. . . I spoke just now of the truth, and folk's fitness to hear
it. Well, the truths contained herein are not for the mass of
folk to hear until they are full ready, until they are capable
of accepting the truth of Arthur the King as he was, not as
the myth in guise of which they choose to see him, cobbling
the lie together out of their own, seemingly everlasting,
need and wishing.

Not they alone are guilty: We see it too in the tales my
own mother brought with her from Earth—I wept to see
Arthur ridiculed and Gweniver slandered—and those were
only prophecies, shadow foretellings of what would come to
be. And so I have written this, as I wrote all the other histories that are perhaps not so intimate a telling as this but
truth even so: the *Deeds of Arthur*, the *Life of Morgan*—who
is being called Morgan Magistra even now by the folk (and
who would slap them senseless for it were she here to do
so). But better I to tell her story, our story, than those not
even born when it unfolded; or who, if they were there for
it, were all the same not *there* for it. . . I am only a bard. I
can command only the words I use in my work, at least
when they are not commanding me. And though the true
index of any man is the manner in which he does, or shirks,
his work, I cannot order the effect that work of mine shall
have on others, nor what form my work shall take in the
minds of those who read it. Much to my displeasure; but
there it is, and I have better things to do than fret about a
thing I cannot change.

After I had been some years at Seren Beirdd, I was joined
there by a young student who showed most promising: a
good ear for music, and as good a one for words. Though I
say it perhaps who should not: for the student was my
granddaughter Cathelin, youngest of Gerrans and Cristant.

Which was not to say the lass got any special treatment,
mind, merely because her grandsir now seemed to be
regarded as some sort of national treasure. Still, having the
Pen-bardd of Keltia for syra-wyn was very like more an
advantage than not; but Cathelin, small and fierce and

brown-haired, like a little woods-wolf, to her credit never traded on the link.

The Dragon Kinship took up most of my time apart from bardery. Arawn the King was building us a fine new brugh of our own, Gwahanlen having grown too small for our burgeoning numbers. The elegant edifice was being raised just a little way away from Seren Beirdd, on the eastern edge of Turusachan's plateau, hard by the entrance to the Way of Souls.

I am proud to say that the Kin to the Dragon now numbered some twenty-seven hundred. As I had planned from the start, they were drawn from all levels of Keltic society—all ranks, trades, crafts and callings—and already we were beginning to make our influence felt. Not to command nor yet to pressure, but to suggest and incline, to prevail by example: We had come into being to stand apart from partisan politics or slanted protocols, however noble or worthy. The oath we had taken, the commitment we had pledged, was to the magic that lay at the heart of Keltia, the magic that had founded and fueled and fostered Keltia since the day Brendan had led the Danaans out from Earth. And because our prime loyalty was to that eternality rather than to a thing more transitory, we would not fail of the oath's keeping, and the well-being, the spirit and soul of Keltdom, would be served thereby.

But after years more than a few—though I will not say how many—I felt myself begin to turn away from even my bards and my Dragons and my much-loved kin, and I knew that the time had come to attend to some last remaining tasks, both here in Keltia and otherwhere. For me, it was time to go.

I made few farewells; few indeed were left to bid good-bye in any case. Only Arawn, the High King, Gerrans my son and Cristant his wife, Sgilti, Anghaud and Cathelin—only these knew my true intent. The rest of Keltia was given a story; and who better than the Pen-bardd to spin it?

My writings were all in order, willed to Cathelin and to the Bardic Library. I had thought I would feel a certain pang at separating from these, but it was not so; more a feeling of freedom. I had done all I could, what I could; the rest was no longer mine to rule, or even to hope. Whatever came next out of those words of mine, it was nothing to do with me.

I took little with me: the portrait of Morgan that had travelled with me wherever I went; the two medallions, the suncross and the sigil, that had belonged first to my mother, and the silver Dragon disk that had been Morgan's alone; the ruby-eyed serpent marriage ring upon my hand; two of the hand-copied little volumes of 'Preithi Annuvin,' bound in Gwynedd blue. I would need little else.

No one had been told the night of my departure from Turusachan, for secrecy's sake; but when I stood on a certain corner of the field at Mardale, where a certain ship had been made ready for me by Gerrans and Arawn himself, a slight, cloaked figure stepped from the shadows.

"I had a feeling it would be tonight," said Cathelin, and embraced me with a whispered blessing.

"You are too like your grandmother sometimes," I said, but I was smiling, and I was glad that she had come. "All is in order?"

She nodded, eyes wide in the depths of her hood. "No fear! By this time tomorrownight all Keltia will be grieving the going of Taliesin Pen-bardd, who died suddenly and was disembodied in secrecy by the scadarc at Caer-na-gael, as was his wish and his kindred's. That is how it shall be. As you have commanded it."

"That is it, right enough," I agreed. "Only you, alanna, and the others of our immediate kin shall know the truth of it. It is best so."

She laughed, but I could see the tears glittering in her eyes that were so like Morgan's.

"Best for you, selfish pig—but we will be left here not knowing. . ."

I gathered her into my arms again. "Oh, lassie, you will know. And you must confess, it has a certain grandeur and rightness about it, not so?"

"Aye, even enough to satisfy bards who must make songs about it after. . ." Cathelin stepped back, and brushed her cheeks, openly but defiantly also.

"This will be hardest on you, I think," I said gently. "Only remember that it is all part of the making; the final dwned has meaning and heart only by grace of what has gone before. Yet that before counts for little if resolution is not made in the last lines."

"Forever bard!" But she knew well I did not speak of bardery alone. . .

"I have somewhat here for you," I said, and lifting a large and well-wrapped bundle from the ground I placed it in her arms.

Cathelin was shaking her head in denial and refusal even as Frame of Harmony settled into her hands, as if it knew its new partner.

"Ah, nay, syra-wyn, not *this*— I cannot let you go music-less from Keltia—"

"The songs are here, and here," I said, touching my temple and my breast. "The rest is gilding on gold. . . We had a long and wondrous chaunt of it, Frame of Harmony and I; now the reel-figure changes. No more."

I kissed her brow, gave a final touch to my harp—my oldest friend, it had been with me before even Arthur had—and heard from within the satchel, though truly this could not have been, a faint whispering chime of the strings as if Frame of Harmony had bidden me farewell. Could not have been; but nice to think it.

And then I turned and entered the ship that stood ready behind me, and closed the door. Its dark-green hull glinting in the moon, the sloop that was the last of Prydwen, that had carried the Seven home from Caer Sidi among the stars, rose up from Tara, and took me with it.

We were not going very far, at least not at first. And as Tara fell behind me—as Arthur before Camlann, I had not been able to forbear a final flight over Caerdroia—and Gwynedd came mistily at me through the ard-na-spéire, I felt the upwelling of a mighty emotion, a tremendous sense of love and joy and tasks accomplished. Not quite all tasks, some yet remained for me to finish; but the task Arthur and I had set ourselves so long ago, down there, in drowned Gwaelod and burned Daars and frozen Coldgates, *that* was well achieved. We had built to last there, we two and the others who had joined us in our building. Arawn and those who would follow had inherited a firm foundation and a strong keep set thereon; the rest of the castle was theirs to raise and hold.

You may be wondering why I did not make one last visit to Morgan's grave, or my mother's, before leaving Keltia as I was now about to do; and indeed, I considered both long and hard before resolving not to visit. Not for lack of love or respect; but I had made my farewells to my mother long since. And as for Morgan, all that I had to say to her, all the work—if I may call it so—I needed to do between us, had been done when we buried her, Gwyn and Birogue and I. Anything more was between her and me alone, and was being done even now. To go back to her grave would be somehow to diminish that farewell and physical parting; I would not do that, and any road she was with me as I went. . .

I came into Gwynedd carefully cloaked by the tirr—that inconvenient quirk of which Artos had so often lamented, that the thing could not be used on a moving ship, had been overcome at last, by the Fianna scientists—and, resisting the temptation of touching down briefly at Tair Rhandir or Caer Dathyl or any of a dozen other places that called out to me now in past voices, I held the little ship on course, straight for Glora and the North.

I set down on the shores of the great inland sea itself. It was just before sunset local time, the mountains that ringed Glora tipped with fire; the sky glowed and throbbed. Across the still water that flamed now like a road to the sun, the island Collimare sailed dark and deserted, the Forest in the Sea. The tall trees rising from its low shores made it seem a galleon of old times, or one of the warships we of the Counterinsurgency had once sailed down these straits, bound for Raven's Rift.

I stepped to the water's edge, my boots crunching loud in the silence on the white pebbled shingle. Even the little wavelets seemed to hush at my coming, as if all around me waited, breathless and expectant, for what was about to happen.

I had a fair idea, myself, as to what that might be, but it remained to be seen. . . I threw back my curtagh and unhooked from my baldric a sword in a leather scabbard worn shiny with age and use, its inlaid tracery of gold and enamel all but flaked away. I held it across my palms, looking at it, remembering.

This was Llacharn, the Sword from the Air and the Sword from the Fire, the Sword from the Water and the Sword from the Stone. Arthur and Morgan and I, working together, had ourselves taken it from the place of its long keeping, deep in the earth beneath Collimare. And now it was going home: The last of the Companions had brought Llacharn with him, or maybe Llacharn had brought him. And it was right and fitting that that last should have also been the first.

The feeling of expectancy deepened around me, and I knew I was waited for. I lifted the sword above my head; then, as once a king had done before me with another, greater Sword, with my left hand I stripped away the scabbard. A shard of blade came with it—Llacharn had never been reforged after Nandruidion where it had broken, in Arthur's hand in defense of Uthyr Ard-rígh—and I caught it before it could fall to the ground.

Hilt-shard, blade-shard. . . I took one in either hand, and with the hand that held the hilt I cast the scabbard from me into the loch. Before it touched the surface it vanished in a flash of flame, and I smiled as a voice cried out from the air itself.

"The hour is here, but not the man!" Three times it cried so, and left behind it a silence even more enormous than before.

I strode forward so that my boots were set in the water's edge. "The hour is come, and the man also!" I shouted into that silence, once only. Then lifting the sword-shards once more, I crossed them above my head in salute, so that catching the fire of the setting Beli, they blazed the suncross symbol that is both a beginning and an end. And I flung the halves of Llacharn mightily out above the waters.

The sparkling shards turned top for tip, revolving with a strange stateliness, spinning like triskells as they reflected the light. They seemed to slow then in the air, and hang there over the center of the waters between Collimare and the shore—Loch Bel Draccon, this arm of Glora was called, the Lake of the Dragon's Mouth, and I wondered suddenly just why it had such a name. . . But then a wind came up, a windfist, a small waterspout, that ruffled Glora's surface and came dancing down the track of the sun. It caught the sword—the sword *reforged*—into itself, bright water spinning everywhere like drops of gold.

And some might say they saw a white hand come up to grasp the hilt, an arm come up out of the dark waters, lifting Llacharn made whole again, an arm clothed in oréadach that held the sword in salute a moment still, then pulled it down without a sound or splash beneath the waters of Loch Bel Draccon, and the sun was gone.

Some might say that. But I myself. . .well, I am a bard. Too many folk already have accused me of embroidering upon the truth. I leave this truth unadorned. Ornament it as you please.

And that was the last of my labors in Keltia, as Gwyn and Birogue and Merlynn—who were ever in my thoughts as I set my ship's nose for the Curtain Wall—had been telling me for so long. I must confess, I had half-hoped to see one or all of them there at Glora for Llacharn's homecoming—and I had no doubt but that it was even now resting once again in its dolmen, where an unknown hand had first set it, in the little cave whence Arthur had brought it up into the light—but, as I had known the grave-visits would be, such farewell was pure superfluity. Our partings had been made, our words had all been said. Anything more would be, well, too much.

As the Wall's pale blue glow began to grow in my ship's viewscreens—you may remember that Morgan had designed it so, to be invisible to direct sight—I began to chaunt, softly at first then in full bardic voice and strength, to sing my way out as a bard will do upon his deathbed; though that for me was yet to come. But I was leaving Keltia for the last time, and if that was not death as I knew it, then naught was; and so I sang.

And also I remembered, and considered: All things had
been left in order, all geisa filled, all tasks accomplished. I
had named Alannagh Ruthven's daughter, Fidais, to be
Pendragon of the Kinship after me. I had passed along
Frame of Harmony to hands full fit to hold it. I had set such
a shield of myth and mystery between Arthur and the truth
of his end that none should ever come at it save that one
who would be born to do so. I had wedded out of love a
lady out of legend, and had loved none other, not even after
she was gone: For, as the great bard Lassarina Aoibhell had
said of her lost mate, the even greater bard Séomaighas
Douglas, and said so well too, 'When the wine is gone, only
a fool would drink seawater; better far to go thirsty, and
remember the wine, however long the drought.'

All this I had done; there was no more in Keltia I
must do.

The Curtain Wall was all but upon me, or I upon it: I
was going beyond the Pale, for the first time and the last.
And it came to me as I looked upon this my wife's monu-
ment and lasting triumph that the Pale was a boundary
between one life and another, a hedge of mist like that one
that is at the end of each span of our days, and before the
beginning of the next. The thought struck me with a sense
of joy and fulfillment renewed, and I knew I should never be
able to set it into song; for I was done with that too, and
well done.

There came around me a light through the ports of the
sloop; the ship shuddered once, twice; then the stars of the
Bawn went dark, and ahead of me the whole sweep of outfrenne space lay open.

Keltia was behind me; but I did not look back.

After an uneventful sail I came to Aojun, where Donah was
now Jamadarin. Majanah had died a few years since: I had
gone to her funeral, accompanied by Gerrans and Arawn
himself, who had wished to pay respects to his lasmathra
whom he had loved, and to see again his halfsister—as
monarchs both, they would have much to share and speak
of. Donah had wedded—Daronwy and Roric's son, of all

people, Harodin—and had now three children, including her heir, Sarinah.

I was met in Mistissyn by the Queen, looking remarkably like herself. She received me as a revered and beloved uncle, with joy only slightly tempered with sorrow, and I spent a month on that world where I had dwelled so long ago.

But Aojun was not my final destination, far from it; and before I left, my sloop refurbished and provisioned for my next world of call, I gave Donah one of the blue leather books in which were written the words I had made on her father's death. She received it gravely and gratefully; though she understood why I must go, all the same she and Harodin and Sarinah—who looked so like her grandmother Daronwy at that age as to unsettle me quite—pressed me both subtly and bluntly to stay on and end my days with them in peace and comfort and love.

Though I was tempted, I refused; those days of mine were running short now, and I had still a thing or two to do before they ran out entirely. So after taking tearful and tender farewell of my niece and her family, and their world that I had grown to love—no chance *here* that Arthur would be forgotten! Artho Kendrion, not entirely to my liking and easiness, had been raised almost to the stature of a minor god—I took ship again, and this time my intended planetfall held no such assurance of felicity.

Kholco looked as dull and dust-veiled as it had the last time I had beheld it—the only time. I spoke briefly with the guardians who had authority over landings, and presently obtained the clearances I sought.

The firemounts across the great lava plain were quiescent this time, though in the greater, the one that had taken Prydwen, a low glow burned, and every now and again a sullen rumble shivered the ground. I put the ship down on a basalt flat as level as a piece of panbread, and waited to see what would happen next.

They came after a reasonable interval, from the cliffs to the west that housed the settlement I knew was called the Ras of Salhi. There were perhaps eight or ten of them all told, mounted on small strong-boned horses with long streaming manes and tails. I had stayed in the sloop to protect myself from the heat that pounded like a fist on the hull, wanting to be let in. I was *not* going to oblige: Kelts do not deal well with heat; seven or eight thousand years of misty cool climes will breed it out of you every time. But the Salamandri had arrived, and I went outside to meet them.

They were a handsome people, saurinoids, with strong blunt features and lightly scaled leathery skin of varying hues. They bowed in answer to my opening courtesies, and the one who stood foremost of them spoke, in a fluent if strangely accented version of the Common Speech.

After an exchange of greetings and words of welcome, I steeled myself to speak of my errand. But I was anticipated.

"We know your reason for coming," said Adamar, who had spoken first. "And we would hear."

I stared, then recovered myself. "How can that be, lord?"

He gave a snort of laughter, immediately stilled. "No—it is not a laughing matter. We knew you would come one day. We saw the ship of your people sink itself in the holy mountain, ori-vech—years ago."

"'Holy mountain'?" I repeated dumbly, first nonplussed and then aghast. "Have we offended?"

One of the other Firefolk jerked up his chin, which I guessed was their signal for Nay. "You do not understand. It is their presence that has made the mountain holy. They were brave folk, and died nobly."

"We could not get home," I murmured. "I was here—I remember."

Adamar saw my thought. "Comfort yourself. There was no way they could have saved themselves. They saved whom they could, and made an end. They did correctly. Even we could not have helped them repair the ship."

"Have you come to take them home, lord?" asked one of the others, of build more slight, though whether this was a sign of youth or gender I did not know. "We understand that you would wish to, and surely would allow it, but it would be best for all if they were left here in peace. No harm will come to them. They are honored."

I hesitated, not sure if I wished to hear an answer; then

asked. "Did you see them—in the ship? Did you look within?"

Adamar nodded slowly. "Once only, when we pulled the craft from the fire, to see if any yet lived or could be saved. The ship had been scanned as it fell—though we have no weapons, we have enough technology for that—and we knew all were dead long before they reached the fire. But still we had hope. Then the mountain began to wake, and we thought it best to move them thence."

"Moved?" I asked, surprised and alarmed. All these years it had been comfort to me, if I can call it that, to think Arthur and the rest lay where I had seen them fall. But now it seemed they had not been there. "Where, then?"

"The Firehorn—the peak where they fell—has a twin," said Adamar. "In their youth both mountains were torches of Earth-heart; then the fire went from Scarva, the elder of the two, and now only the Firehorn, Mount Terror, still burns as of old. We took your folk in their ship and lodged them in Scarva, and there they remain. You may see if you wish. But we never troubled their rest again, and we would not have it troubled now, not even by their own folk and kin."

"There may be another word as to that," I said carefully. "May we speak of it otherwhere?"

He gestured royally. "Come."

We rode to the Ras of Salhi where it loomed in the shade of its rosy cliffs. I was ceremoniously presented to various elders of this particular clann, which seemed to control all the country roundabouts, including the two great volcanoes. Adamar seemed to have been appointed my guide and docent: He took me at once to a spacious chamber with high grilled windows and painted ceilings, and we disposed ourselves on bright-colored patterned pillows and soft deep carpets, to speak of what must be spoken.

In a formal bardic style—these folk seemed to appreciate and respond to formality—I recounted for the Salamandri the story as I knew it, in brief, for it made a long tale even so: of the battle at Camlann and the betrayal that occasioned it, of Arthur's desperate throw that had brought us to the Morimaruse and to Fomor, and to Kholco in the end. And they listened, nodding gravely as my narrative brought guess and supposition into line. Adamar was there, and perhaps a dozen others, some of whom were noting down my words onto clay tablets as I spoke, and other some were using tiny sleek recorders that seemed utterly at variance with the setting.

I remarked on that later to Adamar, when the others had taken leave for the night. The Salamand smiled.

"Well, and a little of both styles is no bad thing, not so? I would wager you have much of a mix on your own worlds."

"And that is a wager you would win," I said lightly. "But, Adamar, I am here for more than storytelling—"

"Indeed. That too shall come. But not tonight." He gestured to the chamber's far corner, where in a deep alcove a deep divan had been made up with soft blankets and more of the ubiquitous cushions. "Tomorrow will be soon enough to begin that."

I bade him goodnight, and then sleepwalked across to the divan, which was looking more and more inviting every moment. You may think it foolhardy of me, to trust so completely so alien a race—I had, as custom demanded, come unweaponed among them—but I was not seeing it so. The Salamandri and the Kelts had been friends of old; only Edeyrn had soured the concord, as he had done with all else. But the chief reason I felt so at ease among the Firefolk was a simpler one: If Artos could sleep safe here, so too then could I. And I did.

I stayed six months among the Salamandri, all of it spent in teaching and being taught. If Arthur and the rest were going to sleep here forever, or at least until that one of my vision came to find them and bring the Treasures home, then it was well that the Firefolk should know all the story, and indeed they were most eager to hear.

Adamar and I became fast friends, and I grew close to all his tribe; they were a most musical people, though their tonal scale was unlike to our own, and we learned much

from one another. But I had not come here to spend my
time so, however pleasant and instructive; my reasons were
rather different, and one night after supper I spoke to
Adamar my heart's truth at last. . .

"So," he said when I had finished; he had not interrupted all my long, long discourse once, but had listened
attentively, at least judging by the half-dozen penetrating
and intelligent questions he put me straightway. I answered
my best, but I was trying to overcome my surprise at his,
well, *lack* of surprise, and finally I put it to him forthwith.

Adamar smiled at my 'stonishment. "Your folk are not
the only ones to have such seeings, Talyos. Nor is much of
what you have told me just now new to us. We have long
guessed more even than you have told me, and now it seems
that we were right."

"The prophecies?" I asked, humbled. "You have Seen
too, then. . ."

"Oh yes; we have seen more than that, even, at least
where it works upon the Firefolk, though that is not your
concern. But we are glad to know for sure, and though it
must be put to a vote, the action you suggest is not unlike
our own thought. I am sure it will be taken up and fall out
as you could wish it."

I leaned back on my pillows after he had gone. My othersense told me I had heard truth here; but, all the same,
unless commanded, I would not leave Kholco—could not
leave—until I had seen my last task at least begun.

I had come to Kholco to give the Salamandri the truth of
Arthur and the Company. Therefore I held nothing back;
not Edeyrn, not the aftermath of Camlann, not the raising
of the Wall, not the visions I had had. And the Firefolk had
confirmed them, and were making them real: In the cavern
just outer of the one in which Prydwen rested, a great work
was beginning.

Given the geology of their harsh and lovely world, it
would have been odd indeed if the Salamandri, or the other
reptile races that ruled here, had not gone in for petro-
graphs, as decoration and teaching tool and mural historical

record all alike. They were an artistic folk, and some of the cave paintings I had seen were extraordinary indeed, combining sculpture with brushwork in an amazing and beautiful way.

And so, already, had Artos and Prydwen been immortalized in stone. . . Upon the rough rock of the cavern walls, places had been melted smooth as water with stonesappers and rockburners, and scenes and images most assuredly not of Kholco had been added to paintings already carved and tinted into the walls: the falling ship, the flaming mountain. Now I had come to give the story new verses, and the walls would have images afresh, and the clues at last suffice.

As I looked on the work already completed, I was minded at once of Gwahanlen, and the tales of Keltic history told on its walls. But there the resemblance ended: These tapestries were woven not of cloth but of the living rock.

I paced round the walls, 'reading' as I went. The lithoglyphs told the story of what had been, and now they were beginning to tell the story of what would be. I saw things I myself had told of, and things to which I had no clue as to their meaning.

But if the Salamandri had secrets of their own to mesh with the one I had given, that was no concern of mine. My task had lain in this, the last thing I had to do for Arthur: to ensure that these signs and signals were left, so that the one, that red-haired queen I had Seen so vividly and so often she seemed by now as one of my kin—as perhaps she would be, or one of my Kin—would know beyond all and any doubt when she came at last that her course was a right and true one. And the Salamandri were a right and true folk to hold this message for her down the years: They might add other seeings to this record for the future, as they Saw, or saw fit, but they would neither alter nor destroy what was here being set down according to my word.

I reached out to brush gentle fingers over the pictoglyph before me: a woman in black, no Salamand but a true Kelt, with hair redder than Morgan's and more golden than Arthur's, the suncross upon which she stood and the crescent sigil above her head the twins of those that still hung around my neck. *Oh aye,* I thought, and hugged myself for certainty and joy, *I think she will know this when she comes, when Gwyn sends her. . .*

Though one thing she would *not* know was how such an image had come here: On that the Salamandri and I were agreed. This tribe alone knew of my coming; and of them, only those of priestly caste and high rank, dwelling at the Ras across the plain from Scarva, had themselves undertaken the labor of creation and execution of the paintings. They alone knew of the message I had brought and would be leaving, here, where the horns of light burned before the gates of Uffern. *How well I had been given to See,* I thought, not for the first time nor yet the last, and how thankful I was for it.

No other word would be left behind here, except perhaps for some songs, and a poem or two, as obscure in their way as my work 'Preithi Annuvin,' which I had read here to great approval, had been in its own. In all ways else, I would be on Kholco—Avilion, Avallin, Afallinn—as dust in the wind. It was my geis, and my honor, and my pleasure to be so.

And I know you are far too polite to ask outright so distressing a question, but are burning to know all the same: Did I, in all the months of my guesting among the Firefolk, so near all that time to my lost and loved ones, ever go within Prydwen and look upon them for myself?

And I tell you now, I did not.

Not for lack of wishing: Nay, not an hour went by when I did not long to look once more upon Artos's face, or Tari's or Betwyr's or Alannagh's—how could I not wish to see them once again? They would be as they had been in life; Arthur had laid a staying-spell upon them all—one of the last things he did—so that their bodies would not suffer the usual fate but would lie forever as if just fallen off to sleep. And I myself reinforced this rann almost immediately after my arrival, with the mightiest spells I knew and sorcerers of the Firefolk to help me; as I had done alone, years since, with Gwain.

And for that, of course, I had had to behold Prydwen as she was, in the inner cavern where the Salamandri had brought her, a steed of the stars in a stabling of earth. But to

behold *them*, nay; that was beyond my strength. For many
reasons, but chiefest among them was that should I look
again upon my friends, upon my brother and my King, my
wish to join them then and there, the wish of my heart ever
since they went, would be too mighty for me to withstand,
and I should give in to it without a fight. No one would
blame me, I knew—no Kelt, and no Salamand either—but I
could not do it. Another dán called me hence.

At last came the day when all was accomplished. I looked
upon the completed glyphs, and again upon Prydwen, and I
was content. This was the last of it: The King slept in the
island Avallinn, with his warriors about him; and upon
Uffern's walls the message waited for the one called to hear
it. I was free to go at last.

So I did. I bade farewell to Adamar and his kin, knowing
the secret would be kept, and I sailed my ship from Kholco
in a direction no Kelt had taken for long and long, not since
my own father had taken it two centuries past.

I was heading to Earth: on a faring, a seeking; a choqa as
Adamar's people, who understood well such things, named
it in their own tongue. One last quest; and, as ever with
quests, I had not the least idea if I would ever come near
achieving that which I sought. But that was not why I did
seek it.

I am going back to Earth to find my mother. Oh, not in
any real sense, for I have seen her peaceful grave among
the Sidhe; but to learn of her, whence she came, what had
made her who and what she was—that in its turn had
made me.

I do not know what I shall find there, or even if I shall
reach it alive, or remain so long thereafter should I come to
it. In our legendry we have many tales of heroes going to
Tir-na-n'-Og or Tir-fo-thuinn or Tir Tairngire—all the tirs
are the same, the Otherworld of many names—and when
they return to our world, if return they ever do, falling down
straightway into a heap of dust. A risk; but I do not care.

Better to be a handful of dust on the shore, having seen the Otherland, than a king breathing who never left home.

The fiction that will go down in the Keltic histories—I know, for I arranged it so—is that Taliesin Pen-bardd died and was disembodied by the scadarc in the neat Fian way, disatomed on the wicker bier above the grave of his wife. But it comes to my mind now that that vision I had at the false corvaen, what time I was on quest for the Cup, showed a fate not unconsonant with any of this. An altar with a form laid upon it, and that myself, and I vanishing: Perhaps it had been a true Seeing in a false place.

Or maybe it was truer even than I can know: Perhaps when I step upon Earth, set foot upon my mother's world, I *shall* fall away to dust, like those heroes in the tales. Considering the paradox of time involved in my father's immram, the reiving that won him my mother, I could well end up on Earth or ever I was born in Keltia; or be born instead a Terran, and have to live all my life, or someone's life, over again—if indeed I lived at all.

But the Hedge of Mist cannot be crossed alive, nor without change; and the nature of mist is that one cannot see through it, to discern aforetime what that change might be. The only way to know is to go; and to accept whatever lies on the Hedge's other side.

It is all one, that is the Mystery of it: the Hedge of Mist, the apple tree, the horn that Geraint blew; Donah with the Cup of all Creation in her two hands, the sun and moon and stars about her head and the radiance of heaven in her face; the Young Goddess, Rhian, at Ashnadarragh; Fionn the Young at the White Ford; the Bhan-reann-ruadh in the Wood of Shapes. Nearer still: Gwyn and Birogue upon the mountain and beneath the hill; Merlynn, my Ailithir, in his cold crystal tomb; Gweniver at Coldgates, when first I set eyes on her, a fourteen-year-old princess, shy and proud and frightened, using the pride to mask the shyness and the fear; Morgan at Collimare, Morgan at the Wall, Morgan my beloved in guises too many to count. . .

And above all others, Arthur: on the October hillside at Daars, in the snows before Talgarth and after Moytura, in the sword-light at Cadarachta and in the torchlight of the

Hall of Heroes and in Scarva's dimness; a matchless spirit in a mighty frame.

All are as one now, in memory and in something beyond memory: The cabin of my little ship is thick with presences, they are all with me now, here, and I cannot tell which were then and which are now and which are yet to be. But this chronicle goes with me to Earth; if it be found, that is dán, and if not, that too is dán.

But a great bard of ours, who began to sing young and shone early, put it thus: 'Darkness and Light contest; but they shall be one at the End, and that one neither Light nor Dark but both together.'

It might be a long way to go to learn that; it might be I shall never reach it. But I am going all the same. Perhaps I shall see you there. In the name of all gods, it may be so.

Maybe even it shall be so.

AFTERTALE

And from that hour none knows where he went; not even I, Cathelin daughter of Geraint, sister of Sgilti and Anghaud who are of the Seven, cousin to Arawn Ard-rígh.

But I shall set down this brief aftertelling in the name and honor of my grandsir, Taliesin Glyndour ac Pendreic gân Morguenna, known as Pen-bardd, fosterer to Arthur the King. Into my hands did he confide the gift of Frame of Harmony; I shall strive to sound it half as well as he did, and perhaps it will help me do so.

It all fell out as he had planned it, of course: The folk have shrouded his ending with as much mystery as they have used to veil Arthur's own, and it was even he who wove those veils for them. Though he told me and a scant few others of his last intent, we do not know if he achieved it, we shall never know: if Taliesin Pen-bardd came to Earth as he purposed, though I for one will ever think so. There is a grand symmetry in it, a closing-off, that is pleasing to the bardic sensibility—like the lastverse and harp-tailing that round off a chaunt.

My grandmother very like would think so also, thinks so where she now is, with him once more; she who is already known as Morgan Magistra among the folk. Indeed, some are even beginning to call her Saint Morgan of the Pale, realizing only now what she did for them, the great gift she gave all Keltia in the raising of the Wall; though I shiver to think what she herself would say to such a title. . .

But it makes no differ, either road. In the books my grandsir left me, the journals his mother, my namesake, brought with her from Earth, there is copied down a poem she much loved, and which he came to love as well. A bard of the Sassenaich (though not to be faulted purely for that), a lord also, set it down centuries since, and it seems to me to be apposite here. It tells of the hero Ulessos, on his own last immram, wondering what may befall him but fearing it not at all, indeed, rejoicing in it: 'It may be that the gulfs will wash us down: It may be we shall touch the Happy Isles, And see the great Achilles, whom we knew. Tho' much is taken, much abides. . .'

Much. Taliesin will come again even as Arthur will, as Morgan will; they shall be together again. Perhaps even Merlynn will awaken to join them, as I know they believed and hoped.

Until then, the songs will live forever. As he himself wrote it:

> 'Their course, their bearing,
>   their permitted way
> And their fate I know:
> until the end.
> Until the end.
> Until the End.'

And what better end could there be for a bard than that?

(Here ends *The Hedge of Mist*, last of *The Tales of Arthur* sequence of THE KELTIAD. The next will be *Blackmantle*, the story of Athyn and Morric.)

Appendices

GLOSSARY

Words are Keltic except where otherwise noted, and follow
Keltic (not Celtic) orthography and grammatical rules.

Abred: "The Path of Changes"; the visible world of everyday existence, within the sphere of which one's various
lives are lived

ac: sponsal affix used with clann name of mate; relative affix
used to indicate consanguinity, linking names of both
parents (birthname takes precedence, and a child will
take the higher-ranking parent's name for surname)

Aengus: one of the **High Dânu** (q.v.); god of winds,
journeys and love

aer: sung satirical verse, employed by bards; can be of such
point and virulence as actually to raise blotches on face of
one satirized

aes dána: (pron. *eyes-dawna*) "folk of skill"; term for artists
and craftsmen

Aes Dânu: "Folk of Dâna"; descendants of the Danaan
race; also, the High Dânu or other associated divinities

Aes Sidhe: (pron. *eyes-shee*) the Shining Ones; a race of
possibly divine or immortal beings; their king at present is
Nudd (or Neith) ap Llyr

ainm-pósta: gamonymic; marriage-name

aircar: small personal transport used on Keltic worlds

aireachtas: hearing-court (cf. Terran *majlis*) presided over
by ruler, lord or local ranking chief

Airts: the four magical directions to which sacred circles are
oriented; as **airts,** mundane compass quarters

alanna: "child," "little one"; Erinnach endearment

Alterator: one of the three High Powers of the Keltic pantheon; neither male nor female, the Alterator works with
the Goddess and the God to effect the changes they
decree and the will of **Kelu** (**Yr Mawreth**)

amadaun: "fool"

Amheraudr, Amheraudraes: Emperor, Empress; titles
used in Keltic Protectorates for the Keltic reigning
monarch (never used in Keltia itself) (also **Imperator,
Imperatrix**)

amhic: (pron. *uh-VICK*) "my son"; used in the vocative
only

anama-chara: "soul-friend"; term for those closest and
most beloved friends of which one has perhaps only one
or two in a lifetime

An Cuach: "The Cup"; another name (Scotic) for the
Graal (q.v.)

an-da-shalla: "the Second Sight"; Keltic talent of
precognition

anfa: "storm"

An Lasca: "The Whip"; ionized northwest wind at
Caerdroia that blows primarily in winter

annat: place of formal public worship or contemplation;
indoors, as opposed to **nemetons** (q.v.); usually attached
to institutions such as convents or monasteries, but frequently found in private homes as well, especially among
royalty or nobility

Annwn: (pron. *Annoon*) the Keltic religion's equivalent to
the Underworld, ruled over by **Arawn,** Lord of the Dead
(q.v.)

an uachdar!: lit., "uppermost"; in salutations (e.g., *Pendreic
an uachdar!*) usually translated as "Long live _____ !"

anwyl, anwylyd: "sweetheart," "darling"; Kymric endearment

Aojun: homeworld of the **Yamazai** (q.v.); has a long and
honorable history of friendship with Keltia (adj.
Aojunni, Aojunese)

ap: "son of"

Arawn Doomsman: one of the **High Dânu;** he is said to
rule Annwn and preside over matters of fate; he has the
power to restore the dead to life

ard-na-spéire: "the height of heaven"; hyperspace, the **overheaven**

Ard-rían, Ard-rígh: "High Queen," "High King"; title of the Keltic sovereign (only actual rulers take this title; consorts are styled plain King or Queen)

Ard-tiarnas: "The High Dominion," "High Lordship"; the supreme rulership of Keltia

Argialla: the innermost, white moon of the Throneworld Tara's two satellites

arva-draoi: "Druid's Fence"; magical spell of binding or hindering

arwydd: (pron. *AR-weethe*) omen, portent

ashling: waking, wishful dream; daydream

athra: "father"; a formal or more adult style

athra-chéile: lit., "mate-father"; father-in-law

athro: "teacher," "master"

Arvor: chief planet of the Brytaned system

Athyn (Cahanagh): Ard-rían of Keltia by acclamation some five hundred years before Arthur's time; her consort was the great Scotan bard **Morric Douglas**

averin: herb averin; healing plant of the sage family, with aromatic, spiky, silver-green leaves; used medicinally and magically, for cleansing (**smudging** or **smooring**: to burn a sprig of this herb to purify tainted persons, things or places; other herbs can be used, but this one is most usual)

Avon Dia: (**Avon** rhymes with "havin'") the great river on Tara that divides the Northwest Continent and flows past Caerdroia

Awen: (usually, **Holy** or **Sacred Awen**) lit., the Muse or sacred gift of inspiration; as used by bards, the personified creative spirit, represented by three lines, the center one vertical, the outer two angling in opposite directions (/|\); creative genius in general

ayont: "beyond"

bach, bachgen: (also **-bach,** added as suffix to male names) denotes affection; used to all ages and ranks, can be translated as "lad" (fem., **fach** or **-fach,** "lass")

Badger-moon: the month of December

bairn: "child"

ban-a-tigh: woman householder (**far-a-tigh,** male householder)

ban-charach: lit., "the loved woman"; term for a woman formally and legally associated with a man short of lawful marriage (cf. **far-charach, céile-charach**)

Ban-draoi: lit., "woman-Druid"; Keltic order of priestess-sorceresses in the service of the **Ban-dia,** the Mother Goddess

banjaxed: stunned, flummoxed, utterly astounded and perplexed

bannock: thick, soft bread or roll, biscuit or muffin

bansha: female spirit, often red-cloaked, that sings and wails before a death in many ruling Keltic (chiefly Erinnach) families; often seen as a wild rider in the air or over water

bard: Keltic order of poets, chaunters, loremasters and musicians; they often function as teachers, mediators, marriage brokers and spies; the Order was founded in the year 347 A.B. (Anno Brendani) by Plenyth ap Alun

Beannacht, beannacht: "blessing"; cap., the formal prayer used universally in Keltia for nearly every occasion requiring such; simple salutation of greeting and farewell

Bear-moon: the month of February

Bellendain: the outer, red moon of Tara's two satellites

Beltane: festival of the beginning of summer, celebrated on 1 May

beneath the Horns: sub rosa, secret; refers to the Horns of the God, the **Cabarfeidh** (q.v.)

Bhan-reann-ruadh: lit., "Red Star Woman"; minor Keltic divinity, or her aspect put on by greater goddesses or the Goddess Herself

birlinn: elegant, galley-type ship, usually both oared and masted

blosc-báis: the mort; the trumpet-call sounded when a quarry is brought down on the hunting field

borraun: wood-framed, tambourine-shaped goatskin drum, played by hand or with a small flat wooden drumstick

braud: "brother"

brehons: Keltic lawgivers and judges

brehon marriage: a type of civil marriage, renewable at pre-specified intervals (a year and a day is most usual); considered less solemn than a **handfasting** (q.v.) or a wedding "at the stones," though equally lawful

Brendan: (Saint) founder of Keltia; **Anno Brendani,** "in the year of Brendan," Keltic year-reckoning (to find the year in Earth Reckoning, add 453)

Brighnasa: feast of the goddess Brigid (pron. *Breed*) or Briginda, celebrated on 1 February (also called **Imbolc**)

Briginda: the goddess Brigid or Bríd in her aspect as Lady of Spring

brugh: fortified manor house, usually belonging to one of the gentry or nobility; in cities, a town-palace of great elegance and size

bruidean: inn or waystation, maintained by local authorities, where any traveller of whatever rank or resources is entitled by law to claim hospitality free of charge

"Bydd i ti ddychwelyd": blessing from Keltic death-ritual, usually spoken by chief mourner or mourner closest to deceased; translates as "There shall be a returning for thee"

Cabarfeidh: personification of the God, the male principle of the universe and the Goddess's mate, as the Hornèd Lord or the Antlered King, a man with the antlers of a stag

caer: fortress, stronghold

Caer Coronach: "Castle Lamentation" or "Crown of the North"; in Keltic theology, the silver-walled castle (also known as **Argetros,** "Silver Wheel") behind the north wind, to which souls journey as the first stop after death; a place of joy, light, refreshment and peace, to which the newly dead soul is guided (and guarded en route) by those who have loved it in life

Caer Dathyl: capital city of the planet Gwynedd and the Kymric system

Caerdroia: capital city of Keltia, on the Throneworld of Tara

cam-anfa: "crooked storm"; violent localized cyclonic disturbance of the sort known to Terrans as a tornado

Cam-Corainn: a name for the **Cup** or the **Graal** (q.v.)

cantred: political division of planets in most Keltic systems, roughly equivalent to a county or shire; province

cantrip: very small, simple spell or minor magic

Caomai: "The Armed King"; a Keltic constellation containing several first-magnitude stars

cariad: "heart," "beloved"; used to a lover

cariadol: "heart," "little love"; used to a child

cariad o'nghariad: "heart of hearts"; used to one's truemate

castaun: chestnut; also, the red-brown color of a chestnut

Cath-Awen: lit., "Head of the Holy Inspiration"; title given at this time in Keltic history to the chief of the Bardic Order

catteran: rebel or other irregular fighter; outlaw

cathbarr: fillet or coronet, usually a band of precious metal ornamented with jewels

céile-charach: lit., "the loved mate"; word for either partner to a legal and formal union short of lawful marriage, or for the partnership itself (cf. **ban-charach, far-charach**)

ceól-mór: "The Great Music"; canon of bardic classical music

chiel: term of opprobrium; roughly translates as "bastard"

Christom: Christian or Christendom, in reference to the Terran political-religious cult

cithóg: port, as on board ship (cf. **deosil**)

clach: sacred crystal or stone used in magical operations

clann: tribe or family (also **Name**)

claymore: huge two-handed broadsword favored by Scotan fighters

Clero: Keltic trading planet; established by Raighne Ardrían as a center for commerce and trade closer to the usual centers of such activities than is Keltia itself (her thought was also to keep outworlders at what she considered a suitable distance)

cliamhan: relation by marriage; generic term that applies to any indirect kinship (wife's niece's husband's father, sister's husband's mother, etc.)

clune: small upland meadow, often used for summer pasturage

Common Tongue: unofficial intergalactic trading language; at the time of Arthur, not based on Englic (as it later became) but on a form of Hastaic, the Coranian mother-language

compall: dueling-ground used by Fianna and others, especially for the **fíor-comlainn** (q.v.)

coney: rabbit

Coranians: ruling race of the Cabiri Imperium, hereditary enemies of the Kelts; they are the descendants of the Atlandean Telchines, as the Kelts are of the Atlandean Danaans

coronach: funeral song; lamentation or dirge

coron-solais: "crown of light"; personal aura

corrigaun: being of the Otherworld; small of stature but powerfully built, usually dark-haired; opinion in Keltia is divided as to whether the corrigauns (also known as **dwarrows**) are indeed a separate race of beings or are actually an aspect of the **Sidhe-folk**

Corryochren: "The Hungry Hollow"; huge and extremely dangerous whirlpool between the two islands Kedria and Carbria, off the south coast of the Northwest Continent on Tara

corvaen: another word for **nemeton** (q.v.); a stone circle

Counterinsurgency: the great resistance movement that arose in Keltia against the Marbh-draoi Edeyrn and his rule

creevies: term of opprobrium; annoying or unworthy persons

cribbins: humble food eaten by travellers, usually a stew of whatever is available or left over, or can be hunted

crimbeul: lit., "droop-mouth"; mustache

Criosanna: "The Woven Belts"; the beautiful rings that circle the planet Tara

crochan: magical healing-pool that can cure almost any injury, provided the spinal cord has not been severed and the brain and bone marrow are undamaged

"Croesawr i mi!": cry of despair; lit., "An hour of adversity to me!"

croi o mo chroi: "heart of my heart"; used to one's true-mate

crossics: unit of Keltic gold money

crystalskin: extremely tough, fine paper used by Keltic bookbinders; it gets its durability from the crystalline structures woven into it, hence the name

Cuchulainn: legendary hero of Celtic Earth

culist: "back-room"; traditional best chamber in Keltic farm-houses, usually behind a free-standing fireplace; very warm and cozy, and therefore offered to guests

curragh: small boat or dinghy; any similarly proportioned starcraft

curtagh: short (knee-length or above) leather mantle with collar and sometimes attached hood

curtal-axe: double-bladed war-axe (also **tuagh**)

dama-wyn: "grandmother," "great-grandmother"

dán: "doom"; fate or karma

Dâna: founding foremother and tutelary goddess of the Kelts

Daynighting: the spring or autumn equinox

deosil: righthandwise or sunwise, clockwise; on a ship, the starboard side (cf. **cithóg**)

Derwydd: "The Trunk of the Oak"; title for the Chief Bard

dolmen: a standing stone, sacred pillar-stone

dreic: "dragon"; ancient word for "warrior"

drench: philtre, potion, compelling drink; commonly, a love potion; *v.*, to offer any sort of drink or liquid to a person who thirsts

Druids: magical order of Keltic sorcerer-priests, in the service of the Ollathair, the Lord-father, the Goddess's mate

dubhachas: "gloom"; deep melancholy characterized by causeless depression and an inexpressible longing for unnameable things (known irreverently as "the Keltic blacks")

dúchas: lordship or holding; usually carries a title with it

duergar: in Kernish folklore, an evil elemental or place-spirit

dwarrow: another name for **corrigaun** (q.v.)

dwimmer: evilly sorcerous (**dwimmercraft,** black magic)

dwned: (pron. *doon-it*) stanza or verse of poem or chaunt

dyster: squall or sudden storm

eacht-grásta: mercy-blow, coup-de-grâce

Ellwand: in the constellation **Caomai,** the stars of the baldric

éraic: "blood-price"; in Keltic law, the payment exacted for murder or other capital crime by the kin of the victim, or, if victim was kinless, by the Crown

ergyd: another word for **eacht-grásta** (q.v.)

Eryri: "Abode of Eagles"; Mount Eagle, below which is situated Caerdroia

esplumeor: in falconry, the cage or place where hawks are kept during their season of moult, to protect them while new feathers are growing in

faha: courtyard or enclosed lawn-space in a castle complex or encampment

far-charach: lit., "the loved man"; term for a man formally and legally associated with a woman short of lawful marriage (cf. **ban-charach, céile-charach**)

faunt: of a child, when he or she becomes a talker and walker

feiching: foul, dirty, disgusting

ferch: (pron. *vairkh,* with guttural "ch") "daughter of"

fetch: the visible form taken by the spirit-guardian of a Keltic person or Keltic family; totem or power animal

fey, feyn: otherworldly, vaguely portentous; capable of precognition

ffridd: (pron. *freethe*) small padded enclosure for a child to play safely in

fiala: "veil"; aura of divinity, or appearance of specific deity, that can come upon an individual whom that deity temporarily "possesses" or indwells; a very holy manifestation

Fianna: Keltic order of military supremacy; **Fian,** officer
    above all other armed forces and ranks

fidchell: chess-style board game

findruinna: superhard, silvery metal used in swords, armor
    and other offensive or defensive applications

Fionn: a major deity of the Keltic pantheon (**Fionn the
    Young**); intermediary between mortals, the lesser gods
    and the **High Dânu;** traditionally well-disposed to and
    extremely protective of humankind; **Fionnasa,** his feast,
    celebrated on 29 September

fíor-comlainn: "truth-of-combat"; legally binding trial by
    personal combat; usually decided when first blood is
    drawn, this combat was in former times to the death

fith-fath: spell of shapeshifting or glamourie; magical
    illusion

flain: laser arrow or bolt fired from balister

Fomori: ancient enemies of the Kelts, inhabiting the planet
    Fomor and many colony worlds

fostern: relation by fosterage; foster-brother or -sister

Fragarach: "The Answerer"; also translated "Retaliator";
    the **Sword** that is one of the Four Chief Hallows of
    Keltia

framachs: brown-skinned root vegetable grown throughout
    Keltia; a food staple

gabhairin-reo: "the little goat of the frost"; common wood
    snipe

gae catha: "battle-frenzy"; temporary state of superhuman
    strength and ability induced by battle (also known as **the
    Red Mist of Doing**)

Gaeloch: language spoken throughout Keltia (in addition to
    the six major planetary languages and numberless dialects
    thereof)

galláin: "foreigners"; sing., **gall,** fem. **gallwyn;** generic
    term for all humanoid non-Kelts (and often used for non-
    humanoids as well)

galloglass: Keltic foot-soldier, infantry fighter; generic term
    for any member of armed forces (also **kern**)

gân: sponsal affix used with mate's forename (*Morguenna gân Taliesin*)

Ganaster: third planet of the Nicanor system; seat of the **High Justiciary,** a voluntary interstellar court to which systems may make petition for arbitrated settlement of grievances short of war; and, very often, to make peace and treaties in war also

garron: small sturdy horse, 13–14 hands high, usually gray in color

gauran: plow-beast similar to ox or bullock

Gavida: Keltic god of fire, lightning, metals and handcraft; known as the Smith of the Gods

geis, pl. **geisa:** (pron. *gesh, gesha*) any prohibition or moral injunction placed upon a person, often at birth or other significant moment; to break geis means certain ill-luck and misfortune, if not worse

glaive: lightsword, laser weapon used throughout settled galaxy

glamourie: temporary illusion, magically placed

glib: forelock of hair; bangs or fringe of hair above forehead

goleor: "in great numbers, overabundance"; Englic word *galore* is derived from this

gossocks: worthless, stupid, feckless persons

graal: shallow, two-handled cup or dish, usually made of precious metals and decorated with jewels and carving; **the Graal,** the sacred **Cup** of the Mysteries, one of the Four Chief Hallows of Keltia

graffit: small sea or earth anchor

gralloch: to disembowel, as a stag or other beast killed in the hunt

gricemite: small misshapen tuber used as pig-food

grieshoch: red-hot flameless fire; embers or low-smoldering fire

Guardians of the Door: great spiritual presences that are invoked at the Airts and that oversee a soul's crossing into the next life

gúna: generic name for various styles of long robe or gown

Gwahanlen: "The Veil of the Temple"; the chamber in which the Companions assembled, noted for its historic tapestries and architectural beauty

Gwencathra: "The White Stanchion of Truth"; seat at the
   Table Rhodaur (q.v.) reserved in Arthur's day for
   Taliesin Pen-bardd; tradition has it that any unworthy
   person attempting to occupy this chair will vanish in
   flame and thunder and never be seen again

gwrach: wild hag-like spirit; **Gwrach y Rhibyn,** The Hag
   of the Dribble, a malevolent spirit of horrifying aspect

Gwynedd: chief world of the system of Kymry

Gwynfyd: "The Circle of Perfection"; eternal afterlife to be
   attained to only after many cycles of rebirth

hai atton: in warfare, the horn-cry that rallies the hosts; lit.,
   "heigh to us"

handfasting: rite of religious marriage (as distinguished
   from civil marriage); a spiritual linking of souls, which is
   symbolized by the making of the third of the **Three Cuts**
   (q.v.)

hearkening-wind: the destructive blast that follows a lull in
   a storm

High Dânu: the eight (or, by other counts, seven, nine,
   twelve or fourteen) gods and goddesses of the general
   Keltic pantheon who are raised up above the rest, to act
   as intermediary Powers between mortals, the lesser
   deities and the Highest God (**Kelu** or **Yr Mawreth,** q.v.)

hilyat-shaar: a blue scarf, folded as a browband and worn
   around the hair, as a sign of mourning on the planet
   Aojun (a blue faceveil is substituted when appearing in
   public, and both men and women follow this custom)

"Hob y deri dan do!": nonsense refrain to Kymric songs;
   lit., "The boar of the wood safely lodged under roof"

Hui Corra: the flagship of Saint Brendan in the first immram to Keltia

Hu Mawr: (**Hu** pron. *hee;* **Mawr** to rhyme with "power")
   Hu the Mighty; father of the gods in the Kymric
   pantheon

immram, pl. **immrama:** "voyage"; the Great Migrations from Earth to Keltia, beginning with Saint Brendan in 453 E.R. and ending around the year 1400 E.R.; also, initiatory trance of Druid and Ban-draoi training sequences

inghearrad: intaglio carving; anything incised or engraved

Inion Durracha: "Daughter of the Darkness"; epithet for Marguessan Pendreic

Inisguidrin: "White Island"; sanctuary of the Graalkeeper in the Marai or Siennega marsh

Iscaroe: Uisge-ruadh, the Red Spring of the sacred well of Saint Clears

(I)'s é do bheatha: (pron. *SHAY doe VA-ha*) lit., "life to you"; traditional Keltic salutation and farewell

Jai: title of the Heir of Aojun

Jamadarin: title of the Queen of Aojun

jurisconsult: brehon engaged in law-court cases

katxa-raika: Coranian word for **eacht-grásta,** mercy-blow

keeve: beaker or barrel

Kelu: "The Crown"; the One High God above all gods, held by Kelts to be both Mother Goddess and Father God together, or neither, or beyond such distinctions entirely; cannot be known in earthly life, though Kelu is frequently besought in prayer as *Artzan Janco,* "Shepherd of Heaven," (and **Yr Mawreth,** "The Highest")

kenning: telepathic technique originally developed (and now used almost exclusively) by Ban-draoi and Druid adepts

kern: noncommissioned warrior; latterly, Keltic starfleet crew member

Kerridwen: aspect of the Goddess as Queen and Mother of the World

khazei'khar: Aojunese word for concept of **dán**

king-torches: flaming brands formerly held by servitors behind the high chairs of rulers at table

lai: unit of Keltic distance measurement, equal to one-half mile

laighen: sharp, leaf-bladed spearpoint

lamh-dia: (pron. *laav-deea*) "hand-gods"; small portable votive statues of various Keltic divinities

landlash: exceptionally powerful rainstorm with destructive winds

lash: limp, strengthless

lasmathra: "half-mother"; stepmother

lasra: laser

leinna: long, full-sleeved shirt usually worn under a tunic

lennaun: lover without benefit of formal arrangement

levin: lightning-bolt

Llacharn: "Flamebright"; the sword Arthur took from the stone on the island of Collimare; it was broken at the battle of Ratherne, and Taliesin returned it to Loch Bel Draccon before he left Keltia; in Arthur's time, the origin of Llacharn—who had made it and who had set it in the stone at Collimare—was a mystery

llan: retreat-place, cell or enclosure for religious anchorite

Llenaur: "Golden Cloak"; The Lady of Heaven's Mantle, Keltic name for the Milky Way

lonna: light war-spear favored by the Fianna; also, hydrofoil-type vessel used by Keltic sea-navy

lorica: mail tunic or breastplate worn in battle

Lughnasa: feast of the light-god Lugh, celebrated on 1 August

lyte: liquid mass of something filthy and disgusting; excrement

machair: "sea-meadow"; wide tracts of salt grassland bordering on the sea and running down to the high-water mark

maenor: hereditary dwelling-place, usually a family seat, in the countryside or city

maeth: foster-father

Maharrion: another name for **Mihangel** (q.v.)

Malen: Kymric name of Keltic goddess of war (usually **Malen Ruadh, Red Malen**)

mamaith: child's word for "mother"; equivalent to "mama" or "mommy"

Manaan: Keltic god of the seas and salt waters; his crystal ship that can sail both land and ocean is called Wavesweeper

marana: deep trance used by Keltic sorcerers

Marbh-draoi: "Death-druid"; universal byname for Edeyrn ap Seli ac Rhûn, usurper, assassin, regicide and Theocrat

marúnad: song or chaunt of lamentation at a death

mataun: mattock or other dull-bladed tool

Mathr'achtaran: "Reverend Mother"; mode of address used to chief priestess of the Ban-draoi order

maukit: filthy; lit., infested with maggots

m'chara: "my friend"; used only in the vocative

Merch Dhu: (pron. *mairkh dee*) "Daughter of the Darkness"; epithet for Marguessan

mether: four-cornered drinking-vessel, usually made of pottery or wood

methryn: foster-mother

mhic: (pron. *vhick*) "son of"

Mi-cuarta: banqueting-hall in Turusachan

Mihangel: Keltic god of battle, known as Prince of Warriors (also **Maharrion**); legend says he will command the forces of Light at the great final battle of Cymynedd, which will decide the fate of the universe between good and evil (also aspected as **Fionn** and **Arawn**, q.v.)

minkler: vagrant; ragamuffin

modryn: "aunt"

Morimaruse: vast electromagnetic void, the Dead Sea of space

Mór-rían: "Great Queen"; title for the Goddess in Her aspect as Lady of Battles, when in shape of a raven She hovers above the field

Moruadha: the merrows, the sea-people; green-haired and red-skinned, of lithe and graceful build, these amphibious people dwell chiefly on Kernow but have since migrated to all the Keltic worlds

muirgha: "harpoon"

Nantosvelta: the secret tunnel, constructed by Brendan's master-builder Gradlon of Ys, that runs beneath the mountain range of the Loom, connecting the palace of Turusachan with Wolfdale, as an escape route at need

nathair: generic term for any of various poisonous snakes of the adder type

nemeton: ceremonial stone circle or henge (also **corvaen**); **Caer-na-gael** is chiefest and oldest of these in Keltia, while **Ni-maen** is the royal nemeton and burial ground above Caerdroia

Nevermas: a time that never comes; used metaphorically

ní, nic, nighean: "daughter of"

nithart: shivering weakling

ollave: master-bard, or anyone with master ranking and supreme command of an art or craft

oréadach: cloth-of-gold (*arghansaweth,* cloth-of-silver)

Otter-moon: month of August

outfrenne: outworld, foreign

oxter: ribcage; angle between side of chest and arm

Pair Dadeni: (pron. *DA-day-nee*) the Cauldron of Rebirth or Cup of Wonder; the **Graal;** one of the Four Chief Hallows of Keltia

palug: graceful, red-furred, ferociously ill-tempered lynx-like feline

pastai: small handmeal; a turnover consisting of a pastry crust filled with gravied meat or vegetables

Pen-bardd: "Head or Chiefest of Bards"; ancient title given to two bards only in all Keltic history—Plenyth ap

Alun, founder of the Bardic Order, and Taliesin ap Gwyddno

Pendragon: title given to head of the Dragon Kinship; Taliesin was the first, as its founder, to be called so

Pheryllt: class of master-Druids who serve as instructors in the order's schools and colleges (**Ro-sai,** head of the Pheryllt or "Great Teacher," a title once held by the Marbh-draoi Edeyrn

piast: large amphibious water-beast found in deepwater lakes on the planets Erinna and Scota; the species was known to Terrans as the Loch Ness Monster

pibroch: battle-song, usually played on war-pipes

pirn: spindle, thread-winder

pishogue: small magic, cantrip

plaisham: small indeterminate or miscellaneous thing; what-you-may-call-it

portune: benevolent place-sprite

Protectorates: confederation of star-systems that have petitioned for Keltia's military and political protection

quaich: low, wide, double-handled drinking vessel; can be made of metal, pottery, wood or leather

Quaternity: the Four Hallows—Spear, Sword, Cup and Stone

quease: person not of strong stomach or nerves

rade: riding-out of the Sidhe-folk at Beltane or Samhain, or in times of war

rann: chanted verse stanza used in magic; spell of any sort

Ravens: Edeyrn's enforcers, used as terror-police

rechtair: steward in royal, noble or merely wealthy households

reiving: "raiding"; expedition traditionally to steal a neighbor's cattle, now any venture of raiding or punishment; kidnapping

Rhên: ancient title meaning "lord"; now used of both genders and chiefly for deities

Rhian: the **Young Goddess;** usually manifests Herself as a slight, lithe, brown-haired girl in her teens

Rhodaur: "Golden Wheel"; the **Table of the Companions** in **Gwahanlen** (q.v.); it is toroid in shape (being circular, it has no head and therefore no seat-precedence need be observed) and seats 144 persons in three rows

Rían-dhuair: "Queen-dowager"; title resultant of Ygrawn Tregaron's marriage and widowhood to Uthyr Pendreic

Rían na Reanna: "Queen of the Stars"; a title of the Goddess

rígh-domhna: members of any of the Keltic royal families, as reckoned from a common ancestor, any of whom may (theoretically, at least) be elected to the Sovereignty

Rocabarra: in Keltic legend, a great gray rock in the seas of Caledon; cursed by a Druid in his wrath to sink beneath the waves, it has risen twice, and the third time will signal the end of the world; used metaphorically ("When Rocabarra rises!") as a time so unimaginably distant as will for all intents and purposes never come

ros-catha: battle-cry; Arthur's of "Lean thusa orm!" is usually translated as "Follow on!" or "Follow thou me!"

rutair: ship's chartbook

saining: ritual of Keltic baptism; first of the **Three Cuts** (q.v.) is made on this occasion; can be held up to a moonyear after a child's birth

sainn-an-rían: (pron. *sawn un REE-un*) "check to the queen"; a game-threatening move in fidchell

Salamandri: saurinoid race dwelling on the planet Kholco

Samhain: (pron. *SAH-win*) festival of the beginning of winter and start of the Keltic year; New Year's Day for Kelts; celebrated on 31 October (Great Samhain) and continuing until 11 November (Little Samhain)

Sassenaich: on Earth, the Anglo-Saxon invaders who displaced the Celtic peoples

scadarc: (pron. *SKY-ark*) crystal used in Fian funerals to disembody the deceased

scranbag: motley assortment of trash or leftovers
seastone: the gem aquamarine
seidean-sidhe: (pron. *SHAY-dawn SHEE*) a small whirl-
    wind that is produced on hot summer days, usually in
    flat lands or farm fields, doing little damage; tradition-
    ally thought by countrydwellers to signal the unseen
    passing-by of one of the Sidhe
Seren Beirdd: "Star of the Bards"; beautiful edifice constructed
    at Turusachan for Bardic Order, at Arthur's command
sgian: small black-handled double-edged knife universally
    worn in Keltia, usually in boot-top
sgian-fish: elongated silvery schoolfish with razor-sharp
    teeth; dangerous and irritable in the extreme
shakla: chocolate-tasting beverage brewed with water from
    the berries of the brown ash; drunk hot or cold through-
    out Keltia as a caffeine-supplying stimulant
sharnclouts: term of opprobrium; *sharn,* cow-dung in a
    semiliquid state
shogglers: delayers and temporizers
Sidhe: (pron. *shee*) the Shining Ones; a race of possibly
    divine or immortal beings; also **Aes Sidhe** (q.v.)
silkies: (also **selchies**) the Sluagh-rón, the Seal-folk;
    phocine race dwelling in Keltia; like the merrows, the
    silkies are on excellent terms with human Kelts and with
    each other
silkwool: luxurious fabric much favored in Keltia
síodarainn: (pron. *shee-dah-RAWN*) "silk-iron"; black
    metal alloy, extremely tough and strong, often used for
    starship hulls
Six Nations: the six star systems of Keltia (excluding the
    Throneworld system of Tara); in order of their founding
    they are: Erinna, Kymry, Scota, Kernow, Vannin and
    Brytaned (or Arvor)
sleekit: smooth in manner, but sly, cunning and not to be
    trusted
slinter: term of opprobrium; roughly, "bastard"
slorach: wet, disgusting mess of something nasty to the senses
sluagh: a hosting, as of an army
smoor: to damp down or cover a fire, so that it smolders to
    grieshoch (q.v.); to produce quantities of smoke with

very little flame; to suffocate; to ritually smudge (bless with smoke) a person or thing

snaoim-draoi: "Druids' Knot"; technique of magical binding

softsauder: to butter up or flatter a person; also, the flattery itself

Solas Sidhe: (pron. *sullis shee*) "The Faery Fire"; natural phenomenon similar to the will-o'-the-wisp but occurring over rocky ground, usually in the spring and fall; also, the magical light or aura sometimes worn by the **Sidhe** (q.v.) themselves in the presence of mortals

Stonerows: lower circles of Caerdroia

stour: uproar, tumult, outcry (rhymes with "poor")

stravaiging: idle wandering about, rampaging

streppoch: term of opprobrium; roughly equivalent to "bitch"

street-town: a town lacking a castle in its midst to defend it

sundog: partial rainbow

sun-shark: species of dolphin, traditionally friendly and helpful to humans in difficulties at sea

Sunstanding: summer or winter solstice

syra-wyn: "grandfather," "great-grandfather"

tailstar: a comet

Tair Rhamant: "Three Romances"; boyhood castle-home of Taliesin Glyndour, destroyed by Edeyrn with all of the province of Gwaelod

Tair Rhandir: (**Tair** is pronounced *tire*) "Three Sharelands"; castle built for Taliesin by his wife Morguenna during his imprisonment by her sister Marguessan; name refers to Taliesin, Morguenna and their son Gerrans

taish, pl. **taisher:** (pron. *tawsh*) magical projection of a person's face or form; common slang for "ghost" or any kind of extraordinary phantom or apparition

talpa: blind, blunt-snouted, sleek-furred digger animal native to the planet Kernow

Tanist, Tanista: designated heir of line to the Keltic throne

Tântad: "The Road of Fire"; a magical discipline, misuse of which can prove fatal

Taoiseach: (pron. *TEE-shaakh*) the Prime Minister of Keltia

tarq-hijar, pl. **tarq-hijarun:** Yamazai (Aojunese) word meaning "leader of a hunting party"

tasyk: "daddy"; a child's word for "father"

telyn: Kymric lap-harp

thole: to endure, to bear a grief or burden

thrawn: stubborn, unreasonably perverse

Three Cuts: tiny ceremonial nicks made on one's wrist with a consecrated sgian, during rituals of saining, fosterance and handfast marriage, to obtain a few drops of blood for the purposes of these three solemn religious rites; the principle being invoked here is courage and willingness to sacrifice—for oneself, a fostern or a mate

tiachán: book-satchel made of leather and adorned with jewels and metalwork, to honor as well as protect ancient and valuable volumes

Timpaun: the plain of the Drumhead on the planet Erinna; an area renowned for its horse-breeding establishments

tinnól: marriage-gift each partner gives the other the morning after the handfasting or wedding

tinnscra: the marriage portion given to a man or woman, or to them as a couple, by their families, clanns or (in the case of royalty or high nobility) by the reigning monarch; generally something substantial, like land or income, with reversion rights vested in each partner in case of subsequent divorce carefully spelled out as to amount due each

tirr: cloaking effect, part magical, part mechanical in nature, used to conceal ships, buildings and the like; until quite recently, did not work on living or moving things

torc: massive neck ornament worn by Kelts of rank; a heavy, open-ended circle usually of gold or silver, sometimes with jewelled terminal-ends

traha: "arrogance"; more than mere arrogance, a wanton pride or hubris

triad: poetic triplet used by bards, in which three similar events, persons or things are linked for instructive purposes

triskell: three-armed (or -legged) device that is the crest of Vannin and symbol of creation

trygariad: "cariad," beloved, with intensifying prefix; "most beloved"

tuagh: small double-bladed war-axe; also **curtal-axe** (q.v.)

Turusachan: (pron. *TOO-roo-SAKH'n*) "Place of Gathering"; the royal palace at Caerdroia; by extension, the entire central government of Keltia; also, the plateau area above the city of Caerdroia, just below Eryri, where the governmental buildings are located

Ulessos: the mythological/historical personage known as Ulysses

usqua: whiskey, generally unblended (**usqueba**, "water of life")

Veils of Aunya: Keltic astronomical name for the Magellanic Clouds

watchpot: greedy person; one overly fond of the table

water-horse: supernatural equine manifestation; beast with fiery eyes and nostrils that lives in lakes and rivers and attempts to lure humans into riding on its back to their destruction

widdershins: lefthandwise or countersunwise; in a counterclockwise direction

Yamazai: dominant race of the planet Aojun; usually refers to the fierce and supremely capable woman warriors of this matriarchal and matrilineal system

Yr Mawreth: "The Highest"; usual name for Keltic Supreme Being

NOTES ON
PRONOUNCIATION

The spellings and pronunciations of the names and words in THE KELTIAD are perhaps unfamiliar to some readers; the Celtic languages (Irish, Scots Gaelic, Welsh, Cornish, Manx and Breton) upon which I have drawn for my Keltic nomenclature are not related to any tongue that might provide a clue as to their derivation or their spoken sound. Outside of loan-words, they have no Latin root as do the Romance languages, and are in fact derived from a totally different branch of the Indo-European linguistic tree. (In case you were curious, Coranian, or Hastaic, is cribbed from Basque, and Aojunese from Arabic.)

Therefore I have taken certain, not always consistent, liberties with orthography in the interests of reader convenience, though of course one may deal with the names any way one likes, or even not at all. But for those who might like to humor the author, I have made this list of some of the more difficult names, words and phonetic combinations.

One further note, to those (and they are legion) whose Celtic linguistic scholarship exceeds my poor own: The words used herein are meant to be Keltic, not Celtic. I have tried to appropriate fairly even-handedly from most of the Celtic languages (well, except for Manx, which is just *too* weird, however phonetically correct)—and from Elizabethan English and Lowland Scots (Lallans) as well where it seemed good to do so—both archaisms and words that are in current modern usage; and in not a few cases I have tampered with them to suit my own purposes and aesthetics. Therefore be not alarmed should familiar words turn out to be not all they seem. Words may be reasonably assumed to change over time and distance; Keltia is very far away by both measures, and who is to say, if not I, what words they shall be speaking and what meaning those words shall have and how they shall be spelled?

But just in case that disclaimer does not avert the wrath of the purists, I hereby claim prior protection under the Humpty-Dumpty Law: "When *I* use a word. . .it means just what I choose it to mean—neither more nor less." Now you are warned.

Vowels:

Generally the usual, though *a* is often pronounced "ah" and *i* never takes the sound of "eye," but always an "ee" or "ih" sound. Thus: *ard-ree* for **Ard-rígh,** not *ard-rye.* Final *e* is always pronounced; sometimes this has been indicated with an accent mark.

Vowel Combinations:

aoi:	"ee" as in "heel"
ao:	"ay" as in "pay"
au:	"ow" as in "cow", never "aw" as in "saw" (except in some Kymric words where it is "eye"; thus, **Tegau:** *TEG-eye*)
ae, ai:	"I" as in "high"
io:	"ih" as in "in" (**Fionn:** *finn*)
ío:	"ee" as in "feet" (**fíor:** *feer*)
á:	accent gives it length; thus, **dán** rhymes with "fawn" (other long vowels: *ú* as in "cool", *é* as in "say")

Consonants:

c:	always a "k" sound. (To avoid the obvious problem here, the more usual **Celt, Celtic, Celtia** have been spelled **Kelt, Keltic, Keltia** throughout; **Seltics** are a basketball team. . .)
ch:	guttural as in the German "ach," never "ch" as in "choose"

g:	always hard, as in "give" or "get" (thus: *Gerrans,* not "Jerrans"; sometimes I have put a *u* amid the *ge-* combination to avoid this)
bh, mh:	"v" (**bhan:** *van;* **amhic:** *avick*) (Note: On occasion *mh* will do bad things to vowels, as in **Samhain:** *sah-win* or *sowen,* where the *ow-* will rhyme with "cow," not "low". I'm sorry.)
th:	"h" (or, sometimes, not pronounced at all!)
dd:	"th" as in "then", not as in "this" (So: **Nudd:** *neethe,* to rhyme with "seethe"; I'll get to that "ee" sound presently)
ll:	I hate to do this to you, you having been so good about reading this far, but. . . Here it comes: The Welsh double-l sound, though feared (and rightly), is bad, but not so bad as it looks. People have been cowering in front of it for centuries: Even Shakespeare chickened out, and went with "Fluellen" as his best shot. We, however, are made of sterner stuff: Put the tip of your tongue behind your upper front teeth, on the hard ridge of the palate, not too far back, and relax the rest of your mouth. Now: With your tongue still in that position, sort of hiss around both sides of the tongue at once; if you do it right, you will get a kind of "chluh" sound. Don't use your voice; just try to pronounce an "s." Believe it or not, that *is* right. I'm very proud of you. Now all you have to do is put other sounds with it.

And two final strange and terrible things: In Kymric (Welsh), *u* (as above, in **Nudd**) will on occasion take an "ee" sound; and *w,* when utilized as a vowel, will be pronounced as "oo" (**Annwn:** *annoon*).

(In case you, like Taliesin in the face of math, have screamed and fled long since, I have given in the Glossary simple pronunciations for some of the more problematic words, and the same in the Character listing for proper names. Thank you. You've been both brave and courteous—true Kelts.)

CHARACTERS

Alannagh Ruthven: Companion; friend to Arthur; went in Prydwen (pron. *RIVV'n,* not *rooth-ven*) (I *promise*. . .)

Allyn mhic Midna: a lord of the Sidhe (*allen vhick MEETHE-na,* more or less)

Amris Pendreic: Prince of Dôn; late Tanist of Keltia, eldest son of Darowen Ard-rían and King Gwain; brother to Leowyn and Uthyr; far-charach to Ygrawn Tregaron; father to Arthur (*pen-drake*)

Anghaud Pendreic: son of Geraint Pendreic; grandson of Morgan and Taliesin; one of the Seven

Arawn Pendreic: son to Arthur and Gweniver, High King thereafter

Arthur Pendreic: known also as **Arthur Penarvon,** his preferred style; Prince of the House of Dôn; son of Amris and Ygrawn; adopted son of Gorlas Penarvon; nephew to Leowyn and Uthyr; foster-brother to Taliesin Glyndour. High King of Keltia, Ard-rígh, by joint rule with Gweniver his second wife; father by her of Arawn and Arwenna; by Majanah of the Yamazai, Queen of Aojun, father to Donah; by Gwenwynbar his first wife, father to Malgan **(Artos)**

Arwenna Pendreic: daughter to Arthur and Gweniver

Avallac'h Pendreic: Graalkeeper; Prince of Dôn; son to Cador, grandson to Alawn Last-king (*uh-VAL-akh*)

Betwyr ap Benoic: Companion; friend to Arthur; went in Prydwen (*BEN-ick*)

the Bhan-reann-ruadh: magical personage; a minor goddess, or a humbler manifestation of a higher deity; "Red Star Woman" (*van-ran-ROO-uh*)

Birogue of the Mountain: a lady of the Sidhe; mate to Merlynn Llwyd (*beer-OAG*)

Cathelin ní Seighin ac Glyndour: Terran; ban-charach to Gwyddno Glyndour; by him, mother of Taliesin

Cathelin Pendreic: daughter of Geraint; granddaughter of Morgan and Taliesin

Cristant Kendalc'hen: wife to Geraint Pendreic; mother of Anghaud, Sgilti and Cathelin

Daronwy Cameron ferch Anwas: Companion; Countess of Endellion; friend to Arthur; wife to Roric Davacho; mother of Harodin; one of the Seven (**Ronwyn, Ronwynna; Daron** on Aojun)

Donah: Heir of Aojun (**Jai Donah**); daughter of Arthur and Majanah; known in Keltia as **Duanagh Penarvon** (**Donayah**)

Edeyrn ap Seli ac Rhûn: Archdruid; known to history as the Marbh-draoi; usurper, murderer, traitor and Theocrat; slain by Arthur at the Battle of Ratherne (Nandruidion); son of the mortal Rhûn and Seli, Queen of the Sidhe

Elen Llydaw: Companion; Duchess of Arvor; known as **Elen Llydawc,** Elen of the Hosts, for her great generalship in battle; friend to Arthur; one of the Seven (**Elenna**)

Elphin Carannoc: Companion; ollave; later Chief Bard, head of the Order; friend to Arthur; chief teacher to Taliesin; went in Prydwen

Ferdia mac Kenver: Companion; Lord of Valtinglas; friend to Arthur; one of the Seven (**Feradach**)

Galeron Pendreic: only daughter and second child of Marguessan and Irian; died in a black working at Caervanogue

Geraint Pendreic: Companion; son of Taliesin and Morgan; husband to Cristant; father of Anghaud, Sgilti and Cathelin (**Gerrans**)

Gorlas Penarvon: Lord of Daars; first husband to Ygrawn Tregaron; adoptive father to Arthur; slain by Edeyrn

Grehan Aoibhell: Companion; Prince of Thomond; latterly Taoiseach of Keltia; friend and warlord to Arthur (**Aoibhell:** *ee-VELL*)

Gwain Pendreic: second son and youngest child of Marguessan and Irian; slain by Taliesin at Marguessan's instigation; restored to life by the Graal at Caervanogue

Gweniver Pendreic: Ard-rían of Keltia; only child of Leowyn Ard-rígh and Queen Seren; niece to Amris and Uthyr; cousin to Arthur, Morgan and Marguessan; High Queen of Keltia by joint rule with Arthur her husband; by him, mother of Arawn and Arwenna; became a Ban-draoi nun after her husband's death, or disappearance (**Gwennach, Gwennol, Gweni, Gwen**)

Gwenwynbar: daughter of Gerwin, Lord Plymon, and Tamise Rospaen; first wife to Arthur by a brehon marriage; mother by him of Malgan; slain by Ysild of Kernow

Gwyddno Glyndour: Lord of Gwaelod; husband to Medeni; far-charach to Cathelin; father of Tegau and five others by Medeni; by Cathelin, father of Taliesin; murdered by Edeyrn (*gwithno glindoore*)

Gwyn ap Nudd: Prince of the Sidhe; heir to Nudd ap Llyr, King of the Sidhe, and Seli his queen; half-brother to Edeyrn Marbh-draoi

Harodin Davacho: son of Daronwy and Roric; mate to Donah, Jamadarin of the Yamazai; by her, father of Sarinah, Heir of Aojun

Irian Locryn: Lord of Lleyn; husband to Marguessan; by her, father to Mordryth, Galeron and Gwain; slain by the Sidhe

Keils Rathen: Companion; Earl of Sulven; warlord and friend to Uthyr and Arthur; lover of Gweniver; murdered by Marguessan's agents

Leowyn Pendreic: Ard-rígh of Keltia; second son of Darowen Ard-rían and King Gwain; husband to Seren Princess of Galloway; father by her of Gweniver; killed by Ravens

Loherin Tregaron: Companion; Graalkeeper to succeed Avallac'h; son of Tryffin and Ysild

Majanah: Jamadarin of the Yamazai, Queen of Aojun; ban-charach to Arthur, by him, mother of Donah; mate of Brone (**Janjan**)

Malgan Pendreic: son of Arthur and Gwenwynbar; reputed son of Owein Rheged; died at Barrendown

Marguessan Pendreic: Princess of Keltia, Duchess of Eildon; elder twin daughter of Uthyr Ard-rígh and Queen Ygrawn; cousin and half-sister to Arthur; cousin to Gweniver; wife to Irian Locryn; by him, mother of Mordryth, Galeron and Gwain; died at Caervanogue

Medeni: Lady of Gwaelod; wife to Gwyddno; mother to Tegau *et al.*; reputed mother to Taliesin (*MED-en-ee*)

Melwas: King of Fomor; kidnapped Donah, precipitating war with Keltia and Aojun

Merlynn Llwyd: Companion; known also as **Ailithir;** Druid; Archdruid; teacher and friend to Arthur and Taliesin (**Llwyd:** *khLOO-id*; the double-l sound is made as described in pronunciation notes, and best of Keltic luck to you)

Mordryth Pendreic: heir of Lleyn; son of Irian and Marguessan; died at Camlann

Morguenna Pendreic: known as Morgan; Companion; Princess of Keltia, Duchess of Ys; younger twin daughter of Uthyr and Ygrawn; cousin and half-sister to Arthur; wife to Taliesin; by him, mother of Geraint; died at Caervanogue and is buried beside Saint Brendan at Caer-na-gael (**Morgan, Guenna**)

Nanteos: predecessor to Melwas as King of Fomor

Nudd ap Llyr: King of the Sidhe; mate to Seli; father of Gwyn

Owein Rheged: Lord of Gwynedd, as the Marbh-draoi's heir and regent; second husband to Gwenwynbar; reputed father of Malgan, until it was proved not so; slain by Edeyrn as Torc Truith

Roric Davacho: Companion; Aojunni; friend to Arthur; warlord to Majanah; husband to Daronwy; by her, father of Harodin; went in Prydwen

Scathach Aodann: Companion; Fian general; teacher to Arthur and Taliesin; inventor of the personal space shield (**skiath**) that bears her name; died in battle (*SKY-ach AY-dan*)

Seli: Queen of the Sidhe; wife to Nudd ap Llyr; by him, mother of Gwyn; onetime mate of the mortal Rhûn, by whom she was the mother of Edeyrn

the Seven: those who went in Prydwen and returned from Kholco—**Taliesin, Daronwy, Elen, Ferdia, Tanwen,** all being original Companions, and **Anghaud** and **Sgilti**

Sgilti Pendreic: son of Geraint Pendreic; grandson to Taliesin and Morgan; one of the Seven

the Six: outfrenne enemies of Keltia, bought hirelings of the Princess Marguessan—**Tembrual Phadaptë** and **Sleir Venoto,** Coranians; the half-Kelts **Kiar mac Ffreswm, Phayle Redshield** and **Rannick of Lissard; Granúmas,** a Voritian of the planet Uxellos; all slain by Taliesin at Barrendown

Taliesin Glyndour ap Gwyddno: narrator; Companion; youngest son of Gwyddno and only child of Gwyddno with his Terran ban-charach Cathelin; fostern to Arthur; Duke of Ys by his marriage to Morguenna Pendreic; by her, father of Geraint; one of the Seven; his end is a mystery (but the pronunciation of his name isn't: It's *tal-YES-in*. It is not *tally-essin*, or *tal-uh-SEEN*, or *tal-LEE-uh-sin*, or anything else) (**Talyn, Talynno, Tal**)

Tanwen Farrach: Companion; Countess of Dyonas; friend to Arthur; one of the Seven

Tarian Douglas: Companion; the Princess of Scots; Taoiseach of Keltia; friend and warlord to Arthur; mate to Graham Strathearn; by him, mother of Shane and Síoda; went in Prydwen (*tahr-YAHN*, please, not *tarry-in*)

Tegau Glyndour: Companion; known as Tegau Goldbreast (see *The Hawk's Gray Feather* for the story); eldest child of Gwyddno and Medeni; sister to Taliesin; wife to Eidier, Lord of Sinadon; both went in Prydwen (*TEG-eye*)

Tryffin Tregaron: Companion; Duke of Kernow; nephew to Ygrawn; cousin and friend to Arthur; husband to Ysild; by her, father of Loherin, the Graalkeeper, and a daughter, Ydain

Uthyr Pendreic: Ard-rígh of Keltia; youngest son of Darowen Ard-rían and King Gwain; brother to Leowyn and Amris; second husband to Ygrawn; by her, father of Marguessan and Morguenna; uncle to Arthur and Gweniver

Ygrawn Tregaron: Queen of Keltia by her marriage to Uthyr Pendreic; by him, mother of Marguessan and Morguenna; ban-charach to Amris Pendreic, by whom she was mother to Arthur (*ih-GRAWN tre-GARRIN*)

Ydain Tregaron: daughter of Tryffin and Ysild; sister to Loherin (*ih-DINE*)

Ysild Formartine: Companion; Lady of Arrochar, Duchess of Kernow by her marriage to Tryffin; by him, mother of Loherin and Ydain (*ih-ZILD*)

NOTES ON
THE TALES OF ARTHUR

The events of the Grail Quest in *The Hedge of Mist* were consolidated from many, many primary and secondary sources into the one presented here, as seemed good to me. Many of the trials Taliesin and Donah encountered in their respective Graal searches were taken from the Breton folk tale "Peronik," as recorded in *Le Foyer Breton* and *Légendes Bretonnes* and as commented on by Emma Jung and Marie-Louise von Franz in their great work *The Grail Legend*. But of course all Quest experiences are common to many tellings and retellings.

A partial bibliography follows; partial in two senses: that it represents perhaps a third of the books to which I had reference during the writing of this trilogy; and that only title and author are given here, since most of the works from which I obtained most assistance are long out of print and largely inaccessible to many readers (though some have been recently reprinted for the wider modern audiences). The works cited here are all from my own library.

The Annals of the Four Masters
The Book of Taliesin
The Fairies in English Tradition and Literature,
    Katharine Briggs
Trioedd Ynys Prydein, Rachel Bromwich, ed.
Encyclopedia of Arthurian Legend, Ronan Coughlan
Celtic Researches, Edward Davies
The High History of the Holy Grail, Sebastian Evans
The Fairy-Faith in Celtic Countries, Y. E. Evans-Wentz
Avalon of the Heart, Dion Fortune

The Gododdin
Hanes Taliesin
The Mystery of King Arthur, Elizabeth Jenkins
The Myvyrian Archaiology of Wales, Owen Jones,
    Edward Williams and William Owen Pughe
English as We Speak It in Ireland, P. W. Joyce
A Social History of Ancient Ireland, P. W. Joyce
The Grail Legend, Emma Jung and
    Marie-Louise von Franz
The Arthurian Encyclopedia, Norris J. Lacy, ed.
A Celtic Quest, John Layard
The Mabinogion
The Winged Destiny, Fiona Macleod
    (The Rev. William Sharp)
Le Morte d'Arthur, Sir Thomas Malory
A Guide to Glastonbury's Temple of the Stars,
    K. E. Maltwood
King Arthur: King of Kings, Jean Markale
Elements of the Arthurian Tradition, John Matthews
Elements of the Grail Tradition, John Matthews
The Flaming Door, Eleanor Merry
The Realms of Arthur, Helen Hill Miller
Iolo Manuscripts, Iolo Morganwg (Taliesin Williams)
The Age of Arthur, John Morris
The Book of Three Dragons, Kenneth Morris (Cenydd
    Morus)
The Fates of the Princes of Dyfed, Kenneth Morris
    (Cenydd Morus)
Brân the Blessed in Arthurian Romance, Helaine Newstead
Celtic Folklore, John Rhys
The Hibbert Lectures (1886), John Rhys
The Welsh People, John Rhys and David Brynmor-Jones
The Mystery of King Arthur at Tintagel, Richard Seddon
British Goblins, Wirt Sikes
The Fairy Tradition in Britain, Lewis Spence
Legends and Folktales of Brittany, Lewis Spence
The Oxford Companion to the Literature of Wales,
    Meic Stephens, ed.
The Idylls of the King and *Complete Poems,*
    Alfred Lord Tennyson

The Glastonbury Legends, R. F. Treharne
The Hidden Church of the Holy Graal, A. E. Waite
From Ritual to Romance, Jessie L. Weston
Guardian of the Grail, John Whitehead
The Black Horsemen, S. G. Wildman
Taliessin through Logres, Charles Williams
Celtic Wonder-Tales, Ella Young
The Tangle-Coated Horse, Ella Young

And no modern author retelling Arthur's story can fail in acknowledging a debt of gratitude to Rosemary Sutcliff for *Sword at Sunset* (my first encounter with a Dark-Ages Artos, as a college freshman in 1963, and heady stuff indeed for a seventeen-year-old with writerly dreams of her own); and to T. H. White for *The Once and Future King,* not so much for the Camelottery that was later laid on it as for the depth of literary scholarship, general erudition and plain joy in language.

—*P.K.M.*

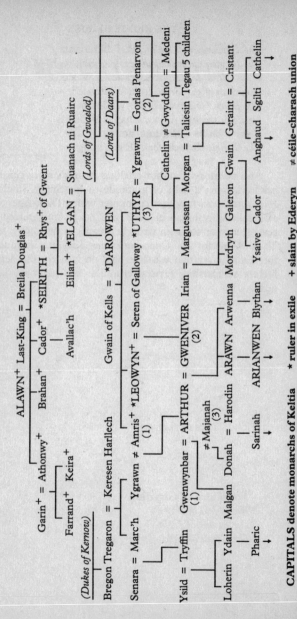

THE ROYAL HOUSE OF DÔN:
Rulers of the Counterinsurgency and Restoration

CAPITALS denote monarchs of Keltia   * ruler in exile   + slain by Ederyn

≠ céile-charach union

THE BOOKS OF
THE KELTIAD

The Tales of Brendan
*The Rock Beyond the Billow
*The Song of Amerguin
*The Deer's Cry

*The Sails of the Hui Corra (A Book of Voyages)

*Blackmantle (The Tale of Athyn)

The Tales of Arthur
The Hawk's Gray Feather
The Oak Above the Kings
The Hedge of Mist

*Lions in the North (Tales of the Douglas)

The House of the Wolf
*The Wolf's Cub
*The King's Peace
*The Beltane Queen

The Tales of Aeron
The Silver Branch
The Copper Crown
The Throne of Scone

The Tales of Gwydion
*The Shield of Fire
*The Sword of Light
*The Cloak of Gold

*forthcoming

To be published 3 July 2021

FIREHEART

THE LOVE POETRY, SONGS, SKETCHES AND LETTERS OF JIM MORRISON TO PATRICIA MORRISON

edited and annotated by Patricia Morrison,

with a foreword by Jim Morrison

On 5 May 1995, the twenty-fifth anniversary of James Douglas Morrison's proposing to me, I began to go over the many letters, drawings, poems and notes he had sent or given me, or had left in my keeping to hold against his return, before he went to Paris to his death on 3 July 1971.

On 24 June 1995, the twenty-fifth anniversary of our handfast wedding ceremony, I completed the anguishing and exalting task of editing (minimally or not at all) and annotating (extensively) this material I had kept so close and cherished so long.

And now, in this twenty-fifth anniversary year of Jim's death, I have the very great honor to announce *Fireheart,* to be published twenty-five years from now on 3 July 2021, half a century since the day he died.

This compilation of Jim Morrison's private communications to me during the years 1969, 1970 and 1971—his *true* 'lost' writings, in a sense, though in point of fact they have never been lost, at least not to him and me—has been set aside in a place of safety, there to await the first instant when I (or my heirs or literary executors) shall finally be able to lawfully publish it without having to beg permission to do so from the controllers of my beloved late consort's literary estate—permission which, given the rancorous hostile contentions that have historically surrounded Jim and his legacies, would without question have been summarily denied me.

During the course of our friendship, love and union, Jim saw fit to honor me with many truths. Save for some confidences which are of such incandescent intimacy as forever to preclude publication (I must keep something for ourselves alone), those truths will all be included here: words about himself, about me, about us; reflections on his childhood and youth; thoughts on his career as a rock star and his ambitions as a writer; observations on his past and present, and hopes for the future he promises we would have shared; poems of rare and, some may think, uncharacteristic lyricism—and unapologetic eroticism also.

Accompanying the letters and poems (many of which will be shown in facsimile) will be some of the drawings Jim made from time to time, as easily and as gracefully as he made his music—including some nude sketches of me and of us together—and several of the hitherto unpublished songs he left with me, perhaps intended for a Doors album that might have followed *L. A. Woman* but more likely meant for his own first solo effort, which he had planned to begin recording here in New York when he came back from Paris.

The Jim Morrison of *Fireheart*, a Jim whom perhaps no one but I was ever privileged to see, *is* Fireheart (as he names himself in one of the last and loveliest of the poems): a man writing the deep secrets of his soul to the woman he calls, in these same writings, his wife, the woman he took to himself in an ancient and beautiful ritual, as he took no other. This is the Jim I know and love and honor, Jim as he was with me and to me and for me.

Owing to the constraints of copyright law, this material has not been mine to release and publish (not even in Jim's own name, the only way in which I would ever have done so), and I would sooner have died myself than have allowed it to be published in the name of his estate, under the control of the managers thereof. Indeed, the very idea of being forced to petition for something that is mine to begin with, given me from Jim's own hand and heart, is hateful and abhorrent in the extreme; but it is, also and alas, the law.

Very little, therefore, of this material has yet been seen, save by my closest friends and associates, and none of it at all has ever been seen by the public. I have chosen to announce its future publication now, in this twenty-fifth anniversary year of Jim's death, out of deepest love and respect, as tribute to him and tribute to the world; but also perhaps as a kind of subtle vengeance, my own way of combatting the rather more dubious "tributes" that other individuals, with little or no personal connection to Jim, or at best, laughably less cause and connection than I have, will doubtless be rushing to produce.

My original, long-held intention was to destroy all this before my own death, and so to take it with me back to Jim. But I have been persuaded away from this course by those who feared that this incomparable legacy might go forever unseen and unshared, and the Jim Morrison it reveals remain unknown. *Fireheart* will surprise many and astonish most, will show a Jim that not even my memoir *Strange Days* could show; and what it will prove most incontrovertibly is that this is a man of matchless spirit and sensitivity, by no means the alcoholic drug-benumbed sadistic catspaw who is the only Jim his various biographers seem able or willing to understand or accept, a man capable of the deepest feeling and the most loving expression thereof.

And, yes, it will also prove, once and for all, just how Jim Morrison felt about me, how he spoke of me both to me and in his own heart, and why he kept our union the secret that it was from the world at large. Quite simply, he thought our love was none of anyone else's business—not his bandmates', not his associates', not the fans'—and considering the public torture that Linda Eastman McCartney and Yoko Ono Lennon were enduring at that very time (it always seems to be open season on rock wives; or at least on the ones who are strong, independent women with creative lives and careers of their own apart from their mates, while the pretty, parasitic, brainless addicts who so often attach themselves to rock musicians are allowed an endless free ride by men and women alike), we were both—for of course I shared his feeling on the matter—quite right to think so.

Jim, in his chivalry and protectiveness, wished only to spare me the pain of ordeal by media, and the harsh, hurtful personal attacks such attention can bring (and indeed has brought). What he and I could never have foreseen was that our silence and our natural wish for personal privacy would, with ghastly irony, work so against me two decades later, resulting in a far more terrible ordeal, far greater pain, nor yet that I would be left to face it alone. If we had, our decision would almost certainly have been very different indeed. . .

Even so, I kept silence in the face of enormity for twenty-one years before finally speaking out in *Strange Days*; no one, I think, can accuse me of rushing to publish, and, with a name and following of my own for my Keltiad, neither can I be accused of being a one-trick author, trading on my association with Jim *ad infinitum* (and *nauseam*) because that is all I have to offer.

Since 3 July 1971 my hands have been tied, my voice (or Jim's voice to and through me) has been stopped. Incredible as it may seem, I do not own publication rights to the love letters sent me by my own mate, nor to the poems he composed for and about me nor the sketches he drew of and for me. Not even in my own autobiography, my memoir of myself with him: not to prove my truth, not to defend his name, not to save us both from honest ignorance and outright lies.

As it is, I must wait out a full half century from the day

he died before that right can be mine: Copyright obtains for the lifespan of the author plus fifty years; thus Jim's estate, in which I have no legal rights, controls even these most deeply personal of missives, and I do not. But the same law that has for so long barred me from making public any of this material will in time free me to do so: If copyright law now holds these writings hostage, as part of Jim's literary estate (even though they were never anything but utterly private, between Jim and me), then on 3 July 2021, by definition, copyright law must likewise let them go.

(Since making these plans, and writing this piece, I have learned that a recent modification in American copyright law states that any unpublished material written before 1978 enters the public domain in 2003; whether I will take advantage of this provision to publish earlier, I have not yet decided, though it is quite likely, and for the moment I will keep to the announced 2021 publication date.)

My one regret is that it shall take so long to happen; but that is a thing I can neither command nor control. Twenty-five years from now, *Fireheart* will at last complete the picture *Strange Days* began to paint. . .and the truth is no less true for being delayed.

Yet perhaps the knowledge that it *will* happen—that Jim's own words are waiting up ahead to point the truth from beyond the grave—may occasion more care and caution as to what people choose to believe or opine in the meantime, may be a warning to future Morrisonographers to get it right for once, may even prompt reconsideration or repentance of certain past wrongful judgments.

I cannot say and dare not hope: But at the very least, come the year 2021, the casual vindictive dismissiveness many have practiced toward me and my part in Jim's life will be considerably more difficult to maintain, and those who did so, or who insist on continuing so to do in the face of this evidence so staggeringly to the contrary, will stand branded, by Jim himself, as the fools and liars they have always been. Nor can I say that the thought much displeases me. . .

By assembling this work, announcing this intent, I break no trust Jim placed in me, have violated no smallest tenet of the covenant we made between us. Indeed, I am all the more confident in my conviction that this but enhances the trust and faith we share, the vows we took, the love that was and is and ever shall be; and it is the way I choose to honor him, by enabling him to speak, for once, for himself, and also, for the first time publicly, for us.

Like *Strange Days* before it, *Fireheart* is a gift of love from me to the man I call my husband, the last I shall give him in this lifetime and perhaps the most enduring. The great, the tremendous difference that changes all is that Jim himself created it, as gift for me; and now at last, at long last, twenty-five years into the future, I can return to him, as one creative artist to another, that wondrous gift of love he bestowed upon me twenty-five years since.

I do not know if, two and a half decades hence, Jim Morrison will still command the same intensity of interest he has aroused in the public during his life and since the undeserved and untimely death that was so murderously dealt him. I realize that many among us may not be around to see published this last loving vindication of a man who has been much and deeply wronged; that I myself, even, may no longer be here in the world to see our triumph but joyfully reunited with Jim according to our vows, moving on together to our next lives, or beyond them.

No matter. What does matter is that whoever may come to read *Fireheart* will find, I think, that it will have been well worth the wait: to meet James Douglas Morrison at last, as he was, and as he was loving enough and coura- geous enough to reveal himself to his mate, face to face, mind to mind, heart to heart.

Or so, at least, he and I both hope. We can wait.

PATRICIA MORRISON
New York, 1996